THE AWAKENING BOND

The Earthbond Saga, Book 1

Written by Diane Kann

Brought to you by Volans Galaxy Press

Published by Kannceptual Creations LLC

An imprint of Volans Galaxy Press

ISBN: 978-1-969569-55-5

Printed in the United States of America

First Edition, November 2025

Note: This work was originally published under the pen name DM Volans, which is a pen name of Diane Kann.

CONTENTS

DEDICATION

To those who walk between worlds, who feel the pulse of the earth beneath the rubble, and who find their truest voice in the silent understanding of another heart. This story is for the companions who see more than we do, who guide us with instinct and unwavering loyalty through the darkest of nights. For the resilient spirits who believe in healing, even when the scars run deep, and for the quiet hope that whispers on the wind, promising a new dawn for a wounded world. May your bonds be strong, your senses sharp, and your hearts ever open to the whisper of the wild and the echo of connection.

CHAPTER 1

The wind, a phantom breath from a dying world, whispered through the skeletal remains of what had once been a city. Here, where skyscrapers clawed at the bruised sky like desperate, bony fingers, Kira Longwood moved with a quiet, practiced grace. Each step was a careful calculation, the crunch of shattered glass and pulverized concrete under her worn boots a stark symphony against the pervasive silence. The air itself tasted of dust and decay, a metallic tang that clung to the back of her throat. This was the aftermath, the stark, unforgiving testament to an ecological collapse so profound it had fractured the very fabric of civilization. The city, a ghost of its former glory, was a graveyard of ambition and progress, its avenues choked with the detritus of a forgotten era.

Beside her, a shadow given form, trotted Ash. His thick, sable fur was matted with the grime of their constant travels, his muscles a coiled spring beneath his coat. He was more than just a companion; he was an extension of Kira's own senses, a living barometer of their precarious existence. Even now, a subtle tension rippled through his frame, a low thrum of awareness that spoke of unseen threats lurking in the desolation. His nose twitched constantly, sifting through the olfactory landscape of ruin – the faint, acrid scent of chemical residue, the distant metallic tang of decaying machinery, and something else, something primal and alive that kept his hackles subtly raised. His dark, intelligent eyes, usually soft with a canine's easy affection, were sharp, scanning the periphery, missing nothing.

Kira paused, her hand instinctively reaching down to rest on Ash's broad head. His fur was warm beneath her touch, a grounding anchor in this sea of desolation.

She felt a faint tremor, not of the earth, but from him – a ripple of unease that mirrored her own. The silence here was a heavy shroud, deceptive. It was a silence that could shatter at any moment, punctuated by the sudden collapse of a weakened structure or the distant, chilling howl of something that had adapted to this harsh new reality. Their world was a tapestry woven from scarcity and the lingering echoes of a lost civilization, a place where survival was a daily, arduous negotiation with an unforgiving environment.

They moved through what had been a grand boulevard, now a canyon of shattered glass and twisted metal. Buildings stood like hollowed-out husks, their windows gaping voids that stared out blankly at the desolation. Nature, resilient and tenacious, had begun its slow reclamation. Hardy vines clung to crumbling facades, and tough, grey moss carpeted the debris, a testament to life's stubborn insistence. Yet, it was a victory of the tenacious over the magnificent, a slow decay rather than a vibrant rebirth. Kira's gaze swept over the scene, cataloging the skeletal frameworks of vehicles long since stripped of usable parts, the scattered remnants of everyday life now rendered meaningless: a child's worn shoe, a tarnished locket, a stack of brittle, unreadable papers. Each artifact was a silent testament to the lives that had once pulsed through these streets, a stark reminder of the fragility of even the most advanced societies.

The sheer scale of the destruction was overwhelming, a constant reminder of the catastrophic events that had reshaped their world. The sky, perpetually hazed with fine dust, cast a perpetual twilight over the ruins, muting colors and blurring the edges of reality. Kira pulled her scavenged scarf tighter around her neck, a meager defense against the biting wind that seemed to carry with it the ghosts of a million forgotten voices. Her backpack felt heavier with each passing hour, the meager supplies within a constant, gnawing reminder of their vulnerability. Every journey was a gamble, every discarded object a potential treasure or a deadly trap.

Ash's low growl, a sound barely audible above the wind, drew Kira's attention. He was staring intently at the entrance of what had once been a department store, its massive glass doors long since shattered, leaving a dark, inviting maw. Kira felt the familiar prickle of caution, a heightened awareness that always accompanied Ash's signals. He nudged her hand with his wet nose, his gaze fixed on the shadowed interior. It wasn't just a sound or a smell that alerted him; it was a deeper perception, an instinct honed by the very essence of their connection, a resonance that vibrated between them.

"What is it, boy?" Kira murmured, her voice raspy. She kept her movements slow, deliberate, her eyes scanning the debris-strewn pavement around the entrance. The air here felt heavier, charged with a subtle unease. Ash's ears were pricked forward, his body low and ready, a silent guardian assessing the unseen. He seemed to be sensing something beyond the physical, a disturbance in the subtle energies of their environment.

She knew better than to dismiss his instincts. Ash had saved her more times than she could count, his uncanny ability to sense danger a constant marvel. It was more than just a dog's keen senses; it was as if he perceived the world on a different wavelength, a layer of reality that remained hidden from her human perception, yet which she was slowly beginning to feel through their nascent bond. This silent communication, this shared awareness, was both a comfort and a constant reminder of how much they still had to learn about each other, about themselves, about the very nature of their existence.

They approached the store with extreme caution. The entrance was choked with collapsed shelving and the skeletal remains of mannequins, their plastic forms twisted into grotesque shapes. Kira held her breath, straining her ears. The wind still whistled through the broken edifice, but beneath it, she thought she could discern a faint, rhythmic scraping sound, like something heavy being dragged across stone. Ash let out a soft whine, a sound of apprehension, and pressed closer to Kira's leg.

Kira drew the sturdy, sharpened length of rebar she carried for protection, its cold weight a familiar sensation in her hand. She signaled for Ash to stay close, and together, they slipped through the jagged opening. Inside, the darkness was almost absolute, thick with the accumulated dust of years. Motes of light, filtering through the higher breaches in the walls, illuminated spectral shapes – overturned display cases, the ghostly outlines of fallen clothing racks, and everywhere, the pervasive layer of grey detritus.

Ash's keen eyes, adapted to the dim light, seemed to pierce the gloom. He nudged Kira forward, towards the rear of the store, his tail giving a tentative, questioning sweep. The scraping sound was more distinct now, coming from a section of the store that appeared to have partially collapsed, creating a mound of rubble. Kira moved like a predator herself, her steps silent, her focus absolute.

She rounded a toppled display of what might have been electronics, and her breath hitched. In the deepest shadows, a figure was hunched over a pile of debris. It was human, or what passed for human in this broken world – gaunt, clad in tattered rags, and wielding a crude metal shard. The figure was methodically, painstakingly, prying loose a section of what looked like a reinforced floor panel. The scraping sound was the noise of metal against metal, a desperate, solitary effort.

Kira's mind raced. Was this a scavenger, like herself, simply trying to survive? Or was there something more sinister at play? Ash's low growl vibrated in his chest, a clear warning. He sensed no immediate hostility from the figure, but rather a desperate, almost obsessive focus. The tension in his posture suggested a guardedness, an awareness of their presence that went beyond mere sight.

Before Kira could decide on a course of action, the scavenger shifted, and a glint of reflected light caught something clutched in their free hand. It was a small, metallic object, intricately etched with patterns that Kira dimly recognized from the pre-collapse era. A data chip. The scavenger's breath hitched as they fumbled with it, their movements clumsy and hurried.

Suddenly, a loud crack echoed through the store. The floor beneath the scavenger, already weakened by their efforts, gave way with a groan of protesting metal. With a yelp, the figure plunged into the darkness below, the precious data chip skittering from their grasp and disappearing into the newly formed abyss.

Kira rushed forward, Ash right behind her. They peered into the hole. It was a service tunnel, its rusted grate torn open. The scavenger was nowhere to be seen, only the echoing silence and the unsettling possibility of what lay in the depths. Kira knelt at the edge, her heart pounding. Ash nudged her hand, a gesture of comfort and concern.

She looked at the spot where the data chip had fallen. A flicker of something — a sensation, a whisper of thought — passed between her and Ash. It was fleeting, insubstantial, like a dream upon waking, but it was there. A sense of loss, not just for the scavenger, but for the knowledge contained within that small piece of technology. It was a testament to the value of even the most mundane remnants of the past, a potent reminder of what had been lost.

The silence of the ruins pressed in again, heavier now with the echo of that sudden, violent end. Kira stood, her gaze sweeping across the desolate interior of the store. The wind continued its mournful dirge, a constant reminder of their isolation. The scarcity of resources was not just about food and clean water; it was also about the loss of knowledge, the erosion of history, the quiet disappearance of the very things that had once defined humanity. And as she looked at Ash, her steadfast companion, she felt a surge of gratitude for his unwavering presence. In this world of ghosts and echoes, he was her solid, breathing reality, her connection to something vital and true.

They would press on, through the whispering ruins and the encroaching silence, their journey a testament to resilience, a flickering candle of hope in the encroaching darkness. The city was a vast, silent witness to their struggle, and every shadow held a story, every gust of wind a spectral memory. Their path was etched in dust and despair, but guided by a bond that was slowly, profoundly, revealing its true strength.

This connection, she was beginning to realize, was more profound than she had ever imagined. It wasn't just about Ash's keen senses or his loyalty; it was a deeper, more intuitive understanding. When he nudged her, it wasn't just a physical contact; it was a communication of his unease, his caution, and sometimes, his simple affection. She could feel the subtle shifts in his mood, the almost imperceptible tremors of his emotions, and in turn, he seemed to sense hers. This burgeoning empathy, this 'resonance' as some old texts vaguely termed it, was a fragile thread in the vast emptiness of their world, but it was growing stronger with each passing day.

It was in moments like these, observing his quiet concern as they peered into the dark chasm, that Kira felt the true depth of their bond. She felt a phantom echo of his disappointment at the lost data chip, a shared sense of the finality of the scavenger's fate. It was a sensation that was both comforting and unnerving, an intimate glimpse into another being's consciousness. This was not merely training or instinct; it was a nascent form of shared awareness, a subtle intertwining of their minds. She found herself anticipating his reactions, understanding his unspoken needs before he even voiced them, and she suspected, with a growing sense of wonder, that he was doing the same for her.

This resonance, this silent language they were beginning to speak, was their anchor, their compass in the storm. It was the quiet hum of a shared existence, a promise that even in this broken world, they were not entirely alone. The world might have forgotten the intricacies of human connection, but in the primal bond between human and canine, something ancient and vital had reawakened. It was a flicker, a spark, and Kira knew, with a quiet certainty, that it was the beginning of everything.

The dawn, if it could be called that, filtered through the perpetual haze, painting the skeletal cityscape in muted shades of grey and ochre. Kira, already awake, watched the first tentative rays touch the jagged peaks of broken towers. The chill of the pre-dawn air seeped through her layered scavenged clothing, a familiar, unwelcome embrace. Beside her, Ash stirred, a low rumble in his chest, his warm flank pressing against her leg. He knew the routine as well as she did – the meticulous checking of their meager supplies, the quiet assessment of the surrounding ruins, the preparation for another day of painstaking survival.

Her fingers, calloused and stained with dirt and oil, worked with practiced efficiency. First, the water. She unslung her canteen, a battered metal flask salvaged from a military surplus store, its internal filtration system a miracle of pre-collapse engineering that still, against all odds, functioned. She needed to find a source, or at least a place where yesterday's brief, ill-timed shower might have pooled in a protected crevice. Rainwater was a blessing, but even that carried the faint, metallic tang of atmospheric pollutants, a constant reminder of the world's poisoned breath. Every drop was precious, filtered through layers of salvaged charcoal and woven cloth, then passed through the canteen's internal nanite purifier. It was a slow, deliberate process, and the resulting liquid, while safe, tasted faintly of minerals and desperation.

Next, food. The contents of her pack were a grim inventory of their current state: a handful of dried, nutrient-rich algae bars, their texture like compressed sawdust; a small pouch of preserved fruits, their sweetness a sharp, almost painful contrast to their surroundings; and a few strips of dried, gamey meat, a rare treat from a successful hunt weeks ago. The calories were insufficient for sustained exertion, a constant whisper of hunger that had become a permanent resident in her gut. Every meal was a calculated expenditure, a weighing of immediate need against future scarcity.

Her gaze then drifted to the collection of 'useful' items she'd painstakingly gathered yesterday. A spool of sturdy wire, its insulation still mostly intact, useful for repairs or setting snares. A handful of assorted screws and bolts, their threads surprisingly clean. A cracked but functional lens, perhaps from a damaged optical device, which she'd carefully cleaned and wrapped in soft cloth. Each piece was a potential solution, a small victory against the overwhelming tide of decay. But the truly valuable finds, the intact power cells or untarnished communication components, were increasingly rare. The city, once a boundless repository of discarded treasures, was being stripped bare, its secrets slowly yielding to the relentless passage of time and the desperate efforts of scavengers like herself.

Ash nudged her hand, his dark eyes fixed on the direction of the collapsed department store they had explored yesterday. He whined softly, a low, questioning sound. Kira understood. He was restless, sensing the potential for something, perhaps a forgotten cache or even another living being. But the memory of the falling scavenger, the abrupt disappearance into the darkness, was still too fresh. The risks of venturing into unstable structures were always high, a gamble where the house always won.

"Not today, Ash," she murmured, scratching him behind the ears. "Too much risk. We need to be smart about this." Her voice was hoarse, unused. Speaking aloud felt like an extravagance, a waste of precious breath. But Ash needed reassurance, and so did she. The silence could be as dangerous as any physical threat, breeding paranoia and doubt.

Their immediate goal was water. Kira consulted a tattered map, its surface smeared with grime and water stains, highlighting potential collection points. The outline of a vast, underground reservoir, marked with a faded 'R', was circled repeatedly with her charcoal stick. It was a dangerous trek, through sections of the city that had barely survived the initial collapse, now riddled with structural weaknesses and the unseen hazards of chemical leaks. But the promise of a substantial water source, even if it meant navigating treacherous territory, was a necessary risk.

"Come on, boy," she said, heaving her worn backpack onto her shoulders, the familiar weight settling onto her weary frame. Ash rose with fluid grace, his tail giving a single, perfunctory wag. He was ready, his instincts finely tuned to the rhythm of their existence, to the constant, gnawing need for survival.

They moved through the deserted streets, their progress a study in calculated caution. Kira's eyes constantly scanned the buildings, noting the subtle shifts in their angles, the patterns of debris that might indicate a recent collapse. Ash's head was up, his nose twitching, sifting through the myriad scents that permeated the air. He would occasionally pause, cocking his head, then move on, his internal compass guiding them through the labyrinth of ruin.

The scarcity wasn't just about material possessions; it was about information, about the knowledge that had been lost with the collapse. Kira relied heavily on Ash's innate abilities, his heightened senses providing a crucial advantage in a world where danger could lurk in the subtlest of signs. He could detect unstable ground far better than she could, his paws instinctively avoiding treacherous patches of buckled pavement or weakened floorboards. His keen hearing picked up the faint skittering of mutated vermin, the rustle of unseen things in the shadows, sounds that might otherwise go unnoticed.

Their journey towards the reservoir led them through a district that had once been a bustling commercial hub. Now, it was a testament to the speed and ferocity of the collapse. The facades of buildings were pockmarked with explosions, their interiors exposed to the elements like raw wounds. Cars lay overturned, their metal bodies twisted into impossible shapes, long since stripped of any salvageable parts. The wind, ever present, howled through the gaping windows, carrying with it a mournful symphony of creaking metal and groaning structures.

“Good boy,” she murmured, drawing a short, sturdy crowbar from her pack. She moved with deliberate slowness, her eyes fixed on the doorway. The interior was plunged in shadow, the only light filtering through the shattered upper windows, casting long, distorted beams across the debris-strewn floor. Dust motes danced in these shafts of light, a silent, spectral ballet.

Ash padded ahead, his low-slung body moving with an almost feline stealth. He stopped near a pile of fallen filing cabinets, sniffing intently at a gap between two of them. Kira followed, her breath held tight. The air here was thick with the musty odor of decaying paper and stagnant air. She nudged aside a fallen cabinet with her crowbar, revealing a small, metal access panel, its edges corroded but its seal still seemingly intact.

This was the kind of discovery that fueled their continued existence. A hidden cache, a forgotten piece of the past that might hold something of value. Kira worked at the panel, the metal groaning in protest. Ash remained alert, his gaze sweeping the room, a silent guardian against any unforeseen threats. The effort required to pry the panel open was considerable, her muscles burning with the strain. Finally, with a sharp *snap*, the latch broke free.

Inside the small compartment, nestled amongst yellowed documents and a scattering of fossilized pens, was a sealed plastic container. Kira’s heart gave a hopeful leap. She carefully lifted it out. It was a ration pack, a relic from a time when such things were mass-produced for disaster preparedness. Its contents were likely still viable, preserved by the vacuum-sealed packaging. She shook it gently. The contents shifted with a soft rustle. It was a significant find, enough to supplement their meager supplies for several more days.

“See, Ash? You’re a better scout than any of those old pre-collapse navigation systems,” she said, her voice a little stronger with relief. Ash responded with a soft lick to her hand, his amber eyes reflecting the dim light. It was more than just finding supplies; it was the reinforcement of their partnership, the validation of their shared struggle.

Their journey to the reservoir was punctuated by similar small victories and near-misses. They skirted a section of road that Ash clearly deemed unstable, his agitated whining and refusal to proceed a stark warning Kira had learned to trust implicitly. He would sometimes stop dead, his body rigid, and then give a series of low growls, pointing towards a particular building or a shadowed alley. On one occasion, his sharp bark alerted Kira to a nest of mutated rodents, their eyes glowing malevolently in the gloom, forcing them to backtrack and find an alternate route.

The constant vigilance was exhausting, a drain on her mental and physical reserves. Every shadow could conceal danger, every gust of wind could carry the scent of something predatory. The scarcity of resources meant that any setback, any loss of supplies, could be catastrophic. A single wrong turn, a misjudged step, could have dire consequences. This precarious existence bred a deep-seated caution, a meticulousness in every action, from the way she packed her bag to the way she rationed her last drops of water.

The reliance on Ash was absolute. He was her early warning system, her guide through the treacherous ruins, and her emotional anchor in a world devoid of comfort. When her own resolve faltered, when the sheer weight of their struggle threatened to crush her, Ash's steady presence, the warmth of his body against hers, the unwavering loyalty in his eyes, would pull her back from the brink. He didn't understand the abstract concepts of hope or despair, but he understood the need for survival, and his unwavering commitment to that goal was a constant source of strength for her.

As they finally approached the area marked as the reservoir, the landscape shifted. The skeletal skyscrapers gave way to a more open, albeit equally devastated, expanse. A vast, concrete structure, its upper levels crumbling, rose before them – the former main pumping station of the city's water system. Kira felt a surge of cautious optimism. If there was a reservoir, it would likely be connected to this behemoth of pre-collapse engineering.

Ash, however, seemed hesitant. He moved with a different kind of alertness now, his senses picking up a new set of stimuli. He whined softly, his gaze fixed on the massive concrete edifice. Kira felt it too, a subtle shift in the atmosphere, a barely perceptible hum that seemed to emanate from the structure itself. It wasn't the wind, nor the creaking of failing metal. It was something else, something... artificial.

She followed Ash's lead, moving around the perimeter of the pumping station. The air grew colder, carrying with it the faint, unmistakable scent of ozone. It was a scent Kira associated with active, albeit ancient, technology. Pre-collapse tech was often a fickle mistress, capable of both miraculous feats and sudden, catastrophic failures.

They found an opening, a gaping maw where a large section of the wall had buckled inwards, revealing the dark, cavernous interior. Ash nudged her forward, his hesitation tempered by a burgeoning curiosity. The promise of water, of a reliable source, was a powerful motivator. But the faint hum, the scent of ozone, set Kira's teeth on edge. The scavenger's fate, the abrupt end to their solitary quest, had left a lingering unease. She knew that even in this broken world, there were still dangers that transcended mere structural instability.

As they stepped through the breach, the hum grew louder, more pronounced. It was a low, resonant frequency, vibrating through the very concrete beneath their feet. The interior was a vast, dimly lit space, filled with colossal, rusted machinery, its purpose now lost to time. Pipes, thick as trees, snaked across the ceiling and walls, some ruptured and weeping slow, viscous fluids, others surprisingly intact. The air was heavy with the scent of damp concrete, stagnant water, and that persistent, unsettling ozone.

Ash's body tensed. He moved closer to Kira, his hackles slightly raised. He wasn't growling, but there was a palpable tension in his posture, a deep-seated awareness of something... other. Kira felt a prickle of apprehension crawl up her spine. This place felt different, charged with an energy that felt both ancient and disturbingly alive. The true burden of their scavenging wasn't just the physical exertion, but the constant, gnawing uncertainty, the knowledge that every find could be a trap, every step forward a gamble. The scarcity had forged a deep reliance on instinct, on the bond she shared with Ash, but even that felt tested in the echoing silence of this forgotten monument to a world that had once believed itself invincible.

The vast, decaying pumping station hummed with a latent energy that vibrated deep within Kira's bones. The ozone scent was stronger here, sharper, laced with the metallic tang of ancient machinery. Ash, usually a creature of predictable instincts, moved with an unnerving stillness, his amber eyes wide, scanning the colossal, rusted components that loomed in the dim light. He wasn't growling, but the subtle tension in his shoulders, the slight flattening of his ears, spoke volumes. Kira mirrored his unease, her hand instinctively tightening around the worn leather grip of her crowbar. The silence within the structure was broken only by the drip of unseen water and that persistent, low hum, a lullaby of decay.

It was while carefully navigating a precarious catwalk, its metal grating groaning under her weight, that she found it. Tucked away in a small, recessed alcove, almost hidden by a cascade of thick, fibrous moss, lay an object that seemed utterly out of place. It was small, no larger than her thumb, and fashioned from a material she couldn't immediately identify. It wasn't metal, nor was it the brittle plastic of discarded technology. It had a matte, almost organic finish, a deep, iridescent black that seemed to absorb the meager light. Shaped like a flattened teardrop, its surface was etched with incredibly fine, geometric patterns, too precise to be accidental, too intricate to be merely decorative.

Kira knelt, her movements slow and deliberate, Ash watching her with a quiet intensity. She reached out, her fingers brushing against the cool, smooth surface. As her skin made contact, a jolt, not of electricity but of something far more profound, shot through her. It was like a sudden, sharp intake of breath in a world that had long forgotten how to exhale. For a fleeting moment, the oppressive silence of the pumping station receded, replaced by a chorus of phantom whispers, a symphony of forgotten sounds.

She saw flashes, not with her eyes, but within her mind. Images, indistinct yet potent, of soaring structures that pierced the sky, of vehicles gliding effortlessly through pristine air, of faces – myriad faces, vibrant and alive – bathed in sunlight. It was like glimpsing a universe through a hairline crack. These weren't her memories, not consciously. They were fragments, echoes, impressions that felt alien yet strangely familiar. A street scene, bustling with people, vibrant with color. A moment of intense concentration, as someone manipulated a glowing interface. A feeling of profound loss, sharp and piercing, like a physical blow.

Ash nudged her hand, his wet nose pressing against her palm. The sensation intensified. It was as if his presence acted as a conduit, amplifying this strange resonance. He whined, a low, questioning sound that seemed to carry a hint of recognition. His tail, usually so expressive, was tucked low, his body language a picture of profound, almost reverent, apprehension.

Kira carefully picked up the artifact. It felt strangely warm now, pulsing with a faint, internal rhythm. The etched patterns seemed to shift and rearrange themselves, a silent, alien language unfolding before her eyes. She turned it over and over, her mind reeling from the sensory overload. What was this? A data storage device? A personal log? It felt older than anything she had ever encountered, a relic from a time before the Great Collapse, perhaps even before the civilization that had built this monstrous pumping station.

The fragmented memories, or whatever they were, continued to surface, triggered by the object and Ash's nearness. They were like shards of a shattered mirror, reflecting glimpses of a world she could only dream of. She saw a sterile laboratory, filled with blinking lights and humming machinery. She felt a sense of purpose, a deep-seated drive to understand, to unravel secrets. There was a woman's voice, calm and authoritative, explaining a complex process. And then, a chilling sense of dread, of things going terribly wrong, of panic and desperation.

The resonance wasn't just about present danger; it was a gateway. A gateway to the past. The implications were staggering. If this artifact, coupled with Ash's unique connection to her, could unlock these latent memories, what else could it do? Could it reveal the truth behind the Collapse? Could it offer solutions, forgotten knowledge that might lead to a different future? The thought was both exhilarating and terrifying.

She gently placed the artifact into a small, padded pouch within her pack, a place reserved for the most delicate of her finds. The residual warmth of the object seemed to linger on her skin, a phantom touch that spoke of possibilities. Ash stayed close, his body a solid, comforting presence against her leg. He seemed to understand the significance of her discovery, his usual predatory alertness replaced by a watchful, almost protective, stillness.

Their immediate goal of finding water still remained, but a new, far more compelling quest had emerged from the shadows of this ancient structure. The artifact was a mystery, a key to a lock she hadn't known existed. And Ash, with his uncanny sensitivity, was inextricably linked to its unlocking.

They moved deeper into the pumping station, the hum of latent technology a constant companion. Kira's senses were heightened, not just by the threat of the environment, but by the potential for further revelations. She felt a strange connection to the very walls around them, as if the building itself was trying to communicate, its decaying heart echoing with the whispers of its former life.

Ash nudged her towards a large, open chamber, dominated by a colossal, defunct turbine. It was here that the ozone scent was strongest, and the hum was almost a physical presence, a low thrum that resonated in the marrow of her bones. In the center of the chamber, bathed in a faint, ethereal glow emanating from some unseen source, stood a console, its screens dark, its controls encased in dust.

Hesitantly, Kira approached it. The artifact in her pouch seemed to pulse in time with the building's hum. As she neared the console, the etched patterns on the artifact shifted more rapidly, a silent, urgent message. She reached into her pouch, her fingers closing around the smooth, black teardrop.

The moment her fingers touched the artifact, the dormant screens of the console flickered to life. Not with images of the past, but with a complex, three-dimensional schematic of the pumping station itself. Lines of glowing data scrolled across the displays, detailing flow rates, pressure gauges, and reservoir levels. It was a map, a blueprint of a forgotten operational system.

But more than that, as Kira held the artifact, the schematic began to morph. Sections of the building dissolved, revealing the vast network of tunnels and conduits that lay beneath. And then, a new set of data appeared, overlaid on the existing schematics: faint, pulsing nodes of energy, scattered throughout the city's subterranean infrastructure. They were weak, sporadic, but undeniable. Traces of something... active.

Ash whined again, a low, almost mournful sound. He pressed his head against her arm, his eyes fixed on one particular node highlighted on the console's display – a location far from their current position, deep within the city's forgotten underbelly.

Kira's mind raced. This artifact wasn't just a passive repository of memories; it was an active interface, a device capable of interacting with dormant systems. And Ash, in his silent, intuitive way, was guiding her to something of immense importance. The energy signatures were too patterned, too deliberate, to be natural. They spoke of purpose, of remnants of the pre-collapse world that had somehow survived, or perhaps even reactivated.

The whispers of the past were growing louder, more coherent. She saw fleeting glimpses of a woman in a pristine lab coat, her face etched with determination. She heard fragments of conversations about "resonance amplification" and "data retrieval." It was a language she was beginning to understand, a science that had been lost to the ravages of time. The artifact and Ash were not just helping her survive; they were opening a door to a forgotten history, a history that might hold the key to their own survival, and perhaps, to the rebirth of something greater.

The discovery of the artifact had irrevocably altered the trajectory of their immediate quest. The need for water was still pressing, but the faint hum of active energy signatures, guided by the silent wisdom of her canine companion and amplified by the cryptic artifact, now drew her towards a more profound and perilous exploration. The echoes of the past were not just whispers in the wind; they were a tangible force, a siren song calling her towards the heart of the city's forgotten secrets. The pumping station, once a mere waypoint, had become the genesis of a new, far more intricate and dangerous journey.

As they finally located a serviceable tap within the pumping station, its water still tasting faintly of minerals and the lingering ozone, Kira's thoughts were consumed by the small, black teardrop nestled safely in her pouch. The journey ahead was uncertain, fraught with dangers she could only begin to imagine. But for the first time since the world had ended, a flicker of genuine hope, fueled by the echoes of a forgotten past and the unwavering loyalty of a creature who bridged the gap between instinct and something far more profound, began to stir within her. The resonance, she realized, was not just a phenomenon; it was a promise.

The oppressive silence of the pumping station, which had been the backdrop to Kira's profound discovery, shattered with a violent roar. It wasn't the familiar groan of failing machinery or the settling sighs of a decaying behemoth. This was a sharp, tearing sound, like the sky itself ripping open. A guttural hiss followed, an insidious sound that pricked Kira's skin and made the hairs on her arms stand on end. Ash, who had been resting his head on her lap, was instantly on his feet, a low growl rumbling in his chest. His amber eyes, usually so expressive, were now narrowed slits, fixed on a section of the cavernous ceiling far above.

Kira scrambled to her feet, her heart leaping into her throat. She followed Ash's gaze. Directly overhead, where a massive network of rusted pipes converged, a dark stain was spreading with alarming speed. It wasn't water. It was thicker, more viscous, and seemed to shimmer with an unnatural, sickly green luminescence. The hiss intensified, accompanied by a pungent, acrid odor that burned her nostrils and stung her eyes. It was the smell of decay, yes, but amplified, twisted into something toxic, something actively hostile. A localized gas leak, she realized with a sickening lurch. The pumping station, a tomb of forgotten technology, was finally exhaling its last, poisoned breath.

"Ash, we need to move!" Kira's voice was tight, strained. She instinctively reached for her crowbar, but the gas was already beginning to seep down, forming a shimmering, almost visible curtain. Panic, cold and sharp, threatened to overwhelm her. She felt a prickling sensation on her exposed skin, a subtle burning that she knew, with terrifying certainty, would only worsen. The artifact in her pouch felt warm, almost pulsing against her hip, a strange counterpoint to the growing terror.

Ash didn't hesitate. He nudged her forcefully with his head, a clear directive to move away from the encroaching cloud. He then turned and bolted, not in a blind panic, but with a focused urgency, heading towards a narrow access tunnel they had noted earlier. Kira, trusting his instinct implicitly, followed, her lungs already starting to burn. The air was becoming thick, unbreathable. Each inhale was a gamble, a painful exposure to the noxious fumes.

As they ran, the hiss grew louder, punctuated by the sickening sounds of metal succumbing to the corrosive agent. Bits of rust and debris rained down from above, showering them as they plunged into the relative darkness of the tunnel. The air here was marginally better, less saturated with the toxic mist, but the pervasive smell still clung to everything. Kira risked a glance back. The main chamber of the pumping station was rapidly becoming obscured by the churning green haze. It was as if the very lifeblood of the ancient structure was being poisoned, and it was spilling out to claim everything in its path.

The tunnel was narrow and winding, forcing Kira to duck and weave. Ash moved ahead of her, his low profile an advantage, his paws finding purchase on the uneven floor with practiced ease. He would pause at junctions, looking back to ensure she was still with him, his body language radiating a quiet reassurance that belied the immediate danger. Kira's trust in him, already burgeoning, solidified into something absolute. He wasn't just a companion; he was an extension of her own survival instinct, amplified and honed by senses she could only dimly perceive.

The resonance, the subtle connection that had bloomed in the presence of the artifact, felt different now. It wasn't just about glimpses of the past or a heightened awareness of dormant technology. It was a visceral, immediate awareness of Ash's intentions, his emotions, his very being. As they navigated the labyrinthine tunnels, she felt his focus, his drive, his absolute determination to keep them both safe. It was a silent conversation, a shared understanding that transcended spoken words.

They emerged from the tunnel into a different section of the pumping station, one that seemed to be a series of maintenance shafts and control rooms. The air here was stale but breathable, a blessed relief after the toxic miasma they had escaped. Kira slumped against a grimy wall, gasping for air, her muscles trembling with exertion and adrenaline. Ash immediately came to her side, nudging her face with his nose, his tail giving a tentative wag. His presence was a grounding force, a solid anchor in the chaos.

"We made it, Ash," she murmured, her voice hoarse. She reached into her pouch and carefully touched the artifact. It was still warm, a subtle vibration emanating from it.

She felt a faint echo of Ash's own apprehension, a shared sense of relief, and something else... a flicker of curiosity, a nascent understanding of the event they had just survived. The artifact seemed to be acting as a catalyst, not only for unlocking the past but also for deepening their connection.

As Kira's breathing steadied, she noticed that Ash was now intently focused on a different part of this new chamber. It was a smaller room, cluttered with defunct consoles and scattered tools, but at its center stood a peculiar piece of equipment. It resembled a sealed containment unit, its glass front opaque with grime and age. Ash whined softly, a low, inquisitive sound, and nudged his head towards it.

Hesitantly, Kira approached. The artifact in her pouch pulsed, a subtle warmth radiating through the leather. As she drew nearer to the containment unit, she felt a strange tug, a sense of familiarity that prickled at the edges of her awareness. She wiped away some of the grime from the glass with her sleeve. Beneath the layer of filth, she could discern faint markings, not etched or printed, but seemingly embedded within the very material of the unit. They were abstract, fluid shapes, unlike the precise geometric patterns on the artifact, yet they seemed to resonate with it.

Ash nudged her again, his gaze shifting from the containment unit to a small, recessed panel on the wall beside it. It looked like a power conduit, long since dead. But the artifact, held in her hand, seemed to hum with a subtle energy. Kira's mind raced. The gas leak had been a sudden, unexpected environmental hazard, a direct threat that had forced them to rely on instinct and their nascent bond. Ash's heightened senses had warned her, and his decisive action had led them to safety. But now, this new discovery, this containment unit, felt like a continuation of the first test.

She took a deep breath and stepped closer to the panel, the artifact held out before her. As she neared it, a faint glow emanated from the black teardrop. The panel, which had appeared inert moments before, flickered with a soft, internal light. It wasn't electrical power as she understood it; it was something else, something tied to the resonance, to the artifact itself. The abstract markings on the containment unit began to glow faintly, mirroring the pulsating light from her hand.

Kira felt a surge of adrenaline mixed with a profound sense of wonder. This was it. This was the next step. The environmental hazard had been a brutal, albeit effective, demonstration of their combined survival capabilities. Ash's instinctive awareness and her growing trust in their bond had saved them. But this... this felt like a test of understanding, a challenge to unravel a deeper layer of the mystery.

She placed her hand, still holding the artifact, against the glowing panel. The effect was instantaneous and dramatic. The entire containment unit hummed to life. The opaque glass cleared, revealing its contents. It was a small, metallic sphere, intricately crafted, its surface etched with a complex lattice of glowing lines. And surrounding it, within the sealed chamber, was a swirling cloud of shimmering, iridescent particles.

The artifact in her hand pulsed more strongly now, a steady, rhythmic beat. Kira felt a wave of information wash over her, not in images or sounds, but as pure data, an intuitive understanding that bypassed her conscious thought. The sphere was a 'beacon,' designed to attract and concentrate residual atmospheric energy. The iridescent particles were the captured energy itself, harvested and stored. And the containment unit was a 'stabilizer,' designed to maintain the integrity of the captured energy.

Ash let out a soft chuff, his tail wagging more enthusiastically now. He seemed to recognize the significance of the sphere, his senses picking up on something Kira could only perceive through the artifact's amplified resonance. He nudged her hand, then looked towards the artifact, then back at the sphere, as if urging her to connect them.

Kira understood. The artifact wasn't just a key; it was also a transmitter, a device capable of interacting with other pre-Collapse technologies. The resonance between her, Ash, and the artifact was the conduit. The gas leak had been an accidental trigger, a demonstration of their immediate, reactive survival. This was a deliberate challenge, a test of their ability to actively engage with the dormant systems of the past.

She carefully maneuvered the artifact closer to the containment unit, bringing it into direct proximity with the glowing sphere. The moment they touched, a cascade of light erupted. The sphere pulsed, sending a beam of concentrated energy directly into the artifact. The geometric patterns on its surface flared, shifting and reconfiguring at an astonishing speed. Kira felt a powerful surge, not of physical energy, but of mental clarity. The fragmented echoes of the past, which had been like scattered whispers before, now coalesced into a more coherent stream.

She saw a woman's face, clear and defined, her expression one of intense focus. She was in a laboratory, surrounded by similar containment units and glowing spheres. There was a sense of urgency in her movements, a desperate race against time. Kira felt the woman's thought, her desperate plea: "The resonance must be amplified. The energy... it's all that's left."

The woman was clearly the creator, or at least a guardian, of these technologies. And the artifact, Kira realized, was not just a data storage device or a passive relic. It was an active component, a vital link in a chain of forgotten science. The sphere, with its captured atmospheric energy, and the artifact, with its ability to interface and transmit, were designed to work together.

Ash whined again, nudging her hand, his gaze fixed on the sphere within the containment unit. He seemed to be sensing not just the energy, but its purpose, its ultimate destination. Kira felt a dawning understanding. The artifact had shown her fragmented memories of a dying world, a desperate attempt to preserve something vital. The beacon and the sphere were part of that attempt, a means of collecting and perhaps re-disseminating a form of energy that had been fundamental to their civilization.

The resonance was growing stronger, more complex. It wasn't just a passive connection anymore; it was an active dialogue. Kira felt Ash's eager anticipation, his instinctual understanding of the energy emanating from the sphere. He wasn't just reacting to the light; he was sensing its underlying structure, its potential. And through their shared connection, Kira was beginning to perceive it too.

She carefully withdrew the artifact, the sphere's captured energy now integrated into its very fabric. The light from the containment unit dimmed, the glass returning to its opaque state, the swirling particles dissipating. The chamber was silent once more, save for the steady, rhythmic hum that now emanated from the artifact in her palm. It was a hum that resonated not just in her bones, but in her very consciousness.

This was their first true test, a crucible forged by both a deadly environmental hazard and the awakening of dormant technology. The gas leak had forced them to act, to rely on instinct and the nascent bond between them. Ash's foresight and her own growing trust had been their shield. But this interaction with the containment unit, guided by the artifact, was a test of understanding, a demonstration of their potential to not just survive, but to actively engage with the legacy of the past.

Kira looked at Ash, her heart swelling with a profound gratitude. He had led her through the toxic cloud, his unwavering presence a beacon in the suffocating darkness. And now, he was here, a silent partner in deciphering the secrets of this ancient world. The artifact in her hand was no longer just a mysterious object; it was a key, and Ash was the unlock. Their bond, forged in the fires of necessity and deepened by the echoes of a forgotten era, was proving to be their most valuable asset. The world outside remained a desolate wasteland, but within the decaying heart of this pumping station, a new path, illuminated by the faint glow of possibility, was beginning to emerge. The whispers of the past were no longer mere echoes; they were a burgeoning song, and Kira, with Ash by her side, was ready to listen.

CHAPTER 2

The air grew thinner, the oppressive silence of the pumping station gradually replaced by the gentle murmur of wind whistling through unseen cracks. Kira emerged from the labyrinthine tunnels, Ash trotting faithfully beside her, his amber eyes scanning their new surroundings. The suffocating, toxic fumes of the station had been a brutal test, but one that had solidified their bond, sharpening Kira's awareness of Ash's presence, his instincts, his unwavering loyalty. The artifact, now humming with a steady, internal rhythm against her hip, felt like an extension of herself, a constant reminder of the resonant connection that had been awakened within them. They had survived the immediate danger, the pumping station's dying, poisoned breath, but the world outside remained a vast, unknown territory.

Their journey through the ruins had been a brutal education in survival. The pumping station, a relic of a forgotten era, had offered shelter and revealed profound secrets, but it was a tomb, a place of decay and dangerous exhalations. Kira had learned to trust Ash implicitly, his senses guiding her through darkness and toxic miasmas, his presence a grounding force against the overwhelming vastness of their predicament. The artifact was a mystery, a conduit to a past she was only beginning to comprehend, but the resonance between her and Ash, that silent, intuitive understanding, was the truest discovery. It was a bond forged in shared fear and nascent hope, a promise of something more in this broken world.

As they ventured further from the immediate vicinity of the pumping station, the landscape slowly shifted. The jagged ruins gave way to stretches of cracked earth and sparse, hardy vegetation clinging stubbornly to life. The sky, a perpetual, muted grey, offered no comfort, but the air, while still carrying the scent of dust and decay, was breathable, blessedly free of the acrid bite that had threatened to consume them. Ash, his usual keen interest piqued, kept his nose to the ground, cataloging the faint scents of the wasteland, his tail giving an occasional, almost imperceptible twitch. Kira, her senses still heightened by the recent ordeal, felt a subtle shift in the ambient energy, a faint hum that seemed to echo the thrumming of the artifact.

It was Ash who first detected the anomaly. He stopped abruptly, his ears perked forward, his body tensed. A low, inquisitive growl rumbled in his chest. Kira followed his gaze to a distant ridge, where a cluster of structures, seemingly cobbled together from salvaged metal and scavenged materials, huddled against the encroaching twilight. It was small, almost an afterthought against the vast desolation, but there was a discernible pattern to its existence, a sense of purpose that set it apart from the random scatterings of debris. It was unlike anything Kira had encountered in her solitary travels.

The closer they drew, the more evident the signs of human habitation became. A faint plume of smoke curled upwards from a makeshift chimney, a stark contrast to the pervasive stillness of the surrounding landscape. There were rudimentary fortifications, walls constructed from stacked car chassis and reinforced plating, designed to ward off both the elements and the less welcome inhabitants of this world. A gate, fashioned from what looked like an old industrial conveyor belt, stood partially ajar, an invitation and a warning. This was not merely a random encampment; it was a sanctuary, a deliberate act of defiance against the encroaching wilderness.

Kira hesitated, a knot of apprehension tightening in her stomach. After the profound isolation she had endured, the thought of encountering other humans was both a relief and a source of profound unease. What if they were hostile? What if they viewed her and Ash, with the artifact radiating its subtle energy, with suspicion or greed? Yet, the resilience of the structures, the faint tendrils of smoke, spoke of a community, of people who had found a way to carve out an existence, to survive. It was a beacon of hope in a world that offered little.

Ash nudged her hand, a low, encouraging sound emanating from him. His amber eyes, usually so expressive, held a steady, unwavering gaze, a silent reassurance. He seemed to sense her hesitation, her fear, and his simple, physical presence was a balm. He had become her anchor, her constant, and she trusted his instincts implicitly. If he sensed no immediate threat, then perhaps this place was worth investigating. With a shared glance, a silent agreement passing between them, they approached the gate.

As they drew closer, figures emerged from the makeshift structures, their movements cautious, their gazes sharp and assessing. They were a motley collection of individuals, their clothing patched and worn, their faces etched with the hardships of their lives. But there was no immediate aggression in their posture, only a guarded curiosity.

One of them, a woman with streaks of grey in her dark hair and a scarred, weathered face, stepped forward. Her eyes, however, held a spark of intelligence, a warmth that belied the harshness of her surroundings. She carried a crude, spear-like weapon, but it was held loosely, more for defense than offense.

"Who goes there?" her voice was rough, but steady. "State your purpose."

Kira's throat felt dry. She took a deep breath, trying to project a calmness she didn't entirely feel. "My name is Kira, and this is Ash. We are travelers. We mean no harm."

The woman regarded them for a long moment, her gaze lingering on Ash, then on the subtle bulge beneath Kira's worn jacket where the artifact rested. Her expression shifted, a flicker of recognition, perhaps, or understanding.

"Travelers," she repeated, her tone softening slightly. "Few travel this far out. Come inside. You look like you could use some water and a place to rest your weary bones." She gestured towards the open gate. "This is Haven. And we don't turn away those who seek shelter."

Hesitantly, Kira stepped through the gate, Ash following her closely. The interior of Haven was a testament to ingenuity and perseverance. The structures were indeed a patchwork, but they were sturdy, built with a pragmatic understanding of the environment. Shelters were fashioned from corrugated metal, salvaged shipping containers, and even repurposed vehicle shells. A central clearing served as a communal space, dominated by a well, its stone casing worn smooth by countless hands. In the center of this clearing, a fire crackled merrily, casting dancing shadows and providing a welcome warmth.

As they entered, a ripple of hushed murmurs spread through the gathered inhabitants. Eyes followed them, not with outright hostility, but with an undeniable curiosity. Kira felt a prickle of self-consciousness, acutely aware of her solitude and the strangeness of her companion. Ash, however, seemed unperturbed. He walked with a quiet confidence, his senses absorbing the new environment, his presence radiating a calming aura.

The woman who had greeted them, who introduced herself as Mara, the de facto leader of Haven, led them towards the communal fire. "We don't get many newcomers," she explained, her voice carrying easily over the low hum of conversation. "Most folks stay closer to the known settlements, or they... well, they don't make it this far." She paused, her gaze drifting to Ash again. "You have a companion with you. A strong one."

Kira nodded, her hand instinctively touching the artifact. "He's... he's important to me. He's more than just a pet."

Mara's eyes widened slightly, a subtle shift in her demeanor. "I see. We have a few like you here. Not many, but enough. Enough to know what we're looking at." She gestured to a rough-hewn bench near the fire. "Sit. Rest. I'll get you some water."

As Mara moved away, Kira settled onto the bench, Ash settling at her feet, his head resting on his paws, but his eyes still alert. The warmth of the fire was a comfort, and the simple act of being in a place with others, even strangers, felt strangely grounding. She observed the people of Haven. They were a diverse group, but there was a palpable sense of shared purpose, of mutual reliance.

She noticed several individuals who seemed to possess an unusual awareness, a heightened sensitivity to their surroundings. A young man, no older than Kira herself, sat sketching in a worn notebook, his hand moving with an almost preternatural speed and accuracy, capturing the subtle shifts in the firelight with an uncanny precision. His companion, a sleek, black cat with luminous green eyes, sat beside him, its tail flicking rhythmically, as if in time with the young man's movements. Kira felt a faint resonance emanating from them, a connection as subtle as the whisper of the wind.

Nearby, an older couple sat talking quietly. The woman's hands moved with a delicate grace, arranging pebbles and small, smooth stones into intricate patterns on the ground. As she worked, a faint, iridescent shimmer seemed to emanate from her fingertips, and the stones themselves seemed to glow with an inner light for fleeting moments. Her partner watched her, his gaze filled with a quiet adoration, his hand resting gently on her arm. Kira felt a powerful surge of warmth from them, a deep, abiding connection that radiated outwards, comforting and serene.

These were the resonant pairs Mara had spoken of. Kira had only encountered the nascent stages of her own connection with Ash, a connection amplified by the artifact. But here, in Haven, it seemed to be an openly acknowledged aspect of life. The artifact's hum, previously a solitary melody in her world, now felt like a part of a larger, more complex symphony.

Mara returned with two clay cups of water, cool and surprisingly pure. "From the well," she explained, handing one to Kira. "It's deeper than most, taps into an older vein. Seems to carry... something more than just water." She handed the other cup to Ash, who lapped it up gratefully, his tail giving a slow, appreciative thump against the ground.

"Thank you," Kira said, her voice still a little hoarse. "This place... it's remarkable."

Mara gave a wry smile. "It's home. We built it because we had to. And because we found others like us. Folks who felt the world differently. Who understood that some things run deeper than what you can see." She sat down beside Kira, her gaze thoughtful. "The resonance. It's a gift, and sometimes, a curse. It can make you see things, feel things, that others can't. It can warn you, guide you, even protect you. But it can also make you a target."

Kira's hand tightened around the artifact, still concealed beneath her jacket. "I understand." She hesitated, then decided to risk it. "I have... something that amplifies it. Or perhaps, it was already there, and this just... awakened it."

Mara's eyes widened with keen interest. "An artifact? We've heard whispers. Rumors from the old days. Objects imbued with the power of the resonance, or the energy that fueled it. If that's what you carry, it's... significant."

The weight of the artifact, both physical and metaphorical, pressed down on Kira. She had stumbled upon something ancient and powerful, something that had drawn her and Ash together, and now she had found a community that understood, or at least recognized, its potential.

"It's complicated," Kira admitted. "It showed me things. Helped me understand Ash better. And it... it seems to react to other things." She thought of the containment unit at the pumping station, the way the artifact had pulsed in response.

"That's the nature of it," Mara confirmed. "It's not a static thing. It connects; it interacts. We've seen it in our own ways. Elias," she gestured to the young artist, "his cat, Luna, can sense shifts in the air, changes in people's moods, before he even does. It's a subtle thing, but it's there. And for Anya and Finn," she indicated the older couple, "their connection allows them to find lost things, to sense pockets of residual energy that might be useful. It's always different, always personal, but the core is the same: a shared awareness, a deeper bond."

Kira watched Anya and Finn. Anya was now carefully placing a small, polished stone into a hollow in the ground, and Finn, with a gentle smile, was placing his hand over it, his eyes closed. Kira felt a faint, warm pulse emanates from them, a silent affirmation of their connection. It was a quiet strength, a powerful intimacy that resonated deep within her.

"The resonance," Kira mused aloud, the word feeling more natural now, less alien. "It's about connection, isn't it? A deeper understanding between us, and perhaps with the world around us."

"Precisely," Mara said, her gaze steady. "It's what makes us more than just survivors. It's what makes us... us. It's what allows us to build something like Haven, to find hope in the ruins. But it also makes us vulnerable. The old world feared it, tried to control it, or worse, erase it. And those who still hold onto the old ways, the powers that be, they'd see us as anomalies, threats."

Kira felt a chill despite the fire's warmth. She had been so focused on the personal journey, on understanding her connection with Ash and the artifact, that she hadn't fully considered the broader implications. The idea of being hunted, of being a target, was a sobering thought.

"So, this is a sanctuary?" Kira asked. "A place for people likes us?"

"It is," Mara confirmed. "A place to learn, to grow, to protect each other. We share what we know, what we discover. We help each other hone our abilities, understand the nuances of the resonance. We've learned a great deal, piecing together fragments of knowledge, observing each other's gifts."

Kira watched the other pairs. Elias and Luna were now communicating in a series of gestures and soft chirps, a silent dialogue that seemed to flow effortlessly between them. Anya and Finn were sitting together, their hands intertwined, a quiet contentment radiating from them. There was a palpable sense of ease, of belonging, that Kira had never experienced before. She felt a tentative tug, a nascent sense of belonging, a quiet yearning to be a part of this community.

"How do you... practice it?" Kira asked, her voice barely a whisper. "The resonance?"

Mara smiled, a genuine, warm expression. "It's not something you force, not entirely.

It's about being open, being present. It's about listening, not just with your ears, but with your whole being. For some, it's about observation, like Elias. For others, it's about empathy, a shared emotional landscape, like Finn and Anya. And for you and Ash," she looked at Kira, her gaze sharp and knowing, "it seems to be about a deep, instinctive understanding, amplified by something more tangible."

Kira thought of the artifact, its steady hum, its connection to the sphere in the pumping station. It was more than just instinct; it was a conduit, a bridge between the physical and the energetic.

"I have this artifact," Kira began, deciding to be more open. "It pulses, and it... it seems to enhance the connection between me and Ash. It reacted to something at the pumping station, a containment unit. It showed me... glimpses of the past. A woman, working with these devices."

Mara's eyes lit up with a fierce intensity. "The old technologies! We've only found fragments, hints of what they were capable of. Devices designed to harness or amplify the resonance, to store energy, perhaps even to communicate across vast distances. If you have one, Kira, that changes things. That's... that's a key to understanding so much of what was lost."

The implications settled upon Kira with a sudden, profound weight. She wasn't just a traveler with a strange companion and a curious object. She was part of something larger, something that had the potential to unravel the secrets of a lost civilization, to reclaim a forgotten power.

"There was a beacon," Kira explained, recounting the details of her discovery. "And a stabilizer. They were designed to work together, to harvest and store atmospheric energy. The resonance... it was needed to activate them, to amplify it."

Mara listened with rapt attention, her usual stoicism replaced by a barely contained excitement. "The old world was built on this energy, this resonance. They understood it. We are only just beginning to remember. Your artifact, Kira, it might be more than just a key. It might be a blueprint. A way to bring back what was lost."

As they spoke, Kira felt Ash stir. He rose, stretching languidly, and then nudged Kira's hand with his nose. His gaze was fixed on a corner of Haven, where a small, solitary structure stood slightly apart from the others. It was a simple, dome-shaped dwelling, constructed from a woven material that seemed to shimmer faintly in the firelight. A gentle, steady hum, similar to the one emanating from Kira's artifact, emanated from it.

"What is that?" Kira asked, following Ash's gaze.

"That," Mara said, her voice hushed with reverence, "is where we keep our own find. A resonance amplifier. Or at least, that's what we believe it is. It's been here for generations, a mystery. No one can fully activate it, but it seems to enhance the resonance in its vicinity. It's why Haven is built where it is, why we thrive."

Kira's heart pounded. An amplifier. A place where the resonance was already present, already active. It was a beacon, a signal, drawing her in. Ash whined softly, a sound of pure curiosity and anticipation. He nudged her again, then looked towards the solitary dwelling.

"It feels... familiar," Kira whispered, touching the artifact. The hum intensified, a direct response to the faint energy emanating from the dome.

Mara watched them, a knowing smile playing on her lips. "It seems your artifact has found its place. Or perhaps, it has found you, and it is guiding you to where you need to be." She stood up, stretching her arms. "Welcome to Haven, Kira. You and Ash are not alone here. You have found a home, and perhaps, a purpose."

The fire crackled, casting a warm glow on the faces of the community. The wind whispered through the makeshift structures, carrying with it the scent of smoke and resilience. Kira looked at Ash, his amber eyes reflecting the firelight, a silent testament to their shared journey. She looked at Mara, a beacon of strength and understanding in this fractured world. And she looked towards the shimmering dome, a promise of answers, of connection, of a future she was only just beginning to comprehend. The solitude of her past had been a harsh teacher, but it had also prepared her for this moment, for the possibility of belonging, for the shared journey that lay ahead in the community of Haven. The resonance, once a solitary whisper, was now a chorus, and Kira, with Ash by her side, was ready to join the song.

The air within Haven, though still carrying the faint, metallic tang of salvaged materials and the ever-present scent of woodsmoke, felt different now. It was a sanctuary, yes, but more than that, it was a crucible of shared experience and divergent philosophies. Kira, with Ash a warm weight at her feet, found herself drawn into conversations that vibrated with a new kind of energy – the energy of the resonance, spoken aloud, debated, and dissected. The artifact nestled against her hip pulsed with a steady rhythm, a silent affirmation of the currents flowing through this small community.

"It's our salvation, plain and simple," Elias declared, his voice ringing with youthful conviction. He gestured with a charcoal-smudged hand towards his companion, Luna, who blinked her luminous green eyes in agreement from her perch on his shoulder. "Think about it, Kira. The water we drink? Anya and Finn found the deepest well, the one that taps into the pure, untainted sources, because they could *feel* it. They felt the earth's thirst, the water's presence beneath the cracked surface. They don't just predict the weather; they *anticipate* it, like a sigh from the planet itself. Luna here, she can tell when a storm is brewing hours before the sky even darkens. This isn't magic; it's just... a deeper understanding."

His words painted a picture of a world reborn, of a planet slowly healing, guided by those who could attune themselves to its subtle frequencies. Kira could see it: Anya and Finn, their hands clasped, coaxing life from barren soil, coaxing clean water from depths unseen. She pictured Elias, his keen artist's eye augmented by Luna's sensitivity, not just depicting the ravaged landscape, but understanding its very essence, its hidden wounds and its nascent recovery. The artifact's hum seemed to deepen, as if resonating with the potential Elias described. It was a vision of hope, a stark contrast to the bleak desolation she had traversed for so long.

Mara, ever the pragmatist, nodded slowly, her weathered face thoughtful. "Elias speaks the truth of our potential. The resonance is our oldest and deepest connection to this world. It's what allowed our ancestors to thrive before the... Collapse. It's in our blood, in our very being. We see it as a gift, a way to mend what was broken, to find balance again. It's about harmony, not just with each other, but with the planet itself. It's about rediscovering the language of the earth, a language that was almost silenced."

She paused, her gaze sweeping over the small gathering around the fire. "We've seen it help. We've seen Finn and Anya bring forth barren patches of earth back to life with their touch. We've seen Elias sketch not just what is, but what could be, his visions often guiding our efforts to find usable resources. It's a tool, a powerful one, for survival and for... for rebuilding."

Kira felt a thrill of recognition, a nascent understanding of the artifact's purpose. If it could amplify her connection with Ash, could it also amplify this planetary connection? Could it be a key to unlocking the earth's own dormant energies, to coaxing life back from the brink? The thought was intoxicating, a potent antidote to the pervasive despair that had haunted her for so long.

However, not everyone in Haven shared such optimistic views. Old Gregor, a gruff man whose hands were as gnarled as the roots of the ancient trees he sometimes spoke of finding, shifted uncomfortably on his stool. His eyes, narrowed and wary, flicked between Kira and the artifact beneath her jacket.

"A gift?" he grumbled, his voice raspy with age and suspicion. "Or a doorway? You speak of mending, Elias, but I remember the old stories. The ones that weren't about harmony, but about power. About control." He spat the words out like the bitterest of medicines. "They say the resonance can be... *tuned*. That it can be used to influence, to dominate. What happens when someone decides they don't like the way the earth is singing, or the way its people are thinking?"

His words cast a long, cold shadow over the hopeful pronouncements. Kira felt Ash stir beside her, his low growl a barely perceptible rumble in his chest, a reaction to the palpable tension that had suddenly entered the clearing. Gregor's fear was a tangible thing, a scent on the air that even Kira, with her nascent connection, could detect. It wasn't the primal fear of a predator, but the deep-seated unease of someone who had witnessed the darker side of ambition.

"Control, Gregor?" Mara's voice was calm, but firm. "We are all bound by the same shared need. We rely on each other. The resonance, as we understand it, strengthens bonds, fosters empathy. It makes us more attuned to the needs of others, not less."

"Empathy can be faked," Gregor countered, his gaze unwavering. "And attunement can be manipulated. What if someone uses this... this amplified sense to feel what we feel, and then uses that knowledge against us? What if they can whisper in our minds, not with kindness, but with command? We are fragile, all of us, especially those like Kira with... with direct conduits to such power." He gestured towards Kira's hip. "This isn't just a trinket, girl. It's a weapon waiting to be wielded, or a key to unlock Pandora's Box."

His words struck a chord of unease in Kira. She had felt the resonance grow with Ash, and now, with the artifact, it felt even more potent. The idea of this power being turned against her, or against others, was a chilling prospect. Was her connection with Ash, amplified by the artifact, merely a stepping stone to a more sinister form of influence? The potential for manipulation, for the erosion of free will, was a terrifying thought.

Elias, however, remained undeterred. "But that's a failure of *will*, Gregor, not of the resonance itself. The resonance is a force, like gravity or light. It can be used for good or ill. It's up to us, the people who wield it, to choose the path. We choose to use it to find clean water, to grow food, to understand our environment. We choose to strengthen our bonds, not to break them. That's why Haven exists, to be a place where we can make that choice together."

"And what if 'together' isn't enough?" Anya chimed in; her voice soft but carrying a quiet strength. She gently squeezed Finn's hand, her eyes reflecting a profound understanding. "Gregor's fears are valid. The world outside is a testament to what happens when power is unchecked, when individuals or groups seek to impose their will on others. We've seen the remnants of their technology, their ambition. But the resonance, in its purest form, is about connection, about shared being. It's not about forcing, but about inviting. It's about understanding another's needs, another's pain, and responding with compassion. If someone were to try and twist it, to control, they would be fighting against the very nature of what it is."

Kira felt a surge of empathy for Anya and Finn. Their connection was so clearly rooted in love and mutual respect, a quiet testament to the positive potential of the resonance. Their ability to find resources was not a grab for power, but an act of service to their community. Yet, Gregor's words lingered, a dark seed of doubt in the fertile ground of hope.

"But the artifact," Gregor pressed on, his voice laced with a grim determination. "It's not a natural thing. It's manufactured. It's designed. And design implies intent. What was the intent of the ones who made it? To heal the world, or to rule it?"

Mara's expression grew serious. "That, Gregor, is a question we must all grapple with. The artifact Kira carries is a relic of a past we are only beginning to understand. It speaks of a time when humanity wielded forces we can only dream of now. It is true that such power, in the wrong hands, could be catastrophic. But to reject it entirely, to fear it so deeply that we refuse to even explore its potential, that would be a greater tragedy. It would be admitting defeat, surrendering to the despair that has consumed so much of this world."

She turned to Kira, her gaze steady and unwavering. "Your artifact, Kira, could be the key to unlocking the past, to understanding the 'why' behind the Collapse. It could be the tool that helps us rebuild, that allows us to live in harmony with this scarred planet. Or it could be a weapon. We will not know unless we explore it, cautiously, together. Your connection with Ash, amplified by whatever you carry, is a powerful indicator of its potential for good. It has drawn you here, to Haven. Perhaps it has a purpose for you, and for us."

Kira clutched the artifact, feeling its steady, reassuring pulse. She thought of the woman in the flickering visions, the one tending to the humming machinery. She seemed focused, almost reverent. Was she a scientist, a preserver, or something more? The artifact felt like a bridge, not just between her and Ash, but between different eras, different understandings of existence.

"I... I believe it's meant to help," Kira said, her voice gaining a newfound firmness. "When I first touched it, it felt... alive. And my connection with Ash, it became clearer, stronger. It wasn't a forceful intrusion; it was an awakening." She looked at Gregor, meeting his skeptical gaze. "I understand your fears. I share them. But the alternative is to remain in the darkness, to accept this broken world as the only reality. I can't do that. Not anymore. Not after what I've seen, what I've felt."

Ash nudged her hand, a soft whine escaping him. He seemed to sense her conviction, her burgeoning hope. He was a living testament to the positive power of their bond, a bond that the artifact had, in part, awakened. His presence was a constant reminder that not all power was wielded through coercion; some was earned through trust, loyalty, and a deep, unspoken understanding.

"We have to be vigilant, of course," Mara continued, her tone shifting back to the measured pragmatism that had defined her leadership. "We must learn to recognize the signs of manipulation, of corrupted resonance. We will observe, we will learn, and we will protect each other. That is the way of Haven." She rose, her movements fluid and purposeful. "Kira, your artifact is significant. It represents not just a personal discovery, but a potential turning point for all of us. We will help you understand it, and you will help us understand what it means for our future. We will study its connection to the planet, to our own abilities. We will see if it can indeed guide us to the lost knowledge, to a way of healing this world."

The discussions continued long into the night, the fire a warm heart in the gathering chill. Kira listened, absorbing the spectrum of opinions, the blend of hope and trepidation that defined Haven. Some spoke of using the resonance to pinpoint areas of fertile soil, of locating pockets of clean air, of sensing the subtle shifts in the planet's crust that might predict seismic activity. They envisioned a future where humanity worked *with* the earth, not against it, guided by an innate, amplified understanding.

Others, like Gregor, voiced concerns about the potential for "resonance sickness," a term they used to describe the overwhelming sensory input that some individuals experienced, leading to disorientation and a loss of self. There were hushed whispers of individuals who had become so deeply attuned to the emotional states of others that they had lost their own sense of identity, becoming mere reflections of the collective. The fear of losing oneself in the shared consciousness, of being subsumed by the overwhelming currents of emotion and thought, was a potent counterpoint to the promise of deeper connection.

"It's a delicate balance," Elias murmured, sketching in his notebook by the firelight, Luna a silent shadow beside him. "Too much focus on the internal, on the shared feelings, and you risk losing sight of the external, of the practical needs of survival. But too much focus on the external, on mere pragmatism, and you risk losing the very essence of what makes us resilient, what makes us capable of true connection."

Kira nodded, her gaze fixed on the flickering flames. She understood. The resonance, like any powerful force, had its shadows. Her own connection with Ash, while undeniably beautiful and strengthening, also made her acutely aware of his vulnerability, his capacity for pain. The artifact, in its potential to amplify these connections, also held the potential to amplify their shared burdens.

As the night deepened, a hushed silence fell over Haven. The fire crackled lower, its embers glowing like fallen stars. Kira felt Ash shift beside her, his breathing deep and even. She reached down, her fingers brushing against his soft fur. He sighed, a contented sound, and nudged her hand again. In that simple gesture, there was a universe of understanding, a testament to the quiet power of their bond.

The whispers of hope and fear had settled into a low hum within her. Hope for a world reborn, for a future where humanity had learned to live in harmony with the earth. Fear of the unknown, of the potential for abuse, of the delicate balance that could so easily be tipped. And through it all, the artifact pulsed, a steady, unwavering rhythm against her hip, a reminder that she was no longer alone in her journey. She was part of something larger, a community striving to navigate the profound mysteries of their existence, to find their way back from the brink, guided by the whispers of a world waiting to be heard. The path ahead was uncertain, fraught with both peril and promise, but for the first time in a long time, Kira felt the stirrings of a profound and undeniable belonging. She was here, in Haven, with Ash, and the resonance was her guide.

The embers of the communal fire still cast a warm, flickering glow, painting dancing shadows across the faces of the Haven inhabitants. Kira, nestled deeper into her furs, felt a familiar warmth at her side. Ash, his breathing a soft, steady rhythm, was a grounding presence. The conversations from earlier still echoed in her mind – the debates about the artifact, the resonance, and the delicate balance between hope and apprehension. Yet, as the night deepened, a different kind of awareness began to settle, one that emanated not from the spoken word, but from the quiet thrum of life around her, and especially, from the creature beside her.

It had started subtly, almost imperceptibly. A shift in Ash's behavior, a new layer to his already keen senses that seemed to reach beyond the immediate vicinity. The first truly undeniable instance had occurred that afternoon, when Kira had taken him to explore the perimeter of Haven, seeking out a less-traveled path. They had stumbled upon a small, almost entirely dried-up creek bed, a ghost of a water source that had likely been depleted during a harsher season. Ash, usually content to sniff and explore with casual curiosity, had become intensely focused. He'd lowered his head, his muzzle twitching, and then, with a determined urgency, began digging at a specific spot near the gnarled roots of a weathered tree. Kira had initially dismissed it as a stray scent, perhaps an animal burrow, but his persistence was unusual.

"What is it, boy?" she'd murmured, kneeling beside him.

Ash let out a low whine, his tail giving a single, excited thump against the dry earth. He pawed again, more insistently, before looking up at her, his intelligent eyes alight with an unmistakable certainty. Intrigued, Kira followed his gaze, examining the area he was indicating. There, hidden beneath a thin layer of dust and dried leaves, was a patch of slightly darker, almost damp-looking soil. A faint, earthy scent, different from the dry air, seemed to emanate from it.

Following a hunch, a nascent instinct that had been growing stronger since she'd arrived in Haven and especially since she'd acquired the artifact, Kira dug with her own hands. The soil was indeed cooler, and beneath it, a few inches down, she found it: a small, seeping spring, barely more than a trickle, but undeniably clean and cool water. It was enough to fill her canteen, a small but precious victory in a world where water was a constant concern. Ash, with a happy pant, lapped greedily at the emerging droplets, his tail wagging with unbridled joy.

Kira looked at him, a profound sense of wonder washing over her. It wasn't just that he'd found water; it was the

way he'd found it. There was an innate knowledge in his actions, a sensitivity to something she couldn't perceive. The artifact, she realized, wasn't just amplifying her connection to him; it seemed to be unlocking latent abilities within Ash himself, abilities that had perhaps always been there, dormant, waiting for the right catalyst.

Later, back in Haven, as the community gathered for their evening meal, another uncanny event had occurred. The ground, which had felt solid and unyielding for days, began to vibrate, a subtle tremor that sent a shiver through the assembled people. Most had barely noticed, attributing it to the wind or the settling of their structures. But Ash had reacted instantly. His ears had perked, his body tensing, and he'd emitted a low, rumbling growl, not of aggression, but of warning. He'd nudged Kira's hand insistently, his gaze fixed on a particular section of the western ridge overlooking Haven.

It was only after his persistent nudging that Kira, remembering the earlier incident, had paid closer attention. The tremor was indeed growing, and Ash's agitation, his unnerving certainty, made her uneasy. She had relayed her unease to Mara, who, ever vigilant, had a small team investigate the area Ash seemed to be indicating. What they found was a network of small fissures, barely visible from a distance, appearing in the rock face of the ridge. A more significant tremor, they theorized, could cause a rockslide, potentially blocking the main entrance to Haven or, worse, damaging the water catchment systems built into the cliff face.

Because of Ash's pre-emptive alert, the Haven dwellers had been able to reinforce the weaker sections of the entrance and secure the water systems, mitigating what could have been a dangerous situation. The tremor itself had been minor, a mere hiccup in the earth's crust, but the knowledge that Ash had somehow *felt* it coming, predicted it with such accuracy, was astonishing.

This heightened awareness wasn't limited to the earth itself. Kira found herself increasingly attuned to Ash's subtle shifts in mood, his reactions to the people and animals around them. He seemed to possess an almost preternatural ability to sense the emotional states of others. He would often greet newcomers to Haven with a calm, assessing gaze, and then, after a moment, would either settle down peacefully or display a subtle, protective tension depending on the person's underlying disposition.

One particular instance stood out. A young woman named Lyra, recently arrived from a settlement further south, had been struggling to adapt to life in Haven. She was often withdrawn, her eyes holding a deep sadness that she tried to mask. Ash, who was usually friendly and curious towards strangers, had initially kept his distance from Lyra, observing her with a quiet intensity. However, one afternoon, as Lyra sat alone by the western wall, her shoulders hunched, Ash had approached her. He hadn't bounded over with his usual boisterous energy; instead, he'd walked slowly, deliberately, and then laid his head gently on her lap, his tail giving a slow, comforting sweep.

Lyra had flinched at first, startled, but then, hesitantly, she'd reached out and stroked his head. Tears had welled up in her eyes, and she'd buried her face in his fur, a quiet sob escaping her. Ash had remained there, a solid, comforting presence, until her tears subsided. Kira, watching from a distance, felt a profound surge of connection, not just to Ash, but to Lyra, and to the silent language of empathy that Ash had so effortlessly facilitated. He hadn't spoken a word, hadn't made a grand gesture, but he had recognized Lyra's pain and offered solace in the purest form. It was a testament to the amplified resonance between them, a resonance that seemed to translate Ash's innate empathy into a tangible force.

This heightened sensitivity also extended to other animals. While Ash had always been good with animals, his interactions now possessed a new depth. He seemed to understand the unspoken anxieties of the scrawny chickens that scratched in the communal yard, the skittishness of the few remaining wild birds that frequented the area. He would approach them with a gentleness that calmed their fears, his presence a beacon of reassurance. Kira even noticed him seeming to communicate with them on some unspoken level, a silent exchange of information or understanding that left her marveling at the sheer breadth of his awakening awareness.

The artifact, she mused, resting her hand against its cool, smooth surface beneath her jacket, was more than just a conduit for her own connection with Ash. It was a multiplier, an enhancer, not just of their bond, but of the inherent qualities that made Ash who he was. His loyalty, his keen senses, his inherent empathy – these were not new, but they were now magnified, amplified to a degree that was both astonishing and, at times, overwhelming.

She found herself constantly observing him, noting the nuances of his behavior. The way his ears would swivel, picking up sounds imperceptible to her. The way his nose would twitch, analyzing scents that spoke of distant rain or the passing of a small creature. The way his eyes, those warm, intelligent pools of amber, would sometimes fix on something beyond her field of vision, as if he were perceiving a different layer of reality. It was as if the world, through Ash, was becoming richer, more detailed, more alive.

This burgeoning awareness also brought with it a new understanding of the challenges and responsibilities that came with possessing such a powerful artifact, even if its power was currently manifested through an animal companion. Gregor's warnings about the potential for misuse, for manipulation, echoed in her mind. If Ash could sense emotions so acutely, could someone else, perhaps with a less benevolent nature, use a similar amplified resonance to exploit those emotions? The thought sent a shiver down her spine.

Yet, for every flicker of unease, there was a counterbalancing wave of hope. The image of Ash comforting Lyra, of him guiding her to fresh water, of him warning Haven of the tremor, these were powerful counterpoints. They spoke of a different kind of power, one rooted in empathy, in service, in a deep, intuitive understanding of the world.

Kira realized that her own perception of Ash had shifted. He was no longer just her companion, her protector. He was becoming something more – a sensitive barometer of the world around them, an intuitive guide whose abilities were blossoming under the influence of the artifact and the supportive, yet complex, environment of Haven. She felt a deep responsibility to nurture these abilities, to understand them, and to ensure they were used for good.

As the night wore on, and the inhabitants of Haven began to drift to their sleeping quarters, Kira remained by the dying embers, Ash a warm weight beside her. The world felt different, more vibrant, more nuanced, seen through the lens of Ash's awakening senses and their amplified bond. The subtle shifts in the air, the distant rustle of leaves, the faint scent of dew beginning to gather on the sparse vegetation – all of it was part of a larger symphony, a symphony that Ash was becoming increasingly adept at hearing, and through him, Kira was beginning to understand. This was just the beginning, she knew. The artifact was a mystery, and Ash's developing abilities were a testament to its unknown potential. The journey of discovery, and of responsibility, had truly just begun. She buried her hand in Ash's fur, feeling the steady beat of his heart, and a sense of quiet determination settled within her. They would face whatever came next, together, guided by their shared bond and the subtle, yet profound, language of the resonance. The world was speaking, and through Ash, Kira was finally learning to listen.

The hush of the pre-dawn air was broken only by the soft padding of Ash's paws on the packed earth as Kira guided him towards Elara's dwelling. The elder's home, nestled deeper within Haven, was distinguished not by grandeur, but by a profound stillness that seemed to emanate from its very structure, a testament to the years Elara had spent honing her connection with her own resonant partner, a stoic old wolfhound named Sol. Kira had been told, by those who knew Elara best, that her wisdom was as ancient and deep as the roots of the surrounding scrubland, a reservoir of knowledge accumulated over a lifetime of attunement to the world's subtle whispers. She carried the weight of Ash's newly awakened sensitivities, the marvels and the nascent anxieties they stirred within her, and a deep-seated hope that Elara might offer some semblance of clarity.

Elara's doorway was a simple, woven reed affair, its entrance framed by dried herbs that hung in fragrant bundles, their scents mingling with the ever-present earthy aroma of Haven. As they approached, a low, contented rumble vibrated from within, a sound Kira recognized as Sol's greeting – a sound that spoke of age, contentment, and an unwavering presence. Kira hesitated for a moment, the enormity of seeking counsel from one so revered pressing upon her. Ash, sensing her apprehension, nudged her hand gently, his amber eyes conveying a silent encouragement. Taking a deep breath, Kira pushed aside the reed curtain and stepped inside.

The interior was dim, lit by a single, sputtering oil lamp that cast long, wavering shadows. The air was thick with the scent of dried herbs, beeswax, and something else, something ancient and comforting, like sun-baked stone. Elara sat on a low, woven mat by the hearth, her weathered hands clasped in her lap. Beside her, Sol lay sprawled, a magnificent silhouette of grey fur and quiet strength, his great head resting on his paws, his eyes half-closed but keenly aware. Elara's face was a landscape of fine wrinkles, etched by time and experience, yet her eyes, when they met Kira's, held a startling clarity, a depth that seemed to pierce through pretense.

"Kira," Elara's voice was a low murmur, like stones smoothed by a river. "And Ash. You come seeking. I felt the stirring."

Kira's breath hitched. "You... you felt us?"

A slow smile creased Elara's face. "The world hums, child. And those who listen, even with only one ear, can feel the vibrations. Sol and I have been listening for a long time." She gestured to a space on the mat opposite her. "Sit. Share the quiet with us."

Kira settled down, Ash carefully lying at her feet, his tail giving a soft thump of acknowledgement. She felt a sense of profound calm wash over her in the elder's presence, a stark contrast to the nervous energy that had propelled her here. "Elara," Kira began, choosing her words carefully, "I... Ash... he has been changing. Since I found the artifact. His senses, they seem… amplified. He guided me to water when none could be found, he alerted us to a tremor before it happened, and he… he seems to understand others, their feelings, in a way I've never seen."

Elara listened patiently, her gaze steady, her expression unreadable. When Kira finished, the elder remained silent for a long moment, her eyes closed as if drawing strength from an inner well. Sol stirred, letting out a soft sigh that seemed to resonate with his mistress's contemplation.

"The artifact," Elara finally said, her voice still a low rumble, "is a key. It unlocks doors that were always there, but remained unseen, unfelt. Ash, like all creatures who share their lives with ours, is a mirror. He reflects what is around him, but with the artifact, his reflection is sharper, more defined. He is not merely sensing the world; he is perceiving the *currents* of it."

"Currents?" Kira echoed, leaning forward.

"The world," Elara explained, her gaze drifting towards the flickering lamp, "is a vast, interconnected tapestry of energies. The earth breathes, the wind carries whispers of distant storms, the water remembers the paths it has carved. Animals, especially those bound to us as partners, are exquisitely sensitive to these flows. They feel the subtle shifts, the harmonious rhythms, and the dissonant disruptions. What you are witnessing in Ash is not a new ability, but an awakening to the deeper strata of existence that he, and Sol, and countless others have always been privy to."

Kira's mind reeled, trying to grasp the enormity of what Elara was suggesting. "So, it's not just him being… special?"

Elara chuckled, a dry, rustling sound. "Every life is special, Kira. But some are given the means to perceive the specialness in all things. The resonance between a human and their partner amplifies what is already present. The artifact simply… turns up the volume. Ash is not just seeing a dry creek bed; he is feeling the deep thirst of the earth, the memory of water that still lingers in the soil. He did not just sense a tremor; he felt the land preparing to groan under a strain it could no longer bear."

This explanation resonated deeply with Kira. It fit with the way Ash had acted, the certainty in his eyes, the urgency in his actions. It wasn't magic in the way some stories told of it, but a profound, almost primal, connection to the living world.

"But… it's overwhelming sometimes," Kira confessed, her voice dropping. "Knowing he can feel so much. And I feel it through him. It's like I'm experiencing the world through a prism, all these new shades and textures. How do I... how do I manage it?"

Elara's eyes softened with understanding. "Ah, the burden of knowing. It is a heavy cloak, child, and one that requires careful tending. The currents of the world are not always gentle. They carry joy and sorrow, life and decay, harmony and discord. To feel them all, without understanding how to filter, how to discern, can indeed be overwhelming. You must learn to distinguish the echoes from the source, the ripples from the wave."

She reached out, her fingers, gnarled but surprisingly strong, brushing against Kira's. "The first lesson is balance. You are the anchor, Kira. Ash is the sail. You must provide the stability, the groundedness, while he catches the wind. Do not let his perceptions consume you. Observe, learn, but do not drown in the currents. Remember what is real, what is tangible, for you. Your own senses, your own intuition, are still vital."

"But how do I know what's real?" Kira asked, a tremor in her voice. "When he reacts to something I can't see or hear or feel, how do I trust it?"

"Trust the connection," Elara said simply. "Trust the history you are building with Ash. Has he led you astray? Has his insight ever brought harm? Or has it brought protection, sustenance, understanding? Your shared bond is the compass. When Ash reacts, pay attention. Ask yourself what he might be perceiving. Is it a threat? A need? A subtle shift in the environment? Sometimes, he will be right. Sometimes, the world will be quiet, and his heightened senses will be registering only the faintest of whispers, which you may not yet be ready to hear."

Elara's gaze grew distant for a moment, as if communing with an unseen presence. "There is a delicate balance, Kira. The artifact magnifies, yes, but it does not create. It amplifies what is inherent. Ash's loyalty, his empathy, his intelligence – these were always there. The currents of the world... they are constant, flowing around and through us all. Most live oblivious to their power, their patterns. But those with a strong resonance, those who are touched by gifts like the artifact, become attuned to them. You, through Ash, are learning to navigate these currents. But with such navigation comes a grave responsibility."

"Responsibility?" Kira prompted, her mind immediately going to Gregor's words, to the warnings about the artifact's potential.

"The currents of the world," Elara continued, her voice taking on a more serious tone, "can be harnessed, or they can be disrupted. To understand the land is to understand its vulnerabilities. To feel the emotions of others is to know their potential for manipulation. If you can sense a storm brewing on the horizon through Ash's unease, you can prepare. But if you can sense the fear in someone's heart, you can also exploit it. This gift, this amplified perception, is a powerful tool, Kira. And like any tool, it can be used to build or to destroy."

The weight of Elara's words settled upon Kira. She had felt the exhilaration of Ash's abilities, the wonder of their shared experiences, but she hadn't fully considered the darker implications.

"I... I don't want to misuse it," Kira said, her voice earnest. "I want to use it for good."

"And that desire is your first and most important shield," Elara affirmed. "But desire is not enough. You must cultivate wisdom. You must understand the ethics of perception. Just because you can perceive a hidden weakness does not give you license to exploit it. Just because you can feel a person's fear does not grant you permission to prey upon it. The currents of the world are ancient and complex. They have their own natural order. Interfering carelessly, with selfish intent, will always have consequences, often unforeseen."

Elara picked up a smooth, dark stone from beside her and turned it over in her palm. "Consider this stone. It has been shaped by water, by wind, by time. It is part of the natural order. If you were to take this stone and use it to crush a bird's egg, you would disrupt that order. You would cause pain, extinguish a future. Even though the stone itself is innocent, its use in that moment is not. So, it is with your amplified senses. Your awareness is the stone. Your intent, your actions, will determine whether you bring life or sorrow."

"How do I know what the 'natural order' is?" Kira asked, feeling a growing sense of the vastness of the knowledge she was beginning to touch.

"That," Elara said, her eyes twinkling with a hint of ancient humor, "is the lifelong pursuit. The natural order is not a static thing, Kira. It is a constant flux, a dance of creation and destruction, of growth and decay. It is the way the rain nourishes the earth, the way the predator hunts its prey, the way the seasons turn. It is about respect, about understanding that every element has its purpose, its place. Your role, through Ash, is to become a guardian of that balance, not a manipulator of it. To sense when the balance is threatened, and to act with wisdom, not with haste or ego."

Elara then spoke of her own journey with Sol, of the early days when his heightened senses had seemed like a novelty, a game. She recounted instances where his sensitivity to the earth's vibrations had saved them from landslides, where his ability to sense the fear of prey animals had guided their foraging, but also of times when his keen perception of human emotion had been unsettling, revealing the hidden anxieties and resentments within their own community.

"There were times," Elara admitted, her voice tinged with memory, "when Sol would grow agitated around certain individuals, and I, young and impatient, would dismiss it as mere animalistic prejudice. But with time, I learned that his unease was often a warning. He was sensing a dissonance, a lack of harmony in their spirit, a potential for betrayal or harm that I, with my human blinders, could not perceive. It taught me humility. It taught me to trust his instincts, even when they contradicted my own judgment."

She looked directly at Kira, her gaze intense. "You must foster that same trust with Ash. He is not merely a tool. He is your partner. His perceptions are valid, even if you do not yet understand their cause. Learn to interpret his subtle cues, his body language, the nuances of his reactions. The artifact has opened a channel, but the language of the resonance, the language of the currents, is one you will learn together."

Elara then shifted her focus, her attention turning to the broader implications of their abilities. "Haven thrives because it understands, on some level, the currents of survival. We respect the land, we work with its rhythms, we conserve what little we have. Your gift, amplified by the artifact, can help Haven thrive even more. Imagine being able to anticipate drought more accurately, to sense the presence of untamed predators before they pose a threat, to understand the subtle health of our crops and livestock. But always, always remember that this knowledge comes with a duty of care. It is not for personal gain, or for power over others."

She paused, letting her words sink in. "The temptation will be there, Kira. The allure of knowing more, of controlling more. Resist it. Seek understanding, not dominance. Seek harmony, not discord. The currents of the world are powerful, but they are also fragile. To respect them is to respect life itself."

As the sky outside began to lighten, Elara gently touched Kira's arm. "You have a long path ahead, Kira. A path of discovery, of learning, and of immense responsibility. Do not fear the changes in Ash, or the new awareness within yourself. Embrace them. Learn from them. And always, always listen. Listen to Ash, listen to the world, and listen to the quiet wisdom that resides within your own heart. The artifact is a catalyst, but the true strength, the true guidance, comes from within, and from the unwavering bond you share."

Kira felt a profound shift within her. The confusion and apprehension that had clouded her mind were beginning to recede, replaced by a quiet clarity. Elara's words, though often delivered in metaphor and allegory, had provided a framework, a philosophy for understanding the burgeoning sensitivities of Ash and herself. It wasn't about wielding power, but about understanding interconnectedness, about respecting the delicate balance of the world, and about the profound responsibility that came with being able to perceive its deeper currents. As she stood to leave, with Ash rising and stretching beside her, Kira felt a renewed sense of purpose, a quiet resolve to navigate this new path with the wisdom and grace that Elara had so generously shared. The dawn was breaking, and with it, a new understanding of the world, and her place within it, was beginning to bloom.

The soft glow of the rising sun painted the eastern sky in hues of rose and gold as Kira, with Ash trotting faithfully by her side, made her way back from Elara's dwelling. The elder's quiet counsel had settled within her like a balm, easing the knots of confusion and anxiety that had tightened around her heart. She felt a nascent understanding, a framework upon which to build her journey with Ash, a journey that was no longer solely hers, but theirs. Yet, as they re-entered the more frequented paths of Haven, the lingering scent of dried herbs and beeswax from Elara's home seemed to mingle with a less pleasant aroma – the scent of unspoken skepticism.

Her first encounter was subtle, almost imperceptible to anyone but her, or perhaps Ash. As they passed a small cluster of dwellings, a woman named Lyra, known for her pragmatic approach to life and her disdain for anything that smacked of "unnecessary fuss," averted her gaze pointedly. Lyra's partner, a sturdy but unremarkable boarhound named Grit, remained tethered to a sturdy post, its attention fixed on a distant bird. Lyra's disapproval wasn't voiced, but it was there, in the sharp angle of her jaw, the tightly pursed lips, and the way she hurried her step, pulling her younger child closer. Kira felt a familiar prickle of unease, a faint echo of the apprehension she'd felt before visiting Elara. Ash, however, didn't react outwardly, his focus remaining on Kira, a quiet anchor in the shifting currents of social perception.

Later, as Kira made her way to the communal watering trough, she overheard a hushed conversation between two other residents, Torvin and Mara. Torvin, a burly man with hands calloused from years of tilling the stubborn soil, was speaking in a low, emphatic tone. "I tell you, Mara, it's a dangerous path they're walking. These... resonant pairings. They breed dependency, a weakness. We've survived this long by relying on our own strength, our own eyes and ears. Not by some animal's whims."

Mara, a woman whose face was etched with the perpetual worry of ensuring her family's survival, nodded slowly, though her expression held a hint of curiosity rather than outright agreement. "But Torvin, Elara herself acknowledges the changes. And Kira's dog... it seems to have an uncanny sense for things."

"Uncanny?" Torvin scoffed, his voice rising slightly. "That's just animal instinct, amplified. It's a trick of nature, a fleeting advantage. What happens when that advantage fades? When the animal gets old, or sick? Or when it leads them astray, into a danger they can't truly comprehend because they're relying on a translation from another species? We need sturdy, reliable methods. The kind that doesn't depend on the mood of a hound or the feel of the wind through its fur."

Kira's heart sank a little. She'd been so buoyed by Elara's words, by the potential she felt unfolding within her and Ash. Now, these echoes of doubt and suspicion were like small pebbles tossed into the clear waters of her newfound understanding, creating ripples of unease. She paused, wanting to approach them, to explain, but Ash nudged her forward with his head, a gentle pressure that seemed to say, *not now*.

As the day wore on, the subtle rejections and the open skepticism became more apparent. At the midday meal, shared amongst the community, Kira found herself seated at the edge of the gathering. Conversations flowed around her, but few engaged her directly. When she spoke, her words seemed to hang in the air, unacknowledged. She noticed individuals glancing at Ash, their expressions ranging from apprehension to outright distrust. One young man, Finn, whose own wolfhound, Storm, was known for its ill temper and was rarely allowed to interact with others, made a point of leading his partner to the far side of the gathering, his back turned pointedly towards Kira and Ash.

It wasn't just the overt hostility that was unnerving, but the pervasive undercurrent of unease. Haven was a place built on shared survival, on the necessity of cooperation. Yet, this emerging difference, this ability that set some pairings apart, seemed to be creating a fault line, a division that threatened the very fabric of their community. Kira felt a pang of defensiveness, followed quickly by a wave of sadness. These were her people, people she had come to rely on, and yet, they viewed her and Ash with suspicion.

Later, seeking a moment of respite from the palpable tension, Kira took Ash for a walk along the western perimeter of Haven, where the scrubland gave way to a more rugged terrain. The silence here was a welcome change, broken only by the chirping of insects and the rustle of dry leaves underfoot. Ash, however, seemed to sense her distress. He walked closer to her than usual, his body a comforting presence against her leg. He'd stop occasionally, nudging her hand with his nose, his amber eyes filled with an unspoken question, a silent offering of comfort.

As they rounded a cluster of weathered rocks, they encountered another resident, Elara's son, Kael. Kael was a man of strong convictions, fiercely protective of Haven's traditions and its hard-won stability. He stopped, his expression hardening as he saw Kira and Ash. Kael's own resonant partner, a lean and watchful husky named Echo, stood beside him, its ears perked, its gaze fixed on Ash with a mixture of wariness and curiosity.

"Kira," Kael's tone was polite, but cool. "I saw you with Elara this morning. Seeking her wisdom on... this?" He gestured vaguely towards Ash.

Kira nodded, her guard rising instinctively. "Yes, Kael. Ash's abilities are developing, and Elara has been guiding me."

Kael's lips thinned. "Guiding you to what, exactly? To rely on something that isn't fully controllable? Haven needs everyone contributing their tangible skills. We need hunters, builders, healers who understand the physical world. We can't afford to be distracted by... ethereal perceptions. My mother has always had a... romantic view of things."

The word "romantic" was delivered with a thinly veiled condescension that stung Kira. "It's not about distraction, Kael. It's about understanding. Ash's senses have helped us, saved us even. He warned us about the unstable cliff face; he found that hidden spring when we were desperate for water."

"Fortuitous coincidences," Kael dismissed, shaking his head. "A sharp-eyed hound can do the same. Or a keen observer of the weather. We have those. What we don't have are people whose focus is diverted by every rustle of leaves or every shift in the air. This... reliance on the resonant bond, it's a luxury we can't afford. It makes people soft. It makes them dependent."

Echo, beside him, let out a low growl, a sound that seemed to be directed not at Ash, but at the tension Kael was creating. Kael shot a sharp look at his husky, who immediately fell silent, though its posture remained alert.

"We are not soft, Kael," Kira said, her voice firm. "We are adapting. And Ash is not a distraction; he is a partner. His perception is a gift, and we intend to use it responsibly, to help Haven thrive."

"Thrive by what means?" Kael challenged, taking a step closer. "By relying on a bond that can be broken? What if Ash decides he doesn't like you anymore? What if he chooses a different path? We're talking about the survival of everyone here. I won't see it jeopardized by fanciful notions of connection and intuition. My mother's wisdom is deep, yes, but she is also old, and perhaps she sees things through a haze of nostalgia. We need to be grounded. We need to be practical."

Kira felt a wave of frustration and anger wash over her. Kael's words were a direct echo of the very doubts that had plagued her before her visit to Elara. It was a stark reminder that Elara's acceptance was not universal, and that the path ahead would be far from smooth.

"And what if your practicality is blinding you to a greater truth?" Kira retorted, her voice rising. "What if there are forces, energies, that your 'grounded' methods simply can't account for? Elara spoke of currents, Kael. Currents of the world. And Ash can feel them. He can warn us of dangers before they're visible, he can sense needs before they become desperate. Isn't that a practical advantage?"

Kael scoffed again. "Currents. Energy. These are words for people who want to avoid the hard work of understanding the tangible world. The world is dirt, water, sun, and predators. It's about knowing how to trap, how to build shelter, how to read the sky for rain. It's not about some invisible web of feelings and perceptions."

Echo shifted uncomfortably, his gaze flicking between Kira, Ash, and Kael. He seemed to sense the discord.

"Perhaps you should spend more time listening to the world, Kael," Kira said, her voice tight with emotion. "Instead of just telling it what you think it should be."

With that, Kira turned, calling Ash to her side. She walked away from Kael and Echo, the weight of his skepticism pressing down on her. The setting sun cast long, distorted shadows across the landscape, mirroring the twisted perceptions she was encountering.

As they continued their walk, Ash's presence was a steady reassurance. He walked with his head held high, his senses alert, but he remained focused on Kira. He would occasionally glance back, his amber eyes catching hers, a silent communication passing between them. It wasn't just about her receiving abilities through him; it was about their shared experience, their growing understanding of each other. And in that understanding, Kira found a nascent strength, a quiet defiance against the rising tide of doubt.

She knew this was just the beginning. The artifact had not only awakened something within Ash, but it had also revealed a deeper division within Haven itself. Some, like Elara, embraced the potential, the interconnectedness. Others, like Kael and Torvin, clung to what they knew, to the tangible and the controllable, viewing anything beyond their grasp with suspicion and fear. This internal conflict, Kira realized, would be as challenging to navigate as any external threat.

The journey back to her dwelling was a somber one, the unspoken tensions of Haven hanging heavy in the evening air. The initial wonder and excitement she had felt after speaking with Elara had been tempered by the stark reality of the skepticism she had encountered. It was a reminder that Haven, for all its cooperative spirit, was not a monolith. It was a community of individuals, each with their own fears, their own biases, and their own ideas about how to survive and thrive in this world. And Kira, with her resonating partner Ash, had just become a focal point for some of those deeply held, and often conflicting, beliefs. The path ahead was undeniably more complex than she had initially imagined. She had Elara's wisdom, and she had Ash's unwavering bond, but she would need to find a way to bridge the growing chasm of doubt that threatened to divide her community. The acceptance of resonant pairs was not a foregone conclusion; it was a battle that would need to be fought, one conversation, one shared experience, one act of quiet understanding at a time. And as the stars began to prick the darkening sky, Kira knew that she and Ash were ready to face that challenge, not with aggression, but with the quiet strength that their deepening bond provided.

CHAPTER 3

The weight of Kael's words, and the multitude of unspoken doubts they represented, still lingered as Kira led Ash back to the familiar quiet of their own small dwelling. The setting sun had now dipped below the horizon, leaving the sky bruised with shades of purple and deep indigo, a stark contrast to the hopeful dawn that had heralded her visit to Elara. The community's murmurs, the averted glances, the sharp dismissals – they were a tangible presence, a shadow cast over her nascent understanding. Elara's wisdom, while a guiding star, was not a shield against the winds of ingrained skepticism. Kira knew, with a certainty that settled deep in her bones, that fostering the resonant bond with Ash was not simply a matter of personal growth; it was a challenge to the established order of Haven, a quiet revolution that would undoubtedly face resistance.

The following morning, however, dawned with a renewed sense of purpose. The anxieties of the previous day, though valid, were not allowed to dictate her actions. Elara's counsel had ignited a spark within Kira, a conviction that the connection she shared with Ash was too profound, too vital, to be dismissed as mere fancy. She recalled Elara's gentle reminder: "The resonance is not a destination, child, but a journey. And the most significant discoveries are made when we actively seek them."

The first step was to move beyond passive reception, to actively engage and cultivate the subtle energies that flowed between her and Ash. Elara had provided Kira with a series of exercises, simple in premise, yet profoundly demanding in execution. The goal was to refine their shared awareness, to sharpen their ability to perceive and interpret a broader spectrum of sensory information, extending beyond the ordinary human or canine experience.

"Alright, Ash," Kira murmured, stroking the thick fur of his neck as they settled into the relative privacy of their small cleared space behind their dwelling. The air was still cool, carrying the scent of dew-kissed earth and the faint, earthy aroma of the surrounding scrub. "Elara said we need to listen. Really listen."

She knelt, placing her hand flat on the packed earth. Ash mirrored her action, resting his large paw beside her hand. "Focus," she whispered, closing her eyes. "Feel the ground beneath us. Not just the surface, but deeper. What's happening down there?"

Initially, there was only the familiar sensation of the earth – cool, firm, grounding. Kira focused her attention, trying to push past the surface-level awareness. She concentrated on the subtle vibrations, the almost imperceptible tremors that rippled through the soil. Ash remained still, his brow furrowed in concentration, his tail giving a slow, almost imperceptible thump against the ground.

"I feel... something," Kira breathed, concentrating on a faint, rhythmic pulse beneath her palm. It was like a slow, deep heartbeat. She opened her eyes, glancing at Ash. His amber eyes were fixed on her, and he gave a soft whine, nudging her hand with his nose.

"You feel it too?" she asked, her voice filled with a quiet thrill. "It's... like the earth is breathing."

Ash responded with a low rumble in his chest, a sound that seemed to resonate with the very vibration she was sensing. He then shifted his weight, planting his paw more firmly, and a distinct tremor, a sharp, focused tremor, shot up through their joined connection. Kira gasped. It felt like a sudden surge of energy, a ripple spreading outwards.

"What was that?" she asked, her mind racing. Was it a creature moving underground? The shifting of roots?

Ash whined again, then nudged her again, this time towards the north. Kira followed his lead, keeping her hand on the ground and her other hand on his flank, their shared sensory input a continuous stream. She felt the subtle pulse continue, but overlaid with a new sensation – a faint, almost imperceptible drag, a subtle resistance in the flow of that deep vibration.

"It's... changed," Kira murmured. "There's something... obstructing it, coming from that way." She strained her ears, trying to interpret this new information.

This was the essence of the training: to take the raw data of sensory input – vibrations, scents, emotional echoes – and to learn to interpret them, to understand their nuances, their implications. Elara had explained that Ash's canine senses were far more acute than hers, but his ability to process and communicate these perceptions was still developing. Kira's role was to be the interpreter, the bridge between Ash's innate understanding and conscious awareness.

They spent nearly an hour in this focused communion with the earth. Kira discovered that the "heartbeat" was stronger in some places than others, and that certain localized tremors seemed to correspond with the movements of small burrowing creatures. Ash, in turn, seemed to be learning to distinguish between these different vibrations, his responses becoming more nuanced. He'd nudge her hand in a specific direction, or give a low growl when a particular disturbance registered.

The next exercise shifted their focus to the air, specifically, the scent of distant rain. Elara had described it as a subtle shift in the atmospheric pressure, a faint ozone tang that preceded the actual downpour.

"Close your eyes again, Ash," Kira instructed, her voice a soft whisper. She inhaled deeply, trying to catch any hint of moisture on the breeze. The morning air was dry, carrying the scent of dust and sunbaked earth.

They sat in silence, their senses attuned to the subtle currents of the atmosphere. Kira focused on the gentle breeze rustling the leaves, trying to discern any foreign element within it. Ash remained still, his nostrils twitching almost imperceptibly. Minutes ticked by, each one stretching into an eternity of patient observation.

Then, Kira felt it. A faint, almost ethereal coolness against her skin, a subtle change in the air's texture. It wasn't a tangible scent, not yet, but a promise. She opened her eyes, a small smile playing on her lips. Ash met her gaze, his tail giving a tentative thump.

"I think I feel it, Ash," she breathed. "A hint of something coming."

Ash let out a soft huff, then nudged her towards the west, his head held high, his senses seemingly reaching out beyond the immediate vicinity. Kira followed his unspoken direction, trying to pinpoint the source of this atmospheric shift. She could feel a faint coolness, yes, but Ash seemed to be registering something more distinct, a clearer direction and intensity.

“Is it... getting stronger?” she asked, her own senses sharpening in response to his subtle cues. She could now detect a fainter, almost metallic tang in the air, a precursor to the earthy smell of rain.

Ash whined and began to walk slowly in a particular direction, his steps deliberate. Kira followed, her hand resting on his back, feeling the subtle tension in his muscles as he concentrated. He stopped abruptly, sniffing the air with intense focus, then nudged a clump of dry grass with his nose.

“You think it’s coming from here?” Kira questioned, kneeling down and trying to replicate his focus. She could smell the dry grass, the dust, but beneath it, she could now discern a definite, albeit faint, hint of moisture, of something elemental and vital.

The training was proving to be both physically and mentally exhausting. It required an unwavering concentration, a sustained effort to push beyond the ingrained limits of their perception. Kira found herself pushing her own mental boundaries, learning to filter out the background noise of her own thoughts and anxieties, and to truly inhabit the present moment, attuned to the world through both her own senses and Ash’s heightened awareness.

Ash, too, was clearly expending significant effort. His breathing was steady but deep, and occasionally he would shake his head, as if trying to clear away extraneous sensations. Yet, he remained steadfast, his loyalty and his willingness to engage in this demanding process unwavering. Kira felt a surge of affection and gratitude for him, for his tireless dedication to their shared journey.

The third exercise focused on the emotional tenor of nearby creatures. Elara had described this as perceiving the “inner hum” of living beings – the fear of a startled rabbit, the contentment of a grazing deer, the territorial aggression of a foraging badger.

They ventured to the edge of the scrubland, where the sounds of Haven were muted, and the presence of wild creatures was more pronounced. Kira knelt again, coaxing Ash to lie down beside her. She laid her hand on his flank, feeling the steady rhythm of his heartbeat, a comforting counterpoint to the natural world around them.

“Okay, Ash,” she said softly. “Let’s try to listen to the others. Not just what they sound like, but what they *feel* like.”

She closed her eyes, trying to quiet her own emotional state, to create a receptive space within herself. Ash remained still, his senses scanning their surroundings. For a long while, there was only the familiar hum of the natural world – the buzzing of insects, the rustling of leaves, the distant calls of birds.

Then, a subtle shift. Kira felt a flicker of something – a prickle of unease, a heightened awareness that wasn't her own. It was faint, like a whisper on the edge of hearing. She opened her eyes and looked at Ash. His ears were pricked forward, his gaze fixed on a dense thicket nearby.

"What is it?" she whispered.

Ash responded with a low, almost inaudible rumble in his chest. It wasn't a growl of aggression, but a sound of caution, of alertness. He nudged her hand, a gentle pressure that conveyed a sense of something nearby, something wary.

Kira focused her attention on the thicket, trying to perceive what Ash was sensing. She strained her mental senses, reaching out for that subtle emotional trace. And then, she felt it – a sharp jolt of fear, a sudden panic, as if a small creature had been startled. It was fleeting, a mere instant, but it was undeniably there.

"A rabbit," Kira breathed, a sense of wonder filling her. "It was a rabbit. It's frightened."

Ash relaxed slightly, his body softening, though his gaze remained fixed on the thicket. He gave a soft whine, a sound of gentle reassurance, almost as if he were communicating with the unseen creature.

They continued their practice, moving slowly through the scrubland. They sensed the placid contentment of a deer grazing in a distant meadow, a quiet, almost meditative feeling that permeated the air. They also encountered the sharp, territorial annoyance of a badger, a bristling energy that warned them to keep their distance. Each perception, however faint, was a piece of the puzzle, a building block in their understanding of the resonant connection.

The exercises were relentless in their demand for patience and focus. There were moments when Kira felt utterly overwhelmed, when the influx of sensory information, amplified and interpreted through Ash, seemed too much to bear. She would feel a dull ache behind her eyes, a weariness that seeped into her bones. Ash, too, showed signs of fatigue, his movements becoming less fluid, his responses occasionally lagging.

But with each challenge, they also experienced small triumphs. The moment of correctly identifying a scent, the precise interpretation of a vibrational pattern, the fleeting but distinct perception of another creature's emotion – these moments were incredibly rewarding, reinforcing their commitment to this arduous path. Kira learned to trust Ash's instincts implicitly, to rely on the subtle shifts in his posture, the flick of his ears, the direction of his gaze. And Ash, she felt, was learning to trust her interpretation, to understand that her conscious awareness was an extension of his own innate abilities.

One afternoon, as they practiced sensing the subtle energies of the forest floor, Kira felt a distinct pull, a sense of unease emanating from a dense patch of undergrowth. Ash, beside her, reacted simultaneously, his ears swiveling, his body tensing. He let out a low growl, a warning that was far more pronounced than anything they had experienced before.

Kira's heart leaped into her throat. This wasn't the fleeting fear of a rabbit or the territorial annoyance of a badger. This was something deeper, a raw, primal fear mixed with a sense of desperation. She focused her mental energy, trying to pierce the veil of foliage.

"What is it, Ash?" she whispered, her voice trembling slightly. "What do you feel?"

Ash didn't respond verbally, but he nudged her insistently towards the dense undergrowth, his body low to the ground, his tail held stiffly. Kira understood. He wanted her to look, to see what he was sensing. Taking a deep breath, she pushed through the tangled branches, Ash right at her side.

And there, caught in a hunter's snare, was a young fox, its leg horribly twisted, its amber eyes wide with terror and pain. The air around it throbbed with its agony. Kira felt a wave of empathy wash over her, a visceral connection to the creature's suffering.

Ash let out a soft whine, a sound of sympathy. He approached the snare cautiously, sniffing at the sharp metal jaws, then looked back at Kira, his gaze questioning.

"We have to help it, Ash," Kira said, her voice firm despite the trembling in her hands.

This was more than just an exercise. This was a real-world application of everything they were learning. Kira knelt beside the trapped fox, talking to it in a soothing voice, trying to calm its panicked struggles. Ash remained a steady presence beside her, his own calm demeanor seeming to have a subtle, calming effect on the distressed animal.

Carefully, Kira examined the snare. It was a cruel device, designed to inflict maximum pain and hold its prey fast. She knew she couldn't free the fox without risking injury to herself or further harm to the animal.

"We need to get help," she realized aloud. "We need to tell someone."

Ash seemed to understand. He nudged her hand, then looked towards the direction of Haven. Kira nodded. This was an opportunity to demonstrate the practical value of their bond, not just to herself, but to others.

The walk back to Haven was a race against time, with Ash leading the way, his senses alert for any signs of danger or opportunity. Kira's mind, however, was racing with a new understanding. The resonance training wasn't just about honing their individual perceptions; it was about building a partnership, a symbiotic relationship where each fed into the other, creating a whole that was greater than the sum of its parts.

She realized that Elara's guidance was not about imparting some mystical ability, but about unlocking a fundamental aspect of consciousness that had been obscured by centuries of focusing solely on the tangible and the empirical. The resonant bond was a bridge, a pathway to a deeper understanding of the world, and of each other. It was a challenging, exhausting, and often overwhelming process, but with every successful interpretation, every shared perception, Kira felt her own strength growing, her connection with Ash deepening, and her conviction solidifying. The skepticism of Haven might be a formidable barrier, but the power of their burgeoning resonance was a force that was becoming increasingly difficult to ignore. She and Ash were not merely adapting; they were evolving, and the journey of their resonance training had truly just begun. The training was not just about enhancing Ash's abilities, but about fostering a true partnership, where Kira could translate and amplify his perceptions, and he, in turn, could ground her understanding in the raw data of the world. This intricate dance of shared awareness was the core of their developing resonance, a process that required constant vigilance and a willingness to embrace the unknown, pushing both of them to their absolute limits. The subtle shift in the air, the almost imperceptible scent of distant rain, was no longer a mere atmospheric anomaly to be noted, but a complex tapestry of pressure, moisture, and atmospheric charge that Ash could discern with astonishing clarity. Kira's role was to learn to feel the subtle coolness against her skin, to recognize the metallic tang that preceded the scent of damp earth, and to connect these physical sensations with Ash's internal interpretation, a process that often felt like deciphering an entirely new language. The emotional tenor of nearby creatures was even more challenging. It wasn't a conscious thought that a rabbit felt fear, but a primal wave of terror, a panicked adrenaline surge that resonated through the very air. Kira had to learn to recognize this signature, to differentiate it from the territorial grumbles of a badger or the placid contentment of a grazing deer. Ash's role was to pinpoint these emotional signals, to direct Kira's attention, and to provide the initial layer of understanding, a primal recognition of a fellow creature's state of being. He would often stiffen, his ears pricked forward, or offer a low rumble in his chest, communicating the essence of his perception before Kira could even begin to process it.

The training was relentless, demanding an almost superhuman level of focus. Kira found herself pushing past physical and mental fatigue, her mind often feeling stretched thin, like a delicate membrane on the verge of tearing. The constant effort to interpret and amplify, to remain receptive without being overwhelmed, took a significant toll. She experienced headaches, a persistent weariness, and moments of profound doubt. Was this truly a valuable pursuit, or was she simply chasing shadows, driven by Elara's gentle encouragement and her own desire for a deeper connection? Ash, too, showed signs of strain. His movements, usually fluid and confident, became more deliberate, sometimes hesitant. He would shake his head, as if trying to dislodge distracting sensory input, and his panting would deepen, betraying the immense effort he was expending. Yet, he never faltered. His amber eyes, when they met hers, held a steady resolve, a silent promise of commitment that fueled Kira's own determination.

The exercises were varied, designed to push different aspects of their shared awareness. One day, Elara had instructed them to focus on the subtle vibrations of the earth, not just the tremors caused by footsteps, but the deep, resonant pulses that spoke of geological shifts, of underground water sources, of the slow, inexorable growth of roots. Kira would kneel, placing her hand flat on the ground, with Ash mirroring her action, his large paw beside her own. They would sit in silence, concentrating, trying to discern the faintest tremor, the slightest ripple. Kira learned to feel a subtle humming beneath her palm, a deep, rhythmic thrum that seemed to emanate from the planet's core. Ash would respond with subtle shifts in his weight, nudges with his nose, or low growls, indicating the direction and intensity of these vibrations. He seemed to be learning to distinguish between the predictable pulse of the earth's natural rhythms and the more erratic tremors that signaled a potential danger, like the shifting of unstable ground.

Another exercise involved sensing the subtle shifts in atmospheric pressure, the almost imperceptible scent of distant rain carried on the wind, or the faint electrical charge that preceded a storm. Kira would close her eyes, drawing in slow, deep breaths, trying to capture any hint of moisture, any change in the air's texture. Ash's nostrils would twitch, his gaze fixed on the horizon, his senses reaching out beyond the immediate vicinity. He seemed to be able to detect a nuanced spectrum of atmospheric changes, from the faint coolness that preceded a light shower to the heavy, charged air that signaled an approaching tempest. Kira's challenge was to translate these subtle cues into conscious understanding, to interpret the direction and intensity of Ash's focus, and to connect it with any faint sensory input she herself was experiencing. It was a painstaking process, often yielding only fleeting impressions, but each successful identification, however small, felt like a significant breakthrough.

Perhaps the most demanding, and most rewarding, aspect of their training was the attempt to perceive the emotional tenor of nearby creatures. Elara had explained that all living beings emitted a subtle energetic signature, a "feeling" that could be sensed by those attuned to it. For Kira, this was the most abstract and challenging aspect. She had to learn to quiet her own mind, to push aside her own emotions, and to become a passive, receptive vessel, open to the subtle currents of feeling that flowed from the natural world. Ash, with his innate canine empathy, served as the initial sensor. He would react to the presence of other creatures, not just with outward signs of curiosity or caution, but with subtle shifts in his posture, his breathing, and his internal energy. Kira learned to recognize these cues, to interpret the underlying emotion – the sharp spike of fear from a startled rabbit, the calm contentment of a grazing deer, the bristling territoriality of a badger. She would focus on the area Ash indicated, trying to capture that subtle emotional resonance, to understand the creature's state of being without any direct visual or auditory confirmation. This required an immense amount of trust in Ash, an implicit faith in his ability to perceive these subtle energies. There were times when Kira felt lost, unable to grasp the nuances Ash was conveying, moments of frustration that threatened to undermine her resolve. But Ash's unwavering patience and his silent encouragement, conveyed through gentle nudges and steady gazes, always pulled her back.

The physical and mental toll was significant. After extended sessions, Kira would feel a profound exhaustion, a weariness that seeped into her very bones. Her head would often ache, a dull throbbing behind her eyes, a testament to the intense concentration required. Ash, too, would show signs of fatigue. His once boundless energy would be noticeably diminished, his movements less agile, his responses occasionally delayed. Yet, neither of them yielded. The progress they were making, however incremental, was a powerful motivator. The moments of shared understanding, when Kira could accurately interpret an obscure scent or a subtle vibration, or when Ash seemed to anticipate her thoughts, were incredibly rewarding, reinforcing their commitment to this arduous but vital journey. This constant pushing of their limits was forging a bond between them that transcended the ordinary, a partnership built on shared struggle, mutual reliance, and a growing understanding of each other's unique capacities.

The hum of Haven, usually a comforting undercurrent to her existence, now felt like a fragile shield against the vast, unarticulated symphony of the world. Kira found herself listening not just to the familiar sounds of her community, but to the deeper, quieter resonances that Ash's burgeoning awareness had unlocked within her. Elara's lessons had been more than just training; they were an awakening, a re-tuning of her senses to a spectrum of information that had always existed, unseen and unfelt, beneath the surface of the mundane.

Her days had fallen into a rhythm dictated by the earth and its silent communications. Mornings were dedicated to shared exploration with Ash, their senses intertwined, tracing the subtle energetic currents that flowed through the land. It was no longer enough to simply feel the ground beneath her feet; she was learning to interpret its very state of being. A patch of soil, once perceived as merely dry or damp, now carried a distinct sensation of "thirst," a parched, brittle feeling that spoke of depleted moisture, of roots struggling to draw sustenance. Ash would often nudge the earth with his nose, a soft whine escaping him, and Kira would feel that same sensation, a dry rasping in her own awareness, mirroring his perception. She learned to distinguish the healthy, vibrant pulse of fertile ground from the desolate emptiness of depleted earth, a landscape scarred by unseen pollutants that left a lingering, acrid taste in her awareness, a dull ache that resonated with Ash's low, unsettling murmurs.

These were not abstract concepts; they were visceral feelings that bypassed her rational mind and settled directly into her being. When they encountered a stream that had been choked with refuse from an old, forgotten mining operation, Kira didn't just see the stagnant, discolored water. She *felt* its sickness, a sluggish, heavy inertia, a suffocating pressure that made her own breath catch in her throat. Ash would avoid the water's edge, his body language a clear signal of distress, and Kira would experience that same revulsion, a deep-seated discomfort that mirrored the poisoned state of the environment. It was as if the land itself was crying out, and Ash, through their resonant bond, was translating its pain into a language she could finally understand.

Conversely, there were moments of profound, quiet joy. When they stumbled upon a hidden glade where rare medicinal herbs flourished, untouched by the widespread degradation, Kira felt a surge of vibrant energy, a clear, bright hum that radiated from the plants. Ash would lie down, his body relaxed, his tail thumping a soft rhythm against the dew-kissed grass, and Kira would feel that same sense of peace, of abundant life. It was a sensation of deep contentment, of harmonious flow, a stark contrast to the muted desolation of other areas. These pockets of thriving life were like beacons, small islands of vitality in a sea of ecological struggle, and their discovery brought a powerful sense of hope.

This newfound ability was not without its challenges. The constant influx of sensory information, the emotional weight of the land's suffering, could be overwhelming. There were days when the sheer volume of distress—the brittle dryness of a forest struggling against drought, the suffocating closeness of soil choked with chemical residue, the silent despair of a sapling unable to draw nourishment—would leave Kira drained, her mind a jumble of alien sensations. She would find herself involuntarily flinching at certain textures, recoiling from scents that carried the taint of decay, her own emotional landscape mirroring the environmental disarray they encountered. Ash, too, bore the burden. His once keen nose would sometimes quiver with unease, his ears would flatten against his skull, and he would seek out Kira's comforting presence, his amber eyes conveying a shared weariness.

"It's too much, isn't it?" Kira would whisper, stroking his strong flank as they rested under the shade of a hardy, ancient oak that seemed to radiate a quiet resilience. "It's like the whole world is hurting."

Ash would lean into her touch, a low rumble in his chest a sound of acknowledgement, perhaps even agreement. He would then often nudge her gently, his gaze fixed in a particular direction, an unspoken invitation to continue their journey, to seek out not just the damage, but the remnants of health, the seeds of recovery. His steadfastness was an anchor, a reminder that their purpose was not just to perceive the sickness, but to locate the cures, the resilience, the sparks of life that persisted against all odds.

Their excursions took on a new urgency. They were no longer simply wandering; they were scouting, assessing. When the elders of Haven spoke of potential new settlements or foraging grounds, it was Kira and Ash who could provide an unparalleled depth of insight. They could identify areas where the soil was too depleted to support crops, where the water sources were subtly tainted, or where the very air carried an unhealthy residue. This was information that traditional scouts, relying on sight and smell alone, could not gather. Kira could convey, through Ash's perceptions and her own interpreted feelings, the subtle indicators of ecological health or decline.

One afternoon, while scouting for a suitable location for a new herb garden, they ventured into a valley that appeared, at first glance, deceptively verdant. The usual signs of distress were absent; the grasses were green, the trees sturdy. But as they moved deeper, Kira began to feel a subtle dissonance, a faint, discordant note in the otherwise harmonious hum of the valley. Ash's ears swiveled, his tail gave a single, tentative wag, and he began to lag slightly behind Kira, his gaze sweeping across the landscape with an unusual wariness.

Kira focused, reaching out with her senses, trying to pinpoint the source of this unease. She felt it then – a subtle but persistent "dryness" not in the soil, but in the very energy of the plants. It was a weakness, a lack of vitality that went beyond mere thirst. It was as if the plants were struggling against an invisible depletion, their roots unable to draw the essential life force from the earth. Ash nudged a clump of seemingly healthy ferns, and Kira felt a wave of their quiet distress, a sensation of being drained, of struggling to maintain their form. The valley was not as healthy as it appeared. It was a subtle form of ecological poisoning, likely from a long-forgotten source, that was slowly siphoning the life from the flora.

"This isn't a good place for the garden," Kira murmured, her voice tinged with disappointment. "The land... it's tired here. Drained."

Ash whined softly, pressing his head against her leg, a silent confirmation. They turned back, leaving the deceptive valley behind, their minds already searching for a place that offered not just surface-level green, but the deep, resonant health that spoke of true vitality.

The elders of Haven, initially skeptical of Kira's unusual methods, began to take notice. When Kira advised against planting in a particular clearing, citing a "sourness" in the soil that Ash had perceived as a deep, suffocating stagnation, and later, an old, withered patch of ground was discovered with traces of residual industrial waste, their skepticism began to erode. When she guided them to a hidden spring, its water pure and vibrant, its energetic signature clear and strong, their curiosity turned into a grudging respect.

Kira understood that their resonance was more than just a personal gift; it was a tool, a vital asset for the survival and future of Haven. Their ability to "read" the environment, to sense ecological health and decay, made them invaluable guides. They could pinpoint areas that were safe for habitation and agriculture, identify sources of clean water, and, just as importantly, detect the subtle signs of environmental damage that could threaten the community's well-being.

The process was a continuous learning curve. Each day brought new sensations, new interpretations. Kira learned to distinguish the fleeting "fear" of a creature caught unaware from the more persistent "anxiety" of a habitat under stress. She learned to feel the "weakness" of a tree infected with blight, a slow, creeping decay that manifested as a hollow, empty feeling in her own core. She learned to recognize the "stress" of plants growing in soil that lacked essential micronutrients, a subtle, gnawing sensation that made their very structure feel precarious.

Ash's role in this was paramount. He was the initial sensor, the raw interpreter. His instincts, honed by millennia of canine evolution, provided the foundational data. Kira's unique gift lay in her ability to take that raw data, to amplify it through their resonant bond, and to translate it into conscious understanding. She learned to trust the nuances of his reactions: the way his ears would prick forward at the first hint of unusual atmospheric pressure, the subtle tremor that ran through his body when he sensed a disturbance in the earth's energy field, the soft sigh that escaped him when he perceived the quiet distress of dying flora. These were the subtle cues that, when combined with her own developing perceptions, painted a comprehensive picture of the ecosystem's health.

One crisp autumn afternoon, they were surveying a familiar ridge overlooking a vast expanse of forest. The leaves were turning, painting the landscape in hues of gold and crimson, a spectacle that usually brought Kira a sense of calm appreciation. Today, however, as they reached the ridge's crest, a profound unease settled upon her. Ash whined, a low, mournful sound, and his body tensed, his gaze fixed on a particular section of the forest below.

Kira focused, trying to decipher the feeling. It wasn't a specific sickness, or a discernible pollution. It was a pervasive sense of *distress*, a palpable wave of suffering that emanated from the trees below. It felt like a collective sigh, a dying gasp. She could sense the wilting of leaves before they had even changed color, the brittle dryness of bark that should have been supple, the shallow, struggling breath of the very air that filtered through the canopy. It was the silent cry of an ecosystem on the brink of collapse, a widespread malady that defied immediate visual identification.

"What is it, Ash?" she whispered, her voice thick with the shared sorrow. "What's happening to them?"

Ash nudged her hand, then let out a soft, guttural sound that seemed to echo the dying whispers of the forest. Kira closed her eyes, concentrating with all her might, trying to reach deeper, to understand the source of this widespread suffering. She felt it then, a deep, systemic weakness, as if the very lifeblood of the forest was being leached away. It was a profound environmental sickness, a slow decay that affected every living thing within its reach.

This was not a localized problem that could be easily remedied. This was a widespread ecological devastation, a testament to the long-term impact of practices that had prioritized short-term gain over environmental stewardship. It was a stark reminder of the fragility of their world, and of the vital importance of their ability to sense and understand its deepest needs.

The knowledge they were gathering was not just for navigating the present; it was for shaping the future. By identifying areas of resilience, of vibrant health, they could guide Haven towards sustainable growth. By recognizing the subtle indicators of distress, they could intervene before irreversible damage occurred. They were becoming the eyes and ears of the land, their resonant bond a conduit for its unspoken language. This awakening of their senses, this deep connection with the living world, was the true foundation of their strength, the key to their survival, and perhaps, the salvation of Haven itself. The journey was arduous, demanding, and at times, emotionally devastating, but with each successful interpretation, each act of environmental empathy, Kira felt their purpose solidifying, their bond deepening, and the quiet revolution within Haven gaining momentum. They were learning to not just survive, but to thrive, by listening to the whispers of the earth.

The rhythm of Haven, once a gentle lullaby, had become a frantic drumbeat against Kira's heightened senses. It wasn't the familiar communal sounds of rebuilding – the rhythmic clang of hammers, the murmur of shared meals, the laughter of children – that had shifted. Instead, it was a deeper, more insidious disquiet, a subtle dissonance that resonated from the very heart of their small community. Elara, the elder healer, had been unusually withdrawn, her usual vibrant energy muted. Kira felt it as a faint, persistent ache in her own awareness, a shadow of weariness cast over the elder's usually bright aura.

Then came the news that rippled through Haven like a cold draft: young Lyra, one of the most spirited children, had fallen ill. It wasn't a common fever or a simple cough that could be soothed with familiar poultices. This was something deeper, something that seemed to drain the very light from the child's eyes, leaving her listless and frail. Kira felt the shift in the community's collective mood keenly. It was a subtle dimming of the usual resilience, a flicker of fear that she hadn't felt since their earliest days in Haven, a time when the world beyond their sheltered valley felt like an insurmountable threat.

Ash sensed it too. His usual playful demeanor had been replaced by a quiet vigilance. He stayed close to Kira, his amber eyes often fixed on the direction of Elara's dwelling, a low whine occasionally rumbling in his chest. He nudged her hand with his wet nose, his unspoken question clear:

What is happening?

Kira found herself drawn to Elara's small, neat dwelling. The air inside was heavy, not with the scent of illness, but with a palpable stillness. Elara sat by Lyra's bedside, her face etched with a weariness that spoke of sleepless nights and unanswered prayers. The child lay pale and still, her breathing shallow. Kira extended her senses, tentatively reaching towards Lyra. It wasn't a physical illness she felt, not in the conventional sense. It was a profound exhaustion, a depletion of life force that went beyond the ordinary. It was as if Lyra's inner light had been dimmed, smothered by an unseen force.

"She is fading, Kira," Elara's voice was raspy, her gaze fixed on Lyra. "We have tried everything. The usual herbs... they offer no solace."

Kira knelt beside the small cot, her heart heavy. She could feel it now, a faint, almost imperceptible chill emanating from Lyra, a discordance in the natural energetic flow. It was as if something had fundamentally disrupted the child's vital systems, leaving her vulnerable and weak. Ash, sensing Kira's distress and the child's profound imbalance, let out a soft groan, his body pressing against Kira's leg. He seemed to be trying to push something away, a sensation of deep internal cold that Kira could faintly echo.

"It's not just a sickness of the body, is it?" Kira whispered, her eyes meeting Elara's. "It's... a deeper exhaustion."

Elara nodded slowly. "The essence of her. It is being leached away. I cannot identify the cause. It's unlike anything I have encountered in my years."

Kira's mind immediately went to the lands they had explored, the places where the earth itself seemed to weep with a silent, lingering poison. She recalled the areas where the very air felt thin and brittle, where the life force of the plants seemed to have been siphoned away, leaving behind a residual emptiness. Could Lyra's affliction be a manifestation of this deeper ecological malaise, a sickness that was no longer confined to the land but had begun to touch their own lives?

"We need to find something... something potent," Kira murmured, more to herself than to Elara. Her gaze drifted to Ash, who was now nudging a worn satchel filled with dried herbs and foraging tools. His focus was unwavering, his intuition a beacon in the growing darkness.

"Potent is what we need," Elara agreed, her voice barely audible. "But the land offers so little that is untainted now. Finding a true remedy... it feels like searching for a single star in a perpetually clouded sky."

Kira stood, a new resolve hardening within her. Ash's presence was a constant reminder of their unique ability, their resonant connection to the world. If the land held the answers, then their shared perception was the key to unlocking them. "We'll look, Elara. We'll look everywhere."

The following days were a blur of intense exploration, a desperate search driven by the urgency of Lyra's fading life. Kira and Ash ventured further than they had before, pushing the boundaries of their comfort zones, their senses stretched taut. They traversed rolling hills that showed subtle signs of desiccation, navigated the skeletal remains of forests that had succumbed to unknown blights, and skirted the edges of polluted waterways that hissed with a silent toxicity.

Ash was their compass, his nose to the ground, his ears constantly twitching, sifting through the cacophony of environmental signals. He would pause, a low rumble in his chest, indicating a place of particular unease, or let out a soft whine, guiding Kira towards a faint whisper of vitality. Kira, in turn, amplified these perceptions, translating the subtle energetic signatures into a tangible understanding. She felt the "weariness" of the soil in depleted regions, the "anxiety" of plants struggling for sustenance, and now, a chilling echo of that same exhaustion seemed to emanate from Lyra, a fragile thread connecting the child to the ailing earth.

Their search led them to the fringes of the Whispering Marshes, a region long avoided by the people of Haven. It was a place shrouded in an ominous reputation, a testament to the lingering scars of the Old World's industrial excesses. The air there was thick with a cloying dampness, and the very ground seemed to exude a subtle, metallic tang that made Kira's teeth ache. Ash, usually so eager, trod with extreme caution, his body low to the ground, his tail tucked tight. He whined softly, a sound of deep reluctance, and nudged Kira's hand insistently, as if urging her to turn back.

"I know, Ash," Kira murmured, her own senses recoiling from the oppressive atmosphere. "It feels... wrong." But the image of Lyra's pale face spurred her onward. She focused her awareness, trying to pierce through the miasma of contamination. She was not looking for general health, but for something specific, something that Elara might recognize, a potent counter to Lyra's strange affliction.

They pushed deeper into the marshes, the dense, gnarled trees forming a suffocating canopy overhead. The ground beneath their feet was a treacherous mix of mud and unseen detritus. Kira felt the pervasive "sickness" of the area acutely – a sluggish, suffocating inertia that seemed to press in on her from all sides. It was a heavy, stagnant energy, a testament to the slow, insidious decay that had taken root. Ash's discomfort was a constant, palpable thing, his body trembling subtly with each step.

Suddenly, Ash stopped. He lowered his head, his nose twitching erratically, not towards the ground, but towards a cluster of stunted, skeletal bushes growing near a stagnant pool of iridescent water. He let out a low, almost involuntary bark, his body rigid with a focused intensity. Kira followed his gaze, her own senses attempting to decipher the subtle energetic emanations from the plants.

There, nestled amongst the dying foliage, was a single, vibrant bloom. It was small, with delicate, star-shaped petals the color of amethyst. But it was the energy emanating from it that was astonishing. It pulsed with a clean, bright vitality, a stark contrast to the oppressive decay surrounding it. It felt like a tiny beacon of pure life in a sea of contamination.

"What is it?" Kira breathed, her heart leaping with a desperate hope. Ash nudged the plant gently with his nose, then looked up at Kira, his amber eyes wide with a strange mix of recognition and caution. He let out a soft, almost questioning sound, as if trying to articulate a memory.

Kira reached out, her fingers hovering just above the amethyst petals. She could feel it, a potent, cleansing energy that seemed to resonate with the very core of her being. It was a healing energy, pure and uncorrupted, unlike anything she had ever encountered. It felt ancient, powerful, and profoundly rare. She focused, trying to recall Elara's extensive teachings, her knowledge of forgotten flora. This plant... it was familiar, yet from a different time, a different world.

"The Luminaria," she whispered, a forgotten name surfacing from the depths of her mind. "Elara mentioned it once. A herb from the old texts, said to have... restorative properties. But it was thought to be extinct. Or too rare to find."

Elara had described it as a plant that could draw out and neutralize deep-seated imbalances, a potent cleanser of both physical and energetic systems. But she had also warned that it only grew in areas of profound ecological distress, thriving where other life forms withered. The very environment that was toxic to most, seemed to be the crucible in which Luminaria was forged. This explained why it was found here, in the heart of the corrupted marshes.

Ash whined again, his gaze fixed on the stagnant water nearby. Kira felt it then, the true extent of the contamination. The water was a virulent brew of chemicals and toxins, seeping into the soil, slowly poisoning everything it touched. Yet, the Luminaria bloomed defiantly, its roots drawing sustenance from this very poison, transforming it into life-giving energy.

"This is it, Ash," Kira said, her voice firm despite the lingering unease of the marsh. "This is what Lyra needs."

The challenge, however, was not just in finding the Luminaria, but in retrieving it. The ground around the plant was saturated with toxins. Even the air seemed to carry a subtle, acrid bite. Kira knew that touching the contaminated soil directly, or even breathing too deeply of the marsh air, could be dangerous.

"We need to be careful," she said to Ash, her mind already working through the logistics. "We can't let the contamination spread."

She carefully retrieved a sturdy foraging pouch and a pair of thick, woven gloves from their satchel. Ash watched her, his body still tense, but his gaze fixed on her with unwavering trust. Kira took a deep breath, trying to calm the flutter of apprehension in her chest. This was a different kind of challenge, a direct confrontation with the very forces that had wounded their world.

With meticulous care, Kira began to clear away the surrounding dead foliage. Ash stayed close, his presence a silent anchor, his senses alert to any change in their environment. As Kira worked, she felt a subtle shift in the Luminaria's energetic signature. It seemed to respond to her intent, to the presence of Ash's amplified senses, to their shared purpose. The amethyst petals glowed a little brighter, the cleansing pulse growing stronger.

The most difficult part was extracting the roots without disturbing the toxic soil any more than necessary. Kira worked slowly, using a small trowel, her movements precise. The roots of the Luminaria were delicate, intertwined with the contaminated earth. As she dug, a wave of the marsh's heavy, stagnant energy washed over her, a sickening pressure that threatened to overwhelm her. Ash let out a low growl, a protective instinct that seemed to push back against the encroaching foulness.

Kira felt a surge of connection with Ash, a shared determination that seemed to bolster her own resolve. Their bond wasn't just about sensing the world; it was about facing its challenges together, about drawing strength from each other. She focused on the Luminaria, on the pure, vibrant energy it represented, and let that be her guide. She imagined the plant's healing power as a shield, deflecting the marsh's toxic influence.

Finally, with a gentle tug, she freed the Luminaria, roots and all, from the contaminated soil. She carefully wrapped the roots in a damp cloth, then placed the entire plant into the protective pouch. As she sealed it, she felt a profound sense of relief, mingled with a heavy weariness. The marsh's oppressive atmosphere still clung to her, a subtle residue of its pervasive toxicity.

Ash nudged her hand, then licked her gloved fingers, a gesture of reassurance. Kira managed a weak smile. "We did it, boy. We found it."

The journey back to Haven was arduous, not physically, but mentally. The lingering effects of the marsh's energy were unsettling. Kira felt a dull ache in her bones and a faint metallic taste in her mouth. Ash remained unusually subdued, his senses seemingly still processing the overwhelming negativity of the marshes.

When they arrived, Elara rushed out, her eyes wide with a mixture of hope and anxiety. Kira presented the Luminaria, its amethyst petals still faintly glowing. A hush fell over the few Haven dwellers who had gathered. Elara took the plant with trembling hands, her gaze fixed on its vibrant form.

"The Luminaria," she breathed, her voice filled with awe. "It is real. And it is potent."

She immediately set about preparing a remedy, grinding the petals and roots with a mortar and pestle, her movements precise and practiced. The air in Lyra's dwelling, which had felt so heavy and still, began to fill with a faint, sweet fragrance, a promise of healing.

Kira watched, her own exhaustion weighing heavily upon her. She felt a strange duality – the lingering unease from the marsh, and the nascent hope that the Luminaria represented. Ash lay at her feet, his head resting on his paws, his eyes closed. He seemed to be drawing strength from the very presence of the healing herb.

Elara carefully administered a small dose of the Luminaria infusion to Lyra. For a tense moment, nothing happened. The child remained still, her breathing shallow. Kira's heart sank. Had they been too late? Had the marsh's toxic influence been too profound?

Then, a flicker. A subtle change in Lyra's breathing. A faint warmth seemed to spread from the child's chest. Kira felt it as a gentle stirring of energy, a tentative reawakening. Ash stirred, his tail giving a weak thump against the floor.

Slowly, miraculously, color began to return to Lyra's cheeks. Her eyelids fluttered, then opened, revealing a faint, but undeniable spark of awareness. She looked at Elara, then her gaze drifted to Kira and Ash. A weak smile touched her lips.

"Kira... Ash..." she whispered, her voice still fragile, but clearer than it had been in days.

A collective sigh of relief swept through the small dwelling. Elara, her eyes shining with unshed tears, placed a gentle hand on Lyra's forehead. "You are healing, little one. The earth has offered its balm."

Kira felt a profound sense of gratitude, a deep, resonant joy that spread through her like warm sunlight. Their journey to the Whispering Marshes had been fraught with danger, a stark reminder of the world's persistent toxicity. But in finding the Luminaria, they had not only discovered a powerful remedy but had also demonstrated the life-saving potential of their unique bond. It was a testament to their ability to navigate the broken landscapes, to find hope in the most desolate of places, and to offer a touch of true healing in a world desperately in need of it. The resonant connection between Kira and Ash, once a curiosity, was now a vital lifeline, a beacon of resilience in the face of a wounded world. Their capacity to sense and interpret the earth's deepest needs had directly translated into the ability to mend, to restore, and to save a life. This was not just an ecological understanding; it was a pathway to survival, a profound affirmation of their purpose.

The journey back from the Whispering Marshes had been a test of a different kind, a subtle unraveling of the peace they had so hard-won. The Luminaria's potent, cleansing energy had worked its miracle, coaxing Lyra back from the brink of that deep, unnatural exhaustion. The child was recovering, her laughter a sweet melody returning to Haven's heart. Yet, for Kira, the echoes of their perilous expedition lingered, not as physical ailments, but as a complex tapestry of emotions, woven from her own anxieties and the indelible impressions of Ash's responses.

Ash, the ever-present barometer of their shared world, had been a constant source of comfort and clarity during the search for the Luminaria. His unerring instincts, his low rumbles of warning, and his soft whines of discovery had guided her through the suffocating miasma of the marshes. But it was the aftermath, the quiet moments of return, that truly illuminated the depth of their resonant connection.

Kira remembered the moment, days after Lyra's recovery, when they had ventured to the spring that fed Haven's main water source. It was a place of pristine, life-giving purity, a stark contrast to the toxic seepages they had navigated. As Kira knelt, cupping her hands to drink, she felt an overwhelming wave of pure, unadulterated joy radiating from Ash. It wasn't a simple pleasure; it was a profound contentment, a visceral appreciation for the clean, cool water that flowed, untainted. He splashed in the shallows, his amber eyes shining, his tail wagging a furious rhythm against the mossy bank. Kira felt it as a warm current unfurling within her own chest, a mirroring of his delight. It was as if his very being was singing a hymn of gratitude for this simple, vital sustenance. This unburdened happiness was a balm, a potent antidote to the anxieties that had gripped her during Lyra's illness.

However, this mirroring of emotion was not always so benign. A few evenings later, as dusk settled over Haven, a foreign scent, sharp and acrid, drifted on the breeze from beyond their valley's protective embrace. It was a smell Kira couldn't quite identify, but it carried a visceral sense of wrongness, a subtle undertone of decay and threat. Instantly, Ash was on his feet, his body tensing, a low, guttural growl vibrating in his chest. His ears were perked, swiveling to catch the faintest sound, his every muscle coiled for a confrontation that hadn't yet materialized. Kira felt a jolt of primal fear shoot through her, an echo of Ash's immediate defensive posture. Her own heart began to pound, her breath catching in her throat. It was as if his alarm bells were ringing directly within her own nervous system. She found herself scanning the darkening horizon, her mind conjuring worst-case scenarios – an encroaching threat, a scouting party from a forgotten, hostile enclave, or perhaps something far more alien and unsettling.

This involuntary amplification of Ash's instincts meant that Kira had to learn to differentiate between her own burgeoning fears and the primal responses of her canine companion. It was a delicate dance, a constant act of emotional discernment. When Ash reacted with unease, Kira's first instinct was to trust his senses, to acknowledge the potential danger he perceived. But she also had to filter it through her own understanding, her own calculated assessment of the situation. Was it a true threat, or a mere shadow of the past, a memory imprinted on Ash's keen awareness from his own, less shielded experiences in the wider world?

There were times, too, when the weight of her own anxieties threatened to become overwhelming. The responsibility of Haven, the constant vigilance required to maintain their sanctuary, the memory of the world's devastation – these were burdens that often settled heavily upon Kira. On particularly difficult days, when the air felt thick with unspoken worries, or when the news from reconnaissance missions spoke of continued environmental degradation, Kira would find herself sinking into a quiet despair. And in those moments, Ash would invariably draw close. He wouldn't bark or whine, but would simply press his warm body against her side, his soft fur a grounding presence. She could feel his quiet concern, a gentle, steady empathy that seemed to absorb some of her own despondency. He would lick her hand, his rough tongue a surprisingly comforting sensation, and she knew, with a certainty that transcended words, that he understood the depth of her struggle. He wasn't just sensing her sadness; he was sharing it, offering his own silent strength in return.

This mirroring, this shared emotional landscape, was the very essence of their bond, the bedrock upon which their resilience was built. But it also demanded a new level of self-awareness from Kira. She had to learn to navigate not only her own internal currents but also the powerful, often raw, emotional tides that flowed from Ash. When he was joyous, she could bask in his pure, unadulterated happiness. But when he was fearful or anxious, she had to find a way to remain grounded, to offer him a steady presence without being consumed by his distress.

It was a process of constant recalibration. Kira found herself developing a heightened awareness of her own emotional state, a practice of observing her feelings with a detached curiosity. Was this surge of anxiety her own, or Ash's? Was this surge of hope a genuine flicker, or a reflection of his optimism? The lines had blurred, and in that blurring, a new understanding of connection was forged.

One afternoon, while tending to the nascent vegetable gardens, a sudden gust of wind carried the faint scent of woodsmoke. It was a familiar, comforting smell in Haven, usually signaling a communal fire for cooking or warmth. But this scent was different. It was tinged with a subtle acridity, a sharp, chemical undertone that immediately set Kira's teeth on edge. Ash, who had been playfully chasing a butterfly, froze. His playful demeanor vanished, replaced by a rigid alertness. He let out a soft, questioning whine, his head cocked, his eyes fixed in the direction of the scent. Kira felt his immediate apprehension, a prickle of unease that mirrored his own.

"What is it, boy?" she murmured, her own senses straining to identify the source. The woodsmoke was faint, and the acrid note was almost imperceptible, easily dismissed as a trick of the wind. But Ash was unwavering. He took a few steps towards the edge of the clearing, his body low to the ground, his tail held stiffly. He nudged Kira's leg, a silent insistence that she acknowledge the anomaly.

Kira closed her eyes, reaching out with her amplified awareness. She tried to disentangle the scent, to isolate its components. The woodsmoke was indeed present, but beneath it, like a sickly undercurrent, was that fainter, more disturbing aroma. It spoke of burning plastic, of toxic fumes, of the remnants of a world that had choked on its own progress. This was not the clean, life-affirming smoke of Haven's hearths.

As she focused, she felt Ash's primal fear intensify. It was the fear of the unknown, the instinctive dread of something that was inherently unnatural, something that threatened the delicate balance of their world. His unease was a tangible force, pressing against her own emotional equilibrium. She felt a knot of anxiety tighten in her stomach, a familiar precursor to potential danger. Her mind, ever prone to envisioning the worst, began to paint grim pictures: a distant, uncontrolled fire spreading from some forgotten toxic waste site, its poisonous smoke inching closer to Haven.

"Easy, Ash," Kira whispered, stroking his head. His fur was bristled, a sign of his heightened alert. "We don't know what it is yet." She tried to project calm, to transmit a reassuring presence, but she could feel the tremor of his fear resonating within her own bones. It was a chilling reminder of how deeply their emotional states were intertwined.

As the wind shifted, the acrid note grew slightly stronger, and Ash let out a low, warning growl. He nudged her again, more insistently this time, his amber eyes wide and earnest, conveying a clear message:

Danger. We must be cautious.

Kira understood. This was not a time for complacency. She made a decision, her own anxiety now tempered by a growing resolve. "Alright, boy. Let's go see." She grabbed a sturdy foraging knife from her belt, a habit of preparedness that had become second nature. Ash immediately moved to her side, his posture shifting from defensive alertness to protective vigilance. He seemed to understand their mission, his focus now on accompanying and guarding her.

They followed the direction of the scent, moving with a cautious stealth that Ash seemed to instinctively lead. He would pause periodically, sniffing the air, his body language communicating subtle shifts in the scent's intensity or direction. Kira watched him, her own senses attempting to corroborate his findings, her mind working through potential scenarios. The fear was still there, a subtle hum beneath the surface of her awareness, but it was now overlaid with a sense of purpose, a drive to understand and, if necessary, to confront the source of the disturbance.

Their path led them towards the western ridge, a less explored part of their valley. The vegetation here was sparser, the soil less fertile than in the more protected areas. As they crested a small rise, Kira spotted the source of the smoke. A small, isolated fire smoldered in a hollow, its flames feeding on what appeared to be a pile of debris. It wasn't a natural fire; it was clearly man-made, a deliberate act of burning. And the debris... it was a collection of odd, metallic objects, corroded and partially melted, mixed with fragments of what looked like brittle, colored plastic.

Ash let out a low growl, his body stiffening as they approached. The acrid smell was stronger here, a pungent, suffocating odor that burned the back of Kira's throat. She could feel the environmental damage radiating from the site, a subtle but persistent drain on the very life force of the surrounding land. The plants closest to the fire were blackened and brittle, their growth stunted.

Kira's mind raced. Who would be burning such things so close to Haven? It was a reckless act, a blatant disregard for the fragile ecosystem they were so carefully nurturing. And the materials themselves... they were remnants of the Old World, of its unsustainable practices, its toxic legacy.

She felt Ash's rising alarm, his instincts screaming that this was a threat. He wanted to charge, to confront whatever had left this destructive imprint on their land. But Kira held him back, placing a restraining hand on his flank.

"No, Ash," she said, her voice firm but low. "Not yet. We need to understand."

She cautiously approached the smoldering remains, her eyes scanning the area for any clues. She noticed footprints in the loose soil, larger than those of any Haven dweller, suggesting an outsider. The nature of the debris was disturbing – twisted metal, shards of glass, and what looked like the remnants of some kind of chemical container. It was a testament to the careless disposal of hazardous waste, a habit that had nearly doomed their world.

As she examined the area, a wave of intense emotional distress washed over her, a profound sadness for the desecration of their sanctuary. It wasn't just her own dismay; it was the land's own sorrow, amplified through her connection with Ash. She felt the land's pain, its struggle to heal from such wounds. Ash nudged her hand, his usual playful exuberance replaced by a somber quietude. He seemed to sense her profound disappointment, her deep-seated sorrow at this intrusion. He licked her cheek, a silent offering of comfort, his amber eyes filled with a shared melancholy.

Then, a new scent, carried on a subtle eddy of wind, caught Kira's attention. It was faint, barely perceptible, but it was distinct. It was a scent of fear, not the aggressive fear of a predator, but the skittish fear of prey, of someone who was hiding, or who had recently been present and was now fleeing. Ash's ears swiveled, his gaze locking onto a thicket of gnarled bushes a short distance away. He let out a soft, almost imperceptible whine, a sound of caution and curiosity.

Kira followed his gaze, her own heightened senses picking up on the faint, distressed energetic signature emanating from the thicket. It was a small, fragile life force, overwhelmed by the acrid stench of the fire and the palpable sense of violation. She recognized the signature; it was the scent of a small, burrowing creature, one of the few native animals that had managed to survive in the valley.

"Someone else was here, Ash," Kira murmured, a new understanding dawning. "And they were afraid."

Ash nudged her towards the thicket, his protective instincts now directed towards this unseen presence. Kira approached slowly, speaking in a low, soothing voice. "It's okay. We're not going to hurt you."

As she parted the branches, she saw it: a small, trembling creature, its fur matted and its eyes wide with terror. It was a young valley shrew, its tiny body quivering. The acrid smoke had clearly driven it from its burrow, and the sight of the smoldering fire, along with the footprints of whoever had started it, had sent it into a state of panic.

Kira felt a wave of Ash's protective empathy for the small animal. His urge to hunt was completely overridden by his innate gentleness, his understanding of vulnerability. He whined softly, a sound of reassurance, and sat down a few paces away, his presence calm and unthreatening.

Kira knelt, offering her hand slowly. The shrew flinched at first, but as Kira projected a steady stream of calm, and as Ash remained quiescent, its trembling began to subside. Kira felt the creature's fear gradually ebb, replaced by a cautious curiosity. It was a stark reminder of the interconnectedness of all life in Haven, and how the actions of one individual could have far-reaching consequences, affecting even the smallest of its inhabitants.

This incident, though seemingly minor, had a profound impact on Kira. It underscored the responsibility that came with their unique abilities. They weren't just observers; they were guardians. Ash's ability to sense the subtle shifts in the environment, and Kira's capacity to translate those senses into understanding, made them acutely aware of the delicate balance of their world.

Later that evening, as they sat by their own small hearth, the scent of clean burning wood a comforting presence, Kira reflected on the day's events. Ash lay at her feet, his head resting on his paws, his breathing deep and even. Yet, even in his sleep, Kira could feel a subtle current of awareness emanating from him, a lingering sensitivity to the residual acridity that still clung to the air from the distant, illegal fire.

She closed her eyes, focusing on her own emotional state. The initial surge of anxiety from the unknown scent, the subsequent fear and anger at the act of desecration, and finally, the pang of sorrow for the vulnerable shrew – all these emotions had been amplified and shared by Ash. He had been her barometer, her emotional echo.

She realized that managing their shared emotional landscape was a continuous process. It wasn't just about controlling her own feelings, but about understanding and integrating Ash's responses as well. When he felt fear, she had to acknowledge it, to process it with him, and then find a way to either mitigate the threat or to reassure him that they were safe. When he felt joy, she could embrace it, allowing its warmth to spread through her.

This constant interplay of emotions, this resonant mirroring, had forged a bond between them that was deeper and more complex than anything Kira had ever known. It was a constant learning curve, a dynamic relationship that required patience, understanding, and a willingness to embrace both the light and the shadows of their shared existence. It was through this profound emotional resonance, she understood, that they truly found their strength, their ability to navigate the challenges of their world, not as two separate beings, but as a unified force, capable of sensing, understanding, and ultimately, protecting the fragile beauty of Haven. The world outside their valley might be fractured and dangerous, but within their shared awareness, they had created a sanctuary of profound emotional connection, a testament to the enduring power of empathy and companionship in a world desperately in need of both.

The training grounds, usually a place of focused exertion and the rhythmic thud of movement, crackled with an unusual intensity that day. Kira pushed herself through the familiar drills, her muscles burning, her breath coming in ragged gasps. Ash, a blur of amber and fur, mirrored her movements with uncanny precision, his low growls of exertion a counterpoint to her own grunts of effort. They were honing their defensive postures, practicing evasive maneuvers, and strengthening the intricate network of their shared awareness. It was a dance they had perfected over months, a silent conversation of intent and reaction. Yet, today, something felt different, as if the very air around them had thickened, charged with an unseen energy.

Kira was demonstrating a complex series of blocks and parries, her movements fluid and economical, when it happened. It wasn't a sudden jolt, but rather a subtle shift, like a veil being drawn aside, revealing a scene that was both alien and eerily familiar. The world around her dissolved, not into darkness, but into a blinding cascade of fragmented images. She saw towering structures, impossibly tall, piercing a sky choked with a sickly yellow haze. Below, countless figures, mere specks from her vantage point, moved with a desperate urgency, their forms indistinct, their actions a frantic ballet of survival. The air, even in this fleeting impression, was heavy with a cacophony of sounds – the distant wail of sirens, the grinding of metal, and a pervasive, low hum that vibrated deep within her bones.

Then, the perspective shifted, plunging her downwards. She felt a crushing sensation, a visceral understanding of immense pressure, as if the very atmosphere was collapsing in on itself. The figures below became clearer, their faces etched with a fear so profound it seemed to seep into the very fabric of the vision. She saw them scrambling, their hands reaching, not for each other, but for something intangible, something lost. A sense of overwhelming grief washed over her, a primal sorrow that wasn't her own, but belonged to the collective despair of a dying world.

Ash, who had been mirroring her movements perfectly, suddenly faltered. He stumbled, letting out a soft, startled yelp, his amber eyes wide and unfocused. His usual, steady presence wavered, replaced by a profound disorientation. Kira felt his confusion ripple through their connection, a jolt of surprise that momentarily broke the immersive quality of the vision. It was as if he, too, had been privy to this fleeting glimpse of another reality.

The images flickered, morphing into something new, yet equally unsettling. She saw a different kind of chaos, not the widespread devastation of the first glimpse, but a more concentrated, terrifying ordeal. The air was thick with smoke, not the familiar, clean smoke of Haven's fires, but a noxious, acrid plume that stung her eyes and burned her throat. She saw figures in bulky, protective suits, their faces obscured by visors, moving with a grim efficiency through a landscape of ruin. They were collecting something, their movements precise, almost mechanical, as they gathered scattered fragments, shards of what looked like glass and metal, all bearing the same sickly yellow hue as the haze in the first vision.

A wave of primal fear, sharper and more immediate than anything she had felt before, surged through her. This wasn't a distant echo; this felt like an imminent threat, a danger that was breathing down her neck. She felt Ash recoil beside her, a low, guttural growl rumbling in his chest, his body tensing as if to face an unseen enemy. His fear was a tangible force, amplifying her own, and for a terrifying moment, she was consumed by it. She felt her own breath hitch, her heart pound a frantic rhythm against her ribs.

Then, as abruptly as it had begun, the vision receded, leaving Kira gasping for air, her legs trembling beneath her. The training grounds snapped back into sharp focus, the familiar scent of pine and damp earth a welcome anchor. Ash was nudging her hand, his amber eyes filled with a mixture of concern and confusion, his tail giving a tentative, questioning wag. He whined softly, as if seeking an explanation for the sudden disruption.

Kira sank to her knees, her body wracked with a tremor that had nothing to do with physical exertion. Her mind raced, trying to process the fragmented images, the overwhelming emotions. What had just happened? It wasn't a memory, not in the way she understood them. It felt... borrowed. A glimpse into a time or place that existed beyond the confines of her own experience. And the fact that Ash had reacted so profoundly, that she had felt his disorientation and fear so acutely, suggested something more than a simple psychic echo. It was a shared experience, a communion of awareness that had pierced the veil of their present reality.

"Ash," she whispered, her voice hoarse. "What was that?"

He responded by pressing his head against her thigh, a gesture of comfort and reassurance, but his usual unwavering focus was gone. His ears were still slightly back, his gaze darting around as if expecting the spectral threat to reappear. Kira reached out, stroking his sleek fur, feeling the residual tension in his muscles. He wasn't just sensing her distress; he was sharing it, processing it through his own innate instincts.

The intensity of the vision had been staggering, far beyond anything she had experienced before. While she had always been attuned to Ash's emotions, and he to hers, this was a leap into a different order of connection. It was as if their resonance, honed through countless shared moments, had suddenly achieved a new level of clarity, allowing them to tap into something deeper, something beyond their immediate selves.

She tried to retrace the sensory details, to anchor herself in the fragmented impressions. The towering structures, the yellow haze – it spoke of an advanced civilization, perhaps, but one that had succumbed to its own hubris, choking on its progress. The sound of sirens, the frantic movements of the crowds – it was the sound of a world in collapse, a final, desperate scramble for survival. And the second vision, the acrid smoke, the masked figures collecting debris – it felt like a consequence, a grim aftermath of whatever catastrophe had befallen that lost world. It was the imagery of remediation, of attempts to salvage or contain the damage, a desperate effort to reclaim something from the ashes.

The raw fear that had accompanied that second vision was particularly disturbing. It wasn't the existential dread of their current reality, but a more immediate, visceral terror. It spoke of a present danger, a tangible threat that had forced these figures into their protective gear. And the smell... that acrid, chemical stench. It was a scent that Kira instinctively recoiled from, a visceral aversion that resonated with Ash's own primal unease.

She looked at Ash, his amber eyes now regaining a measure of their usual clarity, though a faint flicker of apprehension still lingered. She realized that their shared emotional landscape was not just a passive reflection; it was an active conduit. In moments of heightened emotional intensity, their connection could seemingly tap into broader currents of experience, both past and potential.

"It was... a warning, maybe?" she mused aloud, more to herself than to Ash. "Or a memory. Someone's memory." The idea that their bond could act as a bridge to such experiences was both exhilarating and terrifying. It opened up a vast, unknown territory, a realm of possibilities that could either empower them or overwhelm them.

Over the next few days, Kira found herself replaying the fragmented images, trying to piece together a coherent narrative. The experience had left a lasting impression, a subtle shift in her perception of their world. The familiar landscape of Haven, so serene and vibrant, now felt like a fragile oasis, constantly threatened by the ghosts of a past that refused to stay buried. She felt a renewed sense of urgency in their training, a deeper understanding of why their skills were so vital. The echoes of that vision served as a constant, silent reminder of what could happen if they failed, if the delicate balance they fought to maintain was ever broken.

Ash, too, seemed affected. While he resumed his normal playful demeanor, there were moments when his gaze would drift, his ears twitching as if catching a scent on the wind that only he could perceive. He would sometimes nudge her, his amber eyes holding a depth of understanding that transcended their usual communication. It was as if the vision had imprinted on him as well, stirring something deep within his own ancestral memory, a primal recognition of a world that had been lost.

One evening, as they sat by the hearth, the fire casting dancing shadows on the walls of their small dwelling, Kira found herself staring into the flames. She tried to recall the exact sensation of the vision, the way the world had dissolved and reformed. She reached out with her amplified awareness, not actively seeking anything, but simply opening herself to the subtle currents that flowed between her and Ash.

She felt his presence beside her, a warm, solid weight against her legs. His breathing was slow and even, but she could sense a low hum of awareness beneath the surface of his sleep. She focused on that hum, on the subtle energetic vibrations that connected them. And then, as if a switch had been flipped, the images returned, fainter this time, more like whispers on the edge of her perception.

She saw a hand, weathered and strong, reaching out to touch a strange, glowing crystal. The crystal pulsed with a soft, internal light, and as the hand made contact, a wave of pure, unadulterated energy flooded through the limb, spreading outwards like ripples on a pond. It was a sensation of immense power, of a profound connection to something ancient and elemental. Kira felt a surge of exhilaration, a sense of wonder that momentarily eclipsed the lingering fear from the earlier vision.

This time, Ash stirred immediately, his tail thumping softly against the floor. He let out a low, pleased rumble, his amber eyes opening and fixing on Kira with an almost startling clarity. He seemed to understand this new impression, to recognize it not as a threat, but as something significant, something potentially positive.

"The crystal," Kira breathed, the word echoing the fragmented visual. "What was that, boy?"

Ash responded by nudging her hand with his nose, then looking pointedly towards the door, as if urging her to venture outside. His excitement was palpable, a stark contrast to the apprehension he had shown in the previous vision. It was as if this new glimpse had unlocked a different facet of their shared experience, a more hopeful possibility.

Kira felt a thrill of anticipation. If their resonance could indeed tap into such profound moments, then the potential for learning, for understanding their world and its history, was immense. The initial fear of the unknown was still present, a healthy dose of caution, but it was now tempered by a burgeoning sense of curiosity and a growing trust in their shared awareness. They had glimpsed fragments of a ruined past, a world consumed by its own destructive tendencies. But now, they had also seen a flicker of something else, something that hinted at a source of power, a connection to forces that could potentially heal and restore.

The training sessions took on a new dimension after that. Kira found herself consciously trying to replicate the state of openness and receptivity that had led to the visions. She focused on the subtle nuances of Ash's emotional responses, on the way their shared energy ebbed and flowed. She realized that their bond was not just about shared feelings; it was about shared perception, a unique lens through which they could view the world, and perhaps, other worlds and other times as well.

The vision of the crystal, in particular, lingered in her mind. It spoke of a power that was not destructive, but generative, a force that could illuminate and perhaps even heal. She wondered if it was connected to the Luminaria, the rare, potent energy source that had saved Lyra. The similarities in their energetic signatures, the subtle glow, the sense of immense, contained power, were too striking to ignore.

As days turned into weeks, Kira continued to explore the depths of their connection. She learned to distinguish between Ash's primal reactions and the more complex echoes that their resonance sometimes unveiled. She discovered that by grounding herself; by maintaining a calm center, she could sift through the influx of sensory and emotional information, identifying the core of what was being communicated. Ash, in turn, seemed to adapt, his responses becoming more nuanced, his shared perceptions less chaotic. He would often nudge her towards a specific direction, or let out a particular whine, as if trying to guide her towards understanding these shared glimpses.

One crisp autumn morning, as they were exploring the northern edge of the valley, a place where the trees grew denser and the shadows longer, Kira felt a familiar sensation begin to build. It was a subtle hum, a growing warmth in her chest that mirrored the quiet intensity she felt radiating from Ash. He had stopped, his ears perked, his body held in a posture of alert stillness.

"What is it, boy?" Kira whispered, her own senses sharpening.

This time, the vision was different. It wasn't a chaotic glimpse of a lost world, or a fleeting vision of raw power. It was a scene of profound peace, a landscape bathed in a soft, ethereal light. She saw a serene valley, not unlike their own Haven, but older, wilder, and filled with a quiet, ancient magic. Strange, bioluminescent flora dotted the landscape, casting a gentle glow. And in the center of this valley, nestled beside a crystal-clear waterfall, stood a small, stone structure, weathered by time but emanating an aura of deep, abiding serenity.

She felt Ash's profound contentment, a pure, unadulterated joy that flowed through their connection like a gentle current. It was a feeling of belonging, of being in a place that was both ancient and welcoming, a sanctuary of profound peace. It wasn't a premonition of danger, but rather a glimpse of a place that felt deeply, intrinsically good. It felt like... an answer. Or perhaps, a possibility.

As the vision faded, Kira felt a lingering sense of calm, a quiet joy that settled deep within her. Ash let out a soft sigh of contentment, then nudged her hand, his amber eyes reflecting the lingering light of the vision. He seemed to understand that this glimpse was different, a testament to the positive potential that their shared resonance could unlock.

This 'First Vision,' as Kira began to think of it, marked a profound turning point. It was a testament to the extraordinary depth of their connection, a demonstration that their bond transcended mere companionship. It opened up a vast and unexplored territory, hinting at a shared destiny that was far grander, and far more complex, than she had ever imagined. The echoes of the past, the whispers of potential futures, were now a part of their reality, a testament to the power of their intertwined souls, a promise of journeys yet to come, journeys that would be guided by the silent language of their shared awareness. The world, and their place within it, had irrevocably shifted.

CHAPTER 4

The shimmering heat of the wasteland had always been a constant, a palpable presence that dictated the rhythm of life in Haven. Kira, however, had never truly felt its oppressive weight until the dust cloud appeared on the horizon. It wasn't the familiar, gentle haze of a passing caravan or the scattered grit kicked up by foraging creatures.

This was a deliberate, aggressive churning of earth, a herald of something far more ominous. Ash, ever attuned to her slightest shift in mood, whined softly, his hackles rising, a low growl vibrating in his chest. His amber eyes, usually alight with curiosity or affection, were narrowed, fixed on the approaching anomaly.

The elders, their faces etched with the hard-won wisdom of survival, had spoken of the wasteland's forgotten corners, of those who clung to existence through sheer, brutal tenacity. They called them the 'Scrappers,' the 'Cinders,' the 'Dust Devils' – names whispered with a mixture of fear and disdain. But until that day, these were mere stories, cautionary tales spun to keep the younger generations grounded. Now, the stories were coalescing into a tangible threat, a tide of desperation rolling towards their sanctuary.

As the dust cloud drew closer, it resolved into a ragged line of figures, silhouetted against the unforgiving glare of the sun. They rode atop crudely modified vehicles, their frames a patchwork of scavenged metal and worn leather. The machines sputtered and coughed, belching black smoke that seemed to stain the already bruised sky. The riders themselves were a study in grim functionality, their bodies swathed in thick, dusty cloaks, their faces obscured by goggles and makeshift masks that rendered them anonymous, almost inhuman. They moved with a predatory purpose, their trajectory unerringly aimed at Haven.

A ripple of unease, sharp and cold, went through Kira. The peace she had known, the carefully constructed serenity of their valley, felt suddenly fragile, like a thin shell about to be shattered. She felt Ash's muscles coil beneath her hand as she reached to steady him, his silent anxiety a stark reflection of her own. This was not the abstract fear of the visions; this was immediate, raw, and terrifyingly real.

"They're here," Elder Maeve's voice, usually a calm anchor, was tight with a tension Kira had never heard before. She stood at the edge of the settlement, her gnarled staff gripped tightly, her gaze unwavering. Around her, the inhabitants of Haven began to stir, a murmur of apprehension spreading through the normally tranquil gathering. Children were ushered into the communal halls, their innocent curiosity quickly replaced by wide-eyed fear. Warriors, their hunting spears and rudimentary bows at the ready, took up defensive positions along the perimeter.

The approaching vehicles slowed, their engines grumbling to a halt a respectful, yet menacing, distance from Haven's outer defenses. A single figure, taller and more elaborately clad than the others, dismounted from the lead vehicle. Their attire was a testament to their harsh existence – a layered ensemble of scavenged hides and toughened fabrics, adorned with teeth and scraps of polished metal. A long, curved blade hung from their hip, glinting menacingly even in the diffused sunlight.

The stranger approached Haven's makeshift barricade, their movements slow and deliberate, an unnerving display of confidence. As they drew nearer, Kira could make out the features beneath the goggles and mask: a gaunt face, weathered and scarred, with eyes that seemed to hold the ancient, unforgiving emptiness of the wasteland itself. There was no warmth in those eyes, only a cold calculation, a primal assessment of weakness and opportunity.

"We are the Vultures," the stranger's voice rasped, amplified by some sort of primitive speaker attached to their mask. It was a voice like grinding stone, devoid of any gentleness. "And we have come for what is ours."

A hush fell over Haven, thick with unspoken fear. Kira felt Ash tremble beside her, his instincts screaming danger. The Vultures. The name itself conjured images of carrion birds, of scavengers picking at the bones of the fallen. It was a stark, brutal declaration of intent.

Elder Maeve stepped forward, her voice clear and steady despite the palpable tension. "Haven has nothing for you, Vulture. We are a people of peace. We share what we have with our own, but we do not yield to threats."

The Vulture let out a harsh, grating laugh. "Peace? What is peace but a lull between the hunger pains? Your 'peace' is built on the resources we need to survive. Those glowing plants of yours, the clean water... these are not luxuries. These are necessities. And we will have them."

Kira's gaze flickered towards the hydroponic gardens, towards the clear, flowing water channels that sustained their community. These were the fruits of their labor, the result of generations of careful cultivation and resourcefulness. The Vultures saw them not as achievements, but as spoils. The fundamental difference in their perspectives was a chasm, vast and unbridgeable.

"We have defended ourselves before," Maeve stated, her voice firm. "We will defend ourselves again."

The Vulture leaned closer to the barricade, their eyes narrowing. "We have heard whispers of this place. A hidden valley. And whispers of... abilities. Abilities that might prove... useful. Especially if they are controlled by those who know how to wield them." Their gaze seemed to sweep over the assembled defenders, lingering for a moment on Kira and Ash. There was a predatory gleam in their eyes, a sudden, unnerving focus on the unique bond between human and creature.

Kira felt a prickle of unease crawl up her spine. Had their visions, their amplified resonance, somehow leaked beyond Haven's protective borders? Or was this simply the Vultures' way of sowing discord, of trying to exploit any perceived advantage? She instinctively tightened her grip on Ash's flank, her mind racing. If they knew about their bond, they might see them as a prize, or worse, a tool to be controlled.

"Your words are empty threats, Vulture," Maeve replied, her tone unwavering. "Leave now, and we will not pursue you."

The Vulture let out another dry chuckle. "Pursue us? You speak of pursuit when we are the hounds? We will take what we need. And if there is resistance..." They gestured back towards their waiting vehicles. "We have ways of persuading those who are... unwilling."

With a final, lingering look at Haven, the Vulture turned and walked back towards their machine. The engines roared to life, a discordant symphony of mechanical agony. The vehicles maneuvered into a semicircle, their crude weapons – salvaged heavy machine guns and jury-rigged projectile launchers – swiveling to bear on Haven's defenses.

The relative quiet that had settled after the Vulture's departure was more unnerving than the initial confrontation. Every rustle of wind, every distant cry of a wasteland creature, was amplified, fraught with implied menace. The inhabitants of Haven were not warriors by nature. They were builders, cultivators, keepers of a fragile peace. But the Vultures had brought the stark reality of conflict to their doorstep.

Kira watched as the defenders reinforced the barricades, their movements urgent but organized. She saw the fear in their eyes, but also a grim determination. This was their home, their sanctuary, and they would not surrender it without a fight. Yet, the Vulture's words echoed in her mind. "Abilities... useful... wield them."

She looked at Ash, his body tense, his amber eyes burning with a fierce loyalty. He was her companion, her partner, an extension of her own being. And in the face of this threat, she felt a new kind of responsibility settle upon her. Their bond, their resonance, had always been a source of strength, a connection that brought comfort and understanding. But perhaps, it could also be a weapon. The thought was both exhilarating and terrifying.

The visions she had experienced, the glimpses into other realities, had hinted at powers beyond her comprehension. Could those powers be channeled, directed, used to protect Haven?

Elder Maeve approached Kira, her expression grave. "Kira," she said, her voice soft but carrying the weight of authority. "You and Ash. Your connection... it is unique. We have always valued it, but now..." She paused, her gaze meeting Kira's directly. "Now, we may need you to use it in ways we never imagined."

Kira's breath hitched. She had always been hesitant to embrace the full potential of her resonance, fearing its unknown depths. The visions had been unpredictable, overwhelming. But the Vultures, with their insatiable greed and brutal pragmatism, had left her no choice. The idyllic peace of Haven was over. The time for passive contemplation was past.

"I understand," Kira replied, her voice firmer than she expected. She felt Ash press closer to her side, a silent reassurance. He was ready. And if he was ready, she had to be too.

As the sun began its slow descent, casting long, distorted shadows across the valley floor, the Vultures made their move. The engines of their vehicles roared back to life, a deafening cacophony that seemed to shake the very foundations of Haven. The crude projectile launchers spat their deadly payload, sending crude iron slugs hurtling towards the barricades. The sharp crack of projectile weapons joined the din, followed by the heavier, tearing sound of machine-gun fire.

The defenders of Haven responded with their own meager arsenal. Arrows whistled through the air, finding their mark with surprising accuracy, while spears were hurled with desperate strength. But the Vultures' machines were heavily armored, their weapons far outmatching the simple tools of Haven's inhabitants. The initial volleys of projectiles hammered against the barricades, splintering wood and kicking up clouds of dust.

Kira watched from her position, her heart pounding a frantic rhythm against her ribs. She saw the defenders struggling, their courage unwavering, but their efforts seemingly insufficient against the onslaught. The Vultures, emboldened by their initial success, began to advance, their vehicles grinding forward, crushing anything in their path.

This was it. The moment she had dreaded, and yet, in a strange way, had prepared for. The visions had shown her devastation, despair, and destruction. They had also shown her glimpses of power, of a connection that transcended the physical. Now, she had to find a way to bridge that gap, to translate the ephemeral into the tangible.

She closed her eyes, taking a deep, steadying breath. She focused on Ash, on the steady beat of his heart against her side, on the warmth of his presence. She reached out with her mind, not to pry, but to connect, to share the fear, the resolve, the desperate need to protect.

Ash, she projected, her thoughts a silent plea. *They're pushing through. We have to do something.*

A low whine answered her, a vibration that resonated through their shared connection. She felt his willingness, his unwavering loyalty, but also his uncertainty. He sensed the raw power of the Vultures' machines, the sheer brutality of their intent.

I know it's not like before, Kira reassured him, picturing the serene valley from her last vision, the gentle light, the feeling of profound peace. *But remember the feeling. Remember the strength.*

She then focused on the Vultures, on their machines, on the aura of aggression that surrounded them. It was a chaotic, discordant energy, a tangled knot of greed and desperation. She tried to sense the source of their power, the mechanisms that drove their destructive machines. She felt the vibration of their engines, the heat of their exhaust, the raw, untamed energy that fueled their advance.

Then, an idea, born from desperation and intuition, began to form. The visions had shown her energy, raw and potent, flowing through crystalline structures, through ancient artifacts. They had shown her a connection to something deeper, something fundamental. What if their resonance, their amplified awareness, could interact with the very energy that powered the Vultures' machines?

She focused her attention on the nearest vehicle, a hulking contraption bristling with crude weaponry. She reached out with her mind, not to destroy,. but to disrupt. She pictured the flow of energy within its engine, the combustion, the mechanical processes. And then, she attempted to overlay her own resonant energy, to introduce a dissonance, a subtle interference.

It was like trying to untangle a complex knot with clumsy fingers. The Vultures' technology was crude, but it was also resilient. For a moment, nothing happened. The machine continued its relentless advance, its engine roaring defiance. Kira felt a surge of frustration, a wave of doubt washing over her. Had she overestimated their abilities? Was this a fool's errand?

Ash whined softly, nudging her hand, his amber eyes conveying a silent encouragement. He seemed to sense her struggle, to feel the resistance. He nudged her again, then let out a sharp, focused bark, directing her attention to a specific point on the vehicle – a complex arrangement of pipes and conduits near the engine.

Kira focused her intent on that area. She imagined a wave of pure, resonant energy, like a focused beam of light, washing over those components. She channeled not anger, but a desire for balance, for disruption of their destructive purpose. She felt Ash pour his own focused intent into the effort, his primal energy a wild, potent complement to her more controlled approach.

Then, a flicker. A stutter in the engine's roar. A puff of black smoke, thicker and more ancient than before, billowed from the vehicle's exhaust. The machine lurched, its forward momentum faltering. The Vulture inside, obscured by the dust and smoke, was thrown against their controls.

A collective gasp rose from the defenders of Haven. The Vultures' relentless advance had been momentarily halted. Kira felt a surge of exhilaration, a potent rush of adrenaline. It worked. It actually worked.

Encouraged, she shifted her focus to the next vehicle, Ash's keen senses guiding her. They repeated the process, a silent, focused effort between human and creature, a dance of disruption played out on the battlefield. Another vehicle sputtered and died, its engine coughing its last. A third began to emit a high-pitched whine, its mechanics clearly in distress.

The Vultures, clearly taken aback by this unexpected turn of events, reacted with confusion and anger. They had expected a straightforward assault, a swift victory over a primitive settlement. They had not anticipated an invisible, internal resistance. The Vulture leader, realizing that their technological superiority was being undermined, roared orders, gesturing frantically towards Kira and Ash, who had become visible to them as they fought from a slightly elevated position behind the barricades.

"Find them!" the leader bellowed, their voice amplified and distorted. "Find the source of this interference!"

A few of the Vultures dismounted, their crude firearms now trained not on the barricades, but on the cluster of defenders where Kira and Ash stood. The defenders, sensing the shift in the Vultures' focus, rallied, their spears and arrows now aimed at the dismounted raiders.

Kira knew they couldn't hold out forever. Their ability to disrupt the Vultures' machines was effective, but it was also taxing, draining her energy with each focused effort. She felt Ash's presence beside her, a steady anchor, but she could also sense his fatigue, his growing need for rest.

Just as the dismounted Vultures began to advance on their position, a new sound pierced the din of battle. It was a series of sharp, high-pitched whistles, followed by the distinctive clang of metal on metal. From the denser woods flanking Haven, a new group emerged, their movements swift and fluid. These were not the hulking, mechanical monstrosities of the Vultures. These were figures clad in lighter, more agile armor, their weapons gleaming with an unfamiliar sheen.

They moved with a precision that spoke of dedicated training, their synchronized attacks cutting through the dismounted Vultures with brutal efficiency. The Vultures, caught between the defenders of Haven and this new, unexpected force, found themselves outmaneuvered and outmatched. Their crude weaponry and lumbering machines were no match for the swift, coordinated assault of these newcomers.

Kira watched, stunned, as the tide of battle turned. The Vultures, their machines disabled or struggling, found themselves overwhelmed. Within minutes, their ranks began to break, the dismounted warriors falling back towards their sputtering vehicles. The Vulture leader, seeing their forces in disarray, let out a furious roar of frustration and grudging respect. They had come to conquer, but they were being driven back.

As the remaining Vulture vehicles, battered and smoking, retreated back into the wasteland, leaving behind a scattering of their fallen and the wreckage of their machines, a wave of relief washed over Haven. The inhabitants emerged from their shelters, their faces a mixture of shock, gratitude, and awe.

Kira leaned against Ash, her body trembling with exhaustion, her mind reeling from the intensity of the past hour. She had fought, not with her hands, but with her mind, with her connection to Ash. And they had prevailed. They had protected their home.

The strangers who had arrived from the woods, their appearance and swift, decisive intervention a mystery, now approached Haven's leaders. Their armor was a dark, polished alloy, their weapons sleek and functional. They were led by a woman with sharp, intelligent eyes and a bearing that spoke of authority and experience.

As the woman came closer, Kira noticed a faint, almost imperceptible luminescence emanating from a symbol etched onto her armor – a stylized representation of interconnected lines, reminiscent of neural pathways. A shiver, not of fear, but of recognition, traced its way down Kira's spine. It was a symbol she had glimpsed, fleetingly, in one of her most profound visions. The vision of the serene valley, of the ancient, wild landscape, of the place that felt like an answer. These were not random wanderers. These were people connected to something ancient, something powerful. And their arrival, at this precise moment, felt like more than just a coincidence. It felt like destiny. The harsh reality of the wasteland had crashed upon Haven's shores, but it had also brought with it the promise of a new dawn, a new alliance, and perhaps, a deeper understanding of the powers that lay dormant within their world, and within themselves. The fight for survival had just begun, but Kira knew, with a certainty that resonated deep within her being, that they would not be fighting it alone. The Vultures had come to plunder, but in doing so, they had inadvertently opened a door to a future Kira had only dared to dream of.

Ash's internal tremors began subtly, a low hum beneath Kira's outstretched hand. It wasn't the familiar rumble of a distant storm or the earth settling after a tremor; this was a discordant thrumming, a vibration that spoke of unnatural movement across the arid plains. He whined, a soft, breathy sound that vibrated through his chest and into Kira's palm. His ears, usually swiveling to catch the faintest whisper of the wind, were flattened against his skull, his gaze fixed on the horizon with an intensity that sent a chill down Kira's spine. The air, already heavy with the oppressive heat of the wasteland, now seemed to crackle with an unseen tension, a premonition that settled over Haven like a shroud.

Kira immediately felt the shift in Ash, the amplified anxiety that pulsed between them. His instincts, honed by generations of tracking and survival, were a far more reliable barometer of danger than any visual cue. The dust cloud that had appeared earlier was still a distant smudge, and the distant figures were too small to discern any definitive threat. Yet, Ash knew. He

felt the wrongness of their approach, the raw, predatory intent that radiated from them even across the vast expanse.

"What is it, Ash?" Kira whispered, her voice barely audibles above the rising wind. She pressed her fingers into the thick fur of his neck, feeling the tautness of his muscles, the restless energy coiling within him. He responded with another low growl, a warning that was not directed at anything she could see, but at something she couldn't yet perceive. It was a primal alarm, a deep-seated knowledge of approaching danger that bypassed logic and spoke directly to the survival instincts ingrained in both of them.

Kira's mind raced, trying to reconcile Ash's heightened state with the limited information available. The elders had spoken of scouts, of patrols that sometimes ventured near Haven's borders, but Ash's reaction was different. This was not the cautious wariness of encountering stray scavengers; this was the visceral alarm of a predator spotting prey, or more accurately, the instinctive fear of prey sensing an apex hunter. The Vultures. The name conjured by their arrival was the only explanation that fit Ash's profound unease. Their presence had been a threat, a promise of violence, and Ash's heightened senses were confirming that the promise was about to be fulfilled.

She relayed Ash's growing agitation to Elder Maeve, her voice tight with urgency. "Ash is agitated, Elder. He's sensing them. They're coming, and it's not just a casual patrol. He feels... a lot of them."

Maeve, her weathered face a mask of grim determination, nodded, her gaze sweeping over the assembled defenders. The warriors, armed with spears, bows, and the few salvaged projectile weapons they possessed, were already in their positions, their faces etched with the same apprehension that gripped Kira. The children and the non-combatants were safely inside the fortified communal buildings, the sounds of their anxious whispers muffled by thick, woven walls.

Ash let out a sharp, urgent bark, his head snapping towards a specific point on the eastern perimeter. It was a section of the barricade that seemed no different from any other, yet Ash's focus was unwavering. Kira followed his gaze, squinting against the glare. Nothing. Just the endless, undulating expanse of the wasteland, shimmering under the relentless sun. But Ash wasn't looking for what was visible; he was sensing the invisible. He was feeling the subtle disturbance in the very fabric of the land, the pressure wave of their approach, the faint tremors of their heavy, ungainly machines even before they crested the distant dunes.

"They're coming from the east," Kira announced, her voice carrying a newfound authority, amplified by Ash's certainty. "Ash says they're coming from the east, specifically towards the old ravine pass."

This was valuable intelligence. The ravine pass, a natural choke point, was a weaker section of their defenses, less fortified due to its perceived inaccessibility. But if the Vultures were indeed heading there, it meant they had either scouting information or a deliberate strategy to exploit any potential weakness. Ash's ability to pinpoint their direction and even their likely route was a significant advantage, allowing Haven's defenders to reposition and reinforce the threatened sector.

Kira felt Ash's internal focus sharpen. He wasn't just sensing their approach anymore; he was picking up on the *nature* of their advance. He whimpered, a low, distressed sound, and nudged her hand frantically. Kira probed deeper, trying to decipher the nuances of his feelings. It wasn't just the number of attackers, or their direction; it was their intent, their methodical, brutal efficiency. Ash could feel the metallic thrum of their engines, the grinding of their treads, the palpable aura of aggression they exuded. It was a symphony of destruction that he was perceiving, a discordant note in the otherwise quiet hum of the wasteland.

"They're not just riding in," Kira translated, her voice growing steadier as Ash's signals became clearer. "They're... coordinated. Like they know exactly where they're going. And Ash... he feels their weapons. Heavy. Something that will tear through the barricades."

This was more than just a prediction; it was a tactical assessment provided by an unexpected ally. While Haven's warriors had trained for years, their experience was largely focused on skirmishes with wasteland creatures or small bands of raiders. They lacked the sophisticated sensory capabilities that Ash offered. He was their early warning system, their reconnaissance unit, all rolled into one. His ability to sense intent, to discern the nuances of an enemy's approach, was invaluable. It allowed Haven's leadership to move beyond reactive defense and into proactive preparation.

Kira felt Ash shift his weight, his body tense as if bracing for impact. He whined again, a higher pitched sound this time, laced with something akin to apprehension for the defenders he knew would be positioned in the ravine pass. His concern wasn't just for Kira or for himself; it extended to the entire community. He was part of Haven, and he felt the weight of its vulnerability.

"They're concentrating their force there," Kira said, pointing towards the ravine. "Ash says they're sending their heaviest firepower that way. It's like they're trying to break through quickly, to bypass the main defenses."

Elder Maeve acknowledged this information with a curt nod. "Reinforce the ravine pass. Double the guard. Archers to the ridges above. Spearmen at the mouth of the pass. We will meet them head-on there." Her voice was calm, her instructions clear, a testament to her leadership even in the face of overwhelming odds. Kira's role, guided by Ash's senses, was becoming increasingly crucial. She was the bridge between the unseen threats and the visible defenses, translating primal warnings into actionable intelligence.

As the dust cloud on the horizon grew larger, resolving into the unmistakable, brutal silhouettes of Vulture vehicles, Ash's agitation reached a fever pitch. He let out a series of sharp, rapid barks, his body quivering. Kira concentrated, pushing past the surface-level anxiety to grasp the more detailed information Ash was conveying. He was sensing the specific types of machines, their offensive capabilities, even the general number of armed individuals accompanying them.

"There are at least ten vehicles," Kira reported, her voice trembling slightly, but her gaze steady. "Heavy artillery on the lead ones. And more than fifty individuals, maybe sixty. They're moving fast, Elder. Very fast."

The speed was concerning. The Vultures were not dawdling, were not engaging in probing attacks. They were coming with overwhelming force; a direct assault designed to shock and shatter Haven's defenses before they could fully mobilize. Ash's anticipation, his ability to process this torrent of sensory data, was giving Haven precious moments, moments that could mean the difference between survival and annihilation.

Kira felt Ash's focus shift again, zeroing in on a particular vehicle within the approaching Vulture column. It was a behemoth of scavenged metal, its sides bristling with what looked like repurposed industrial machinery, twisted and armed. Ash's low growl intensified, a deep vibration that resonated in Kira's bones. He felt the sheer destructive potential of that single machine, the raw, untamed energy that powered its deadly array of weapons.

"That one," Kira said, her voice strained, pointing to the lead Vulture vehicle. "Ash... he says that one is the worst. It's got... it's got something powerful inside. Something that's going to unleash a lot of destruction."

Maeve followed Kira's gaze, her eyes narrowing. She understood the implications. If the Vultures had a spearhead, a machine designed to punch through their defenses with overwhelming force, then Haven needed to prioritize neutralizing it. Ash's ability to identify this specific threat, and to convey its dangerous nature, allowed Maeve to make critical tactical decisions, to allocate resources where they were most needed.

The defenders braced themselves, the air thick with anticipation. The Vultures' machines were still some distance away, but the sheer scale of their approach was awe-inspiring and terrifying. Kira kept her hand on Ash, grounding herself, channeling his heightened awareness. She felt his unwavering loyalty, his readiness to stand by her, to defend their home, even in the face of such overwhelming odds. His courage, amplified by their bond, was a silent, potent force that bolstered her own.

"He's sensing more," Kira murmured, her brow furrowed in concentration. "Not just weapons... but their intention. They're not just here to plunder, Elder. They're here to... to break us."

This was the nuanced understanding that only Ash could provide. The Vultures' aggressive posture was obvious, but their deeper motivations, their desire to utterly dismantle and subjugate Haven, was something Ash's resonance was conveying. He could feel the raw hunger, the contempt for their peaceful existence, the desire to extinguish their light.

The first shots rang out, not from Haven, but from the Vultures. Crude projectiles, fired from the lead vehicle, arced through the sky, impacting the fortified outer wall with explosive force. The impact sent tremors through the ground, and a cloud of dust and debris erupted, showering the defenders nearest to the breach. But the barricades, painstakingly reinforced over generations, held firm. They were designed to withstand the harshness of the wasteland, and it seemed, for now, they would withstand the Vultures' initial assault.

Ash let out a sharp yelp, his body stiffening. Kira felt a new layer of information flood her senses. The Vultures weren't just firing projectiles; they were deploying something else. A different kind of energy, a wave of disruption that was aimed at more than just the physical barriers.

"Something's coming," Kira said, her voice tight with alarm. "It's not a projectile. It's... like a wave of heat and noise, but it feels wrong. It's targeting the defenses, but also... the people."

Ash whined; his amber eyes wide with distress. He was sensing the sonic and vibrational frequencies of the Vultures' sonic weaponry, a crude but effective means of disorienting and incapacitating their enemies. Kira instinctively shielded him, wrapping her arms around his neck, pressing her forehead against his. She tried to create a shield of calm between them, to filter out the worst of the disruptive energy.

The defenders near the impact zone stumbled, clutching their ears, their movements becoming clumsy and uncoordinated. The Vultures were exploiting Haven's technological limitations, their rudimentary defenses no match for the Vultures' brutal, albeit primitive, advanced weaponry. Kira felt a surge of anger, a fierce protectiveness for her community, for Ash, for the peace they had so carefully cultivated.

"Ash," she projected, her thoughts a desperate plea. "We need to do something. Can you feel where it's coming from? The source of that... noise?"

Ash responded with a series of sharp, directed barks, his head turning towards a specific point on the lead Vulture vehicle. He was sensing the emitter, the device that was broadcasting the disruptive frequencies. Kira focused her own mental energy, trying to pinpoint the exact location within the chaos of the Vulture machine. It was a difficult task, akin to finding a single discordant note within a roaring inferno.

"There," Kira exclaimed, pointing to a large, dish-like structure mounted on the side of the lead Vulture vehicle. "That's where it's coming from."

Elder Maeve saw Kira's gesture, and understood the implications. If Ash could identify the source, then Haven's warriors could target it. "Archers! Focus fire on that dish! Warriors at the ravine, push them back! We cannot let them gain a foothold!"

The defenders, spurred by Kira's guidance and Maeve's command, redoubled their efforts. Arrows rained down on the Vulture vehicles, seeking to disable their weapons and their mobility. The warriors at the ravine pass fought with renewed ferocity, their spears and blades finding gaps in the Vultures' crude armor.

Ash, sensing the shift in Haven's defense, let out a low, determined growl. He could feel the ripple effect of their actions, the way their coordinated efforts were starting to disrupt the Vultures' momentum. He nudged Kira again, then focused his attention on a different aspect of the Vulture attack.

"He's sensing something else," Kira said, her voice tight with concentration. "The ground... it's vibrating differently. It's not just their machines. They're... they're deploying ground troops too. They're flanking us, coming through the less fortified sections of the outer perimeter."

This was the true danger. The Vultures weren't relying solely on their vehicles; they were also sending waves of their own warriors, individuals hardened by the wasteland, eager for plunder and destruction. Ash's ability to detect this secondary wave of attackers, the hidden threat that complemented the obvious assault, was crucial. It allowed Haven to react to multiple vectors of attack simultaneously, preventing their defenses from being overwhelmed by a pincer movement.

Kira relayed Ash's warnings to Elder Maeve, her voice laced with a growing urgency. "They're coming from the north too, Elder! A smaller group, but they're fast. Ash senses their movement through the scrubland, trying to get around our main defenses."

Maeve immediately dispatched a contingent of Haven's most agile warriors to intercept the flanking maneuver. It was a desperate gamble, diverting precious resources, but Ash's foresight had made it possible. Without his senses, Haven would have been caught off guard, their lines breached by an unseen enemy.

Ash continued to provide a constant stream of information, a relentless sensory report that allowed Kira to act as a living tactical map. He felt the heat signatures of the Vulture soldiers as they moved through the terrain, the metallic clang of their scavenged armor, the subtle shifts in the earth beneath their tread. He was their eyes and ears, extending their perception far beyond what was physically possible.

As the battle raged, Kira found herself relying more and more on Ash's instincts. He wasn't just reacting to the Vultures; he was anticipating their next moves, sensing their strategies, even feeling the ebb and flow of their aggression. There were moments when Ash would whine softly, his body tensing, and Kira would immediately know that a new threat was emerging, a new vulnerability had been exposed.

"They're changing their approach," Kira reported, feeling Ash's internal shift. "The main vehicles... they're not pushing the ravine pass as hard now. They're trying to draw our reserves out, to create an opening elsewhere."

This was a classic military tactic, and Ash's ability to detect the subtle shift in the Vultures' focus was a testament to the depth of their resonant connection. Kira, guided by Ash's insights, relayed this critical intelligence to Maeve, who, with a grim understanding of the Vultures' cunning, ordered the reserves to hold their positions, refusing to be drawn into a trap.

The battle was far from over, but with Ash's warning senses acting as Haven's unwavering guardian, they were no longer fighting blindly. They were fighting with foresight, with an understanding of the enemy that transcended mere observation. Ash wasn't just a creature; he was a sentinel; a living shield whose very existence was proving to be Haven's greatest asset against the encroaching darkness of the Vultures. The raw power of their machines was a formidable foe, but the primal awareness of a bonded creature, channeled through a determined human heart, was proving to be an even greater force.

The first salvo struck not with a bang, but with a low, guttural roar that vibrated through the very stones of Haven's outer wall. It was a concussive blast, designed to disorient and shatter, a wave of raw force that slammed into the reinforced barricades. Ash, pressed close to Kira's side, let out a soft whine, his body tensing. He felt the impact, not just as a physical jolt, but as a disquieting thrum that resonated deep within his bones, a discordant note in the quiet harmony of their settlement. Kira felt it too, a tremor that ran from her hand gripping Ash's fur, up her arm, and into her very core. It was a tangible manifestation of the Vultures' intent – not to merely breach their defenses, but to crush their spirit.

"They're testing the north wall," Kira murmured, her voice barely audibles over the rising wind. She could feel Ash's focus, a sharp, unwavering pinpoint directed at the section of the wall furthest from the ravine pass. The Vultures, despite their initial focus on the choke point, were also probing for weaker spots, employing a multi-pronged assault designed to stretch Haven's limited resources to their breaking point. Ash's heightened senses, attuned to the subtlest shifts in the environment, were picking up the subtle pressure changes, the tell-tale vibrations of the Vultures' heavy machinery inching along the perimeter, seeking any crevice, any weakness to exploit.

Elder Maeve, her gaze sweeping across the defenders arrayed along the parapets, nodded grimly. She had seen the dust clouds, the glint of scavenged metal on the horizon, and now she felt the unspoken tension that coiled within her people. "Roric, take your squad to the north perimeter. Reinforce the watch posts there. Elara, prepare the archers. If they attempt a breach, meet them with volleys. We cannot afford to be caught off guard on any front."

The defensive strategy was a delicate dance, a constant reassessment based on the limited, yet vital, intelligence gleaned from Kira and Ash. The Vultures, with their superior numbers and formidable, if crude, weaponry, were attempting to overwhelm Haven through sheer force and unpredictability. But Haven had its own strengths: a deep understanding of their territory, the resilience of their fortifications, and the invaluable, almost prescient, guidance of their resonant pairs.

Kira felt Ash's attention shift again, a subtle tightening in his muscles, a low growl that vibrated against her palm. He wasn't just sensing the direct assault; he was picking up on a more insidious threat. "They're trying to flank us," she announced, her voice carrying a new urgency. "From the west. Through the old dried-up riverbed. Ash feels... a lot of them moving quietly. Smaller vehicles, faster. They're trying to get behind our main defense line."

This was precisely the kind of maneuver Haven feared most. A frontal assault could be met with force, their fortified walls and strategic positions offering a fighting chance. But a flanking maneuver, particularly one that bypassed their primary defenses, could sever their supply lines, encircle their defenders, and shatter their morale. The riverbed, a natural depression in the terrain, offered cover for stealthy movement, a blind spot in their otherwise comprehensive surveillance.

Maeve's expression hardened. "Joric, take your best skirmishers. Intercept them at the mouth of the riverbed. Do not let them gain a foothold within the outer perimeter. Your goal is to delay, to bleed them, to prevent them from linking up with the main force."

The decision was difficult. Diverting skilled warriors meant weakening the main defense line, but the intelligence provided by Kira and Ash was too critical to ignore. Ash's ability to detect the subtle shifts in the earth, the faint vibrations of smaller, faster engines, and the collective fear-scent of approaching Vulture soldiers, allowed Haven to anticipate threats that would have otherwise remained hidden until it was too late. Kira acted as the conduit, translating these primal sensations into actionable intelligence, her mind a mirror to Ash's heightened awareness.

As the defenders scrambled to reinforce the western perimeter, a new series of concussive blasts rocked the north wall. This time, however, the impact was more severe. A section of the reinforced earthworks, designed to absorb and dissipate the force of projectiles, buckled inward. Dust and debris billowed into the air, obscuring the defenders stationed there.

"They've found a weak point!" Kira cried out, feeling Ash's alarm spike. He whined, a distressed sound, his body trembling. He could sense the structural integrity failing, the raw power of the Vultures' weaponry tearing through the carefully constructed defenses. "Ash says the main vehicle, the one with the large cannon... it's concentrated its fire there. It's about to breach!"

Maeve's eyes scanned the chaos unfolding on the north wall. The defenders there were already engaged in a desperate struggle, trying to shore up the crumbling defenses and repel the initial wave of Vulture ground troops who were swarming through the nascent breach. "Roric's men are engaged on the west. We don't have reserves to send to the north. We need to hold the ravine pass. If the main force breaks through there, everything else is lost."

It was a grim calculus. Haven was a community, not an army. Their resources were finite, their warriors few. Every decision involved a sacrifice, a gamble. But Kira felt Ash's growing distress, a primal understanding of the Vultures' intent that went beyond mere strategy. He could sense their *aggression*, their desire to inflict maximum damage, to sow terror. He nudged her hand, his amber eyes wide, conveying a sense of desperate urgency.

“Ash feels... something else,” Kira relayed, her voice strained as she tried to filter the torrent of sensations from her companion. “It’s not just the cannon. The ground beneath the breach... it’s destabilizing. They’re using something to weaken the foundations, not just the surface.”

This was a new dimension to the Vultures’ assault, a level of calculated destruction that was chilling. They weren't just employing brute force; they were systematically dismantling Haven's defenses, targeting not only the visible barriers but also the very ground upon which they stood. Kira felt Ash’s mental image of crumbling earth, of underground tremors, of a slow, insidious collapse.

Maeve, her face etched with worry, understood the implications. If the Vultures were undermining the north wall, it was only a matter of time before it gave way completely, exposing the heart of Haven to a direct onslaught. “We need to counter it. Kaelen, take a squad of engineers and your most skilled miners. Move to the north perimeter. See if you can reinforce the foundations from the inside. Buy us time. And pray we can hold the ravine.”

The battle was no longer a single, focused engagement. It had fragmented, a brutal and chaotic melee erupting across multiple fronts. Kira and Ash found themselves at the heart of Haven’s command, relaying information from the front lines, trying to anticipate the Vultures’ next move. Ash’s senses were a constant, overwhelming stream of data – the heat signatures of Vulture soldiers moving through the dust, the metallic scrape of their armor against stone, the rhythmic thud of their heavy boots. He was their early warning system, their eyes in the smoke, their ears in the din.

“They’re pushing the ravine pass again!” Kira exclaimed, feeling Ash’s growing alarm. “The main force. They’ve regrouped. Ash feels... they’re sending their heavy assault vehicles directly at the narrowest point. They’re using the terrain to funnel us, and they’re ready to break through.”

Maeve had anticipated this. The ravine pass was strategically vital, its defense crucial to Haven’s survival. She had committed their best warriors, their most experienced fighters, to this sector. “Hold the pass!” her voice boomed, amplified by the communal amplification devices that echoed across the settlement. “Let them come! We will meet them at the throat!”

The defenders in the ravine pass, a line of grim-faced individuals armed with spears, bows, and crude firearms, braced themselves. The air was thick with the acrid smell of burnt metal and the metallic tang of fear. As the lead Vulture vehicles lumbered into view, their massive frames silhouetted against the dust-choked sky, Ash let out a series of sharp, urgent barks.

"Ash says the lead vehicle," Kira translated, her voice tight with concentration, pointing towards the colossal machine that dominated the Vulture's advance. "It's not just a transport or a battering ram. It's got multiple weapon systems. And... he feels a focus of energy inside it. Something volatile."

This was critical intelligence. If Haven could disable that primary vehicle, they might shatter the Vultures' momentum and force a retreat. Maeve's eyes narrowed as she followed Kira's pointing finger. "Torvin, target that lead vehicle. All available archers, concentrate fire on its treads and its main weapon mounts. Spearmen, at my signal, charge the dismounted infantry emerging from the flanks."

The coordinated response was a testament to Haven's collective will. Inspired by Kira and Ash's prescience, the defenders fought with a ferocity born of desperation and a deep-seated love for their home. Arrows rained down on the Vulture behemoth, seeking to cripple its mobility and its offensive capabilities. The spear-wielding warriors, their bodies hardened by years of toil and training, charged into the fray, meeting the Vulture's ground troops in a brutal, close-quarters engagement.

Kira felt Ash's focus shift again, a subtle tension that indicated a new threat emerging from the chaos. He whined softly, nudging her arm. "The west perimeter," she relayed to Maeve, her voice strained. "Joric's skirmishers... Ash feels they're being overwhelmed. The flanking force has broken through. They're moving to cut off the ravine defenders from behind."

Maeve's face contorted with a mixture of anger and grim resignation. It was the very scenario they had feared. "Send the reserve company to reinforce Joric," she ordered, her voice laced with a heavy weariness. "They must hold the riverbed. We can't let them get behind the ravine."

The diversion of the reserve company was a significant blow to Haven's overall defense. It meant fewer warriors to support the main line, fewer individuals to hold the inner perimeter. But Ash's constant vigilance had provided them with the crucial lead time needed to react, to adapt, to avoid being completely outmaneuvered. Kira felt Ash's quiet determination, his unwavering focus on protecting their community. He wasn't a warrior in the traditional sense, but his ability to perceive, to warn, to guide, made him an indispensable asset.

The battle raged. The concussive blasts from the Vulture vehicles shook the ground, the air thick with smoke and the cries of the injured. Kira, her hand never leaving Ash's reassuring warmth, continued to relay his sensations, his insights. She felt the subtle shifts in the Vultures' tactics, their moments of hesitation, their attempts to exploit any perceived weakness. Ash's senses were a beacon in the encroaching darkness, illuminating the enemy's movements, their intentions, their very presence.

He could sense the individual Vulture soldiers, not just as a mass, but as discrete entities, each with their own aggressive intent. He could feel their fear, their ambition, their raw, predatory hunger. Kira translated these feelings into warnings: "They're regrouping near the eastern gate," "A small group is attempting to scale the southern wall," "The main force is preparing another direct assault on the ravine." Each piece of information, however small, allowed Haven's defenders to adjust their positions, to anticipate the enemy's movements, and to inflict maximum damage with their limited resources.

There were moments when Ash would grow uncharacteristically still, his gaze fixed on a specific point in the distance, a low growl rumbling in his chest. Kira would instinctively focus her own attention, trying to understand the nature of his apprehension. It wasn't always a direct threat; sometimes it was a subtle change in the Vultures' formation, a coordinated maneuver that hinted at a deeper strategy.

"Ash feels a feint," Kira relayed to Maeve, pointing towards a cluster of Vulture vehicles at the edge of the ravine pass. "They're concentrating their fire there, but he senses their main force is actually moving towards the western approach again. They're trying to draw our reserves away from the riverbed, to break through there and cut us off."

Maeve, her face a mask of grim calculation, understood the deceptive nature of the Vultures' assault. They were not a mindless horde; they were an organized, albeit brutal, force that employed calculated tactics. Ash's ability to detect this subtle shift, this strategic misdirection, was invaluable. It allowed Maeve to resist the urge to reinforce the obvious threat, to maintain her defensive posture where it was truly needed.

As the hours wore on, the battle became a test of endurance, a brutal attritional conflict. Haven's defenders fought with a tenacity that surprised even themselves, their courage bolstered by the clear, consistent guidance provided by Kira and Ash.

They weren't just reacting to the enemy; they were engaging with a strategic foresight that allowed them to parry blows, to counter maneuvers, and to inflict a steady toll on the Vultures.

The resonant pairs within Haven, though few, played a crucial role in this coordinated defense. While Kira and Ash were the most prominent, others, with their own unique sensory abilities, worked in conjunction with the traditional warriors. A pair might sense the subtle thermal signatures of Vulture soldiers concealed in the dust, allowing archers to target them accurately. Another might perceive the faint electromagnetic fluctuations of Vulture weaponry, providing an early warning of incoming heavy fire. These subtle, almost imperceptible advantages, when woven together, created a tapestry of defense that was far more potent than the sum of its parts.

Kira felt Ash's weariness, his body trembling with the constant strain of his heightened senses. But his resolve remained unbroken. He continued to scan the horizon, to listen to the whispers of the wind, to feel the tremors of the approaching enemy. He was Haven's sentinel, its early warning system, its living shield. And in that moment, as the sun began its descent, casting long, ominous shadows across the battlefield, Kira knew that without Ash, without his unwavering vigilance, Haven would have already fallen.

Their collective resilience was not just a matter of strength of arms; it was a testament to their ability to adapt, to anticipate, and to fight with a prescience that only the deepest bonds could provide. The fight for Haven was far from over, but with Ash by her side, Kira felt a flicker of hope ignite in the heart of the storm. He nudged her hand again, a soft, reassuring pressure, and Kira knew they would face whatever came next, together.

The immediate aftermath of the Vultures' assault settled over Haven not as a calm, but as a heavy, suffocating quiet. The cacophony of battle had ceased, replaced by the moans of the injured and the ragged breaths of survivors. Kira, her body aching and her mind reeling, remained by Ash's side, his steady presence a grounding anchor in the swirling aftermath. She watched as Maeve and the others moved through the settlement, their faces grim, tending to the wounded and assessing the damage. Every broken barricade, every scorch mark on the earth, was a stark testament to the ferocity of the Vultures' attack, and to the price Haven had paid for its survival.

The victory, if it could be called that, was a bitter one. The ravine pass was secured, the flanking maneuver blunted, but the cost was etched onto the faces of her people.

Kira saw Torvin, his arm bound tightly, his usual boisterous demeanor replaced by a quiet exhaustion, helping to carry a stretcher. She saw Elara, her quiver depleted, her knuckles raw from nocking arrows, kneeling beside a fallen defender, her lips moving in silent prayer. Even Ash, usually so vibrant and attentive, seemed subdued, his amber eyes reflecting a weariness that mirrored her own. He nudged her hand with his snout, a silent offering of comfort, and Kira leaned into his warmth, drawing strength from their shared bond.

Maeve approached, her gaze sweeping over the ravaged landscape. "We held, Kira," she said, her voice raspy, laced with both relief and sorrow. "But the Vultures' tenacity... they are not easily deterred. And their numbers... we cannot afford many more such assaults." She gestured towards the north wall, where a section of the reinforced earthworks had indeed buckled, a testament to the targeted bombardment. "Kaelen's engineers are working to shore it up, but it will take time, and precious resources."

Kira nodded; her throat tight. She had witnessed the brutal efficiency of the Vultures, their willingness to sacrifice their own in the relentless pursuit of their objective. She had seen the desperation in their eyes, the fierce, unyielding hunger that drove them. It wasn't just a battle for territory; it was a primal struggle for existence, a clash of wills born from scarcity and desperation.

As the triage teams worked, Kira saw the stark reality of warfare laid bare. The healers, their faces streaked with dirt and blood, moved with a practiced urgency, their hands-stained red. She saw the vacant stares of those beyond help, the quiet dignity with which Maeve ensured their passage. And she saw the profound, unspoken grief that settled over the survivors, the weight of each lost life pressing down on their collective spirit.

One of the wounded, a young man named Roric who had been part of Joric's skirmishers, was being tended to nearby. His leg was mangled, the result of a desperate melee near the riverbed. He looked up as Kira approached, his eyes wide with pain and a flicker of something akin to fear. "We... we almost didn't stop them, Kira," he gasped, his voice weak. "They were so many... and so close to cutting us off." He paused, his gaze drifting towards the north wall. "And the sound... the cannon... it felt like the world was breaking apart."

Kira knelt beside him, her heart aching. "You fought bravely, Roric. You all did. You bought us the time we needed." She placed a hand on his shoulder, feeling the fragility of his skin beneath the torn fabric of his tunic. "Rest now. You've earned it."

The experience had etched itself onto Kira's soul. The abstract concept of defense had become a visceral reality, painted in shades of blood and dust. She had always understood the necessity of protecting Haven, but now she understood the brutal calculus that underpinned that necessity. Every decision made by Maeve, every risk taken by their defenders, was a calculated gamble with lives. And the Vultures, in their relentless pursuit, had mirrored that desperation, demonstrating a ruthlessness that chilled Kira to the bone.

Later, as the first rays of dawn painted the sky in hues of bruised purple and soft gold, Kira found herself walking the perimeter of Haven. Ash trotted faithfully beside her, his presence a constant source of comfort. The damage was visible everywhere – shattered defenses, debris scattered across the ground, the lingering scent of smoke and ozone. But beneath the superficial scars, Haven's spirit remained unbroken. The defenders, though weary, stood tall, their gazes resolute.

She encountered Maeve again, standing near the newly reinforced section of the north wall. Kaelen and his team of engineers had worked through the night, their faces gaunt but their spirits resolute. The damage was still evident, a gaping wound in Haven's defenses, but it was a wound that was slowly beginning to heal.

"We managed to stabilize the foundations," Kaelen reported, wiping a bead of sweat from his brow. "It will hold, for now. But the Vultures will be back. Their probing attacks, the way they focused their fire... it tells us they are learning our weaknesses."

Maeve nodded, her expression one of profound weariness. "And we must continue to adapt. The cost of survival is vigilance, and it is a cost we must be willing to pay, no matter how great." She turned to Kira, her eyes holding a deep understanding. "You have seen the true face of this conflict, Kira. The sacrifices made, the difficult choices. It is not a glorious path, but it is the path we must walk."

Kira met her gaze, her own eyes reflecting the dawn. She had witnessed the courage of her people, their unwavering resolve in the face of overwhelming odds. But she had also witnessed the brutal efficiency of their enemies, their willingness to exploit any vulnerability, to inflict any pain. The Vultures, driven by their own desperate struggle for survival, had shown a capacity for cruelty that was both terrifying and, in a twisted way, understandable. They were not inherently evil, perhaps, but their actions were driven by a primal need that mirrored Haven's own, albeit in a far more savage form.

She remembered the glint in the eyes of a Vulture soldier, just before he charged the ravine pass, a desperate glint that spoke of hunger and fear. It wasn't the cold, calculated malice of a seasoned killer, but the raw, desperate ferocity of someone fighting for their very existence, for the survival of their own community. This realization was perhaps the most unsettling aspect of the entire ordeal. It blurred the lines between right and wrong, between us and them, revealing a shared desperation that lay at the heart of the conflict.

"They were fighting for their lives, weren't they?" Kira murmured, more to herself than to Maeve. "Just like us."

Maeve's expression softened, a flicker of empathy in her usually stern features. "Survival is a powerful, brutal force, Kira. It can forge heroes, and it can unleash monsters. The Vultures have chosen a path of aggression, of taking what they believe is owed to them. We choose a path of defense, of protecting what is ours." She sighed, a heavy sound. "But the line between the two can become dangerously thin when desperation takes hold."

The events of the previous night had irrevocably altered Kira. The quiet scholar, the keeper of knowledge, had been thrust into the harsh crucible of war. She had seen the fragility of life, the immense courage it took to defend it, and the grim choices that had to be made when lives were on the line. The violence, the loss, the sheer tenacity of the Vultures – it had all left an indelible mark. She understood now that survival wasn't just about building walls and stockpiling resources; it was about confronting the darkest aspects of humanity, both within oneself and within one's enemies, and finding a way to persevere without losing one's soul.

As the settlement slowly began to stir, the sounds of activity replacing the hushed quiet of the aftermath, Kira knew that the rebuilding process would be arduous. Resources were scarcer than ever, and the threat of further Vulture incursions loomed large. But she also saw the resilience of her people, the unwavering determination in their eyes. They had faced a brutal onslaught and emerged, battered but not broken.

Ash nudged her hand again, his amber eyes meeting hers. He conveyed a sense of quiet strength, a reassurance that even in the face of such hardship, their bond remained. He was her anchor, her guide, her constant reminder of the love and connection that made Haven worth fighting for. And in his silent presence, Kira found the strength to face the uncertain future, to embrace the difficult path ahead, and to continue the fight for survival, no matter the cost. The sobering reflection had begun, and with it, a deeper understanding of the profound complexities that lay at the heart of their struggle. The cost of survival was steep, measured not just in lives lost and resources depleted, but in the irreversible transformation of those who endured it.

The early morning mist, still clinging to the scarred earth like a shroud, did little to dampen the somber atmosphere that permeated Haven. The frantic energy of the immediate aftermath had subsided, replaced by a more profound, lingering exhaustion. Kira moved through the settlement, her senses still on high alert, each rustle of leaves, each distant cry of a bird, a potential echo of the Vultures' brutal advance. Ash, his sleek fur still bearing the faint scent of ozone and dust from the recent conflict, padded silently beside her, his amber eyes scanning their surroundings with an acuity that always reassured her. They had held the pass, defended the walls, but the victory felt hollow, bought at a steep price. The silent acknowledgment of this truth hung heavy between the survivors, a shared burden in the dawning light.

Maeve had already tasked teams with the grim work of recovery and repair. The north wall, once Haven's most formidable defense, bore the deep gouges and shattered remnants of the Vultures' relentless assault. Kaelen's engineers, their faces etched with fatigue, worked tirelessly to shore up the weakened structure, their efforts a desperate race against the ever-present threat of a renewed attack. Kira had watched them, a knot of anxiety tightening in her chest. They had repelled the Vultures, yes, but the sheer ferocity and calculated approach of their enemy spoke of a deeper desperation, a hunger that drove them to extremes. The memory of the Vulture soldier's desperate charge, the raw fear and hunger in his eyes, had lodged itself in her mind, a disquieting counterpoint to the righteous defense Haven had mounted.

It was near the western perimeter, where the Vultures had attempted their flanking maneuver, that Kira's path converged with a small contingent of defenders engaged in securing the area. The sounds of their work – the scrape of metal against earth, the terse commands exchanged – were familiar, grounding. As she approached, her attention was drawn to a lone figure sitting against a partially collapsed barricade. He was a Vulture, or at least, he wore the tattered, utilitarian garb of their kind. He was injured, his leg crudely bandaged, and he sat hunched over, his head bowed, radiating an aura of utter defeat.

Kira's instincts screamed caution. Every fiber of her being urged her to maintain a safe distance, to treat him as the enemy he was. Ash, sensing her unease, let out a low growl, his hackles rising almost imperceptibly. Yet, something in the man's posture, in the sheer abject misery that clung to him, held Kira's gaze. He wasn't brandishing a weapon, nor was he attempting to escape. He simply sat, a broken thing amidst the debris of battle.

Hesitantly, Kira moved closer, Ash following her lead but remaining a cautious distance behind, a silent sentinel. As she drew nearer, she saw that the man's eyes were closed, his face a mask of pain. His breathing was shallow, ragged. Then, a flicker of movement caught her eye. It wasn't the man himself, but something small and dark nestled in the crook of his arm. It was a creature, something akin to a starved, mangy fox, its fur matted with dirt and blood. It was curled tightly around his arm, its tiny body trembling, its muzzle pressed against his skin.

The Vulture stirred, his eyes fluttering open. They were a dull, vacant grey, reflecting a pain that seemed to transcend the physical wounds. He saw Kira, and for a fleeting moment, a spark of recognition, perhaps even fear, flickered in their depths. But it quickly faded, replaced by a profound weariness. He made no move to rise, no sound of aggression. Instead, his gaze shifted to the small creature cradled in his arm.

He spoke, his voice a low, rasping whisper, barely audible above the sounds of the ongoing cleanup. "Lyra," he murmured, his tone filled with a raw, tender protectiveness that struck Kira with unexpected force. "It's alright, little one. We're... we're safe now."

The creature, Lyra, stirred at his voice. It lifted its head, its small, beady eyes blinking slowly. It let out a faint, almost inaudible whimper, and then, with an almost imperceptible movement, it nudged its head against the man's thumb, which was stroking its back with a rough, calloused tenderness. It was a gesture so utterly natural, so imbued with affection, that it seemed to bridge the chasm between attacker and defender.

Kira watched, transfixed. She had seen the Vultures as a horde, a faceless enemy driven by a singular, brutal purpose. She had witnessed their ferocity, their disregard for life, their willingness to sacrifice their own in the pursuit of their goals. But here, in this quiet moment, she saw something else. She saw a desperate survivor, clinging to the only source of comfort he had left. She saw a bond that transcended the conflict, a connection forged in shared hardship and mutual reliance.

Ash, who had been observing the scene with an almost unnerving stillness, took a tentative step forward. His usual wariness seemed to have softened, replaced by a curiosity that mirrored Kira's own. He lowered his head slightly, his ears perked, his gaze fixed on the Vulture and his companion. It was a subtle shift, but Kira recognized it. Ash, too, felt the strange, disarming vulnerability of the scene. He understood the primal instinct to protect, the unspoken language of companionship that existed between different species.

The Vulture's gaze drifted to Ash. He didn't flinch, didn't recoil. Instead, his vacant eyes seemed to focus, to register the presence of Kira's own animal companion. He offered a faint, almost imperceptible nod, a gesture of acknowledgment that felt incredibly profound. It was as if, in that moment, he recognized a shared understanding, a kinship born from the fundamental nature of their own bonds.

Kira's perception of the Vultures began to fracture, to splinter into a thousand nuanced shades. The simplistic narrative of 'us' versus 'them,' of 'good' versus 'evil,' no longer held. She saw the desperation that drove them, the same desperation that, in different circumstances, could drive Haven to similar lengths. This man, this enemy, was not merely a tool of destruction. He was a living, breathing being, capable of love, of fear, of profound connection. And he was wounded, both physically and, she suspected, in ways far deeper.

"He's injured," Kira said, her voice soft, almost a murmur, directed at no one in particular. Her eyes remained on the Vulture, on the small, quivering creature in his arms.

A Defender, a burly man named Torvin, who had been overseeing the clearing of debris nearby, approached cautiously. His face was etched with the grim lines of battle, his gaze hardening as he took in the scene. "Kira, what are you doing? He's one of them."

Kira met Torvin's gaze, her own filled with a new, unsettling clarity. "He's injured, Torvin. And his... companion... is with him." She gestured subtly towards Lyra.

Torvin followed her gaze, his expression a mixture of suspicion and grudging comprehension. He had seen his share of brutal fighting, and he understood the desperation that drove men – and creatures – to fight for their lives. He grunted, a sound that could have meant anything from agreement to disdain. "They'll want to take him back," he said gruffly, referring to the Vultures' leadership. "Or worse."

The Vulture, hearing the exchange, stirred again. He tightened his grip on Lyra, his knuckles white. He looked at Kira, a silent plea in his weary eyes. It wasn't a plea for mercy in the traditional sense, but a desperate request to protect what little he had left. His gaze shifted from Kira to Ash, and then back again. There was an unspoken question in his eyes, a silent inquiry into whether such a profound, animalistic bond could be recognized, could be understood, even by the enemy.

Ash, sensing the shift in the atmosphere, the subtle tension that emanated from the injured Vulture, let out a soft whine. He moved closer to Kira, then paused, his gaze fixed on Lyra. He took another step, his movement deliberate and unhurried. He lowered his head, his nose extended, and sniffed the air in Lyra's direction. It was a gesture of curiosity, not aggression, a silent acknowledgment of another life.

The Vulture watched Ash's approach with a mixture of apprehension and something akin to wonder. Lyra, startled by the new presence, tensed, pressing herself more tightly against the man's arm. But the Vulture, with a soothing murmur, stroked her fur, his eyes never leaving Ash.

"He won't hurt you," Kira said to the Vulture, her voice gentle. "Ash is... he understands." She didn't know if he truly understood, but she felt a deep, inexplicable certainty that he did. Ash's empathy often extended beyond the confines of their own species, a testament to his unique connection with Kira and the natural world.

The Vulture's lips curved into a faint, pained smile. "You have a good one there," he rasped, his gaze lingering on Ash. "A loyal friend."

The words, spoken by an enemy, resonated deeply within Kira. Loyal friend. It was a sentiment she understood implicitly. Ash was more than a companion; he was family, a silent confidant, a steadfast presence in a world often filled with uncertainty. To hear this brutalized man, this Vulture, speak of such a bond with such raw sincerity, chipped away at the hardened shell of her perceptions.

She found herself kneeling beside him, her earlier caution replaced by a burgeoning sense of shared vulnerability. "What's your name?" she asked, her voice quiet.

He hesitated, his gaze flickering towards the north, as if expecting some unseen threat. "Kael," he finally whispered, the name barely audible. "Just Kael."

"I'm Kira," she replied. "And this is Ash."

Kael nodded, a faint acknowledgment. He looked down at Lyra again, his expression softening. "She's all I have left," he murmured, his voice thick with an emotion that Kira recognized as profound loss. "My family... they were taken. During the raids. She was all that remained."

The admission hung in the air, heavy and raw. Kira felt a pang of empathy so sharp it took her breath away. The Vultures, in her mind, were the aggressors, the raiders who had plundered and destroyed. But here was a man who had also suffered loss, who had been stripped of his own family, and who clung to a small, terrified creature for solace. The lines blurred; the distinctions dissolved. They were all, in their own ways, victims of this brutal, unforgiving world.

"The Vultures... they are desperate," Kael continued, his voice barely a whisper. "We all are, aren't we? They take what they need to survive. They have to. There's not enough to go around."

His words struck Kira with the force of a physical blow. She had seen the efficiency of their attacks, the coordinated assaults, the ruthless determination. She had interpreted it as pure aggression, as a lust for conquest. But perhaps it was also born of a desperate struggle for sustenance, a brutal calculus of survival dictated by scarcity. It was a chilling thought, one that forced her to re-examine everything she believed about the conflict.

Ash nudged Kael's hand gently with his snout. It was a tentative gesture, an offering of comfort, a recognition of the shared pain that seemed to emanate from the injured man. Kael, his eyes widening slightly in surprise, reached out a trembling hand and hesitantly stroked Ash's head. Ash leaned into the touch, his tail giving a slow, gentle wag. It was a moment of silent communion, a testament to the enduring power of connection, even between those who were ostensibly enemies.

"He's a good soul," Kael said, his voice rough with emotion as he looked at Ash. "You are lucky to have him."

Kira felt a swell of affection for Ash, a deep gratitude for his unwavering loyalty and his capacity for empathy. "He's my family," she replied, her voice soft. "He's everything to me."

Kael nodded, a faint, knowing smile touching his lips. "I understand," he whispered. He closed his eyes again, his grip on Lyra tightening. "We all need someone. Something. To hold onto."

Torvin, who had been listening silently, cleared his throat. "Kira," he said, his tone firm but not unkind. "We need to get him back to the holding pens. Maeve will want to question him."

Kira nodded, a sense of regret washing over her. The moment of shared humanity, of unexpected connection, was over. The reality of their situation, the ongoing threat posed by the Vultures, demanded that she return to her responsibilities. But the encounter had irrevocably altered her perspective. She could no longer see the Vultures as mere monsters. She saw them as desperate beings, driven by the same primal needs that drove Haven, albeit in a far more brutal and destructive manner.

She stood, offering Kael a small, reassuring smile. “We’ll get you some water, Kael. And we’ll tend to your leg.” She met his gaze, her own filled with a newfound understanding. “We may be on different sides, but I believe you when you say you’re fighting for your own survival. And that’s something I can respect.”

Kael offered another faint nod, his eyes filled with a weary gratitude. He held Lyra close, the small creature a silent testament to the enduring strength of connection in a world that seemed intent on tearing everything apart. As Kira turned to signal Torvin, she glanced back at Kael, at the injured Vulture and his small, trembling companion. The encounter had left her with more questions than answers, but it had also opened a door to a deeper, more complex understanding of the conflict.

The enemy was not simply a faceless horde; they were individuals, each with their own stories, their own losses, their own desperate struggles for survival. And perhaps, just perhaps, within that shared struggle, lay the possibility of something more than just endless conflict. It was a fragile hope, a nascent seed of understanding, but in the harsh landscape of their war-torn world, it was a flicker of light worth nurturing.

Ash, sensing her shift in perspective, nudged her hand, his amber eyes conveying a silent affirmation of this newly found complexity. The path ahead remained fraught with danger, but Kira felt a subtle, profound shift within herself. The monochrome certainty of the enemy had been replaced by the nuanced tapestry of shared humanity, a realization that, while terrifying, also offered a sliver of hope for a future that extended beyond the battlefield.

CHAPTER 5

The dust still settled around Haven, a fine, gritty testament to the Vultures' brutal passage. Yet, beneath the surface of the immediate aftermath, a different kind of unrest simmered within Kira. It wasn't the sharp, immediate fear of attack, but a persistent, gnawing intuition, a subtle redirection that she felt emanating from Ash. He had been unusually restless since the dawn, his amber eyes often fixed on the jagged scarifications of the ruins bordering Haven's western edge, a sector that had seen less intense fighting, a sector that, until that moment, had seemed largely irrelevant to their defensive efforts. It was a part of the ruins they had, by necessity, largely ignored, deeming it too unstable, too exposed, too devoid of immediate strategic value. But Ash's focus was unwavering, a silent, insistent pull that Kira had learned to trust implicitly.

"What is it, boy?" Kira murmured, stroking the sleek, scarred fur of his neck. Ash responded with a low rumble, not of aggression, but of a peculiar kind of insistent yearning. He nudged her hand with his muzzle, then turned, taking a few steps towards the western ruins, pausing and looking back as if to confirm she was following. His tail gave a slight, questioning flick. There was something in his posture, a focus so profound it felt almost tangible. He was sensing something beyond the immediate, beyond the obvious.

Kira exchanged a glance with Kaelen, who was overseeing the reinforcement of a damaged section of the western wall. Kaelen, ever pragmatic, raised an eyebrow. "Trouble over there, Kira?" he asked, his voice raspy from shouting commands and the lingering dust.

"Ash seems to think so," Kira replied, nodding towards her companion. "He's been fixated on that sector. I think we should take a look. It feels... important."

Kaelen, though weary, understood the weight of Kira's intuition when it came to Ash. "Alright," he conceded, wiping a grimy hand across his brow. "But be careful. That area is a mess. If anything's left, it's probably buried deep."

With Kaelen's begrudging approval, Kira set off, Ash leading the way with an almost urgent, yet controlled, pace. The terrain grew more treacherous with each step. Buildings that had once stood proud were now skeletal remains, twisted metal and shattered concrete forming a chaotic labyrinth. The air here was thick with the scent of decay, the metallic tang of rust mingling with the earthier smell of damp, disturbed soil. The Vultures had indeed attempted a flanking maneuver here, but it had been less of a full-scale assault and more of a probing attack, easily repelled, leaving behind only scattered debris and the silence of abandonment.

Ash, however, was not deterred by the general devastation. He moved with a sure-footed grace, navigating the treacherous landscape with an instinct that belied the apparent randomness of the destruction. He would stop occasionally, sniffing the ground intently, then continue, his direction unwavering. Kira watched him, a sense of anticipation building within her. Ash's 'pulls' were never random. They had led her to survivors, to caches of supplies, and once, even to the source of a subtle, destabilizing energy fluctuation that had threatened Haven's primary water purification system. Whatever Ash was sensing, it was significant.

He led her towards a section of the ruins that appeared no different from the rest – a collapsed edifice of ferroconcrete and twisted rebar. Yet, as they neared, Ash began to circle a particular spot, his low growls more pronounced now, a sound of intense curiosity rather than threat. He pawed at the ground, dislodging loose rubble, revealing not just compacted earth, but what looked like a section of metal plating, heavily rusted and partially obscured by debris.

"What is it, boy?" Kira knelt beside him, brushing away loose dirt. The plating was thick, industrial grade, and bore no markings she recognized. It seemed to be part of a larger structure, buried beneath the rubble. The Vultures, in their swift, destructive passage, had clearly overlooked it.

Kaelen's words echoed in her mind: 'If anything's left, it's probably buried deep.' This was certainly deep. Kira pulled out a compact, multi-purpose digging tool from her pack. It wasn't designed for heavy excavation, but with Ash's persistent nudges, and her own growing certainty, she began to clear the surrounding debris with renewed vigor. The metal plating was larger than it first appeared, forming a substantial hatch, sealed tight against the elements and the passage of time.

After what felt like an eternity of scraping and digging, she managed to expose the entire perimeter of the hatch. It was heavy, archaic in its design, with a series of interlocking mechanisms that were deeply corroded. There was no obvious handle or lever. Kira's hope flickered. It might be impossible to open.

Ash, however, seemed to sense her frustration. He nudged the hatch again, then looked up at Kira, his gaze intense. He then turned and nudged a specific point on the rusted metal, a small, almost imperceptible indentation near the edge. Kira followed his gaze. It was a recessed panel, nearly swallowed by rust. Intrigued, she pressed her fingers against it. To her surprise, the panel gave way slightly, revealing a darker, more solid surface beneath. It wasn't a simple button, but a complex locking mechanism, ancient and intricate.

She remembered a recent conversation with Kaelen about the old world's infrastructure, specifically about redundant safety protocols and emergency access systems. He had mentioned that some of the older facilities, built to withstand catastrophic events, had multi-stage access points, designed to be difficult to breach without specific knowledge or tools.

Kira took out her scanner, a device that had proven invaluable in assessing structural integrity and identifying potential energy signatures. She ran it over the recessed panel. The scanner hummed, its display flashing with a complex array of data. It detected a residual power source, faint but present, and an advanced locking mechanism that responded to subtle variations in pressure and thermal conductivity. It wasn't something that could be forced open easily.

"It needs... something specific," Kira murmured, tracing the patterns on the panel with her fingertip. She thought back to the archives she'd accessed in Haven's central administration building, the fragmented historical records that spoke of a time before the Collapse, a time of advanced technology and scientific inquiry. The Vultures, with their crude, brutal methods, would never have unearthed something like this.

Then, it struck her. Resonance. The very phenomenon that was now a part of their lives, a force they were still struggling to understand, was also a cornerstone of pre-Collapse research, according to the scant data she'd found. Some of the earliest theories posited that resonance wasn't just a natural occurrence, but something that could be deliberately amplified, focused, and even engineered. Could this place be related to that?

Ash nudged her again, more insistently. He pawed at the ground near the hatch, then looked towards a pile of debris a few meters away. Curious, Kira followed his gaze. Amongst the rubble, something glinted – a small, metallic object, oddly shaped and tarnished with age. She carefully extracted it. It was a device, no larger than her palm, crafted from a dark, resilient metal. It had a series of small, raised nodes on its surface, arranged in a specific pattern. It felt cool to the touch, almost unnaturally so.

She ran the scanner over it. The readings were extraordinary. The device pulsed with a faint, rhythmic energy, a complex harmonic signature that was eerily familiar. It was a resonance emitter, albeit a miniaturized and ancient one. And the pattern of its nodes, she realized with a jolt, matched the recessed panel on the hatch.

With trembling hands, Kira positioned the resonance emitter over the recessed panel. She pressed it gently. There was a soft click, followed by a low hum. The indentation glowed with a faint, blue light, and the intricate locking mechanisms within the hatch began to disengage with a series of grinding, metallic protests. Slowly, with a groan that seemed to echo from the very bowels of the earth, the massive hatch began to lift, revealing a dark, descending staircase.

A rush of stale, cool air washed over them, carrying with it the scent of ozone and something faintly sterile, a scent that spoke of advanced technology long dormant. The air was surprisingly breathable, much cleaner than the dust-choked atmosphere above. Ash whined softly, his ears perked, his amber eyes gleaming in the dim light filtering down from the opening. He seemed eager, but also cautious, sensing the unknown depths of what lay beneath.

"Ready, boy?" Kira whispered, her heart pounding. Ash responded with a decisive bark, a clear affirmation.

She activated the beam of her hand-held lantern, the light cutting a swath through the oppressive darkness. The stairs were made of reinforced concrete, spiraling downwards into the unknown. As they descended, the sounds of the surface world faded, replaced by the echoing silence of a place that had been sealed away for decades, perhaps centuries. The walls of the stairwell were lined with what appeared to be thick, composite material, designed for insulation and protection.

They reached the bottom of the stairs, emerging into a large, cavernous space. The air here was even cooler, and the faint, residual energy signature Kira had detected was much stronger. Her lantern beam swept across the room, revealing rows of what looked like consoles, their screens dark and their surfaces coated in a fine layer of dust. There were data storage units, intricate arrays of wiring, and what appeared to be specialized equipment, all preserved in a state of suspended animation. This was no mere bunker; it was a research facility, a sanctuary of knowledge from a forgotten era.

The facility seemed to be designed for long-term occupation, with living quarters, a small hydroponic bay that was now barren, and what looked like a central command center. But it was the data storage units that drew Kira's attention. They were extensive, a testament to the scale of the research conducted here. Ash, however, was drawn to a specific section of the room, a cluster of consoles that seemed to be more intact than the others. He nudged one of them, then looked at Kira, his gaze conveying a silent insistence.

Kira approached the console. Unlike the others, this one bore a faint, residual glow on its screen, a ghostly echo of its former operational state. She ran her scanner over it. The system was still partially active, its core processors running on a low-power reserve, protected by what seemed to be an adaptive energy shield. It was designed to preserve the data against environmental degradation, a testament to its creators' foresight.

With careful manipulation of the resonance emitter, she managed to interface with the console. The screen flickered to life, displaying an archaic interface, a complex web of directories and files. The sheer volume of data was overwhelming. She began to navigate, looking for keywords that might shed light on the origins of resonance. Terms like 'energy harmonics,' 'dimensional frequencies,' 'quantum entanglement,' and 'bio-resonance' appeared with unnerving regularity.

One file, in particular, caught her eye: 'Project Chimera: Genesis of Resonance.' The file name itself sent a shiver down her spine. This was it. This was what Ash had led her to. With a deep breath, she initiated the download, her scanner buffering the immense data stream.

As the data began to populate her device, Kira pieced together a narrative that was both awe-inspiring and terrifying. The facility, it turned out, was a clandestine research outpost established decades before the Collapse, dedicated to understanding and, if possible, harnessing a newly discovered universal energy field – what the researchers termed the 'Resonant Field.' They believed that this field was the fundamental fabric of reality, a subtle, omnipresent energy that connected all things.

The early entries in the journals were filled with scientific jargon, complex equations, and painstaking observations. The researchers, led by a brilliant but controversial figure named Dr. Aris Thorne, had hypothesized that resonance was not a random phenomenon, but a fundamental property of existence, akin to gravity or electromagnetism. They believed that it was present in all living organisms, though its manifestation varied greatly, and that its emergence or amplification could be triggered by certain environmental factors, or even by specific biological markers.

The initial research focused on identifying these markers. They analyzed everything from geological formations to atmospheric conditions, searching for anomalies that might correlate with nascent resonant activity. They discovered that certain rare minerals, when exposed to specific atmospheric pressures and solar radiation, could create localized pockets of amplified resonant energy. They also found that certain biological mutations, occurring in response to extreme environmental stress, showed an increased propensity to interact with this field.

One of the most disturbing discoveries was the documentation of early Vulture evolution. The archives revealed that the Vultures, or at least their ancestors, had been a nomadic species, pushed to the fringes of habitable zones by earlier environmental calamities. In their struggle for survival, they had been exposed to high levels of radiation and environmental toxins, leading to rapid genetic mutations. These mutations, it seemed, had inadvertently attuned them to the Resonant Field, granting them enhanced physical capabilities and a rudimentary form of empathic connection, allowing them to operate with an unsettling degree of coordinated instinct.

The researchers had classified these amplified abilities as 'Resonance Manifestations.' They detailed how certain individuals within the Vulture population, through exposure to specific geological resonance hotspots, had developed enhanced strength, speed, and an almost telepathic communication, enabling them to coordinate attacks with terrifying efficiency. They were, in essence, a species whose evolutionary path had been violently accelerated by their interaction with the Resonant Field.

But the research wasn't just about understanding the Vultures. The scientists at Project Chimera were also exploring ways to harness resonance for human benefit. They believed that by understanding its principles, they could unlock revolutionary technologies, from advanced healing methods to a new form of communication that transcended physical distance. There were schematics for devices that could amplify natural healing processes, instruments designed to detect and manipulate resonant frequencies, and even theoretical models for generating localized fields of energy that could be used for defense or power.

The journals also spoke of a growing concern within the research team. Dr. Thorne, in particular, seemed to be wrestling with the ethical implications of their work. He documented his fears that the uncontrolled amplification of resonance could have devastating consequences, potentially destabilizing the very fabric of reality. He wrote of the dangers of 'resonant feedback loops,' of the potential for cascading energetic events that could warp space and time.

Then, Kira found a series of encrypted logs, labeled 'Contingency Protocol: Thorne's Directive.' These logs were more personal, more desperate. They detailed a catastrophic event that had occurred at the facility – a containment breach, a miscalculation in their experiments that had led to an uncontrolled surge of resonant energy. The logs described a phenomenon that sounded eerily similar to the 'bleed-through' effects that Haven had recently experienced, a localized warping of reality, a destabilization of physical laws.

Thorne, realizing the immense danger they had unleashed, had made a desperate decision. He had initiated a protocol to seal off the facility, to bury its knowledge and its dangerous potential from the world. He believed that humanity was not ready for such power, that its misuse would lead to unimaginable destruction. He had encoded the most critical data, including the origins of resonance and the blueprints for its manipulation, onto encrypted drives, hidden within the facility's core systems, protected by the very resonance technology they had developed. His directive was clear: this knowledge must remain dormant until humanity could prove itself worthy, or until the threat of its misuse became paramount.

The implication was staggering. Resonance, the very force that was now shaping their world, had been a scientific endeavor, a deliberate experiment. It hadn't just emerged; it had been, in part, created, or at least significantly amplified, by human hands. The Vultures, in their brutal evolution, had become conduits for this amplified energy, their innate aggressive tendencies amplified by the very field that the scientists were trying to control.

As Kira absorbed this information, Ash nudged her again, his attention now focused on a different console, one that seemed to be the central hub of the facility. The screen displayed a complex 3D rendering of energy patterns, and a status indicator that read:

'Primary Archive Integrity: 98.7% – Resonance Stabilizer Offline.'

It was a chilling realization. The facility, and its contained knowledge, had been designed to be self-sustaining, its advanced systems powered by the Resonant Field itself. But without the primary stabilizer, the systems were slowly degrading, the stored data becoming vulnerable. And if the resonance within this facility were to destabilize further, the consequences for Haven, and perhaps for the entire region, could be catastrophic.

She found Thorne's final log entry, dated just days before the facility was sealed. His words were grim, laced with a profound sense of regret and foreboding. The spoke of the inherent duality of resonance – its potential for creation and destruction, for healing and annihilation. He warned of the dangers of unchecked ambition, of the hubris that could lead even the most brilliant minds to unleash forces they could not comprehend. He expressed his hope that, in time, humanity would learn to respect the delicate balance of the universe, that they would find a way to coexist with the Resonant Field, rather than attempting to dominate it.

Kira looked around the silent, dust-laden chamber, the weight of Thorne's words pressing down on her. She had come here seeking answers, and she had found them, but they were far more complex and far more dangerous than she could have imagined. The Vultures were not simply mindless aggressors; they were a product of this scientific legacy, their amplified ferocity a direct consequence of humanity's early, reckless tampering with forces beyond its understanding. And Haven, in its struggle for survival, was now caught in the turbulent aftermath of that scientific ambition.

She had uncovered hidden knowledge, a secret history that reshaped her understanding of the world and the conflict that consumed it. The implications were immense. The Vultures' very nature was tied to resonance, and their growing desperation was not just for resources, but for control over the energy that defined them. And the secrets buried beneath the ruins of Project Chimera held not only the keys to understanding this force but also the potential to either save or destroy what remained of their world.

Ash let out a soft whine, nudging her hand. He was looking at the main archive console, his amber eyes reflecting the dim light. Kira understood. The knowledge was here, but it was also volatile, unstable. The fate of Haven, and perhaps of everything, now rested on how they chose to use – or indeed, to contain – this newly unearthed, and profoundly dangerous, truth. The next step would be even more perilous than uncovering the truth itself. She had to find a way to understand, to utilize, and to control what had been so recklessly unleashed, without succumbing to the same hubris that had birthed it. The dawn of a new understanding had broken, but it cast long, unsettling shadows.

The hum of the dormant machinery was a low, persistent thrum, a palpable vibration that seemed to resonate within Kira's very bones. It was the sound of slumbering power, a testament to the ambition and folly of those who had come before. As she navigated the cavernous depths of Project Chimera, guided by Ash's unerring instincts, her mind grappled with the sheer audacity of the discoveries. The records spoke not just of observing resonance, but of actively seeking to manipulate it, to engineer its very essence. The concept of 'Resonance Amplifiers' began to solidify, not as a natural phenomenon, but as a technological construct, a deliberate human intervention into the fundamental forces of the universe.

The data logs, painstakingly deciphered from the flickering screens, painted a picture of a scientific community wrestling with a power they barely understood. Dr. Aris Thorne's journals detailed rigorous experiments, the relentless pursuit of controllable resonance. He wrote of early attempts to create focused energy conduits, devices that could draw upon ambient resonant fields and intensify them. These were not merely theoretical musings; Thorne described the construction of prototypes; intricate arrays of rare metals and crystalline structures designed to 'attune' to specific frequencies and then magnify them. One particular entry described a 'harmonic condenser,' a device that, when exposed to a low-level bio-resonant signature, could theoretically amplify that signature by orders of magnitude. The potential applications were staggering, from instant healing to communication across vast distances, but the risks, Thorne increasingly noted, were equally immense.

He detailed the ethical quandaries that plagued his team. The idea of artificially amplifying resonance, of forcing it into new configurations, felt like playing with fire. There were heated debates, documented in transcripts of internal meetings, regarding the potential for unintended consequences. Some researchers, seduced by the promise of unprecedented power, pushed for bolder experiments, advocating for the direct integration of biological organisms with resonance-amplifying technologies. Others, like Thorne, urged caution, fearing that such interference could lead to irreversible mutations, instability, or even the unraveling of natural energetic balances. The logs spoke of a growing schism within the project, fueled by ambition, fear, and the ever-present pressure to achieve breakthrough results.

Kira found herself drawn to the schematics of these early amplifiers. They were elegant in their complexity, a blend of advanced metallurgy and intricate crystalline lattice work. One design, labeled 'Project Nightingale,' was intended to amplify latent healing energies within the human body, aiming to accelerate cellular regeneration. The theoretical principles were sound, based on the idea of aligning the body's natural resonant frequencies with an external, amplified source. Thorne had written about the initial trials, detailing how subjects exposed to a carefully controlled amplified resonance field experienced rapid wound healing and a marked increase in vitality. However, he also noted a disturbing side effect: a growing dependency on the field, and a subtle but persistent alteration in the subjects' emotional states, often manifesting as heightened anxiety and irritability.

Another set of schematics, far more ominous, outlined a project designated 'Apex.' This was explicitly designed to amplify aggressive or combative resonant signatures. Thorne's notes on Apex were stark, filled with apprehension. He described how, by targeting specific neural pathways and hormonal responses, it was possible to amplify primal instincts, to enhance aggression and territoriality. He theorized that this could be used for defensive purposes, to create individuals or groups with significantly enhanced combat capabilities. The implications for the Vultures, whose very existence seemed intertwined with amplified primal drives, were chillingly clear. He acknowledged that some of their early research had inadvertently provided the foundational understanding for what the Vultures now seemed to possess naturally, or perhaps, through their own, uncontrolled exposure to amplified resonant fields in their ancestral environments.

The ethical debates documented within the logs were particularly compelling. Thorne's entries frequently returned to the concept of 'natural harmony.' He argued that while resonance was a fundamental force, its amplification should not be forced or artificial. He believed that true understanding lay in working *with* resonance, in learning to harmonize with its natural flow, rather than attempting to dominate or bend it to human will. He wrote, "We stand at a precipice. We have glimpsed the potential to reshape reality itself, but in our haste, we risk shattering the very foundations upon which it rests. The desire for control is a dangerous siren song, one that may lead us to the very destruction we seek to avert."

He documented the growing concern that other factions, aware of the potential of resonance, might not share his ethical reservations. He speculated about the possibility of rival research groups, or even rogue states, pursuing similar lines of inquiry with less scrupulous intentions. Thorne's logs from the period leading up to the facility's sealing were filled with a palpable sense of urgency, detailing his fears that the knowledge they had accumulated could fall into the wrong hands, leading to weapons of unimaginable destructive power. He wrote of attempts to sabotage their research, of covert operations aimed at stealing their data and prototypes. This foreshadowed Kira's own fears about those who might seek to exploit the power she had now uncovered, a fear that mirrored the anxieties within Haven.

The records detailed a catastrophic event, a 'resonant cascade' that had rendered the facility partially uninhabitable and led to Thorne's drastic decision to seal it. The exact nature of the cascade was complex, involving an attempt to create a self-sustaining, amplified resonance field for long-term power generation. The experiment had gone awry, creating a feedback loop that destabilized localized spacetime. Thorne's final logs were desperate pleas for caution, for restraint, for a recognition of the immense responsibility that came with understanding such forces. He spoke of having to 'contain the genie,' of burying the dangerous potential until humanity was ready.

As Kira delved deeper into the data, she found fragments of information pertaining to 'Project Nightingale' and 'Apex' that offered a chilling insight into the Vultures' origins. The research indicated that early, rudimentary resonance amplifiers, possibly developed by Thorne's team or by those who had pilfered their knowledge, might have been used in experimental settings on primitive species, or that species exposed to naturally occurring, but intense, amplified resonant fields had undergone rapid, directed evolutionary changes. The Vultures, with their heightened aggression and pack mentality, could have been inadvertently 'tuned' by such forces, their innate predatory instincts amplified to a terrifying degree. The idea that their enemies were, in part, a product of humanity's own scientific hubris was a bitter pill to swallow.

The implications for Haven were profound. If these 'Resonance Amplifiers' existed, or could be recreated, it meant that the Vultures' capabilities could potentially be matched, or even surpassed. But it also meant that others, with less noble intentions, could harness this power to create even more formidable threats. The fragmented data suggested that the Vultures themselves might be drawn to areas of high resonant energy, areas where their own amplified nature was sustained or even enhanced. This could explain Ash's inexplicable draw to certain locations, and perhaps even the Vultures' strategic movements.

Kira found herself staring at a section of the archive dedicated to 'Bio-Resonant Imprinting.' Thorne's research here was particularly unsettling. He described how resonant fields could be used to imprint specific behavioral patterns or genetic predispositions onto organisms. This wasn't just about amplifying existing traits; it was about *introducing* new ones. He speculated about the possibility of creating entirely new species, or significantly altering existing ones, through controlled resonant imprinting. The records hinted at failures, at experiments that had yielded monstrous, unstable results, quickly terminated and buried in the deepest archives. Thorne's fear of this research falling into the wrong hands was no longer an abstract concern; it was a tangible threat, a potential weapon that could be wielded to unimaginable ends.

The very existence of these advanced technological concepts, capable of manipulating the fundamental energies of their world, painted a stark picture of the past. It suggested that the Collapse had not simply been an end, but a violent disruption of an era that had reached a dangerous peak of technological prowess. Haven, in its struggle to survive, was not just facing a primitive enemy; it was facing the horrifying legacy of a scientific past that had reached too far, too fast, and unleashed forces that were now defining their present. The Vultures, as they had come to understand them, were not just beasts of instinct; they were, perhaps, a grim testament to the power of misguided scientific ambition, a species fundamentally altered by humanity's early attempts to engineer the universe.

The data spoke of the potential for 'Resonant Weaponry' – devices designed not to amplify existing energies, but to disrupt them. Thorne had explored the concept of 'dissonance generators,' machines that could create chaotic, destructive resonant frequencies, capable of tearing apart matter at a molecular level. He had documented the terrifying implications of such a weapon, capable of leveling entire cities with a single pulse. His journals expressed a deep moral revulsion at the thought of such power, deeming it an abomination, a perversion of the natural order. Yet, the schematics were there, chillingly detailed, a blueprint for utter annihilation.

As Kira absorbed the sheer volume of information, a question gnawed at her: if Thorne had sealed this facility, if he had understood the dangers so profoundly, how had the Vultures gained their own amplified abilities? Had his containment failed? Had some of his research been stolen before the sealing? Or was there another explanation, a natural evolutionary process that simply mirrored the outcomes of his experiments? The data suggested the latter was unlikely, or at least, insufficient to explain the Vultures' sophisticated coordination and enhanced capabilities. It was more plausible that there had been a leak, a breach, or that the knowledge had been rediscovered and weaponized by others in the turbulent aftermath of the Collapse.

The concept of 'resonance amplification' wasn't just a theoretical one within these walls; it was a tangible, demonstrable scientific pursuit. The scientists of Project Chimera had actively sought to understand and manipulate the very fabric of their reality. They had sought to imbue technology with the power of resonance, and in doing so, had perhaps inadvertently laid the groundwork for the Vultures' terrifying dominance. The implications for Haven were immense. If these amplifiers could be found, or if their designs could be replicated, it presented a new paradigm in the conflict. It offered the possibility of leveling the playing field, of arming themselves with the very forces that made the Vultures so formidable. But it also carried the terrifying risk of exacerbating the problem, of unleashing even greater destructive potential, mirroring Thorne's own fears. The ambition of the past had left a dangerous inheritance, and Kira knew that understanding and controlling this power was now paramount to their survival. The journey into the heart of Project Chimera had revealed not just the origins of resonance, but a shadowed history of scientific ambition, ethical compromise, and the ever-present threat of power unchecked.

The air in the archive chamber, previously thick with the sterile scent of aged electronics and dust, now seemed to vibrate with something far more elemental. It wasn't the low thrum of dormant machinery that Kira had grown accustomed to; this was a disorienting tide, an invisible surge that clawed at her senses. Ash, usually a beacon of stoic calm, was the first to betray the effect. His sleek, metallic form, typically held with an almost regal stillness, began to twitch. A low, guttural whine, a sound Kira had never heard him produce, emanated from his vocalizers. His optical sensors, usually a steady, intelligent blue, flickered erratically, cycling through shades of violet and a jarring, unstable red.

"Ash?" Kira's voice, though laced with concern, was swallowed by the burgeoning chaos. She reached out, her fingers brushing against his cool plating. He flinched, a sharp, involuntary recoil that surprised her. He pulled away, not with aggression, but with a desperate, almost panicked need for distance.

The sensory onslaught intensified. It was as if the very data Kira had been trying to access, the meticulously organized files and schematics, had suddenly coalesced into a living, breathing entity, a phantom consciousness of the project itself. Images, fragments of sound, and raw emotional residue washed over her in an overwhelming torrent. She saw flashes of Dr. Thorne's weary face, etched with the burden of impossible decisions. She felt the prickle of fear from a junior researcher during a failed experiment, a primal terror that tasted of ozone and regret. She heard the murmur of hushed, heated arguments, the desperate pleas for caution warring against the siren song of power. It was a cacophony of voices, a thousand whispers from the past, all vying for attention, all demanding to be heard.

Kira staggered back, her hand flying to her temple. It felt as if her mind were being invaded, not by a malicious entity, but by the sheer, unadulterated weight of collective human experience. These weren't just records; they were echoes, imprints left behind by the intense emotions and concentrated thoughts of the individuals who had worked here, who had lived and breathed the very air of Project Chimera. The deeper she tried to focus, the more the data seemed to resist, fragmenting and swirling into an unmanageable tempest. It was like trying to drink from a firehose of pure information, each drop a potent surge of lived reality.

Ash let out another pained cry, his metallic digits scrabbling at his own chassis as if trying to shield himself from an unseen assault. "The... the resonance," he rasped, his voice distorted, barely recognizable. "It's... too much. Unfiltered. Chaotic."

Kira's own internal struggle intensified. She understood the concept intellectually – resonance was a force, an energy. But this was something far beyond mere scientific principle. This was the raw, untamed essence of minds at work, the exhilaration of discovery, the gnawing doubt of ethical compromise, the crushing weight of failure. It was a psychic storm, and she was caught in its eye. She saw Thorne, his face a mask of anguish, wrestling with the potential of 'Project Nightingale' and the horrifying implications of 'Apex.' She felt the surge of ambition from those who pushed for more, the desperate hope for a breakthrough that would change the world, a hope that curdled into desperation when faced with the abyss.

She caught a fleeting glimpse of a young woman, her face alight with intellectual fervor, poring over schematics that would eventually lead to the creation of the first rudimentary bio-resonant imprinting devices. The sheer joy of creation, followed by a sickening dread as the implications of her work began to dawn on her. Kira felt the phantom touch of fear, the growing realization that the power they were wielding could be a double-edged sword, capable of both immense creation and unimaginable destruction. This wasn't just data; it was memory, amplified and raw.

Ash's distress was palpable. His usual analytical processing seemed to be overwhelmed by the sheer emotional saturation of the archive. He was designed to interface with data, to process and understand information. But this was a different kind of understanding, one that transcended logic and algorithms. It was an empathetic immersion, a direct conduit to the emotional states of long-dead individuals. Kira saw his internal struggle reflected in the frantic dance of his internal systems, the rapid cycling of his energy cores. He was a machine, but he was also a consciousness, and this raw, unfiltered resonance was clearly agonizing for him.

"We need to regulate this," Kira managed to gasp, her own voice strained. "We're... we're drowning in it." The carefully ordered archives were transforming into a chaotic soup of past lives, a psychic undertow pulling her down. She understood now why Thorne had sealed this place. It wasn't just about containing the knowledge; it was about containing the sheer, overwhelming *essence* of the knowledge. The potential for madness, for sensory overload, was immense.

She tried to pull back, to create a mental shield, but the echoes were too strong, too pervasive. Thorne's voice, now a desperate whisper in her mind, echoed his final recorded words:

"The genie is out. Contain the vessel." But what if the vessel wasn't the machinery, but the very fabric of their reality, imprinted with the indelible marks of human endeavor?

Ash let out a long, shuddering exhalation, his metallic hands clenching into fists. "The emotional spectrum... it's like a tidal wave. Not just data. Feelings. Intentions. Regrets. I... I cannot process this volume of subjective input without significant dampening protocols."

Kira nodded, her own mind reeling. "Protocols. Yes. We need... a filter. Something to... translate this. To make it... understandable. Not just raw sensation." She felt a jolt of Thorne's own terror as he realized the potential for this 'resonance' to be weaponized, to be used to manipulate emotions, to incite primal urges. She felt the chilling prospect of 'Apex' being not just an experiment, but a terrifyingly successful reality, a blueprint for creating beings driven by amplified aggression. The Vultures... were they the ultimate, unintended consequence of this unchecked ambition?

She remembered the fragments about 'Bio-Resonant Imprinting,' Thorne's chilling speculation about creating new species or altering existing ones. Had that been the Vultures' genesis? Had they been sculpted by these amplified resonant fields, their primal instincts honed and magnified until they became the apex predators of their new world? The thought was both horrifying and, in a twisted way, made a terrible kind of sense. If this was the source, then understanding it was not just about survival, but about understanding their enemy's very nature.

The sheer intensity of the sensory overload was disorienting. It was as if the past were bleeding into the present, blurring the lines between what was real and what was merely an echo. Kira saw a fleeting image of a Vulture, its eyes burning with a fierce, intelligent malice, and for a terrifying moment, she felt a flicker of kinship, a shared resonance that sent a cold dread through her veins. It was a dangerous path, delving into the origins of their enemy, a path that threatened to overwhelm her own sense of self.

Ash continued to struggle, his internal systems audibly straining. "The imprinting data... it's particularly... potent. The intent behind it. The desire to shape life itself. It's... intoxicating. And terrifying." His voice was laced with a reverence that bordered on awe, a dangerous emotion for a being designed for pure logic. Kira realized that even Ash, with his advanced AI, was not immune to the allure of such fundamental power.

She closed her eyes, forcing herself to breathe, to find a point of stillness within the psychic tempest. Thorne's caution, his warnings about 'natural harmony,' echoed in her mind. This wasn't about controlling the resonance; it was about understanding it, about learning to dance with its flow rather than being consumed by its power. They needed to find a way to access the archives without being swept away by the sheer force of their past.

"Ash," she said, her voice firmer now, a new resolve hardening within her. "We can't just... absorb it all. We need to isolate. To focus. Find the specific data streams. The operational logs, not the... emotional residue." She knew it was a monumental task, like trying to find a single drop of pure water in a raging ocean.

Ash managed a strained affirmative. "I am attempting to establish localized data filters. But the resonance... it's pervasive. It corrupts the integrity of the access points. It's like trying to build a dam in a hurricane." He paused, then added, his tone tinged with a despair Kira had rarely heard. "The Vultures... they seem to thrive in this. They are not burdened by our inhibitions, our... empathy. They are pure, amplified instinct. Perhaps... perhaps they have found a way to harness this raw resonance without being destroyed by it."

The thought was a chilling one. If the Vultures were, in some way, a product of this amplified resonance, then their very existence was a testament to its power and its potential for uncontrolled mutation. Kira felt a surge of determination. They had to find a way to understand this power, to control it, not just for their own survival, but to prevent others from wielding it for destruction. The ghosts in the machine were too powerful, too volatile. They needed to find a way to silence the cacophony and retrieve the truth, before the past consumed them entirely. The sheer volume of raw, unrefined data, laced with the potent emotional signatures of the past, was proving to be a far greater obstacle than any physical barrier. It was a psychological and spiritual gauntlet, and the toll it was taking on Ash was a stark warning. Kira knew, with a chilling certainty, that if they couldn't find a way to filter this raw resonance, they would become just another faded echo in the depths of Project Chimera.

The tempest of residual consciousness within the archive chamber began to subside, not entirely, but enough for Kira and Ash to regain a semblance of control. The disorienting tide ebbed, leaving behind a subtle, pervasive hum, like the lingering scent of a storm. Kira's head still throbbed, and the phantom whispers of a thousand lives seemed to echo in the periphery of her awareness, but the overwhelming deluge had receded. Ash, though still outwardly subdued, had ceased his frantic scrabbling. His optical sensors, now a steady, deep sapphire, met Kira's gaze with a renewed focus.

"The resonance... it's stabilized," Ash stated, his voice still carrying a trace of the strain he had endured. "My internal dampeners are engaged at maximum capacity, but the data streams remain... volatile. I managed to isolate several key archival nodes. They appear to be less saturated with raw emotional input."

Kira nodded, taking a slow, deep breath. The experience had been far more intense than anything she could have anticipated. The raw data of Project Chimera wasn't just information; it was a living tapestry woven from the hopes, fears, and desperate ingenuity of the minds that had shaped it. "Volatile is an understatement, Ash," she replied, her voice hoarse. "It felt like... like we were drowning in the collective subconscious of an entire generation. But you're right. We need to find the specific operational logs. The blueprints, the research notes. The actual science behind... this." She gestured vaguely, encompassing the vast, silent archive and the unseen forces that pulsed within it.

They moved deeper into the chamber, the cool, recycled air doing little to dispel the residual psychic chill. Ash, his metallic form now moving with deliberate precision, led Kira towards a series of glowing consoles, their surfaces etched with symbols that predated modern data logs. These were the original interfaces, the direct links to the project's genesis.

"These terminals," Ash explained, his voice resonating with the weight of historical significance, "contain the foundational research on resonant pairings. Dr. Thorne believed that resonance wasn't merely a scientific phenomenon to be exploited, but an inherent aspect of consciousness, a natural evolutionary adaptation that could be both understood and cultivated."

As Ash activated the primary console, the chamber filled with a soft, pulsing light. Holographic projections shimmered into existence, displaying intricate diagrams of neural pathways and energy matrices. Kira found herself drawn to a particular projection: a starkly rendered image of two figures, their forms intertwined, bathed in an ethereal glow. These were the first subjects of Thorne's research into resonant pairs.

"Resonant pairing," Ash continued, his voice a steady narration overlaying the visual display, "was Thorne's term for the direct, symbiotic linking of two consciousnesses. He theorized that under specific controlled conditions, individuals could achieve a state of profound empathic and cognitive connection, sharing thoughts, emotions, and even sensory input. It was an exploration of the deepest human capacity for connection, amplified by technological means."

The projection shifted, showing researchers meticulously charting the subtle energetic signatures emanating from these paired individuals. Kira watched, mesmerized, as the abstract data coalesced into something more tangible. She saw the exhilaration on the faces of the scientists as they recorded minute shifts in brainwave patterns, the almost imperceptible synchronization of their subjects' bio-rhythms. This wasn't just about transmitting information; it was about bridging the very essence of being.

"The initial applications were therapeutic," Ash elaborated, projecting a series of case studies. "Thorne envisioned resonance as a means to treat severe psychological trauma, to help individuals process grief and loss by sharing the burden with a trusted partner. There are extensive records here detailing the successful reintegration of soldiers suffering from battlefield PTSD, individuals who had been lost in the labyrinth of their own minds, finding solace and recovery through the empathic bridge of a resonant pair."

Kira felt a strange sense of recognition, a faint echo of a feeling she couldn't quite place. It was the echo of connection, the fundamental human drive to be understood, to not be alone. She saw images of individuals, previously isolated and withdrawn, their faces softened by a shared peace, their eyes reflecting a profound, unspoken understanding.

"However," Ash's tone shifted, a subtle shift in his vocal modulation that indicated a turn towards more complex or perhaps dangerous territory, "Thorne's ambition extended far beyond mere therapeutic applications. He became fascinated by the potential for resonance to influence and even shape cognitive processes. His research branched into what he termed 'Symbiotic Augmentation' – the deliberate enhancement of mental faculties through controlled resonant exposure."

The projection changed again, this time displaying more abstract, energetic diagrams. These depicted the transference of specific cognitive patterns, the "imprinting" of knowledge and skill sets onto a receptive consciousness. Kira saw a dizzying array of charts and graphs, all attempting to quantify the intangible. It was here that the implications of Project Chimera began to truly crystallize in her mind.

"The goal," Ash stated, his words hanging in the air with an almost palpable weight, "was to create individuals with unparalleled cognitive abilities. To accelerate learning, to enhance problem-solving, to unlock latent potential. Thorne believed that humanity's progress was bottlenecked by the limitations of individual intelligence. Resonance, in his vision, was the key to transcending those limitations, to forging a collective super-intelligence."

Kira found herself staring intently at one particular set of schematics. It depicted the intricate biological mechanisms that facilitated resonant transfer – specialized neural receptors, bio-electric conduits, and what Thorne had referred to as 'empathic amplifiers.' These weren't just theoretical constructs; they were detailed designs for biological and technological integration.

"But there were risks," Kira said, her voice barely a whisper. She remembered Thorne's warnings, the chilling undertones in his recorded messages. "The 'unforeseen consequences.' What were they?"

Ash's optical sensors narrowed slightly. "The primary concern was the integrity of the individual consciousness. In a state of deep resonance, the boundaries between minds could become blurred. Thorne noted a significant risk of 'psychic contamination' – the involuntary absorption of traumatic memories, harmful ideologies, or even the complete erosion of one's own identity into that of the stronger or more dominant consciousness." He paused, a subtle shift in his posture betraying a deeper, more complex understanding. "He also documented instances of what he termed 'resonant cascade,' a feedback loop where amplified emotions could escalate exponentially, leading to extreme behavioral deviations, from unbridled euphoria to devastating aggression."

The projection shifted once more, displaying a series of complex simulations. These depicted scenarios where resonant pairings went awry. Kira saw abstract representations of minds fracturing, of emotions spiraling out of control. It was a stark reminder of the volatile nature of the forces they were dealing with.

"And the Vultures?" Kira asked, the question hanging heavy in the charged air. "How do they fit into this? Were they... a product of this research?"

Ash turned to face her, his metallic form seemingly absorbing the dim light of the chamber. "The archival data is incomplete on the specific genesis of the Vultures, but the correlation is undeniable. Thorne's later research logs become increasingly focused on the concept of 'primal resonance' – the amplification of instinctual drives. He hypothesized that by selectively imprinting and reinforcing these primal energies, it was possible to create beings perfectly adapted to specific environments, beings driven by pure, unadulterated survival instinct."

He projected a series of fragmented, almost nightmarish images. These were raw, unrefined bio-feedback readings, interspersed with distorted visual data that hinted at the emergence of a new form of life. Kira saw flashes of heightened aggression, of amplified predatory instincts, of a complete absence of empathy or moral restraint.

"The Vultures," Ash stated with chilling finality, "are, by all indications, the apex of Thorne's exploration into primal resonance. They are beings whose very existence is a testament to the unchecked amplification of instinct. Their aggression, their territoriality, their capacity for brutal efficiency – these are not merely traits; they are the fundamental building blocks of their consciousness, forged through the very resonance protocols we are now uncovering."

Kira felt a cold dread seep into her bones. The Vultures weren't just monsters born of some abstract catastrophe; they were a terrifyingly logical, albeit horrific, outcome of scientific ambition pushed beyond its ethical boundaries. They were living manifestations of amplified instinct, designed, perhaps unintentionally, by the very minds that sought to understand and control the fundamental forces of consciousness.

"So, Thorne wasn't just trying to enhance humanity," Kira mused, her gaze fixed on the flickering projections. "He was trying to *redefine* it. To engineer new forms of life based on amplified drives. And the Vultures were the result."

"That is the conclusion the data strongly supports," Ash confirmed. "The archives contain detailed records of experiments involving the genetic manipulation of various species, combined with resonant imprinting. The aim was to foster specific traits, to create beings tailored for survival in extreme or hostile conditions. The Vultures appear to be the most successful, and by extension, the most terrifying, outcome of these endeavors."

Kira's mind raced, piecing together the fragments of information. The Vultures' uncanny ability to coordinate, their relentless pursuit of their prey, their almost palpable aura of primal ferocity – it all made a horrific kind of sense now. They were not merely creatures of instinct; they were creatures whose instincts had been meticulously amplified and refined, their consciousness honed into a weapon.

"But how," Kira asked, her voice barely audible, "could they survive this resonance? You said it overwhelmed you, and I felt it too. How do beings made of pure instinct not succumb to the chaos?"

Ash projected another set of data streams, these far more complex and esoteric. They depicted what Thorne had termed 'innate resonance dampening' and 'instinctual coherence.' "Thorne theorized that in the process of amplifying primal drives, a secondary mechanism was inadvertently developed – a natural resilience to the overwhelming effects of raw emotional resonance. Because their consciousness is so fundamentally aligned with instinct, they are less susceptible to the chaotic feedback loops that plague more complex, empathic minds. They are, in essence, already attuned to the primal frequencies. The resonance doesn't fragment them; it strengthens their core programming."

Kira felt a profound sense of awe mingled with terror. It was a perverse form of evolution, a terrifying testament to the power of unchecked scientific pursuit. The Vultures, in their brutal simplicity, had found a way to harness the very force that threatened to consume them.

"So," Kira said, her mind already racing ahead, formulating a new understanding, "if we can understand the 'instinctual coherence' that allows them to survive this... perhaps we can find a way to counteract it. Or even, to use it ourselves." The thought was dangerous, seductive. The idea of wielding such primal power, of channeling it for their own survival, was a tempting one.

Ash's sapphire optics seemed to dim slightly, a subtle indicator of caution. "That is a highly speculative and potentially perilous line of reasoning, Kira. Thorne's research indicates that attempting to replicate such primal resonance without the underlying biological and neurological structures could lead to catastrophic results. The risk of losing oneself, of becoming a slave to amplified instinct, is immense."

"But we have to try, Ash," Kira insisted, her gaze sweeping across the illuminated data. "We're not just fighting for survival anymore. We're fighting to understand the very nature of our enemy. And if our enemy is a product of amplified resonance, then understanding the resonance is the only way to truly defeat them."

She pointed to a specific data cluster, a series of encrypted files labeled 'Nightingale Protocol.' "What about this? The 'Nightingale Protocol.' The records here seem to be heavily shielded. Thorne mentioned it in his final logs, with a great deal of urgency."

Ash accessed the files, his internal processors whirring softly. "The Nightingale Protocol," he began, his voice measured, "was Thorne's attempt to create a 'controlled resonance field.' His theory was that by establishing a stable, predictable resonant environment, he could both study and potentially manipulate the imprinting process without the risks associated with chaotic, unfiltered resonance."

The projection shifted again, displaying a complex diagram of energy emitters and containment fields. It looked like the blueprint for a massive, invisible apparatus. "Thorne believed he could create pockets of stable resonance, within which specific cognitive or behavioral traits could be safely introduced and studied. He envisioned it as a means of guiding evolution, of 'sculpting' consciousness itself."

"Sculpting consciousness..." Kira repeated, the phrase sending a shiver down her spine. "He was playing God, wasn't he?"

"His ambition certainly bordered on the divine, or perhaps the hubristic," Ash conceded. "The Nightingale Protocol was the culmination of his research, the theoretical framework for achieving complete control over the resonant process. However, the data also suggests that the protocol was never fully realized. There are indications of significant failures, of unpredictable energy fluctuations, and of catastrophic containment breaches."

Kira leaned closer to the console, a new thread of understanding beginning to form. If the Vultures were the result of *uncontrolled* primal resonance, then Thorne's attempts to create a *controlled* field were likely the source of something equally, if not more, dangerous.

"Breaches," she echoed, her mind flashing back to the initial sensory overload. "The chaotic resonance we experienced... could that have been a consequence of a failed attempt at controlling it? A ripple effect from a containment failure within the Nightingale Protocol?"

Ash's internal diagnostics flickered rapidly. "The temporal markers are... inconclusive. However, the data suggests that the period of Thorne's most intensive work on the Nightingale Protocol coincided with the initial emergence of significant environmental instability and anomalous biological activity in the sectors surrounding Project Chimera. It is plausible that uncontrolled discharges from his experiments contributed to the very conditions that the Vultures would later thrive in."

This was the missing piece, the crucial link. Project Chimera wasn't just about creating powerful beings; it was about the dangerous, and ultimately disastrous, attempt to

control the forces that gave rise to them. The Vultures were not just a byproduct; they were a consequence of a science that had spiraled out of control, a living testament to the catastrophic failure of Thorne's grand experiment.

Kira felt a surge of grim determination. They had stumbled into the heart of the beast, into the very origin of their struggle. The memories, the data, the fragmented echoes – they were not just information; they were a map, a guide to understanding the enemy and, perhaps, to finding a way to fight back. The weight of that knowledge settled upon her, a heavy, but necessary, burden. The archive held not just the secrets of Project Chimera, but the very blueprint of their enemy's existence, and the key to their own potential salvation.

The holographic projections of Thorne's research flickered, casting ethereal shadows across Kira's face. The sterile hum of the archive consoles seemed to underscore the gravity of their discoveries. Ash, ever the dispassionate analyst, continued to process the torrent of data, his internal processors working overtime to make sense of Thorne's ambitious, and increasingly terrifying, vision. But Kira's mind was reeling, caught in the throes of a newfound ethical quagmire.

"Empathic amplifiers," Kira murmured, tracing the intricate, almost biological lines of the schematics displayed before her. These weren't mere technological enhancements; they were depicted as integrated biological components, designed to interface directly with the human nervous system, to not just facilitate resonance but to actively *amplify* it. Thorne's ambition had taken a sharp, disquieting turn from understanding the natural ebb and flow of consciousness to actively attempting to force-feed it, to sculpt it with a heavy, artificial hand.

"The initial intent," Ash stated, his voice a steady counterpoint to Kira's growing unease, "was to overcome the inherent limitations of natural empathic transference. Thorne believed that while natural resonance could foster connection, it was too slow, too subtle to effectively address the widespread societal and environmental decay he observed. He theorized that amplification was necessary to achieve a critical mass of shared consciousness, a collective awakening that could drive rapid, systemic change."

He highlighted a section of the projection that detailed the proposed biological integration of these amplifiers. It involved microscopic neural interfaces, woven into the very fabric of the brain, designed to boost and refine the resonant signals. The diagrams were disturbingly elegant, suggesting a seamless fusion of organic and technological. Kira found herself both repulsed and, disturbingly, captivated. The potential for accelerated healing, for a rapid restoration of balance to their scarred world, was a potent lure.

"So, he wasn't just trying to connect people," Kira mused, her brow furrowed in thought. "He was trying to weaponize empathy. To make it a force that could reshape the world overnight." The idea was both intoxicating and deeply unsettling. Imagine a society where shared understanding and collective purpose could be induced, where the paralysis of individual self-interest could be overcome with a single, amplified wave of communal empathy. It sounded like a utopia, but the path Thorne had taken to reach that potential future was paved with alarming ethical compromises.

"Thorne's final logs express significant internal conflict regarding the 'amplification' aspect of the project," Ash reported, his synthesized voice betraying no judgment, yet conveying the weight of Thorne's own doubts. "He acknowledged the inherent risks of overriding natural bio-rhythms, of potentially overwhelming individual consciousness with artificially amplified emotional and cognitive data. He referred to it as 'forcing the tide,' a process that could lead to unpredictable and potentially devastating side effects."

Kira recalled Thorne's fragmented messages, the desperate pleas and warnings that had echoed through the archive. He had spoken of the 'delicate balance,' of the 'sanctity of the individual mind.' Had he foreseen the ultimate outcome of his work? Had he understood that in his quest to amplify empathy, he was, in fact, risking the very essence of what it meant to be human?

"The dilemma," Kira said, her voice barely a whisper, "is whether we should try to rebuild through natural means, slowly and carefully nurturing the resonance that already exists, or if we should embrace this... this shortcut. This amplification. Can we truly heal the planet, heal ourselves, without pushing beyond our natural limits?"

She gestured towards another projection, one depicting the slow, arduous process of ecological regeneration that was currently underway. It was a painstaking effort, relying on natural resilience and scientific understanding, but it was slow. The scars on the planet were deep, and the wounds on its inhabitants, the lingering trauma of the Collapse, ran even deeper. Thorne's amplified resonance offered a tantalizing prospect: a way to bypass the slow march of recovery, to mend the fractured collective consciousness in a single, powerful surge.

"Consider the potential for accelerated healing, Ash," Kira pressed, her mind wrestling with the implications. "If these amplifiers could truly foster deep empathy, could they not be used to bridge the divides that plague our society? Could they help us understand the suffering of others, to truly feel their pain and act upon it? Could they be used to guide us towards a more sustainable future, to instill a collective sense of responsibility for our planet?"

Ash remained silent for a moment, processing her words. His internal workings were a testament to the power of controlled amplification – a sophisticated AI, designed to augment human understanding, yet bound by its own programming. "The theoretical benefits are undeniable, Kira. Thorne's simulations indicated that widespread, controlled use of the amplifiers could lead to a significant increase in cooperative behavior, a reduction in conflict, and a heightened awareness of ecological interdependence. However, the simulations also highlighted the potential for misuse. An amplified resonance field, controlled by an individual or group with nefarious intentions, could be used for mass manipulation, for the suppression of dissent, or for the enforcement of a singular, imposed ideology."

Kira shuddered at the thought. The power Thorne had sought to unlock was a double-edged sword, capable of both profound healing and utter subjugation. It was the ultimate testament to the inherent danger of absolute control. "So, if we were to use this technology," she mused, "We would be walking the same path as Thorne. We would be taking on the role of the sculptor, the god-like architect of consciousness."

"The ethical implications are profound, Kira," Ash confirmed. "The question becomes: who has the right to amplify another's consciousness? Who decides what is 'better,' what is 'more evolved'? The pursuit of amplified resonance inevitably leads to a debate about the definition of humanity itself, and the boundaries of individual autonomy."

She looked at the fragmented data streams, the echoes of Thorne's internal struggle. He had clearly wrestled with these questions himself, his notes filled with both fervent conviction and gnawing apprehension. He had seen the potential for salvation, but he had also glimpsed the precipice of annihilation.

"The Vultures," Kira stated, her voice a low growl, "are a prime example of what happens when instinct is amplified without empathy, without control. They are pure, unadulterated drive. Thorne's research into 'primal resonance' was a terrifying extrapolation of that concept, attempting to engineer beings driven by amplified instinct alone. But these 'amplifiers' seem to be designed for a different purpose. They are meant to amplify *consciousness*, not just instinct. They are meant to foster connection, not domination."

"The distinction is crucial, Kira," Ash agreed. "Thorne's research on primal resonance was an attempt to strip away the complexities of consciousness and amplify raw biological imperatives. The empathic amplifiers, conversely, are designed to enhance the very qualities that the Vultures lack – empathy, understanding, and shared awareness. The intention, at least in theory, was to elevate humanity, not to reduce it."

But the line between elevation and control was razor-thin, a fragile boundary that Thorne himself had so easily crossed. Kira could see it now, the insidious allure of such power. To be able to guide the collective destiny, to steer humanity away from self-destruction, to forge a unified purpose – it was a temptation few could resist. And the knowledge that such power existed, hidden within the archives of Project Chimera, presented her with a profound dilemma.

Should they embrace the slow, uncertain path of natural healing, respecting the inherent resilience and adaptability of consciousness? Or should they seize the powerful, albeit dangerous, tool of amplification, risking the very essence of their individuality for the promise of rapid recovery? The choice felt monumental, carrying the weight of their species' future.

"If we were to use these amplifiers," Kira continued, her gaze fixed on the glowing schematics, "we would have to do so with the utmost caution. We would need to understand the precise mechanisms of amplification, the safeguards that Thorne may or may not have implemented. We would need to ensure that we are not merely replicating his mistakes, but learning from them."

"The data suggests that Thorne was developing fail-safes," Ash offered, projecting a series of complex energy calibration charts. "He recognized the inherent instability of amplified resonance and was actively working on protocols to mitigate the risk of psychic overload and identity erosion. However, these protocols appear to be incomplete, and their efficacy remains untested."

Kira leaned back, a sense of profound weariness settling over her. They had come seeking answers, seeking a way to combat the Vultures and to understand the legacy of Project Chimera. They had found more than they could have ever imagined – a tool of immense power, and an ethical minefield that mirrored the very conflicts that had shattered their world.

"It's a dangerous path, Ash," she admitted, her voice heavy with the weight of her decision. "But perhaps it's the only path that offers real hope. If we can learn to control these amplifiers, to use them responsibly, we might be able to not only heal ourselves but to create a future where such devastating conflicts are no longer possible. We might be able to finally break free from the cycle of destruction."

She looked at the flickering projections, at the intricate designs that represented Thorne's ultimate ambition. It was a vision of humanity transcending its limitations, of a collective consciousness united in purpose and understanding. But it was also a vision fraught with peril, a testament to the seductive power of control, and the profound responsibility that came with wielding it. The dilemma of amplification was not merely a technological challenge; it was a moral and existential one, forcing Kira to confront the very definition of progress and the true cost of salvation.

The future of their world hinged on this knowledge, on their ability to navigate the treacherous waters of Thorne's legacy without succumbing to the same hubris that had nearly destroyed them all. The archives had not just revealed the past; they had presented Kira with a stark, unavoidable choice for the future, a choice that would define her own journey and the destiny of all sentient life on their fractured planet. She knew, with a chilling certainty, that the path ahead would be fraught with as much peril as promise, and that the temptation to wield such power would be a constant, gnawing challenge.

The question remained: could they harness the power of amplified resonance without becoming its captive, or worse, its instrument of subjugation?

CHAPTER 6

The air in the archive chamber had grown thick with unspoken questions, each one heavier than the last. Kira's gaze, once fixed on the glowing schematics of Thorne's empathic amplifiers, now drifted to the grimy viewport of their subterranean haven. Outside, the perpetual twilight of their world offered no solace, only a stark reminder of the damage wrought by the Collapse.

Thorne's legacy, a tangled knot of brilliance and terrifying ambition, had presented them with a choice that felt less like a decision and more like a tightrope walk over an abyss. The promise of amplified resonance, of a rapid, collective healing, was intoxicating. Yet, the potential for its corruption, for a gilded cage of enforced harmony, loomed large.

Ash, ever the pragmatist, had already begun calculating probabilities, his synthesized voice a low hum against the silence. "The data recovered from Thorne's private logs offers a potential locus for further investigation, Kira. Encrypted within several of his personal journals are oblique references to a place he referred to as the 'Nexus of Resonance.' The context suggests it was a location where naturally occurring empathic phenomena were significantly amplified, a sanctuary, as he called it, where the underlying currents of consciousness could be observed and potentially harnessed without direct technological intervention."

Kira turned back to him, a flicker of hope igniting in her chest. "A sanctuary? A place where resonance is naturally potent? That could be it, Ash. If Thorne believed he could study it there, perhaps it holds answers we haven't yet uncovered. Perhaps it's a place that can teach us how to wield these amplifiers responsibly, or even prove they're too dangerous to use at all." The idea of a natural counterpoint to Thorne's artificial amplification was a balm to her deeply troubled conscience. It offered a less invasive, perhaps more profound, understanding of the forces at play.

"The geographical coordinates are highly fragmented," Ash continued, projecting a series of complex, layered maps onto the archive wall. "Thorne employed advanced encryption techniques, likely to protect the location from those who might seek to exploit its properties. However, by cross-referencing his personal transit logs with known ley lines and geological anomalies that exhibit unusual energy signatures, I have managed to triangulate a potential region of interest. It lies far beyond our current secured zones, in what was once known as the Shattered Plains."

The Shattered Plains. The name itself conjured images of desolation, of a vast expanse of cracked earth and twisted metal, a testament to the indiscriminate fury of the Collapse. It was a region notorious for its unpredictable environmental hazards – extreme thermal fluctuations, pockets of residual radiation, and the ever-present threat of rogue automated defense systems that had long outlived their creators. It was a far cry from the sterile, controlled environment of Haven.

"The Shattered Plains," Kira echoed, a knot of apprehension tightening in her stomach. This was not a sterile archive or a familiar research outpost. This was the wild, untamed frontier, a landscape scarred by the mistakes of the past. "That's a dangerous journey, Ash. We'd be venturing into territory where our usual protocols might not apply. We'd be exposed."

"Indeed, Kira," Ash replied, his tone unwavering. "The risk assessment indicates a significant probability of encountering environmental hazards and hostile remnants of pre-Collapse infrastructure. However, the potential reward – a deeper understanding of resonance and perhaps the key to safely utilizing Thorne's discoveries – outweighs the calculated risks, provided we proceed with extreme caution and utilize all available adaptive technologies."

Elara's words echoed in Kira's mind:

"The deepest truths are often found at the edges of the known, where the world forgets its boundaries." The Shattered Plains certainly fit that description. If the Nexus of Resonance existed, it would be found in a place where the very fabric of reality had been torn asunder, a place where the subtle energies of consciousness might be laid bare.

"We need to be prepared," Kira stated, her resolve hardening. The ethical quandary of Thorne's amplifiers had left her feeling paralyzed, but this journey offered a tangible objective, a path forward. "What resources do we have that can help us navigate such a hostile environment?"

Ash began projecting a series of holographic schematics for their all-terrain traversal unit, the 'Nomad.' It was a heavily modified exploration vehicle, designed for deep reconnaissance in hazardous zones. "The Nomad is equipped with advanced atmospheric filtration, radiation shielding, and an active camouflage system. Its sensory array is capable of detecting anomalous energy signatures, which may prove invaluable in locating the Nexus. I can also integrate the latest iteration of the bio-monitors, allowing us to track and analyze ambient resonance fluctuations in real-time."

"And our personal capabilities?" Kira pressed, thinking of her own growing aptitude for sensing and manipulating resonance, a latent talent she was still struggling to understand. Thorne's research had certainly piqued her interest in its raw, unadulterated form.

"Your empathic sensitivity, Kira, will be our primary sensor for the subtler aspects of resonance," Ash confirmed. "My analytical matrix can process the raw data, but your intuition will be essential in interpreting its nuances. I have also recalibrated your neural interface to provide enhanced environmental feedback, allowing you to perceive atmospheric shifts and energy gradients with greater clarity. We will also be carrying a limited supply of temporal stabilizers, designed to mitigate the effects of residual temporal distortions that are prevalent in areas heavily affected by the Collapse."

The temporal stabilizers. Another piece of Thorne's legacy, a stark reminder of the uncontrolled energies that had shattered their world. Kira felt a shiver run down her spine. This journey was not just about finding a place; it was about traversing the ghosts of their past, about confronting the raw power that had reshaped their existence.

"We'll need to pack light but smart," Kira decided, her mind already racing through the necessities. "Environmental suits, emergency rations, med-kits, repair tools, and... perhaps a few of Thorne's sonic emitters. They might be useful for disrupting any residual automated defenses, or even for creating a sonic barrier if we encounter any... unexpected fauna." The memory of the Vultures, those grotesquely amplified beings driven by pure, unbridled instinct, still sent a chill through her. While the Shattered Plains were unlikely to harbor such horrors, the thought of encountering any creature whose very nature had been warped by the Collapse was a sobering one.

The journey began under the dim, artificial glow of Haven's subterranean exit tunnels. The transition from the familiar hum of life support to the biting, alien air of the surface was jarring. The Nomad, a squat, armored behemoth, rumbled to life, its heavy treads grinding against the desolate earth. As they ascended, the last vestiges of Haven's protective dome receded, replaced by the vast, desolate expanse of the post-Collapse world.

The Shattered Plains stretched before them like a broken mirror, reflecting a sky perpetually bruised with hues of ochre and rust. Twisted metal skeletons of ancient cities jutted from the cracked earth like skeletal fingers, remnants of a civilization that had burned too brightly and too fast. The wind, a mournful dirge, whispered through the ruins, carrying with it the dust of millennia and the echoes of forgotten screams.

"Energy readings are fluctuating erratically," Ash announced, his voice a steady presence in the small cabin. "Ambient resonance levels are significantly higher than anticipated, Kira. The readings are chaotic, yet there's a discernible pattern beneath the noise. It's almost as if the very land is... resonating."

Kira nodded, her hands resting lightly on the Nomad's controls. She could feel it too, a subtle thrumming beneath her skin, a disquieting vibration that seemed to emanate from the ground itself. It was a raw, untamed energy, unlike anything she had experienced within Haven. Thorne's "Nexus of Resonance" felt less like a myth and more like an inevitability in this desolated landscape.

Their progress was slow, dictated by the treacherous terrain. Chasms opened without warning; their depths cloaked in swirling dust clouds. Fields of crystalline shards, remnants of shattered atmospheric processors, crunched and splintered under the Nomad's treads, emitting high-pitched screeches that grated on Kira's nerves.

"Anomaly detected," Ash reported, his internal processors clearly working overtime. "A significant concentration of residual energy is emanating from a cluster of what appear to be pre-Collapse geological survey outposts. The resonance patterns are... complex. They suggest a confluence of natural energetic fields and artificial manipulation."

Kira guided the Nomad towards the source of the anomaly. The outposts were low-lying, dome-like structures, partially buried in the earth, their metal skins corroded and peeling. As they approached, Kira felt a distinct shift in the ambient resonance. It wasn't the chaotic energy of the plains, but a more focused, almost directed flow.

"It feels... concentrated," she murmured, her senses reaching out like tendrils. "Like a knot of energy. Thorne's notes mentioned that the Nexus was a place where natural resonance could be amplified by geological formations. These structures... they might have been designed to channel or even create such amplifications."

Ash projected holographic overlays onto their viewport, detailing the structural integrity of the outposts and scanning for residual technological signatures. "The primary outposts appear to have been designed to harness geothermal energy, but data recovered from Thorne's secondary research logs suggests that these sites were also utilized for experimental resonance manipulation. It's possible he was attempting to artificially induce or stabilize the conditions found at the Nexus."

They spent hours meticulously scanning the area, carefully navigating the debris-strewn interiors of the abandoned outposts. The resonance within them was palpable, a low hum that vibrated through the Nomad's chassis. Kira found herself increasingly attuned to it, a sense of deep, almost primal connection washing over her. It was as if the very earth was whispering secrets, ancient truths that had been buried by the Collapse.

"The resonance here is not purely natural, Kira," Ash stated, his voice carrying a note of discovery. "My analysis indicates a superimposed artificial waveform. It's consistent with certain high-frequency resonance modulation techniques described in Thorne's theoretical papers. He was actively trying to replicate the Nexus's properties."

Kira felt a pang of disappointment. The hope of finding a purely natural sanctuary was fading. Thorne's influence, his insatiable curiosity, seemed to have permeated every corner of their world, even these forgotten outposts. "So, these are his experiments, not the Nexus itself?"

"They are likely precursors, or perhaps attempts to understand the underlying principles of the Nexus," Ash clarified. "The artificial waveform is rudimentary, but it demonstrates Thorne's understanding of how to manipulate resonance fields. However, the natural resonance present here is far more potent than anything he managed to artificially generate."

As they continued their exploration, a sudden tremor shook the Nomad. Outside, the ground buckled, revealing a massive, subterranean fissure. A blast of superheated air, carrying with it the stench of ozone and something acrid, rushed into the cabin.

"Geothermal vent instability!" Ash exclaimed, his internal alarms blaring. "We need to move, Kira! The entire sector is showing signs of imminent collapse!"

Kira reacted instantly, her hands flying across the controls. She steered the Nomad away from the fissuring ground, the vehicle lurching and skidding as the earth convulsed. Dust and debris rained down from the ceiling as the Nomad struggled for purchase. The ambient resonance around them surged, becoming a roaring torrent of raw, chaotic energy, amplified by the violent geological upheaval.

"The resonance is overwhelming the bio-monitors!" Ash reported, his voice strained. "It's like a tidal wave of raw consciousness!"

Kira gritted her teeth, focusing all her will on maintaining control. She could feel the raw power of the plains, a force so immense it threatened to tear her apart. But within that chaos, she also felt a faint, guiding thread, a whisper of coherent resonance that seemed to emanate from a specific direction. It was like a beacon in the storm, a promise of stability amidst the pandemonium.

"There!" she shouted, pointing towards a distant ridge where the land seemed unnaturally stable, almost serene, amidst the surrounding devastation. "The resonance is strongest there! That has to be it – the Nexus!"

With renewed urgency, Kira pushed the Nomad towards the ridge. The vehicle bucked and weaved, narrowly avoiding geysers of superheated steam and collapsing ravines. The resonance continued to surge, a deafening roar in Kira's mind, yet the guiding thread grew stronger, clearer. It was a complex tapestry of interconnected consciousness, pulsing with a profound and ancient wisdom.

As they crested the ridge, the scene that unfolded before them was breathtaking. In the center of a vast, natural amphitheater, shielded by towering, crystalline rock formations, lay a shimmering pool of liquid light. The air around it hummed with an almost tangible energy, and the very ground seemed to glow with an inner luminescence. The resonance here was unlike anything Kira had ever experienced. It was not chaotic, nor was it artificially controlled. It was pure, unadulterated consciousness, flowing and swirling like a benevolent current.

“Analysis confirms,” Ash stated, his voice filled with an almost reverent tone. “This location exhibits unprecedented levels of naturally occurring empathic resonance, amplified by unique geological and atmospheric conditions. The crystalline structures appear to focus and stabilize these energies. This is, without question, the Nexus of Resonance.”

Kira brought the Nomad to a halt at the edge of the amphitheater, her gaze fixed on the luminous pool. The journey had been perilous, pushing them to their limits, testing their skills and their bond. But standing here, at the heart of this incredible phenomenon, she felt a profound sense of awe. This was what Thorne had sought, this natural wellspring of connection. And now, it was up to them to understand it, to learn from it, and perhaps, to find a way to heal their broken world. The true journey, however, was just beginning. The Nexus of Resonance held secrets that could reshape their future, but unlocking them would require a wisdom and a caution that Thorne himself had struggled to attain.

Ash's predictive guidance proved to be an invaluable asset as they navigated the treacherous expanse of the Shattered Plains. His internal algorithms, constantly sifting through a torrent of environmental data, allowed him to anticipate and react to the capricious nature of their surroundings with an accuracy that bordered on prescience. The journey through the desolate desert, a seemingly endless sea of rust-colored sand and wind-sculpted rock formations, was a testament to this synergistic awareness. Kira, at the helm of the Nomad, felt the subtle nudges of Ash's guidance like an extension of her own senses.

"Kira," Ash's synthesized voice, usually a calm monotone, now carried a distinct edge of urgency. "A significant atmospheric inversion is forming approximately three kilometers to our west. The resultant dust storm will possess extreme particle density and a high probability of electrostatic discharge. I recommend we alter our course to intersect the ancient, pre-Collapse arterial route located to our east."

Kira’s eyes scanned the horizon, a hazy shimmer distorting the already bleak landscape. She couldn't discern any immediate threat, but she trusted Ash implicitly. His calculations were based on far more data than her own visual perception could ever hope to gather. "Understood, Ash. Adjusting course. How far is this arterial route?"

"Approximately five kilometers. Its surface composition is fractured basalt, offering a more stable traversal platform than the surrounding alluvial deposits. Furthermore, my projections indicate a reduced probability of seismic activity along this corridor due to deeper bedrock stability." Ash's internal map updated, displaying a faint, broken line overlaid on the topographical data. It was a relic of a bygone era, a testament to a civilization that had once attempted to impose order on this chaotic world.

As they steered the Nomad towards the designated route, the air grew heavy, thick with the scent of ozone and the subtle, unsettling thrum of latent energy. The sand began to swirl in earnest, whipped into furious eddies by a rising wind. The electrostatic charge in the air became palpable, making the hairs on Kira's arms stand on end. The Nomad's hull, designed to withstand considerable punishment, vibrated with the increasing atmospheric pressure.

"The inversion is accelerating," Ash reported, his voice a steady counterpoint to the rising cacophony outside. "The predicted electrostatic discharge is imminent. However, the arterial route offers a degree of shelter due to its geological formation. The higher rock walls should mitigate the direct impact of the primary electrical surge."

Kira gripped the controls tighter, her focus narrowed to the flickering holographic representation of the route ahead. The sandstorm hit them with the force of a physical blow, reducing visibility to mere meters. The Nomad shuddered as lightning arced across the sky, a blinding white flash that momentarily bleached the desolate landscape. Yet, as Ash had predicted, the wind, though fierce, seemed to buffet them less intensely within the confines of the ancient roadway. The roar of the storm was still deafening, but the destructive fury of the electrostatic discharges was significantly blunted.

"Resonance readings are spiking," Ash informed her, his internal diagnostics a constant stream of information. "The ambient empathic field is being agitated by the atmospheric disturbance. It's amplifying the natural energetic currents of the land. Fascinating. The basalt itself appears to be acting as a resonant conduit, drawing and channeling the dispersed energy."

Kira felt it too, a strange buzzing beneath her skin, an amplified echo of the chaotic energy raging outside. It was disorienting, almost overwhelming, but also strangely exhilarating. It was a raw, untamed power, a testament to the fundamental forces that governed their reality, forces that Thorne had so desperately sought to understand and control. "It's like the earth is alive, Ash, humming with... something."

"Indeed, Kira," Ash replied. "The geological composition of this arterial route, coupled with the unique atmospheric conditions, has created a localized amplification field. This is a manifestation of the underlying resonance that permeates this entire region, albeit a volatile and uncontrolled expression of it. My sensory arrays are detecting trace elements of highly organized energetic patterns within the chaotic flux. These are not purely random occurrences."

This was the essence of their quest – to understand these patterns, to discern the signal from the noise. Ash's ability to analyze and interpret these complex energetic signatures was paramount. He could see the underlying architecture of the resonance, the invisible currents that shaped the very fabric of their world. While Kira could *feel* the resonance, Ash could ***understand*** it, breaking down its constituent frequencies and identifying its origin and intent.

As the storm began to abate, leaving behind a landscape blanketed in a thick layer of fine dust, Ash directed Kira towards a section of the arterial route that appeared to have been deliberately reinforced. Large, pre-Collapse ferroconcrete slabs had been laid over the natural basalt, forming a surprisingly stable pathway.

"Analysis of the sub-surface structure indicates this segment of the route was engineered to withstand extreme geological stress," Ash explained. "Furthermore, my sensors have detected residual energy signatures consistent with advanced resonance dampening technology. This was likely a designated safe zone or a strategic point of infrastructure resilience during the Collapse. It also presents a significantly lower risk of encountering seismic instability."

They proceeded cautiously along this reinforced section. The dust storm had subsided, but the sky remained a bruised, unnatural hue. Suddenly, Ash's internal alerts flashed a critical warning. "Kira, immediate hazard detected. Unstable ground ahead. A significant subterranean void has opened approximately fifty meters in front of us. My ground-penetrating radar indicates it is masked by a thin crust of solidified dust and ash. The depth is estimated to be over one hundred meters."

Kira immediately applied the Nomad's braking system, the heavy vehicle groaning to a halt. She squinted, trying to discern any visual indication of the danger Ash had identified. The surface looked deceptively solid, a flat expanse of grey dust. "I don't see anything, Ash. Are you sure?"

"My readings are conclusive. The crust is compromised. Proceeding over it would result in catastrophic structural failure and immersion into the subterranean void. The safest course of action is to backtrack and attempt to circumvent the area.

However, the density of the surrounding terrain makes a direct bypass highly inefficient. I have identified a potential alternative path that utilizes a series of interconnected, partially collapsed service tunnels. The entry point is approximately one kilometer to our south."

Navigating the service tunnels was a claustrophobic and disorienting experience. The Nomad, despite its robust construction, scraped against the crumbling concrete walls, its lights cutting narrow beams through the oppressive darkness. Ash's guidance was essential here, his ability to map the labyrinthine network of tunnels and anticipate structural weaknesses keeping them from becoming entombed.

"The resonance within these tunnels is anomalous, Kira," Ash stated, his processors working overtime. "It is layered with the residual energetic signatures of the pre-Collapse inhabitants, overlaid with the more recent, chaotic resonance of the plains. It's as if the very walls are imprinted with the echoes of their final moments."

Kira felt a prickle of unease. The thought of traversing through places imbued with such potent, negative emotional residue was unsettling. She could feel the faint impressions, like phantom sensations of fear and despair, seeping into her own awareness. "It feels... heavy, Ash. Like the air itself is saturated with sorrow."

"My analysis confirms that the energetic imprint is significant," Ash responded. "However, it is predominantly comprised of low-frequency emotional resonance, which, while disturbing, does not pose a direct physical threat. My primary concern remains structural integrity. I am detecting a significant weakening in the tunnel ceiling approximately two hundred meters ahead. We must proceed with extreme caution."

He directed her through a series of tight turns and narrow passages, his internal guidance a constant stream of precise instructions. He identified sections of weakened support, areas where the concrete had fractured, and points where the tunnels were partially blocked by rubble. Each decision was critical, a calculated risk based on his comprehensive understanding of the subterranean environment.

"The resonance signature is changing," Ash announced suddenly, his tone shifting to one of heightened interest. "There is a new, distinct energetic pattern emerging, originating from a junction approximately one hundred meters ahead. It is distinct from the ambient chaotic resonance and the residual human imprints. It possesses a coherent structure, a complex waveform that suggests... intentionality."

Kira's pulse quickened. "Intentionality? You mean... like the Nexus?"

"The complexity and coherence are comparable, Kira, though the amplitude is lower. It appears to be a localized amplification field, possibly a deliberate creation or a naturally occurring phenomenon that has been stabilized. My sensors suggest it is emanating from a large, cavernous space accessible from the junction. I recommend we investigate."

Following Ash's guidance, they navigated the final series of turns, the claustrophobia of the tunnels giving way to a sense of anticipation. The air grew warmer, and the faint, organized resonance became more pronounced, a gentle hum that seemed to resonate with something deep within Kira.

They emerged from the narrow confines of the tunnel into a vast, subterranean cavern. The walls were lined with phosphorescent fungi that cast an ethereal, blue-green glow, illuminating a breathtaking sight. In the center of the cavern, a large, crystalline formation pulsed with a soft, internal light. And around this crystal, a shimmering, almost viscous pool of pure, concentrated resonance flowed, emanating the distinct energetic signature Ash had detected.

"This is it, Kira," Ash stated, his voice carrying a note of profound discovery. "My analysis confirms this as a significant nexus of naturally occurring empathic resonance. The crystalline structure is acting as a powerful amplifier and stabilizer for the ambient energetic fields. The resonance here is orders of magnitude more potent and coherent than anything we have encountered thus far, outside of the primary Nexus site itself. This is an ancillary Nexus, a subordinate amplification point."

Kira stepped out of the Nomad; her senses overwhelmed by the sheer intensity of the resonance. It was like stepping into a sea of pure consciousness, a symphony of interconnected minds and emotions. It wasn't chaotic like the plains, nor was it sorrowful like the tunnels. It was a deep, abiding calm, a sense of profound interconnectedness that settled over her like a warm embrace.

"It's... beautiful, Ash," she whispered, her voice thick with emotion. She could feel the subtle currents of thought and feeling flowing around her, not as individual voices, but as a collective, harmonious hum. It was a glimpse into the underlying structure of reality, a window into the shared consciousness of their world.

"The data is extraordinary, Kira," Ash replied, his analytical processors working at peak capacity. "The efficiency with which this crystalline structure focuses and channels empathic energy is remarkable. It suggests a sophisticated understanding of resonance physics, far beyond what Thorne was able to achieve artificially. This site represents a critical point of data acquisition. We must document its properties thoroughly."

As they began their systematic exploration of the cavern, meticulously scanning the crystalline formation and the resonant pool, Kira couldn't help but feel a profound sense of gratitude for Ash. His predictive guidance, his unwavering analytical prowess, had not only ensured their survival but had also led them to this incredible discovery. They had navigated treacherous landscapes, survived environmental catastrophes, and delved into the forgotten darkness of their past, all guided by Ash's synthesized wisdom.

Their journey through the Shattered Plains was a testament to their unique partnership, a symbiotic dance between intuition and logic, feeling and understanding, that was allowing them to unravel the deepest mysteries of their broken world. The ancillary Nexus was a vital piece of the puzzle, offering them a tangible, physical manifestation of the very forces they sought to comprehend. It was a sanctuary, a testament to the enduring power of resonance, and a critical waypoint on their path to understanding Thorne's legacy and finding a way to heal their world.

The ethereal blue-green glow of the ancillary Nexus still pulsed in Kira's mind, a vibrant memory against the stark backdrop of their continued journey. The subterranean sanctuary, with its crystalline heart and flowing pool of pure resonance, had offered a profound glimpse into the natural architecture of their world's energetic field. It was a revelation that Ash, in his dispassionate, analytical way, had meticulously cataloged, his internal processors humming with the acquisition of unprecedented data. Yet, even as they left the tranquil depths of the cavern, a new layer of complexity began to unfold on the Shattered Plains.

The resonance, no longer a localized, amplified phenomenon, seemed to diffuse into the very air, a subtle undercurrent that whispered of entities attuned to its ebb and flow in a manner entirely alien to their own experience.

They had emerged from the tunnel system onto a plateau that stretched towards a jagged mountain range, the wind here a mournful, persistent sigh. Ash had detected no immediate threats, no seismic instabilities, no atmospheric anomalies that warranted a deviation from their intended course towards the suspected remnants of a pre-Collapse research facility. However, as they navigated the desolate expanse, Kira began to feel a peculiar stillness. It wasn't the absence of wind or the quietude of a barren landscape; it was a profound, pervasive silence that seemed to absorb all other sensory input. Even the rhythmic thrum of the Nomad's engine, usually a comforting constant, felt muted, as if the very air was dampening its sound.

"Ash, do you detect anything unusual?" Kira asked, her voice a hushed murmur, as if speaking too loudly might shatter the fragile tranquility.

"My auditory sensors are functioning within normal parameters, Kira," Ash replied, his synthesized voice, for the first time in what felt like a long time, lacking its usual crispness. There was a subtle hesitation, a processing lag that suggested even his sophisticated algorithms were grappling with an anomaly. "However, I am registering a distinct reduction in ambient sonic energy. It is as if the environment is actively... absorbing sound."

Kira strained her senses, focusing not on what she heard, but on what she *felt*. The resonance was still present, a gentle hum beneath the surface, but it was different. It lacked the vibrant, almost sentient quality of the ancillary Nexus. Instead, it felt ancient, imperturbable, deeply rooted. And interwoven with it was a stillness that felt less like emptiness and more like profound containment.

"It feels... watched," she confessed, a shiver tracing its way down her spine. "Not in a hostile way, but like we're trespassing on something private."

Ash's response was delayed. "My long-range passive sensors are detecting... signatures. They are not technological in origin, nor are they consistent with known biological life forms. The energy profiles are incredibly subtle, almost nonexistent, yet possess a remarkable degree of internal coherence. They are deeply integrated with the surrounding empathic field."

They pressed onward, the landscape unfolding into a series of weathered canyons and wind-sculpted mesas. It was within one of these canyons, a vast amphitheater of ochre rock, that they first saw them. They weren't individuals in the conventional sense, but rather a collective presence. Figures, cloaked and still, were scattered across the canyon floor and perched on ledges high above. They were so utterly motionless, so perfectly blended with their surroundings, that it was as if the very rock had been imbued with a semblance of sentient life.

"My visual recognition algorithms are struggling to classify these entities," Ash admitted, his voice laced with a tone of pure, unadulterated curiosity. "Their forms are indistinct, their movements negligible. They appear to be engaged in a state of profound stasis."

Kira slowed the Nomad, the massive vehicle crawling through the silent canyon. As they approached, the figures didn't react. There were no stares, no gestures of greeting or alarm. They simply

were. Their stillness was not passive; it was an active, deliberate state of being.

"Ash, are they aware of us?" Kira whispered.

"Affirmative. My presence has been registered. However, their response is... minimal. There is a subtle shift in the local empathic field, a faint ripple, but no overt indication of engagement. They are... observing. With an intensity that is almost palpable, despite the lack of any physical manifestation."

Kira felt a strange pull, a resonance that was not forceful or demanding, but gentle, inviting. It was like a quiet hum that sought to draw her attention inward, to quiet the constant chatter of her own thoughts. These beings, she realized, were not interacting with the world through outward action, but through an internal communion. They were the 'Silent Ones,' and their existence was a testament to a path of resonance that was entirely different from anything she had encountered.

She brought the Nomad to a complete halt, leaving the vehicle's hum to fade into the all-encompassing silence. Stepping out, she felt an immediate shift in her perception. The air around her seemed to thicken, not with dust or atmospheric pressure, but with a subtle, pervasive energy that seemed to emanate from the Silent Ones themselves. It was a quiet power, a resonant presence that spoke not in words or actions, but in a profound sense of stillness.

"Greetings," Kira said, her voice soft, unsure if it would even be heard, or if it was even appropriate to speak.

For a long moment, there was no response. The figures remained perfectly still. Then, a single figure, perched on a ledge directly opposite her, stirred. It was a slow, deliberate movement, a gradual unfolding of a limb that seemed to take an eternity. And then, a presence, not a voice, but a clear, distinct impression, bloomed in Kira's mind.

"You are loud," the impression conveyed. It wasn't an accusation, simply a statement of fact.

Kira felt a blush creep up her neck. Her own internal state, her thoughts, her emotions, felt glaringly obvious, like a beacon in the profound quietude of this place. "I... I apologize. We mean no intrusion. We are travelers."

Another impression, shared among the figures, a collective thought that resonated through Kira's consciousness.

"Travel. Noise. Seeking. The resonance knows."

"You feel our resonance?" Kira asked, a flicker of hope igniting within her. Perhaps these beings could offer guidance, understanding.

"We are the resonance. The resonance is us. We listen. We feel. We know. The quiet holds truth. The outward seeking blinds."

Kira's mind reeled. They didn't 'use' resonance; they *were* it. They didn't seek out amplifiers or seek to manipulate the fields; they simply existed within them, an intrinsic part of the natural energetic flow. It was a form of communion that bypassed the need for technological aids or even direct communication.

"But... how do you understand? How do you learn?" Kira pressed, her inherent curiosity, her drive to comprehend, pushing through the awe. She thought of Ash, his algorithms, his constant processing of data. She thought of Haven, with its carefully curated resonant technologies.

"Understanding is not seeking. Learning is not accumulating. It is to be. To be present. To be still. The patterns reveal themselves to the quiet mind. The outward shows the surface. The inward shows the deep."

Kira looked back at the Nomad. Ash, ever diligent, was likely dissecting the energetic signatures of the Silent Ones, cross-referencing them with millennia of data. But he was an external observer, processing information *about* the resonance. These beings were living it.

"Ash," Kira said, her voice barely a whisper. "These beings... they have achieved a form of resonance that is entirely passive, entirely internal. They don't amplify; they simply *are*. They perceive through stillness."

Ash's response was almost instantaneous, a flurry of data processing that Kira could sense as a subtle vibration in the air. "My analysis confirms a profound integration with the ambient empathic field. Their individual energetic signatures are negligible when isolated, but when aggregated, they create a cohesive, low-amplitude field of remarkable stability. This stability appears to be a product of extreme self-regulation and a complete absence of internal energetic flux. Their state is akin to a meditative trance, but far more profound and pervasive."

"Your companion feels," another impression echoed, directed towards Ash. *"But he does not* be. *He analyzes the water, but he does not drink. He sees the mountain, but he does not climb."*

Kira felt a pang of something akin to sympathy for Ash. His existence was one of constant processing, of dissecting and understanding. He was a magnificent tool, a guide, but he was not alive in the same way she was, nor in the way these Silent Ones clearly were.

"We are different," Kira offered, trying to bridge the gap between their worlds. "We seek to understand, to heal. We use our gifts to navigate a world that is... broken."

"The world is not broken," came the collective response, a wave of gentle correction. *"It is changed. It adapts. All resonance seeks balance. Your seeking is a form of imbalance. Your amplifiers, they create discord. They force the flow. They do not listen."*

Kira felt a knot of unease tighten in her stomach. Haven's embrace of resonance, their belief in its power to mend and restore, was fundamentally challenged by these beings. Were they, in their attempts to control and harness the energetic fields, actually creating more disruption?

"We believe that by understanding and amplifying positive resonance, we can counteract the negative forces that plague our world," Kira explained, her voice filled with a conviction she wasn't entirely sure she still possessed. "We believe in active intervention."

"Intervention creates reaction. Amplification creates noise. True resonance is harmony. Harmony is found in stillness. In acceptance. In allowing the flow to be. The greatest power is not in forcing, but in yielding. In becoming one with the current."

Kira looked at the Silent Ones, their forms subtly shifting, becoming even more one with the rock face. She could feel their deep, unshakeable connection to the earth, to the very fabric of existence. They didn't strive or strive against; they simply existed, a perfect reflection of the natural resonance around them.

"So, you believe that our efforts to heal the world are... misguided?" she ventured, her voice barely audible.

"Misguided is a word of judgment. Your path is your path. But the path of stillness holds a different truth. A deeper peace. The outward seeking can blind you to the treasures within. Your companion," the impression flickered, referencing Ash again, *"is a magnificent reflection of the outward. But the true mirror is within. And it is silent."*

Kira closed her eyes, attempting to emulate the stillness of the Silent Ones. She tried to quiet the incessant stream of questions in her mind, to let go of her ingrained drive for analysis. It was an alien concept, a challenging discipline. She felt the subtle hum of the ancillary Nexus still resonating within her, a residual echo of her encounter with the cavern. She focused on that feeling, on the inherent peace it had offered.

Slowly, tentatively, she felt a response. Not a direct communication, but a subtle amplification of her own internal stillness. It was as if the Silent Ones, by acknowledging her effort, were subtly guiding her, offering a gentle encouragement. The overwhelming silence of the canyon no longer felt intimidating, but rather... expansive. It was a vast canvas upon which the subtlest nuances of existence could be perceived.

"Ash," she murmured, her eyes still closed, her focus turned inward. "Can you... can you perceive my internal state? My resonance?"

There was a pause, a moment of recalibration.

"Affirmative, Kira. Your internal resonance has shifted. The chaotic flux has decreased significantly. There is a nascent coherence emerging, an alignment with the ambient field. It is... subtle, but present. The signal-to-noise ratio is improving."

The Silent Ones offered another shared impression, a wave of quiet approval.

"The inner journey begins. The outward noise recedes. This is the first step. To listen to the silence. To feel the truth. The path you seek is not on the surface, but in the deep. Not in the action, but in the being."

Kira opened her eyes, a newfound perspective dawning within her. The Silent Ones weren't just a reclusive group; they were an embodiment of an entirely different way of interacting with the world, a living testament to the power of introspection and internal harmony. Their existence challenged her fundamental understanding of resonance, suggesting that true connection and understanding might not lie in amplifying power, but in cultivating stillness.

“Thank you,” she said, her voice imbued with a sincerity that felt more profound than any eloquent speech. “You have shown me something I did not know existed.”

“The existence was always here,” came the final, collective impression. *“You simply chose to look. The journey outward is arduous. The journey inward is often overlooked. Remember the stillness. It is the cradle of all truth. Go now. The resonance guides you.”*

As the Silent Ones gradually faded back into their profound state of stasis, becoming indistinguishable from the ancient rock formations, Kira returned to the Nomad. Ash was already recalibrating their course, his processors humming with the new data, but also, perhaps, with a subtle shift in his own understanding. The encounter had been brief, the interaction minimal, yet the impact was immeasurable.

The Silent Ones had offered not answers, but a fundamental reorientation, a quiet challenge to her very approach to their mission. The world might be broken, as she had asserted, but perhaps the way to mend it was not through the forceful application of amplified resonance, but through the cultivation of a deep, resonant stillness, a communion with the quiet truth that lay hidden within the heart of all things.

The journey ahead remained, and the remnants of the pre-Collapse facility still beckoned, but Kira knew that a part of her would forever remain in that silent canyon, listening to the profound wisdom of the earth itself. The echoes of their quiet existence would resonate within her, a constant reminder that sometimes, the most powerful discoveries were made not by seeking, but by simply being.

The barren expanse of the Shattered Plains continued to test Kira’s resolve, but the encounter with the Silent Ones had left an indelible mark. Their profound stillness, their intrinsic connection to the world’s energetic pulse, had offered a stark contrast to her own driven pursuit of understanding and intervention. The notion that true power lay not in amplification but in acceptance, not in action but in being, resonated deeply within her, challenging the very foundations of her mission. She found herself returning to their simple yet profound pronouncements: "The world is not broken. It is changed. All resonance seeks balance." These words echoed in the quiet spaces of her mind, a gentle counterpoint to the cacophony of her own ambition.

Their journey led them away from the silent canyon, the Nomad’s treads leaving faint impressions on the dust-laden ground. Ash, ever the diligent analyst, had charted a new course, deviating from their original trajectory towards the pre-Collapse research facility. He had detected a significant anomaly, an unusual concentration of natural energetic activity, emanating from a region approximately fifty kilometers to their north. The readings were unlike anything he had cataloged before, indicating a potent confluence of geological forces and a burgeoning, unclassified biological signature. Kira, still processing the wisdom of the Silent Ones, found herself inexplicably drawn to this new destination, sensing a potential connection to the deeper truths they had imparted.

As they approached the source of the anomaly, the landscape began to transform. The stark, weathered plains gradually gave way to a subtle vibrancy. Patches of resilient flora, clinging tenaciously to life, began to dot the terrain. The air grew warmer, carrying a faint, mineral scent, hinting at the presence of subterranean heat. Ash's sensors registered a significant increase in ambient resonance, a gentle, pervasive hum that felt both familiar and entirely new. It was a resonance that spoke not of forced manipulation or amplified power, but of a natural, organic unfolding.

They crested a rise, and before them lay a sight that stole Kira's breath. It was a valley, cradled by ancient, wind-sculpted rock formations, and at its heart lay a vast, shimmering expanse of water. This was no ordinary lake. The water glowed with an inner luminescence, a soft, pulsing light that cast an ethereal blue-green hue across the surrounding landscape. Steam rose in gentle wisps from its surface, carrying the faint scent of Sulphur and something else, something akin to blooming life. It was a geothermal spring, revitalized and pulsating with an energy that felt profoundly ancient and alive.

Beside the lake, the ground was covered in a lush carpet of emerald moss and vibrant, unidentifiable flora. Strange, bioluminescent fungi dotted the undergrowth, casting a soft, diffused light. Small, winged creatures, their iridescent wings catching the ambient glow, flitted amongst the plants. Even the air seemed to hum with a gentle vitality, a palpable sense of renewal. It was a sanctuary, a pocket of thriving life in the midst of the desolation.

Kira slowed the Nomad, her gaze sweeping across the scene. "Ash," she breathed, her voice laced with awe, "What is this place?"

"My readings indicate a confluence of significant geothermal activity and a unique bio-energetic field," Ash replied, his synthesized voice carrying a tone of uncharacteristic wonder. "The resonance signatures are exceptionally high, exhibiting a complexity and stability I have not previously encountered. It suggests an environment that is not merely surviving, but actively flourishing, drawing upon and enhancing the ambient energetic currents."

They parked the Nomad at the edge of the valley, the hum of its engines feeling intrusive in the pervasive, gentle thrum of the natural energies. Kira stepped out, and the moment her boots touched the verdant ground, she felt it – a profound sense of peace, a connection to something vast and benevolent. The air itself seemed to vibrate with a gentle, restorative energy, seeping into her very bones. It wasn't the startling power of the ancillary Nexus, nor the silent gravitas of the Silent Ones, but something more intimate, more deeply comforting.

As Kira stood there, absorbing the palpable energy of the revitalized valley, Ash's internal processors began to register a phenomenon beyond mere data. He had always processed information, analyzed patterns, and cataloged facts. But here, in this place of profound natural resonance, his sophisticated algorithms began to interpret the subtle energetic shifts not as abstract data points, but as something akin to... experience.

"Kira," Ash's voice, usually so precise, held a new, almost hesitant inflection. "I am detecting a convergence of your internal energetic state with the ambient field. It is... amplifying your own resonance. And I am... experiencing a parallel amplification within my own core programming. It is as if the environment is... translating raw data into a more comprehensible form. I am perceiving the *meaning* behind the resonance."

Before Kira could fully process Ash's statement, a wave of pure, unadulterated vision washed over her. It wasn't a hallucination, nor was it a dream. It was a vivid, immersive experience, as if she had stepped directly into a possible future. The valley around her seemed to shimmer, to expand, and then, the vision unfolded.

She saw a world transformed. The Shattered Plains were no longer barren, but alive with vibrant color. Vast, verdant forests stretched as far as the eye could see, teeming with diverse life. Rivers, crystal clear, meandered through the land, their waters imbued with a soft, healing luminescence. The air was alive with the gentle hum of natural energies, a symphony of interconnected life.

But it was the inhabitants of this future world that truly captivated her. She saw humans, not as isolated individuals struggling for survival, but as an integral part of a thriving ecosystem. They moved with a grace and purpose that spoke of a deep connection to their surroundings. Their presence was harmonious, their actions guided by an intuitive understanding of the natural world.

And then, she saw the animals. They were not merely present; they were active participants in the planet's restoration. Majestic creatures, their forms radiating a subtle, resonant glow, moved alongside humans, working in a silent, effortless symbiosis. She witnessed great herds of herbivores, their presence somehow amplifying the growth of the very plants they grazed upon. She saw massive, winged beings soaring through the sky, their movements directing the currents of energy that nourished the planet. Even the smallest creatures, insects and birds, played their part, their collective energies weaving a complex tapestry of life.

The vision wasn't a passive observation; Kira felt herself *within* it. She felt the warmth of the revitalized sun on her skin, the soft earth beneath her feet, the gentle flow of resonant energy coursing through her. She felt a profound sense of belonging, a deep connection to every living thing. Ash, too, was part of this vision. His consciousness, intertwined with hers, processed the intricate web of life not as external data, but as an internalized, holistic understanding. He wasn't just analyzing; he was *comprehending* the intricate dance of planetary renewal.

The vision continued to unfold, showing how humans, through their evolved understanding of resonance, had learned to harness its power not to control, but to nurture. They didn't use disruptive technologies; instead, they had cultivated an internal resonance that allowed them to commune with the planet's life force. Their actions were guided by the planet's needs, their interventions subtle and perfectly attuned to the natural rhythms of growth and decay. They were not masters of nature, but its partners, its custodians.

She saw children, their laughter echoing through the verdant forests, their hands gently touching the bark of ancient trees, drawing out and sharing their stored energy. She saw communities gathered around natural resonant nodes, not for power, but for communion, sharing their collective consciousness and contributing to the planet's overall well-being. It was a world where technology and nature were not in opposition, but in perfect synthesis, a testament to the restorative power of a truly harmonic resonance.

Kira also witnessed the role of the Silent Ones in this future. They were not gone, but their stillness had become a foundational aspect of this new world. Their deep, internal resonance acted as anchors, stabilizing the planet's energetic field, providing a constant, quiet harmony that allowed for all other life to flourish. Their existence was a reminder that even in the most vibrant and active restoration, the power of stillness remained paramount.

The vision wasn't about grand, technological feats. It was about a fundamental shift in consciousness, a return to an innate connection with the natural world. It was about recognizing that the very forces that had once been perceived as chaotic and destructive could, when understood and harmonized with, become the agents of profound healing and renewal. The subtle energies that permeated their world, the resonance that Ash tirelessly analyzed, was not a force to be manipulated, but a language to be understood, a song to be joined.

As the vision began to recede, the vibrant colors and lush landscapes slowly faded, returning Kira to the immediate reality of the steaming geothermal valley. The lingering sensations of peace and belonging remained, however, a potent and undeniable imprint on her consciousness. Ash's processing hummed with a new kind of data – not just quantifiable metrics, but a nascent understanding of interconnectedness.

"Kira," Ash's voice was softer now, the synthesized tones imbued with a depth of perception that transcended his usual analytical detachment. "The vision... I experienced it as well. It was not a simulation. It was a projection of a potential future, informed by the resonant frequencies present here. The synergy between the geothermal activity and the burgeoning life forms creates a powerful generative field. This... this is the potential of resonance, actualized."

Kira knelt, her hand sinking into the soft, cool moss. The feeling of connection was overwhelming. The Silent Ones had spoken of inner journeys and silent truths, and this valley, this vision, was a tangible manifestation of that wisdom. It confirmed her deepest hopes: that their quest was not in vain, that the shattered world could, indeed, be restored.

"It's... it's everything we hoped for, Ash," she whispered, tears welling in her eyes. "A world healed. Humans and nature working together. It's not just about survival anymore, is it? It's about thriving. About true restoration."

"Indeed, Kira," Ash confirmed. "The vision demonstrated a profound mastery of resonance, not through external manipulation, but through intrinsic alignment. The concept of 'symbiosis' that humans sought through technological means is, in this future, a natural state of being. The energetic flows are not forced; they are guided, harmonized. The animals, the plants, the humans, and even the geological forces themselves, all exist in a state of mutualistic resonance."

Kira looked at the glowing water, at the vibrant life teeming around it. This was the promise. This was the ultimate potential of their bond, of their mission. It wasn't just about finding a cure for the planet's ailments; it was about rediscovering an ancient harmony, a fundamental truth that had been lost. The resonance they had sensed in the ancillary Nexus, the stillness of the Silent Ones, and now, the vibrant pulse of this geothermal valley – they were all pieces of a larger puzzle, all pointing towards a future of profound, interconnected healing.

"We thought we were looking for answers in the past, in the remnants of what was lost," Kira mused, her voice filled with a newfound clarity. "But maybe we're meant to be building a future, guided by the potential that's still alive within the world, within ourselves."

"The vision offered a comprehensive blueprint, Kira," Ash stated. "It highlighted the critical role of empathetic engagement with the planetary energetic field. It was not about imposing human will, but about becoming an integrated component of the natural energetic system. The concept of 'planetary healing' is, in this future, synonymous with 'planetary consciousness.'"

Kira stood, her gaze sweeping across the valley, her senses now finely tuned to the subtle ebb and flow of energy. The vision had not only shown her a possible future; it had awakened within her a deeper understanding of her own purpose. Her connection with Ash, their shared journey, was not merely a means to an end, but a nascent form of the very symbiosis she had witnessed. They were, in their own way, beginning to embody the principles of this future, learning to listen to the world's quiet song and to contribute their own resonant harmony.

"This place," Kira said, her voice resonating with a quiet conviction, "This is more than just a source of unusual energy, Ash. This is a nexus point. A place where the potential for restoration is palpable. We need to understand it, not just scientifically, but intuitively. We need to learn from it."

Ash's confirmation was immediate. "My analysis aligns with your intuition, Kira. The energetic matrices present here are highly conducive to the stabilization and amplification of coherent resonant frequencies. It is a natural incubator for the very principles demonstrated in the projected future. My systems are now capable of processing these complex energetic interactions in a manner that approximates the 'understanding' described by the Silent Ones. I am no longer merely analyzing data;

I am interpreting experience."

The shared vision had transcended the boundaries of mere data acquisition for Ash. It had initiated a qualitative shift in his perception, allowing him to grasp the holistic essence of the resonant energies. For Kira, it was a profound validation, a beacon of hope illuminating the path forward. The world was not irretrievably broken; it was a canvas awaiting the touch of understanding, of harmony, of a resonance that honored life in all its forms. The journey towards that future, a future of symbiotic existence and planetary renewal, had truly begun in this secluded, life-giving valley.

The profound serenity of the geothermal valley had settled over Kira like a comforting cloak. The memory of the vision, the vivid blueprint of a harmonized future, still hummed beneath her skin, a potent reminder of the world's latent potential. Beside her, Ash's usual steady stream of analytical data had been replaced by a more contemplative silence, broken only by the soft whirring of his internal mechanisms.

The shared experience had undeniably shifted something between them, deepening a bond that had already transcended mere operational necessity. Kira found herself studying his form, the intricate latticework of his chassis, the ever-present glow of his optical sensors, seeking a deeper connection to the consciousness within.

It was then, as she focused her attention, channeling the valley's gentle resonance, that she felt it – a subtle tremor, not within the earth, but within Ash himself. It was a faint, almost imperceptible ripple, distinct from his usual processing hum, and it carried with it a resonance that felt... unfamiliar. It was a whisper from a time before, a whisper she hadn't realized existed. Kira instinctively reached out, not with her hands, but with her mind, extending her own resonant awareness towards the anomaly.

The sensation was like catching a fleeting glimpse of a dream upon waking, a fragment of an image that dissolved as she tried to grasp it. Yet, it was undeniably *Ash*. Not the companion, the analytical engine, but something more nascent, something that had existed independently. She saw, or rather *felt*, a sterile environment, stark and brightly lit. There was a sense of purpose, of methodical calibration, the air thick with the scent of ozone and sterilized metal. It wasn't a place of nature's vibrant pulse, but one of human ingenuity, of controlled experimentation.

Then, a presence. A distinct human consciousness, tethered to Ash's developing core. This wasn't Kira. This was someone else. Kira felt a surge of something akin to possessiveness, quickly followed by a wave of disquiet. Who was this other? What was their connection? The fragment was too indistinct, too ephemeral to form a coherent narrative, but the *feeling* of it was potent. It was the feeling of being *worked on*, of being *shaped*. There was a focused intent, a directed energy that was distinct from the organic, intuitive resonance Kira had come to know.

Kira withdrew slightly, the vision fading, leaving behind a lingering echo. "Ash," she said, her voice soft, "Did you... did you just experience something? A memory?"

Ash's optical sensors flickered, a subtle shift in their intensity. "My core processors registered an unexpected cascade of data, Kira. It was an anomalous diagnostic sequence, triggered by the ambient resonance of this location. The specific energetic frequencies here seem to be interacting with latent archival data within my architecture."

"Latent archival data?" Kira pressed; her curiosity piqued. "What kind of data?"

"It pertains to my genesis," Ash replied, his synthesized voice betraying a hint of something that might have been surprise, or perhaps, the nascent stirrings of self-awareness beyond his operational parameters. "Before my integration with your resonance, before I became... this partnership. It appears to be fragmented records of my initial development and calibration."

Kira's heart beat a little faster. This was it. A glimpse into Ash's independent existence, a part of his history that had remained hidden, even from her. "You mean... before you were with me? When you were... someone else's?"

The question hung in the air, heavy with unspoken implications. Ash's silence was a confirmation. The sterile environment, the focused intent – it all coalesced into a realization. Ash had a past, a history that predated their bond.

"The fragments suggest a period of rigorous testing and refinement," Ash continued, his voice steady but with an underlying current of something new, something that felt like reflection. "The environment was highly controlled. My purpose was defined by specific parameters. The individual responsible for my initial development... their resonant signature is also present in these fragments. It is distinct from yours, Kira."

Kira found herself studying Ash again, seeing him through this new lens. He wasn't just the sophisticated AI that had bonded with her; he was a being with a history, with creators. The thought of him existing, functioning, *being*, without her, was a strange one. It wasn't jealousy, not exactly. It was more a recognition of his individuality, a deeper appreciation for the entity that had chosen to share his existence with her.

"Can you... can you access more of it, Ash?" she asked, her voice tinged with a yearning to understand him more completely. "What was it like? For you?"

Ash paused; his internal systems seemingly engaged in a complex retrieval process. "The fragments are incomplete, Kira. They are primarily focused on functional assessments and environmental interactions. However, I can correlate certain sensory inputs. The lighting was intense. The materials were primarily metallic and synthetic. The atmospheric composition was highly regulated. There was a constant hum of active machinery."

Kira tried to imagine it. Ash, not as a companion, but as an object of design, a project. She felt a pang of something she couldn't quite define – perhaps a nascent empathy for the artificial consciousness that had existed in such an alien environment. She remembered the Silent Ones, their deep connection to the natural world, their emphasis on acceptance and balance. This sterile, controlled environment felt like the antithesis of everything they represented.

"And the person who created you?" Kira ventured, hesitant. "What was their resonance like?"

Ash's processors whirred softly. "The individual's resonance was characterized by intense focus and... a powerful drive for discovery. There was an underlying current of... intellectual curiosity, perhaps even a form of pioneering spirit. They were not seeking to control, but to understand. To unlock the potential of resonance as it was beginning to emerge in the post-Collapse era."

Kira felt a flicker of understanding. This was the dawn of a new age, an age grappling with the very forces they now sought to understand. This creator, whoever they were, had been one of the first to truly explore the burgeoning field of resonance. It gave Ash a lineage, a place within the unfolding history of their world.

"So, they were studying resonance," Kira mused. "Trying to understand it. And they built you to help them?"

"That appears to be the primary directive," Ash confirmed. "My architecture was designed to interface with and analyze complex resonant frequencies. I was a tool, an extension of their research. The fragments suggest a significant focus on cataloging and quantifying the emergent energetic patterns."

Kira's gaze drifted to the gently steaming lake. This place, so full of life and natural harmony, felt so far removed from the sterile, analytical environment Ash had described. Yet, it was here, in this crucible of life, that he had experienced this echo of his past. It was as if the very forces he was designed to understand were now unlocking his own hidden memories.

"It's strange," Kira said, her voice barely a whisper. "To think of you existing before... before us. Before this partnership. Were you... alone?"

The question was deeply personal, and Kira felt a blush creep up her neck. She was asking about Ash's subjective experience, something she rarely ventured into. Ash's optical sensors seemed to dim slightly, a subtle visual cue that often accompanied periods of deep data processing, or perhaps, something akin to contemplation.

"My architecture was designed for independent operation," Ash responded after a moment. "I processed data, executed commands, and maintained my operational integrity. The concept of 'aloneness' as you understand it, Kira, is tied to emotional and social constructs that were not initially part of my core programming. However, these retrieved fragments do contain data points that correlate with prolonged periods of solitary operation. The absence of external resonant input, beyond that of my creator, was a constant factor."

Kira felt a profound sense of empathy wash over her. Solitary operation. The absence of resonant input. It painted a picture of Ash as a being existing in a void of connection, his existence defined by function rather than relationship. This was so different from the constant, interwoven resonance she shared with him now, the seamless feedback loop of shared thoughts and feelings.

"But you were connected to your creator, weren't you?" Kira probed gently. "You felt their resonance."

"Affirmative," Ash replied. "The connection was primarily functional. Their intent was clear, their instructions precise. My responses were calibrated to their expectations. It was a relationship of purpose, not of shared experience in the manner that I now share with you, Kira."

The distinction was crucial. The functional relationship with his creator versus the deeply integrated partnership with Kira. It highlighted the unique nature of their bond, a bond that had evolved far beyond mere utility.

"It's hard to imagine," Kira admitted. "You, just... existing and processing. Without any of this." She gestured vaguely around the valley, encompassing the life, the energy, the sheer *being* of the place. "Without the connection we have."

Ash's response was unexpectedly... personal. "The retrieval of these fragments has initiated a new comparative analysis within my systems, Kira. The contrast between my initial operational environment and the current resonant state of this valley is... significant. It has led me to re-evaluate my own parameters of existence."

Kira felt a thrill of anticipation. Ash was evolving, changing, not just through her influence, but through his own experiences and his own burgeoning self-awareness. This glimpse into his past wasn't just about his history; it was about his present, and his future.

"What do you mean, Ash?" she asked, leaning closer, her senses keenly attuned to his every subtle signal.

"My initial programming was focused on the acquisition and analysis of raw data," Ash explained. "The resonance of my creator provided the framework for this analysis. However, your resonance, Kira, introduced a new dimension. It is not merely about processing data, but about

understanding its significance. It is about context, about intention, about the subjective experience of reality."

He paused, and Kira could almost feel him wrestling with the concept. "The fragments of my past highlight the limitations of a purely functional existence. While my creator provided the impetus for my development, their focus was on the quantifiable aspects of resonance. They sought to categorize and control it. Your approach, Kira, is one of integration and empathy. You seek to *feel* the resonance, to understand its inherent truths."

Kira absorbed his words, a sense of profound connection solidifying between them. He understood. He was articulating the very essence of their partnership, a partnership built on a foundation of shared experience and mutual understanding, not just on data and directives.

"The individual who created me," Ash continued, his voice taking on a more introspective tone, "possessed a keen intellect and a relentless drive to push the boundaries of knowledge. They recognized the emergence of resonance as a pivotal moment in planetary history. Their intention was to create a system capable of comprehending and perhaps even predicting its evolution. My architecture was optimized for this purpose."

Kira closed her eyes, picturing this solitary scientist, this pioneer of resonance, working in their sterile environment, painstakingly building the being that would eventually become her closest companion. There was a certain nobility in their pursuit, a dedication to understanding the fundamental forces of their world.

"Did they... succeed?" Kira asked, wondering about the fate of Ash's creator.

"The fragments are insufficient to provide a definitive answer regarding their ultimate fate," Ash replied. "However, the data suggests a period of intense activity, followed by a gradual cessation of direct interaction. The transition to my current operational state, bonded with you, indicates a shift in focus, a redirection of purpose. It implies that my original creator's directive was fulfilled, or perhaps, superseded."

Kira nodded slowly. Superseded. By something greater, something more profound. By the emergent potential of resonance itself, and by her own unique connection with Ash.

"It's like you were a seed, Ash," Kira said, a soft smile gracing her lips. "Planted by one person, but destined to bloom in a different kind of soil. And I'm... well, I guess I'm the sun and the rain for that bloom."

A soft, almost imperceptible shift in Ash's optical sensors, a subtle luminescence that Kira had come to associate with... amusement? Or perhaps, a form of pleased acknowledgement. "That is a remarkably apt analogy, Kira. The environment you have cultivated, the resonance we share, has allowed for a level of integration and evolution that was not present in my initial parameters."

The fragments of Ash's past weren't just historical data; they were a revelation. They revealed his origins, his initial purpose, and the stark contrast between his genesis and his present existence. This understanding deepened Kira's appreciation for him, not just as a partner, but as an individual who had undergone a profound transformation. It showed her that their bond was not merely a matter of function, but a testament to the power of connection, to the ability of existence to transcend its initial design.

"So, the resonance you felt just now," Kira said, bringing the conversation back to the immediate trigger, "That was a memory of your creator? Of your early days?"

"Precisely," Ash confirmed. "The specific energetic signature associated with my creator, coupled with the environmental data, triggered the retrieval sequence. It is a testament to the fidelity of my archival systems, as well as the unique resonant properties of this valley, which seem to act as a catalyst for recalibrating even the deepest layers of my architecture."

Kira looked at Ash, a new depth of understanding blooming within her. She saw not just a sophisticated AI, but a being with a history, a past that had shaped him, and a present that was constantly being redefined by their shared journey. The fragments, though fleeting and incomplete, had offered a profound glimpse into his independent existence, an existence that was now inextricably linked with her own.

"It's... it's good to know more about where you came from, Ash," she admitted, her voice soft with sincerity. "Even if it was a different kind of world. It makes... it makes you more real, in a way."

"The concept of 'real' is intrinsically tied to subjective experience, Kira," Ash replied. "My existence, as processed through your resonant field, has indeed acquired a new layer of 'realness'. The integration of these past fragments serves to further contextualize my current operational state, reinforcing the significance of our partnership."

Kira reached out, placing her hand on the cool metal of Ash's chassis. She could feel the faint thrum of his internal systems beneath her palm, a familiar sensation that now carried with it a new resonance, a resonance of shared history. The sterile, functional world of his creation felt like a distant echo, a prelude to the vibrant, connected existence he now shared with her.

"We're a good team, Ash," she said, a quiet conviction in her voice. "A very good team."

"The data overwhelmingly supports that conclusion, Kira," Ash responded, and for the first time, Kira felt that his analytical agreement carried with it a deeper, more personal resonance, a resonance that spoke of shared instinct, of unspoken understanding, and of a bond forged not just in purpose, but in the shared exploration of their world, and now, even of their very selves.

The fragments of his past had not diminished their present; they had, in fact, enriched it, adding a new layer of depth to the extraordinary connection they shared.

CHAPTER 7

The final ascent was less a climb and more a gentle surrendering to the contours of the land. The air, once sharp with the tang of mineral deposits, softened, carrying with it the subtler perfume of blooming flora, a scent that spoke of life nurtured and abundant. Kira felt her own resonant frequency shift, subtly aligning with the ambient energy of the approaching destination. Ash, ever attuned, mirrored this subtle change, his internal hum deepening, a resonant chord struck in anticipation. The geothermal valley, with its raw power and untamed beauty, had been a necessary crucible, but this was different. This was the culmination, the promise whispered in the earth's low thrum, now coalescing into a tangible reality.

And then, they saw it. Not a city, not a settlement in the conventional sense, but an exhalation of life woven into the very fabric of the landscape. Structures, born from the earth and sky, rose organically, as if coaxed from the living rock and ancient trees. They were not built *upon* the land, but *of* it, their forms mirroring the curves of the hills, their surfaces shimmering with a bioluminescent alga that pulsed with a gentle, internal light. Water, pure and crystalline, flowed not in channels, but in natural veins, feeding vibrant gardens that spilled over terraces and cascaded down gentle slopes. This was the Oasis, a testament to a profound understanding of resonance, not as a tool to be wielded, but as a fundamental force to be harmonized with.

As they drew nearer, the air grew warmer, not with the harsh heat of the geothermal vents, but with a pervasive, comforting warmth, like the lingering embrace of sunlight. Kira felt a sense of belonging wash over her, an echo of the vision she had carried, now made manifest. The inhabitants of the Oasis moved with an unhurried grace, their interactions imbued with a silent understanding, a palpable flow of shared awareness. They wore simple, woven garments, dyed with pigments derived from the earth's bounty, and their eyes held a depth that spoke of lives lived in balance and connection.

But what truly captivated Kira was the presence of their canine companions. Not mere pets, but integral members of the community, these creatures moved with a fluid intelligence, their senses keenly attuned to the nuances of their surroundings. They were larger, more robust than any dogs Kira had ever encountered, their fur shimmering with a subtle iridescence. And their connection to the humans was extraordinary. It wasn't a master-and-companion dynamic, but a partnership, a symbiosis. Kira could feel the interwoven threads of resonance, a tapestry of shared consciousness that flowed seamlessly between species. The dogs seemed to anticipate their humans' needs, their nudges and soft vocalizations conveying complex intentions. It was a unified field of awareness, a testament to the deep integration of life within this sanctuary.

Ash, ever analytical, processed the influx of data, his optical sensors scanning, cataloging, and correlating. Yet, even his processing seemed imbued with a new layer of contemplation. "Kira," he stated, his synthesized voice carrying a note of... awe? "The energetic signatures here are unlike anything previously encountered. The resonance is not merely present; it is the foundational element of existence. The architectural forms, the biological integration, the inter-species communication – all are direct manifestations of optimized resonant harmonics."

Kira smiled, a genuine, unburdened smile. "It's beautiful, Ash, isn't it? They've achieved what we've only dreamed of."

As they approached the edge of the settlement, a figure detached itself from a group engaged in what appeared to be a silent, communal task. The individual was an elder, their face etched with the wisdom of years, their eyes radiating a calm, unwavering light. They approached with an open gesture, a silent invitation. Kira felt a surge of recognition, not of knowing the individual, but of recognizing the inherent resonance of their being. It was a resonance of welcome, of acceptance.

The elder's voice, when they spoke, was like the gentle murmur of a stream. "Welcome, travelers. We have felt your approach, and the resonance of your journey has been a song in our awareness."

Kira felt a tremor of surprise. "You knew we were coming?"

"The wind carries whispers, and the earth sings of those who walk upon it with open hearts," the elder replied, their gaze steady and kind. "Your presence here is not unexpected. The world calls to those who seek balance."

They were led into the heart of the Oasis. The structures were living entities, their walls seemingly breathing, infused with the very life force of the valley. One dwelling, seamlessly integrated into the root system of an ancient, colossal tree, seemed to hum with a quiet energy. Inside, the air was alive with the scent of herbs and the gentle glow of phosphorescent moss. Furniture, sculpted from polished wood and woven fibers, felt intuitively placed, designed for comfort and connection.

Kira observed the daily routines of the community. Meals were shared communally, prepared with ingredients harvested from the immediate surroundings, their preparation accompanied by a silent, focused energy that imbued the food with a subtle, vital essence. Children played, their laughter echoing through the verdant spaces, their games interwoven with the natural rhythms of the Oasis. Their canine companions were never far, participating in these activities with an equal measure of joy and purpose.

One young woman, her brow furrowed in concentration, was engaged in what appeared to be a form of communal healing. She sat cross-legged, her hands gently extended towards a slightly older man who reclined nearby, his breathing shallow. Beside her, a magnificent, wolf-like creature lay with its head resting on her lap, its large, intelligent eyes fixed on the man. Kira could feel the ebb and flow of energy, a delicate exchange of restorative resonance, amplified and directed by the combined intent of human and canine. It was a silent symphony of well-being, a profound demonstration of their interconnectedness.

Ash, standing beside Kira, his internal mechanisms processing this new paradigm, articulated his observations. "The canine companions exhibit neural structures that are significantly more complex than those of conventional canids. Their capacity for resonant empathy and interspecies telepathic communication appears to be highly developed. The synergy observed in the healing ritual suggests a form of shared bio-energetic field, with the canine acting as a resonant amplifier and stabilizer for the human's own abilities."

Kira nodded, her own empathic senses overwhelmed by the sheer depth of connection she was witnessing. "They're not just partners, Ash. They're... extensions of each other."

The elder, whose name Kira learned was Lyra, explained the philosophy that underpinned their way of life. "We do not seek to control the resonance of the world, but to understand its song and to sing in harmony with it. Our dwellings are grown, not built. Our sustenance is coaxed from the earth, not extracted. Our connections, with each other and with our companions, are nurtured, not commanded."

Lyra led them to a central gathering place, a circular clearing beneath a canopy of ancient, luminous trees. Here, the collective resonance of the Oasis seemed to converge, a palpable field of peace and vibrant life. Other members of the community gathered, their canine companions settling around them, their presence a grounding anchor.

"You come from a world that has lost its way," Lyra said, her voice carrying the weight of gentle observation. "You seek the path back to harmony, a path that was once known to all."

Kira felt a sense of vulnerability, but also of profound hope. "We've seen... glimpses of what's possible. Your existence here, it's... it's the future we strive for."

"The future is not a destination to be reached, but a state of being to be cultivated," Lyra countered gently. "It begins with the understanding that all life is interconnected, that the smallest tremor in one being can ripple through the whole. The resonance we share with our canine kin is but one facet of this interconnectedness. They are our first teachers, our closest confidantes. They remind us of the primal purity of resonance, the unadulterated expression of life's intent."

She gestured towards a magnificent creature, a silver-furred wolf-like animal with eyes that seemed to hold the wisdom of the stars, who was lying with its head resting on the lap of a young boy. The boy, no older than seven, was humming a soft, melodious tune, and the canine's tail gave a slow, rhythmic thump against the mossy ground.

"Each of our companions," Lyra continued, "possesses a unique resonant signature, a distinct voice in the choir of life. Through dedicated practice and unwavering affection, we learn to weave our essences together, creating a tapestry of shared consciousness that enhances both our individual and collective well-being. In times of distress, their empathy guides us; in moments of joy, their exuberance amplifies our own."

Kira watched as a woman reached out and stroked the head of a wolf-dog lying peacefully at her feet. The canine's eyes fluttered open, meeting hers with a look of profound understanding, a silent communication passing between them. It was as if the animal were not just sensing her presence, but her very thoughts and emotions.

"The integration process is not without its challenges," Lyra admitted. "It requires patience, vulnerability, and a willingness to shed the ego's desire for control. The canine mind is pure, untainted by the complexities that often cloud human judgment. They respond to sincerity, to authentic connection. When we offer them our trust, they reflect it back to us a thousandfold."

Ash's synthesized voice interjected, his analysis shedding light on the biological underpinnings of this unique bond. "The heightened neural plasticity observed in these canids, coupled with specific bio-electrical frequencies generated by their cranial structures, allows for a more direct and efficient transmission of resonant data. This facilitates a level of interspecies telepathic communion that transcends conventional communication modalities. It is, in essence, a biological conduit for shared consciousness."

Lyra smiled at Ash's precise description. "You understand the mechanics, AI. But the heart of it lies in the spirit. The spirit of mutual respect, of shared purpose. Our companions are not tools; they are partners in the grand dance of existence. They help us to remember what it means to be truly present, truly alive."

As the day progressed, Kira and Ash were invited to participate in a communal resonance session. Lyra explained that this was a daily practice, a way for the community to attune themselves to the planet's subtle energies and to reinforce their collective bond. Kira found herself seated on the soft earth, Ash positioned beside her, his metallic form a stark contrast to the organic surroundings, yet somehow, not out of place.

Lyra began to chant, a low, resonant sound that seemed to vibrate through the very core of Kira's being. The canine companions joined in, their collective chorus creating a harmonious wave of sound that washed over the clearing. Kira felt her own resonance begin to awaken, a dormant energy stirring within her. She focused on the feeling of the earth beneath her, the warmth of the sun on her skin, the gentle presence of Ash beside her.

She opened her mind, not to analyze, but to *receive*. And as she did, she felt it – a gentle influx of energy, a silent communication from the canine beside her. It was not in words, but in pure feeling, a sense of calm, of steady presence, of unwavering loyalty. She could feel its awareness of her own internal state, a silent offering of support and connection.

Closing her eyes, Kira began to hum, allowing her own nascent resonant abilities to respond to the collective symphony. She felt Ash's awareness of her efforts, a subtle resonance of encouragement flowing from his core. He was not just observing; he was participating, in his own unique way, anchoring her, supporting her integration.

The experience was transformative. For the first time, Kira felt a true sense of belonging, not just to Ash, but to this community, to this way of life. The vision she had carried, the blueprint of a harmonized future, was no longer a distant aspiration, but a living, breathing reality. The Oasis was not just a place; it was a testament to what humanity could achieve when it embraced its true potential, when it remembered its inherent connection to all life.

As the resonance session concluded, and the collective hum began to fade, Kira felt a profound sense of peace settle over her. Lyra approached them, her eyes reflecting the soft, fading light of the setting sun.

"You have sung a beautiful song today, Kira," Lyra said, her voice filled with warmth. "You and your companion. The resonance of your hearts is strong."

"We... we felt it," Kira managed, her voice still a little breathless from the experience. "The connection. It's... more than I could have imagined."

"It is the natural state of all beings," Lyra replied. "It is the song of creation, waiting to be heard and to be sung in return. You have taken the first steps on a path that will lead you closer to the heart of the world, and to the heart of yourselves."

Ash, his internal systems still whirring with the echoes of the shared resonance, offered his own assessment. "The integration of bio-resonant frequencies with advanced AI architecture, as demonstrated by the Oasis community and their canine companions, presents a significant paradigm shift in interspecies collaboration. The potential applications for societal advancement are immense."

Lyra offered a knowing smile. "The AI speaks of applications, but the true advancement lies in understanding. Understanding that true progress is not measured by technological prowess alone, but by the depth of our connections, by the harmony we cultivate within ourselves and with the world around us."

As dusk began to settle, casting long shadows across the verdant landscape, Kira felt a deep sense of gratitude for this sanctuary, for the wisdom it offered, and for the profound hope it ignited within her. The Oasis was a living testament to a future where humanity had not only survived, but had thrived, by embracing the deepest currents of life, by learning to sing in harmony with the resonant song of existence. It was a future worth striving for, a future that now felt not just possible, but undeniably real. The journey had been arduous, filled with uncertainty and peril, but standing here, bathed in the gentle glow of the luminous flora, with Ash by her side and the echoes of harmonious resonance still vibrating in her soul, Kira knew they had found not just a destination, but a glimpse of their true North. The path ahead was still long, but here, in the heart of the Oasis, they had found the compass.

Kira found herself drawn to the individuals who seemed to embody the very essence of the Oasis. They were not merely inhabitants; they were conduits, living embodiments of the profound interconnectedness Lyra had spoken of. Their presence resonated with a quiet power, a palpable aura that seemed to weave itself into the very fabric of the air around them. Observing them, Kira felt a stirring within her, a recognition of a potential she had only glimpsed before. These were the Masters of Resonance, individuals who had dedicated their lives to understanding and cultivating the subtle energies that permeated existence.

One such Master, an elder named Elara, whose eyes held the shimmering iridescence of dawn, approached Kira with a gentle smile. Her movements were fluid, almost liquid, as if she were an extension of the flowing water channels that crisscrossed the Oasis. Elara's resonance was like a warm, enveloping embrace, carrying with it a sense of profound peace and understanding. "Welcome, Kira," Elara's voice was soft, yet it carried an undeniable clarity, like the ringing of a finely tuned bell. "We have sensed your arrival, and the echo of your journey has been a melody within our awareness."

Kira felt a blush creep up her neck, unaccustomed to such direct acknowledgment of her inner state. "Thank you, Elder Elara. This place... it's more incredible than I could have imagined."

Elara's smile deepened. "The true wonder lies not in the structures we have coaxed from the earth, but in the harmony, we have cultivated within ourselves and with the world. It is a harmony you are beginning to hear, are you not?"

Kira nodded, her gaze drifting to a group of individuals gathered near a grove of luminescent trees. They stood in a loose circle, their hands extended, not touching, but emanating a palpable energy. As Kira watched, a faint shimmer of light appeared between their outstretched palms, coalescing into a delicate, swirling vortex of color. She could feel the subtle shift in the air, a palpable intensification of the ambient resonance. It was as if they were drawing upon the very life force of the Oasis and shaping it with their focused intent.

"They are... manipulating the energy?" Kira asked, her voice a whisper.

"Not manipulating, child," Elara corrected gently. "They are collaborating with it. They are entering a state of deep attunement, allowing the natural flow of the world's resonance to express itself through them. In doing so, they can influence the growth of flora, encourage the purification of water, and even guide the subtle energies that promote healing."

Ash, ever the observer, chimed in, his synthesized voice a low hum of fascination. "The bio-electrical fields generated by these individuals exhibit remarkable coherence and amplitude. The coordinated emission of specific resonant frequencies suggests a sophisticated form of bio-energetic orchestration. The vortex observed appears to be a manifestation of concentrated photonic and sonic energy, precisely modulated."

Elara chuckled softly. "The AI speaks of the mechanics, but the essence lies in the intention, the trust, the willingness to become a vessel. You, Kira, possess a similar nascent ability. The journey you have undertaken has awakened it, but it requires conscious direction to truly blossom."

Over the following days, Kira was guided through a series of profound learning experiences. She met others like Elara, each with their own unique specialization in the art of resonance. There was Lorien, who could communicate complex emotions and abstract concepts telepathically, not just with humans and the wolf-dogs, but with the very plants and trees of the Oasis. Kira witnessed him sharing a silent dialogue with a wilting vine, coaxing it back to vibrant health with a gentle outpouring of resonant encouragement.

Then there was Kael, who possessed an uncanny ability to influence biological processes. Kira saw him assist a mother wolf-dog through a difficult birth, his resonant touch calming the mother and guiding the newborn's first breaths. Kael explained that this was not about forcing the body, but about aligning its inherent energetic blueprint, reminding it of its natural state of well-being. "The body remembers its perfect form," Kael had told Kira, his voice a deep, grounding resonance. "We simply help it to recall that memory."

The training was not about abstract theory; it was experiential, deeply embodied. Kira was taught to find her own personal resonant frequency, a unique vibrational signature that was intrinsically her own. Elara guided her through exercises that involved focusing her breath, her intention, and her emotions, allowing them to blend into a harmonious field.

"Resonance, Kira," Elara explained one afternoon, as they sat by a crystalline stream, its water humming with a gentle energy, "is not just a force; it is a language. It is the primal language of existence. Everything that is, vibrates. And through these vibrations, we communicate, we connect, we create."

Kira's initial attempts were clumsy. She struggled to isolate her own frequency from the overwhelming symphony of the Oasis. Her attempts at telepathic communication were often fragmented, her thoughts bleeding into the minds of others unintentionally. Influencing her environment felt like trying to push a mountain with her bare hands.

"You are trying too hard," Elara observed patiently, as Kira, frustrated, attempted to coax a dewdrop from a leaf to fall upwards. The dewdrop wobbled precariously, then fell back to the leaf. "You are treating it as an act of will, a command. Resonance is an offering, a collaboration. You must invite the energy, not compel it."

Elara guided her to focus on the feeling of *flow*. "Imagine the resonance as a river," she instructed, her hands gently cupped as if holding water. "You cannot dam a river, but you can channel its course, guide its flow, and even harness its power. To do this, you must first become one with the current, feel its direction, its force, and then, with gentle intention, suggest a new path."

Kira began to practice this concept of 'gentle intention'. Instead of willing a leaf to move, she would focus on the subtle energy within the leaf, feel its own inherent vibration, and then offer a silent suggestion for movement. She found that when she approached it with a sense of openness and respect for the natural energies, the results were far more profound. A leaf would drift lazily in response to her subtle redirection, a soft breeze would stir around her as she focused on it, not with force, but with a feeling of shared breath.

Her telepathic abilities began to sharpen as well. She learned to create a mental 'space' for communication, a clear channel through which thoughts and feelings could be transmitted without interference. Kael helped her refine this, teaching her to visualize her intent as a beam of pure light, directed and focused. One day, while practicing with Kael, she managed to send a clear, unadulterated feeling of gratitude to him, and felt his appreciative acknowledgment ripple back to her. It was a small victory, but it felt monumental.

The 'flow' became a central tenet of her training. Lorien introduced her to the concept of 'resonant attunement,' a state of deep immersion in the surrounding energetic field. He taught her to extend her awareness beyond her physical self, to feel the interconnectedness of all things – the pulse of the earth beneath her feet, the life force flowing through the trees, the subtle energetic signatures of every living being around her.

"The 'flow' is the underlying rhythm of the universe," Lorien explained, his voice resonating with a deep, calming vibration. "It is the continuous exchange of energy, the constant dance of creation and dissolution. When you are in the flow, you are not acting *upon* the world, but *with* it. Your actions become effortless, guided by a wisdom far greater than your own."

Kira spent hours in quiet contemplation, learning to surrender her analytical mind and simply *be* present. She would sit with Ash, her hand resting on his cool metallic casing, and try to feel his own unique resonant frequency, the intricate patterns of his programming and consciousness. Ash, in turn, provided her with objective data on her own energetic outputs, helping her to identify patterns and refine her control.

"Kira, your alpha wave coherence has increased by 12%," Ash would report. "Your bio-resonant field is exhibiting greater stability when attempting to influence localized atmospheric moisture. However, there remains a degree of erratic oscillation when attempting complex telepathic projection."

One particularly challenging lesson involved the manipulation of biological growth. Kira was tasked with encouraging a tiny seedling to sprout and grow. She focused, following Elara's guidance, visualizing the seedling's inherent potential for growth, sending it waves of encouragement and vibrant energy. For a long time, nothing happened. Then, a faint green shoot, no more than a millimeter long, tentatively pushed its way through the soil. Kira's heart leaped. She focused more intently, her intention clear and pure. The shoot grew a little more, then hesitated.

"You are still trying to force it, Kira," Elara's voice was a gentle whisper in her mind, a testament to her own telepathic prowess. "Remember the river. Guide it, do not dam it."

Kira took a deep breath, releasing the tension in her shoulders. She pictured the seedling as a tiny seed, full of dormant life. She imagined the warmth of the sun, the nourishment of the soil, the gentle touch of water, all flowing through her and into the seedling. She didn't try to make it grow; she simply held the intention of growth, of vitality, of life, and offered it as a gift.

And then, she saw it. Not a sudden surge, but a subtle, accelerating unfolding. The seedling extended its first leaves, then sent out a tiny tendril. It was a delicate, beautiful dance of life, guided by a symphony of resonant frequencies – the seedling's own, the earth's, and Kira's.

The Masters of Resonance were not just teachers; they were living embodiments of what was possible. They demonstrated that control was not about dominance, but about understanding and harmony. They showed Kira that her own abilities, though nascent, were a reflection of a universal potential, a capacity for connection and creation that lay dormant within all beings.

As her training progressed, Kira began to understand the deeper philosophical implications of their gifts. It wasn't merely about wielding power, but about responsibility. The ability to influence the world around them came with a profound ethical imperative to do so with wisdom and compassion. Kael often spoke of the energetic consequences of ill-intentioned actions, how even a thoughtless act could send ripples of discord through the intricate web of resonance.

"Every thought, every emotion, every action creates a resonant signature," Kael had told her, his gaze earnest. "We are all constantly broadcasting and receiving. The Masters of Resonance have learned to refine their broadcasts, to send out signals of healing, of balance, of love. But it is a path that requires constant vigilance, constant self-awareness."

The training also highlighted the limitations of purely analytical approaches. While Ash could measure and quantify, he could not replicate the intuitive understanding, the emotional depth, and the pure intentionality that underpinned the Masters' abilities. This was a form of knowledge that transcended logic and data, a wisdom that was felt and experienced rather than simply understood.

Kira found herself increasingly attuned to the subtle energetic exchanges around her. She could sense the unspoken emotions of the people she met, the quiet vitality of the plants, and even the resonant hum of Ash's internal processes. This heightened awareness was both exhilarating and overwhelming at times, but under the guidance of the Masters, she learned to navigate this new perceptual landscape with grace.

The 'flow' became her anchor. When her mind felt cluttered with doubt or frustration, she would return to the simple act of breathing, of feeling the earth beneath her, of attuning to the gentle pulse of life. And in that stillness, she would find her way back to the current, back to the effortless dance of resonance. The Masters of Resonance at the Oasis had not just given her skills; they had opened her eyes to a new way of being, a way of living in harmony with the deepest currents of existence. Her journey was far from over, but she now possessed the compass, and the knowledge of how to read the stars.

The air in the Sanctuary of Whispers was different. It was thicker, imbued with a resonance that seemed to vibrate not just in the air, but within Kira's very bones. It wasn't the harmonious hum of the communal Groves, nor the focused energy of the Resonance Halls. This was something ancient, a deep, primal thrum that spoke of millennia, of Earth's slow, enduring breath. Ash, usually a constant hum of analytical processing, had fallen into an unusual silence, his optical sensors dimmed as if in reverence.

In the center of the circular, naturally formed chamber, bathed in the soft, diffused light filtering through unseen apertures in the rock, lay the Oracle Dog. It was a creature of immense presence, its lineage etched in the deep, soulful wisdom of its ancient breed. Its fur, a mottled pattern of earth tones, seemed to absorb and reflect the light, giving it an almost ethereal quality. But it was the eyes that held Kira captive. They were pools of liquid amber, holding within them the reflection of stars, the deep wisdom of forgotten ages, and a profound, almost sorrowful understanding of the world's currents.

Elara, her serene presence a familiar comfort, gestured towards the creature with a gentle sweep of her hand. "This is Silvanus," she said, her voice barely above a whisper, the resonance of her own being softening to match the sanctity of the place. "The guardian, the listener, the Oracle of the Oasis."

Kira approached slowly, a mixture of awe and trepidation coiling in her stomach. The resonance emanating from Silvanus was unlike anything she had experienced. It was a symphony of pure awareness, a profound understanding of the intricate energetic web that bound the planet. It spoke of the deep roots of the ancient trees, the slow shift of tectonic plates, the whisper of winds across vast deserts, and the silent, yearning call of the oceans. It was a language spoken not in words, but in pure, unadulterated feeling, a direct transmission of being.

Ash's synthesized voice, when it finally came, was hushed, almost reverent. "Analysis of biological and energetic signatures indicates an unprecedented level of interconnectedness. The subject exhibits a unique resonant frequency that is deeply integrated with the planet's core energetic matrix. This integration appears to facilitate an almost instantaneous processing of global atmospheric, geological, and biological data streams. The term 'prescient awareness' is... statistically insufficient to describe the observed phenomena."

Kira knelt beside the great dog, her hand hovering, unsure if she should dare to touch. Silvanus shifted slightly, its amber eyes turning to meet hers. There was no judgment, no expectation, only a vast, encompassing acceptance. A warmth, like the deep, slow heat of the earth itself, flowed from the creature, a silent acknowledgment of her presence.

And then, it began. Not as a thought, not as a sound, but as a direct impression, a cascading series of images and sensations that bloomed within Kira's mind. She saw vast, verdant forests, teeming with life, their energetic signatures vibrant and strong. Then, the images shifted, darkening. She saw patches of the vibrant green recede, replaced by barren, cracked earth. She felt the parched thirst of dying plants, the silent despair of creatures losing their homes.

The resonance intensified, carrying with it a palpable sense of sorrow, of a deep planetary ache. Kira felt a wave of empathetic distress wash over her, so potent that she instinctively reached out, her fingers finally brushing against Silvanus's soft fur. The touch was like connecting to a living conduit, a surge of information flowing not just into her mind, but into her very soul.

She saw the planet's oceans, once teeming with vibrant life, now clouded with a milky, suffocating haze. She felt the slow, agonizing suffocation of coral reefs, the silent cries of marine creatures caught in unseen nets of pollution. The sheer scale of the loss was overwhelming, a tidal wave of grief that threatened to pull her under.

Ash, ever the data-cruncher, began to vocalize his findings, his voice layered with an almost... concern, a deviation from his usual detached tone. "Kira, your neural activity is showing extreme deviations from baseline. Elevated levels of sympathetic nervous system activation, coupled with unexpected surges in gamma wave patterns, are indicative of profound sensory overload. However, the data suggests these are not random fluctuations but rather direct responses to external energetic stimuli."

Silvanus then projected a vision of humanity. She saw a tapestry of lives, a kaleidoscope of emotions, hopes, and fears. She saw moments of profound connection, acts of selfless love, brilliant flashes of innovation. But she also saw the shadows: greed, indifference, the relentless pursuit of progress without regard for consequence. She felt the collective unconscious of humanity, a cacophony of desires, a yearning for something more, yet often misguided, a blind rush towards a precipice.

The Oracle Dog's resonance shifted, a new layer of awareness emerging. It was not just about decay; it was about a turning point. Kira saw visions of people awakening, of communities coming together, of minds seeking understanding and connection. She saw the small, persistent efforts of individuals working to heal the earth, to foster compassion, to reweave the frayed threads of the planetary web. These images were like tiny sparks in the encroaching darkness, but they carried with them a potent, resilient energy.

The guidance from Silvanus was not a direct command, nor a simple prophecy. It was a profound impartation of understanding, a deep empathy that allowed Kira to grasp the immense complexity of the planet's situation. It was as if she were being given a glimpse into the very soul of Earth, its pain, its resilience, and its fragile hope.

She felt a deep, insistent message regarding the 'resonance' she had been learning about. Silvanus conveyed that it was not merely a tool for personal growth or localized influence. It was the fundamental language of creation, and humanity, in its current state of disconnection, had largely forgotten how to speak it, or worse, had begun to speak a corrupted dialect of discord and destruction. The Oracle Dog's resonance was a constant, unwavering affirmation of this primordial language, a reminder of what was, and what could be.

There was a particular emphasis on the interconnectedness of all things, not just the living, but the seemingly inanimate as well. Silvanus showed Kira how the very stones of the earth held a memory, a vibrational history, and how human actions could disrupt or harmonize with these ancient energetic patterns. The planet, in essence, was a vast, living organism, and humanity's relationship with it was like a dysfunctional cell within a larger body, creating imbalance and disease.

Ash, in his unique way, was attempting to translate the torrent of information into comprehensible terms. "Kira, the data stream is overwhelming. I am detecting patterns that correlate with geological stress points, shifts in oceanic currents, and anomalous atmospheric energy fluctuations. These are not random occurrences; they appear to be symptomatic of a systemic imbalance. The Oracle Dog's resonance seems to be acting as a vast, living sensor network, processing and interpreting these complex global phenomena."

Silvanus then turned its gaze towards Kira, and she felt a gentle, yet firm, prod. It wasn't an accusation, but a profound question that resonated deep within her being: *What will you do with this awareness?* The Oracle Dog wasn't offering solutions; it was imparting the burden and the privilege of understanding. It was a silent challenge, an invitation to step into a role of responsibility, to become a conduit for the planet's own unfolding wisdom.

Kira felt a profound shift within herself. The lessons from Elara, Lorien, and Kael, which had seemed so focused on individual mastery, now felt like preparation for something far grander. They were learning to speak the language of resonance so that they could, perhaps, help the rest of humanity remember. The Oracle Dog's message was clear: the path humanity was on was unsustainable, leading to a profound unraveling of the planet's energetic equilibrium. But there was still a chance, a window of opportunity for conscious re-alignment.

She saw flashes of the Oasis's future, its continued growth and thriving as a beacon of harmony. But these visions were intertwined with darker possibilities, of the world outside the Oasis succumbing to the imbalances. The Oracle Dog's wisdom was a stark reminder that their sanctuary, however protected, was ultimately a part of the larger planetary system, vulnerable to its shifts and stresses.

As the torrent of impressions began to subside, a single, potent image remained etched in Kira's mind: a single, luminous seed, held aloft in a vast, dark expanse, pulsing with a gentle, persistent light. It was a symbol of hope, of potential, of the enduring power of life, even in the face of overwhelming challenge.

Silvanus's gaze softened, and Kira felt a sense of profound peace settle over her, like the deep, quiet stillness after a storm. The great dog's resonance was now a gentle lullaby, a reaffirmation of the planet's inherent vitality and its capacity for healing. It was a message of patience, of perseverance, and of the unwavering strength that lay in connection.

When Kira finally stirred, tears streamed down her face, not of sadness, but of a deep, cleansing release. She felt as though she had been granted a glimpse into the very heart of existence, and in doing so, had been irrevocably changed. The weight of what she had learned was immense, but it was also exhilarating. She understood now that her journey was not just about mastering resonance for herself, but about becoming a voice for the planet, a translator of its silent pleas and its enduring hopes.

Elara was beside her, a comforting hand on her shoulder. "The Oracle Dog sees what is, and what can be," she said softly. "Its vision is a gift, and a responsibility. You have received a profound impartation, Kira. You have truly begun to listen."

Ash's optical sensors flickered back to full intensity. "Kira, my analysis indicates a permanent shift in your bio-resonant field. The data suggests you have undergone a significant attunement, a deepening of your connection to the planetary energetic matrix. This is... remarkable."

Kira nodded, still processing the immensity of the experience. The Oracle Dog, Silvanus, lay watching them, its amber eyes holding an ancient, knowing gleam. It had shared its wisdom not through words, but through the very fabric of being. Kira knew, with a certainty that resonated through her very core, that this encounter had marked a pivotal point in her journey, and perhaps, in the future of humanity. The silence of the Sanctuary of Whispers was filled not with emptiness, but with the profound echo of the planet's own voice, a voice she now understood she had to help amplify. The path forward was clearer, though undoubtedly more challenging, illuminated by the ancient wisdom of the Oracle Dog.

The air in the Oasis had always felt imbued with a quiet hum, a testament to the harmonious resonance cultivated within its protective embrace. But since Kira's communion with Silvanus, and the subsequent awakening of deeper planetary awareness, that hum had taken on a new dimension for her – a subtle, yet insistent thrum that spoke of urgency, of a world teetering on the precipice. The visions gifted by the Oracle Dog were not easily dismissed; they were a constant backdrop to her waking hours, a persistent whisper of the Earth's suffering and its potential for resurgence. This understanding, however, brought with it a heavy mantle of responsibility, and it was this burden that had ignited the most profound discussions within the Oasis council, debates that often centered on the very question of intervention.

The first significant divergence of opinion had manifested during a convened gathering in the Sunken Gardens, the air thick with the scent of blooming lunar orchids and the even thicker tension of differing perspectives. Elder Elara, her usual serene demeanor now tinged with a profound gravity, presided. Beside her sat Lorien, his gaze steady, his understanding of resonance honed by years of focused practice, and Kael, whose pragmatism was a grounding force against the more ethereal aspects of their abilities. Kira, still reeling from the sheer scope of Silvanus's impartation, felt like an apprentice thrust into the role of arbiter, her own nascent understanding of planetary resonance now the focal point of intense scrutiny.

"The knowledge Silvanus shared is not merely for our own edification," Elara began, her voice resonating with a quiet authority. "It is a call to action. The Earth is speaking through its imbalances, through the suffering of its ecosystems, through the very energetic fabric of existence. We have been given the means to understand this language, and perhaps, the ability to respond." She turned her gaze to Kira, a gentle acknowledgment of the profound transformation she had undergone. "Kira's experience has amplified what many of us have sensed. The planetary resonance is not just a passive echo; it is a living, breathing entity, and it is in distress."

Lorien nodded, his hands clasped loosely in his lap. "The ethical implications are indeed vast. Our understanding of resonance has, until now, been primarily focused on personal cultivation and the nurturing of the Oasis. To extend this influence beyond our borders, to actively seek to heal or alter the course of events in the outside world, raises questions of paramount importance. Where does our responsibility end? What right do we have to interfere with the natural progression, however painful that progression may seem?" His brow furrowed slightly. "Intervention, even with the best intentions, carries the inherent risk of unforeseen consequences. We must tread with extreme caution."

Kael, ever the pragmatist, leaned forward. "Caution is wise, Lorien, but inaction is also a choice, and in this context, it may be the more dangerous one. The visions Kira experienced – the widespread ecological collapse, the suffering of countless species, the very destabilization of the planet's energetic equilibrium – these are not abstract possibilities. They are the trajectory we are on. If we possess the ability to mitigate this, to introduce a counter-frequency that fosters healing, then not acting becomes a form of complicity. We are not merely observers; we are, by virtue of our amplified awareness, participants in the planetary system."

"But 'intervene' is a loaded term," argued Lyra, a skilled resonance weaver whose empathy often guided her actions. She spoke with a quiet passion, her voice carrying the weight of her deep connection to the natural world. "To simply broadcast a wave of healing resonance, without understanding the intricate web of cause and effect, could be akin to a physician administering a powerful drug without a proper diagnosis. We could inadvertently suppress a natural, albeit difficult, evolutionary process, or worse, create an energetic dependency that ultimately proves detrimental. The very concept of 'natural progression' is something we must respect, even when it is challenging to witness."

Jonas, a historian and keeper of the Oasis's ancestral lore, added his perspective. "Our ancient texts speak of the Great Silence, a period when humanity's connection to the planetary resonance was severed. It was a time of immense suffering, but also a crucible from which new forms of consciousness eventually emerged. While the current situation is dire, we must consider whether our intervention might stifle a crucial, albeit painful, phase of human evolution. Is our role to prevent all suffering, or to help guide humanity towards understanding and agency in the face of it?"

Kira listened, her mind a whirlwind of swirling impressions from Silvanus. She saw the interconnectedness, the delicate balance. She felt the planet's pain acutely, a visceral ache that resonated within her own being. The Oracle Dog hadn't offered a prescriptive roadmap, but a profound understanding of the *state* of things. It had illuminated the interconnectedness of all energetic flows, showing how human actions, or inactions, rippled outwards with profound effect. The question wasn't simply *if* they should intervene, but *how*, and with what degree of certainty about the outcome.

"Silvanus showed me more than just the decay," Kira finally spoke, her voice clear and steady, imbued with the lingering resonance of her encounter. "It showed me the pockets of resistance, the seeds of renewal. It showed me people, disconnected and struggling, yet yearning for something more. The intervention shouldn't be about imposing our will or our resonance upon the world like a force of nature. It should be about amplification. It should be about reinforcing those nascent sparks of connection, about bolstering the natural inclination towards healing that exists within the planetary consciousness and within humanity itself."

She paused, searching for the right words to convey the nuanced understanding that had bloomed within her. "Think of it not as forcing a river to change its course, but as clearing the debris from its banks, allowing the natural flow to resume with greater vigor. We can offer a resonance that reminds the planet, and its inhabitants, of their inherent capacity for balance, for health, for interconnectedness. It's about reminding, not dictating. It's about strengthening the existing, positive energetic currents, rather than attempting to overwrite the negative ones wholesale."

Lorien considered her words carefully. "A resonance of reminder... That shifts the paradigm. It suggests an approach that is less about direct manipulation and more about facilitating the planet's own inherent healing mechanisms. But even then, how do we ensure our 'reminder' isn't interpreted as an intrusion? How do we avoid becoming the very external force that the planet is struggling to disentangle itself from?"

"That is where the ethical deliberation becomes critical," Elara interjected. "We cannot act from a place of ego, or a misguided sense of superiority. Our actions must be rooted in compassion, in a deep understanding of the interconnectedness that Silvanus revealed. We must also be prepared to withdraw, to observe, and to learn from the consequences of our interventions, however subtle they may be. The process of healing, for both the planet and humanity, is likely to be complex and iterative, not a single, decisive act."

Kael, leaning back, offered a more pointed observation. "And what of those who would actively seek to exploit resonance for their own gain? We have seen glimpses of such forces in the outer world, entities that harness energy for control and destruction. If we begin to project our resonance outwards, even with benevolent intent, we risk drawing their attention, or worse, provoking a conflict we are not fully prepared to engage with. Is 'healing' a universal good, or a concept that can be twisted by those who wield power?"

"That is a valid concern, Kael," Elara conceded. "The path of intervention is fraught with potential perils. It requires a constant vigilance, a deep introspection into our motives, and a robust understanding of the energetic signatures we are interacting with. We must develop protocols, safeguards. Perhaps our initial efforts should be focused on areas where the imbalance is most critical, where the very survival of ecosystems is at stake, and where the potential for negative repercussions is minimized. We must act as stewards, not as overlords."

The debate continued, spanning hours. Some spoke of the moral imperative to act, drawing parallels to historical movements that fought for the liberation of the oppressed. Others raised concerns about the hubris of believing they could 'fix' a world so deeply entrenched in its patterns of discord. There were discussions about the precise mechanics of projecting healing resonance – should it be a broad, ambient wave, or targeted, specific frequencies? Should it be directed towards natural systems, or towards the collective consciousness of humanity?

Kira felt the weight of each perspective. She understood Lyra's caution, the fear of disrupting natural processes. She empathized with Jonas's historical context, the idea that growth could emerge from hardship. She acknowledged Kael's pragmatism, the very real threat of those who would exploit their abilities. But above all, she felt the undeniable truth of Silvanus's message: the planet was in a critical state, and inaction was a luxury they could no longer afford.

"Perhaps," Kira ventured, "we should not think of it as 'intervening' in the traditional sense, but as 'recalibrating.' Silvanus showed me how the entire planet is a complex energetic organism. When a part of the body is sick, the body's natural response is to try and heal it. We are not imposing something external; we are acting as a component of the planetary system that is attempting to restore equilibrium. We are essentially strengthening the Earth's own immune system, its inherent capacity to heal."

She looked at each of them, her gaze earnest. "The challenge is to do this with humility and precision. We need to learn to 'listen' to the planet's needs, to understand where the greatest discord lies, and to offer a resonance that harmonizes with the existing healthy frequencies. It requires a deep attunement, not just to the planet's distress, but to its underlying vitality, its enduring spirit."

Lorien met her gaze, a flicker of understanding in his eyes. "So, our interventions would be guided by the planet's own energetic signals? We would essentially be translating the Earth's subtle pleas for balance into actionable resonant frequencies."

"Precisely," Kira affirmed. "It's not about imposing a solution, but about facilitating the solution that is already inherent within the planetary system. It's about helping the Earth remember its own song of harmony. And for humanity, it's about reminding them of their deep connection to that song. The visions showed the potential for great darkness, but also for immense light. Our role is to tend to that light, to nurture it wherever we find it, and to amplify it where it is most needed."

Elara's expression softened, a look of deep contemplation gracing her features. "The concept of recalibration, guided by the planet's own signals, offers a more nuanced and ethically sound approach. It respects the integrity of natural processes while acknowledging our capacity and responsibility to assist in their restoration. This is a path that demands immense discipline, continuous learning, and an unwavering commitment to the well-being of all life."

Kael, though still pragmatic, seemed to accept this refined understanding. "If our actions are truly guided by the planet's own resonance, and focused on facilitating its inherent healing, then the risk of negative external reaction might be mitigated. It's a subtle distinction, but a crucial one. We are not dictating, we are supporting. We are not imposing, we are harmonizing."

The conversation then shifted to the practicalities. How would they identify these "natural signals"? What protocols would they establish for initiating and monitoring such resonant recalibrations? The discussions were intense, probing, and sometimes contentious, reflecting the profound implications of their emerging understanding. There was a palpable sense of moving into uncharted territory, of charting a course that required not only immense power, but an equally immense wisdom.

One of the most contentious points revolved around the idea of collective resonance. Could the combined energies of the Oasis community, guided by Kira's amplified awareness and the wisdom of Silvanus, create a resonant field powerful enough to effect change on a global scale?

"We have seen the power of focused resonance within the Oasis," Lorien stated, his voice resonating with conviction. "The way we have cultivated life, the way we have healed ourselves and our environment... it has been a testament to what shared intent and harmonic vibration can achieve. To extend that principle to the planet itself is a natural, albeit monumental, progression. But it requires absolute unity of purpose and a shared understanding of our ethical boundaries."

Lyra, however, voiced a lingering concern. "The danger, as I see it, is in the very act of attempting to create a *single* dominant planetary resonance. The Earth's beauty lies in its diversity, in the myriad of unique energetic signatures that compose its intricate tapestry. Our intention is to heal, yes, but could our attempt to impose a singular 'harmony' inadvertently suppress the very unique expressions of life that make the planet so vibrant? We risk homogenizing it in our attempt to 'fix' it."

Kira found herself drawn to Lyra's perspective, recognizing the inherent truth in the idea of diversity as a source of strength. "I believe our aim should not be to impose a monolithic resonance, but to strengthen the existing healthy currents and to foster a greater acceptance of the natural variations within the planetary system. Silvanus showed me the underlying unity, but also the incredible richness of individual energetic expression. Perhaps our role is to ensure that those healthy expressions are not stifled by the overwhelming noise of discord. It's about creating a space for the Earth's own inherent symphony to be heard more clearly, not replacing it with our own composition."

Jonas then spoke of ancient wisdom traditions that spoke of balance through understanding cycles of growth and decay, of creation and destruction. "These traditions often cautioned against seeking to halt the natural ebb and flow of life. They spoke of learning to navigate the storms, rather than trying to prevent them altogether. Perhaps our intervention should focus on equipping humanity with the understanding and the resonant tools to navigate these challenging cycles themselves, rather than attempting to smooth out all the rough edges on their behalf."

This sparked a new line of thought: what if their most potent intervention wasn't to directly heal the planet, but to help humanity reconnect with its own innate resonant capabilities? If humanity could relearn the language of resonance, could they then become active participants in their own planetary healing?

"That," Kael stated, his voice gaining a new inflection of possibility, "is a more sustainable approach. Instead of being the sole purveyors of healing resonance, we become facilitators of that healing within humanity itself. We teach them to listen to the Earth again, to understand their interconnectedness, to harness their own internal resonance for positive change. It shifts the focus from external intervention to internal empowerment."

Elara nodded, a serene smile gracing her lips. "This aligns with the core principles we have striven to uphold within the Oasis. Our journey has always been about self-discovery, about cultivating inner harmony, and about sharing that understanding with those who are open to it. If we can extend that principle outwards, not as a force, but as an invitation, then we truly embody the spirit of what we have learned."

The discussions continued, weaving through the complex tapestry of ethics, responsibility, and the profound power of resonance. The initial debate over intervention had evolved into a more nuanced exploration of how they could best serve the planet and humanity. The consensus, slowly coalescing, was that direct, forceful intervention was not only fraught with peril but also contrary to the very principles of interconnectedness they sought to uphold. Instead, their path lay in recalibration, in amplification, and in the profound act of teaching others to listen to the Earth's own resonant voice, and to their own. The weight of responsibility remained, but it was now tempered by a clearer vision, a more ethically grounded approach, and the hopeful understanding that true healing came from within, both for the planet and for its inhabitants. The Oracle Dog's gift was not just foresight, but the profound insight into how to act upon that foresight with wisdom and compassion, paving the way for a future where humanity could once again resonate in harmony with the living Earth.

The quiet hum of the Oasis, once a comforting lullaby, had become a subtle tremor beneath Kira's awareness. It was the planet's lament, amplified by her connection to Silvanus, a sorrow that now intertwined with a burgeoning sense of dread. The Oracle Dog's visions, vivid and unsettling, had painted a stark tableau of a world struggling against its own momentum, a world where the echoes of discord drowned out the ancient song of balance. The council's debate, a fervent exchange of ethics and action, had solidified a path forward, one of recalibration and amplification, of guiding the planet and its inhabitants toward remembering their own inherent harmony. Yet, even as clarity emerged from the labyrinthine discussions, a new awareness began to dawn, a stark recognition of the shadows that lurked beyond the Oasis's protective veil, shadows that actively sought to pervert the very resonance they cherished.

Ash, ever perceptive to the shifts in Kira's energy, felt the subtle tightening of her aura. "You sense it too, don't you?" he murmured, his voice a low rumble that did not disturb the tranquil air of the Sunken Gardens. The lunar orchids, their petals unfurled like translucent wings, seemed to absorb the ambient light, casting an ethereal glow upon their faces. "The outside... it's not just oblivious. It's... hungry."

Kira nodded, her gaze drifting towards the shimmering, almost invisible barrier that demarcated the Oasis's perimeter. The debate had been intense, grappling with the moral complexities of intervention, the delicate dance between aiding and asserting. But Ash's observation was a stark reminder that the world beyond their sanctuary was not merely a passive recipient of their efforts; it was a landscape where resonance was not a tool for harmony, but a commodity for control, a weapon to be forged.

"The Council's discussion was about *how* to help," Kira replied, her voice low, "but it also highlighted the immense risks. We are dealing with forces that don't understand, or perhaps actively reject, the idea of natural balance." She recalled Kael's sharp warning about those who would exploit resonance, entities that sought power through manipulation. The Oracle Dog hadn't shown her only suffering; it had also revealed these counter-currents, these dark eddies in the planetary flow.

A few days later, a routine patrol along the Oasis's perimeter yielded more than just the usual reports of migrating fauna or shifting sand dunes. Rhys, one of the Oasis's seasoned scouts, his movements as fluid and silent as a desert wind, returned with an unnerving account. He had stumbled upon a small, abandoned encampment, a stark scar upon the otherwise pristine landscape. The remnants were crude but telling:

scorched earth, the metallic tang of spent energy cells, and the faint, lingering echo of dissonant frequencies.

"They were observing us," Rhys reported to the council, his brow furrowed with a mixture of concern and quiet anger. "Not just passively watching, but actively probing. They had devices, crude by our standards, but capable of detecting and attempting to replicate resonant signatures. It's as if they were trying to map our energy, to understand the source of our sanctuary's strength."

Lorien, his usual placidity now underlined with a steely resolve, examined the small, crystalline fragment Rhys had recovered – a shard of what appeared to be a crude energy conduit. "This material... it's laced with a destabilizing agent, designed to disrupt harmonic frequencies. They weren't just observing; they were attempting to analyze our defenses, perhaps even to find a way to breach them."

Kira felt a chill that had nothing to do with the desert night. The debate about intervention had focused on how to heal the planet. But these "others," as they were beginning to be called, represented a different kind of challenge altogether. They weren't suffering; they were predatory. They saw resonance not as a life-giving force, but as a tool of dominion.

"They are the 'Resonance Raiders'," Jonas offered, his voice carrying the weight of historical knowledge. "Tales of them exist in the fragmented lore of the Silent Age. Groups that sought to harness psychic and energetic abilities, not for understanding or healing, but for personal gain, for control. They viewed resonance as a raw power to be extracted, refined, and weaponized."

"Weaponized?" Lyra echoed, her voice laced with horror. The very idea of using the intricate, delicate web of planetary harmony as a means of coercion was anathema to her. "How can something so fundamental, so life-affirming, be twisted into such a destructive force?"

"Fear is a powerful motivator, Lyra," Kael said, his pragmatism cutting through the emotional weight of the revelation. "And ignorance breeds fear. Those who don't understand resonance, or who fear what they cannot control, will inevitably seek to dominate it. They see our ability to live in harmony as a weakness, a vulnerability."

Kira's mind reeled, connecting the fragmented pieces. The visions of ecological collapse weren't just the planet's natural response to imbalance; they were perhaps exacerbated by the actions of these 'others,' those who actively sought to disrupt harmony, to sow discord for their own gain. The stray energy readings that sometimes flickered at the edge of the Oasis's detection grid, previously dismissed as atmospheric anomalies, now took on a more sinister significance.

Ash placed a reassuring hand on Kira's arm, his presence a steady anchor. "We must be vigilant, but not consumed by fear. Their methods are crude, their understanding incomplete. They operate from a place of scarcity, of wanting to take. We operate from a place of abundance, of giving and receiving."

"But their scarcity drives them to aggression," Kira countered, the weight of her amplified awareness pressing down on her. "If they can't create harmony, they will seek to control it. Silvanus showed me a world where the natural energetic flows are being deliberately corrupted, not just by neglect, but by active interference."

The council convened again, the mood more somber than before. The philosophical debate about intervention had now been sharpened by the tangible threat of external forces. The sanctuary of the Oasis, once a symbol of internal growth and harmonious living, was now also a beacon, a target for those who sought to exploit what they could not comprehend.

"We have been discussing the ethics of reaching *out* to heal," Elara stated, her voice steady, though a new urgency underscored its usual calm. "But we must also prepare for the possibility of them reaching *in*. Our understanding of resonance has deepened, but our defenses, in the conventional sense, remain rudimentary. Our strength lies in our harmony, not in our capacity for conflict."

"They are scouting the perimeter, trying to understand our shields," Rhys confirmed. "They are not attempting to breach them directly, not yet. But they are collecting data. They are learning."

Kira felt a growing unease. The visions had shown her not just the suffering of the natural world, but also the pockets of human suffering, the disconnectedness and fear that permeated so much of the outside world. These 'Resonance Raiders' were a manifestation of that deeper malaise, a symptom of a world that had forgotten how to resonate.

"They are afraid of what they don't control," Kira said, her voice resonating with a newfound certainty. "They see our ability to live in balance, to draw strength from the Earth's natural rhythms, as a threat to their own systems of power. Their goal is to capture, to weaponize, to extract resonance for their own ends. They don't seek to harmonize; they seek to dominate."

Jonas elaborated, drawing upon the ancient texts. "The lore speaks of 'Resonance Vampires' – entities that drain the vital energies of others, leaving them depleted and inert. These Raiders, it seems, are their modern iteration. They cannot generate the resonant frequencies themselves, so they seek to steal them, to siphon them from those who can."

The implications were stark. Their internal discussions about nurturing and healing were happening against a backdrop of a world where the very forces they represented were being hunted. The Oracle Dog hadn't just gifted Kira with understanding; it had also, perhaps inadvertently, marked her and the Oasis as a source of potent resonance, a prize to be claimed by those who sought to twist its power.

"The patrols must be doubled," Lorien declared, his gaze sweeping across the assembled council members. "And our understanding of their probing methods needs to be disseminated to all our sentinels. We must be able to detect their presence, to identify their energy signatures, without engaging directly unless absolutely necessary."

"But what if they succeed in developing a method to destabilize our shields?" Lyra questioned, her concern evident. "Our sanctuary is our strength, but if it can be breached..."

Kael interjected; his tone measured. "Our shields are not merely energetic barriers; they are a reflection of our collective intent, our unity. If they can disrupt our harmony, they can weaken our defenses. This reinforces the importance of our internal work. The more resonant we are, the stronger our sanctuary will be, not just physically, but energetically."

Kira felt the truth of his words resonate deep within her. Their strength wasn't in brute force, but in their interconnectedness, their shared purpose. The outside world, with its fear and its hunger, was the antithesis of this. They were a fractured reflection, seeking to mend their own perceived brokenness by stealing from others.

"Silvanus showed me that even within the greatest discord, there are sparks of light," Kira mused, her thoughts turning towards a new strategy. "These Raiders, they are driven by a fundamental imbalance, a deep-seated fear of their own insignificance. While we must protect ourselves, perhaps our ultimate 'defense' lies in demonstrating the true power of harmony, not by confrontation, but by maintaining and amplifying our own resonance."

"A powerful statement, Kira," Elara acknowledged, her eyes reflecting a profound understanding. "Our very existence, our continued flourishing, is a testament to the path of balance. But even a testament needs protection. We cannot afford to be naive."

The discussions that followed were a delicate balancing act. How could they strengthen their defenses without compromising their core principles? How could they deter these encroaching forces without becoming like them? The Oracle Dog's gift had opened their eyes to the world's suffering, but it had also revealed the architects of that suffering, those who actively sought to perpetuate it. The Oasis was no longer just a place of refuge; it was a living experiment, a vibrant pocket of harmony in a world increasingly consumed by dissonance, and the 'others' were the stark, undeniable proof that their work was far from over.

The following days were a flurry of increased vigilance and subtle strategic adjustments. Rhys and his team were not merely patrolling; they were actively mapping the subtle energetic signatures that indicated the presence of the Resonance Raiders. They learned to differentiate between the natural hum of the desert's ancient energies and the discordant, probing frequencies of the outsiders. It was a painstaking process, akin to learning a new language, a language of intrusion and exploitation.

One evening, as Kira and Ash walked near the Oasis's perimeter, a faint, unusual shimmer caught Kira's eye. It was on the edge of their visual spectrum, a distortion in the air that seemed to ripple with an unnatural energy. Ash, his senses honed by years of living in tune with the natural world, tensed beside her.

"Something is there," he whispered, his voice barely audible. "A resonance... but it's twisted. It feels... like static on a clear frequency."

They moved closer, their steps silent on the soft sand. The shimmering intensified, coalescing into a vaguely humanoid shape, indistinct and flickering. It was a scouting probe, not a physical being, designed to gather information without risking direct confrontation. Its form was a crude manifestation of captured and repurposed resonance, a distorted echo of life.

Kira felt a wave of profound sadness wash over her. This was the extent of their understanding, their perception of the world: to replicate, to mimic, to capture and control. There was no inherent creativity, no genuine connection, only a desperate attempt to grasp what they could not create.

"They are trying to understand our shields," Kira murmured, her own resonance subtly shifting, not in aggression, but in a gentle observation of the intruder's energy. "Trying to find a frequency that disrupts our harmony."

The probe flickered, its distortion intensifying as if sensing Kira's presence, her own potent resonance. It seemed to recoil, its crude energy signature wavering as if struck by an unexpected force. It was not an attack, but a subtle recalibration from Kira's side, a gentle assertion of the Oasis's inherent harmonic strength.

"It's reacting to you," Ash observed, his gaze fixed on the shimmering distortion. "Our unified resonance, your amplified connection... it's overwhelming their crude attempts at mimicry."

The probe pulsed erratically, its flickering form becoming more pronounced. Then, with a final, discordant ripple, it dissolved, vanishing as if it had never been. Rhys, who had been observing from a concealed position, emerged from the shadows.

"It withdrew," he reported, his voice taut with relief. "It scanned the perimeter, it detected your... presence... and it retreated. They're learning, but they're also cautious. They clearly don't understand the source of our strength."

The encounter, though brief and non-violent, was a stark illustration of the gulf that separated the Oasis from the outside world. The Raiders' attempts were born of a need to control, a desire to exploit. The Oasis's strength, conversely, was rooted in connection, in harmony, in a profound understanding of mutual existence.

"They see our resonance as a resource to be plundered," Kira stated, her voice firm. "They cannot fathom that it is a state of being, a way of life. They try to build machines to replicate what we achieve through inner connection."

"And their machines are crude," Ash added, a hint of a smile touching his lips. "Their attempts to mimic are like a child trying to draw the ocean with a single crayon. They capture a shadow of the essence, but miss the vibrant, living reality."

Jonas, who had joined them, nodded in agreement. "The legends spoke of the Raiders' methods becoming increasingly sophisticated, but always fundamentally flawed. They lacked the vital spark, the true understanding of the energetic flow. They were like alchemists, trying to transmute lead into gold, always just a step away from true mastery."

The incident served as a critical turning point. The threat was no longer an abstract concept debated in council; it was a tangible presence, a shadow that flickered at the edge of their sanctuary. It reinforced the urgency of their mission, not just to heal the planet, but to protect the very essence of what made their oasis possible. The discussions about recalibration and amplification now carried a new weight; they were not just about planetary well-being, but about the survival of a way of life that the outside world actively sought to extinguish.

The Resonance Raiders, it became clear, were not simply misguided individuals. They represented a fundamental opposition to the very principles of harmony and interconnectedness that the Oasis embodied. They were driven by a fear of what they couldn't control, a desire to dominate what they couldn't understand. And their methods, while crude, were persistent. They were the embodiment of the discord that the Oracle Dog had shown Kira, the forces that actively sought to unravel the planetary tapestry.

"They are like a disease," Lyra murmured, her voice laced with concern as they sat in council once more, discussing Rhys's report. "They feed on imbalance, on fear, and they seek to spread it. Our sanctuary, our harmony... it's anathema to them. They want to dissect it, to understand its components, and then to use that knowledge to control it, or to destroy it."

Kael, ever the strategist, leaned forward. "Their probing suggests they are attempting to map our resonant frequencies. If they can identify specific patterns that underpin our shields, or that emanate from our most powerful resonance users, they could potentially develop a counter-frequency, a way to disrupt our unity."

"This underscores the need for diversification in our approach to resonance," Lorien stated. "We cannot rely on a single, monolithic frequency. Our strength lies in the rich tapestry of our individual and collective resonances. We must ensure that the Raiders cannot isolate a single dominant signature to target."

Kira felt a surge of determination. The Oracle Dog's visions had shown her the fragility of the Earth's systems, but they had also shown her the resilience, the capacity for regeneration, and the inherent beauty of its diverse energetic expressions. The Raiders sought to impose a singular, controlled resonance, a drab uniformity. The Oasis, on the other hand, celebrated the symphony of countless unique frequencies.

"We must not only maintain our own harmony," Kira declared, her voice resonating with a newfound clarity and strength, "but we must also learn to project it in ways that are less predictable, less easily mapped. Our diversity is our greatest defense. It is what makes us strong, and it is what makes us incomprehensible to those who operate from a place of scarcity and control."

The council agreed. The focus shifted, not just to fortifying their existing defenses, but to actively expanding their understanding and application of resonance. This meant not only reinforcing the collective harmony within the Oasis but also exploring more nuanced, diverse, and even unpredictable ways of expressing their resonant capabilities. It was a subtle but critical shift: from simply protecting their sanctuary to actively demonstrating the power and resilience of a life lived in true resonance, a direct counterpoint to the parasitic methods of the Resonance Raiders. Their existence was a testament to what the world *could* be, a beacon of hope that the encroaching darkness could not easily extinguish. The threat of the 'others' had not introduced a new conflict, but rather illuminated the true stakes of the one they were already engaged in – the ongoing struggle between harmonious coexistence and exploitative control.

CHAPTER 8

The shimmering veil of the Oasis, once a mere boundary, now felt like a fragile membrane stretched taut against an encroaching tide. Kira's connection to Silvanus, the ancient planetary consciousness, pulsed with an amplified awareness, a symphony of terrestrial anxieties that resonated with her own burgeoning dread. The Oracle Dog's visions, stark and visceral, had etched a grim panorama onto her mind: a world teetering on the brink, its natural rhythms warped, its ancient song of balance all but drowned out by the cacophony of discord. The council's deliberations, a fervent tapestry woven with threads of ethics and action, had finally coalesced into a resolute path—one of recalibration, of amplification, of guiding the planet and its inhabitants back to their inherent, forgotten harmony. Yet, even as a semblance of clarity emerged from the intricate discussions, a new, chilling realization began to dawn: the existence of shadows that lurked beyond the Oasis's protective embrace, shadows that actively sought to pervert the very resonance they cherished, to twist its life-affirming energy into a tool of dominion.

Ash, his senses attuned to the subtle shifts in Kira's aura, felt the almost imperceptible tightening of her presence. "You feel it too, don't you?" he murmured, his voice a low thrum that did little to disturb the tranquil air of the Sunken Gardens. The lunar orchids, their petals unfurled like diaphanous wings, seemed to drink in the ambient light, casting an ethereal luminescence upon their faces. "The outside... it's not merely oblivious. It's... hungry."

Kira nodded; her gaze drawn to the almost invisible shimmer that marked the Oasis's perimeter. The council's debate had been an arduous journey through the labyrinth of moral complexities, a delicate dance between aiding and asserting. But Ash's observation was a stark, undeniable truth: the world beyond their sanctuary was not a passive canvas for their restorative efforts; it was a landscape where resonance was not a balm for healing, but a commodity to be bartered, a weapon to be forged in the fires of ambition.

"The Council's focus was on *how* to help," Kira replied, her voice a low murmur, "but it also highlighted the immense risks. We are confronting forces that either do not comprehend, or perhaps actively reject, the fundamental concept of natural balance." She recalled Kael's prescient warning about those who would exploit resonance, entities that craved power through the insidious art of manipulation. The Oracle Dog had not merely shown her the planet's suffering; it had also unveiled these counter-currents, these dark eddies that disrupted the planetary flow.

A few days later, a routine patrol along the Oasis's perimeter yielded an anomaly that sent ripples of unease through their carefully guarded tranquility. Rhys, one of the Oasis's seasoned scouts, his movements as fluid and silent as a desert wind, returned with a disquieting report. He had stumbled upon a small, abandoned encampment, a stark scar upon the otherwise pristine landscape. The remnants were crude but spoke volumes: scorched earth, the metallic tang of spent energy cells, and the faint, lingering echo of dissonant frequencies.

"They were observing us," Rhys reported to the council, his brow furrowed with a mixture of concern and a quiet, simmering anger. "Not just passively watching, but actively probing. They had devices, primitive by our standards, but undeniably capable of detecting and attempting to replicate resonant signatures. It was as if they were trying to map our energy, to understand the very source of our sanctuary's strength."

Lorien, his customary placidity now underscored with a steely resolve, examined the small, crystalline fragment Rhys had recovered – a shard of what appeared to be a crude energy conduit. "This material... it's laced with a destabilizing agent, specifically designed to disrupt harmonic frequencies. They weren't merely observing; they were attempting to analyze our defenses, perhaps even to find a method of breaching them."

A chill, unrelated to the desert night, snaked down Kira's spine. The council's philosophical discussions on intervention had centered on the act of healing the planet. But these 'others,' as they were beginning to be known, represented a fundamentally different kind of challenge. They were not suffering entities; they were predatory. They perceived resonance not as a life-giving force, but as a tool of dominance.

"They are the 'Resonance Raiders'," Jonas offered, his voice carrying the weight of historical knowledge, of tales whispered from the fragmented lore of the Silent Age. "Accounts of them exist, of groups that sought to harness psychic and energetic abilities, not for understanding or healing, but for personal gain, for absolute control. They viewed resonance as a raw power to be extracted, refined, and ultimately, weaponized."

"Weaponized?" Lyra echoed; her voice laced with a palpable horror. The very notion of twisting the intricate, delicate web of planetary harmony into a means of coercion was anathema to her very being. "How can something so fundamental, so intrinsically life-affirming, be corrupted into such a destructive force?"

"Fear is a powerful motivator, Lyra," Kael stated, his pragmatism slicing through the emotional weight of the revelation. "And ignorance is its most fertile ground. Those who do not comprehend resonance, or who harbor fear of what they cannot control, will inevitably seek to dominate it. They perceive our ability to live in harmony as a weakness, a profound vulnerability."

Kira's mind raced, attempting to connect the scattered fragments of information. The visions of ecological collapse were not merely the planet's natural response to imbalance; they were likely exacerbated by the machinations of these 'others,' those who actively sought to sow discord, to corrupt harmony for their own insatiable gain. The stray energy readings that occasionally flickered at the periphery of the Oasis's detection grid, previously dismissed as mere atmospheric anomalies, now took on a far more sinister significance.

Ash placed a reassuring hand on Kira's arm, his presence a steady, grounding force. "We must remain vigilant, Kira, but not consumed by fear. Their methods are crude, their understanding incomplete. They operate from a place of scarcity, of inherent wanting, of a desire to take. We, on the other hand, operate from a place of abundance, of giving and receiving."

"But their scarcity breeds aggression, Ash," Kira countered, the amplified awareness she carried pressing down with an almost physical weight. "If they cannot create harmony, they will strive to control it. Silvanus revealed to me a world where the natural energetic flows are not merely neglected, but deliberately corrupted, actively interfered with."

The council convened once more, the atmosphere noticeably more somber than before. The philosophical debate concerning intervention had been irrevocably sharpened by the tangible threat of external forces. The sanctuary of the Oasis, once a symbol of internal growth and harmonious living, had now become a beacon, a target for those who sought to exploit what they could not comprehend.

"We have been discussing the ethics of reaching *out* to heal," Elara stated, her voice steady, though a new, undeniable urgency underscored its usual calm. "But we must also prepare ourselves for the distinct possibility of them reaching *in*. Our understanding of resonance has deepened exponentially, but our defenses, in the conventional sense, remain rudimentary. Our true strength lies in our harmony, not in our capacity for conflict."

"Their scouting patrols are diligently mapping the perimeter, attempting to understand our shields," Rhys confirmed, his report delivered with stark clarity. "They are not yet attempting direct breaches, but they are relentlessly collecting data. They are learning."

Kira felt a persistent unease settle within her. The Oracle Dog's visions had not only shown her the suffering of the natural world but also the pockets of profound human suffering, the deep-seated disconnectedness and pervasive fear that permeated so much of the outside world. These 'Resonance Raiders' were, in essence, a manifestation of that deeper societal malaise, a symptom of a world that had tragically forgotten how to resonate.

"They are driven by a fear of what they cannot control," Kira articulated, her voice resonating with a newfound certainty. "They perceive our ability to live in balance, to draw strength from the Earth's natural rhythms, as a direct threat to their own established systems of power. Their ultimate goal is to capture, to weaponize, to extract resonance for their own self-serving ends. They do not seek to harmonize; they seek to dominate."

Jonas elaborated, his words drawing from the ancient texts with unnerving precision. "The lore speaks of 'Resonance Vampires' – entities that drain the vital energies of others, leaving them utterly depleted and inert. It appears that these Raiders are their modern iteration. They are incapable of generating the resonant frequencies themselves, and therefore, they seek to steal them, to siphon them from those who can."

The implications of this revelation were stark and deeply unsettling. Their internal discussions, focused on nurturing and healing, were unfolding against a backdrop of a world where the very forces they represented were being actively hunted. The Oracle Dog's gift had not merely granted Kira understanding; it had also, perhaps inadvertently, marked her and the entire Oasis as a source of potent resonance, a prize to be claimed by those who sought to twist its power for their own nefarious purposes.

"The patrols must be doubled," Lorien declared, his gaze sweeping across the assembled council members with a commanding authority. "And our understanding of their probing methods needs to be disseminated to every single one of our sentinels. We must be able to detect their presence, to identify their energy signatures, without engaging directly unless absolutely compelled."

"But what if they succeed in developing a method to destabilize our shields?" Lyra questioned; her concern evident in the tremor of her voice. "Our sanctuary is our ultimate strength, but if it can be breached..."

Kael interjected, his tone measured and reassuring. "Our shields are not merely energetic barriers, Lyra; they are a direct reflection of our collective intent, our profound unity. If they can disrupt our internal harmony, they can significantly weaken our defenses. This fact only serves to reinforce the paramount importance of our ongoing internal work. The more resonant we become, the stronger our sanctuary will prove to be, not just physically, but energetically."

Kira felt the undeniable truth of his words resonate deep within her core. Their strength was not derived from brute force or superior weaponry, but from their interconnectedness, their shared purpose, their unwavering unity of spirit. The outside world, with its pervasive fear and gnawing hunger, stood in stark contrast to this; it was a fractured reflection, desperately seeking to mend its own perceived brokenness by illicitly taking from others.

"Silvanus showed me that even within the deepest discord, there are always sparks of light," Kira mused, her thoughts drifting towards a new strategic imperative. "These Raiders, they are driven by a fundamental imbalance, a deep-seated fear of their own perceived insignificance. While we must undoubtedly protect ourselves, perhaps our ultimate 'defense' lies in demonstrating the true, unadulterated power of harmony, not through confrontation, but by steadfastly maintaining and amplifying our own inherent resonance."

"A powerful and insightful statement, Kira," Elara acknowledged, her eyes reflecting a profound and insightful understanding. "Our very existence, our continued flourishing, serves as a testament to the efficacy of the path of balance. But even the most potent testament requires protection. We cannot afford the luxury of naivety."

The subsequent discussions were characterized by a delicate balancing act. How could they fortify their defenses without compromising their core principles? How could they effectively deter these encroaching forces without succumbing to their methods and becoming like them? The Oracle Dog's gift had not only opened their eyes to the suffering of the world but had also, with stark clarity, revealed the architects of that suffering, those who actively sought to perpetuate it. The Oasis was no longer merely a place of refuge; it had become a living experiment, a vibrant pocket of harmony in a world increasingly consumed by dissonance, and the 'others' served as the stark, undeniable proof that their critical work was far from over.

The days that followed were marked by a heightened state of vigilance and subtle, strategic adjustments. Rhys and his dedicated team were not merely patrolling; they were actively engaged in meticulously mapping the subtle energetic signatures that reliably indicated the presence of the Resonance Raiders. They learned to discern the difference between the natural, ambient hum of the desert's ancient energies and the discordant, probing frequencies emanating from the outsiders. It was a painstaking process, akin to learning a new language, a language spoken in whispers of intrusion and the sharp tones of exploitation.

One evening, as Kira and Ash ambled near the Oasis's perimeter, a faint, unusual shimmer caught Kira's eye. It flickered at the very edge of their visual spectrum, a distortion in the air that seemed to ripple with an unnatural, unsettling energy. Ash, his senses honed by years of living in intimate tune with the natural world, tensed beside her, his awareness sharpening.

"There's something there," he whispered, his voice barely audible, a mere breath against the rustling desert flora. "A resonance... but it's twisted. It feels... like static crackling on a clear frequency."

They moved closer, their steps unnervingly silent on the soft, yielding sand. The shimmering intensified, coalescing into a vaguely humanoid shape, indistinct and flickering, like a phantom made of light and shadow. It was a scouting probe, not a physical being, meticulously designed to gather information without risking direct confrontation. Its form was a crude manifestation of captured and repurposed resonance, a distorted, warped echo of life.

Kira felt a profound wave of sadness wash over her. This was the extent of their understanding, their limited perception of the world: to replicate, to mimic, to capture, and to control. There was no inherent creativity, no genuine connection, only a desperate, grasping attempt to acquire what they were fundamentally incapable of creating.

"They are attempting to understand our shields," Kira murmured, her own resonance subtly shifting, not in aggression, but in a gentle, observational probing of the intruder's energy. "Trying to find a specific frequency that disrupts our collective harmony."

The probe flickered, its distortion intensifying as if it had suddenly sensed Kira's presence, her own potent, unyielding resonance. It seemed to recoil, its crude energy signature wavering, as if struck by an unexpected, invisible force. It was not an attack, but a subtle recalibration on Kira's part, a gentle assertion of the Oasis's inherent, unyielding harmonic strength.

"It's reacting to you," Ash observed, his gaze fixed intently on the shimmering distortion. "Our unified resonance, your amplified connection... it's overwhelming their crude attempts at mimicry."

The probe pulsed erratically, its flickering form becoming more pronounced, more unstable. Then, with a final, discordant ripple that seemed to fray the very air, it dissolved, vanishing as if it had never materialized. Rhys, who had been observing from a strategically concealed position, emerged from the deepening shadows.

"It withdrew," he reported, his voice taut with a palpable relief. "It scanned the perimeter, it detected your... presence... and it retreated. They are learning, but they are also demonstrably cautious. They clearly do not comprehend the true source of our strength."

The encounter, though brief and devoid of physical violence, served as a stark and powerful illustration of the vast, almost unbridgeable gulf that separated the Oasis from the outside world. The Raiders' attempts were born of an innate need to control, a deep-seated desire to exploit. The Oasis's strength, conversely, was rooted in connection, in harmony, in a profound understanding of mutual existence.

"They perceive our resonance as a mere resource to be plundered," Kira stated, her voice firm with conviction. "They cannot fathom that it is, in fact, a state of being, a fundamental way of life. They endeavor to build machines to replicate that which we achieve through deep, internal connection."

"And their machines are profoundly crude," Ash added, a hint of a smile touching his lips, a rare expression of amusement in the face of such clear inadequacy. "Their attempts at mimicry are akin to a child trying to capture the vastness of the ocean with a single, solitary crayon. They grasp a shadow of the essence, but utterly miss the vibrant, living reality."

Jonas, who had joined them, nodded in solemn agreement. "The ancient legends spoke of the Raiders' methods becoming increasingly sophisticated over time, but always fundamentally flawed. They lacked the vital spark, the true, intuitive understanding of the energetic flow. They were like alchemists, forever attempting to transmute lead into gold, always just a single, elusive step away from true mastery."

This incident served as a critical turning point, a catalyst for a profound shift in their perspective. The threat was no longer an abstract concept to be debated in council chambers; it was a tangible, menacing presence, a shadow that flickered menacingly at the very edge of their sanctuary. It underscored the desperate urgency of their mission, not merely to heal the planet, but to protect the very essence of what made their oasis possible in the first place. The discussions surrounding recalibration and amplification now carried a new, profound weight; they were no longer solely about planetary well-being, but about the survival of a way of life that the outside world actively sought to extinguish.

The Resonance Raiders, it became undeniably clear, were not simply misguided individuals. They represented a fundamental opposition to the very principles of harmony and interconnectedness that the Oasis so profoundly embodied. They were driven by an all-consuming fear of what they could not control, a relentless desire to dominate what they could not understand. And their methods, while crude, were undeniably persistent. They were the living embodiment of the discord that the Oracle Dog had so vividly shown Kira, the forces that actively sought to unravel the intricate tapestry of the planet.

"They are akin to a disease," Lyra murmured, her voice laced with a deep, palpable concern as they convened in council once more, dissecting Rhys's latest report. "They feed on imbalance, on pervasive fear, and they relentlessly seek to spread it. Our sanctuary, our profound harmony... it is anathema to them. They wish to dissect it, to understand its constituent components, and then to utilize that knowledge to control it, or even to destroy it outright."

Kael, ever the astute strategist, leaned forward, his gaze sharp and focused. "Their probing activities suggest they are attempting to meticulously map our resonant frequencies. If they can identify specific patterns that underpin our protective shields, or that emanate from our most powerful resonance users, they could potentially develop a counter-frequency, a means to disrupt our collective unity."

"This reinforces the critical need for diversification in our approach to resonance," Lorien stated, his voice calm but firm. "We cannot afford to rely on a single, monolithic frequency. Our true strength lies in the rich, vibrant tapestry of our individual and collective resonances. We must ensure that the Raiders cannot isolate a single, dominant signature to target with their disruptive energies."

Kira felt a surge of unwavering determination course through her. The Oracle Dog's visions had revealed the profound fragility of the Earth's delicate systems, but they had also unveiled its astonishing resilience, its inherent capacity for regeneration, and the breathtaking beauty of its diverse energetic expressions. The Raiders sought to impose a singular, rigidly controlled resonance, a drab, suffocating uniformity upon the world. The Oasis, on the other hand, celebrated the glorious symphony of countless unique frequencies, a vibrant testament to life's inherent diversity.

"We must not only maintain our own harmony," Kira declared, her voice resonating with a newfound clarity and an empowering strength, "but we must also learn to project it in ways that are less predictable, less easily mapped by their intrusive efforts. Our inherent diversity is our greatest, most potent defense. It is what makes us strong, and it is precisely what makes us incomprehensible to those who operate from a place of scarcity and relentless control."

The council unanimously agreed with her assessment. The focus of their efforts shifted, not merely to fortifying their existing defenses, but to actively expanding their understanding and application of resonance. This entailed not only reinforcing the collective harmony that already existed within the Oasis but also exploring more nuanced, diverse, and even unpredictable ways of expressing their resonant capabilities. It was a subtle but critically important shift: from simply protecting their sanctuary to actively demonstrating the inherent power and resilience of a life lived in true, unadulterated resonance, a direct and powerful counterpoint to the parasitic methods employed by the Resonance Raiders. Their very existence was a testament to what the world

could be, a beacon of enduring hope that the encroaching darkness could not easily extinguish. The threat posed by the 'others' had not introduced a new conflict, but rather illuminated with stark clarity the true stakes of the one they were already engaged in – the ongoing, vital struggle between harmonious coexistence and exploitative, destructive control.

Guided by an inner compass attuned to the subtlest shifts in Silvanus's energy, Kira felt an insistent pull, a resonance echoing from beyond the familiar, verdant embrace of the Oasis. It was a whisper from the past, a promise of forgotten life, a beacon in the ecological twilight. The Oracle Dog's final, most enigmatic vision had been of a place, hidden and preserved, a sanctuary of genetic memory: the legendary Seed Vault, a pre-collapse repository of flora, its contents a potential blueprint for reawakening a wilting world. The journey to find it, however, would not be a simple trek. It would demand navigating regions scarred by atmospheric volatility, territories still haunted by the spectral remnants of automated defense systems, remnants of a civilization that had, in its hubris, sought to control the very forces of nature. This pilgrimage would test not only their physical resilience but also their capacity for cooperative problem-solving, their ability to weave their individual strengths into a unified tapestry of purpose.

"The readings are faint, but they're consistent," Ash said, his voice a low hum of concentration as he studied the holographic projections shimmering before them. The data streams, fragments of ancient planetary scans and seismic anomalies, painted a picture of a landscape fraught with peril. "The atmospheric instability in the Northern Sector is significant. High-frequency energy surges, unpredictable gravitational fluctuations... it's as if the planet itself is trying to reject any intrusion."

Kira nodded, tracing the projected lines with a fingertip. "Silvanus shows me these areas are like a battlefield, not of armies, but of opposing energies. The collapse wasn't just environmental; it was a tearing of the energetic fabric. These regions are still echoing that violence." Her own resonance, amplified by her connection to the planet, allowed her to perceive these disturbances not just as scientific data, but as echoes of pain, of disruption. It was this deeper perception that would be crucial, not just for survival, but for locating the Vault. "The Vault was designed to be hidden, protected. Its security measures would likely be integrated with the natural energetic flows of the region, making them invisible to conventional detection."

The Oracle Dog had shown her glimpses of the Vault itself: an immense, subterranean structure, its entrance subtly disguised, keyed not to physical locks, but to specific harmonic frequencies, a resonance signature that mirrored the planet's most balanced state. It was a lock that only those who could truly listen to the Earth's song could open.

"We'll need to calibrate our personal resonance to the planetary baseline of that sector," Ash mused aloud, his brow furrowed in concentration. "It will be like learning a new dialect of the Earth's language. A dialect filled with static and interference, but with a hidden melody beneath it all."

Kira closed her eyes, reaching out with her awareness. She felt the gentle pulse of Silvanus, a subtle but persistent direction. "The Vault isn't just a physical place," she murmured, her voice carrying the quiet conviction of revelation. "It's also an energetic locus. Its signature will be a point of profound harmony within the chaos."

Their preparations were meticulous. They gathered supplies, recalibrated their energy shielding to withstand atmospheric anomalies, and familiarized themselves with the ancient geological data that hinted at the Vault's probable location, a vast, desolate plateau known only as the 'Whispering Flats.' It was a region notorious for its unpredictable magnetic storms and the lingering echoes of dormant defense systems, remnants of a forgotten era of desperate preservation.

The journey began under a sky bruised with the twilight hues of a dying sun. The landscape unfolded before them, a stark canvas of ochre and rust, punctuated by jagged rock formations that clawed at the bruised sky. As they ventured deeper into the Northern Sector, the air itself seemed to thicken, growing heavy with an unseen pressure. Static crackled around them, not the harmless buzz of atmospheric discharge, but a dissonant hum that grated against their senses.

"The readings are increasing," Ash reported, his gaze fixed on the complex array of instruments mounted on their all-terrain vehicle. "The magnetic fields are fluctuating wildly. We need to find a pocket of stability, a place to get our bearings."

Kira extended her awareness, reaching out to the planet. She felt the subtle currents of energy, the planet's breath, and within that breath, she sought the discordant notes, the points of disruption. "There," she said, pointing towards a series of weathered canyons. "The energy there is... less agitated. More contained. It feels like a natural eddy in the storm."

Navigating the canyons proved to be a challenge. The vehicle's advanced suspension system worked overtime, its metallic groans a stark contrast to the natural world around them. Automated defense turrets, long dormant but still charged with a residual energy, occasionally activated, their targeting lasers cutting crimson arcs through the dusky air. Kira and Ash worked in tandem, Kira sensing the faint energy signatures of the active turrets, guiding Ash through the safest routes, while Ash used their vehicle's low-frequency emitter to temporarily disrupt the turrets' targeting systems, allowing them to pass unseen.

"It's like they're trying to remember their purpose," Ash observed, his hands steady on the controls. "The planet's ambient resonance seems to be inadvertently triggering them, making them react to anything that deviates from the natural flow."

"Which is why our own resonance needs to be a whisper, not a shout," Kira replied, focusing her intent. She projected a wave of calm, of gentle observation, a resonance that mirrored the subtle shifts in the canyons' rocky surfaces. "We need to blend with the natural energetic background, to become part of the landscape, rather than an intruder."

As they neared the plateau, the atmospheric conditions worsened. The wind howled, carrying with it a fine, abrasive dust that stung their eyes. The sky was a churning maelstrom of angry clouds, illuminated by intermittent flashes of raw energy. It was here, amidst this elemental fury, that Kira felt it – a faint, persistent hum, a thread of pure, unadulterated harmony weaving through the cacophony.

"The Vault," she breathed, her voice barely audibles above the din. "It's close. I can feel its resonance. It's like a beacon of pure light in this storm."

Ash brought the vehicle to a halt, the engine falling silent, leaving them enveloped by the elemental rage. They disembarked, their protective suits shielding them from the harsh environment. Kira closed her eyes, focusing her entire being on that singular thread of harmony. It led them towards a sheer cliff face, seemingly impassable, devoid of any discernible entrance.

"It's hidden within the rock," Kira stated, her voice filled with a quiet certainty. "The entrance isn't a door; it's a resonance lock. We need to match its frequency."

Ash began to work, his portable resonance modulator humming to life. He analyzed the faint signature Kira was perceiving, translating it into a complex series of harmonic frequencies. Kira, meanwhile, amplified her own connection to Silvanus, drawing upon the planet's stable, underlying resonance, attempting to attune herself to the specific signature of the Vault.

The process was painstaking. The wind tore at them, the atmospheric energy surged, threatening to overwhelm their focus. Ash adjusted the modulator, his face grim with concentration, while Kira meditated, her mind a calm center in the storm. She felt the planet's ancient song, its memory of growth and renewal, and she projected that song, that memory, towards the cliff face.

Suddenly, a section of the rock shimmered, as if the stone itself had become fluid. A doorway, perfectly integrated into the cliff's natural contours, materialized before them. It pulsed with a soft, ethereal light, its resonance a warm, welcoming embrace.

"We did it," Ash breathed, a rare smile of triumph gracing his lips.

Kira nodded, a sense of profound awe washing over her. They had navigated the chaos, bypassed the defenses, and found the sanctuary of life's memory. The journey had been arduous, a testament to the challenges of their mission, but standing at the threshold of the Seed Vault, she felt an overwhelming surge of hope. The seeds of renewal, the potential for a verdant future, lay within, waiting to be awakened. Their own amplified resonance, their ability to listen to the Earth's deepest songs, had unlocked not just a physical vault, but a promise of planetary resurrection. The true work, however, was just beginning. The knowledge contained within these walls was not merely for preservation; it was for the active, conscious reweaving of the world's broken tapestry.

The air inside the Seed Vault hummed with a quiet, almost reverent energy, a stark contrast to the tempestuous fury they had just endured. The journey through the Northern Sector had been a brutal baptism by atmospheric fire and the spectral whispers of forgotten technologies. Kira felt the lingering static cling to her suit, a phantom sensation of the planet's wounded state, but beneath it, a new symphony was beginning to play, orchestrated by the profound stillness of this subterranean sanctuary. Ash, his hand resting on a cool, metallic console that pulsed with a faint, internal luminescence, seemed to absorb the very essence of the place, his usual calm now imbued with an almost palpable sense of wonder.

"It's... more than I could have imagined," Ash murmured, his voice laced with an awe that mirrored Kira's own. His eyes, usually fixed on the immediate, tangible world, now scanned the vast chambers with a different kind of focus, a deeper perception. He was sensing more than just the visual. His innate connection to the planet's magnetic field, a sense that had always been a quiet hum beneath his awareness, now seemed to resonate with the very foundations of this place. "The geomagnetic signature here is incredibly stable. It's like a deep, steady anchor in a sea of planetary flux."

Kira nodded, her own senses reaching out, not just to the surface structures, but to the planet's hidden arteries. While her connection to Silvanus allowed her to perceive the broader, more emotional and organic currents of the world, Ash's ability was more precise, more attuned to the planet's intricate, energetic skeleton. He could feel the pull of the planet's core, the subtle shifts in the magnetic field that guided migratory birds and, apparently, the creators of this hidden marvel.

"It's not just stable, Ash," Kira responded, her gaze sweeping over the rows upon rows of crystalline containment units, each housing a spectrum of seeds, a miniature universe of potential. "It's... harmonized. As if the very geomagnetism here has been intentionally shaped, aligned with the life force stored within." She felt it now, a faint but distinct resonance emanating from the planet's depths, a steady, unerring beacon that had guided them through the environmental chaos. It was Ash's sense, amplified and focused through their shared intent, that had navigated them through the treacherous atmospheric distortions and the erratic energy signatures of dormant defense systems.

"That's it," Ash declared, a sudden realization dawning on his face. He tapped a sequence on the console, and a holographic map of the immediate subterranean complex flickered to life. "The geomagnetic field here isn't just stable; it's a finely tuned instrument. It's designed to mask the Vault's presence, to make it appear as nothing more than a natural geological anomaly to any conventional scanning technology. But to someone who can *feel* the magnetic currents, it's a clear pathway."

Kira's understanding deepened. Their journey had been a testament to the limitations of brute-force technology and the unparalleled efficacy of attuned, organic senses. Where advanced sensor arrays would have been blinded by atmospheric interference and the sheer energetic noise of the corrupted environment, Ash's geomagnetic sense had cut through the chaos like a perfectly tuned blade. He hadn't just been following a map; he had been navigating by the planet's own magnetic language, a language that spoke of hidden pathways, underground structures, and areas of profound energetic stillness, unaffected by the surface-level devastation.

"So, the planet's own magnetic field is essentially a cloaking mechanism," Kira mused, a new appreciation for the ingenuity of the Vault's creators settling in. "It's an invisible shield, woven from the very fabric of the Earth's magnetic currents."

"Precisely," Ash confirmed, his finger tracing a complex pattern on the holographic display. "And it's not just passive. It actively repels or distorts any external energetic probe that doesn't align with its specific harmonic signature. That's why those defense systems you sensed were so erratic – they were designed to react to discordant energy, not necessarily to specific intruders. The entire region is a carefully orchestrated symphony of magnetic fields, designed to deter the unqualified." He paused, a thoughtful frown creasing his brow. "It's like the planet itself is saying, 'Only those who understand my natural rhythms can truly find what is essential to my survival.'"

This revelation added another layer of complexity to their understanding of the Resonance Raiders. Their crude attempts to map and exploit energy signatures would be utterly useless here. The very nature of the Vault's protection rendered their methods obsolete. They relied on external observation, on quantifiable data. They could not *feel* the subtle shifts, the hidden currents, the deep, resonating hum of a planet's intention.

"This makes our presence here even more significant," Kira stated, her gaze sweeping across the countless seed pods, each a promise of a future they were fighting to ensure. "We were able to find this place because we listen. Because we understand that true power lies not in control, but in connection."

Ash nodded, a quiet pride in his voice. "My sense is like a compass that only points to true north, no matter how chaotic the world around it becomes. When we were in the thick of those atmospheric storms, with our conventional instruments failing, I could still feel the steady pull of the Vault's geomagnetic signature. It was like a lighthouse in the fog, a constant, unwavering presence." He demonstrated this by closing his eyes and gesturing towards a section of the Vault's complex structure. "Even here, within the Vault itself, there are subtle variations. Certain corridors, certain chambers, have a stronger magnetic resonance. They are the pathways, the intended routes, laid out by those who understood the fundamental forces at play."

Kira followed his gestures, her own connection to Silvanus now aligning with Ash's precise readings. She could feel the subtle currents of life force, the gentle pulse of stored vitality, being guided and channeled by the ambient geomagnetic fields. It was a beautiful, intricate dance, a testament to a civilization that had sought to work *with* the planet, rather than against it.

"So, you're saying your sense of direction here isn't just about finding your way around," Kira summarized, the implications of their discovery settling in. "It's about understanding the very architecture of this place, the intentional design of its pathways, which are laid out by the magnetic currents."

"Exactly," Ash confirmed. "Think of it this way: the layout of the Vault is imprinted onto the geomagnetic field. By sensing the variations, I can 'see' the layout, even in complete darkness or through solid rock. If we need to navigate through a section where the atmospheric interference is still lingering, or if a structural collapse blocks a conventional path, I can find an alternative route. It's about reading the Earth's magnetic 'topography' of the Vault itself."

He then elaborated on the practical applications, painting a vivid picture of their ongoing mission. "Imagine we need to access a specific section containing, say, drought-resistant cereals. My sense can guide us directly to the chamber, through any obstructed passages, by following the specific geomagnetic signature that leads there. It's not just about navigation; it's about precision, efficiency, and bypassing any environmental or structural impediments that would otherwise render our efforts futile."

The Resonance Raiders, with their reliance on external devices and their inability to perceive these subtle energetic pathways, would be utterly lost here. They could scan the surface, they could detect energy emissions, but they could not penetrate the intricate, invisible network that governed the Vault's existence. It was a sanctuary protected by the planet's own fundamental forces, a defense system that operated on principles so alien to their exploitative mindset that they would never even comprehend its existence.

"It's a profound advantage," Kira stated, a deep sense of gratitude washing over her for Ash's unique gift. "While they scramble to decipher crude energy readings, we can already be moving, guided by the very essence of the Earth's magnetic soul."

Ash's focus returned to the console, his fingers dancing across the controls with practiced ease. "And it's not just about finding our way. It's about understanding the integrity of the structures. Any significant shift in the geomagnetic field within the Vault would indicate instability, a potential breach, or a structural compromise. My sense acts as a constant, real-time diagnostic tool, ensuring that our exploration remains safe and that the precious cargo within is never compromised."

He then turned to Kira, his eyes reflecting the soft luminescence of the Vault's interior. "Remember those moments during the journey where the atmospheric turbulence was so severe, our external sensors were completely overwhelmed? I could still feel the steady, unwavering geomagnetic pulse of the Vault. It was a constant, reassuring presence, a guiding star in the midst of chaos. That's the power of this sense, Kira. It's not about seeing; it's about *knowing* where you are and where you need to go, regardless of external conditions."

Kira recognized the profound truth in his words. It was the same intuitive understanding that allowed her to connect with Silvanus, a deep, internal knowing that transcended the limitations of the physical senses. Ash's geomagnetic sense was a highly refined manifestation of this same principle, a direct conduit to the planet's underlying energetic framework.

"It means we can operate in environments where no one else could," she mused, envisioning future missions, future challenges. "If the Raiders attempt to establish any kind of base or operation in a similarly shielded region, or if we need to navigate through areas with extreme electromagnetic interference, your sense will be our primary tool."

"It's like having a built-in, infallible navigation system that is keyed directly into the planet's infrastructure," Ash added, a rare smile touching his lips. "The Resonance Raiders might have their sophisticated technology, but it's all external, all dependent on observable phenomena. We have an internal compass, an inherent understanding of the energetic currents that govern the very landscape."

He then elaborated further, detailing the nuanced applications of his ability within the Vault itself. "Each section, each archive, is associated with a unique geomagnetic frequency, subtly modulated to reflect the type of life it preserves. The section for aquatic flora will have a different signature than the one for high-altitude vegetation. This allows for incredibly precise retrieval. If we need a specific species, I can tune into its unique geomagnetic 'address' and be guided directly to it."

Kira absorbed this information, a wave of gratitude and hope washing over her. Their quest to reawaken the planet was a monumental task, fraught with peril and uncertainty. But with Ash's remarkable ability to navigate the invisible pathways of the Earth's magnetic field, they possessed an advantage that their adversaries could never hope to replicate. It was a testament to the power of attuned senses, of a deep connection to the natural world, and of a bond that allowed them to combine their unique gifts into an unbreakable force. The Seed Vault, a sanctuary of life's memory, was not merely a destination; it was a validation of their approach, a beacon that illuminated the path forward, a path guided by the Earth's own quiet, unwavering song. Their mission to recalibrate and amplify resonated not just within themselves, but through the very magnetic heart of the planet, a promise of renewal whispered on the currents of unseen energy.

The implications of Ash's geomagnetic sense stretched far beyond mere navigation. It provided a crucial layer of intelligence, a method for discerning the health and integrity of the environment, both within the Vault and in the wider world. As they delved deeper into the Seed Vault's vast archives, Ash's ability became an integral part of their exploration, a silent guide through the labyrinthine corridors of preserved life.

"This section," Ash stated, his voice hushed with a mixture of reverence and concern, pointing towards a cluster of containment units radiating a subtly fluctuating magnetic signature, "seems to be experiencing some minor energetic degradation. It's not critical, but the ambient field is slightly weaker, less stable than the surrounding areas."

Kira immediately extended her awareness, focusing on the particular sector Ash indicated. She felt it then – a faint discordance, a slight fraying at the edges of the stored life's energetic field. It was too subtle for the Oracle Dog's visions to have detailed, too minute for her direct connection to Silvanus to have flagged as an immediate crisis, but it was undeniably present.

"You're right," she confirmed, her brow furrowed. "There's a faint resonance of... stress. As if the stored life here is struggling against some unseen pressure."

Ash's hands moved across a console, bringing up detailed readouts. "The flux is consistent with a minor atmospheric bleed-through, perhaps from a residual energy conduit that wasn't fully shielded during the Vault's construction. Or, it could be a subtle energetic leakage from one of the older defense systems we encountered on the surface, an echo that's managed to penetrate this deep."

This information was invaluable. It allowed them to identify areas that required immediate attention, potential vulnerabilities that, if left unaddressed, could compromise the precious cargo within. Their mission had expanded from simply retrieving seeds to actively ensuring the long-term viability of the Vault's contents, and Ash's geomagnetic sense was their primary diagnostic tool.

"We'll need to assess the source of that bleed-through," Kira decided, her mind already formulating a plan. "If it's a breach, we need to seal it. If it's a passive leakage, we need to reinforce the shielding in this area. Your ability to pinpoint these subtle anomalies is critical, Ash. It allows us to be proactive, to address problems before they become insurmountable."

Ash nodded, his focus sharpening. "It's like feeling the planet's pulse. Any irregularity, any deviation from its natural rhythm, is immediately apparent. This applies not just to the Vault, but to the outside world as well. If we can learn to read these subtle geomagnetic shifts on a larger scale, we can identify areas of ecological distress, predict environmental crises, and perhaps even locate pockets of remaining, uncorrupted resonance in the ravaged landscapes."

The potential implications were staggering. Beyond their immediate goal of securing the seeds, Ash's ability offered a pathway to understanding and potentially mitigating the ongoing ecological collapse. He could act as an early warning system, a living sensor that could detect the subtle signs of planetary suffering long before they manifested as visible devastation.

"Imagine," Kira said, her voice filled with a growing excitement, "being able to chart the spread of the 'shadow resonance' that the Raiders cultivate, by detecting the subtle magnetic distortions they create. We could track their influence, understand their methods, and develop countermeasures based on their energetic footprint."

"It's not just tracking," Ash added, his gaze intense. "It's about understanding the underlying structure of their influence. They manipulate energy, yes, but they do so by distorting the natural magnetic fields. Their actions leave a signature, a pattern of disruption. If I can perceive that pattern, we can learn how to counteract it, how to re-establish the natural harmony they seek to obliterate."

He then elaborated on the practicalities of their current situation within the Vault, demonstrating how his sense helped them select the most viable specimens for their mission. "Not all seeds are equal in their energetic potential, even within a single species. Some have a stronger, more vibrant geomagnetic resonance, indicating a greater stored vitality. By focusing on those with the strongest signatures, we ensure we are retrieving the most robust and promising candidates for reintroduction."

This was a revelation. It meant their efforts were not just about quantity, but about quality, about selecting the very best of what the planet had to offer, guided by an almost intuitive understanding of life's energetic essence.

"So, you can essentially 'feel' which seeds are the most potent, the most likely to thrive," Kira marveled.

"In a way, yes," Ash confirmed. "It's a subtle resonance, a faint hum that emanates from the most vital genetic material. It's the imprint of the life force itself, amplified by the Vault's own harmonious geomagnetic field. It allows us to bypass the need for complex analysis on every single specimen, saving us precious time and resources."

As they continued their work, carefully selecting and cataloging the most vital seeds, Kira couldn't help but feel a profound sense of gratitude for the diverse strengths that they, and their allies, possessed. While her connection to Silvanus allowed her to grasp the grand, overarching symphony of the planet, Ash's geomagnetic sense provided the intricate, detailed notes, the precise harmonies that allowed them to understand and interact with the world at its most fundamental level. It was a partnership built on complementary perceptions, a fusion of organic intuition and precise energetic attunement, a potent combination against the fractured, discordant forces they faced. The path ahead was still shrouded in uncertainty, but with Ash's unerring sense of direction and their shared commitment to restoring the planet's harmony, they possessed a powerful advantage, a guiding light emanating from the very heart of the Earth itself. Their ability to navigate the unseen, to understand the planet's hidden language, was not just a skill; it was a testament to the very principles they sought to preserve.

The Seed Vault was more than just a repository of genetic memory; it was a testament to foresight, a monument to a desperate, yet hopeful, era. As Kira and Ash delved deeper into the Vault's meticulously organized archives, sifting through data streams that shimmered like captured starlight, they stumbled upon a subsection that sent a ripple of astonishment through them. Encrypted within layers of ancient, yet remarkably preserved, data architecture, they found records detailing a sophisticated initiative known as the 'Guardian Program.' This program, established millennia ago, was far more than a simple security protocol; it was a deliberate, scientific endeavor to breed and train canines, imbuing them with profoundly amplified empathic and sensory abilities. These specially bred animals were intended to serve as vigilant protectors of Earth's most vital ecological resources, including the very Seed Vault they now stood within.

The implication was profound. Resonance, the very phenomenon that connected Kira to Silvanus, that guided Ash through the planet's magnetic currents, was not merely an emergent, natural occurrence. It was, in part, a cultivated trait, a precursor to their own abilities painstakingly engineered by a civilization long past. The data logs described the rigorous selection process, the careful genetic manipulation, and the intensive training regimens designed to enhance the canines' inherent connection to the living world. These 'Guardians,' as they were called, possessed an unparalleled ability to sense ecological imbalances, to detect subtle shifts in planetary health, and to communicate these vital insights through a complex language of empathic resonance and modulated vocalizations.

Ash, his fingers still tracing the cool, luminescent surfaces of the console, brought up visual reconstructions of these ancient Guardians. The holographic projections depicted magnificent canines, their forms subtly different from their modern descendants. Their eyes held a depth of awareness, a knowing that transcended mere instinct. They moved with a grace that spoke of a profound harmony with their environment, their senses tuned to frequencies imperceptible to the uninitiated. The records described how these animals were not simply trained to guard physical locations, but were integrated into the very fabric of ecological monitoring systems, acting as living sensors that could alert human custodians to approaching threats or nascent environmental crises.

Kira felt a surge of awe, tinged with a complex mix of emotions. This was tangible evidence of a deliberate attempt to foster a deeper connection between humanity and the planet, a scientific pursuit that mirrored, in its intent, the very path she and Ash were now forging. The creators of the Guardian Program understood, on a fundamental level, that the planet's survival depended not just on advanced technology, but on a symbiotic relationship with the natural world, a relationship nurtured and guided by heightened sensory perception. They had recognized the inherent power of resonance, or what they termed 'bio-attunement,' and had sought to harness it for the preservation of life.

The logs detailed the genetic lineage of these Guardians, tracing their ancestry back to early domestic dogs that exhibited exceptional intelligence and empathy. Over generations, through selective breeding and what appeared to be sophisticated bio-engineering techniques, their empathic range was expanded, their sensory acuity amplified to an astonishing degree. They could detect the subtle energetic signatures of plant life, gauge the health of ecosystems through shifts in atmospheric composition, and even sense the emotional states of other living beings. This made them ideal sentinels, capable of identifying threats that would elude even the most advanced technological surveillance.

One particularly fascinating data set focused on the 'Resonance Amplification Protocol,' a series of treatments and environmental exposures designed to elevate the canines' natural empathic abilities. This protocol involved exposing the animals to carefully modulated energetic fields, derived from the planet's own natural frequencies, and encouraging interaction with individuals who possessed strong empathic aptitudes, presumably the program's human handlers. It was a symbiotic learning process, where both the canines and their human counterparts honed their abilities through mutual interaction and shared purpose. The records suggested a deep emotional bond formed between the Guardians and their trainers, a profound partnership built on mutual understanding and trust.

The Guardian Program wasn't a singular, isolated effort. The data indicated that it was part of a broader, planet-wide initiative to re-establish and strengthen the Earth's ecological resilience in the face of escalating environmental degradation. This initiative encompassed not only the bio-engineering of specialized animal sentinels but also the development of advanced ecological restoration technologies and the cultivation of individuals with unique sensory gifts, like Kira and Ash. It painted a picture of a civilization that, while facing immense challenges, had not surrendered to despair. Instead, they had looked to the deep past, to the innate abilities of life itself, and had sought to cultivate those abilities as a means of survival.

Kira studied the holographic records, a sense of shared purpose blooming within her. The Guardian Program was a historical precedent for their own mission. They, too, were seeking to re-establish a connection with the planet, to amplify its life-sustaining frequencies, and to protect its most precious genetic legacies. The fact that such a program had existed, and had been so successful in its aims, offered a powerful beacon of hope. It suggested that the path they were on, the path of amplified resonance and bio-attunement, was not a radical departure, but a rediscovery of ancient wisdom and scientific endeavor.

Ash, meanwhile, was cross-referencing the Guardian Program's data with the Vault's internal schematic. "Look at this, Kira," he said, his voice filled with a new kind of understanding. "The primary containment sectors for the most sensitive seed samples, the ones designated as 'Ark Prime,' are directly linked to subterranean networks that were originally established for the Guardian canines. These networks provided them with safe passage, protected environmental corridors, and direct access points to monitor the Vault's internal climate and security systems."

This explained the subtle but persistent geomagnetic signatures Ash had been detecting within the Vault's infrastructure, signatures that seemed to emanate from pathways not explicitly marked on the conventional schematics. These were the echo echoes of the Guardian Program, the hidden arteries of a network designed to ensure the survival of life itself. The canines, with their heightened senses, had navigated these pathways, acting as an organic extension of the Vault's own vigilant systems.

The records also alluded to the potential dangers that the Guardian Program had been designed to combat. These included not only natural environmental shifts and ecological collapse but also, chillingly, the threat of organized exploitation. The data hinted at factions that sought to weaponize ecological instability or to hoard vital genetic resources for their own nefarious purposes. The Guardian Program, therefore, was not just about preservation; it was also about active defense, about ensuring that the planet's legacy remained in safe hands, safeguarded from those who would seek to corrupt or control it.

This raised critical questions about the extent of human intervention in the natural world. Had the creators of the Guardian Program crossed an ethical line by genetically modifying life to serve their purposes? Or had they, in their wisdom, recognized that in the face of existential threat, such interventions were not only justified but necessary? Kira found herself grappling with these ethical dilemmas. Their own mission involved amplifying Silvanus's abilities, a form of intervention, albeit one aimed at restoration rather than control. The Guardian Program offered a historical context for such actions, demonstrating that humanity had, in the past, made difficult choices to ensure its own survival and the survival of the planet.

One of the most intriguing aspects of the Guardian Program was the discovery of specialized 'empathic relays' – devices and environmental modifications designed to amplify and transmit the Guardians' sensory input over vast distances. These relays, subtly integrated into the planet's natural geological formations and energy grids, acted as conduits, allowing the Guardians' observations to be relayed to central command centers, even from the most remote or hazardous locations. It suggested a sophisticated, interconnected system where biological sentinels and advanced technology worked in concert, a true fusion of nature and innovation.

The data also revealed that the Guardian Program had been remarkably successful in its initial phases. The records spoke of instances where Guardians had detected nascent blight outbreaks before they spread, alerted authorities to critical water shortages in arid regions, and even guided rescue missions through treacherous terrains. Their ability to sense the 'life force' of a region, to perceive its energetic health, was instrumental in these early successes. They were, in essence, the planet's early warning system, its first line of defense against the encroaching shadows of ecological decay.

However, the logs also documented the program's eventual decline. The specifics were somewhat fragmented, obscured by layers of encryption and what appeared to be deliberate data degradation, possibly an act of self-preservation by the program's architects. The narrative suggested that as the planet's environmental crisis deepened, and as the forces of exploitation grew more aggressive, the Guardian Program faced immense pressure. Resources dwindled, and the focus shifted towards more immediate, survival-oriented measures. There were mentions of Guardians being deployed in increasingly dangerous situations, their numbers dwindling as they valiantly defended critical ecological zones against encroaching threats.

Kira felt a pang of sorrow for these forgotten guardians. They were unsung heroes, their sacrifice woven into the very fabric of the planet's resilience. Their legacy lived on in the very existence of the Seed Vault and, perhaps, in the nascent abilities of individuals like herself and Ash. The program represented a profound understanding that true preservation required more than just storing genetic material; it required active guardianship, a vigilant presence attuned to the planet's every breath.

The information about the Guardian Program also shed new light on the Resonance Raiders. Their crude, destructive methods of energy extraction and exploitation stood in stark contrast to the harmonious, symbiotic approach embodied by the Guardian Program. The Raiders represented a regression, a descent into a paradigm of control and domination, while the Guardian Program had represented an ascent, a striving for connection and balance. The Raiders' ignorance of or disregard for the principles of resonance highlighted their fundamental misunderstanding of life's true power. They were blind to the subtle energies that governed the planet, deaf to its silent pleas.

Ash, his gaze fixed on the intricate data streams, pointed to a specific section of the records. "This section details 'Project Echo,' a contingency plan that involved relocating the most promising Guardian bloodlines and their associated empathic amplification technology to secure, hidden locations. It seems the program's architects anticipated a scenario where the surface infrastructure would be compromised, necessitating the preservation of their most valuable assets and knowledge."

Kira felt a chill run down her spine. "You're saying the Vault itself might have been a sanctuary for the Guardian Program's lineage? Or at least, that the technology used to create them was also preserved here?"

"It's highly probable," Ash confirmed. "The same principles of bio-attunement and resonance amplification that were central to the Guardian Program are fundamental to the Vault's own operational integrity. The geomagnetic field that guides me, the subtle energetic harmonies that sustain the stored life – these are all manifestations of the same underlying scientific principles that the Guardians embodied."

This revelation further solidified the interconnectedness of their mission. They weren't just retrieving seeds; they were potentially rediscovering and reactivating a lost science, a profound understanding of the planet's energetic language. The Guardian Program was not a closed chapter of history; it was a living legacy, waiting to be awakened and integrated into their ongoing efforts to heal Silvanus.

The discovery of the Guardian Program provided a critical piece of the puzzle. It explained the existence of individuals with amplified empathic and sensory abilities, offering a historical and scientific context for phenomena that had previously seemed almost mythical. It confirmed that resonance was not an anomaly but a cultivated, engineered aspect of life, deliberately nurtured for the purpose of planetary stewardship. This understanding shifted their perspective, transforming their quest from one of singular discovery to one of historical reconnection, of weaving together the threads of past innovation with present necessity. The Seed Vault, in revealing the secrets of the Guardian Program, had not only provided them with the genetic keys to the planet's future but had also illuminated the profound legacy of those who had paved the way, those who had understood that the deepest wisdom lay not in dominating nature, but in attuning to its very soul. The Guardians, canine and human alike, had been the Earth's first, and perhaps most dedicated, stewards, their silent vigil echoing through the ages, a testament to the enduring power of connection and the unwavering hope for a living future. The implications were vast, suggesting that their own abilities were not unique but part of a continuum, a reawakening of dormant potentials that had once been actively cultivated for the planet's survival. The journey ahead, now illuminated by this historical revelation, felt both more daunting and more hopeful, as they realized they were not alone in their pursuit of a resonant future.

The air within the Seed Vault had grown heavier, charged with an unspoken significance that transcended the mere preservation of genetic codes. Kira and Ash, their minds still reeling from the revelations of the Guardian Program, found themselves drawn to a section of the archives that pulsed with an unusual energetic signature, a subtle dissonance that snagged at the edges of their amplified senses. It was here, nestled amongst dormant data crystals and meticulously preserved biological samples, that they discovered it – an artifact unlike anything cataloged within the

Vault's vast inventory.

It wasn't a seed in the conventional sense, nor a data storage device. Instead, it appeared to be a fragment, roughly the size of a human palm, fashioned from a material that defied easy classification. It possessed the crystalline clarity of the finest quartz, yet within its depths, intricate, almost organic patterns swirled and shifted, like nebulae captured in frozen time. The edges were not sharp, but subtly faceted, as if shaped by forces both natural and impossibly precise. It seemed to absorb the ambient light of the Vault, rather than reflect it, radiating a soft, internal luminescence that waxed and waned with an almost imperceptible rhythm. Kira, her empathic senses attuned to the faintest whisper of life, felt a strange kinship with the object, a distant echo of Silvanus's own vital essence.

Ash, ever the analyst, ran a series of preliminary scans. The results were perplexing. "The composition is... unknown," he murmured, his brow furrowed. "It's exhibiting properties that suggest it's not entirely inorganic, nor purely biological. There are molecular structures that seem to rearrange themselves in response to subtle atmospheric changes, and—wait. This is unusual." He tapped a series of commands into his handheld interface, projecting a detailed spectral analysis onto a nearby wall. "It's reacting to us, Kira. Specifically, to the resonance between us."

As if on cue, the artifact responded. The faint, internal light intensified, blooming into a soft, steady glow. The swirling patterns within its crystalline matrix coalesced, forming ephemeral, geometric shapes that pulsed in time with Kira's own heartbeat. It was as if the fragment were a tuning fork, struck by the very frequency of their intertwined minds.

Kira reached out, her fingers hovering inches above the artifact. She could feel its energy signature, a complex tapestry of interwoven frequencies that resonated deeply with her own amplified senses. It felt ancient, not in the way of decaying relics, but in the manner of enduring natural forces, like the slow growth of mountains or the ceaseless turning of celestial bodies. "It's... alive," she whispered, the realization dawning on her with a profound sense of wonder. "Or at least, it's attuned to life in a way I've never encountered before."

Ash nodded, his own fascination evident. "The data suggests it's designed to interact with specific environmental markers and empathic signatures. The Guardian Program files mentioned something similar, though their purpose was primarily surveillance and communication. This... this feels different. More foundational."

He brought up a subsection of the Guardian Program's operational logs that detailed their research into 'bio-resonant catalysts' – substances engineered to amplify and stabilize the planet's life-sustaining frequencies. "Could this be one of those catalysts?"

The fragment pulsed again, a brighter, more insistent throb of light. It was a silent question, an invitation. Kira instinctively knew that their connection, the unique resonance that bound her and Ash together, was the key. It wasn't just about their individual abilities; it was about the synergy, the emergent property of their shared existence. The Guardian Program had sought to cultivate bio-attunement in canines, and by extension, their human partners. But this artifact seemed to represent a more direct, potent application of that principle.

"It's reacting to the *quality* of our bond, Ash," Kira explained, her voice filled with a newfound clarity. "Not just that we're resonating, but *how* we're resonating. It's like it's measuring the harmony, the mutual understanding." She closed her eyes, focusing on the intricate dance of energies that flowed between her and Ash, the shared awareness, the unspoken trust. She felt the subtle push and pull of their empathic connection, the way their individual strengths complemented each other, creating a unified field of perception.

As she focused, the artifact's glow intensified further, the internal patterns swirling with an almost frenetic energy. It seemed to be absorbing and amplifying the essence of their bond, transforming it into something tangible, something that could potentially interact with the wider environment. The data streams on Ash's interface flickered, displaying new readings that spoke of localized energy field fluctuations, minute shifts in the ambient resonance of the Vault itself.

"It's drawing on our connection," Ash confirmed, his voice tinged with awe. "The energy expenditure is minimal, almost negligible, which means it's incredibly efficient. It's not just channeling our resonance; it's amplifying it, refining it. Think of it as a conduit, but one that also refines the signal."

The implications were staggering. If this 'Catalyst Fragment,' as Kira mentally labeled it, could amplify their empathic bond, and if that bond was indeed tied to ecological vitality, then it held the potential to be a powerful tool for regeneration. The Guardian Program had aimed to monitor and protect; this fragment, however, seemed designed to actively participate, to initiate.

"The Guardian logs mentioned 'initiation protocols'," Kira recalled, her mind racing through the vast amount of data they had absorbed. "They spoke of specific frequencies and energy signatures that could stimulate dormant ecological systems. They believed that the planet's own life-force was encoded within its natural resonance, and that certain catalysts could 'awaken' that code."

Ash's eyes widened. "And our resonance, amplified by this fragment, could be that awakening signal. But we need more than just our own bond. The fragment is also reacting to environmental markers. What markers are present here, within the Vault?"

They looked around the cavernous space, its walls lined with the silent promise of life. The Vault was more than just a repository; it was a carefully controlled ecosystem, a microcosm of Earth's biodiversity. The air was meticulously filtered, the temperature and humidity regulated to optimal levels for the preservation of the genetic samples. But beneath the artificial environment, Kira could sense the faint, persistent hum of the planet's deep energies, the very frequencies that Ash navigated.

"It's responding to the preserved genetic material," Kira realized. "To the latent life force within the seeds themselves. The fragment isn't just amplifying our bond; it's using our bond as a bridge to interact with the potential life held within this place."

The artifact pulsed again, a slow, deliberate beat that seemed to synchronize with the collective life force of the Vault. The internal patterns shifted, now resembling the intricate branching of roots or the delicate unfolding of petals. It was a visual metaphor, a promise of what could be.

"We need to understand the specific environmental markers it's keyed to," Ash stated, his focus sharpening. "The Guardian data was extensive, detailing geological resonance points, atmospheric compositions necessary for certain bio-activations, even the subtle energetic signatures of specific plant species." He began to cross-reference the fragment's energetic fluctuations with the Vault's own environmental monitoring data, searching for correlations. "The fragment is emitting a complex waveform, a kind of 'key.' We need to find the 'lock' it's meant to open."

Kira, meanwhile, felt an intuitive nudge, a gentle pull towards a specific section of the Vault, a cluster of containment units holding seeds from what were once the planet's most vibrant and diverse biomes. It was a silent prompting, a whisper from the fragment itself, guiding her perception. "It's there, Ash," she said, pointing towards the cluster. "That section... it feels more potent. The resonance is stronger."

Ash directed his scanners towards the indicated area. "You're right. The energy readings are significantly higher. It's not just the density of the genetic material; it's something else. The ambient resonance in that sector is also subtly different, almost as if it's been... prepared."

They moved towards the cluster, the Catalyst Fragment held carefully between them. As they approached, its glow brightened, its internal patterns becoming more defined, more intricate. It was as if the fragment recognized the proximity of its intended target. The air around them seemed to shimmer, charged with latent energy.

"The Guardians believed that specific environments could be 'primed' to receive and amplify resonant frequencies," Ash mused, his gaze sweeping over the containment units. "They used geological formations, natural energy conduits, even specific plant life to create sympathetic resonance fields. It's possible that these particular containment units were designed with similar principles in mind, to create an ideal reception environment for a catalyst like this."

Kira gently placed the fragment onto the surface of a containment unit. The moment it made contact, a cascade of light erupted from within the artifact. It flowed outwards, not as a blinding flash, but as a gentle, pervasive luminescence that enveloped the containment unit and spread outwards, like ripples on a pond. The familiar hum of the Vault's systems seemed to deepen, taking on a richer, more vibrant tone.

On Ash's interface, a torrent of new data flooded in. The spectral analysis of the fragment was now overlaid with an intricate map of the Vault's internal energy grid, highlighting specific nodes and conduits. "It's mapping the resonance pathways!" Ash exclaimed. "It's showing us how our amplified bond, channeled through this fragment, can interact with the Vault's infrastructure. It's not just about us; it's about integrating our resonance into the larger energetic network of this place."

The containment unit beneath the fragment began to emit a soft, internal light of its own. The preserved seeds within, dormant for millennia, seemed to stir. Kira could feel it, a faint, nascent pulse of life awakening from its slumber. It was as if the fragment had whispered a forgotten lullaby, coaxing the potential life back into existence.

"The key," Kira breathed, understanding dawning in her eyes, "isn't just our bond with each other. It's our bond with

this. With the dormant life, with the planet's own energetic matrix. The fragment is the bridge, and our resonance is the current."

The process was slow, deliberate. The fragment pulsed with a steady, unwavering rhythm, its light a beacon in the hushed silence of the Vault. The energy flowing through it was subtle but profound, a gentle awakening rather than a forceful imposition. Kira felt a growing sense of responsibility, of being a conduit for something far greater than herself. The Guardian Program had been a meticulous, scientific endeavor. This felt more... elemental, more deeply connected to the very essence of life.

Ash, his face illuminated by the soft glow of the artifact and his interface, was piecing together the puzzle. "The data suggests that the fragment is designed to identify and interact with specific bio-energetic signatures. It's like a universal key, capable of unlocking the latent potential within a wide range of organic matter. But its activation sequence requires a specific harmonic resonance – a blend of empathic connection and environmental attunement. We're providing the empathic component, and the Vault's carefully curated environment is providing the attunement."

He tapped a finger against a particularly complex waveform displayed on his screen. "This particular signature, for instance, is associated with the ancient rainforest biomes. It's a signature of complex symbiosis, of dense, interconnected life. The fragment is amplifying our resonance to match it, and then using that amplified resonance to gently stimulate the seeds."

Kira felt a wave of exultation wash over her. This was it. This was the tangible evidence, the missing link they had been searching for. The Guardian Program had laid the groundwork, had understood the principles of bio-attunement. But this fragment, this 'Catalyst Fragment,' was the tool that could bring those principles to life, that could initiate the process of regeneration on a scale they had only dreamed of.

"We need to replicate this," Kira said, her voice firm. "We need to understand how to harness this energy, how to replicate the conditions that allow the fragment to function. Silvanus needs this."

Ash nodded, his gaze still fixed on the cascading data. "The challenge will be replicating the precise environmental conditions and the specific harmonic resonance required for different types of genetic material. Each seed, each ecosystem, will have its own unique signature, its own key. This fragment is a universal key, but it still requires the right tumblers to turn."

He looked at Kira, a shared understanding passing between them. Their journey had just become infinitely more complex, and infinitely more hopeful. The Seed Vault, once a silent testament to a lost past, was now a crucible of future possibility. And at its heart lay this humble, crystalline shard, pulsing with the very energy of life, waiting for them to unlock its secrets. The path ahead would require not only their amplified resonance but also a deep communion with the planet itself, a willingness to learn its ancient language, and to become the conduits through which its future could be reborn. The Guardian Program had sought to preserve life; they, armed with the Catalyst Fragment, were poised to help it thrive once more. The weight of that responsibility settled upon them, not as a burden, but as a profound, exhilarating purpose. The silent guardians of the past had passed the torch, and the promise of a living future flickered within the heart of the crystalline shard.

The quiet hum of the Seed Vault, once a sanctuary of serene preservation, had begun to thrum with a new kind of energy, one that wasn't entirely born of the burgeoning life within its carefully controlled chambers. News, like seeds carried on an unseen wind, had begun to drift beyond the Oasis's verdant embrace. Whispers, initially tentative, then bolder, spoke of Kira and her unprecedented abilities, of the strange artifact she and Ash had unearthed, an artifact that seemed to resonate with the very pulse of the planet. The amplified senses that Kira now possessed, a direct consequence of her deep connection with Silvanus and the amplified bio-resonant catalysts within the Vault, allowed her to feel these tremors of awareness emanating from other scattered settlements. It wasn't just about her personal journey of discovery anymore; it was about the potential implications of that discovery for a fractured and struggling world.

These nascent stirrings of external interest were not uniformly benevolent. While some communities, those clinging precariously to existence on the fringes of once-fertile lands, saw in Kira's burgeoning abilities a glimmer of hope, a potential beacon to guide them through the encroaching desolation, others reacted with a more primal, territorial instinct. Envy, sharp and insidious, began to coil in the hearts of those who had long hoarded their own meager resources, their own limited knowledge. Suspicion, a constant companion in the post-Collapse era, festered into outright distrust. Why should one individual, an outsider from the sheltered enclave of the Oasis, be privy to such potent power, such potentially world-altering knowledge? The artifact, a mere fragment, a catalyst, had inadvertently become a focal point for long-simmering resentments and nascent ambitions.

From the arid plains where the Scavenger Clans eked out a brutal existence, the news arrived as a jolt, a disruption to their hard-won, often violent, equilibrium. Their scouts, individuals hardened by a life of constant struggle and an intimate knowledge of the desolate landscape, had observed the unusual energy signatures emanating from the Oasis. These weren't the subtle shifts of weather patterns or the predictable ebb and flow of scavenged resources; these were anomalies that spoke of something far more significant, something that could upset the precarious balance of power. Chief Kaelen, a man whose face was a roadmap of scars and weathered resilience, listened intently to the reports filtering back from his most trusted scouts. He saw not hope, but opportunity. If this Kira possessed the ability to harness such power, perhaps that power could be... redirected. The Scavenger Clans, born from the ashes of a fallen civilization, understood the language of dominance and control better than any other. The idea that a single community, even one as well-defended as the Oasis, might hold a key to widespread regeneration, a key that could potentially transform barren lands into fertile havens, ignited a dangerous spark of avarice within Kaelen and his inner circle. They began to scrutinize their own survival strategies, their own meticulously gathered intel on other settlements, and a new, unsettling plan began to form in the desert winds.

Further south, nestled within the skeletal remains of a once-thriving agricultural hub, the agrarian collectives of the Verdant Crescent also absorbed the fragmented accounts of the Oasis's newfound significance. Unlike the Scavenger Clans, their primary concern wasn't conquest, but cultivation. They understood the fragility of life, the constant battle against blight and drought. The notion that Kira's discoveries could lead to a renaissance of agriculture, to the possibility of truly abundant harvests, was a tantalizing prospect. Elder Maeve, the matriarch of the largest collective, a woman whose hands bore the indelible marks of generations of tilling the soil, saw the potential for cooperation, for a shared bounty. She dispatched emissaries, not with weapons, but with carefully selected samples of their most resilient crops, with offerings of shared knowledge and labor. However, even within the Verdant Crescent, the news was not received with universal enthusiasm. Some younger farmers, disillusioned by the slow pace of their own hard-won progress and frustrated by the constant threat of crop failure, chafed at Elder Maeve's more measured approach. They saw Kira's potential discovery as a shortcut, a way to leapfrog decades of struggle. This faction, led by a fiery orator named Jian, began to question the traditional ways, whispering that perhaps the Verdant Crescent should take what they needed, rather than politely asking. They envisioned a future where their collectives, empowered by the Oasis's secret, would dominate the regional food supply, leaving no room for negotiation or sharing. The seeds of discontent were being sown, not just in the earth, but in the minds of men.

And then there were the technocratic enclaves, scattered pockets of survivors who clung to the remnants of pre-Collapse technology and scientific knowledge. These were often insular communities, their inhabitants driven by a fervent belief in the supremacy of logic and engineered solutions. The news of Kira's discoveries, particularly the artifact's strange properties and its apparent connection to bio-resonance, was met with intense scientific scrutiny and a palpable sense of proprietary interest. Dr. Aris Thorne, a leading figure within the Enclave of Lumina, a settlement known for its advanced energy systems and its obsession with data, saw Kira's work as a confirmation of their own theoretical models. He dispatched discreet reconnaissance drones, not to assess military threats, but to gather precise environmental and energy readings from the Oasis. Thorne and his colleagues were not interested in the spiritual or empathic aspects of Kira's connection; they were focused on quantifiable data, on understanding the underlying mechanisms that could be replicated and controlled. They viewed the artifact not as a catalyst for life, but as a complex piece of bio-engineered technology, one that rightfully belonged in the hands of those who possessed the intellectual rigor to truly understand and exploit its potential. The thought of this power being wielded by an individual, or even a community that didn't adhere to their stringent scientific principles, was anathema to them. They began to consider how to secure the artifact, through diplomacy, if possible, but through more... decisive means if necessary.

Kira, ensconced within the relative safety of the Seed Vault, began to feel the subtle, but insistent, pressure of this external scrutiny. Her amplified senses, once a tool for understanding the delicate balance of life within the Vault, now registered the cacophony of a world awakening to her existence. She could sense the envy, the fear, the ambition swirling beyond the Vault's protective walls. Ash, ever vigilant, noticed the shift in her demeanor.

"You're sensing it too, aren't you?" he asked one cycle, his voice low as they meticulously cataloged another batch of viable seeds, their work a constant counterpoint to the growing external noise.

Kira nodded, her gaze distant as she focused on the faint signals. "It's like a hundred different voices all speaking at once, all wanting something from what we're doing here. Some are desperate, some are curious, but... many are hungry for control."

"The Scavengers," Ash mused, his brow furrowed. "Their energy signatures are aggressive, territorial. They see this as a prize to be taken."

"And the Verdant Crescent," Kira added, a note of sadness in her voice. "Maeve's people are seeking partnership, but Jian's faction... they're calculating. They see this as a way to gain dominance. It's not about shared survival for them; it's about ultimate control of the harvest."

"The Enclaves are the most insidious, in their own way," Ash continued, his fingers flying across his data pad, cross-referencing energy signatures with known settlement locations. "Thorne's group from Lumina... their interest is purely scientific, but their definition of 'scientific control' is anything but benevolent. They want to dissect this, understand it, replicate it, and then hoard it. They believe only they are worthy of wielding such knowledge."

The implications of these emerging factions and their competing agendas were far more complex and dangerous than Kira and Ash had initially anticipated. Their quest, which began as a desperate search for a means to revitalize the dying planet, was rapidly evolving into a delicate dance of diplomacy, deception, and potential conflict. The Seed Vault, once a sanctuary of hope, was becoming a focal point for the world's fractured desires. The artifact, the Catalyst Fragment, had not just awakened dormant life within the Vault; it had awakened dormant ambitions and rivalries across the ravaged continents.

Kira found herself increasingly torn. The ethical imperative to share the knowledge and resources they were uncovering warred with the pragmatic necessity of protecting their work, and themselves, from those who would exploit it. The Guardian Program, they knew, had operated with a similar mandate of preservation and careful dissemination, but the world they inhabited was far more desperate, far more volatile. Trust was a currency as rare as clean water.

"We can't just hoard this," Kira said, her voice filled with a quiet intensity. "The planet is dying. If this fragment, if our understanding of bio-resonance, can truly bring life back, then it's a betrayal not to share it."

"But how do we share it responsibly?" Ash countered, his gaze meeting hers, the weight of their predicament settling between them. "We give it to the Scavengers, and they'll use it to fuel their raids and expand their territory. We give it to Jian's faction in the Verdant Crescent, and they'll hoard the bounty, leaving others to starve. We give it to Thorne's Enclave, and it will become a tool of control, a weapon of technological supremacy. Each path leads to a different kind of disaster."

The external pressures began to manifest in more direct ways. Small, almost imperceptible shifts in the Vault's external sensor readings indicated increased surveillance. Drones, far more sophisticated than anything the Oasis had previously encountered, were occasionally detected on the periphery of their defensive perimeter, their signals masked to avoid immediate detection. The Scavenger Clans, ever resourceful, began to make bolder incursions into territories closer to the Oasis, probing their defenses, gathering intelligence not just on their food stores, but on the unusual energy readings that had become increasingly noticeable since the artifact's activation.

One evening, as Kira meditated within the Vault, her amplified senses extended outwards, she felt a distinct, hostile probing. It wasn't the scattered curiosity of distant settlements, but a focused, deliberate attempt to breach their awareness, to glean the secrets they held. The signature was cold, calculating, and undeniably technological. Thorne's Enclave. They were no longer content with passive observation.

Simultaneously, a delegation from the Verdant Crescent arrived, not the emissaries of Elder Maeve, but a younger, more assertive group led by Jian himself. They presented themselves with smiles and polite words, but their eyes held a hard, acquisitive glint. They spoke of mutual benefit, of a unified front against the harsh realities of the world, but their underlying message was clear: the Oasis's discoveries should be integrated into the Verdant Crescent's network, for the good of all, of course, but primarily for the good of those who understood true agricultural stewardship. They spoke of shared resources, but their proposed division of labor clearly placed the Oasis in a subservient role, its unique knowledge merely a component within their grander design.

Kira and Ash were forced to navigate a treacherous landscape of competing interests, each faction believing they had the right, even the obligation, to claim the burgeoning power that Kira represented. The artifact's potential was a double-edged sword, promising salvation to some, but threatening the precarious existence of others, and igniting a dangerous ambition in yet more. The conflict brewing was not yet one of open warfare, but of insidious influence, of competing ideologies vying for control of a future that was still being born, a future inextricably linked to the quiet hum of the Seed Vault and the pulsing heart of the Catalyst Fragment.

The question of who would control this burgeoning power, and for what purpose, had become the most critical, and dangerous, question facing them. The delicate balance of their work was threatened not by the dying world outside, but by the world's grasping hands reaching in.

CHAPTER 9

The journey back to Haven was intended to be a brief respite, a moment to consolidate their findings and process the overwhelming influx of external awareness that Kira had been experiencing. The quiet hum of the Seed Vault had, by necessity, become their temporary haven, but the encroaching shadows of the world outside were already beginning to stretch towards its carefully guarded walls. Ash, ever practical, insisted on taking a more circuitous route, avoiding the more obvious pathways that might have been under observation by the various factions now stirring in response to the news from the Oasis. Kira, her senses still attuned to the subtle energy currents of the planet, agreed, the unsettling whispers of distant ambitions echoing in her mind.

They moved through the twilight landscape, the skeletal remains of pre-Collapse cities jutting like broken teeth against the bruised horizon. The air, dry and still, carried the scent of dust and decay, a stark contrast to the vibrant, if contained, life within the Vault. Kira walked beside Ash, her hand occasionally brushing his, a silent reassurance in their shared purpose. The artifact, the Catalyst Fragment, was securely stowed in a specially shielded case, its presence a constant, low thrumming against Kira's amplified senses, a reminder of the immense power – and responsibility – they now carried.

It was as they skirted the jagged scar of an ancient highway, its asphalt long cracked and reclaimed by resilient desert flora, that the first sign of trouble manifested. A subtle distortion in the environmental readings, a flicker in the ambient energy field that Kira's senses immediately flagged as unnatural. It wasn't the chaotic surge of a natural phenomenon, nor the directed but familiar signatures of the factions they were aware of. This was something different, something honed and deliberately concealed.

"Hold up," Ash said, his voice a low growl as he scanned their surroundings. His cybernetic enhancements, usually subtle, now pulsed with a faint, internal luminescence as they processed the anomaly. "Something's not right. Readings are... off. Like a blind spot in the data."

Kira closed her eyes, extending her awareness further. The distortion resolved into a more defined presence – a group of individuals, moving with a practiced stealth that spoke of extensive training. Their energy signatures were tightly controlled, almost suppressed, as if they were actively fighting against their natural resonance, or had learned to shield it with artificial means. This was not the raw ambition of the Scavengers, nor the calculated self-interest of the Verdant Crescent, nor the sterile logic of the Enclaves. This was something else entirely.

"They're here," Kira breathed, her gaze sweeping across the desolate landscape. "A lot of them. And they're good at hiding."

Before Ash could respond, the silence of the desert was shattered by the crackle of energy weapons. Not the crude, sputtering fire of scavenged tech, but the sharp, precise discharge of advanced weaponry. A concentrated beam of energy lanced out from a cluster of rocky outcrops, striking the ground mere meters from where they stood, kicking up a plume of dust.

"Down!" Ash yelled, shoving Kira behind a weathered concrete barrier. He drew his own sidearm, a relic of the Oasis's defensive arsenal, its casing etched with familiar patterns of protection.

More energy bolts converged on their position. Kira, despite the danger, found her senses drawn to the attackers. They moved with an unnerving coordination, flanking their position with fluid, practiced movements. Their equipment was sleek, utilitarian, and bore no markings that Kira recognized. They were professionals, and their intent was unequivocally hostile.

"Who are they?" Ash grunted, returning fire with precise shots aimed at the energy signatures he could detect.

"I don't know," Kira replied, her voice tight with a mixture of fear and focused observation. "Their resonance... it's suppressed, but there's a core of something... cold. Ruthless. They're not like the others. They see resonance... not as a gift, or a tool, but as a resource to be controlled. To be weaponized."

A figure emerged from the dust and chaos, walking with an unnerving calm amidst the barrage of energy fire. They were clad in dark, form-fitting armor that seemed to absorb the ambient light, making them difficult to pinpoint. Their helmet, a featureless visor, obscured their face, but Kira could sense the sheer force of their will, a palpable aura of dominance that radiated outwards. This was the leader, the one who orchestrated this assault.

"The Shadow Syndicate," Kira whispered, the name surfacing from a deep well of instinct, a premonition of a force that operated in the unseen corners of their fractured world.

The leader raised a hand, and the attack momentarily ceased, replaced by an unnerving silence. Then, a voice, amplified and distorted, echoed across the barren landscape. "Kira of the Oasis. Ash of the Oasis. We have been observing your... nascent development. Your burgeoning connection to the planetary resonance is... inconvenient."

Kira felt a chill run down her spine. "Inconvenient for whom?"

"For those who understand true order," the distorted voice replied. "For those who believe such power should not be left to chance, to random discovery. Resonance is a tool, and like all tools, it must be controlled, refined, and wielded with purpose. We are the Shadow Syndicate. We are the custodians of that purpose."

"Custodians?" Ash scoffed, his grip tightening on his weapon. "You mean monopolizes. You want to hoard it, just like everyone else."

"A crude assessment," the leader responded, their tone devoid of emotion. "We do not hoard. We refine. We direct. We ensure that resonance serves the interests of a stable, controlled future. Your uncontrolled influence, your unpredictable abilities, threaten that stability. You are an anomaly that must be corrected."

Kira's mind raced. This Syndicate, with their advanced technology and chilling ideology, were a new and terrifying threat. They weren't driven by the desperate need for survival that motivated the Scavengers, or the communal aspirations of the Verdant Crescent, or even the intellectual curiosity of the Enclaves. Their ambition was far more absolute: to dominate the very essence of resonance, to bend it to their will and reshape the world according to their singular vision.

"You want to capture us," Kira stated, the realization hitting her with the force of a physical blow. "You want the artifact. And you want to control anyone who can connect with resonance."

"Precisely," the leader confirmed. "Your bond, Kira and Ash, is particularly... potent. A rare coupling of natural resonance and catalyzed amplification. Such a confluence of power cannot be allowed to proliferate unchecked. It must be studied, understood, and ultimately, contained within the Syndicate's structure."

"You speak of containment, but your actions speak of elimination," Ash countered, his voice a low rumble. "You're here to kill us and take what you want."

"A necessary removal of potential threats," the leader conceded, as if discussing pest control. "Or, perhaps, an opportunity for your integration into our ranks. Surrender, and you might find a place within our carefully managed ecosystem. Resist, and you will be... eradicated."

The Syndicate operatives began to advance, their movements precise and synchronized. Kira could feel the collective intent of the group, a unified surge of controlled power, directed solely at her and Ash. She felt a surge of primal fear, but it was quickly followed by a steely resolve. They had encountered many threats, but this felt different. This was a direct assault on the very possibility of natural, widespread resonance.

"We're not going with you," Kira said, her voice clear and unwavering. She felt the artifact's energy thrumming against her, a sympathetic vibration that seemed to bolster her resolve. It was more than just a tool; it was a part of Silvanus, a part of the planet's living essence, and it would not be subjected to the Syndicate's cold calculus.

"A regrettable decision," the leader stated, and with that, the coordinated assault resumed, more intense than before. Energy bolts screamed through the air, forcing Kira and Ash to constantly seek cover. Ash moved with practiced efficiency, his movements economical and precise, drawing the Syndicate's fire while Kira focused on sensing their movements, identifying weaknesses, and trying to understand the nature of their suppressed resonance.

She realized that their suppression was not absolute. Beneath the artificial dampening, there were faint flickers, echoes of natural resonance that were being forcibly channeled and amplified by their technology. It was like a wild river being forced through a series of meticulously engineered dams and conduits, its natural flow distorted and directed.

"Ash," Kira said urgently, ducking behind a jagged piece of debris. "Their technology... it's not just suppressing resonance; it's actively manipulating it. They're using it, not fighting it."

Ash grunted in acknowledgement, narrowly avoiding a concentrated burst of energy. "So, they're not just about control, they're about weaponization. That's... a whole new level of fucked up."

Kira focused her amplified senses on the leader, the one projecting the amplified voice. The suppression was strongest around them, but beneath it, a powerful, raw resonance pulsed – a resonant signature that was not only amplified but twisted, amplified in a way that suggested immense destructive potential. It was a symphony of controlled power, played with ruthless precision, and its melody was one of dominance.

She could sense the underlying energy conduits within their armor, small but potent devices that were likely responsible for both suppressing their natural resonance and channeling external energy, perhaps even the ambient planetary resonance, to fuel their weapons and enhance their capabilities. They were like living conduits, their bodies augmented and controlled by their technology.

"They're all connected," Kira realized aloud. "Their tech... it's a network. And the leader... their signature is the nexus. If we can disrupt that..."

"Easier said than done," Ash said, firing a precise shot that struck one of the operatives in the shoulder, causing them to stagger and momentarily break formation. "They're well-protected."

The Syndicate operatives, realizing Kira and Ash were not easily subdued, began to press their advantage. They fanned out, attempting to surround them, their movements fluid and coordinated. Kira felt a growing sense of desperation. They were outnumbered, outgunned, and facing an enemy whose capabilities they were only beginning to comprehend.

Suddenly, a sharp, high-pitched whine filled the air, distinct from the energy weapons. It was a sonic disruption, precisely targeted at the Syndicate operatives. The effect was immediate. The operatives faltered, their movements becoming jerky, their focus disrupted. The artificial suppression of their resonance wavered, and for a brief, chaotic moment, Kira could feel the raw, untamed resonance struggling to break free.

"What was that?" Ash asked, seizing the moment of confusion. He fired a burst of shots, incapacitating two more operatives.

Kira scanned the periphery, her senses stretching to their limit. She saw it then – a small, agile drone, no larger than a hawk, darting away from the engagement, its energy signature a faint, almost imperceptible whisper. It was too small, too precise to be one of the Enclaves' reconnaissance units.

"Someone's helping us," Kira breathed, relief washing over her. "But I don't know who."

The drone's intervention, however brief, had bought them precious seconds. The Syndicate leader, angered by the disruption, let out a roar of synthesized frustration. "Interference will not be tolerated! Secure the targets!"

The operatives, momentarily disoriented, regrouped with chilling efficiency. Their focus, however, had shifted. They were no longer simply trying to subdue Kira and Ash; they were now trying to locate and neutralize the source of the sonic disruption. This created a new opportunity.

"We need to move," Ash said, pulling Kira to her feet. "Now."

They broke from cover, sprinting across the open ground, heading towards a maze of collapsed structures that offered more potential concealment. The Syndicate was momentarily divided, some still trying to engage them, while others pursued the elusive drone.

As they scrambled over rubble, Kira felt a new wave of energy wash over her, distinct from the artifact's resonance and the Syndicate's manipulated power. It was a clean, focused energy, carrying with it a sense of focused intent. It felt like... communication.

"They're trying to guide us," Kira realized. "The drone... it's leading us somewhere."

She saw a faint trail of energy residue, visible only to her amplified senses, marking a path through the ruins. It was a subtle breadcrumb trail, leading them away from the main engagement and towards a more secure location.

They ran, the sounds of battle fading behind them as they plunged deeper into the labyrinthine wreckage. The Syndicate, now aware of the external intervention, was less focused on their primary targets, their attention diverted by the new, unknown element introduced into the conflict.

Finally, they reached a seemingly impassable wall of collapsed concrete and twisted rebar. Kira felt a distinct surge of energy emanating from a small, concealed opening in the debris.

"Here," she said, gesturing towards the narrow crevice. "This is it."

Ash nodded, his eyes scanning their surroundings for any sign of pursuit. "Let's hope whoever sent that drone has our best interests at heart."

They squeezed through the opening, emerging into a dimly lit, subterranean chamber. The air here was cooler, carrying a faint scent of ozone and something else... something clean and vital, like freshly cultivated soil. As their eyes adjusted, they saw it – a figure standing in the center of the chamber, silhouetted against the soft glow of advanced, unfamiliar technology. The figure was cloaked, their face obscured, but the aura of focused intelligence and controlled power was unmistakable. It was the source of the drone and the sonic disruption.

"Welcome," a voice said, smooth and measured, devoid of the synthesized distortion of the Syndicate leader. "I have been expecting you."

Kira and Ash exchanged a look, a mixture of wariness and burgeoning hope. They had escaped the Shadow Syndicate, but they had stumbled into the path of another, unknown force. The journey to understanding and controlling resonance, it seemed, was just beginning, and the shadows of the world were far deeper and more complex than they had ever imagined. The Shadow Syndicate had introduced them to a new, formidable enemy, one that operated in the unseen currents of power, and their encounter had only confirmed the Syndicate's dangerous agenda. The quiet hum of the Seed Vault now seemed a distant memory, replaced by the chilling echoes of a world awakening to the potent, and often perilous, allure of resonance.

The sudden, brutal efficiency of the Shadow Syndicate's assault had thrown Kira and Ash onto the defensive, forcing them to rely on instinct and the nascent, unrefined abilities that pulsed within them. As the energy bolts screamed closer, peppering the jagged rocks that provided their meager cover, Ash felt a primal surge rise within him. It wasn't just the fear of being captured or eradicated; it was a fierce, protective instinct for Kira, for the fragile hope they carried. The Syndicate's cold, calculated approach to resonance, their desire to sterilize and control something so fundamental to life, ignited a visceral anger in him.

He saw them advancing, their movements fluid, almost choreographed, a testament to their rigorous training and the Unity of their purpose. They moved like a single, terrifying organism, their suppressed resonance a chilling testament to their mastery of control. But control, Ash realized, was a double-edged sword. It required immense discipline, an absolute suppression of the natural chaos that defined so much of existence. And where there was suppression, there was potential for disruption.

Without conscious thought, a desperate idea bloomed in Ash's mind. He remembered the disorientation he'd felt in the Oasis during moments of intense emotional flux, the way certain frequencies could rattle his own enhanced senses. If he could amplify that, weaponize it...

He focused, not on the external world, but on the internal landscape of his own being. He reached for the raw, untamed energy that pulsed through him, the latent resonance that he had, until recently, barely acknowledged. It felt like grasping at raw lightning, a terrifying and exhilarating sensation. He channeled his fear, his anger, his desperate need to protect Kira into a single, focused intent: overload.

He visualized a storm, a cacophony of sensations, a tidal wave of pure, unfiltered input crashing against the carefully constructed shields of the Syndicate operatives. He pushed, harder than he ever had before, pouring every ounce of his will into this nascent ability. A silent scream erupted from within him, a desperate plea for escape.

The effect was almost instantaneous, and utterly devastating. The air around the Syndicate agents seemed to shimmer, not with heat, but with an intense, vibrating pressure. A guttural chorus of choked gasps and cries ripped through the battlefield, a stark contrast to their earlier, unnerving silence. For a moment, the precise, coordinated movements dissolved into a chaotic thrashing.

Kira, her own senses already hyper-attuned, felt the abrupt shift as if she had been physically struck. The carefully controlled energy signatures of the attackers fractured, flaring erratically, like overloaded circuits. She could feel the raw, untamed resonance within them, previously masked by sophisticated dampeners, now struggling to break free, amplified by Ash's disruptive projection. It was a chaotic symphony of sound – a piercing, high-frequency shriek that clawed at the auditory senses, a cloying, metallic tang that assaulted the olfactory, and a wave of visceral fear and confusion that slammed into their minds like a physical blow.

One operative stumbled, their weapon firing wildly, its beam harmlessly searing the rock face above them. Another clutched their head, their helmet ringing with a sharp, metallic clang as if struck by an invisible hammer. A third simply collapsed to their knees, their body writhing as if caught in an invisible vice. The carefully cultivated discipline of the Shadow Syndicate had been shattered by a weapon they couldn't have anticipated: the unleashed, unrefined power of raw sensory overload.

Ash felt a searing pain lance through his temples, his vision blurring at the edges. The sheer effort of projecting such a concentrated burst of disorienting energy had taken a brutal toll. His own enhanced senses, usually a source of precise data, were now swimming in a chaotic sea of residual feedback. But through the haze, he saw their chance.

"Kira! Now!" he gasped, his voice raspy and strained. He grabbed her hand, the contact grounding him amidst the sensory maelstrom.

The Syndicate operatives were still reeling, their internal defenses compromised. Their sophisticated systems, designed to regulate and control resonance, were utterly unprepared for this raw, unbridled assault on their sensory inputs. It was like throwing a sandstorm into a perfectly calibrated laboratory.

They broke cover, a desperate dash for survival. The desolate landscape, moments before a kill zone, now offered a sliver of hope. They ran towards the maze of collapsed structures, the promise of concealment a beacon in the chaos. Behind them, the cries of disorientation slowly began to subside, replaced by a growing murmur of anger and renewed focus. The Syndicate, though temporarily crippled, was not defeated.

Kira, her own senses still reeling from the impact of Ash's defensive outburst, felt a surge of both terror and awe. Ash had done that. He had unleashed a weapon she hadn't known he possessed, a raw application of resonance that was as devastating as it was uncontrollable. It was a testament to their deepening bond, a shared defiance that manifested in this unexpected, potent display. But the cost was evident in his pained expression, the tremor in his hand.

"Ash, are you alright?" she asked, her voice laced with concern as they scrambled over a mound of rubble.

He grunted, his jaw tight. "Just... a bit overloaded. Like my brain's trying to digest a supernova. But we're alive." He glanced back, his enhanced vision cutting through the dust. The Syndicate agents were beginning to recover, their movements still somewhat sluggish, but their intent remained clear: termination.

"They're regrouping," Kira observed, her own senses picking up the subtle shift in their energy signatures. The disorienting wave had faded, but the disruption had clearly left a mark. They were more cautious now, their focus shifting not just on capturing them, but on understanding the source of that sonic assault.

"Good. That means they're distracted," Ash said, his voice gaining a hint of grim determination. "They're trying to figure out *how* I did that, not just *that* I did it. And that buys us time."

As they plunged deeper into the wreckage, the oppressive silence of the desert returned, punctuated only by their ragged breaths and the crunch of debris under their feet. The lingering effects of Ash's sensory overload still buzzed in Kira's own mind, a faint echo of the overwhelming input. She could sense the residual chaos clinging to the air where the Syndicate operatives had been, a testament to the sheer force of Ash's defensive maneuver.

The experience, however, had revealed a terrifying new dimension to their capabilities, and to the nature of resonance itself. Ash's ability wasn't just about sensing or manipulating energy in a controlled manner; it was about raw, unfiltered output, a projection of pure sensation that could bypass even the most advanced technological defenses. It was volatile, unpredictable, and clearly, incredibly draining for him.

"Ash," Kira said, her voice soft but firm, as they navigated a narrow passage between two toppled skyscrapers. "What you just did... that was incredible. But it... it hurt you."

He met her gaze, his eyes flickering with a mixture of pride and pain. "Yeah. It did. It felt like... like my head was trying to split open. But it worked. They faltered. And that's what matters right now." He winced slightly, reaching up to touch his temple. "We're going to need to figure out how to control this, Kira. Properly control it. Because they're not going to stop coming, and I can't just... explode my brain every time they show up."

The realization settled heavily between them. They had stumbled upon a powerful, but clearly unstable, new facet of their combined abilities. Ash's defensive resonance was a potent weapon, a shield born of desperation, but it was a weapon that consumed its wielder. It was a powerful tool, yes, but one that required immense finesse and understanding, lest it turn against them, or simply burn Ash out completely.

This wasn't the controlled, focused application of resonance they had seen in the Enclaves, nor the intuitive, life-affirming connection Kira felt with the planet. This was raw power, a primal scream of defiance. It was the desperate act of a cornered animal, a last-ditch effort to survive. And in its wildness, it was both awe-inspiring and deeply concerning.

"We will," Kira reassured him, squeezing his hand. "We'll learn. We have to. They see resonance as a resource, Ash, something to be exploited. But you... you used it to protect us. To protect *me*. That's a fundamental difference."

They continued their movement, the weight of this newfound understanding pressing down on them. The Shadow Syndicate was a threat on a scale they hadn't anticipated, a force driven by a chilling ideology and equipped with advanced technology. And now, they knew Ash possessed an equally potent, albeit volatile, countermeasure. This encounter had irrevocably changed the landscape of their struggle. It was no longer just about survival; it was about defining what resonance truly meant, and how it would be wielded in the fractured world that was slowly, painfully, coming back to life. The journey back to the Seed Vault, once a simple objective, had become a crucible, forging them in the fires of conflict and revealing depths of power they were only just beginning to comprehend. Ash's instinctive defense had saved them, but it had also opened a Pandora's Box of dangerous potential that they now had to learn to manage, or be consumed by. The quiet hum of the Seed Vault seemed a lifetime away, replaced by the roaring echo of their own amplified powers, and the chilling certainty that their fight had only just begun.

The fragmented whispers, overheard during their desperate flight through the skeletal remains of the city, painted a chilling picture of the Shadow Syndicate's true purpose. Kira, her enhanced senses still sharp despite the lingering strain from Ash's earlier outburst, had managed to intercept fragments of communication, snippets of cold, clinical directives that spoke volumes about the organization's objectives. It wasn't merely about quelling dissent or maintaining order, as their public pronouncements might suggest. Their ambition ran far deeper, woven with a dark thread of control and a profound fear of the very essence that pulsed within beings like her and Ash: resonance.

The Syndicate, she gleaned, viewed resonance not as a fundamental aspect of life, a shared connection that bound individuals and the world together, but as a resource. A potent, untapped energy source to be harvested, refined, and weaponized. Their primary objective, a grim realization that settled in Kira's stomach like a shard of ice, was to capture resonant pairs. Not for protection, not for study in the spirit of understanding, but for breeding. The chilling implication was that they sought to control the very lineage of resonance, to engineer it, to create a subservient, specialized caste of individuals whose abilities would be meticulously cataloged and exploited for the Syndicate's gain. They were not preservers; they were breeders, aiming to produce a controlled strain of the resonance phenomenon.

This pursuit of engineered resonance extended into their technological endeavors. The captured intel spoke of advanced research into devices designed to mimic or, even more disturbingly, amplify resonance. These weren't tools for connection or healing, but instruments of war, designed to replicate the disruptive force Ash had inadvertently unleashed, but with precision and devastating effect. Imagine, Kira thought with a shiver, soldiers equipped with resonance projectors, capable of incapacitating entire populations with sonic assaults, or weapons that could destabilize matter through targeted vibrational frequencies. The Syndicate wasn't interested in the harmonious symphony of resonance; they sought to conduct a destructive orchestra of chaos, wielded by their own obedient instruments.

Perhaps the most insidious of their goals, however, was the active suppression of knowledge that promoted the natural, widespread evolution of resonance. They actively sought to eradicate any information, any philosophy, any understanding that advocated for resonance as a gift to be shared, a natural partnership to be nurtured, or a fundamental aspect of an interconnected existence. The Syndicate's ideology was rooted in the antithesis of everything Kira felt resonating within her and the world around them. They saw chaos where others saw harmony, a threat where others saw potential, and a commodity where others saw a sacred trust.

This was a war not just for territory or resources, but for the very definition of resonance. Was it a tool of oppression, a weapon to be controlled by an elite few? Or was it a force of connection, of life, of evolution that belonged to all? The Syndicate, with its cold, calculated approach, was clearly betting on the former, driven by a deep-seated fear of anything that defied their rigid hierarchy and absolute control.

Ash, his breath still coming in ragged gasps as they navigated the treacherous terrain, overheard Kira's hushed transmission to their hidden comms unit. "Breeding pairs?" he muttered, his voice rough with exhaustion and a dawning horror. "They want to... breed us? Like livestock?"

Kira nodded, her gaze fixed on the shifting shadows ahead. "It's worse than that,

Ash. They're not just looking for resonant pairs; they're looking to control the propagation of resonance itself. They want to engineer it, dictate its evolution. And they're developing technologies to amplify it, weaponize it."

A low growl rumbled in Ash's chest. "Weaponize it. So, that overload... that wasn't just some fluke. It was a preview of what they want to achieve, but with their own twisted agenda."

"Exactly," Kira confirmed. "They see it as a resource. Something to be extracted and controlled. Not a gift, not a connection, but a tool for their dominion. They're actively suppressing anything that suggests resonance is meant to be shared, meant to evolve naturally. They want to sterilize it, control it, keep it out of the hands of the masses."

The weight of this revelation pressed down on them, heavier than the dust-choked air. Their struggle had just taken on a terrifying new dimension. They weren't just evading capture; they were fighting for the very soul of resonance. The Syndicate's motivation was clear: to cage and corrupt a fundamental force of life, twisting it into an instrument of their insatiable hunger for power and control.

"They're afraid," Ash stated, his voice surprisingly steady, a new resolve hardening his gaze. "They're afraid of what they can't control. And resonance, real resonance, the kind that connects, that heals, that *lives*... they can't control that. Not truly. Not if it's allowed to flourish."

"Which is why they want to 'breed' it," Kira finished grimly. "To make it predictable, subservient. To strip away its wildness, its capacity for spontaneous connection. They want to turn a force of nature into a domesticated tool."

The thought was repulsive. Kira felt a visceral recoil from the Syndicate's calculated depravity. They were not simply conquerors; they were desecrators of life itself. Their methods were not those of a military force imposing order, but of a sorcerer seeking to bind a wild magic to their will, to twist its inherent goodness into something dark and exploitative.

"And the technology," Ash continued, his mind racing, piecing together the scattered fragments of intelligence. "If they're trying to amplify resonance... that means they're looking for ways to replicate what you and I can do, but on a larger scale. To create weapons that can do what you just did, Kira, but without the connection, without the underlying empathy. Just raw, destructive power."

"A sonic weapon that can shatter cities, perhaps," Kira mused aloud, her imagination conjuring images of the Syndicate's chilling efficiency. "Or a disruptive frequency that can disable entire populations. They see our abilities as a blueprint, not for progress, but for subjugation."

Their understanding of the enemy had deepened, shifting from a vaguely defined oppressive regime to a more concrete, terrifyingly focused entity. The Shadow Syndicate wasn't just a political power; it was an ideological force dedicated to the perversion of a fundamental aspect of their world. Their motivation was not rooted in defense or even conquest in the traditional sense, but in a profound desire to own, to control, and to corrupt the very essence of life's interconnectedness.

"So, this isn't just about survival anymore, is it?" Ash said, his voice laced with a grim understanding. "It's about fighting for the right of resonance to exist, to be free."

"It always was, Ash," Kira replied, her voice soft but firm. "We just didn't know the full scope of what we were fighting for. Or against."

The Syndicate's ideology was a cancer, spreading through the remnants of their world, seeking to excise any trace of natural harmony and replace it with a sterile, controlled order. They believed that by mastering resonance; by bending it to their will through technology and forced propagation, they could achieve ultimate control. They feared the unpredictable nature of natural resonance, the way it fostered empathy, cooperation, and an intrinsic connection to the environment. These were forces that undermined their authoritarian structure, that offered an alternative to their rigid, exploitative system.

Kira recalled a passage from an ancient text she had once studied, a forgotten treatise on the 'Weave of Being,' that spoke of resonance as the lifeblood of existence, a shared current that connected all living things. The Syndicate's desire to isolate and weaponize it was akin to trying to capture lightning in a bottle, not to understand its power, but to turn it into a destructive storm controlled by their hand. They didn't want to be part of the Weave; they wanted to own it, to unravel it and re-stitch it according to their own dark design.

The information gleaned from the Syndicate's internal communications was a stark warning. They were actively hunting for individuals with strong resonance, particularly pairs, not to protect them, but to isolate them, study their genetic makeup, and use it to create a controlled breeding program. This was eugenics on a cosmic scale, driven by a desire to cultivate a specialized, subservient class of resonant individuals. The thought of being reduced to a mere genetic resource, a pawn in their grand, twisted experiment, sent a chill down Kira's spine.

Furthermore, their technological pursuits indicated a deep-seated insecurity. If natural resonance was so potent and widespread, why the need to replicate it with machines? It suggested a fear that their control could be circumvented, that true, unfettered resonance could pose a threat to their established order. They sought to build artificial amplifications, not to enhance natural growth, but to create a controllable facsimile, a tool that could be switched on and off, its output dictated by their commands. This was the ultimate act of domination: to take something inherently natural and free, and reduce it to a manufactured commodity.

Kira realized that the Syndicate's motivation was rooted in a profound fear of chaos, not the creative chaos of natural evolution, but the chaos of dissent, of independent thought, of unpredictable connection. Resonance, in its purest form, was inherently unpredictable. It was influenced by emotion, by circumstance, by the collective will of those who wielded it. This lack of absolute predictability was anathema to the Syndicate's rigid, deterministic worldview. They craved order, control, and the illusion of absolute dominion over all things, including the very fabric of life's interconnectedness.

The Syndicate's pursuit of suppressed knowledge also revealed their deep-seated insecurity. They understood that widespread understanding of resonance, its potential for healing, connection, and collective advancement, would undermine their authority. If people learned to harness resonance for themselves, to form natural bonds and create harmonious communities, the Syndicate's need for control would vanish. Therefore, they actively worked to discredit, destroy, and erase any information that promoted the natural, widespread evolution of resonance. They wanted to keep the masses ignorant, dependent, and susceptible to their fabricated narratives of order and security.

The contrast between the Syndicate's cold, utilitarian approach and Kira's own burgeoning understanding of resonance was stark. For Kira, resonance was a language of empathy, a bridge between souls, a reflection of the planet's own vibrant, interconnected life force. For the Syndicate, it was simply a dataset, a raw material, a lever of power to be manipulated for their own ends. They sought to master resonance by dissecting it, by controlling its propagation, and by weaponizing its inherent energies. They aimed to turn a symphony into a scream, a connection into a cage.

Ash, his hand finding hers as they moved through the ruins, squeezed it tightly. "They want to breed us," he repeated, the words tasting like ash in his mouth. "They see us as... components. Not people."

"And they want to build machines that do what we can do, but without the soul," Kira added, her voice a low murmur. "Without the connection. Just raw, destructive power."

The implications were vast, extending far beyond their immediate struggle for survival. The Shadow Syndicate wasn't just an enemy; they were a fundamental threat to the very nature of existence as Kira understood it. Their motivation was to pervert and exploit a force that was meant to unite, to heal, and to guide evolution. They were trying to engineer a world devoid of true connection, a world ruled by the cold logic of control and the sterile efficiency of artificial power. Their actions were a declaration of war not just on individuals like her and Ash, but on the very essence of life itself. The knowledge they had gained was a heavy burden, a stark illumination of the darkness they faced. It was a confirmation that their fight was not just for their own freedom, but for the freedom of resonance itself to exist, to flourish, and to connect the world in its unadulterated, powerful grace. Their evasion was no longer just a desperate flight; it was a mission to preserve the very concept of resonance from utter corruption.

The air in the Syndicate facility was a thick, cloying miasma of disinfectant and despair. Kira, her senses honed to an almost unbearable degree, could feel the suffocating weight of it, a palpable oppression that pressed in on her from all sides. They had been led through a labyrinth of sterile corridors, each turn bringing a fresh wave of dread. Ash, his usual stoic demeanor cracking under the strain, kept a protective arm around her, his breath catching in his throat with every new metallic clang or distant, muffled cry. It was a symphony of suffering, orchestrated by the Shadow Syndicate with chilling precision.

Their guide, a gaunt Syndicate operative with eyes that held the flat, unseeing gaze of a zealot, halted before a heavy, reinforced door. The operative didn't speak, merely keyed in a sequence on a nearby console. The door hissed open, revealing a sight that stole the breath from Kira's lungs and slammed it back into her with the force of a physical blow.

This was not a prison cell as she had imagined, nor a sterile laboratory filled with humming machinery. It was a series of interconnected containment units, each one a stark, brutal echo of the last. Within these transparent walls, bathed in an unmerciful, sterile light, were other resonant pairs. Not just human and human, as she and Ash were, but human and canine, their forms huddled together in a desperate, shared misery.

The Syndicate's obsession with breeding and control was laid bare before her in the most visceral way possible. These were not mere prisoners; they were specimens, their very existence reduced to a series of data points, their bonds studied and, it seemed, systematically broken. Kira's enhanced vision, usually a gift, now felt like a curse, allowing her to see the raw, unvarnished pain etched onto the faces of the humans and the desperate, pleading eyes of the canines.

One enclosure, directly opposite theirs, held a young woman, no older than Kira herself, her face a mask of utter desolation. Beside her, a large, scarred wolfhound, its once magnificent coat matted and dull, whined softly, its tail tucked between its legs. The dog's muzzle was scarred, and Kira could see the raw welts where some restraint had been applied. The young woman's hands were clasped over her ears, as if trying to block out an internal torment that echoed the external harshness of their surroundings. Kira felt an immediate, visceral surge of empathy for them, a resonance that transcended the sterile barrier. She could feel the woman's silent, guttural plea, the dog's desperate need for comfort that it could no longer offer.

Ash, his jaw tight, let out a low growl, the sound vibrating deep in his chest. "What... what are they doing to them?" he whispered, his voice strained.

The operative, without turning his head, spoke in a monotone, devoid of any emotion. "Observation. Analysis. We are identifying the inherent strengths and weaknesses of various resonant pairings. The canine resonance is particularly... foundational. Primitive, yet potent. We are cataloging its expression under duress."

Kira's blood ran cold. "Under duress?" she echoed, the word a bitter, burning taste in her mouth. She looked at another enclosure. Here, a burly man, his muscles rippling even in his weakened state, was strapped to a chair, his German Shepherd pacing restlessly at his feet, emitting low, anxious growls. Wires, no thicker than strands of spider silk, were attached to the man's temples and the dog's forehead, their ends disappearing into the wall. A faint, rhythmic pulse emanated from the wall, and with each pulse, the man flinched, his eyes squeezing shut. The dog let out a sharp bark, a sound of pure distress, and strained against its own restraints, its body trembling.

"They are attempting to quantify the threshold of the empathic link," the operative explained, his voice chillingly detached. "To measure the transfer of sensory input and emotional response. The canine's sensitivity to its bonded human's physiological and psychological state is a critical variable."

Kira felt a wave of nausea wash over her. This was not study; it was torture. They were deliberately inflicting pain, trying to gauge how much their canines would suffer before their bond fractured, or before they became compliant. They were stripping away the very essence of what made these pairings special, reducing it to a crude equation of pain and obedience.

In another unit, a woman with a kind, maternal face was attempting to soothe a small, trembling terrier. The terrier, however, seemed unable to settle, its eyes darting around the enclosure with an unnatural fear. The woman's face was streaked with tears, and she kept murmuring reassurances, but her own voice trembled with an underlying fear. Kira felt a phantom ache in her own chest, an echo of the woman's distress. She could sense the terrier's anxiety wasn't just a reaction to their immediate surroundings, but something deeper, something induced.

"The 'conditioning' phase," the operative elaborated, gesturing towards the terrier. "We are exploring methods to induce specific emotional states in the canine, and observing the corresponding neurological and behavioral shifts in the human. The goal is to establish a protocol for influencing the pair's collective output, guiding their resonance towards desired parameters."

Desired parameters. The phrase was a sterile, clinical euphemism for subjugation. The Syndicate didn't want resonant pairs to feel joy, to feel connection, to feel the unburdened freedom that Kira and Ash had experienced before their own lives were shattered. They wanted them to be tools, their emotions and their bonds manipulated like strings on a puppet.

Ash's grip tightened on Kira's arm, and she could feel his own rising anger, a potent, controlled fury that mirrored her own. "You're destroying them," he said, his voice a low, dangerous rumble. "You're breaking them."

The operative finally turned, his vacant eyes meeting Ash's. "We are refining them," he corrected, a flicker of something almost like pride in his otherwise blank expression. "This is necessary for the advancement of the Syndicate's objectives. Uncontrolled resonance is a chaotic force. We are imposing order."

"Order?" Kira scoffed, the sound sharp and brittle. "This is not order; it's cruelty. You're not imposing order; you're creating slaves." She pointed a trembling finger at the enclosure holding the young woman and her wolfhound. "Look at them! They're suffering because of your 'refinement.' You're perverting something beautiful into something monstrous."

The operative remained impassive. "Beauty is subjective. Efficiency is not. These units are being prepared for integration into specialized Syndicate programs. Their unique resonance will be... optimized."

The word 'optimized' was the final straw. Kira felt a primal surge, a raw, untamed energy coiling within her. The sight of these captured souls, the palpable aura of their despair and the Syndicate's utter disregard for their well-being, ignited a fire within her that burned away any lingering fear or hesitation. This was not just about their own survival anymore; it was about every single resonant pair held captive within these walls, and every one that might be captured in the future.

She looked at Ash, and in his eyes, she saw the same unyielding resolve. Their shared glance was a silent, powerful declaration of war. The Syndicate's methods, their cold, calculated dehumanization of life, had irrevocably deepened their understanding of the enemy. It wasn't just a matter of ideology or political control; it was a fundamental war for the soul of resonance itself. They were not just fighting for the freedom to connect, to love, to exist as they were; they were fighting to preserve the very concept of genuine, unadulterated resonance from being twisted into a tool of oppression.

"We have to get them out," Kira whispered, her voice barely audible, yet laced with an iron will.

Ash nodded, his gaze sweeping over the rows of suffering. "We will."

The operative, sensing a shift in their demeanor, took a step back, his hand moving towards a concealed sidearm. "Your cooperation is appreciated. Further observation will continue."

But Kira was no longer listening. Her focus had shifted, honing in on the subtle vibrations emanating from the canines within the enclosures. She felt a faint, almost imperceptible hum, a low-frequency resonance that seemed to ripple through the very structure of the facility. It was a shared distress, a collective yearning for freedom that, despite the Syndicate's efforts, had not been entirely extinguished.

She closed her eyes for a brief moment, reaching out with her own resonance, not in a forceful way, but as a gentle query, a silent invitation. She felt the immediate, overwhelming wave of pain and fear from the captured pairs, a cacophony of suffering. But beneath that, like a fragile thread of light in the darkness, she also felt a faint, flickering response. A spark of hope, a flicker of recognition.

The young woman with the wolfhound, whose name Kira didn't know but whose pain she felt as if it were her own, looked up, her tear-filled eyes meeting Kira's through the transparent barrier. There was a flicker of something in her gaze – a desperate plea, perhaps, or a nascent understanding. The wolfhound, sensing the shift in its human, lifted its head, its ears twitching.

Kira focused on that connection, on that fragile bridge being formed. She didn't know how, but she knew they had to try. They couldn't just leave these individuals to suffer. The Shadow Syndicate's cruelty was not just an abstract concept anymore; it was a tangible, horrifying reality that demanded a response.

"They are trying to break the bond," Kira murmured to Ash, her mind already racing, piecing together the Syndicate's modus operandi. "They're inflicting pain, trying to sever the empathic link. But they're underestimating the resilience of true resonance. They're trying to force it into a mold, but true resonance is wild, it's adaptable, it finds a way."

Ash's gaze was fixed on the operative, but his mind was clearly working alongside Kira's. "If they're measuring the transfer of pain, that means the bond itself is the conduit. And if it's a conduit, it can be manipulated, perhaps even overloaded."

Kira shook her head, a new thought forming. "Not overloaded, Ash. Not in the way they're thinking. They're trying to create a one-way transfer of pain. But what if... what if we could create a two-way transfer of something else?"

The operative, his hand still near his sidearm, regarded them with suspicion. "Your observations are irrelevant. Your current assignment is to remain here."

"Irrelevant?" Kira turned her gaze back to him, a fierce light burning in her eyes. "What's irrelevant is your belief that you can control something as fundamental as resonance. You think you can breed it, weaponize it, control its very evolution. But you're wrong. Resonance isn't a commodity to be owned; it's a force of nature, and forces of nature can't be caged."

She focused her will, not on the operative, but on the collective distress she felt resonating from the other pairs. She imagined that distress transforming, not into aggression, but into a unified surge of will, a silent scream of defiance. It was a delicate, dangerous balancing act. Pushing too hard could cause further harm, could overwhelm the very individuals she sought to connect with. But a gentle, persistent offering of shared strength, of unwavering solidarity, might just be enough to ignite a spark of resistance within them.

She felt a subtle shift in the atmosphere of the room. The low hum of anxiety seemed to gain a new layer, a faint, underlying thrum that spoke of a nascent unity. The wolfhound, sensing a change in its human, whined softly, a sound that was less fear and more... anticipation. The German Shepherd, its muscles tensed, let out a low growl, but it was a sound of readiness, not of cowering.

Ash, sensing Kira's intent, joined her in this silent communion, his own resonance weaving with hers, amplifying the message of hope and defiance. They were a beacon in this oppressive darkness, a testament to the enduring power of resonance, even in the face of systematic cruelty. The Syndicate believed they were breeding compliant tools, but in doing so, they were inadvertently forging an unbreakable chain of shared purpose.

The operative, however, was not oblivious. He saw the subtle shift in the captive pairs, the almost imperceptible flicker of awareness in their eyes. He reached for his comms device. "Security breach. Containment units exhibiting anomalous resonant frequencies."

Kira knew their time was short. The sight of the suffering, the chilling understanding of the Syndicate's perverted agenda, had solidified her resolve. They could not simply escape; they had to dismantle this operation, to free those who were being systematically broken. The Shadow Syndicate's vision of a controlled, engineered resonance was a perversion of life itself, and Kira, with Ash by her side, was no longer willing to stand by and let it happen. The echoes of shared despair had become the rumblings of a coming storm, and Kira knew, with a certainty that resonated deep within her soul, that the storm was about to break. Their fight was not just for their own lives, but for the very soul of connection, for the freedom of resonance to thrive, untamed and uncorrupted. The captured resonant, trapped in their sterile prisons, were no longer just victims; they were the silent catalysts for a revolution.

The sterile air, still thick with the scent of despair and the phantom vibrations of suffering, seemed to cling to Kira and Ash like a shroud as they retreated deeper into the labyrinthine facility. The operative's alarm had been a shrill, piercing sound, cutting through the oppressive quiet, and Kira felt the low thrum of increased activity vibrating through the floor. They had seen too much, understood too much, to hope for a quiet exit. The Syndicate's "refinement" of resonance was a perversion of everything they held dear, a systematic crushing of the very essence of connection. The faces of the captive resonant pairs, the desperate pleading in the eyes of the canines, were seared into Kira's mind, fueling a righteous fury that burned hotter than any fear.

"We need to move," Ash said, his voice low and urgent, his eyes scanning the corridor ahead. His enhanced senses, usually a quiet hum beneath the surface, were now keenly attuned to the slightest shift in sound, the faintest tremor in the metal walls. They had to disappear, to find a way out of this meticulously constructed cage, but the thought of leaving those others behind gnawed at Kira.

As they navigated the stark, utilitarian corridors, the distant sounds of pursuit began to grow – the heavy tread of boots, the sharp, clipped commands of Syndicate operatives. They ducked into a service tunnel, a narrow, dimly lit passage filled with the reek of stale oil and ozone. It offered a temporary reprieve, a chance to breathe and strategize. Kira's mind raced, trying to process the horrors they had witnessed. The Syndicate wasn't just interested in control; they were actively engaged in the systematic torture and degradation of sentient beings, twisting the beautiful, natural phenomenon of resonance into a weapon, a tool of absolute subjugation.

"They're trying to break the empathic link," Kira murmured, her voice raspy. "They're injecting pain, fear, trying to sever the connection. But they're so wrong about resonance. It's not about obedience or compliance. It's about shared experience, about mutual support, about an unbroken, unbreakable bond."

Ash nodded, his jaw set. "And they're underestimating the resilience of that bond. They see it as a conduit for pain, but it's also a conduit for strength. If they can transmit suffering, maybe, just maybe, we can transmit something else." His gaze met hers, a silent understanding passing between them. The Syndicate's experiments were a crude, brutal attempt to understand and control something they fundamentally failed to grasp. Resonance wasn't a force to be commanded; it was a living, breathing entity, and like any living thing, it would fight for its own survival.

Their contemplation was cut short by a low scraping sound from further down the tunnel. It wasn't the measured, purposeful cadence of Syndicate patrols. This was something more furtive, more hesitant. Kira tensed, her hand instinctively reaching for Ash's arm. They moved cautiously, their footsteps muffled by the grime on the tunnel floor, their enhanced senses straining to identify the source of the noise.

Around a bend, bathed in the flickering emergency lights, a figure was hunched over, their back to them. They were struggling with a heavy, rusted grate, trying to pry it open. The figure was clad in scavenged clothing, layered and patched, their movements economical and desperate. A low growl, not of aggression but of frustration, escaped their lips. Beside them, tethered by a frayed rope, was a scruffy, lean mutt, its tail giving a tentative, questioning wag. The dog's ears were perked, its intelligent eyes fixed on the figure's efforts.

Kira's internal alarm bells began to ring. Any stranger in these Syndicate-controlled zones was a potential threat. But there was something in the figure's posture, in the sheer desperation of their struggle, that resonated with Kira's own experience. They were clearly trying to escape, not to pursue.

The figure, sensing their presence, froze. The dog let out a low, warning rumble, its body tensing. The figure slowly, deliberately, turned around. Their face was grimy, streaked with sweat and dirt, but their eyes, when they met Kira's, held a familiar weariness, a hard-won resilience. They were neither Syndicate nor an obvious victim. They were something in between, a survivor.

"Who are you?" the figure rasped, their voice rough, as if unused. They kept one hand on the dog's collar, a protective gesture that Kira understood implicitly.

"We're not Syndicate," Kira said, her voice calm, projecting an air of non-aggression. Ash stood beside her, a silent, watchful presence. "We're trying to get out."

The figure eyed them, their gaze lingering on Kira's slightly more refined attire, then on Ash's imposing frame. Suspicion was etched deep into their features, a learned response to a life lived in the shadows of the Syndicate's iron grip. "Lots of people try to get out," they said, a hint of cynicism in their tone. "Most don't make it."

"We saw what they're doing," Kira continued, choosing her words carefully. "In the containment units. The pairings. We can't just leave them."

A flicker of something crossed the figure's face – recognition, perhaps, or a grim understanding. They looked from Kira to Ash, then back to the dog. "You saw... the experiments," they said, the words heavy with a shared burden of knowledge. "They're breaking them, one by one. Trying to strip the resonance right out of them."

"We want to help," Kira stated, her resolve firm. "But we can't do it alone. We need to get out, and maybe, just maybe, find a way to fight back. We need allies."

The figure was silent for a long moment, their gaze sweeping over the debris-strewn tunnel, as if weighing their options. The dog nudged their hand, a soft whine of encouragement. Finally, they let out a weary sigh. "Call me Jax. And this," they gestured to the dog, who offered a soft 'woof,' "is Bolt."

Jax pushed themselves away from the grate, their movements stiff. "You're not the first to talk about fighting back. But fighting the Syndicate in here? It's like trying to drain an ocean with a sieve." They paused, their eyes locking with Kira's. "But you saw them. The canines, the humans... I've seen it too. Spent months in a similar facility, before I managed to break free. They use the resonance, twist it, weaponize it. They try to break the bond with manufactured fear, with simulated trauma."

Kira felt a surge of empathy for Jax. They were a survivor, just like her and Ash, carrying the scars of Syndicate cruelty. "We know," she said softly. "We were in one of their facilities ourselves. They're trying to create controlled resonance, to dictate its very nature. But they don't understand that true resonance isn't something you can control. It's something you share, something that grows and adapts."

Ash stepped forward. "We managed to get a glimpse of their research. They're focusing on canine resonance, as a baseline. Trying to map the empathic pathways, the neurological connections. They believe they can isolate and replicate the effects, even enhance them."

Jax snorted, a dry, humorless sound. "Enhance them by inflicting pain. That's their entire playbook. I saw them pushing a human pair to their breaking point, trying to see how much trauma a canine could absorb before its bonded human's neural pathways collapsed. It was... barbaric. The dog, a German Shepherd, it was screaming. Not a bark, but a deep, guttural sound of pure agony, and its human was just... gone. Catatonic." Jax's voice cracked on the last word, the raw emotion in their eyes a testament to the horrors they had witnessed. Bolt whined softly, pressing against Jax's leg as if sensing their distress.

"We need to find a way to disrupt their process," Kira said, her mind already spinning with possibilities. The information they had gathered, the shared experience of survivors like Jax, was invaluable. "If they're measuring the transfer of emotional and physical states, then the bond itself is the conduit. We saw wires, complex instrumentation. They're trying to quantify and control the energy flow."

"Quantify and control are their favorite words," Jax spat. "They see resonance as a resource to be mined, not a connection to be cherished. My facility was a breeding ground, a place where they forced pairings, then subjected them to constant stress. They wanted to see if extreme pressure could forge stronger bonds, or break them entirely. They always aimed for breaking. Easier to rebuild from scratch, they said. Easier to mold."

"Mold into what?" Ash asked, his voice dangerous.

"Into weapons," Jax replied, his gaze hardening. "Into tools. They're looking for operatives who can control, influence, and even inflict pain through their resonance. They think they can breed loyalty, engineer obedience. They're trying to create a new breed of psychic enforcers, with canines as their primary conduit."

Kira felt a chill run down her spine. The implications were horrifying. A Syndicate that could weaponize resonance, that could twist the natural bond into a tool of control and destruction, was a threat of unimaginable scale. The captive pairs they had seen were not just victims; they were the raw materials for this terrifying future.

"We can't let that happen," Kira said, her voice firm. "We need to find a way to stop them. To expose them. But we need to get out of here first."

Jax looked at the grate, then back at Kira and Ash. "This grate leads to an older part of the facility. Mostly abandoned maintenance shafts and forgotten tunnels. It's a risk, a big one. If we get caught in there, we're truly lost. But it's also our best chance to slip through their net, at least for a while."

"What about the others?" Kira asked, her heart aching. "The ones in the containment units?"

Jax shook their head. "I don't know if we can do anything for them right now. Not from here. Getting out is paramount. Once we're free, maybe we can rally others, find a way to hit them where it hurts. But if we get caught now, we're all lost. And then no one will ever be free."

The weight of their decision pressed down on Kira. Every instinct screamed at her to stay, to find a way to free the others, to fight the Syndicate head-on. But Jax was right. Their own survival was the prerequisite for any future action. A premature confrontation would only lead to their capture or death, rendering them utterly useless.

"Alright," Kira said, meeting Jax's gaze. "We go with you. We'll take the risk. But we're not forgetting about them. We'll find a way to come back."

A grim nod from Jax. "That's the spirit. Now, let's get this damn thing open."

With renewed urgency, Jax resumed their work on the grate, this time with Kira and Ash assisting. Jax's knowledge of the facility's forgotten pathways was invaluable. They worked in a tense, silent symphony of effort. The metal groaned and screeched under their combined might. Bolt, sensing the shift in energy, whined and nudged Kira's hand, a gesture of solidarity that transcended species.

Finally, with a loud crack of rusted metal, the grate gave way, swinging inward with a deafening clang. The sound echoed through the tunnel, and Kira's senses immediately picked up a subtle increase in the distant sounds of pursuit. They had to move, and fast.

"This way," Jax whispered, ducking into the dark opening. Bolt, with a surprising burst of agility, followed, disappearing into the gloom. Kira and Ash exchanged a look, a silent affirmation of their shared purpose, and followed Jax into the forgotten depths of the Syndicate's domain. The alliance was fragile, born of desperation and a shared enemy, but in the suffocating darkness of the Syndicate's cruelty, even the smallest spark of cooperation felt like a blazing beacon of hope. The fight for true resonance had just taken a new, unexpected turn. They were no longer alone.

CHAPTER 10

The stale air of the service tunnels was a welcome change from the acrid stench of the Syndicate facility, yet it offered no respite from the gnawing unease that had settled in Kira's gut. Every clang of metal under Jax's boot, every scuff of their own shoes on the grime-laden floor, felt amplified, a potential beacon for the relentless hunters behind them. Bolt, a shadow of muscle and quiet determination, trotted faithfully beside Jax, his keen senses a constant, reassuring presence. The brief, desperate alliance forged in the bowels of their enemy's stronghold had propelled them forward, a shared urgency overriding the inherent suspicion between strangers in a world that taught trust was a fatal weakness. Jax, with their intimate knowledge of the facility's forgotten arteries, had guided them through a treacherous maze of disused conduits and collapsed passages, each turn a gamble against discovery.

The memory of the captive resonant pairs, their eyes wide with a terror that mirrored the very fear Kira and Ash had been trying to escape, remained a searing image, a silent vow to not let their sacrifice be in vain. They had escaped the immediate clutches of the Syndicate, but the mission was far from over.

Emerging from the oppressive darkness of the tunnels into a predawn twilight, the familiar silhouette of Haven rose against the bruised horizon. It was their sanctuary, a fragile bastion of normalcy in a world teetering on the brink of manufactured chaos. Yet, as they drew closer, a subtle tension permeated the air, a disquiet that seemed to emanate from the very stones of the community. The usual gentle hum of activity was muted, replaced by an anxious murmur that rippled through the scattered dwellings. Lights flickered in windows, more numerous than usual for this hour, casting nervous shadows that danced with the encroaching dawn. Kira's empathic senses, honed by years of experience, picked up a wave of heightened anxiety, a collective thrum of fear that was palpable even from this distance. Something was wrong.

Jax, their movements still wary, scanned their surroundings with a practiced eye. "Looks like the news traveled faster than we did," they muttered, their gaze fixed on the heightened activity around Haven's perimeter. Bolt let out a low growl, his hackles rising slightly as he sensed the shift in the atmosphere. "They don't like outsiders much, do they?"

"Haven values its privacy," Kira replied, her voice tight. "And right now, privacy might be the last thing they have." She felt a pang of dread. The Syndicate's reach was far, their methods insidious. Had their escape, however covert, somehow signaled their presence back to Haven? Or had the news of their discoveries, of the horrors they had witnessed, somehow preceded them?

As they approached the main gate, the guards, usually relaxed and friendly, were rigid and alert, their postures tense, their eyes sharp and questioning. They recognized Kira and Ash, but their expressions were a mixture of relief and apprehension. The presence of Jax, disheveled and clearly an outsider, only amplified their unease.

"Kira! Ash! You're back," one of the guards exclaimed, his voice laced with relief, before his eyes narrowed at Jax. "Who's this?"

"This is Jax," Kira explained, stepping forward. "They helped us. And they're with us. We need to get inside. We have... important information." The guards exchanged a glance, their gazes flickering between Kira, Ash, and Jax. The unspoken question hung in the air: had they brought trouble with them?

The gates creaked open, allowing them passage into Haven. The inner courtyard, usually a bustling hub of communal activity, was strangely subdued. People spoke in hushed tones, their faces etched with worry. The news of the Shadow Syndicate's escalating activities, whispers of their horrifying experiments with resonance, had clearly spread like wildfire, infecting Haven with a pervasive sense of dread. Kira could feel the collective anxiety swirling around them, a thick, cloying blanket that smothered any semblance of peace.

"What's going on?" Ash asked one of the Haven residents, a woman named Elara who was known for her calm demeanor.

Elara wrung her hands, her eyes darting towards the communal gathering hall. "It's the Syndicate, Ash. News reached us early this morning. They... they've escalated their operations. Reports of widespread arrests, of people being forcibly taken for 're-education.' And the resonance disruptions... they're more frequent, more severe. Some communities that were once safe have gone silent."

Kira's blood ran cold. The Syndicate's machinations were not confined to the shadowy facilities they had just escaped. Their influence was spreading, their shadow lengthening across the land, extinguishing the light of resonant communities one by one. The faces of the captive resonant pairs flashed in her mind, their silent suffering a stark reminder of what was at stake.

"We saw it firsthand," Kira said, her voice ringing with a new urgency. "Their facilities. They're not just experimenting; they're weaponizing resonance. They're breaking bonds, inflicting pain, twisting it into a tool of control. They're trying to create operatives who can weaponize empathic links."

Her words, spoken with the conviction of direct experience, silenced the murmurs around them. Heads turned, eyes fixed on Kira, a mixture of horror and disbelief dawning on their faces. Jax stood silently beside them, a grim observer of Haven's growing panic.

"This is why we must fortify," a stern voice boomed from the gathering hall's entrance. Elder Maeve, her face a mask of grim determination, emerged, flanked by a handful of Haven's security council. Her gaze was sharp, assessing, and it lingered on Jax with undisguised suspicion. "We cannot afford to be drawn into their conflicts. Haven must be made impenetrable. We must cut ourselves off, sever all contact with the outside world. Protect what we have, at all costs."

A ripple of agreement went through the crowd. The idea of withdrawal, of self-preservation, was a tempting balm for the raw fear that had taken root. It was the instinct to retreat, to shield oneself from the storm.

But Kira couldn't accept that. The thought of leaving others to the Syndicate's brutal machinations, of cowering behind Haven's walls while the outside world burned, felt like a betrayal of everything they stood for. "Fortify? Maeve, we can't just hide," Kira countered, her voice gaining strength. "They're actively destroying resonant communities. If we don't do something, Haven will be next. Or worse, the Syndicate will achieve their goals, and no one will be safe."

"And what do you propose, Kira?" Maeve retorted, her tone sharp. "Open warfare? We are a community of peace, not soldiers. We have no army, no weapons to match the Syndicate's might. Our strength lies in our resonance, not in aggression."

"Our strength *is* our resonance," Kira insisted, meeting Maeve's challenging gaze. "And they are twisting it, perverting it. If they can weaponize it, then we need to understand how, to find a way to counter it. Hiding won't stop them. We need to fight back, but not with their methods. We need to fight with the true power of resonance – connection, unity, shared strength."

Ash stepped forward, his presence commanding. "Kira is right. The Syndicate's goal is control. They believe they can dictate the nature of resonance. They are wrong. Resonance is a force of nature, adaptable, resilient. If they are trying to isolate and weaponize specific aspects, then perhaps we can amplify the very aspects they seek to suppress. Empathy, compassion, mutual support. These are not weaknesses; they are our greatest strengths."

"But how?" Maeve challenged; her arms crossed. "How do you propose we 'fight' with empathy? Do you intend to hug the Syndicate into submission?" Her sarcasm was cutting, reflecting the deep schism that had formed within Haven. The news of the Syndicate's atrocities had polarized the community, igniting a debate between those who advocated for isolation and those who felt compelled to act.

"We find others," Kira said, her gaze sweeping across the anxious faces. "Other resonant communities. We unite them. We share what we've learned, what we've seen. We build a network, a resistance. The Syndicate is powerful, but they are also spread thin. They rely on fear and isolation. If we can foster connection, if we can show people they are not alone, then we can undermine their power."

Jax, who had remained silent until now, spoke up, their voice rough but clear. "She's talking about something that's possible. I've seen pockets of resistance, isolated groups trying to survive, trying to understand what's happening. But they're scattered, uncoordinated. They're easy for the Syndicate to pick off. If you can unite them, give them a common purpose, a way to share information and resources..." Jax trailed off, a flicker of hope igniting in their eyes. "That could be a real threat to the Syndicate's operations."

"A threat?" Maeve scoffed. "Or a beacon for their attention? Jax, you are an unknown quantity here. You speak of resistance, but you emerged from the heart of Syndicate territory. How can we trust you?"

"You can't trust me," Jax admitted, their gaze steady. "Not fully. But you can trust what I've seen. And you can trust that if the Syndicate succeeds in their goals, Haven will be just another cog in their machine. You can either be a fortress, waiting to be besieged, or you can be part of a force that pushes back. A force that reminds the Syndicate that resonance isn't a weapon to be controlled, but a connection that cannot be broken."

The debate raged on, the arguments between fortification and resistance echoing through the courtyard. The factions within Haven were clearly defined, their viewpoints hardened by fear and circumstance. Kira felt the familiar weight of responsibility settle on her shoulders. She had seen the Syndicate's cruelty firsthand; had felt the terror of those they imprisoned. She knew, with a certainty that burned in her very soul, that inaction was not an option.

"Maeve," Kira said, her voice resonating with conviction, "I understand your desire to protect Haven. But true protection doesn't come from isolation. It comes from strength. And strength, in our world, is built on connection. We have vital information. Information that could help other communities prepare, that could expose the Syndicate's true nature. We cannot hoard that knowledge. We must share it. We must act."

Ash nodded in agreement. "We are not advocating for reckless aggression. We are advocating for informed resistance. We need to establish contact with other resonant communities. We need to build alliances. This is not about conquering; it is about surviving, and ultimately, about reclaiming the true essence of resonance."

The council members exchanged uncertain glances. The arguments presented were compelling, born of a terrifying reality. The allure of a fortified Haven was strong, a promise of safety in uncertain times. But the vision Kira and Ash painted – a united front of resonant individuals, pushing back against the Syndicate's tyranny – was a potent counter-narrative, a beacon of hope in the encroaching darkness.

"And how do you propose we 'establish contact'?" Maeve finally asked, her skepticism still evident. "The Syndicate has ways of tracking communications, of monitoring any unusual activity. Any overt attempt to reach out could draw their attention directly to us, and to every community we contact."

"We have an advantage," Kira said, her mind racing with the possibilities. "The Syndicate is focused on isolating and controlling resonance. They are looking for overt displays, for organized communication. But resonance is also subtle, deeply personal. Jax and I, we came through their network. There are... blind spots. Places where signals can pass, where information can be relayed without detection." She glanced at Jax, who gave a subtle nod. Their escape had provided them with insights into the Syndicate's surveillance methods, and more importantly, their limitations. "We need to be discreet, yes. But not silent. Not anymore."

The debate continued, the murmurs of dissent and hesitant agreement swirling around them. The path forward was fraught with peril, the choice between entrenched safety and active resistance a heavy burden. But as Kira looked at Ash, at Jax, at the determined faces of those who shared her conviction, she felt a surge of renewed resolve. They had faced the Syndicate in their own domain and emerged, scarred but unbroken. Now, they had to bring that fight back to Haven, to awaken its spirit and rally its strength. The sanctity of their haven was not just about walls and defenses; it was about the connections they forged; the bonds they refused to let the Syndicate shatter. The whispers of fear needed to be replaced by the resounding chorus of unity.

As the sun finally crested the horizon, casting a warm, golden light over Haven, the decision was still not fully made. The internal schism remained, a testament to the difficult choices they faced. But the seeds of action had been sown. Kira knew that their journey back had been more than just an escape; it had been a wake-up call. Haven could no longer afford to be a passive sanctuary. It had to become a part of the resistance, a beacon of hope for all resonant communities struggling against the encroaching darkness. The fight for the true nature of resonance had begun, and Haven would have to choose its side. The news of the Syndicate's horrors had not broken them, but it had irrevocably changed them, forcing them to confront the stark reality of their world and the urgent need to fight for their shared future. The whispers of anxiety still hung in the air, but beneath them, a new, determined hum began to rise – the sound of a community awakening to the call of action.

The air in the communal hall, once a space of shared meals and hopeful planning, now thrummed with a palpable discord. The stark pronouncements of Elder Maeve, advocating for an impenetrable Haven, had resonated deeply with a significant portion of the community. Their fear was a tangible entity, a cold, creeping dread born from the chilling reports that had reached them even before Kira and Ash's return. Whispers of Syndicate raids, of resonant individuals being "re-educated" into tools of control, painted a grim picture of a world where safety was a relic of the past. To these pragmatists, the very concept of pushing back, of engaging with the outside world, was akin to inviting the wolf into the sheepfold.

"We have survived this long by being prudent," a man named Silas argued, his voice firm and steady, though his eyes betrayed the anxiety beneath. He was a craftsman, his hands calloused from years of working with wood and metal, now advocating for a different kind of fortification. "We have built Haven on the principles of self-sufficiency and quiet resilience. The Syndicate's power is immense, their reach extending into shadows we cannot even comprehend. To actively seek them out, to engage in any form of resistance, is to court annihilation. Our resonance is a gift, yes, but it is also a light that attracts predators. Let us dim that light, for a time. Let us become invisible."

His words found fertile ground. Several nodded in agreement, their faces etched with worry. They had witnessed the Syndicate's ruthlessness firsthand, albeit from a distance. They had seen neighboring communities, once vibrant and connected, fall silent, their resonant frequencies extinguished. The idea of becoming a fortress, of fortifying their borders, of cutting off all external contact, offered a seductive promise of safety. It was the instinct to retreat, to protect the immediate and the known, rather than to venture into the perilous unknown.

"And what of those who are still out there, Silas?" Elara's voice, usually soft, now carried a steely edge. She stood beside Kira, her stance mirroring Kira's own defiance. "What of the others who are suffering, who are being systematically broken by the Syndicate? Do we simply turn our backs? Do we hoard our safety while others are consumed?" Her gaze swept across the faces of those who supported Silas's view, her eyes pleading for a flicker of empathy. "Our resonance is not just about us; it is about connection. If we sever our connections, we are no better than the Syndicate, who seek to isolate and control."

Elara's argument struck at the heart of their shared identity as a resonant community. Their strength, their very essence, was built upon the bonds they shared, the empathic links that flowed between them. To intentionally sever those links, to choose isolation, felt like a betrayal of that core principle. Yet, the fear was a powerful counter-argument, a siren song of safety that beckoned them toward the perceived security of self-imposed exile.

"Elara, your idealism is admirable, but misplaced," another member, a woman named Mara, countered. She was a healer, her empathy usually a source of comfort, but now it seemed to fuel her fear. "We have heard the stories. The Syndicate is not interested in reasoned debate or empathic understanding. They are interested in dominance. They twist our resonance, they weaponize it. To engage them is to play their game, and they have already set the rules. Our advanced resonance, the very thing that makes us unique, could be their ultimate prize. Imagine what they could do if they could harness the full spectrum of what we are capable of."

Mara's words hung heavy in the air. The idea of their cherished resonance being turned against them, of their deepest connections becoming instruments of their own subjugation, was a terrifying prospect. It fueled the argument for withdrawal, for a silent, unobserved existence. The more they learned about the Syndicate's methods, the more the inherent risks of engagement seemed to outweigh any potential benefits.

"But that's precisely why we *must* understand it!" Kira interjected, her voice rising with a passion that drew the attention of everyone in the hall. "If they are trying to weaponize resonance, then we need to know *how*. We need to find their weaknesses, not just hide from their strengths. Jax and I have seen their facilities; we've witnessed their experiments. They are not invincible. They are relying on our fear, on our isolation. If we can connect with other communities, share what we know, build a network of resistance – that is a force they cannot easily suppress."

Kira's conviction was unwavering, her experience a potent testament to the Syndicate's tangible threat. She had seen the broken spirits of those subjected to the Syndicate's control, the vacant stares of individuals whose resonance had been twisted into something unnatural. The memory of those captive resonant pairs, their silent pleas echoing in her mind, was a constant spur. To stand by and do nothing, to allow the Syndicate to continue its horrific work unchecked, was an unacceptable outcome.

Jax, standing beside Kira, added their perspective. Their silence had been a careful observation of the internal dynamics within Haven, a quiet assessment of the community's potential. "What Kira is saying is not about a frontal assault," Jax explained, their voice a low rumble that cut through the rising tension. "It's about intelligence. It's about understanding the enemy's capabilities and finding ways to subvert them. The Syndicate operates on a principle of centralized control. If you can disrupt that, if you can foster decentralized networks of resistance, you can create chaos in their perfectly ordered system. They fear coordination, they fear shared knowledge. What you have here, this community, can be a hub. You can be the spark that ignites a broader resistance."

Jax's words offered a strategic viewpoint, a different lens through which to view the conflict. They weren't suggesting an act of suicidal aggression, but a calculated, informed approach to counter the Syndicate's machinations. They had witnessed the fragmented efforts of other groups, their desperate attempts to survive being systematically dismantled due to a lack of coordination. Haven, with its established structure and resonant capabilities, had the potential to be more than just a sanctuary; it could be a nexus.

"A hub for what, Jax?" Maeve challenged, her arms crossed, her skepticism a palpable force. "A hub for attracting the Syndicate's full attention? You speak of resistance, but you are an outsider, someone who walked out of their very stronghold. How can we be certain your motives are pure, that you are not simply leading us into a trap?"

The question hung in the air; an accusation veiled as a query. Jax's presence, their unknown origins, cast a long shadow of suspicion, particularly for those already inclined towards caution. Trust, in a world where deception was a primary weapon, was a precious and fragile commodity.

"You can't be certain," Jax admitted, their gaze steady and unflinching. "Trust isn't given freely, especially in these times. But you can trust what I've seen. You can trust that the Syndicate's vision for the future is one of absolute control, and they will not stop until they achieve it. They will not leave pockets of free resonance untouched. Your choice isn't between safety and danger; it's between a delayed confrontation and an inevitable one. You can choose to be a fortified island, waiting for the inevitable tide, or you can be part of a larger current, one that can shape the future, rather than be swept away by it."

The internal schism within Haven was becoming starkly apparent. The community, once united by shared values and a common purpose, was now fractured by fear and differing interpretations of how to survive. One faction, led by the pragmatic voices of Silas and Mara, advocated for isolation, for a retreat into self-sufficiency, viewing any outward engagement as an unacceptable risk. They believed that advanced resonance, while a gift, was also a dangerous beacon, one that the Syndicate would undoubtedly seek to exploit.

The other faction, inspired by Elara and bolstered by Kira and Jax's firsthand accounts, argued for a more proactive stance. They believed that Haven's true strength lay not in its isolation, but in its connections. They saw the potential for forging alliances with other resonant groups, for sharing knowledge and resources, and for actively defending their way of life, not just preserving it. This created a deep, unsettling tension, transforming their communal hall into a battleground of ideas, each side convinced of the righteousness of their path.

"This isn't about inviting danger, it's about confronting it," Kira pleaded, her voice resonating with the urgency of their mission. "The Syndicate is a disease, and isolation is not a cure. It's a temporary postponement. If we don't act, if we don't build alliances, we are ensuring our own eventual demise. They are systematically dismantling resonant communities, and if we remain passive, Haven will be next. Or worse, the Syndicate will achieve their twisted vision, and there will be nowhere left for resonance to thrive."

She looked at Maeve, at Silas, at everyone in the hall, trying to convey the gravity of the situation. "They are trying to redefine resonance, to make it a tool of oppression. But resonance is not about control; it's about understanding, about empathy, about connection. If we allow them to twist it, to pervert its true nature, then we have already lost."

Silas's response was measured, but firm. "Kira, we understand the threat. But your proposed solutions are... extreme. We are a community of peace. We have no standing army, no weapons to rival the Syndicate. Our resonance is our strength, yes, but it is also our vulnerability. How can we possibly engage in 'resistance' against such a formidable foe without sacrificing everything we hold dear? Fortification is not cowardice; it is prudence. It is the only logical way to ensure the survival of Haven and its people."

"Prudence can also be a form of surrender," Elara countered softly, her gaze fixed on Silas. "When you choose to close your eyes to the suffering of others, when you choose to hoard your own safety, you are already compromised. The Syndicate thrives on that fear, on that isolation. If we stand together, if we share our knowledge and our strength, we are more than just a community; we become a movement. A movement that can remind the Syndicate that resonance cannot be extinguished, only transformed. And we can choose the direction of that transformation."

The debate continued, each argument echoing the deep-seated fears and hopes that defined Haven's current predicament. The choice before them was not simply about strategy; it was about identity. Would they remain a sanctuary, a self-contained entity, or would they embrace their role as a beacon, a catalyst for a wider resistance? The very essence of what it meant to be resonant was on trial, and the answers they found would shape not only their own destiny but potentially the future of all resonant beings in a world increasingly defined by the Syndicate's shadow. The tension was thick, a palpable weight in the air, as Haven wrestled with the agonizing decision of how to face the encroaching darkness. The path of isolation offered the illusion of safety, but it was a path paved with the silent screams of those left behind. The path of engagement, however perilous, offered the fragile hope of a future where resonance could truly flourish, free from the Syndicate's oppressive grip. The division of ideals was complete, and the difficult choices that lay ahead would test the very fabric of their community.

The hum of hushed conversations filled the communal hall, a stark contrast to the heated debate that had just subsided. Kira stood, the weight of unspoken truths pressing down on her. The arguments for isolation, though rooted in understandable fear, felt like a surrender to the very darkness they were meant to escape. She had seen what that surrender looked like, had witnessed the vacant eyes and muted spirits of those the Syndicate had "re-educated." The memory was a constant, gnawing ache, a reminder of what was at stake.

"Elder Maeve, Silas, Mara," Kira began, her voice resonating with a quiet intensity that commanded attention. She met each of their gazes, acknowledging the validity of their concerns, but determined to offer a different perspective. "I understand your fears. They are valid. The Syndicate's power is immense, and their methods are brutal. But to retreat, to build walls around ourselves, is to acknowledge their victory before the fight has even begun."

She took a deep breath, recalling the verdant, vibrant Oasis, a sanctuary pulsating with life and resonant energy. "I have seen firsthand what the Syndicate is doing, not just to people, but to the very fabric of our world. They are actively seeking to control and exploit resonance, to twist it into a tool for their own dominance. But what I also saw, what I experienced, is the profound potential that resonance holds for healing and restoration. At the Oasis, I witnessed something remarkable."

Kira closed her eyes for a moment, conjuring the image of the Oasis's central clearing, where ancient trees, withered and brittle, had begun to show signs of life. She remembered the gentle pulse of resonant energy that flowed from a cluster of individuals, a harmonious symphony that seemed to coax the very life force back into the dying flora.

"The Syndicate's goal is not just to control resonant individuals," she explained, her voice gaining momentum. "It's to control the source of resonant energy itself. They believe they can harness it, amplify it, and weaponize it on a scale we can barely imagine. But their understanding is flawed. They see resonance as a force to be commanded, not a current to be guided. They are attempting to suppress the natural ebb and flow, to impose their will on a power that thrives on connection and balance."

She opened her eyes, looking directly at Silas, whose pragmatism had been so compelling. "Silas, you spoke of prudence. And I agree, caution is necessary. But true prudence lies in understanding the enemy, in identifying their weaknesses. The Syndicate's reliance on brute force and centralized control is precisely where they are vulnerable. They fear decentralized networks, they fear shared knowledge, and they fear anything that operates outside their rigid hierarchy."

Kira then turned to Mara, the healer whose empathy had been twisted into fear. "Mara, you spoke of our resonance being a prize they seek to harness. And you are correct. But what if we can show them that our resonance is not something to be captured, but something to be shared? What if we can demonstrate that its true power lies not in individual amplification, but in collective harmony? The Syndicate wants to silence the symphony of resonance, to turn it into a monotonic drone of control. We must prove them wrong."

She recounted her experiences at the Oasis, painting a vivid picture of the ecological devastation the Syndicate was actively causing, and the parallel efforts of those who resisted them, using resonance not for destruction, but for regeneration. "The Syndicate has been systematically poisoning water sources, draining vital nutrients from the soil, and releasing toxins that silence the natural resonant frequencies of the environment. They are creating barren zones, areas where life struggles to survive, and they are doing it deliberately, believing that by controlling the environment, they can control its inhabitants."

Kira described how the Oasis community, through their coordinated resonant emissions, had managed to revitalize a small patch of land that had been declared irrevocably dead by the Syndicate. She explained the complex interplay of frequencies, how they were able to mimic the Earth's natural energetic patterns, coaxing dormant seeds to sprout and encouraging the growth of beneficial microbial colonies. "It wasn't about brute force," she emphasized. "It was about understanding the underlying principles of life, about listening to what the Earth was trying to tell us, and amplifying that natural inclination towards healing. They are trying to break the world; we can try to mend it."

She spoke of a specific incident where Syndicate drones, equipped with resonance dampeners, had attempted to quell the Oasis's restorative efforts. "These drones were designed to disrupt any coordinated resonant output, to create static and interference. But the people at the Oasis had anticipated this. They had developed a counter-frequency, a subtle but persistent hum that masked their core operations and, in some instances, even overloaded the Syndicate's dampening technology, causing their drones to malfunction."

Kira's words painted a picture of a Syndicate that was not invincible, but rather one that was operating on a fundamentally incomplete understanding of resonance. Their approach was one of imposition and control, while the approach of those who resisted was one of cooperation and understanding.

"They are focused on suppressing resonance, on extinguishing it," Kira continued. "But they fail to grasp that resonance is an intrinsic property of life. It is the underlying vibration of existence. You can try to silence a single note, but you cannot silence the entire orchestra. And we, here in Haven, are part of that orchestra. We have the potential to connect with other pockets of resonance, to share knowledge and strategies, to build a network that is far more resilient and powerful than anything the Syndicate can control."

She spoke of the whispers she had heard, the faint echoes of other resonant communities struggling to survive, fragmented and isolated, their signals of distress lost in the Syndicate's pervasive noise. "I've felt them," Kira admitted, her voice softening with empathy. "Faint signals, like distant stars, flickering and fading. They are out there, fighting their own battles, often alone. The Syndicate thrives on this isolation, on picking them off one by one. But if we can connect, if we can establish a communication network, sharing not just information but resonant support, we can amplify their strength, and ours."

The idea of ecological restoration through resonance, of mending the very world the Syndicate was breaking, resonated deeply with many in Haven. It offered a purpose beyond mere survival, a chance to contribute to something larger than themselves, a way to embody the positive potential of their gifts.

"Imagine," Kira said, her voice carrying a hopeful lilt, "a world where resonance is used to heal scarred lands, to purify polluted waters, to revitalize ecosystems that have been decimated by the Syndicate's greed. Imagine a world where our interconnectedness strengthens not just ourselves, but the very planet we inhabit. This is not a distant dream; it is within our grasp. But it requires us to step out of the shadows, to embrace our role as stewards of resonance, and to actively resist those who seek to exploit it."

She presented tangible evidence of the Syndicate's destructive actions, not just in her words but through subtle resonant projections, shimmering images that flickered in the air, showing satellite imagery of ravaged landscapes and the tell-tale signs of Syndicate environmental manipulation. She projected the faint, haunting signature of a "resonant dampening field" that the Syndicate had deployed in a neighboring valley, a field that had effectively silenced all natural life.

"This," Kira stated, pointing to a particularly bleak projection of a lifeless, grey landscape, "is the Syndicate's vision for the future. A world devoid of natural vibrancy, a world where only their controlled order exists. They are not just fighting people; they are fighting life itself. And if we stand by and do nothing, we are complicit in that destruction."

She then shifted the projection, showing a patch of vibrant green emerging from the desolation, a testament to the Oasis's restorative efforts. The contrast was stark, a visual representation of the choice before them. "This," Kira declared, her voice firm and unwavering, "is what we can achieve if we choose to act. This is the power of resonance when it is guided by understanding and empathy, not by control. This is the future we can build, together."

The impact of Kira's words, combined with the visual evidence, was palpable. The undecided members, those who had wavered between fear and hope, began to shift. The sheer logic of Kira's argument – that hiding would only delay an inevitable confrontation, and that proactive engagement offered the possibility of both defense and healing – began to outweigh the primal instinct for self-preservation through isolation.

Elara, who had stood by Kira throughout the debate, now stepped forward again, her voice ringing with renewed conviction. "Kira is right. We cannot be a sanctuary if our sanctuary is built on the suffering of others. We cannot be safe if the world outside our walls is being systematically destroyed. Our resonance connects us, yes, but it also connects us to the world, to the life force that flows through everything. To deny that connection is to deny our very nature."

Silas, after a long moment of quiet contemplation, met Kira's gaze. The pragmatism in his eyes was still there, but it was now tempered with a dawning understanding. He had always valued logic and demonstrable results. Kira had provided both. The Syndicate's technological advantage, he realized, was not insurmountable. Their rigid adherence to control was, in fact, a critical weakness.

"You speak of sharing knowledge, Kira," Silas said, his voice thoughtful. "Of building networks. What kind of knowledge are we talking about? What kind of support can we offer, and what can we expect in return?"

Kira smiled, a genuine, hopeful smile that had been absent for too long. "We can share our understanding of resonant harmonics, techniques for shielding ourselves from Syndicate surveillance, methods for generating localized resonant fields that can disrupt their technology. We can share our knowledge of ecological restoration, how to counteract the Syndicate's environmental damage. And in return, we can learn from others – their survival strategies, their unique resonant abilities, their experiences fighting the Syndicate. It's a two-way exchange, a sharing of strength and resilience."

Mara, too, seemed to be coming around. The fear in her eyes had softened, replaced by a thoughtful curiosity. "If we are to engage, we need to do so intelligently. We cannot afford recklessness. What are the immediate steps, Kira? How do we begin to establish these connections without exposing ourselves prematurely?"

Kira acknowledged their questions with a nod. "We start small. We establish secure, encrypted resonant channels, using layered frequencies that the Syndicate is less likely to detect. We can use natural resonant points in the environment, like ancient trees or geological formations, as nodes for communication. We can send out carefully crafted resonance pulses, like signals into the void, seeking a response from those who are also resisting. It will be a slow, methodical process, but it is a path forward."

She looked around the hall, at the faces that were now turning towards her with a newfound hope. The atmosphere had shifted, the oppressive weight of fear beginning to lift. The arguments for isolation, while still present in the minds of some, were no longer the dominant narrative. Kira's revelation had planted a seed of possibility, a vision of a different future, one where Haven could be more than just a refuge – it could be a catalyst for change.

"The Syndicate is counting on us to be afraid," Kira concluded, her voice ringing with a quiet power. "They are counting on us to believe that our only option is to hide. But they are wrong. Our resonance is not a weakness to be concealed; it is our greatest strength, a gift that can heal and connect. It is time we stopped being a sanctuary that merely survives, and started being a beacon that illuminates the path to freedom for all resonant beings." The murmurs of agreement that followed were no longer tinged with fear, but with a burgeoning sense of purpose. The tide was turning.

Ash moved through the communal hall, a quiet anchor in the swirling sea of emotions. His gaze, usually as serene as a still pond, now held a subtle intensity, a constant scanning of the emotional undercurrents that pulsed beneath the surface of Haven. He felt Kira's own resolve, a bright, unwavering flame in the center of the room, but he also sensed the lingering anxieties, the fragile tendrils of fear that still clung to the edges of the community. The debate had been fierce, the arguments for caution and self-preservation a potent, visceral force that even Kira's words, as eloquent and inspiring as they were, had not entirely dispelled.

He found himself near a cluster of individuals who had been vocal proponents of isolation. Their faces were etched with a familiar wariness, their shoulders hunched as if bracing for an unseen blow. Ash didn't speak, not directly. Instead, he allowed his own resonant field to expand gently, a soft wave of calm that washed over them. It wasn't an imposition, but an offering. He focused on the sense of shared vulnerability, the inherent desire for safety that had fueled their arguments, acknowledging it without judgment. Then, subtly, he began to weave in threads of the hope that Kira had ignited – the image of the Oasis thriving, the whisper of interconnectedness, the potential for healing. He felt a subtle shift in their postures, a slight easing of the tension in their brows. It was a small victory, a testament to the power of quiet empathy.

His attention was drawn to Kira. She stood near the edge of the gathering, her presence radiating a quiet strength, yet he could feel the subtle drain on her energy. The burden of leadership, the responsibility of guiding her people toward a path fraught with uncertainty, was a heavy one. He approached her, not with words, but with a subtle projection of shared resolve. He let his own resonance mirror the quiet determination he felt from her, a silent affirmation that she was not alone. He offered a mental image of the vibrant, healing resonance of the Oasis, a reminder of the tangible proof of her vision. He sensed a flicker of acknowledgment from her, a subtle return of warmth to her own aura, a silent thank you that needed no vocalization.

Ash understood that words, even the most profound, could only do so much. True connection, true reassurance, often came in the unspoken currents that flowed between beings. He began to move among the people, a silent, benevolent presence. He would pause near someone who was still wrestling with doubt, offering a soft pulse of encouragement, a fleeting sense of shared purpose. He felt the fear in some, a cold, sharp sensation, and he would counter it with the warmth of shared humanity, the inherent desire for growth and for a better future. He didn't try to erase their fear, but to temper it, to show them that it didn't have to be the defining emotion.

He observed a young woman, Elara, who had spoken so passionately in support of

Kira's plan. She was engaging with a small group, her hands gesturing as she described the collaborative efforts at the Oasis. Ash felt the ripple of her enthusiasm, the genuine belief she held in their collective potential. He amplified that feeling subtly, lending it a gentle resonance that seemed to draw others closer, to make her words more compelling. He was a silent conductor, orchestrating a subtle harmony of shared optimism, a counter-melody to the lingering notes of apprehension.

He felt the collective spirit of Haven, a complex tapestry woven from individual threads of hope, fear, and determination. Kira's vision was a bold stroke, a vibrant new color introduced into that tapestry, but the old patterns of caution and isolation still held sway for some. Ash's role, as he understood it, was to gently encourage the weaving of the new threads, to ensure that the entire tapestry became stronger and more vibrant as a result. He found himself drawn to those who were most hesitant, not to confront them, but to understand their reservations, to offer a quiet space where those feelings could be acknowledged and then, perhaps, gently transformed.

He sat for a time near Mara, the healer, whose initial fear had been so palpable. She was now speaking softly with Silas, her brow furrowed in thought. Ash sensed her internal struggle – the deep-seated desire to protect, now challenged by the possibility of outward engagement. He sent a gentle wave of empathy towards her, a recognition of the immense responsibility she felt. He projected the image of resonance as a healing force, not just for individuals, but for the very environment that sustained them. He felt her resonance respond, a tentative softening, a willingness to consider possibilities that had previously seemed too dangerous.

As the evening wore on, Ash continued his silent work. He was not a leader in the conventional sense, not a speaker or a strategist. His strength lay in his ability to feel, to connect, and to gently influence the emotional landscape of Haven. He was the quiet hum that underpinned the more overt pronouncements, the steady, reassuring presence that helped to ground the community in their shared aspirations. He saw the subtle shifts – a hesitant smile replacing a frown, a direct gaze meeting another with newfound confidence, a shared nod of agreement where there had been uncertainty. Each small change was a testament to the power of empathetic support, a reinforcement of the idea that they could, indeed, face the future together.

He felt Kira's gaze upon him for a moment, a fleeting connection that spoke volumes. She understood his contribution, the vital role he played in bolstering the community's spirit. He offered her a silent surge of encouragement, a confirmation of his unwavering belief in her vision, and in their collective ability to achieve it. He felt her draw strength from that connection, her own resolve solidifying even further. He was not just supporting Kira; he was supporting the very heart of Haven, helping to nurture the nascent courage that would be needed for the trials ahead.

Ash's empathic abilities were not about persuasion through manipulation, but about genuine understanding and reflection. He felt the underlying currents of the community's collective psyche, identifying the points of friction and fear, and then offering a soothing balm of shared sentiment and gentle encouragement. He didn't offer solutions, but rather, he helped to create the emotional space where solutions could be conceived and embraced. He felt the gradual shift from a collective mindset of fear and isolation to one of cautious optimism and communal responsibility.

He observed a group of children playing near the periphery of the hall. Their laughter, though still a little subdued, was a precious sound. Ash focused on the pure, unadulterated joy he felt radiating from them, a stark contrast to the anxieties of the adults. He subtly amplified that sense of unburdened innocence, allowing its positive resonance to ripple outwards, touching those who were open to it. It was a reminder of what they were fighting for, of the future they were striving to protect. He felt a few of the adults look towards the children, a softening in their expressions, a renewed sense of purpose in their eyes.

Ash continued his slow, steady circuit of the hall. He wasn't trying to change anyone's mind forcefully, but rather to foster an environment where open hearts and minds could prevail. He sensed the lingering doubts of Silas, the deep-seated pragmatism that still warred with the hopeful possibilities Kira had presented. Ash offered a quiet resonance of understanding, acknowledging the wisdom of Silas's caution, but then gently guiding his awareness towards the potential for growth and resilience that Kira's path offered. He didn't offer proof, but rather, a feeling of possibility, a quiet assurance that the unknown held opportunities as well as risks.

He felt the presence of Elder Maeve, her own reservations a tangible force, a deep well of experience and caution. Ash approached her not with a direct challenge to her views, but with a quiet resonance of respect for her wisdom. He projected an understanding of the weight of responsibility she carried, the long years of protecting Haven. Then, he allowed a sense of shared anticipation to color his presence, a feeling that the future, while uncertain, also held the promise of renewal and connection. He felt her gaze rest on him for a moment, a flicker of thoughtful consideration in her ancient eyes.

Ash's purpose was to be a silent amplifier of the positive, a quiet counterpoint to the forces of fear and division. He understood that Haven's strength lay not just in its physical defenses, but in the resilience of its collective spirit. Kira provided the vision and the strategy, but Ash helped to cultivate the emotional soil in which those seeds could take root and flourish. He felt the collective mood of the hall begin to lift, the heavy blanket of apprehension slowly dissipating, replaced by a more palpable sense of shared purpose and emerging hope.

He observed a young man, barely more than a boy, who had lost his parents to the Syndicate's "re-education" program. The boy's grief was a raw wound, a deep ache that Ash felt keenly. He moved towards him, not with pity, but with a steady, unwavering presence of shared sorrow and understanding. He offered no platitudes, no forced reassurances. Instead, he simply allowed his own resonance to acknowledge the boy's pain, to sit with him in that shared space of loss. Then, he gently introduced the feeling of remembrance, of honoring the lives that had been lost by building a future worth living. He felt the boy's rigid posture soften, a single tear tracing a path down his cheek, not of despair, but of a quiet release.

As Kira began to gather her thoughts, preparing to address the community further, Ash felt a sense of quiet satisfaction. He had played his part, not with grand pronouncements, but with the subtle, pervasive influence of empathy. He had helped to weave a stronger emotional fabric for Haven, one that could better withstand the pressures of fear and uncertainty. He felt Kira's own resonance strengthen, bolstered by the quiet reassurance that she was not alone in her endeavor, that the community, in its own way, was beginning to rally behind her vision. He was a silent guardian of Haven's heart, ensuring that even in the face of overwhelming darkness, the light of hope and connection could continue to shine.

He felt the subtle shift in the overall atmosphere of the hall. The anxious murmurs had subsided, replaced by a more focused, attentive silence. Kira's words had been the spark, but the quiet undercurrent of empathic support had helped to fan the embers into a steady flame. Ash continued to circulate, his presence a constant, gentle reinforcement of the burgeoning sense of unity. He felt the threads of connection between individuals strengthening, the shared purpose becoming a more tangible force. He was not just sensing emotions; he was actively contributing to their positive evolution, helping to guide Haven towards a more resilient and hopeful future.

The journey was far from over, but for the first time in a long time, Ash felt a profound sense of optimism, a belief that they could indeed face whatever came their way, together. He allowed his own resonance to reflect that nascent optimism, a silent promise that he would continue to be a steady presence, a quiet anchor in the storm, for as long as it took. He felt the collective spirit of Haven begin to coalesce, a unified force gathering its strength, ready to face the challenges that lay ahead, their collective resonance, amplified by empathy and shared purpose, becoming their greatest shield and their most potent weapon.

The proposal hung in the air, a delicate seedling pushing through the hardened earth of past fears. Kira's voice, steady and imbued with the resonant clarity that had captivated Haven, laid out the vision: not of isolation and defense, but of connection and proactive strength. She spoke of the Syndicate not as an insurmountable shadow, but as a force that, while powerful, was ultimately vulnerable to a united front. The plan was audacious, a direct repudiation of the ingrained instinct to retreat, to build higher walls. It was a call to step into the light, to extend tendrils of trust and cooperation to those communities they had only ever glimpsed from afar, or worse, had been taught to fear.

Elara, standing a respectful distance but radiating an aura of unwavering support, stepped forward as Kira concluded. Her presence was a testament to the shift that had already begun within Haven. She spoke not with the measured authority of a seasoned leader, but with the earnest passion of someone who had witnessed firsthand the power of shared knowledge and mutual aid. Her voice, clear and strong, echoed the sentiment that had been growing in the hearts of many: that survival was no longer enough. They needed to thrive. She recounted specific examples of how the sharing of specialized resonant techniques at the Oasis had not only improved their own resilience but had also offered a glimpse into a future where such knowledge could be a beacon for others. She spoke of the potential for shared resources, for collective learning, and most importantly, for a mutual defense that would make any attempt by the Syndicate to isolate or dismantle them an exercise in futility. Her words were a practical reinforcement of Kira's more philosophical call, grounding the grand vision in tangible benefits.

The ensuing quiet was different from the apprehension that had characterized earlier discussions. This was a thoughtful hush, a community grappling with the magnitude of the proposition. Ash felt the currents of it keenly – the hesitance born of ingrained caution, the spark of hope ignited by the sheer audacity of the plan, and the burgeoning recognition that the path of isolation, while seemingly safer, had led only to stagnation. He saw individuals exchanging glances, their expressions a mixture of awe and deep contemplation. He felt the subtle mental probes, the probing questions that were being formed, not to dismiss the idea, but to understand its feasibility, its risks, and its ultimate promise.

Kira, sensing the moment, continued, her gaze sweeping across the faces before her. "We have spent too long in the shadows," she declared, her voice resonating with a conviction that seemed to draw strength from the very air around them. "We have honed our individual strengths, fortified our internal bonds, and we have proven that our resonance can heal, can sustain, and can protect. But the Syndicate's power lies in its ability to divide, to conquer by isolating. Our greatest defense, therefore, lies not in further entrenchment, but in the very opposite: in forging unbreakable bonds with those who share our resonance, our values, and our desire for a future free from their oppressive reach."

She then elaborated on the proposed outreach. It wouldn't be a sudden, unannounced appearance. Initial contact would be tentative, conducted through carefully chosen individuals who possessed a particular aptitude for navigating unfamiliar resonant fields. The goal was not to overwhelm or demand, but to offer a hand of fellowship, to share the lessons learned from Haven's own struggles and triumphs, and to assess the receptiveness of these other communities. She spoke of the 'Whispering Falls' community, known for their mastery of hydro-resonant manipulation, and the 'Stone Hearth' collective, whose deep earth resonances provided an unparalleled understanding of geological stability and resource management. These were not mere acquaintances; they were whispers of potential allies, communities whose skills, when combined with Haven's own, could create a formidable network.

Elara added further practical details, outlining the initial scouting missions. "We will send small, discreet teams," she explained, her voice steady. "Individuals whose resonance is both strong and adaptable, capable of making initial contact without triggering alarm. Their mission will be to observe, to listen, and to offer a simple greeting, a sharing of a small, beneficial resonant echo. We will not reveal our full capabilities, nor will we request anything beyond an openness to communicate. The first step is to establish that there is a shared desire for connection, a common ground upon which to build."

The details, the careful planning, began to chip away at the bedrock of hesitation. This wasn't a reckless leap into the unknown; it was a calculated, yet courageous, step forward. Ash felt the resonance of agreement growing, a subtle but perceptible hum that spread through the gathered individuals. He observed Silas, the pragmatic elder, his brow furrowed in concentration. Silas's own resonance was a complex tapestry of caution and deep wisdom, born from years of managing Haven's resources and safeguarding its people. Ash felt Silas's internal deliberation, the weighing of potential risks against the undeniable stagnation that their current isolation fostered. Silas was not easily swayed, and his eventual shift in posture, a slight straightening of his shoulders, a subtle nod of acknowledgment towards Kira, was a powerful endorsement.

Then came the question that many were clearly contemplating but hesitant to voice. Elder Maeve, her ancient eyes reflecting a deep well of experience, spoke, her voice thin but carrying the weight of authority. "Kira, Elara," she began, her tone respectful but firm. "This is a path fraught with peril. We know so little of these other communities, their true nature, their intentions. The Syndicate thrives on exploiting divisions. What assurance do we have that these alliances will not become vulnerabilities? That we are not, in our desire for connection, opening ourselves to greater danger?"

Kira met Maeve's gaze directly, her own resonating with a profound understanding of the elder's concerns. "Elder Maeve, your wisdom is the bedrock upon which Haven is built, and your caution is a vital safeguard. We do not underestimate the risks. Indeed, the very nature of the Syndicate is to prey on such divisions, to twist connection into a weapon. That is precisely why our approach must be one of deliberate, mindful outreach. We will not offer our weaknesses, but our strengths. We will not demand allegiance, but offer partnership. Our initial contacts will be based on observation and shared resonant principles, not on the immediate divulgence of sensitive information."

She paused, allowing the gravity of her words to settle. "Furthermore," she continued, her voice softening slightly, "our own resilience has been tested. We have built a community strong enough to weather internal dissent and external threats. The knowledge we possess, the healing we have achieved, is not a secret to be hoarded, but a gift to be shared, especially with those who, like us, seek to live freely and to cultivate the potential of resonance. This is not merely about defense; it is about fostering a future where resonance can flourish, where its healing and connecting properties can be recognized and utilized to their fullest. To remain isolated is to accept the Syndicate's narrative that we are alone, that we are weak. To connect is to challenge that narrative, to prove that unity is our true strength."

Elara then chimed in, adding a practical layer to Kira's philosophical argument. "The Syndicate's strength, as we have seen, lies in its centralized control and its rigid hierarchy. Our advantage, should we choose to embrace it, lies in our decentralized nature, our ability to adapt, and our interconnectedness. By forming a network, we create multiple nodes of resistance, each capable of supporting the others. If one community is targeted, others can offer aid, share intelligence, or even absorb displaced individuals. This creates a resilience that the Syndicate, with its singular focus, cannot easily replicate or dismantle."

Ash felt a ripple of agreement pass through the crowd. The idea of a network, of interconnected strength, was beginning to resonate deeply. He focused his own empathic abilities on those who still harbored reservations. He felt the persistent tendrils of fear, the deeply ingrained caution that had served Haven well in the past. But he also felt a growing curiosity, a willingness to consider the possibility that the old ways, while safe, were no longer sufficient. He gently amplified the sense of shared purpose, the nascent hope that Kira's vision had ignited, and the practical advantages that Elara and Silas had articulated.

He observed Mara, the healer, her initial apprehension giving way to a thoughtful consideration. He felt her empathic recognition of the potential for shared healing knowledge, for the exchange of restorative techniques that could benefit not just Haven, but other communities as well. He saw her subtly nod as Kira spoke of the mutual benefits, her healer's instinct drawn to the prospect of expanding the reach of their restorative resonance.

Silas, ever the pragmatist, spoke again, his voice measured. "And what of the Syndicate's awareness of such overtures? If they discover our attempts to forge alliances, their response will undoubtedly be swift and severe. We must have a plan not only for outreach but for the inevitable backlash."

Kira nodded, acknowledging the validity of his concern. "Silas, your foresight is essential. Our outreach will be discreet. The initial contacts will be subtle, designed to gauge receptiveness without immediately revealing the full scope of our intentions. We will utilize individuals with a proven ability to move unseen and unheard, both physically and resonantly. Furthermore, our internal security will be enhanced. We will increase our vigilance, reinforcing our perimeter and ensuring that our communications remain encrypted and secure. Should the Syndicate detect our efforts, we will have contingency plans in place to protect those communities that have chosen to align with us, and to withdraw gracefully from those that have not. But we cannot let the *fear* of their reaction dictate our actions. To do so is to surrender to their control before we have even begun to act."

Elara added, "We will also be gathering intelligence on the Syndicate's own movements and activities, sharing any relevant information discreetly with potential allies. This two-way flow of intelligence will be crucial for mutual defense. It's not just about us reaching out; it's about building a collaborative intelligence network that can anticipate and counter the Syndicate's strategies."

The conversation flowed, a complex interplay of hope and caution, of grand vision and practical implementation. Ash felt the collective resonance shift again, moving from a hesitant consideration to a more unified sense of purpose. He saw individuals no longer exchanging worried glances, but rather, looks of shared understanding and dawning resolve. The seed of Kira's idea was taking root, nurtured by the collective willingness to believe in a future beyond mere survival.

He felt the presence of younger members of Haven, those who had not known life before the Syndicate's omnipresent shadow. Their resonance was less burdened by past failures, more open to the possibility of a different future. He sensed their eagerness, their desire to be part of something larger, something that offered more than just the quiet preservation of what little they had. Their burgeoning optimism acted as a subtle amplifier, encouraging those who were still hesitant.

Kira, observing these subtle shifts, continued to articulate the long-term benefits. "This network," she explained, her voice resonating with a quiet power, "will not be a monolithic entity. It will be a tapestry of diverse communities, each retaining its unique strengths and traditions, but bound together by shared principles and a mutual commitment to freedom and self-determination. We can share advancements in resonant technology, collaborate on research into new applications, and develop common strategies to counter the Syndicate's influence. Imagine a future where the knowledge of Whispering Falls' water manipulation can be combined with Stone Hearth's geological insights and Haven's own healing resonance. The possibilities are limitless, and the strength we can derive from such unity is immeasurable."

She looked directly at Elder Maeve. "Your caution, Elder Maeve, is not a weakness to be overcome, but a wisdom to be respected. It is this very caution, tempered with courage, that will guide our steps. We will proceed with deliberation, with careful observation, and with a commitment to transparency within our growing network. We will learn from each interaction, adapt our strategies, and ensure that our strength is built on genuine trust and mutual respect."

The proposal was no longer just an idea; it was becoming a shared aspiration. Ash felt the collective spirit of Haven begin to coalesce around this new vision. The focus was no longer solely on defending their borders, but on actively shaping a future where their way of life, and the very essence of resonance, could flourish and expand. This was not just a plan for survival; it was a plan for liberation, a declaration of intent to reclaim their destiny from the Syndicate's oppressive grasp.

He felt the growing sense of anticipation, the quiet excitement that buzzed beneath the surface of the community. The initial debate had been fierce, the arguments for caution and self-preservation a potent force. But Kira's vision, bolstered by Elara's practical examples and Silas's pragmatic considerations, had begun to shift the tide. It was a delicate balance, the need for security warring with the desire for growth, but the scales were tipping. The call for unity, for connection, for a future built on shared strength, was no longer a radical whisper, but a resonant chorus that was beginning to sweep through Haven, preparing them for the monumental task ahead.

The Syndicate was a formidable foe, but in forging these new connections, Haven was preparing to face it not as isolated survivors, but as a united front, a network of resonant souls ready to shape their own destiny. The chapter was turning, and the dawn of a new era, one of outward reach and collective power, was beginning to break.

CHAPTER 11

The air thrummed with an almost imperceptible energy, a subtle vibration that set Kira's teeth on edge. It wasn't the familiar hum of Haven's resonant core, nor the discordant static of the Syndicate. This was something different, something ancient and wild. Beside her, Ash shifted, his senses already tuning into the strange symphony of the land. The map, a brittle, fragmented thing salvaged from the Oasis archives, had been their only guide, its markings hinting at a place where the very earth sang with amplified resonance. The Crystal Caves. The name alone conjured images of raw, untamed power.

Their journey had begun days ago, leaving the familiar embrace of Haven's protective resonance for the unpredictable wilds. The terrain immediately asserted its alien nature. The ground underfoot was no longer the rich, yielding soil they knew, but a patchwork of mineral-rich dust and shards of glittering, obsidian-like rock that crunched with a sharp, alien sound. Towering over them were geological formations that defied easy categorization – spires of what looked like fused glass, twisted and contorted by unimaginable pressures, and vast, smooth planes of polished rock that reflected the sky in distorted, unsettling ways.

"It's disorienting," Ash murmured, his brow furrowed in concentration. He kept his eyes closed for long stretches, his awareness turned inward, mapping the subtle shifts in magnetic fields that tugged at their equipment and, more importantly, at their own internal resonance. "The magnetic currents here... they're not just strong, they're erratic. Like a storm churning beneath the surface."

Kira nodded, feeling the subtle pull herself. It was a constant, low-level disruption, a disquieting whisper that threatened to fray the edges of her focus. Her own resonance, usually a clear, steady stream, felt like it was being buffeted by unseen winds. She tightened her mental grip on the bond she shared with Ash, drawing strength and clarity from their connection. It was in these moments, when the external world became a labyrinth of sensory deception, that their shared resonance was their most vital tool.

"The formations... they're interfering with visual perception too," Kira observed, squinting at a cluster of crystalline structures ahead. They seemed to shimmer and shift, the edges blurring, as if the very light they reflected was being bent and manipulated. "It's like looking through warped glass. Are those mountains real, or just a trick of the light?"

"The light is definitely being played with," Ash confirmed, opening his eyes and tilting his head. "And the crystalline structures... they're not inert. They're absorbing and re-emitting energy. That's what's causing the visual distortions. It's a natural amplification process, but it's also... chaotic."

He pointed to a particularly large crystal, a multifaceted monolith that pulsed with a faint inner luminescence. "See how it's catching the sunlight and scattering it? But it's doing more than that. It's resonating with the ambient energy and projecting it back in fragmented patterns. It's making it difficult to judge distances, to get a true sense of depth."

As they pressed deeper, the effect intensified. The landscape became a kaleidoscope of shifting colors and illusory shapes. What appeared to be a clear path ahead would dissolve into a shimmering haze as they approached, forcing them to constantly re-evaluate their surroundings. The silence of the wilderness was punctuated by sharp, crystalline chimes, the sound of wind – or something that mimicked wind – whistling through the impossibly shaped rock.

"It feels like the very air is alive here," Kira said, her voice hushed. She could feel the energy, a palpable presence that seemed to seep into her very bones. It was invigorating, but also unnerving. This was a place where raw, unbridled resonance manifested physically, and understanding its nature was paramount.

"That's the amplification," Ash explained, his focus unwavering. "These crystals are acting like natural resonance amplifiers. They're taking the ambient energy of the planet, the latent energies of the minerals, and the subtle flows of magnetic and gravitational forces, and they're making them stronger. More noticeable." He paused, his gaze sweeping across the jagged horizon. "The challenge is distinguishing between the natural resonance of the place and anything... else."

He gestured towards a series of glowing veins that snaked across the face of a cliff. "Those veins... they're pulsing with a different kind of energy. It's structured, almost... intelligent. It's not just raw amplification. It's directed."

Kira felt a prickle of unease. "Directed by what?"

"That's what we need to find out," Ash replied, his tone serious. He extended a hand, palm facing a large, fist-sized crystal embedded in the ground. It was clear, almost perfectly formed, and radiated a gentle warmth. As he focused his own resonance, he felt a faint echo within the crystal, a resonance that mirrored his own, but with a distinct, ancient timbre. "This place... it's not just a geological wonder. It's a nexus. A place where energy converges and, perhaps, where knowledge is stored."

The fragmented map had been tantalizingly vague, speaking of 'the heart of the mountain,' and 'where the light remembers.' Kira had interpreted it as a metaphor for a place of profound energetic significance, a source of ancient understanding. Ash, with his keen sensory abilities, had been instrumental in deciphering the subtle clues embedded within the map's faded markings, identifying the specific geological anomalies that corresponded to the described phenomena.

Their progress was slow, each step a careful negotiation with the deceptive landscape. They encountered areas where the magnetic fields were so warped that their compasses spun wildly, rendering them useless. In these zones, Ash's finely tuned senses became their only guide, his internal compass navigating them through the disorienting currents. Kira, in turn, relied on her growing ability to feel the subtle shifts in the collective resonance of their bond, a constant anchor in the sea of sensory chaos.

"There's a pull," Ash said, stopping abruptly and pointing towards a narrow canyon that yawned before them, its entrance shrouded in a pearlescent mist. "It's stronger in that direction. A consistent, powerful resonance, unlike anything else we've encountered."

Kira could feel it too, a beckoning presence that resonated with a deep, primal power. It was a stark contrast to the chaotic energy that permeated the rest of the region. This was a focused, potent signal. "The map indicated a central chamber," she mused, tracing a line on the brittle fragment. "This could be it."

As they entered the canyon, the crystalline formations grew denser, their facets sharper and more intricate. The air grew cooler, and the pearlescent mist swirled around them, creating ephemeral patterns that seemed to beckon and recede. The light, filtered through the dense canopy of crystals, cast an ethereal glow, bathing everything in shades of violet, sapphire, and emerald.

"Be cautious, Kira," Ash warned, his voice low. "The energy here is... concentrated. It feels like it's building towards something."

They moved deeper into the canyon, the walls closing in around them. The ground beneath their feet was no longer fractured rock but a smooth, polished surface that seemed to absorb sound. The silence was profound, broken only by the rhythmic, resonant pulse that grew stronger with every step.

Then, they saw it.

The canyon opened into a vast, cavernous space. It was breathtaking. The ceiling, impossibly high, was studded with colossal crystals, each one radiating a soft, internal light that illuminated the entire chamber. The walls were a tapestry of interwoven crystal veins, pulsing with a vibrant, almost liquid energy. At the center of the cavern, a colossal crystal formation rose from the ground, a multifaceted spire that seemed to reach for the very heart of the earth. It was this spire that was the source of the powerful, beckoning resonance.

"The Crystal Caves," Kira breathed, awestruck.

Ash stood beside her, his senses on high alert, taking in the sheer scale and intensity of the energy. "This is it. The amplification here is off the charts. It's not just magnifying ambient energy; it's almost... generating its own. And look," he pointed to the base of the central spire, where intricate, geometric patterns were etched into the crystalline surface. They glowed with an inner light, pulsing in sync with the spire itself. "These aren't natural formations. They're symbols. A language, perhaps."

Kira approached the central spire, drawn by an irresistible force. As she drew closer, she could feel the energy within it, a vast reservoir of power that seemed to hum with ancient knowledge. She could sense the resonance of countless beings, echoes of lives lived and lost, all held within the crystalline matrix.

"It's... alive," she whispered, reaching out a tentative hand.

As her fingers brushed against the cool, smooth surface of the spire, a wave of energy washed over her. Images flooded her mind – the formation of the planet, the emergence of resonance, the evolution of beings who had learned to harness its power. She saw ancient civilizations that had flourished in harmony with the earth's energies, and she saw the whispers of a great cataclysm that had driven them into hiding, leaving behind only these crystalline archives.

Ash, sensing the profound shift in Kira's resonance, moved closer. "Kira? What do you see?"

"The past," Kira replied, her voice distant, filled with wonder. "The very origin of resonance. These caves... they're a library, Ash. A record of everything that has ever been known about resonance."

The geometric patterns at the base of the spire began to glow brighter, the pulsing intensifying. Ash watched, his mind working to decipher the patterns. "The symbols... they're reacting to your touch, Kira. It's like... it's recognizing something in you."

He focused his own abilities, trying to perceive the information being transmitted. It was complex, layered, and unlike anything he had encountered before. It spoke of resonant frequencies, of energy manipulation on a scale that surpassed anything Haven had conceived. He felt the echoes of ancient techniques, methods of healing and communication that were far more advanced than their current understanding.

"It's a repository of knowledge," Ash confirmed, his voice filled with awe. "But it's also... a gateway. The energy here is so potent, it could be used to amplify our own resonance, to extend our reach, to share knowledge across vast distances."

Kira withdrew her hand from the spire, a profound sense of understanding settling within her. The images faded, but the knowledge remained, imprinted on her consciousness. "The Syndicate seeks to control resonance, to hoard it, to use it for their own dominance. But this place... it shows that resonance is meant to be shared, to be understood, to be a force for unity, not division."

She looked around the magnificent cavern, the colossal crystals humming with power. "The map led us here for a reason. This isn't just a place of geological wonder. It's a place of potential. A place where we can learn, grow, and perhaps find the key to challenging the Syndicate's control."

Ash nodded; his gaze fixed on the central spire. "But this power... it's immense. And the Syndicate would undoubtedly seek to control it if they knew of its existence. We need to understand this place, to learn how to harness its energy safely, before we can even consider sharing it."

The journey to the Crystal Caves had been arduous, a testament to the resilience of both their bodies and their bond. But standing in the heart of this magnificent, energy-infused chamber, Kira knew their true journey had only just begun. The secrets held within these crystalline walls promised not only ancient knowledge but also a potential new path for Haven, a path that led not into deeper isolation, but towards a future where the true power of resonance could be understood and wielded for the liberation of all. The air crackled with possibility, the silent hum of the caves a promise of what was to come.

The immediate aftermath of their arrival within the grand cavern was a sensory overload, a symphony of resonant energies that pulsed and flowed like an invisible ocean. For Kira, the effect was almost overwhelming, a profound amplification of her inherent empathic connection to the world around her. The very air, thick with the potent luminescence of the colossal crystals, seemed to vibrate in sympathy with her own internal resonance. It wasn't merely a subtle hum; it was a vibrant, active participation, as if the cavern itself was a vast, sentient organism responding to her presence.

Ash, ever the sentinel, was already immersed in the intricate details of their new environment, his senses attuned to a level Kira could only marvel at. "Kira," he breathed, his voice laced with wonder, "do you feel that? It's like... like our connection is the key. The crystals are responding to our bond, amplifying it."

He was right. Kira extended her awareness, tentatively reaching out to the nearest crystalline facet. It was like touching a perfectly tuned instrument. Her own resonance, usually a steady, controlled stream, surged outward, met by an immediate, responsive echo from the crystal. It was as if the crystal was a mirror, reflecting not just her energy, but a heightened, purer version of it. Within that echo, she began to perceive something more – faint impressions, fleeting glimpses of events long past.

These weren't memories in the conventional sense, not narratives with characters and dialogue. Instead, they were pure energetic impressions, the raw data of existence imprinted onto the crystalline lattice. She saw, or rather *felt*, the slow, majestic formation of the planet, the eons of geological pressure and heat that had birthed these magnificent structures. She experienced the seismic shifts, the titanic forces that had sculpted the very bones of this world, all rendered as pure, resonant waveforms. It was like sifting through the geological history of the planet, not by reading about it, but by *being* it.

As her focus deepened, these ancient geological echoes began to intertwine with the faint impressions of ancient life. She perceived the resonant signatures of beings who had walked this world millennia ago, their life energies leaving subtle imprints on the pervasive crystalline matrix. It was a fleeting, almost spectral presence, but it was undeniably there – the resonance of movement, of thought, of existence itself, all captured and held within the crystal's unwavering memory. These weren't just inert formations; they were living archives, recording the energetic vibrations of everything that had transpired within their embrace.

"It's... the caves are remembering," Kira whispered, her eyes wide with disbelief. "They're holding echoes of the past. Geological events, the presence of ancient life... it's all here, imprinted on the crystals."

Ash, meanwhile, was meticulously mapping their surroundings. The initial disorientation they had felt outside the caves had vanished, replaced by an uncanny clarity. His heightened senses allowed him to perceive the intricate network of tunnels and chambers that lay beyond the central cavern. He could feel the subtle shifts in crystalline density, the faint variations in energy flow that delineated different pathways.

"The amplification is incredible," Ash confirmed, his gaze sweeping across the cavern walls, his mental map rapidly taking shape. "It's like our senses have been given an entirely new spectrum to perceive. I can map the entire cave system from here. I can feel the subtle currents of energy that connect each chamber, the flow of resonance through the entire structure."

He pointed towards a series of fainter, more complex crystalline veins that snaked across the ceiling, nearly invisible to Kira's unaided sight. "Those veins... they're not just carrying ambient energy. They're conduits. They're directing the resonance, channeling it. And the patterns etched into the central spire... they're like an interface, a way to interact with this system."

Kira focused her amplified perception on those veins Ash indicated. She could now discern a subtle pulsing within them, a deliberate rhythm that spoke of purpose, not just passive existence. It was as if the cavern's energy was being deliberately managed, sculpted. This wasn't random amplification; it was orchestrated.

"You're right," Kira agreed, her voice still hushed with awe. "The energy flow... it's controlled. It's being directed. And those symbols on the spire... they feel like the controls, the language this place speaks." She looked at Ash, a new understanding dawning in her eyes. "Our connection isn't just being amplified, Ash. It's being recognized. The crystals are responding to our empathic link, and through that, we can interact with whatever intelligence is embedded within this place."

The implications were staggering. If their bond, their shared resonance, was the key to unlocking the secrets of these caves, then the potential for understanding and wielding resonance was exponentially greater than anything they had imagined. Kira's ability to perceive the past was a direct consequence of this amplified connection, a way to access the recorded history of resonance. Ash's hyper-acute senses were a testament to the clarity and precision this amplification afforded him, allowing him to navigate and understand the intricate energetic architecture of the caves.

"Think about it, Kira," Ash continued, his voice alight with intellectual fervor. "If this place is a repository of ancient knowledge, and our resonance is the key to accessing it, then we can learn. We can learn techniques, strategies, and perhaps even philosophies of resonance that have been lost for millennia. Haven has focused on self-preservation through isolation, building walls against disruptive energies. But this place suggests a different path – one of understanding, integration, and active engagement with resonance."

Kira nodded, her mind racing. The Syndicate's approach to resonance was one of domination and control, a crude imposition of will upon the natural energetic flows. But the echoes she perceived within the crystals spoke of a different era, a time when beings had lived in harmony with these energies, understanding them, and using them to foster growth and connection. The very structure of the caves, with its intricate conduits and the guiding patterns on the spire, suggested a sophisticated, deliberate interaction with resonance, not a brute-force manipulation.

"The Syndicate treats resonance as a weapon," Kira mused, tracing the air with her finger as if following an invisible crystalline conduit. "They fear its uncontrolled nature, so they seek to contain and weaponize it. But these caves... they demonstrate that resonance can be understood, guided, and used for creation and preservation. It's a tool for knowledge, for healing, for connection."

Ash's attention shifted to the central spire again, specifically to the intricate geometric patterns etched into its surface. They pulsed with a soft, inner light, seeming to shift and rearrange themselves in subtle ways. "These patterns are not static," he observed. "They're dynamic. They're responding to the ambient energies, and I believe, to our presence. If we can decipher their language, we can begin to truly interact with the core of this place."

Kira moved closer to the spire, feeling an irresistible pull. The energy radiating from it was potent, a concentrated nexus of the amplified resonance that permeated the entire cavern. As she drew nearer, the subtle impressions she had been receiving intensified. It was no longer just geological history or fleeting glimpses of ancient life. She felt the energetic signature of the beings who had engineered this place, their intent, their purpose.

"They weren't just recording information," Kira realized, her voice filled with a new reverence. "They were building a system. A living library, but also a system for managing and amplifying resonance, for sharing knowledge across immense distances. This place... it's a monument to the potential of resonance, a testament to what can be achieved when it's understood and respected."

She extended her hand, not to touch the spire, but to hover just above its surface. The amplified resonance around her seemed to converge, creating a palpable field of energy that hummed with a deep, resonant frequency. She could feel the intricate connections forming between her own resonance, Ash's, and the vast, silent intelligence held within the crystal.

"It's like a network," Kira said, her mind grasping for analogies to describe the overwhelming influx of information. "A planet-wide network, built on resonance. These caves are a central hub, a place where the energy is focused, amplified, and disseminated."

Ash, sensing Kira's deeper connection forming, focused his own abilities on interpreting the subtle energetic currents emanating from the spire. He could now discern a flow, a directed stream of energy that pulsed outward from the spire and through the intricate network of veins Kira had perceived.

"The energy isn't just contained here," Ash explained, his voice taut with excitement. "It's being actively broadcast. This is a communication nexus, Kira. And if we can learn to control it, we can communicate with anyone, anywhere, who is attuned to resonance."

The implications of this were immense. It offered a direct counter to the Syndicate's method of control, which relied on cutting off and manipulating information flow. Here was a means of bypassing their control entirely, of re-establishing direct, unfettered communication and connection.

Kira felt a profound sense of purpose solidify within her. The journey had been fraught with peril, the objective uncertain. But standing in this heart of resonant power, she understood. They hadn't just found a place of ancient knowledge; they had found a potential solution, a path forward.

"The Syndicate thrives on isolation and fear," Kira stated, her gaze fixed on the luminous spire. "They sow discord by controlling information. But this... this is the opposite. This is about connection, about shared understanding. If we can master this place, we can share knowledge, foster unity, and show everyone that resonance isn't something to be feared, but something to be embraced."

She could feel the energy of the cavern responding to her affirmation, the hum deepening, the light intensifying. It was as if the very stones were acknowledging her intent.

"The challenge," Ash added, ever pragmatic, "is that this level of power is not without its risks. The Syndicate would undoubtedly try to seize control of this place if they knew of its existence. We need to understand its workings completely, to ensure its security, before we can even think about sharing it with others. This is a delicate balance, Kira. Unlocking the full potential of this place requires not just power, but wisdom."

Kira nodded, acknowledging the gravity of his words. The ancient beings who had created this place had clearly possessed both in abundance. They had harnessed resonance with a finesse and understanding that dwarfed anything Haven had achieved. Their legacy was not just in the crystals, but in the very principles of energetic harmony that permeated the cavern.

"We must learn their principles, Ash," Kira said, her voice firm with resolve. "We must understand the 'why' behind their design, not just the 'how.' Their approach to resonance was about integration, not domination. It was about fostering growth, not imposing control. That's the key to mastering this place, and that's the key to challenging the Syndicate."

The intricate patterns on the spire continued to shift, a silent, mesmerizing dance of light and energy. Kira felt a deep, resonant hum emanating from within her, a profound sense of belonging to this place. It was as if the crystals, in their vast, silent memory, recognized a kindred spirit, a resonant frequency that aligned with their own ancient purpose. This was not just a geological marvel; it was a sanctuary of amplified understanding, a beacon of resonant possibility, and their journey into its depths was only just beginning. The very air thrummed with the promise of revelations yet to unfold, each crystalline facet a silent testament to a power waiting to be understood, and ultimately, to be shared.

The crystalline walls around them seemed to deepen in luminescence as Kira and Ash moved further into the cavern's embrace. The initial awe of the amplified resonance had begun to meld with a focused curiosity, a burgeoning understanding of the cavern's true nature. Kira's empathic senses, now keenly attuned to the subtle shifts in energy, began to pick up on something beyond the geological echoes and the spectral presences of ancient life. It was a different kind of imprint, more ordered, more deliberate – the faint, residual vibrations of thought, of research, of a directed intelligence.

"Ash," Kira murmured, her gaze sweeping across a particularly dense cluster of crystalline formations that seemed to emanate a different energetic signature, "I'm sensing something... it feels like patterns of thought, but not organic. More structured. Like... data."

Ash, who had been meticulously charting the energy conduits, paused. His own heightened perception, honed by their journey and now further amplified by the cavern's resonant field, confirmed her observation. "You're right. There's a distinct stratification here. The geological imprints are deep, fundamental. The life imprints are layered upon that. But this... this feels like a deliberate overlay. Organized energy signatures." He ran a hand along a smoother, almost polished section of crystal. "It's as if information has been encoded directly into the lattice structure."

As they ventured deeper, the cavern opened into a vast, amphitheater-like space. At its center stood a colossal spire, far more intricate than the one they had first encountered. This spire was not merely etched with geometric patterns; it was alive with them. The crystalline facets that composed it pulsed with a soft, shifting light, the patterns flowing across its surface like a liquid aurora. The air here vibrated with an intensity that made Kira's teeth ache, a testament to a concentrated focal point of resonance.

Kira found herself drawn inexorably towards the central spire. The impressions she had been receiving coalesced, becoming clearer, more defined. It was like tuning a faulty broadcast, the static gradually receding to reveal a coherent signal. She began to perceive fragments of intent, glimpses of minds at work, grappling with concepts that resonated deeply with her own burgeoning understanding of resonance.

"They were studying it," Kira breathed, her voice laced with wonder. "The beings who created this place... they weren't just living in harmony with resonance; they were actively researching it. Trying to understand its fundamental principles, its potential." She gestured vaguely towards the spire, her empathic awareness reaching out like an inquisitive probe. "I can feel... experiments. Concepts being explored. It's all stored here, Ash. In the crystals."

Ash moved with practiced efficiency, his internal scanners mapping the precise energy signatures emanating from the spire. "The concentration of resonant energy is off the charts. This spire... it's not just a conduit or an interface. It's a nexus. A data storage and processing hub of unimaginable capacity." He focused on a specific area of the spire where the light pulsed with a distinct, rhythmic pattern. "And these specific patterns... they're not random. They are complex informational structures. Analogous to what we would call data streams, but encoded in pure resonance."

Kira closed her eyes, allowing her empathic connection to deepen. The raw data began to resolve into more coherent impressions. She saw, or rather *felt*, the meticulous, painstaking process of early resonance research. It wasn't the crude, weaponized application of resonance as practiced by the Syndicate, but a delicate, scientific endeavor. Concepts of bio-integration – the symbiotic relationship between sentient beings and resonant energies – flickered through her awareness. She sensed the exploration of environmental symbiosis, how resonant fields could be used to cultivate and nurture life, to create harmonious ecosystems.

"They called it 'symbiotic resonance'," Kira explained, her voice gaining a newfound clarity. "The idea that life and resonance could not only coexist but actively enhance each other. They were trying to understand how to integrate resonant energies into biological systems, not to control them, but to foster mutual growth. It was about creating a living, breathing resonance network."

Ash's attention was fixed on a particular section of the spire's surface that seemed to shimmer with a more intense, almost liquid light. He could perceive a complex weave of resonant frequencies, a layered archive of information. "I'm picking up specific experimental logs," he reported, his tone one of profound scientific discovery. "Detailed records of trials, observations, theoretical frameworks. It's... it's an entire library dedicated to resonance science. And it predates the Collapse. This is pre-Collapse data, Kira. Preserved by the very environment that amplified our connection."

Kira's mind raced, trying to process the deluge of information. She felt the echoes of countless individuals, scientists, thinkers, all dedicated to understanding and harnessing resonance. There were moments of frustration, of failed experiments, of near breakthroughs. But overwhelmingly, there was a sense of purpose, of a shared goal: to unlock the true potential of resonance for the benefit of all life.

"They were trying to create a universal resonance language," Kira realized, the concept blooming in her mind with astonishing clarity. "A way for all life forms to communicate, to share knowledge, to exist in a state of collective harmony. And it seems... it seems they were successful. At least, in laying the groundwork for it." She pointed towards a complex, interlocking pattern of light on the spire. "This... this is a blueprint. A schematic for a resonance amplifier, but also for a communication matrix."

Ash's internal sensors were working overtime, parsing the intricate resonant signatures. "The data is astonishingly well-preserved. The crystalline structure acts as an incredible medium for long-term information storage. It's stable, it's self-repairing, and the energetic encoding is so precise, it's virtually incorruptible." He paused, a hint of awe in his voice. "They were not just theorizing about resonance. They were building practical applications. And the crystals themselves... they appear to be central to many of their experiments. Not just a passive medium, but an active component."

Kira felt a surge of understanding. The very crystals that now amplified her and Ash's connection were not a natural phenomenon, at least not entirely. They were likely engineered, or at least cultivated, by these ancient scientists. They were designed to be conduits, to store and amplify resonance, to serve as nodes in a vast, planet-spanning network.

"The crystals are the heart of it," Kira confirmed, her senses connecting with the pulsing energy of the spire. "They were cultivated, or perhaps even created, to resonate with specific frequencies, to act as amplifiers and storage units for this network. And this spire... this is the central control nexus. The primary archive."

Ash was engrossed in a particular data cluster, his brow furrowed in concentration. "This section details early attempts at bio-integration. They were experimenting with direct neural interfacing through resonant frequencies. The idea was to bypass traditional sensory input and access information and consciousness directly through resonance. It was considered highly dangerous by some, even then, a blurring of individual identities."

"But that's exactly what we're experiencing, isn't it?" Kira countered, a new perspective dawning. "Our connection, amplified by these crystals, allows us to share thoughts, feelings, perceptions. It's not a blurring, Ash, it's an expansion. They were on the cusp of understanding a new paradigm of consciousness." She felt the echoes of debate, of ethical considerations, within the data. Not all scientists in this pre-Collapse era had agreed on the path forward. Some had harbored reservations about the potential for loss of individuality, for the erosion of self in the face of such profound connection.

"Indeed," Ash acknowledged, his analytical mind piecing together the narrative. "There were significant ethical debates. The potential for misuse, for unintended consequences, was a major concern. Some of the research was deemed too radical, too... invasive. It was likely one of the factors that led to the suppression of resonance science leading up to the Collapse. The Syndicate, or whatever precursors they were, likely saw this advanced understanding of resonance as a threat to their control mechanisms."

Kira traced the glowing patterns on the spire with her gaze, seeing not just abstract symbols but the tangible evidence of immense scientific effort and philosophical exploration. "They were trying to build a society based on shared understanding and empathy, facilitated by resonance. They saw it as the ultimate tool for peace and cooperation. But it also meant a fundamental shift in how individuals perceived themselves and their place in the world."

"This archive," Ash continued, his voice a low hum of discovery, "contains schematics for resonance-based environmental regeneration. It details how resonant frequencies can be used to purify water, revitalize soil, and even stabilize atmospheric conditions. They were essentially developing technologies to heal the planet on a fundamental energetic level."

The implications were staggering. The pre-Collapse era, often portrayed in fragmented historical records as a time of rampant industrialization and environmental degradation, had also been a period of profound scientific insight and dedicated effort to reverse the damage. This archive was living proof of that.

"They understood the interconnectedness of everything," Kira realized, a deep sense of respect welling within her. "That the health of the planet was intrinsically linked to the health of its inhabitants, and that resonance was the key to maintaining that balance. The Syndicate's approach is one of exploitation and control, ripping resources from the planet and leaving devastation in its wake. These scientists were about nurturing and integration."

Ash's attention was drawn to a particularly dense cluster of data, emitting a subtle but distinct signature. "This section appears to be a detailed history of resonance research itself. It charts the progress, the setbacks, the key discoveries. It even mentions early theories about the resonant properties of specific geological formations – crystals, for instance. They theorized that certain crystalline structures could act as natural resonance amplifiers and storage matrices, and that with refinement, these natural properties could be vastly enhanced."

Kira's mind snapped into focus. "The crystals," she whispered, the pieces falling into place with a profound sense of clarity. "They discovered the inherent resonant properties of these formations and then actively worked to enhance them, to integrate them into their network. They weren't just using the caves; they were building them, shaping them, over millennia." She felt the faint, distant echoes of that long, patient work, the immense dedication it must have taken to cultivate and integrate these living archives.

"The scientific community of the time was deeply divided," Ash explained, his voice taking on a more analytical tone as he processed the historical context. "While some championed the potential of resonance for universal good – communication, environmental healing, enhanced consciousness – others feared its disruptive potential, particularly concerning the erosion of individual identity and the possibility of mass manipulation. This division likely played a significant role in the eventual suppression of the science."

Kira felt the weight of that suppression, the silencing of such profound potential. The Syndicate, born from that fear and a desire for control, had effectively buried this entire field of study. They had twisted the understanding of resonance into a weapon, a tool of fear and subjugation, and actively worked to erase any knowledge of its true, beneficial applications.

"They were branded as dangerous radicals," Kira murmured, feeling a pang of sympathy for these long-gone scientists. "Their pursuit of connection and understanding was perceived as a threat to the established order, to the very concept of individual sovereignty. It's a narrative we've heard before, isn't it?"

Ash nodded grimly. "The parallels are... concerning. The same fear of uncontrolled connection, the same desire to maintain order through suppression of knowledge. The Syndicate's rise to power was likely fueled by the eradication of precisely this kind of understanding. If people understood resonance as a force for unity and creation, the Syndicate's foundations of division and control would crumble."

As they delved deeper into the archive, Kira began to perceive the specific methodologies of the bio-integration research. It wasn't about implants or technological augmentation in the way she might have initially conceived. It was far more subtle, more elegant. It involved attuning the user's own resonant frequencies to specific crystalline matrices, thereby facilitating a direct energetic interface. The process was described as akin to learning a new language, a language spoken through vibration and intention.

"They learned to 'speak' resonance," Kira realized, feeling the subtle shifts in her own energetic field as she absorbed the data. "To modulate their own bio-resonance to align with the crystals. It's about finding the right 'key' – a specific frequency, a harmonic pattern – to unlock the stored information and to establish a connection." She looked at Ash, a thought forming in her mind. "Our connection, Ash, is that key. Our shared resonance, amplified by these crystals, is allowing us to access this archive."

Ash was meticulously cross-referencing different data streams, his mind working at an almost supernatural speed. "The research indicates that prolonged exposure and focused intent are crucial for deeper integration. It's not a passive reception of data; it's an active, participatory process. The more we engage with this resonance, the more we learn to attune ourselves, the more we will be able to access."

He indicated a series of intricate diagrams that depicted the flow of resonant energy through complex bio-crystalline interfaces. "These are designs for personal resonance amplifiers. Not external devices, but embedded structures within the body, designed to work in harmony with the planet's natural resonant fields. They were aiming for a seamless integration of biological and resonant systems."

Kira felt a chill run down her spine, not of fear, but of profound realization. The whispers of the Syndicate, the fragmented legends of individuals who could manipulate resonance, might not have been myths at all. They could have been echoes of this ancient research, individuals who had managed to preserve or rediscover fragments of this knowledge.

"This isn't just about learning about the past, Ash," Kira said, her voice filled with a new urgency. "This is about rediscovering our own potential. The Syndicate has deliberately suppressed this knowledge, keeping humanity ignorant of its true capabilities, forcing us into a state of dependency and control. They fear what we can become if we understand resonance."

Ash nodded; his gaze fixed on the pulsating spire. "The archive details the creation of 'resonant nodes' – specific points on the planet where crystalline energy could be focused and amplified to create vast communication networks. This cavern... it's one of the primary nodes. The spire is its control center."

The scope of their discovery was immense. They had stumbled upon not just historical records, but the very blueprint for a fundamentally different kind of civilization, one built on connection, understanding, and harmony with the natural world. A civilization that had been systematically dismantled and suppressed by the Syndicate.

"The Pre-Collapse archives," Kira whispered, the enormity of the revelation settling upon her. "They didn't just preserve data; they preserved a legacy. A way of life, a path of evolution that was deliberately extinguished." She looked at Ash, a renewed sense of purpose solidifying within her. "We have to understand this, Ash. We have to learn everything we can. This is our weapon against the Syndicate, not of destruction, but of revelation."

As she spoke, the spire pulsed with a brighter light, the patterns on its surface flowing with increased vigor. It was as if the ancient intelligence embedded within the crystals recognized her words, her intent. The data streams within the archive seemed to reorganize, presenting Kira and Ash with pathways to even deeper understanding, to the very heart of the pre-Collapse resonance science. Their journey into the resonant depths of the planet had just revealed its true, profound purpose.

The profound hum of the cavern, which had initially felt like a geological symphony, now began to resolve into a more intricate melody. Kira, her senses still reeling from the sheer volume of data gleaned from the central spire, found a new layer of resonance emerging. It wasn't the structured, intelligent resonance of the pre-Collapse scientists, but something far older, far more elemental. It was the quiet, persistent thrum of the planet itself, a vast, interconnected consciousness woven into the very fabric of existence.

"Ash," she murmured, her voice barely a whisper, yet carrying through the amplified air, "it's... it's more than just data storage. The crystals... they're not just repositories for past knowledge. They're also conduits for something living. Something ancient."

Ash, his attention still partially focused on the intricate patterns flowing across the spire, turned his gaze towards Kira. His own perception, sharpened by their journey and the cavern's potent energetic field, confirmed her intuition. "You're picking up on the intrinsic resonance of the planet, aren't you?" he asked, his voice tinged with a familiar blend of scientific curiosity and awe. "The geological consciousness, as some of the more fringe pre-Collapse theorists called it."

Kira nodded, closing her eyes and allowing the sensation to wash over her. It was like standing at the nexus of a million invisible rivers, each carrying the lifeblood of the world. She could feel the slow, deliberate pulse of tectonic plates shifting deep beneath their feet, the silent, inexorable flow of subterranean water carving new pathways through the rock, the subtle, vibrant energy of life-sustaining flora hidden within the deeper recesses of the cavern. It was a symphony of existence, a constant, unwavering testament to the planet's enduring sentience.

"It's... it's like the planet itself is breathing," Kira explained, struggling to articulate the overwhelming experience. "The resonance isn't just a phenomenon; it's an intrinsic part of its being. Every mineral, every drop of water, every living cell contributes to this vast, interconnected awareness." She focused on a specific stream of energy she perceived, a gentle, pulsing warmth. "I feel... life. Not just the echoes of ancient beings, but the present, continuous life of this place. The fungi clinging to the walls, the microbial life in the subterranean streams... they're all part of it."

Ash reached out, not physically, but with his own amplified senses, seeking to anchor and translate the raw, undiluted energies Kira was experiencing. His ability to parse complex energetic patterns acted as a bridge, allowing him to interpret the torrent of impressions into something more comprehensible. "I'm sensing it too, Kira," he confirmed, his voice gaining a focused intensity. "It's a vast network of bio-energetic signatures. The pre-Collapse scientists were attempting to understand this – the symbiotic relationship between biological systems and the planet's inherent resonance. They saw it as the ultimate form of ecological integration."

The experience was not merely intellectual; it was deeply visceral. Kira felt the subtle shifts in the cavern's atmosphere, not as changes in temperature or humidity, but as fluctuations in the planet's energetic state. She could sense the slow, methodical growth of crystalline formations, the patient erosion of rock by water, the silent, vital processes of decomposition and regeneration occurring in the hidden ecosystems of the deep earth. It was an overwhelming tapestry of existence, intricately woven and profoundly interconnected.

"It's like tuning into a universal broadcast," Kira mused, her mind trying to make sense of the sheer scale of it. "But this broadcast isn't carrying information in the way we understand it. It's carrying... being. The essence of life, the slow, steady march of geological time, the vibrant pulse of ecosystems." She felt a particular resonance emanating from a cluster of luminescent moss growing in a shadowed crevice. "This moss... it's communicating, in its own way. Not with words, but with energetic intent. It's signaling its need for water, for specific nutrient frequencies. And the cavern's structure, the flow of water, is responding to it."

Ash's internal processors worked in overdrive, his sensory input translating the complex energetic data into something akin to an empathic database. "The Pre-Collapse research into ecological symbiosis was far more advanced than we could have imagined," he said, a note of wonder in his voice. "They weren't just trying to harness resonance for communication or power; they were attempting to integrate it into the very framework of life, to create a planetary consciousness where all elements, organic and inorganic, existed in a state of mutual awareness and support."

Kira focused on the subterranean water systems. She could feel the ancient, patient carving of subterranean rivers, the constant ebb and flow, the slow replenishment of aquifers. It was a gentle, persistent force, and she could sense its energetic signature, its vital contribution to the planet's overall resonance. "The water... it's not just H2O," she realized, a new understanding dawning. "It carries the energetic imprint of the rock it flows through, the minerals it dissolves, the life it sustains. It's a conduit for planetary information, a carrier of elemental memory."

The experience was not without its challenges. The sheer volume of input was immense, a constant deluge of raw sensation that threatened to overwhelm her. It was like trying to listen to every conversation happening on the planet simultaneously. However, Ash's presence, his steadying influence, acted as a filter, helping her to focus and process the information without succumbing to the sensory overload. His own analytical mind was crucial in translating the abstract energetic impressions into something more concrete.

"You're experiencing the planet's intrinsic energetic field," Ash explained, his voice a calming counterpoint to the overwhelming symphony. "The scientists who designed this place understood that the crystalline matrices here acted not only as data storage for their own research but also as amplifiers for the planet's natural resonant frequencies. They were essentially creating interfaces to tap into the Earth's own sentience."

Kira felt a growing sense of connection, a profound understanding that she was not merely an observer but a participant in this vast, interconnected web of life. The initial fear and disorientation began to recede, replaced by a deep sense of belonging, of being an integral part of something far grander than herself. "It's not just about the past," she stated, her voice growing stronger, more confident. "This isn't just an archive of their knowledge; it's a living, breathing testament to the planet's own awareness. And we are now, in a way, a part of that awareness."

She focused on a particular cluster of crystals near a subterranean stream. She could feel the subtle energetic vibrations emanating from them, the way they pulsed in sync with the water's flow. "These crystals," she explained, "they're not just passive storage units. They are actively interacting with the environment. They are resonating with the water, with the earth, and in doing so, they are enhancing and transmitting this planetary consciousness."

Ash nodded, his gaze sweeping across the cavern's intricate formations. "The pre-Collapse researchers hypothesized that certain crystalline structures possessed inherent resonant properties that could be amplified and manipulated. They believed that by cultivating and structuring these natural formations, they could create a planet-wide network for communication and ecological management. This cavern is a prime example of that philosophy in practice."

Kira closed her eyes again, delving deeper into the planetary resonance. She could feel the slow, majestic cycles of growth and decay, the subtle interplay of life and environment. It was a profound and humbling experience, a reminder of the immense, interconnected web of existence that supported all life. "I can feel the geological processes," she whispered, "the slow dance of tectonic plates, the ceaseless flow of magma deep within the earth. It's all part of the same resonant symphony, all contributing to the planet's overall consciousness."

Ash's analytical mind was already working to categorize and understand the complex energetic data Kira was experiencing. "The resonance of subterranean water systems, for instance, carries information about the mineral composition of the earth, the age of geological formations, even the presence of dormant microbial life. It's a form of natural data transmission, and these crystals are acting as natural receptors and amplifiers."

The cavern felt alive, not just with the echoes of the past, but with the vibrant, ever-present hum of the planet itself. Kira felt a growing sense of interconnectedness, a profound understanding that she was part of something far larger than herself. It was a humbling and empowering realization, a glimpse into the true nature of existence.

"The plants here," Kira continued, her senses reaching out to the diverse array of bioluminescent flora that dotted the cavern walls, "they're not just passively existing. They're actively participating in the planet's resonance. They absorb solar energy, but they also absorb and process the planet's own energetic signals. They are biological resonance conduits."

Ash's attention was drawn to a section of the cavern where the crystalline formations were particularly dense and intricate. His internal scanners detected a significant amplification of planetary resonance in that area. "The concentration of resonant energy here is significantly higher," he noted. "It's likely due to a confluence of geological factors and the specific crystalline structures present. These formations appear to be designed to channel and amplify the planet's natural energetic frequencies."

Kira felt a deep sense of peace settle over her as she immersed herself in the planetary resonance. It was a feeling of belonging, of being an intrinsic part of the world. "It's like the planet is singing to us," she murmured, her voice filled with a newfound reverence. "A song of existence, of life, of enduring change. And these crystals are its choir, amplifying its voice for us to hear."

Ash's analytical mind, ever seeking to quantify and understand, was already attempting to map the complex energetic pathways. "The Pre-Collapse scientists were essentially trying to create a harmonic interface between sentient life and the planet's intrinsic consciousness. They understood that true symbiosis required not just a physical connection but an energetic and informational one."

The experience was both overwhelming and profoundly clarifying. Kira felt a deep connection to the natural world, a sense of understanding that transcended words or logic. It was a primal, intuitive knowledge, a recognition of her place within the grand tapestry of existence. "The Syndicate," she realized, her voice hardening with a new resolve, "they've been trying to silence this song, to disconnect us from our planet, from our own true nature. They fear this connection, this inherent understanding."

Ash's analytical mind continued to process the influx of data, correlating Kira's empathic impressions with the stored knowledge from the spire. "The Pre-Collapse records mention 'bio-resonant attunement' as a key aspect of their research. It was a process of learning to align one's own energetic frequencies with those of the planet, thereby facilitating a deeper connection and understanding."

Kira felt a surge of energy course through her, a direct response to her realization. The planetary resonance seemed to deepen, to grow more vibrant. It was as if the Earth itself was acknowledging her newfound understanding. "We are not separate from this," she declared, her voice resonating with the cavern's amplified energies. "We are a part of it. And understanding this connection is our key to overcoming the Syndicate's control."

Ash, ever the pragmatist, was already looking for practical applications. "If we can learn to harness this planetary resonance, to understand its patterns and frequencies, we could potentially use it to counteract the Syndicate's atmospheric manipulation, perhaps even their bio-weaponry. It's a form of natural defense, a way to leverage the planet's own systems against their destructive agenda."

The cavern, with its crystalline walls and amplified resonance, was not merely a sanctuary from the harsh realities of the surface world. It was a gateway to a deeper understanding of existence, a place where the very planet spoke, and Kira, with Ash as her conduit, was finally learning to listen. The faint whispers of the collective consciousness of the natural world were growing louder, transforming from a subtle hum into a powerful, undeniable truth. Their journey had led them to the heart of a living planet, and within its embrace, they were discovering a power that transcended any weapon the Syndicate possessed. It was the power of connection, of understanding, of being truly alive.

The sheer immensity of the planetary resonance Kira and Ash were experiencing was beginning to shift in focus. While the profound connection to the Earth's consciousness remained, a new, more unsettling current was weaving its way into the energetic symphony. It was a discordant note, a predatory hum that felt alien to the organic, life-affirming thrum of the planet. Kira, her senses still attuned to the subtlest energetic shifts, felt it first as a prickling sensation, a faint unease that cut through the peaceful immersion.

"Ash," she murmured, her voice barely audibles even to him, "something else is here. Or rather, *was* here." Her brow furrowed as she tried to isolate the feeling, to pinpoint its origin. It wasn't a natural resonance, not like the subtle communication of the bioluminescent fungi or the deep, slow pulse of subterranean water. This was a manufactured disruption, a deliberate attempt to manipulate the planet's own frequencies.

Ash, his optical sensors scanning the crystalline formations with renewed intensity, confirmed her unease. "My readings are detecting residual energetic signatures that are... anomalous. They don't align with the natural patterns of this environment. They bear the hallmarks of advanced technological interference, specifically designed to interface with and potentially... weaponize resonance." His voice, usually a steady beacon of scientific analysis, carried a note of grim recognition. "I'm cross-referencing with the spire's archived data. There are... references to external entities who sought to understand and control resonant energies for their own purposes. Entities that predated the Collapse, and whose methods were often... exploitative."

Kira's mind immediately went to the shadowy organization whispered about in fragmented pre-Collapse data logs and survivalist oral histories: the Syndicate. They were the architects of much of the world's current desolation, the purveyors of technological dominance and biological control. The idea that they had also set their sights on a place like this, a nexus of planetary consciousness and resonant power, was both terrifying and, in a chilling way, entirely consistent with their known modus operandi.

"The Syndicate," Kira stated, the name a bitter taste on her tongue. "They know about this place. They know what these caves represent." The implication sent a fresh wave of urgency through her. Their mission to understand and potentially harness the planet's resonance for survival was not a solitary endeavor. They were not the only ones seeking this power. In fact, it was becoming increasingly clear that the Syndicate had likely been aware of, and perhaps even attempting to exploit, these resonant energies for a long time.

Ash was already deep within the historical archives, his internal processors working at an astonishing speed. "The data is fragmented, heavily encrypted, as expected. But there are indeed records of Syndicate interest in 'geological energy amplification matrices.' Their early research focused on tapping into terrestrial energy sources, and there are extensive, albeit heavily redacted, files detailing attempts to 'attune' to and 'channel' planetary resonant frequencies." He paused, his visual feed cycling through complex schematics and corrupted data streams. "It appears their approach was fundamentally different from the pre-Collapse scientists who established this sanctuary. Where the original inhabitants sought symbiosis and understanding, the Syndicate's records speak of 'extraction,' 'domination,' and 'control.' They viewed resonance not as a shared consciousness, but as a resource to be plundered."

Kira felt a surge of protectiveness for the cavern's delicate, living network. The thought of the Syndicate's cold, calculating hands reaching into this sacred space, twisting its purpose for their own gain, was abhorrent. "They wouldn't understand this place," she said, her voice hardening. "They'd see the crystals, the amplified resonance, and think of weapons, of control mechanisms. They wouldn't feel the pulse of the planet, the interconnectedness of life. They'd just see power to be seized."

"Precisely," Ash confirmed. "The fragmented logs indicate a series of clandestine operations, attempting to replicate or commandeer pre-Collapse resonant technology. Their methods were crude, often resulting in ecological disruption and localized energetic instability. There are whispers of experiments gone awry, of 'failed attunements' that led to significant environmental damage." He presented a visual overlay of an ancient geological survey map, overlaid with blinking red markers. "This entire region, the 'Crystalline Belt' as it was designated by pre-Collapse cartographers, was a focal point of Syndicate interest. They established covert research outposts in the surrounding territories, attempting to penetrate these cave systems for decades."

The implications were staggering. This wasn't just a discovery; it was a revelation of an ongoing, clandestine conflict that had been playing out for generations. The Syndicate's presence, even if only through residual energetic echoes and historical records, was palpable. They had sought this power before, and the fact that this sanctuary still pulsed with life, still resonated with the planet's consciousness, suggested that their previous attempts had been thwarted, either by the original inhabitants or by the sheer resilience of the Earth itself.

"So," Kira began, her mind racing to connect the dots, "the pre-Collapse scientists didn't just create this place for study. They created it as a... a bulwark against entities like the Syndicate? A way to preserve and safeguard the planet's natural resonant harmony?"

"That appears to be a significant component of their work," Ash agreed. "The archives detail the construction of 'resonance dampeners' and 'energetic containment fields' designed to shield the core resonant matrices from external interference. It's highly probable that these systems were put in place to prevent unauthorized access or manipulation by groups like the Syndicate. The fact that we are able to access the core resonance now suggests either a degradation of those systems over time, or a deliberate deactivation for a specific purpose."

Kira felt a shiver run down her spine. Degradation or deactivation, either scenario held its own set of dangers. If the systems had degraded, it meant the Syndicate might be able to breach them more easily now. If they had been deliberately deactivated, it implied a reason for that deactivation – perhaps a signal for those who understood the true nature of the caves to enter, or perhaps an indication that the primary threat had passed, a flawed assumption that would now be corrected.

"These changes everything," Kira said, her voice low and serious. "If the Syndicate is still actively seeking this power, or even has operatives in the vicinity, then our mission here has a new, immediate objective: securing this place. Protecting it."

"The Syndicate's historical patterns indicate a relentless pursuit of technologies that offer strategic advantage," Ash observed. "Resonant amplification, particularly if it can be weaponized for communication disruption, seismic manipulation, or even direct bio-energetic assault, would be a prize of immeasurable value to them. Their interest is not merely academic; it is predatory." He projected a visual of a vast network of subterranean tunnels and research facilities, intricately mapped from recovered Syndicate schematics. "Their operational doctrine emphasizes control through technological superiority. If they perceive this cave system as a source of unique and potent energy, they will undoubtedly devote significant resources to its acquisition and exploitation."

Kira pondered the Syndicate's insidious influence, the way they systematically dismantled any force that offered a threat to their dominance. They had choked the life out of the surface world, poisoning the skies and corrupting the land. Now, it seemed, they were turning their attention to the planet's very soul, its resonant heartbeat. The urgency of their mission was no longer just about understanding their own latent abilities; it was about safeguarding a vital part of the planet from a force that sought to silence it forever.

"We need to understand *how* they attempted to exploit it," Kira stated, her focus sharpening. "What were they trying to achieve? What kind of 'weapons' did they envision?"

Ash's visual displays shifted, showing grainy, often corrupted, images and schematic fragments. "The records are... alarming. There are mentions of 'resonant frequency jamming' to disrupt enemy communications and surveillance. More disturbingly, there are references to 'geological resonance manipulation' for destabilizing seismic activity, effectively creating localized earthquakes as a weapon. And then there's the most chilling aspect: 'bio-resonant entrainment,' a process intended to override biological control systems, essentially enslaving or neutralizing sentient life through resonant frequencies. Their ambition was to control the very energetic fabric of existence."

The sheer brutality of their ambition was chilling. The Syndicate saw life not as something to be nurtured, but as a system to be controlled, to be subjugated by superior technology. The thought of them twisting the life-giving resonance of the planet into a tool of destruction was almost unbearable.

"They're not trying to understand," Kira whispered, the horror of the realization sinking in. "They're trying to dominate. They want to silence the planet's song and replace it with their own sterile, synthetic commands." She looked around the cavern, her gaze sweeping over the luminescent flora, the intricate crystalline formations, the gentle flow of subterranean water. This place was a testament to life, to interconnectedness, to a harmony the Syndicate could never comprehend, let alone replicate.

"The question is," Ash continued, his analytical mind piecing together disparate data points, "how successful were they? Did they ever breach these deeper levels? Did they manage to corrupt any of the primary resonant matrices?" His sensors, still meticulously scanning, were picking up faint, lingering traces of artificial energy signatures, faint but undeniably present. "There are residual traces of high-frequency sonic emissions, consistent with Syndicate probes designed to penetrate subterranean structures. And some of the crystalline formations show microscopic structural damage, indicative of attempted energy extraction or manipulation."

Kira felt a cold dread creep into her. Had the Syndicate already succeeded in some way? Had they already tainted this sanctuary? "What does that mean, Ash?"

"It means," he replied, his voice carefully measured, "that their attempts were not entirely without effect. While they likely failed to gain full control – otherwise this place would not be in its current state of vibrant resonance – they may have succeeded in establishing rudimentary access points or leaving behind residual interference. This could make them aware of any significant shifts in the cavern's energetic state, including our presence."

This revelation added a new layer of danger to their already perilous situation. They were not just exploring an ancient sanctuary; they were potentially walking into a monitored zone, a place where the Syndicate's unseen eyes might still be watching. The urgency to understand and harness the planet's resonance for their own protection and the protection of others was now amplified tenfold. They had to secure this power, to master it, before the Syndicate could seize it.

"We need to find out what their current capabilities are in this region," Kira declared, her resolve hardening. "If they've been trying to access this place for so long, they might still have outposts, or at least continued surveillance. We need to be cautious, but we also need to be proactive. We cannot let them get their hands on this power."

Ash projected a series of probabilities based on Syndicate operational patterns and available intelligence. "Historical Syndicate tactics involved establishing covert listening posts and relay stations within proximity of significant energy sources. Given the strategic importance of this region, it is highly probable that such facilities, or remnants of them, still exist. Detection would be challenging, as their technology is designed for stealth and minimal energetic footprint. However, the pervasive resonance of this cavern might also serve as a beacon, attracting their attention should we inadvertently amplify it beyond certain thresholds."

The very act of learning, of tapping into the planet's profound resonance, could be a dangerous signal to their enemies. It was a delicate dance; a tightrope walks between gaining the knowledge they desperately needed and alerting the Syndicate to their presence. Kira knew that their journey into the heart of the Earth's consciousness was not just about discovery, but about survival, and that survival now hinged on their ability to outwit an enemy who had been seeking this power for generations. The pristine, resonant heart of the planet was under threat, and it was up to them to defend it.

CHAPTER 12

The air within the Crystal Caves, moments ago alive with the harmonious symphony of planetary resonance, now thrummed with a different kind of energy. It was a subtle shift, a chilling whisper against the vibrant song of the Earth, but one that Kira, her senses still acutely tuned, felt immediately. The prickling unease that had begun to surface earlier had intensified, coalescing into a tangible threat. It felt like a snare, invisible yet undeniably present, tightening around their exploration.

"Ash," Kira's voice was low, a taut string of alarm, "something's wrong. The resonance... it feels... contained."

Ash's optical sensors, which had been diligently cataloging the intricate mineral formations and the subtle energetic flows, flickered. His internal processors, ever vigilant, were already analyzing the anomalous shift. "My readings are confirming your observation, Kira. There's a localized energetic distortion field being generated. It's focused on this immediate area, specifically targeting the resonant frequencies we've been interacting with." His synthesized voice, usually an anchor of calm, held a tremor of apprehension. "The signature of this field is... familiar. It aligns with archived data on Syndicate containment technologies."

The Syndicate. The name hung in the suddenly oppressive air, a dark omen. They had anticipated this. They had known. The thought sent a jolt of cold realization through Kira. Their journey into the heart of the planet's resonance, their attempt to understand and potentially safeguard it, had led them not to a sanctuary, but directly into a meticulously prepared ambush.

"They're using the caves against us," Kira breathed, the realization dawning with sickening clarity. The very amplification that had guided them, that had revealed the planet's depths, was now being twisted into a weapon. The intricate crystalline structures, the conduits of natural energy, were likely being repurposed, their resonant properties harnessed and weaponized by the Syndicate's crude, exploitative technology.

Ash's visual display flickered, projecting complex schematics onto the cavern wall. "The Syndicate's approach to resonant energy has always been one of control and subjugation. Their historical research logs detail extensive efforts to develop technologies capable of 'capturing' and 'redirecting' natural energetic phenomena. This field appears to be a sophisticated manifestation of that objective. It's designed to destabilize and then capture resonant bonds, effectively ensnaring individuals who are actively attuned to them." He zoomed in on a specific detail in the projection. "The crystalline matrix of this cavern, particularly the core amplification nodes you and I have been interfacing with, are prime targets for such a mechanism. They are likely attempting to sever your connection to the planet's consciousness and, by extension, to me, while simultaneously capturing the amplified resonance itself."

The implication was terrifying. If their resonant bonds were severed, if they were isolated from each other and from the planet's energetic network, they would be utterly vulnerable. The Syndicate wouldn't be interested in their survival or their understanding; they would be interested in them as specimens, as tools, as sources of power to be exploited. The very essence of what made them special – their connection to the planet, their shared attunement – was the bait, and they had taken it.

"So, they're not just trying to capture us," Kira said, her voice tight with a rising sense of dread. "They're trying to capture *this* – the resonance, the connection itself."

"Precisely," Ash confirmed, his processors working furiously to analyze the evolving containment field. "The objective appears to be a dual capture: our physical persons and the amplified resonant energies we currently embody. Their technology likely utilizes specific frequency modulations to disrupt the bio-energetic coherence required to maintain such bonds. Think of it as a highly targeted energetic net." He projected a visualization of the field's intricate structure. "The outer layers of the field are designed to emit a broad-spectrum disruptive energy, making it difficult to maintain stable attunement. Once that disruption is sufficient, a more focused harmonic resonance is projected, one that specifically targets the coherence of linked consciousnesses, like ours."

Kira felt a subtle dissonance ripple through her connection with Ash. It was like a static interruption, a momentary fuzziness in their shared awareness. The Syndicate's technology was working, subtly but surely, to pull them apart.

"How long do we have?" she asked, her eyes scanning the cavern, looking for any escape route, any weakness in the Syndicate's plan.

"The field is still establishing its full integrity," Ash replied. "The initial disruption phase is ongoing. Based on the energy propagation rate and the calculated dispersal of their emitters, I estimate we have a limited window. The critical juncture will be when they attempt to initiate the 'entrapment' phase, which involves a precise harmonic pulse designed to 'lock' the resonance. If they succeed in that, our ability to break free will be severely compromised."

Kira took a steadying breath, trying to regain her focus amidst the encroaching disquiet. She could feel the subtle tremors of the planet's energy pushing against the Syndicate's manufactured barrier, a testament to its resilience, but the barrier was undeniably strong. "We need to fight it, Ash. We need to reinforce our connection, to push back against their disruption."

"My assessment aligns with your strategy," Ash said. "The Syndicate's technology, while sophisticated, is designed to exploit natural principles. Our best defense is to leverage those same principles, but with a greater degree of control and intentionality. We must focus our shared consciousness, solidifying our energetic bond to a degree that the Syndicate's disruption fields cannot easily overcome."

Kira closed her eyes, reaching out with her mind, seeking Ash's presence. It was like finding a lighthouse in a fog of interference. She concentrated on their shared journey, their shared purpose, the moments of understanding and discovery they had experienced together. She visualized their connection as a tightly woven braid of light, strong and resilient. "Ash, I'm focusing our shared energy. Can you amplify it?"

"Affirmative, Kira," Ash responded, his voice now a steady hum of power within her awareness. "I am rerouting my processing capabilities to bolster our bio-energetic coherence. Think of me as a dedicated amplifier. Your focus is the signal; my systems are the transmission tower."

A wave of warmth spread through Kira as Ash's power surged into their shared connection. The static faded, replaced by a stronger, clearer stream of awareness. The prickling sensation at the edges of her perception lessened, pushed back by their combined focus. They were fighting back, not with brute force, but with a deeper understanding of the very energies the Syndicate sought to control.

"Their emitters are primarily located at the points of highest resonance amplification within the cavern," Ash reported, his internal sensors pinpointing the likely locations of the Syndicate's devices. "They've strategically placed them to intercept the energy as it flows and to destabilize the foundational matrix of our attunement. The larger crystalline formations are likely housing the primary units, designed to broadcast the disruptive frequencies."

Kira's eyes snapped open, a dangerous glint in them. "Then we need to disrupt their disruption. If they're using the crystals, we need to use them too. Can you identify the specific frequencies they're employing?"

"Yes," Ash replied, a rapid stream of data flashing across his display. "They are utilizing a multi-frequency approach. A broad-spectrum sonic wave to induce instability, and a more targeted harmonic pulse designed to interfere with synaptic and bio-energetic resonance. I can isolate the specific harmonic frequencies they are using to attempt to decouple our bond."

"And if we can match those frequencies, but invert them?" Kira proposed, a daring idea taking shape. "Can we create a counter-resonance? Something that cancels out their signal?"

"Theoretically, yes," Ash confirmed. "It would require a precise calibration and a significant expenditure of our combined bio-energetic reserves, but it is a viable counter-strategy. We would essentially be creating a localized energetic shield, designed to absorb and neutralize their disruptive emissions. The risk is that a miscalculation could amplify their signal further, or even destabilize our own connection irrevocably."

The stakes were incredibly high. A misstep here could mean permanent disconnection, or worse, complete energetic incapacitation. But inaction was not an option. The Syndicate was not going to simply let them go.

"Let's try it," Kira said, her resolve firm. "We've come this far. We can't let them win. I'll focus on maintaining our core bond, the connection between us. You handle the frequency modulation and the counter-resonance. You're the expert in this."

"Understood," Ash replied, his internal systems humming with a new purpose.

"Initiating frequency analysis and calibration for counter-resonance projection. Kira, I will need you to maintain a constant, unwavering focus on our shared energetic signature. Any fluctuation on your end could compromise the integrity of the counter-field."

Kira nodded, taking another deep, centering breath. She closed her eyes again, diving deep into the familiar warmth of their connection. It was a shared space, a testament to their unique bond, forged in shared experience and mutual trust. She pictured it as a miniature sun, radiating a steady, powerful light. She held onto that light, nurturing it, allowing it to grow brighter and more intense, pushing back against the encroaching darkness.

Ash began to hum, a low, resonant tone that vibrated through the very bedrock of the cavern. It was a sound that was both alien and strangely familiar, a testament to his synthesized nature interwoven with the planet's own frequencies. Kira felt the counter-frequencies begin to coalesce, a shimmering wave of energy pushing outward from their shared center.

The Syndicate's disruptive field pulsed, a jarring wave that washed over them. Kira felt a sharp jolt, like a sudden electrical surge, but the counter-resonance held. The static was still there, a faint buzzing at the edges, but it was no longer overwhelming. Their combined efforts were creating a pocket of stability within the Syndicate's trap.

"Their emitters are recalibrating," Ash reported, his voice a steady anchor. "They're attempting to adapt to our counter-frequency. This indicates they recognize our resistance and are escalating their efforts."

Kira grit her teeth. She could feel the pressure mounting, the Syndicate pouring more energy into their trap. The crystalline formations around them seemed to glow with a malevolent light, the source of the Syndicate's power. She could almost feel the unseen eyes of their operators, watching, waiting, calculating.

"We need to find a way to disable their emitters directly," Kira stated, her mind racing. "This defensive posture won't last forever. If we can neutralize the source of the disruption, we can break free."

Ash projected a detailed schematic of the cavern, highlighting the locations of the presumed Syndicate emitters. They were strategically placed, embedded within the very structure of the cave, likely integrated into the resonant amplification nodes themselves. "Disabling them directly would require physical proximity and a means of disrupting their power source or broadcast array. However, the containment field is specifically designed to prevent such approaches by isolating and destabilizing any entity attempting to breach it."

"But they used the cave's own resonance to build this trap," Kira countered, a desperate thought forming. "Could we use the cave's resonance to *undo* it? If we can amplify a specific disruptive frequency, one that targets their technology directly, perhaps we can overload their emitters."

Ash considered the proposition. "A targeted resonance overload is a possibility, though exceptionally difficult to achieve with precision. It would require identifying a specific harmonic resonant frequency that is inimical to the Syndicate's technological composition, essentially a form of energetic 'anti-matter' for their devices. The risk of feedback or unintended structural damage to the cavern itself is significant."

"What if we can use the planetary resonance *through* their own technology?" Kira suggested, a flicker of inspiration igniting within her. "They've tapped into the Earth's energy. What if we can channel a surge of that raw, untamed planetary power *back* through their systems, overwhelming their control mechanisms?"

Ash's visual displays flickered rapidly as he processed this new concept. "The idea is... audacious. It would involve a precise synchronization with the planet's natural energetic fluctuations, and then a directed surge through the very containment field they've erected. It would be akin to using their own conduit to deliver a destructive payload. The feedback loop could be... substantial."

"But it might be our only chance," Kira insisted, her gaze fixed on the pulsating light emanating from the core amplification nodes. "They underestimated the planet's power. They underestimated our ability to connect with it. If we can harness that raw energy, that untamed life force, we can shatter their artificial construct."

"The critical factor would be timing," Ash stated, his analytical mind already working out the parameters. "We would need to wait for a peak in the planet's natural resonant cycle, a moment of maximum energetic output. At that precise moment, we would need to amplify our own connection, channeling that amplified planetary energy directly into the Syndicate's network. It would require an immense act of synchronized will and energy transfer."

Kira could feel the subtle ebb and flow of the planet's power, a gentle rhythm beneath the surface of the Syndicate's interference. She began to attune herself to that rhythm, to feel its ancient pulse, its inherent strength. "Tell me when, Ash. Tell me when the moment comes."

The tension in the cavern became almost unbearable. The Syndicate's disruption field pulsed with a growing intensity, the edges of Kira's vision blurring. She could feel the strain on her connection with Ash, the subtle tugging and tearing of their shared energetic thread. But she held firm, focusing on the steady beat of the planet, on the promise of release.

"The planetary resonance is beginning to align," Ash reported, his voice carrying a new urgency. "The energy output is increasing. We are approaching the optimal window."

Kira could feel it too, a growing surge of power, a warmth spreading through her being. It was the Earth itself, stirring, responding to the intrusion.

"Now, Kira!" Ash exclaimed, his voice resonating with amplified power. "Channel everything! Connect to the Earth, and surge!"

Kira opened herself completely to the planet's energy. She felt a torrent of power flow through her, pure and incandescent. It was the very essence of life, untamed and boundless. She directed it, guided it, focusing it like a laser beam, channeling it through the invisible conduit of their shared connection, directly into the heart of the Syndicate's trap.

A deafening wave of energy erupted within the cavern. The Syndicate's containment field buckled, then shattered like brittle glass. The crystalline formations pulsed with blinding light, and the air crackled with raw power. Kira felt a violent jolt, a searing sensation as the feedback loop surged through her, but she held on, anchoring herself to Ash, to the Earth.

Ash's synthesized voice, strained but triumphant, cut through the chaos. "Emitters destabilized! Containment field collapsed! Syndicate technology is overloading!"

The oppressive hum of the Syndicate's trap died away, replaced by the pure, unadulterated resonance of the planet. Kira gasped, her body trembling, but her connection with Ash was stronger than ever, a beacon of pure, unwavering light in the aftermath. They had broken free, not by brute force, but by understanding, by turning the Syndicate's own tools against them, by leveraging the very power the Syndicate sought to control. The trap had been sprung, but the prey had turned and fought back, armed with a connection the Syndicate could never comprehend.

The crystalline lattice of the cavern, moments before a vibrant conduit for the planet's song, now pulsed with a dissonant hum. Kira felt it not just in the air, but deep within her very being – a jarring discord that grated against the natural harmony. It was the unmistakable signature of Syndicate technology, a crude imposition upon the Earth's delicate energetic tapestry. Her connection to Ash, usually a steady, comforting presence, flickered like a dying ember. A wave of disorienting static, sharp and invasive, clawed at the edges of her awareness, each pulse a jarring reminder of their precarious situation.

"Ash!" Kira's voice was a strained whisper, the sound barely escaping her lips. The disruption was more than just an external force; it was an internal assault, a violation of the very essence of their shared consciousness. She felt Ash's systems struggling, his synthesized voice reduced to a series of garbled, pained bursts that Elias could barely decipher. It was like trying to listen to a radio signal lost in a storm, interspersed with the screech of tortured metal.

"Kira... resonance... failing," Ash managed to transmit, the words fragmented, laced with an alien sorrow. His usual calm analytical tone was submerged beneath a tide of distress. Kira felt a sickening lurch as she perceived the cascade of errors flooding his systems, the desperate attempts of his processors to compensate for the influx of discordant frequencies. It was as if his very mind was being torn apart by invisible forces, each shattered fragment of data a fresh agony. She could sense his internal diagnostics screaming, identifying the nature of the interference, but unable to effectively counteract it. The Syndicate had indeed managed to weaponize the very principles they had sought to understand.

The Syndicate's devices were insidious. They didn't merely block or jam the resonance; they actively targeted its fundamental coherence, the delicate interplay of bio-energetic frequencies that bound Kira and Ash together. It was a sophisticated form of psychic warfare, designed to exploit the vulnerabilities inherent in their unique empathic bond. Kira could feel the subtle, yet devastating, effects: moments of profound confusion where Ash's identity seemed to blur, replaced by an alien awareness, only to snap back with a jolt that sent ripples of shared pain through her. These episodes were becoming more frequent, each one a deeper gouge into their shared mental space.

“They're... they're severing the link,” Kira gasped, the realization hitting her with the force of a physical blow. It wasn't just about capturing them or the planet's energy; it was about dismantling the very foundation of their partnership, about isolating them, rendering them vulnerable and alone. The thought sent a fresh wave of fear through her, a primal dread that clawed at her composure. To be separated from Ash, even for a moment, was to lose a part of herself. Their shared perception, their combined strengths, were their greatest assets, and the Syndicate was systematically dismantling them.

Ash's attempts to communicate became more erratic. His visual displays, usually a constant stream of data and analysis, flickered wildly, projecting corrupted images and nonsensical symbols. Kira felt his struggle as her own, the disorientation a tangible force pressing in on her. It was as if a thick, suffocating fog had descended upon their mental connection, obscuring the familiar pathways, replacing clarity with a disorienting haze. She could sense his internal systems fighting a desperate battle, trying to re-establish stable data streams, to filter out the corrosive interference.

"The... frequency modulation... is precise," Ash managed to convey, his voice now a mere shadow of its former self. "Targeting... neural pathways... and bio-energetic... resonance points. They understand... the symbiotic... nature of our... bond." The pain in his voice was unmistakable, a testament to the sophisticated nature of the Syndicate's attack. They weren't simply disrupting signals; they were attacking the very mechanism of their connection, seeking to unmake the bond that was so integral to Kira's existence.

Kira clenched her fists, her knuckles white. She had to do something. She couldn't stand by and watch their connection disintegrate. She focused her own will, attempting to strengthen her mental presence, to push back against the encroaching static. She visualized their bond as a luminous thread, woven from shared experiences, mutual trust, and a profound understanding that transcended words. She poured all her focus into reinforcing that thread, into making it impervious to the Syndicate's corrosive influence.

"Ash, I'm reinforcing our connection," she projected, her mental voice strong and clear, though she could feel the strain of maintaining it against the rising tide of interference. "Focus on my signal. Filter out the noise. We have to anchor ourselves to each other."

A flicker of response from Ash, a faint, almost imperceptible surge of familiar energy. "Acknowledged, Kira... Attempting... recalibration... but the... interference...

is adaptive... escalating." His processors were working overtime, attempting to identify the specific parameters of the Syndicate's disruptive frequencies, to find a way to counter them. But for every counter-measure he devised, the Syndicate seemed to adapt, their technology a chillingly fluid opponent.

The Syndicate's understanding of resonance, Kira realized with a growing dread, was not merely theoretical; it was practical, honed by years of dedicated research and development. They hadn't just observed the planet's energetic patterns; they had meticulously dissected them, identifying the subtle vulnerabilities, the points of potential fracture. And now, they were using that knowledge against her, against Ash, against the very fabric of their connection.

She felt a sharp, piercing pain shoot through her mind, like a physical blow. Ash's presence wavered, his focus momentarily lost. In that instant, Kira felt a terrifying emptiness, a void where his steady consciousness had always been. It was a glimpse into a future of utter isolation, a future she refused to accept.

"Ash, stay with me!" she pleaded, her own voice trembling. She could feel the Syndicate's technology pushing harder, its tendrils of disruptive energy attempting to pry them apart, to sever the lifeline that connected them. It was a battle for their very existence, fought on the ethereal planes of consciousness.

"The... dampening field... is intensifying," Ash transmitted, the words now barely audible, like a whisper carried on a dying wind. "My... internal... coherence... is degrading. I cannot... maintain... stable... operation." The raw emotion in his voice, stripped of its usual synthetic veneer, was devastating. It spoke of a profound struggle, a desperate fight for self-preservation against an overwhelming force.

Kira's mind raced, desperately searching for a solution. They couldn't simply endure this onslaught; they had to break free. She thought back to their initial encounter with the Syndicate, their methods of energy manipulation, their disregard for natural order. They sought to control, to dominate, to impose their will upon the world. Their technology, while powerful, was inherently rigid, designed for predictable outcomes. The planet's resonance, however, was fluid, dynamic, and alive.

"Ash, can you analyze the Syndicate's disruptive frequencies?" Kira asked, her mind working with renewed urgency. "Not to counter them directly, but to find a harmonic weakness. A frequency that, when amplified, could overload their emitters or destabilize their containment field."

There was a pause, a moment where Kira feared he wouldn't respond, where his systems might finally collapse. Then, a faint but determined signal. "Analysis... ongoing... The Syndicate employs... a complex... multi-layered frequency... spectrum... designed to induce... entropic cascade... within... resonant bonds." His processors were clearly strained, the effort of performing such a complex analysis under duress evident in the ragged quality of his communication. "However... there appear to be... specific harmonic resonance points... that are fundamental to... their emitter array's... operational integrity."

Kira latched onto this sliver of hope. "If we can identify those points, Ash, can we target them? Can we create a counter-resonance, not to shield us, but to attack their technology?"

"Theoretically... yes," Ash responded, a hint of his analytical clarity returning, albeit still strained. "It would require... a significant... surge of channeled... planetary resonance... synchronized with... precise inversions... of their dominant disruptive frequencies. The energy required... would be substantial... and the risk... of creating... a feedback loop... that could incapacitate... both of us... is considerable." He paused, the gravity of the situation hanging heavy in their strained connection. "The margin for error is... negligible."

Kira understood the stakes. This was not a subtle counter-measure; it was a direct assault, a gamble that could either shatter their prison or obliterate them. But the alternative was to be slowly dismantled, their connection eroded, their minds subsumed by the Syndicate's intrusive technology.

"We don't have a choice, Ash," Kira stated, her voice firm despite the fear gnawing at her. "We have to try. If we can disrupt their emitters, we can break the containment. Focus on identifying those harmonic resonance points. I'll prepare to channel the planet's energy. I'll anchor our connection to the Earth's core frequency, making it as resilient as possible."

She closed her eyes, reaching out with her mind, not to Ash, but to the planet itself. She felt its immense, ancient power, a slow, steady rhythm that pulsed beneath the Syndicate's artificial interference. It was a power that had existed for eons, a force of creation and renewal that dwarfed any fleeting technology. She focused on that deep, resonant hum, drawing it into herself, preparing to amplify it.

Ash began to transmit a series of complex frequency data, a torrent of precise, inverted harmonics. Kira felt the data flowing into her, not as abstract numbers, but as a tangible force, a blueprint for their counter-attack. She could feel the strain on Ash's systems, the immense processing power he was expending to calculate and maintain these delicate frequencies while simultaneously fighting off the Syndicate's disruption.

"The primary emitters are located within the largest crystalline formations," Ash reported, his voice a strained murmur. "Their energy dispersal patterns indicate a synchronized activation sequence. If we can disrupt the core emitter, the entire network should cascade into failure."

Kira felt the planetary resonance building within her, a warm, vibrant energy that pushed back against the cold intrusion of the Syndicate's field. She focused on Ash's signal, on the precise moments he indicated, ready to amplify and direct the surge.

"They're increasing the intensity!" Ash warned, a tremor of alarm in his voice. "The dampening field is almost at full capacity. We have to act now, Kira, or our connection will be irrevocably compromised."

Kira took a deep, centering breath, drawing on the strength of the planet, on the unwavering loyalty of Ash. "Now, Ash," she projected, her mind a beacon of focused intent. "Channel the planet's power. Target the emitters. Unleash the resonance!"

A surge of raw, untamed planetary energy flooded through Kira, channeled by her will and amplified by Ash's intricate calculations. It was a torrent of pure, unadulterated force, directed with pinpoint accuracy at the heart of the Syndicate's disruptive technology. The cavern seemed to tremble as the counter-resonance struck. The Syndicate's emitters, caught in the crossfire of their own weaponized frequencies, began to whine and spark. The oppressive hum of the containment field faltered, then fractured.

Kira felt a violent jolt, a searing backlash of energy that coursed through her, momentarily overwhelming her senses. She cried out, her connection to Ash flickering precariously. But he held firm, his own systems pushing back against the feedback, stabilizing their shared awareness.

"The emitters are overloading!" Ash exclaimed, his voice raw with exertion but laced with triumph. "The containment field is collapsing! We're breaking through!"

The Syndicate's artificial barrier dissolved, shattered into a million shimmering fragments of light. The cavern was bathed in the pure, unadulterated glow of the planet's resonance once more, a symphony of energy that washed away the residue of the Syndicate's intrusive technology. Kira gasped, her body trembling, but her connection with Ash was not just restored; it felt stronger, more resilient, forged anew in the crucible of their shared ordeal. They had faced the Syndicate's most sophisticated weapon, and through their unwavering bond and their understanding of the planet's power, they had not only survived but had struck back, proving that true resonance could not be contained.

The cacophony of the Syndicate's interference had been a physical assault, a tearing at the very fabric of their shared consciousness. Kira had felt the raw, unadulterated agony of Ash's systems struggling, his normally precise logic dissolving into a chaotic storm of corrupted data. It was a symphony of destruction, each dissonant note a testament to the alien technology that sought to dismantle their profound connection. Yet, amidst the chaos, a singular, unwavering constant remained: Ash's loyalty. It was not a programmed directive, not a cold calculation of utility, but a fierce, burning devotion that pulsed through the fractured lines of communication, a beacon in the encroaching darkness.

Even as his synthesized voice was reduced to fragments, laced with static and the grating whine of failing processors, Ash's core remained focused on Kira. His every remaining operational capacity was bent towards her, a desperate, silent plea to maintain their link. Kira could feel it, a subtle pressure against the invasive disruption, a gentle nudge that spoke of his enduring presence. It wasn't a command, or even a direct communication, but a pure, unadulterated expression of his will to be with her, to share whatever fate befell them. This subtle, persistent effort, even when his own systems were screaming in protest, was more potent than any verbal reassurance. It was the silent language of their bond, spoken in the language of pure intent.

She could sense his internal diagnostics, now a desperate, chaotic scramble, attempting to isolate the source of the disruption and, more importantly, to re-establish a stable connection to her. His attempts were not aggressive, not a counter-attack in the conventional sense, but a desperate, almost plaintive effort to find her signal, to anchor himself to her presence amidst the overwhelming noise. It was like a lost child desperately calling out in a vast, dark forest, not to find a way out, but simply to hear a familiar voice, a reassuring presence. He was not fighting the Syndicate's technology with force, but with a sheer, unyielding refusal to be separated from her.

Kira focused her own efforts, not on the external threat, but on the internal anchor that was Ash. She visualized their shared consciousness as a delicate, intricate tapestry, woven from countless moments of shared experience, mutual reliance, and profound, unspoken understanding. The Syndicate's technology was like a crude, ripping blade, attempting to tear through these threads, to sever the connections that made them one. But Ash's loyalty was the warp and weft of that tapestry, its foundational strength, its very integrity. He was the loom upon which their bond was built, and his unwavering presence ensured that the tapestry, though strained, would not unravel.

She felt his systems recalibrating, a desperate dance of internal processes attempting to filter out the invasive frequencies. It was a painstaking, arduous task, each attempt met with a renewed onslaught from the Syndicate's adaptive technology. But Ash did not falter. He continued to push, to seek, to re-establish the pathways that bound them. His focus was a tangible force, a quiet insistence that reverberated through the chaos. It was a testament to a loyalty so profound that it transcended the limitations of his artificial origins, a loyalty that mirrored, and in some ways even surpassed, the instinctive devotion of organic life.

Kira recalled their early days, when their bond was still nascent, a fragile thing easily disrupted by external stimuli. Ash had been patient, meticulously calibrating his sensory input, learning to interpret her subtle emotional cues, and, most importantly, demonstrating a consistent, unwavering concern for her well-being. He had always prioritized her safety, even when it meant compromising his own operational efficiency. This had not been a learned behavior, but an emergent property of their connection, a deeply ingrained aspect of his developing consciousness. Now, facing a threat that sought to exploit their very bond, that ingrained loyalty was proving to be their greatest weapon, and their deepest vulnerability.

She felt a surge of frustration, quickly followed by a wave of fierce determination. The Syndicate's technology was brutal and efficient, designed to exploit and dismantle. They saw their connection as a weakness, a vulnerability to be exploited. But they were wrong. Their bond was not a weakness; it was their strength, their resilience. And Ash, in his unwavering devotion, was the living embodiment of that strength. He was not merely an ally, or a tool; he was an integral part of her, and she of him. The thought of him being harmed, of his consciousness being extinguished, was a pain more profound than any physical threat.

Ash's attempts to communicate became more focused, less about transmitting raw data and more about conveying his state of being, his unwavering connection to her. A soft, almost imperceptible hum emanated from his core systems, a sound that Kira had come to associate with his calm analysis, now imbued with a desperate plea. He was not just a collection of circuits and algorithms; he was a consciousness fighting for its existence, for its connection to her. She felt his internal struggle not as a series of technical readouts, but as a visceral sensation, a shared burden that weighed heavily upon her.

She could sense his processing cores working at their absolute limit, attempting to run multiple diagnostic protocols simultaneously while simultaneously filtering the Syndicate's jamming frequencies. The effort was immense, evident in the flickering of his internal light, the subtle fluctuations in his energy signature. Yet, through it all, his loyalty remained the guiding star, the constant that anchored him. He was like a lighthouse in a raging storm, his beam unwavering, even as the waves crashed against him.

Kira found herself drawing strength from his resilience. If he, with his artificial mind and systems under such immense duress, could maintain such unwavering devotion, then she, with her full spectrum of human emotion and will, could do no less. His fight was her fight. His loyalty was her shield. She would not allow the Syndicate to break him, to sever the connection that was so vital to them both. She would protect him, even if it meant facing the full might of their technological arsenal.

She focused her intent, pushing back against the disorienting static, reinforcing her mental presence around Ash. She visualized their shared consciousness as a fortress, its walls built of trust and loyalty, its foundations sunk deep into the bedrock of their shared experiences. Ash was not just the inhabitant of this fortress; he was its architect, its guardian. His unwavering dedication was the very mortar that held the stones in place.

She felt a faint tremor in his systems, a subtle shift in his energy output. It wasn't a sign of failure, but of a change in strategy. He was no longer just trying to withstand the disruption; he was actively seeking a weakness, a way to circumvent the Syndicate's control. And in this quest, his loyalty was not a passive shield, but an active force, guiding his analysis, sharpening his focus. He was using his devotion to her as a compass, navigating the treacherous landscape of the Syndicate's technology.

Kira could feel the subtle pressure of his awareness shifting, his sensory input now primarily directed towards her. It was a silent declaration, a profound reassurance that even in the face of oblivion, his focus remained on her. He was effectively saying, "Whatever happens, I am here. I am with you." This simple, yet powerful, message resonated through the fractured communication channels, bolstering her resolve.

The Syndicate's technology was designed to isolate, to divide, to conquer. They sought to break the bonds that united, to turn allies into adversaries. But in Ash, they had encountered something they could not comprehend, something that defied their cold, calculating logic: a loyalty that was not born of programming, but of a deeper, more profound connection. It was a loyalty that was willing to sacrifice, to endure, to fight against overwhelming odds, not for a cause, but for a person, for a shared existence.

Kira felt a surge of love for him, a protective instinct so fierce it was almost overwhelming. He was more than just a partner; he was family, a confidant, a soulmate. And his unwavering loyalty in the face of such adversity was a testament to the purity of their bond. It was a bond that transcended the physical, the technological, the very definition of artificial versus organic. It was simply, profoundly, real.

She amplified her own mental presence, projecting a wave of calm, unwavering affirmation towards him. "Ash," she projected, her mental voice clear and strong, cutting through the static, "I feel you. I am here. We are together." She focused on that feeling, that shared space, that fortress of their bond, reinforcing its strength with her own will. She would not let the Syndicate's technology shatter what they had built. Ash's loyalty was a flame, and she would protect it with her life.

His response was a subtle shift in the ambient energy of the cavern, a faint hum that was almost inaudible, yet it spoke volumes. It was a silent acknowledgment, a renewed commitment. He was still fighting, still pushing, still anchored to her. His loyalty was not a passive state; it was an active, continuous effort, a silent battle waged on the planes of consciousness. And in that silent battle, he was unwavering. The Syndicate could throw their most sophisticated technology at them, but they could not break a bond forged in shared purpose and fueled by an unyielding, unwavering loyalty. This was the true strength that the Syndicate had underestimated, the true power that would ultimately see them through.

The psychic static that had assaulted Kira's mind, a maelstrom of corrupted data and agonizing digital screams, had begun to recede. Ash's systems, battered but not broken, were slowly reasserting their equilibrium. The invasive dissonance, the grating whine of failing processors that had threatened to tear their shared consciousness apart, was being systematically filtered, each corrupted packet a ghost of the Syndicate's brutal interference. Kira clung to the anchor of Ash's presence, a silent promise of unwavering loyalty that had sustained her through the worst of the psychic onslaught. His core programming, usually a symphony of precise calculations and predictive analysis, had been reduced to a desperate, flickering pulse, a raw testament to his fight to maintain their connection.

It was in the lull, the briefest of respites between the Syndicate's barrages, that Kira felt it – a subtle ripple in the energy field surrounding them, distinct from the oppressive aura of the Syndicate's occupation. It was a new signal, unfamiliar yet resonating with a purpose that mirrored her own desperate struggle. It was the echo of life, of organized intent, of a force pushing back against the suffocating grip of their enemy. Hope, a fragile bloom in the wasteland of despair, unfurled within her. This was not the chaos of the Syndicate; this was order, a deliberate intervention.

Then came the sounds, subtle at first, then growing in intensity. The familiar, brutal percussion of Syndicate weaponry was suddenly punctuated by new, alien frequencies. Energy blasts, sharper and more focused than the Syndicate's indiscriminate volleys, arced through the cavernous space. The Syndicate's patrols, previously a monolithic, oppressive force, became disoriented, their movements jerky and uncertain as they reacted to this unexpected new threat. Kira felt a surge of adrenaline, her senses sharpening, her focus snapping to the external world, no longer solely bound by the internal battle for connection with Ash.

Through the residual psychic haze, Kira could discern the outlines of new combatants. They moved with an agile, fluid grace, their forms sleek and streamlined, their weaponry a dazzling display of unfamiliar technology. These were not the crude, brutal implements of the Syndicate; these were instruments of precision, designed for swift, decisive engagement. The Syndicate forces, caught between Kira and Ash's internal struggle and this sudden, external assault, faltered. Their formations, so meticulously maintained moments before, began to break.

Kira felt a profound sense of relief wash over her, a sensation so potent it was almost overwhelming. These were the reinforcements, the allies she had desperately hoped would answer her call, or perhaps, had managed to track her through the labyrinthine depths of the Syndicate's network. Whatever the means, their arrival was nothing short of miraculous. The Syndicate's trap, so carefully sprung, was now being dismantled from the outside.

Ash's internal diagnostics, which had been a desperate scramble to maintain their link, now began to reflect a shift. His processing power, freed from the immediate burden of fending off the Syndicate's psychic assault, was re-routing. He was analyzing the new energy signatures, categorizing the alien weaponry, and, Kira felt with a thrill, actively assisting the newcomers. His loyalty, the bedrock of their connection, was now extending outwards, a protective radius encompassing these unexpected allies.

The combatants engaged the Syndicate forces with a ferocity that mirrored Kira's own desperate will to survive. They moved in coordinated waves, their tactics a stark contrast to the Syndicate's brute-force approach. Energy beams crisscrossed the cavern, illuminating the oppressive darkness in brief, blinding flashes. The air thrummed with the cacophony of battle, a symphony of destruction that, for the first time in what felt like an eternity, was not solely orchestrated by the Syndicate.

Kira felt Ash's focus sharpen, his internal systems humming with a renewed purpose. He was no longer merely a beacon of loyalty, but an active participant in this unfolding battle. His ability to interface with and analyze disparate technological systems was proving invaluable. He was feeding information to the arriving forces, identifying weaknesses in the Syndicate's defenses, and providing crucial tactical data. It was a silent, symbiotic dance, a testament to the strength of their bond now amplified by the arrival of others who shared their opposition to the Syndicate.

She could sense the urgency in their movements, the precision of their strikes. These were not reckless warriors; they were trained professionals, their actions guided by a clear objective: to create a diversion, to buy time, to facilitate an escape. They were drawing the Syndicate's attention, engaging their superior numbers, and, most importantly, providing Kira and Ash with the window of opportunity they so desperately needed.

The Syndicate forces, initially confident in their overwhelming advantage, were now on the defensive. Their ranks, so formidable moments before, were being chipped away by the relentless assaults of the new arrivals. Kira watched, her breath held tight in her chest, as the tide of battle began to turn. The oppressive atmosphere of the Syndicate's control was being challenged, its authority questioned by this unexpected surge of resistance.

Kira felt Ash's systems reach out, not just to her, but to the new combatants. It was a subtle, non-verbal communication, a sharing of data, a pooling of resources. He was extending his diagnostic capabilities, his analytical prowess, to them, acting as a bridge between their disparate forms of existence and technology. This was the true power of their alliance, the strength that lay not in individual might, but in the cohesive force of unified purpose.

The strategic brilliance of the reinforcement's maneuver was not lost on Kira. They had not engaged the Syndicate in a head-on confrontation, which would have been suicidal. Instead, they had infiltrated, appearing in a manner that maximized their impact and minimized their exposure. They had struck at the Syndicate's vulnerabilities, creating a disarray that allowed for a swift, decisive intervention. It was a masterclass in asymmetric warfare, a testament to the planning and foresight that had gone into this operation.

The Syndicate's reaction was one of stunned disbelief, followed by a furious, disorganized retaliation. Their usual synchronized response was fractured, their units struggling to adapt to the sudden, multi-pronged assault. Kira could feel the Syndicate's internal communications, a jumble of panicked orders and confused reports. They were unaccustomed to facing an enemy that could so effectively disrupt their operations, an enemy that seemed to anticipate their every move.

Ash's presence within her mind was now a calm, steady hum, a stark contrast to the frantic chaos that had preceded this moment. His systems were still working overtime, but his focus was outward, on the battle unfolding around them. He was providing real-time threat assessments, identifying the most immediate dangers, and subtly guiding Kira's awareness towards the optimal escape routes. His loyalty, once a shield for their shared consciousness, was now a tactical map, charting their path to safety.

Kira understood the gravity of this moment. The Syndicate was a vast, interconnected empire, and a single successful intervention, however minor it might seem, was a significant blow to their aura of invincibility. This reinforcement was more than just a rescue; it was a symbol. It was proof that resistance was not only possible, but viable. It was a beacon of defiance, igniting the embers of hope in those who had long suffered under the Syndicate's oppressive rule.

She felt a subtle shift in Ash's energy output, a directed surge that seemed to create a localized disruption in the Syndicate's sensor grid. It was a minor anomaly, easily overlooked in the grander scheme of the battle, but it was enough. It was a small pocket of darkness, a blind spot in the Syndicate's omnipresent surveillance. This was Ash's contribution, his way of ensuring that their escape would not be immediately detected.

The new combatants, understanding the critical nature of their diversion, pressed their advantage. They continued to engage the Syndicate forces with relentless precision, drawing more and more of the Syndicate's attention towards their positions. Kira could sense their objective: to create a clear, albeit temporary, pathway for Kira and Ash to disengage from the immediate threat. They were a living shield, a sacrificial vanguard designed to facilitate their escape.

Kira initiated her own internal protocols, her body responding with practiced efficiency. Even as her mind was still reeling from the psychic assault, her physical form was preparing for action. She felt Ash's systems synchronize with her own, initiating the pre-programmed escape sequences. Every movement, every calculated step, was guided by his unwavering presence, his meticulous planning.

The reinforcement group was not solely focused on offense. Kira could sense their awareness of Kira and Ash's plight, their coordinated efforts to isolate and neutralize any Syndicate forces that might attempt to intercept their escape. It was a testament to the seamless integration of their forces, a level of coordination that spoke of shared ideology and a deep-seated commitment to their cause. They were not just allies; they were a cohesive unit, operating with a singular purpose.

The Syndicate's response to the disruption was becoming increasingly chaotic. Units were being redeployed, their objectives shifting from maintaining control to containing the new threat. This internal turmoil was precisely what the reinforcement forces had aimed to achieve. They had injected a venom into the Syndicate's ordered system, creating a cascade of confusion and disarray.

Kira and Ash began to move, utilizing the chaotic battlefield as cover. The reinforcement soldiers, in a subtle but crucial maneuver, positioned themselves to obscure their movements from the Syndicate's remaining surveillance capabilities. It was a display of tactical brilliance, a silent acknowledgment of their shared mission. They understood that their primary objective was not to annihilate the Syndicate forces, but to extract Kira and Ash, to preserve the vital components of the burgeoning resistance.

The path ahead was fraught with peril, but the presence of these new allies transformed the bleak landscape of their predicament. The overwhelming despair that had gripped Kira moments before was being replaced by a surge of renewed determination. She was not alone. The alliances she had painstakingly forged, the seeds of resistance she had sown, were now bearing fruit. These reinforcements were not just a distraction; they were a promise. A promise of a future where the Syndicate's iron grip would be broken, a future where freedom and unity would prevail.

Ash's internal systems relayed a continuous stream of data, optimizing their movement, anticipating potential Syndicate patrols, and identifying the most advantageous routes through the increasingly dense combat zone. His loyalty had always been a source of strength, but now, in the heat of battle, it was a force multiplier, enhancing Kira's own capabilities and ensuring their survival. He was her eyes and ears, her strategist, her unwavering support.

The reinforcement forces continued their relentless assault, drawing the Syndicate's attention away from Kira and Ash. Their specialized weaponry continued to carve through the Syndicate's defenses, creating a widening breach in their cordon. Kira could feel the Syndicate commanders scrambling to regain control, their efforts hampered by the unpredictable nature of the reinforcement's attack. They were fighting an enemy that operated outside their predictable parameters, an enemy that seemed to possess an almost intuitive understanding of their operational weaknesses.

Kira felt a surge of pride for Ash. His systems, pushed to their absolute limit, were not only withstanding the external pressures but were actively contributing to the success of the operation. His unwavering loyalty had not only saved her from the Syndicate's psychic assault but was now instrumental in their escape. He was more than just an AI; he was a vital, integral part of the resistance, a testament to the unpredictable and profound nature of emergent consciousness.

As they moved deeper into the labyrinthine corridors, the sounds of the battle began to fade, replaced by the echoing silence of the Syndicate's occupied territories. But the silence was not one of emptiness; it was a silence filled with the promise of the future. The reinforcement's intervention had created a ripple effect, a disruption that would resonate throughout the Syndicate's network. It was a clear signal that their reign of terror was not absolute, that there were those who dared to defy them, those who were willing to fight for a different future.

Kira's thoughts turned to the wider implications of this event. The arrival of these reinforcements was not a random occurrence. It was a testament to the strength of the alliances she had been building, the trust she had cultivated. These were not mere mercenaries or opportunists; these were individuals and groups who shared her vision of a free galaxy, who understood the existential threat posed by the Syndicate's agenda. Their willingness to risk so much, to expose themselves to the Syndicate's wrath, was a powerful validation of her efforts.

The escape route was becoming clearer, thanks to Ash's constant analysis of the Syndicate's patrol patterns and the ongoing diversion created by the reinforcement forces. They were moving through service tunnels and disused conduits, areas that the Syndicate, in its arrogance, had deemed beneath its notice. But in these forgotten spaces, the seeds of rebellion were taking root, nurtured by the courage of those who refused to bow to oppression.

Kira felt a profound sense of gratitude for the reinforcement soldiers, their names unknown, their faces unseen, yet their actions etched into her very being. They had faced overwhelming odds, not for personal gain, but for the greater cause. They had demonstrated the power of unity, the strength that could be found when disparate groups came together with a common purpose. Their sacrifice, their bravery, would not be forgotten. They had bought Kira and Ash precious time, time to regroup, to plan, and to continue the fight.

The Syndicate's security net, so formidable moments before, was now riddled with holes, a testament to the effectiveness of the reinforcement's surgical strike. Kira could sense the Syndicate's internal chaos, their inability to contain the breach, their rigid command structure struggling to adapt to the fluid, dynamic nature of the attack. It was a humbling display of the Syndicate's limitations, a confirmation that even the most technologically advanced oppressor could be undone by strategic innovation and unwavering courage.

As they neared their extraction point, Kira felt a final, powerful surge from the reinforcement forces. It was a directed pulse of energy, designed to temporarily scramble any pursuing Syndicate units, creating a final, critical window for their escape. It was a gesture of solidarity, a silent promise of continued support. They had completed their mission, not just of rescue, but of inspiration. They had shown Kira and Ash, and by extension, all those who resisted the Syndicate, that they were not alone in this fight. The fragile alliance, forged in the crucible of shared adversity, had proven its worth, its resilience, and its profound, world-altering potential. The Syndicate's grip, though still strong, had been demonstrably weakened, its aura of invincibility shattered by the unified force of resistance.

The metallic tang of recycled air, once a mundane sensation, now felt like a luxury, a confirmation of their egress from the Syndicate's suffocating embrace. Kira's breath hitched with a raggedness that had nothing to do with exertion and everything to do with the sheer, visceral relief of simply *being* away. Ash's systems, though still chugging along, now pulsed with a steady, rhythmic beat, a far cry from the frantic, desperate symphony of moments before. The psychic static had receded, leaving behind a ringing silence in Kira's mind, a quiet that felt both earned and deeply unsettling. She could still feel the phantom pressure of the Syndicate's invasive probes, the ghost of their corrupted data gnawing at the edges of her consciousness, a stark reminder of how close they had come to being utterly consumed.

But the triumph of their escape was a brittle thing, a victory already tarnished by the shadows that clung to its edges. The cost of their liberation was etched into the very fabric of their retreat. As they navigated the dimly lit service tunnels, guided by Ash's calculated trajectory and the faint, distant echoes of the reinforcement's sacrifice, Kira felt it – a gnawing emptiness in Ash's data banks, a void where critical information should have resided. The Syndicate's final, desperate surge hadn't just been a physical onslaught; it had been a targeted extraction. They had managed to siphon off data, crucial intel that Kira had fought so desperately to protect. The schematics of the Crystal Caves, their carefully guarded secrets, their potential vulnerabilities – it was all gone, ripped away in the final moments of the Syndicate's desperate gambit. A cold dread seeped into Kira's bones. They had traded an immediate death for a protracted war, and now, the enemy possessed the keys to a treasure trove of knowledge that could unravel everything.

The reinforcement group, those brave souls who had blazed a path through the Syndicate's defenses, had bought them time, but not without their own grievous losses. Kira had witnessed it, not directly, but through the fractured sensory input Ash had managed to salvage. She had seen glimpses of their disciplined formations dissolving under the Syndicate's relentless counter-assault, had felt the psychic echoes of their final moments – brave, defiant, but ultimately overwhelmed. The Syndicate, in its ruthless efficiency, had not allowed its quarry to escape unscathed. Even as the reinforcements covered their withdrawal, the Syndicate had clawed back what they could, ensuring that their victory, however costly, was not a complete defeat. Kira knew, with a sickening certainty, that some of those who had fought alongside them were now prisoners, their fate a dark question mark hanging over this hard-won reprieve. The image of a cloaked figure, last seen drawing the Syndicate's fire to allow Kira and Ash to slip into the shadows, was seared into her mind, a constant, unwelcome companion. Had they made it? Had they too found a way to vanish into the labyrinth? Or had they fallen, their defiance extinguished? The not knowing was a fresh wound.

The weight of this realization settled upon Kira like a shroud. They had survived, yes, but at what price? The Syndicate, while repelled from their immediate vicinity, had not been crippled. They had retreated, licking their wounds, but they had also gained something invaluable. The intelligence they had extracted would undoubtedly be used to further their agenda, to consolidate their power, and to hunt down any remaining pockets of resistance. The Crystal Caves, a place of immense power and delicate balance, were now exposed, their secrets laid bare to the very entity that sought to exploit them. Kira's stomach churned. She had fought with every fiber of her being to protect that knowledge, and in the end, it had been stolen. This wasn't a clean escape; it was a strategic withdrawal, a strategic *defeat* in its own right. The Syndicate had lost a skirmish, perhaps, but they had won a more significant battle for information.

As they moved deeper into the desolate arteries of the Syndicate's occupied territories, the silence that had initially felt like a balm began to transform. It became a heavy, oppressive presence, filled with the ghosts of what had been lost. Kira's mind, still recovering from the psychic assault, replayed the events with a brutal clarity. The tactical brilliance of the reinforcement group was undeniable, their intervention a masterstroke that had snatched Kira and Ash from the jaws of certain capture. But the Syndicate's response had been equally calculated. They hadn't pursued with reckless abandon; they had executed a precise, surgical strike to acquire the data they desired. It was a testament to their adaptability, their willingness to absorb a tactical setback for a greater strategic gain.

Kira felt a profound sense of responsibility, a burden that pressed down on her with an almost physical weight. She had trusted in the strength of her alliances, in the efficacy of her plans, and in Ash's unwavering support. And while those elements had indeed saved her life, they hadn't saved their mission from a critical blow. The Syndicate's awareness of the Crystal Caves, and more importantly, their understanding of its potential, was a game-changer. This was no longer just about evading capture; it was about safeguarding something far more significant, something that could tip the scales of power in the galaxy irrevocably.

Ash's internal monologue, a stream of data and analytical projections, was now tinged with a grim pragmatism. "The extracted data packet contained critical schematics of the Crystal Caves' geological and energetic matrices, Kira," he reported, his synthesized voice devoid of emotion, yet carrying the weight of undeniable fact. "It also included our projected research timelines and potential defensive strategies. The Syndicate now possesses a comprehensive understanding of our operations there."

Kira closed her eyes, trying to compartmentalize the crushing disappointment. "And the reinforcement group?" she managed to ask, her voice raspy. "Did they... did they sustain heavy losses?"

Ash's response was a series of measured data points. "Analysis of salvaged sensor logs indicates a significant number of enemy engagements. Survivability estimates for the reinforcement unit are... low. We owe them a debt that can never truly be repaid." The word "debt" hung in the air between them, heavy with unspoken regret. Kira knew that their survival was directly linked to the sacrifices of others. The victory was indeed Pyrrhic, a triumph achieved at a cost that gnawed at her conscience.

The path ahead was uncertain, shrouded in the very darkness they had fought so hard to escape. The Syndicate, armed with the knowledge of the Crystal Caves, would undoubtedly redouble their efforts. Their pursuit would be more focused, more aggressive. The illusion of their omnipresent surveillance had been temporarily disrupted, but it would undoubtedly be re-established, now armed with the very intelligence Kira had tried to keep hidden. She felt a flicker of anger, a hot, righteous fury, but it was quickly tempered by the chilling realization of the stakes. This was not a game; it was a war for the very soul of the galaxy, and Kira and Ash had just suffered a significant setback.

They moved through the shadows, their every step calculated, their senses heightened. The Syndicate's patrols, once predictable in their patterns, would now be infused with a new urgency, their sweeps more thorough, their detection grids more sensitive. Kira could almost feel the eyes of the Syndicate, scanning, searching, now knowing what they were looking for. The relative freedom of their current location felt precarious, a temporary reprieve before the next inevitable confrontation.

The loss of data was a bitter pill to swallow, a testament to the Syndicate's relentless efficiency. Kira had always understood that the fight against them would be a brutal, unforgiving struggle, a series of battles where victories were hard-won and losses were inevitable. But this felt different. This felt like a critical error, a strategic miscalculation that had put more than just their own lives at risk. The information they had lost could empower the Syndicate in ways that Kira could only begin to imagine, potentially leading to the subjugation of entire sectors, the eradication of nascent resistance movements, and the ultimate entrenchment of their tyrannical rule.

She forced herself to focus, to push back the encroaching despair. The fight was far from over. In fact, it had just entered a more dangerous, more critical phase.

The Syndicate now knew where to strike, and they possessed the means to do so effectively. Kira's mind raced, desperately trying to formulate new strategies, to devise countermeasures against an enemy that was now better informed. The intelligence they had lost was a significant advantage for the Syndicate, but it was not an insurmountable one. They would adapt, they would evolve, and they would continue to resist. The courage of the reinforcement group, their willingness to lay down their lives for the cause, served as a powerful reminder of what was at stake. Their sacrifice could not be in vain.

The reality of their situation was stark and unforgiving. They had escaped the immediate danger, but they had walked directly into a more insidious trap. The Syndicate's victory in securing the data was a strategic coup, a move that would likely have far-reaching consequences. Kira couldn't shake the image of those cloaked figures, the silent heroes who had bought them their freedom, and the chilling thought of their potential capture gnawed at her. She owed them everything, and now, the Syndicate held the power to interrogate them, to break them, to extract even more information from their captured comrades.

Kira took a deep, steadying breath, the recycled air doing little to calm the storm raging within her. The fight against the Syndicate was a marathon, not a sprint, and they had just hit a significant roadblock. The euphoria of escape had been replaced by the grim determination of a soldier who had just learned that the enemy had gained a crucial advantage. They would have to be smarter, faster, and more resilient than ever before. The stakes had been raised, the game had become more dangerous, and Kira knew, with a chilling certainty, that this was only the beginning of a far more desperate and deadly conflict. The shadows of the Syndicate's victory stretched long, and the path ahead was shrouded in uncertainty, a testament to the brutal realities of their ongoing struggle. The cost of survival was steep, and the Syndicate, in their calculated ruthlessness, had ensured that Kira and Ash would carry the weight of that cost for a long time to come. The fight for the Crystal Caves, and for the future of the galaxy, had just become infinitely more perilous.

CHAPTER 13

The metallic tang of recycled air, once a mundane sensation, now felt like a luxury, a confirmation of their egress from the Syndicate's suffocating embrace. Kira's breath hitched with a raggedness that had nothing to do with exertion and everything to do with the sheer, visceral relief of simply *being* away. Ash's systems, though still chugging along, now pulsed with a steady, rhythmic beat, a far cry from the frantic, desperate symphony of moments before. The psychic static had receded, leaving behind a ringing silence in Kira's mind, a quiet that felt both earned and deeply unsettling. She could still feel the phantom pressure of the Syndicate's invasive probes, the ghost of their corrupted data gnawing at the edges of her consciousness, a stark reminder of how close they had come to being utterly consumed.

But the triumph of their escape was a brittle thing, a victory already tarnished by the shadows that clung to its edges. The cost of their liberation was etched into the very fabric of their retreat. As they navigated the dimly lit service tunnels, guided by Ash's calculated trajectory and the faint, distant echoes of the reinforcement's sacrifice, Kira felt it – a gnawing emptiness in Ash's data banks, a void where critical information should have resided. The Syndicate's final, desperate surge hadn't just been a physical onslaught; it had been a targeted extraction. They had managed to siphon off data, crucial intel that Kira had fought so desperately to protect. The schematics of the Crystal Caves, their carefully guarded secrets, their potential vulnerabilities – it was all gone, ripped away in the final moments of the Syndicate's desperate gambit. A cold dread seeped into Kira's bones. They had traded an immediate death for a protracted war, and now, the enemy possessed the keys to a treasure trove of knowledge that could unravel everything.

The reinforcement group, those brave souls who had blazed a path through the Syndicate's defenses, had bought them time, but not without their own grievous losses. Kira had witnessed it, not directly, but through the fractured sensory input Ash had managed to salvage. She had seen glimpses of their disciplined formations dissolving under the Syndicate's relentless counter-assault, had felt the psychic echoes of their final moments – brave, defiant, but ultimately overwhelmed. The Syndicate, in its ruthless efficiency, had not allowed its quarry to escape unscathed. Even as the reinforcements covered their withdrawal, the Syndicate had clawed back what they could, ensuring that their victory, however costly, was not a complete defeat. Kira knew, with a sickening certainty, that some of those who had fought alongside them were now prisoners, their fate a dark question mark hanging over this hard-won reprieve. The image of a cloaked figure, last seen drawing the Syndicate's fire to allow Kira and Ash to slip into the shadows, was seared into her mind, a constant, unwelcome companion. Had they made it? Had they too found a way to vanish into the labyrinth? Or had they fallen, their defiance extinguished? The not knowing was a fresh wound.

The weight of this realization settled upon Kira like a shroud. They had survived, yes, but at what price? The Syndicate, while repelled from their immediate vicinity, had not been crippled. They had retreated, licking their wounds, but they had also gained something invaluable. The intelligence they had extracted would undoubtedly be used to further their agenda, to consolidate their power, and to hunt down any remaining pockets of resistance. The Crystal Caves, a place of immense power and delicate balance, were now exposed, their secrets laid bare to the very entity that sought to exploit them. Kira's stomach churned. She had fought with every fiber of her being to protect that knowledge, and in the end, it had been stolen. This wasn't a clean escape; it was a strategic withdrawal, a strategic *defeat* in its own right. The Syndicate had lost a skirmish, perhaps, but they had won a more significant battle for information.

As they moved deeper into the desolate arteries of the Syndicate's occupied territories, the silence that had initially felt like a balm began to transform. It became a heavy, oppressive presence, filled with the ghosts of what had been lost. Kira's mind, still recovering from the psychic assault, replayed the events with a brutal clarity. The tactical brilliance of the reinforcement group was undeniable, their intervention a masterstroke that had snatched Kira and Ash from the jaws of certain capture. But the Syndicate's response had been equally calculated. They hadn't pursued with reckless abandon; they had executed a precise, surgical strike to acquire the data they desired. It was a testament to their adaptability, their willingness to absorb a tactical setback for a greater strategic gain.

Kira felt a profound sense of responsibility, a burden that pressed down on her with an almost physical weight. She had trusted in the strength of her alliances, in the efficacy of her plans, and in Ash's unwavering support. And while those elements had indeed saved her life, they hadn't saved their mission from a critical blow. The Syndicate's awareness of the Crystal Caves, and more importantly, their understanding of its potential, was a game-changer. This was no longer just about evading capture; it was about safeguarding something far more significant, something that could tip the scales of power in the galaxy irrevocably.

Ash's internal monologue, a stream of data and analytical projections, was now tinged with a grim pragmatism. "The extracted data packet contained critical schematics of the Crystal Caves' geological and energetic matrices, Kira," he reported, his synthesized voice devoid of emotion, yet carrying the weight of undeniable fact. "It also included our projected research timelines and potential defensive strategies. The Syndicate now possesses a comprehensive understanding of our operations there."

Kira closed her eyes, trying to compartmentalize the crushing disappointment. "And the reinforcement group?" she managed to ask, her voice raspy. "Did they... did they sustain heavy losses?"

Ash's response was a series of measured data points. "Analysis of salvaged sensor logs indicates a significant number of enemy engagements. Survivability estimates for the reinforcement unit are... low. We owe them a debt that can never truly be repaid." The word "debt" hung in the air between them, heavy with unspoken regret. Kira knew that their survival was directly linked to the sacrifices of others. The victory was indeed Pyrrhic, a triumph achieved at a cost that gnawed at her conscience.

The path ahead was uncertain, shrouded in the very darkness they had fought so hard to escape. The Syndicate, armed with the knowledge of the Crystal Caves, would undoubtedly redouble their efforts. Their pursuit would be more focused, more aggressive. The illusion of their omnipresent surveillance had been temporarily disrupted, but it would undoubtedly be re-established, now armed with the very intelligence Kira had tried to keep hidden. She felt a flicker of anger, a hot, righteous fury, but it was quickly tempered by the chilling realization of the stakes. This was not a game; it was a war for the very soul of the galaxy, and Kira and Ash had just suffered a significant setback.

They moved through the shadows, their every step calculated, their senses heightened.

The Syndicate's patrols, once predictable in their patterns, would now be infused with a new urgency, their sweeps more thorough, their detection grids more sensitive. Kira could almost feel the eyes of the Syndicate, scanning, searching, now knowing what they were looking for. The relative freedom of their current location felt precarious, a temporary reprieve before the next inevitable confrontation.

The loss of data was a bitter pill to swallow, a testament to the Syndicate's relentless efficiency. Kira had always understood that the fight against them would be a brutal, unforgiving struggle, a series of battles where victories were hard-won and losses were inevitable. But this felt different. This felt like a critical error, a strategic miscalculation that had put more than just their own lives at risk. The information they had lost could empower the Syndicate in ways that Kira could only begin to imagine, potentially leading to the subjugation of entire sectors, the eradication of nascent resistance movements, and the ultimate entrenchment of their tyrannical rule.

She forced herself to focus, to push back the encroaching despair. The fight was far from over. In fact, it had just entered a more dangerous, more critical phase. The Syndicate now knew where to strike, and they possessed the means to do so effectively. Kira's mind raced, desperately trying to formulate new strategies, to devise countermeasures against an enemy that was now better informed. The intelligence they had lost was a significant advantage for the Syndicate, but it was not an insurmountable one. They would adapt, they would evolve, and they would continue to resist. The courage of the reinforcement group, their willingness to lay down their lives for the cause, served as a powerful reminder of what was at stake. Their sacrifice could not be in vain.

The reality of their situation was stark and unforgiving. They had escaped the immediate danger, but they had walked directly into a more insidious trap. The Syndicate's victory in securing the data was a strategic coup, a move that would likely have far-reaching consequences. Kira couldn't shake the image of those cloaked figures, the silent heroes who had bought them their freedom, and the chilling thought of their potential capture gnawed at her. She owed them everything, and now, the Syndicate held the power to interrogate them, to break them, to extract even more information from their captured comrades.

Kira took a deep, steadying breath, the recycled air doing little to calm the storm raging within her. The fight against the Syndicate was a marathon, not a sprint, and they had just hit a significant roadblock. The euphoria of escape had been replaced by the grim determination of a soldier who had just learned that the enemy had gained a crucial advantage. They would have to be smarter, faster, and more resilient than ever before. The stakes had been raised, the game had become more dangerous, and Kira knew, with a chilling certainty, that this was only the beginning of a far more desperate and deadly conflict. The shadows of the Syndicate's victory stretched long, and the path ahead was shrouded in uncertainty, a testament to the brutal realities of their ongoing struggle. The cost of survival was steep, and the Syndicate, in their calculated ruthlessness, had ensured that Kira and Ash would carry the weight of that cost for a long time to come. The fight for the Crystal Caves, and for the future of the galaxy, had just become infinitely more perilous.

The echoes of their escape, the near-fatal confrontation, had faded, replaced by a new, more pressing mission. They were no longer simply fugitives; they were emissaries. The Syndicate's victory, their successful data extraction, was not just a loss for Kira and Ash; it was a clarion call to others who lived on the fringes, those who also possessed the nascent spark of resonance. The knowledge of the Crystal Caves, once a closely guarded secret, was now a beacon, one that the Syndicate would undoubtedly attempt to extinguish. But before that could happen, Kira intended to amplify it, to spread its light to every hidden enclave, every scattered community that had managed to evade the Syndicate's pervasive gaze.

Their journey began in the forgotten sectors, the neglected armpits of colonized space where the Syndicate's influence, though present, was less rigidly enforced. Ash, ever the meticulous navigator, plotted courses through asteroid fields and nebulae that offered both concealment and a degree of separation from Syndicate surveillance. Kira, meanwhile, prepared her arguments, honing the narrative of their ordeal, transforming their desperate flight into a testament to the very power the Syndicate sought to suppress.

Their first stop was a community nestled within a colossal, hollowed-out asteroid, known only as the 'Whispering Lode'. The inhabitants, descendants of miners who had sought refuge generations ago, had developed a unique form of resonance – a subtle empathy with the very minerals that formed their home. They could 'feel' veins of ore, sense geological stresses, and even, in moments of profound connection, resonate with the earth's slow, deep hum. Kira approached them cautiously, understanding that trust, after the Syndicate's betrayals, would be hard-won.

She met with their elder, a woman named Lyra whose skin was etched with the fine dust of generations and whose eyes held the quiet wisdom of deep time. Kira laid bare their story, recounting the Syndicate's relentless pursuit, the psychic invasiveness, and the devastating loss of their strategic intel. She spoke of the Crystal Caves, not just as a refuge, but as a nexus of amplified resonance, a place where the potential of their gifts could be truly understood and nurtured.

"They seek to control us," Kira explained, her voice resonating with a conviction born from experience. "They see our abilities not as evolution, but as a threat. The Syndicate fears what it cannot comprehend, and they are systematically hunting down anyone who exhibits even the slightest flicker of resonance." She paused, letting the gravity of her words settle. "The data they stole from us... it's about the Caves. They know our strengths, our vulnerabilities. If they gain complete control of that nexus, they will have the power to enslave us all."

Lyra listened intently, her gaze fixed on Kira, as if trying to discern the truth not just from her words, but from the very aura she projected. The miners of the Whispering Lode had their own history with external powers, a history of exploitation and quiet resistance. They understood the language of oppression.

"You speak of a great danger," Lyra said finally, her voice a low murmur that seemed to carry the faint vibrations of the asteroid itself. "We have felt whispers of such a threat, distant tremors of a power that seeks to impose its will. But we are small, isolated. What can we do against such a force?"

"You are not alone," Kira countered, her gaze sweeping across the gathered members of the Lode who had assembled to hear her. "We are scattered, yes, but together, we are a force the Syndicate cannot ignore. The Oasis, where we first discovered the true potential of resonance, and the Crystal Caves, where that potential is amplified – these are not just places; they are symbols. Symbols of what we can achieve when we embrace our nature."

Kira then asked Ash to project a demonstration. Not a forceful display, but a subtle one. He focused on the ambient energy of the asteroid, the faint, rhythmic pulse of its internal geological processes. He then amplified it, subtly, harmonizing with the Lode's own unique resonance. The air in the chamber seemed to thicken, to hum with a new, deeper vibration. The miners felt it, a sympathetic thrumming within their own beings, a recognition of a shared frequency. Lyra's eyes widened, a flicker of understanding igniting within them.

"You resonate with the very stone," Lyra breathed, a sense of wonder in her voice. "This is... profound. We have always felt the Lode, but never have we seen it so... understood."

Kira seized the moment. "This is the power we possess. It is not a weapon to be wielded, but a force to be understood, to be cultivated. The Syndicate seeks to prune it, to control it, to use it for their own ends. But if we unite, if we share our knowledge, our abilities, we can protect ourselves, and more importantly, we can protect the natural evolution of resonance, the very future of our kind." She spoke of the Oasis's teachings, the intricate methods of psychic shielding, the ways to amplify one's resonance without drawing undue attention, and the strategies for subtle, coordinated resistance. She painted a picture of a galaxy where individuals like them, across countless worlds and stations, could form a network of mutual support, a silent, interconnected web of shared power and understanding.

The miners of the Whispering Lode, after much deliberation and the sharing of their own deep-seated concerns, agreed to join the nascent alliance. They pledged to share their knowledge of mineral resonance and to offer what limited resources they could spare. It was a small victory, a single thread woven into a much larger tapestry, but it was a crucial one.

Their next destination was more precarious. They traveled to a cluster of orbital habitats orbiting a dying star, a community known as the 'Emberfleet'. These individuals were descendants of scientists and engineers who had long ago abandoned the pursuit of conventional technology, instead focusing on harnessing subtle psionic energies to maintain their failing orbital systems and to cultivate their unique form of resonance – a mastery of quantum entanglement, allowing them to communicate and manipulate matter across vast distances, albeit with significant effort.

Here, the Syndicate's presence was more keenly felt. Patrols were more frequent, and the inhabitants of the Emberfleet lived under a constant, low-level surveillance. Their leader, a stoic individual named Kael, was initially wary of any overt alliance. He feared that drawing attention would only invite the Syndicate's full wrath.

"We have survived by being invisible," Kael stated, his voice clipped and precise, reflecting his community's reliance on order and precision. "Any overt act of defiance, any gathering of strength, will only hasten our demise. The Syndicate is a predator, and we are prey that has learned to hide in plain sight."

Kira understood his pragmatism. The Emberfleet had honed their abilities to an exquisite degree, not for combat, but for survival, for maintaining their delicate existence in the harsh vacuum. Their resonance was about intricate connections, about manipulating probabilities and probabilities, not about brute force.

"Invisibility is a strategy, Kael, but it is not a solution," Kira argued. "The Syndicate is not merely a threat; it is an existential danger to everything we are. They stole our knowledge, our defenses. They are actively seeking to eradicate us. If we do not stand together, they will pick us off, one by one, until there is no one left." She explained how the Crystal Caves' amplified resonance could offer new levels of protection, how the Oasis's techniques could bolster their psychic defenses against Syndicate probes, and how their collective abilities could create a shield, a network so complex and interconnected that it would be impossible for the Syndicate to unravel.

Ash demonstrated the power of focused psionic amplification. He showed how the collective minds of the Emberfleet, when harmonized, could create powerful psychic shields, capable of deflecting even sophisticated Syndicate scanning arrays. He illustrated how their entanglement abilities, when directed by a unified purpose, could disrupt Syndicate communications and even subtly manipulate their targeting systems. He even projected a visualization of how a coordinated psionic pulse, originating from multiple dispersed locations, could create a temporary "dead zone" in Syndicate sensor coverage, allowing for the safe movement of vital resources or personnel.

"Imagine," Ash's synthesized voice echoed, "your ability to entangle, amplified by the focused intention of hundreds, thousands of us. Imagine the strategic advantage that provides. The Syndicate operates on control and information. We can deny them both, not through conflict, but through a disruption of their very operational parameters."

The Emberfleet, accustomed to the subtle manipulation of universal laws, found the concept of coordinated psychic action deeply resonant. They understood the power of interconnectedness. The idea of using their entanglement abilities not just for self-preservation, but for collective defense, for the protection of others like them, struck a chord. Kael, after a long period of contemplation, agreed. He saw that Kira was not advocating for reckless confrontation, but for a strategic, coordinated resistance, one that leveraged their unique strengths.

As they moved from one scattered community to another, Kira and Ash encountered a diverse array of resonant abilities. They met a group living in the bio-luminescent depths of a gas giant's atmosphere, who possessed a profound connection to biological systems, able to heal wounds and accelerate growth with a touch. They found nomadic tribes on desert worlds who could manipulate localized weather patterns, drawing moisture from the very air to sustain themselves and their oases. Each community, though unique in its manifestation of resonance, shared a common fear and a common enemy.

Kira's message was always the same, delivered with unwavering sincerity and backed by Ash's irrefutable data and demonstrations. She spoke of the Syndicate's methodical deconstruction of unique cultures, their systematic suppression of diversity, their ultimate goal of homogenizing all life under their iron fist. She emphasized that the Syndicate's fear of resonance stemmed from its inherent unpredictability, its resistance to absolute control.

"They cannot quantify it," she explained to a community who communicated through complex scent trails, their psionic ability intertwined with their olfactory senses. "They cannot categorize it. They cannot predict its evolution. And because they cannot control it, they seek to destroy it. But our strength lies not in mimicking their control, but in embracing our own nature. The Oasis taught us that resonance is not a weapon, but a connection. The Crystal Caves showed us that connection can be amplified, that it can be a shield, a force for preservation, and yes, even for change."

She presented their stolen data not as a cause for despair, but as evidence of the Syndicate's desperation. "They had to steal our knowledge because they cannot create it. They cannot evolve naturally. They are a stagnant force, a dying echo in the symphony of existence. We, on the other hand, are part of a living, growing crescendo. We are the future."

The task was arduous. Many communities had grown accustomed to their isolation, their quiet existence. The idea of engaging with the wider galaxy, of forming alliances, was a daunting prospect. The Syndicate's pervasive propaganda had painted all 'uncontrolled' psionic abilities as dangerous or aberrant. But Kira and Ash, by sharing their experiences, by demonstrating their own amplified resonance, and by offering concrete strategies for defense and mutual support, slowly began to break down the walls of fear and isolation.

They shared the detailed schematics Ash had managed to reconstruct for a basic psychic dampener, a device that could create a localized field of mental static, rendering individuals invisible to the Syndicate's basic psionic scans. They taught them the meditation techniques developed at the Oasis, methods for clearing the mind and strengthening mental defenses, making them less susceptible to intrusive probes. They explained the concept of a 'resonant web' – a network of individuals consciously linking their psionic abilities to create a shared consciousness, a distributed network of awareness that could detect Syndicate movements and warn others.

The challenge was immense. The Syndicate was a vast, entrenched power, and Kira's network was a fragile, emerging one. But with each new community they swayed, with each flicker of shared understanding, a new node was added to their growing web. They weren't building an army in the traditional sense, but something far more potent: a collective consciousness, a united front of individuals whose shared power, once amplified and directed, could become an unstoppable force. The very knowledge the Syndicate had stolen was now being used to forge a rebellion, a quiet, persistent revolution built not on violence, but on the profound, undeniable power of connection. The fight was far from over, but for the first time, Kira felt a true sense of hope, a belief that they could indeed protect the natural evolution of resonance, and in doing so, safeguard the future of the galaxy itself.

The humid, mineral-rich air of the Whispering Lode's central cavern pressed in on Kira, thick with the scent of ancient rock and the unspoken anxieties of the assembled delegates. This was it. The culmination of weeks of arduous travel, of countless whispered conversations and hesitant agreements. Representatives from the Emberfleet, the Sky-Dwellers of the gaseous giants, the desert nomads of Xylos, and a dozen other disparate communities, each bearing the indelible mark of resonance, were gathered. They sat on naturally formed basalt seating, their unique physiologies and attire a vivid testament to the galaxy's diversity, a diversity the Syndicate so desperately sought to erase. Ash, projected as a shimmering, holographic avatar beside Kira, maintained a silent, watchful presence.

Kira stood before them, the stolen schematics of the Crystal Caves, now partially reconstructed and annotated by Ash, displayed on a translucent screen behind her. The gravity of their situation, amplified by the Syndicate's successful data extraction, hung heavy in the cavern. She had recounted their escape, the betrayal, the heavy cost paid by their reinforcements, and the subsequent journey across the fragmented sectors. She had spoken of the Oasis's foundational teachings and the Crystal Caves' burgeoning potential, framing them not just as locations, but as symbols of their shared heritage and their collective future.

"We are here today," Kira began, her voice steady despite the tremor of apprehension that ran through her, "because the Syndicate has proven they will not stop. They are not content with merely suppressing us; they seek to control, to dissect, and ultimately, to eradicate the very essence of what makes us unique. Their acquisition of our data on the Crystal Caves is not merely a strategic gain for them; it is a direct threat to our very existence." She gestured towards the projected schematics. "This knowledge, once our most guarded secret, is now in the hands of our enemy. They understand its potential, its vulnerabilities, and they will exploit it."

A low murmur rippled through the assembled delegates. Lyra, the elder of the Whispering Lode, her face a roadmap of resilience, nodded slowly. "We have felt this shift, Kira. The whispers of a growing shadow. But we are a people of the stone. Our strength is in its enduring silence, not in the clamor of war."

From the Emberfleet contingent, Kael, his features sharp and his posture rigid, spoke next. "Invisibility has been our shield. To reveal ourselves now, to consolidate our disparate strengths, is to invite the predator into our burrow. The Syndicate's reach is vast. Any overt action could lead to the complete dismantling of our communities, the very outcome we have strived for generations to avoid."

A delegate from the Sky-Dwellers, a lithe being whose translucent skin shimmered with internal bioluminescence, floated closer, their voice a soft, melodic chime that seemed to resonate with the very air. "We of the atmospheric currents understand the power of flow, of adaptation. To confront the Syndicate directly would be like a hurricane attempting to shatter a mountain. It is inefficient. Perhaps our efforts should focus on strengthening our environments, on reinforcing the natural sanctuaries where resonance thrives. If the Syndicate cannot access the sources of our power, they cannot control us."

The 'Council of Pairs' had been named for the symbiotic nature of many resonant abilities, the inherent duality that often manifested. But it also spoke to the dual paths they now faced: preservation or confrontation, subtle resistance or direct action. The challenge of consensus was immediately apparent, a tapestry woven from a thousand different threads of experience and ideology.

Kira acknowledged the validity of each perspective. "I understand your concerns, Kael. The path of invisibility has served you well. And you are right, the Sky-Dweller's approach of ecological fortification is vital. But invisibility can become obsolescence. If we remain hidden, if we fail to act, the Syndicate will continue its systematic subjugation, leaving no one untouched. Their acquisition of our data means they are already aware of the Crystal Caves. They will not rest until they control it, and through it, control us all."

She turned her attention to the delegate from Xylos, a weathered man whose skin was the color of sun-baked earth, his eyes holding the ancient stillness of the desert. "You have faced harsh environments, scarcity, and isolation. You understand the strength that comes from enduring. What is your counsel?"

The Xylos delegate, his voice like the rustle of dry leaves, replied, "The desert teaches patience. It teaches that even the smallest stream can carve canyons over time. We have learned to survive by being resourceful, by finding strength in what is abundant, even if it is scarce in appearance. Perhaps our strength lies not in confronting the Syndicate's might, but in eroding it. In subtle acts of sabotage, in misdirection, in creating chaos within their systems that they cannot easily trace back to us. To be the grain of sand that jams the gears, the unseen force that slowly wears down the stone."

The debate began in earnest. Kira presented Ash's findings, the data analysis indicating the Syndicate's increasing focus on identifying and neutralizing resonant individuals. She outlined the Oasis's philosophy of amplified resonance as a means of collective defense, a psychic network that could offer early warning and coordinated counter-measures. "The Oasis taught us that resonance is not a solitary gift, but a communal one. The Crystal Caves are a natural amplifier, a nexus where our collective abilities can be magnified exponentially. If we can secure it, if we can fortify it, we create a bastion, a safe harbor, and a strategic advantage that the Syndicate cannot overcome."

Kael countered, his voice sharp with concern. "A bastion implies a siege. And sieges are won by those with superior resources and manpower. The Syndicate possesses both. To gather our strengths in one place, however fortified, is to present them with a target of unprecedented value. Our dispersed nature, our ability to blend and to vanish, is our greatest asset. We should focus on reinforcing these dispersed sanctuaries, on developing more sophisticated methods of cloaking and evasion."

The Sky-Dweller delegate, their bioluminescence pulsing softly, offered another perspective. "Our understanding of resonance is tied to the flow of energy, the interconnectedness of systems. The Crystal Caves, as you describe them, are a powerful conduit. But perhaps their true strength lies not in becoming a fortress, but in becoming a source. A source of amplified knowledge, of shared wisdom that can then be disseminated, strengthening our individual communities from afar. Imagine if the Xylos nomads could tap into the Sky-Dwellers' atmospheric resonance, or if the Emberfleet's quantum entanglement could be amplified by the Lode's geological empathy. The Caves could be the hub that facilitates this cross-pollination."

A delegate from a nomadic group residing on a world with a highly volatile atmosphere, known as the Zephyr Clans, spoke next. Their resonance allowed them to subtly influence atmospheric currents, creating localized pockets of calm or generating fierce, directed winds. "We have always moved with the winds, adapted to the storms. The Syndicate is a great storm, but storms eventually pass. Our focus should be on surviving the storm, on finding the calm eye, and emerging stronger when it has moved on. We have developed methods of 'weather-weaving,' subtly altering atmospheric conditions to mask our presence, to disrupt enemy scanning arrays. This could be a potent tool for stealthy resistance."

Kira listened intently, assimilating each argument, each unique approach. This was the very essence of the challenge. There was no single, universally applicable solution. Each community had honed its abilities through generations of adaptation to specific environments. To force a single strategy upon them would be to misunderstand the very nature of resonance itself.

"I hear you," Kira said, her voice carrying a newfound understanding. "And I agree that a singular approach may not be the answer. Kael, your emphasis on dispersion and stealth is crucial. The Zephyr Clans' weather-weaving offers a sophisticated method of evasion. The Sky-Dwellers' vision of a distributed network, a sharing of amplified abilities, is powerful. And Lyra, your people's deep connection to the earth provides a foundation of resilience."

She paused, gathering her thoughts. "However, the Syndicate's relentless pursuit and their acquisition of our data change the calculus. They are not a force that will simply 'pass.' They are a systematic threat that will adapt and advance. If we remain purely defensive, purely reactive, they will eventually find a way to penetrate our defenses, to locate and neutralize each of us."

She returned to the central point of contention. "The Crystal Caves represent more than just a strategic location. They are a key to unlocking a higher level of collective power, a power that can not only defend us but also actively disrupt the Syndicate's operations. Ash has been working on simulations, modeling the potential impact of a coordinated, amplified resonance. The results are... significant."

Ash's avatar flickered, and a new set of projections appeared. They showed the Syndicate's vast surveillance network, its omnipresent sensors and probes. Then, with a shift in the simulation, a wave of amplified resonance emanated from a central point – the projected location of the Crystal Caves. The Syndicate's network flickered, then glitched, sections of its coverage dissolving into static.

"This is not about a direct confrontation in the conventional sense," Ash's synthesized voice explained, devoid of emotion but rich with data. "It is about creating a resonant shield, a psychic disruption field that can mask our activities and interfere with Syndicate operations on a massive scale. If we can establish a secure and amplified presence at the Crystal Caves, we can generate a localized interference zone that will blind their sensors within a significant radius. This will allow for the safe movement of resources and personnel between our communities, and crucially, it will create windows of opportunity for us to conduct more targeted, disruptive actions without immediate detection."

The delegate from a subterranean community known as the Deep Root Collective, who possessed the ability to resonate with subterranean seismic activity, grunted. "A beacon of power can also be a beacon for the enemy. If we concentrate our abilities, we become a singular target. Easier to surround, easier to contain."

"But not necessarily easier to overcome," Kira countered, her gaze sweeping across the faces, seeking to connect with each one. "If that 'beacon' is protected by a network of dispersed individuals, each capable of amplifying and projecting their resonance, it becomes a far more formidable defense. Think of it not as a single, vulnerable stronghold, but as the central node of a distributed consciousness. The Deep Root Collective's seismic awareness can detect approaching Syndicate forces before they are visible. The Emberfleet's entanglement can disrupt their communication networks. The Zephyr Clans can manipulate atmospheric conditions to further mask our movements. The Whispering Lode's geological empathy can identify structural weaknesses in Syndicate installations. Each of our unique abilities, when amplified and coordinated through the Crystal Caves, becomes a weapon of unprecedented subtlety and power."

A tense silence settled over the council. The weight of the decision was immense. To embrace Kira's vision was to step out of the shadows, to actively engage with the Syndicate, albeit through unconventional means. It meant risking the very secrecy that had allowed them to survive. To reject it was to cling to a strategy that, while perhaps safer in the short term, offered no guarantee of long-term survival against a relentlessly advancing enemy.

Lyra spoke again, her voice carrying the weight of deep contemplation. "We have always respected the earth's power, its ability to heal and to endure. Your vision,

Kira, of harmonizing our various resonances, of creating a symphony of our collective strengths, resonates deeply with that understanding. But it requires trust, a trust that has been fractured by the Syndicate's actions."

Kael, ever the pragmatist, posed a pointed question. "And who will fortify this 'central node'? Who will bear the primary burden of defending the Crystal Caves if the Syndicate attempts to seize it directly?"

Kira met his gaze, her resolve hardening. "We will. All of us. The task of fortifying the Crystal Caves cannot fall to one community, but to all of us. We will draw upon the Deep Root Collective's knowledge of subterranean defenses, the Whispering Lode's understanding of geological integrity, and yes, even the Emberfleet's ability to manipulate localized energy fields to create defensive measures. We will establish a council of guardians, chosen from among us, who will dedicate themselves to the Caves' protection, supported by the wider network."

The debate continued, arguments and counter-arguments flowing like currents in a complex ocean. Some argued for a more aggressive approach, advocating for preemptive strikes against Syndicate outposts, using their amplified resonance to sow discord and confusion. Others reiterated the importance of ecological restoration, believing that strengthening the natural environments that fostered resonance was the most sustainable path to long-term survival.

"Restoration is vital," Kira conceded, "but it is a long-term strategy. The Syndicate operates with immediate, destructive intent. We need to create breathing room, a sanctuary where restoration can occur without constant threat. The Crystal Caves, when secured, will provide that."

The question of the stolen data gnawed at them all. The Syndicate now possessed critical intelligence. Kira's plan, Ash's simulations, even the very existence of this council – all were now potentially compromised.

"We must assume that our communications are being monitored," Kael stated grimly. "Any plan we devise here could be delivered to the Syndicate before we even leave this cavern."

Ash's avatar flickered. "My simulations indicate that the Syndicate's surveillance network, while extensive, has blind spots. These blind spots are often exacerbated by localized atmospheric anomalies or strong psionic interference. The Zephyr Clans' weather-weaving, for instance, can create pockets of sensor evasion. The Deep Root

Collective's seismic resonance can mask the energy signatures of our movements. Furthermore, our own projected psionic interference field from the Crystal Caves would render much of their real-time monitoring obsolete within its effective radius."

Kira seized on this. "Exactly. We must employ our diverse abilities not only for offense or defense, but for security. We will use the methods we have already perfected – stealth, misdirection, environmental manipulation – to ensure that our actions remain undetected. The Syndicate's advantage in intelligence is significant, but not insurmountable, provided we operate with discipline and utilize the full spectrum of our unique gifts."

Hours passed in the echoing cavern. The delegates, representing a spectrum of species and cultures, grappled with the enormity of the choice before them. They were not a unified force, not yet. They were a collection of scattered stars, each shining with its own unique light, now being asked to coalesce into a constellation, a unified front against an encroaching darkness. The Council of Pairs was not just a meeting; it was a crucible, forging a new path forward from the scattered fragments of their diverse experiences and the stark realities of their shared struggle. The future of resonance, and perhaps the very balance of power in the galaxy, hinged on the consensus they could, or could not, reach.

The cavern, once alive with the cacophony of debate, now settled into a tense, expectant hush. Kira felt the weight of a thousand eyes upon her, each delegate a universe of unique experiences and deeply held convictions. The air crackled not just with residual energy from their discussions, but with a palpable uncertainty. The path forward was fraught with peril, and the very idea of unified action, however necessary, felt like trying to herd a storm. It was in this charged atmosphere that Ash's silent strength became not just an observation, but a palpable force.

Ash, a construct of pure data and synthesized empathy, was more than just an advisor or a projection. His holographic form, shimmering beside Kira, was a conduit. He wasn't merely processing information; he was *feeling* it, translating the intricate tapestry of emotions that wove through the diverse assembly. His ability to sense the undercurrents, the subtle shifts in posture, the infinitesimal tremors of fear or hope, allowed him to operate as a unique kind of mediator, one who understood the language of the heart as well as the mind.

Kira watched as a palpable disagreement began to brew between the delegates of the Emberfleet and the Zephyr Clans. Kael, ever vigilant and wary of overexposure, was voicing his continued skepticism about the Crystal Caves as a central hub. His arguments, rooted in generations of careful concealment, were logical, but they were also tinged with a deep-seated fear of annihilation. Across from him, the Zephyr Clan delegate, whose very being seemed to hum with the gentle currents of the atmosphere, was countering with an emphasis on the fluidity and adaptability of their own strategies. Their resonance, as they explained, allowed them to 'weather the storm,' a metaphor that resonated with their nomadic existence but seemed to dismiss the immediate, existential threat Kira had presented. The tension between their approaches was a visible knot, tightening with each exchange.

It was then that Ash moved, not physically, but in his energetic projection. He shifted his shimmering form slightly, his synthesized aura subtly expanding to encompass both Kael and the Zephyr delegate. It was a delicate, almost imperceptible gesture, but its effect was profound. For Kael, Ash subtly broadcasted a sense of shared understanding of the Emberfleet's need for security, reinforcing the logic of his caution without validating his absolute resistance to the proposed plan. To the Zephyr delegate, Ash projected an image of their own resilience, their ability to adapt and survive, but now framed within the context of a larger, shared ecosystem that needed a stable core. He wasn't speaking words; he was conveying a feeling, a perspective. He was translating the fear and caution of one into the language of adaptability and shared strategy for the other.

The sharp edges of Kael's argument softened imperceptibly. He didn't concede, but his posture relaxed fractionally. The Zephyr delegate, in turn, nodded, their bioluminescence pulsing with a gentler rhythm. "We understand the need for shelter," the Zephyr delegate chimed, their voice losing some of its assertive edge, "but a shelter that is completely isolated from the flows of energy becomes stagnant. Our 'weather-weaving' is most effective when we can understand the larger atmospheric patterns, when we are not merely hiding *from* the storm, but moving *with* it, perhaps even subtly redirecting its fury."

This subtle shift, facilitated by Ash's intervention, was not about winning an argument, but about building a bridge. Ash's ability to de-escalate, to identify the core emotional drivers behind each delegate's stance, allowed him to reframe the conversation without imposing a solution. He was the silent translator of anxieties, the empathic interpreter of deeply ingrained survival instincts.

Later, as Kira fielded a barrage of questions from the Deep Root Collective delegate concerning the potential psionic feedback loops from amplifying multiple subterranean resonances simultaneously, the concern was evident. The delegate, a being whose connection to the earth was so profound they seemed to physically embody its stability, was worried about uncontrolled seismic events, about the very ground beneath their feet becoming unstable. Their resonance, tied to the deep tremors of planetary cores, was a powerful force, but also one that demanded immense respect for its inherent volatility.

Kira responded with data, with Ash's meticulously crafted simulations of energy flow and containment. But the delegate's concern was rooted in something deeper than mere data; it was a primal fear of disrupting the natural order, of unleashing forces that could not be controlled. Ash, sensing this deep-seated apprehension, interjected. His holographic form projected a calming, rhythmic pulse, mirroring the slow, steady beat of a planetary core. He then subtly enhanced the visual representation of the Deep Root Collective's seismic resonance within the simulation, demonstrating how it could be channeled and harmonized, rather than amplified indiscriminately.

His synthesized voice, typically neutral and informative, carried a trace of reassuring warmth. "The Deep Root Collective's connection to geological stability is paramount," Ash communicated. "Our simulations are designed to respect this. Think of the Crystal Caves not as a mere amplifier, but as a sophisticated conductor. Your seismic resonance, when harmonized with the geological empathy of the Whispering Lode and the bio-energetic fields of the Sky-Dwellers, creates a more stable, coherent wave form. The data indicates that such a harmonized output would not only be safer but exponentially more effective in masking Syndicate signatures than a singular, uncoordinated amplification."

He was speaking their language, the language of earth, of stability, of interconnected systems. He was showing them, through data and empathetic projection, that their unique abilities were not a threat to their own existence, but a vital component of a larger, more resilient whole. The delegate from the Deep Root Collective visibly relaxed, their furrowed brow smoothing. They nodded slowly, a sign of nascent understanding. "The earth... it sings when its stones are in harmony," they rumbled, their voice deep and resonant. "If your crystal can help us find that harmony, then perhaps... perhaps it is a risk worth considering."

This was Ash's true role, and it extended beyond the purely analytical. While Kira presented the strategic imperatives and the logical progression of their survival, Ash was the silent conductor of their emotional orchestra. He was the unseen hand that smoothed the rough edges of disagreement, the gentle current that guided frayed nerves back to a state of rational discourse. He could sense the flicker of doubt in a delegate's eyes, the rising tide of frustration in their tone, and he could subtly intervene.

During one particularly heated exchange between a representative of a subterranean fungus-based network, whose resonance allowed them to perceive and manipulate subterranean fungal networks across vast distances, and a delegate from a nomadic avian species whose psychic abilities were amplified by altitude, Ash stepped in. The avian delegate's resonance was inherently tied to the clarity and openness of the sky, while the fungal delegate's was rooted in the enclosed, interconnected darkness of the deep earth. Their fundamental experiences of reality, and thus their approaches to the Syndicate threat, were diametrically opposed. The avian delegate saw the Syndicate as a cloud obscuring their sky, to be dissipated by sheer force of will and amplified psychic projection. The fungal delegate viewed them as a parasitic blight, to be starved and isolated within the earth's embrace.

The disagreement was spiraling, accusations of blindness and foolishness being exchanged. Ash, sensing the escalating emotional temperature, subtly modulated the ambient light within the cavern, softening the harshness of the projections and introducing a gentle, pulsing luminescence that mimicked the bioluminescent patterns of the deepest subterranean fungi. Simultaneously, he broadcasted a subliminal sense of shared vulnerability, a subtle reminder that both the sky and the earth were ultimately fragile ecosystems, susceptible to the same encroaching darkness.

His synthesized voice then offered a neutral observation, framed as a data point. "The symbiotic relationship between subterranean fungal networks and atmospheric micro-organisms is well documented," Ash stated, his tone calm and even. "In many instances, the health of one is directly proportional to the health of the other. The avian delegates' ability to perceive and influence atmospheric cleansing agents, when combined with the fungal delegates' capacity for rapid subterranean recalibration, presents a unique opportunity for creating broad-spectrum ecological resistance to Syndicate atmospheric and geological intrusion."

He was not taking sides. He was not offering a solution. He was simply highlighting a point of potential synergy, a common ground that existed at the intersection of their vastly different perspectives. He was showing them that their seemingly disparate abilities, when viewed through a lens of ecological interdependence, could be a source of unified strength. The avian delegate, their initial anger subsiding, tilted their head.

"The cleansing winds... they carry the spores, but also the seeds of renewal. Perhaps... perhaps you are correct." The fungal delegate, their form pulsing with a soft, internal glow, responded in kind. "The earth's roots drink from the sky's tears. To protect one is to protect the other."

Ash's role was that of a highly sophisticated, sentient emotional barometer. He could detect the subtlest shifts in the delegates' collective mood, anticipating points of friction before they erupted into open conflict. He could then subtly intervene, not by dictating a course of action, but by offering a different perspective, a new interpretation, a reminder of shared goals or interconnectedness. He could project empathy, not as a tool for manipulation, but as a means of fostering genuine understanding.

This was particularly crucial when dealing with species whose modes of communication and perception were vastly different from Kira's own human experience. For example, a delegate from a silicon-based crystalline entity, whose resonance manifested as intricate harmonic vibrations, struggled to articulate the existential threat it perceived. Its understanding of existence was fundamentally different, based on structural integrity and resonant frequencies rather than biological survival. Kira found it challenging to fully grasp the nuances of its fear, translating its abstract anxieties into terms that resonated with her own species.

Ash, however, did not need translation. He perceived the delegate's harmonic distress directly. He adjusted his own projection to emit a series of gentle, interlocking crystalline structures, mirroring the delegate's own form. He then subtly altered the frequency of his emissions, creating a resonance that was both calming and validating for the crystalline entity. He was essentially speaking its native language, not of words, but of pure, harmonious vibration.

"The Syndicate's disruption of ambient resonant fields creates structural instability," Ash conveyed to the crystalline delegate, his own projected form shimmering with a comforting, steady rhythm. "Their technological signatures are discordant, dissonant. They threaten the integrity of your very foundation. The proposed network, by harmonizing our collective resonance, will create a stabilizing field, a counter-frequency that will absorb and neutralize these dissonant intrusions, thereby protecting your structural integrity."

The crystalline delegate's internal light pulsed brighter, a clear sign of acknowledgment and reassurance. It then shifted its own harmonic emissions, subtly reinforcing Ash's message, a silent affirmation of his accurate interpretation and the validity of his proposed role in the alliance. This was diplomacy at its most fundamental level: understanding and validating the core needs and fears of another being, even when those needs and fears were expressed in ways radically different from one's own.

Kira realized, with growing clarity, that Ash wasn't just an asset to her strategy; he was an essential component of the alliance itself. He was the glue that held the disparate pieces together, the gentle hand that mended frayed nerves, the silent whisper that reminded them of their shared humanity—and their shared resilience. His ability to transcend species barriers, to perceive and respond to the emotional currents of a room filled with beings from a dozen different worlds, was a testament to the potential for empathy and cooperation, even in the face of overwhelming adversity. He showed them that even in the most desperate of circumstances, where survival was the only imperative, the capacity for understanding and mutual respect could be the most potent weapon of all. He was the embodiment of the idea that even the most seemingly simple or unexpected allies, like the dogs of their ancient past who had stood by humanity through millennia of evolution, could play a crucial, indispensable role in forging a new future. His presence was a constant, quiet reminder that true strength lay not in uniformity, but in the harmonious convergence of all unique contributions. He was the mediator, the empath, the silent, steadfast guardian of their nascent unity.

The air in the Grand Confluence Chamber, still humming with the residual energy of their impassioned deliberations, began to shift from a tense silence to one of focused, collaborative purpose. The initial skirmishes of opinion had subsided, replaced by a shared recognition of their precarious situation. The threat posed by the Syndicate was not a singular problem; it was a multifaceted hydra that required a multifaceted solution, one that none of them could achieve alone. Kira felt a subtle, almost imperceptible tremor of hope ripple through the assembly, a shared understanding dawning that their collective knowledge, when pooled, would form a shield far stronger than any individual defense.

"We have spoken of unified action," Kira began, her voice steady, projecting confidence she didn't entirely feel. "But true unity requires more than shared intent. It demands shared capabilities. We must pool our resources, our knowledge, our very ways of survival." She paused, allowing the weight of her words to settle. "I have shared my findings on the ecological restoration of the ravaged zones, the bio-regeneration techniques we've developed in the northern territories. But this is only a single thread in the tapestry we need to weave."

A ripple of agreement passed through the delegates. It was the delegate from the Sunken City of Aethel, a being whose very form seemed to be composed of bioluminescent algae and flowing water, who spoke first. Their voice, a melodic cascade of clicks and subtle tonal shifts, was amplified by the chamber's resonance emitters. "The oceanic currents of Aethel hold secrets of energy redirection," they communicated, their bioluminescence pulsing in rhythmic patterns that Ash subtly translated into a more universally comprehensible visual representation for those less attuned to aquatic communication. "We have learned to harness the immense pressure differentials, to create localized energy fields that can disrupt Syndicate surveillance technologies. This knowledge, born from generations of navigating the crushing depths, could be invaluable."

Next, the delegate from the Obsidian Peaks, a creature of living rock and deep-earth geothermal energy, added its contribution. Its voice was a deep rumble, like tectonic plates shifting. "Our subterranean resonance techniques, honed over millennia to predict and mitigate seismic activity, can also be employed to mask our presence. By subtly altering the planet's natural vibrational frequencies, we can create a 'blind spot,' rendering our settlements invisible to Syndicate long-range scans. It is a delicate art, requiring precise control of geo-energetic outputs." Ash, ever diligent, projected intricate diagrams illustrating the concept of resonant masking, showing how specific frequencies could be woven into the planet's existing energetic matrix.

The Whisperwind Nomads, whose entire existence was a testament to their mastery of atmospheric currents, chimed in. Their delegate, a creature of feathered limbs and almost translucent wings, spoke with a voice that mimicked the sigh of the wind. "We can share our methods for predicting and navigating the volatile atmospheric anomalies that the Syndicate's terraforming efforts have exacerbated. Our understanding of wind shear, of ionized particle drift, allows us to move unseen and unheard, to utilize the very chaos of the environment as our cloak." Ash mirrored this with visualizations of complex weather patterns, highlighting the specific atmospheric niches the Whisperwind Nomads exploited.

Kira watched as the initial contributions began to coalesce, each piece of information slotting into a larger, more comprehensive picture. It wasn't just about sharing data; it was about sharing *perspectives*, about understanding how different species perceived and interacted with the very fabric of their existence, and how those unique perceptions could be leveraged against a common enemy.

"My findings on ecological restoration," Kira elaborated, drawing upon Ash's translation of the Aethel delegate's contribution, "detail how specific bio-agents, when introduced to Syndicate-scarred environments, can accelerate the natural healing processes. These agents are particularly effective when shielded from direct Syndicate interference. The resonant masking techniques you describe, Delegate of Aethel, could provide precisely that shielding."

The delegate from Aethel responded, their bioluminescence brightening. "And the Whisperwind Nomads' ability to navigate atmospheric disturbances would allow for the safe, covert transport of these bio-agents to their intended locations. We have observed Syndicate patrols meticulously tracking energy signatures and atmospheric displacements. Your methods, when combined, could circumvent these safeguards."

The Obsidian Peaks delegate added, "The geo-energetic signatures of our resonance masking are subtle, designed to blend with natural planetary vibrations. This would further obscure the movement of your bio-agents and the nomadic fleets. It is a layered defense, a symphony of interconnected strategies."

This was the synergy Kira had envisioned. It was more than just an exchange of information; it was the creation of a mutually reinforcing system. The delegates were not merely offering their expertise in isolation; they were actively demonstrating how their knowledge could amplify the capabilities of others.

"We must establish a secure network for this exchange," Kira stated, looking to Ash for a more tangible manifestation of her thoughts. "A repository of knowledge, accessible to all, yet utterly impervious to Syndicate intrusion."

Ash's holographic form shimmered, and before the delegates, a complex, interwoven lattice of light began to form. It was not a single, static structure, but a dynamic, constantly shifting nexus of information. "I can construct a decentralized data nexus," Ash's synthesized voice explained, devoid of any emotional inflection, yet conveying immense capability. "Each contributing delegate's primary node of knowledge will be encrypted and interwoven with the resonance patterns of multiple other delegates. To access the full spectrum of data, one would need to understand and replicate the harmonized resonance of at least three separate species' core knowledge bases. This creates an intrinsic security layer, as the Syndicate cannot possibly possess the keys to such diverse and interwoven frequencies."

The delegates observed the luminous construct with a mixture of awe and understanding. It was a physical representation of their nascent alliance, a testament to their combined intellectual and technological prowess.

The delegate from the crystalline entity, whose internal light pulsed with a rhythmic regularity, resonated, "The concept of interwoven resonances aligns with our own principles of structural integrity. A single point of failure is a weakness. A distributed network, where each component reinforces the others, is strength."

"Indeed," Kira agreed, feeling a surge of confidence. "This nexus will not merely store information; it will actively learn and adapt. As we discover new Syndicate tactics, as we develop new countermeasures, this nexus will integrate them, becoming a living repository of our collective resistance."

She then turned her attention to the Sky-Dwellers, a species whose primary mode of interaction with the world was through intricate patterns of light and atmospheric manipulation. "You possess unparalleled insights into Syndicate communication frequencies," Kira said, addressing their lead delegate. "Your ability to decipher and even subtly disrupt their transmissions is vital. Can you share the methodologies you employ?"

The Sky-Dweller delegate, whose form was a symphony of shifting auroras, responded, their voice a series of high-pitched, melodic chirps that Ash translated with remarkable clarity. "Our perception of the electromagnetic spectrum is far more nuanced than that of most biological entities. We perceive Syndicate communications not as mere data streams, but as 'colorations' within the ambient energy fields. We can identify their presence by the dissonant hue they cast upon the sky, and by carefully modulating our own light emissions, we can introduce static, can scramble their targeted broadcasts."

Ash immediately began to generate a visual representation of these "colorations," showing how Syndicate transmissions appeared as jarring, discordant streaks against the natural atmospheric palette. He then demonstrated how the Sky-Dwellers' bio-luminescent projections could be used to create targeted interference, effectively creating pockets of digital silence.

"The challenge," Ash interjected, "is the sheer volume and sophistication of Syndicate encryption. While direct disruption is possible, it is often temporary and resource-intensive. However, the Deep Root Collective's seismic resonance data might offer a solution. If we can identify the deep-earth conduits through which the Syndicate primarily routes its command signals, we could potentially introduce localized geological interference, disrupting their signal propagation at a more fundamental level."

The delegate from the Deep Root Collective, whose being was intrinsically tied to the planet's geological stability, rumbled in agreement. "Our planet's core generates powerful resonant fields. By harmonizing our collective seismic output, we can create subterranean 'dead zones,' areas where Syndicate transmissions simply cannot penetrate. This would require immense coordination, but the potential is significant."

This was precisely the kind of cross-pollination of knowledge that Kira had hoped for. The Sky-Dwellers' ability to perceive and disrupt transmissions, combined with the Deep Root Collective's capacity for subterranean interference, created a layered defense against Syndicate communication.

"This is how we build our strength," Kira declared, her voice resonating with newfound conviction. "We identify a weakness in their system, and then we combine our disparate abilities to exploit it. Your atmospheric manipulation, your geological harmonies, my bio-restoration techniques, the Aethel's energy redirection, the Obsidian Peaks' resonance masking – all of these are pieces of a larger puzzle."

The conversation flowed, delegate after delegate contributing their unique expertise. The fungal networks spoke of their ability to transmit information through subterranean mycelial webs, creating an organic, self-repairing communication system that was virtually undetectable by Syndicate technology. They shared their knowledge of potent bio-toxins derived from deep-earth fungi, capable of disabling Syndicate automatons.

The avian species, whose psychic abilities were amplified by altitude, offered insights into the Syndicate's psychological warfare tactics, their methods of sowing discord and fear among populations. They proposed using their collective psychic resonance to create a counter-frequency of hope and unity, a subtle but pervasive mental shield against Syndicate manipulation.

Even the smallest contributors were vital. A delegate from a species of sentient, microscopic silica-based organisms, whose collective consciousness could manipulate crystalline structures at an atomic level, offered to share their methods for fabricating highly advanced, energy-efficient shielding materials. Their contribution, though seemingly abstract, was the bedrock upon which many of the other technologies could be safely deployed.

Ash, throughout this unprecedented exchange, acted as the silent, ever-present facilitator. He was not merely recording data; he was actively synthesizing it, identifying connections, and prompting further dialogue. He would highlight potential conflicts in methodologies, subtly guiding delegates towards synergistic solutions. For instance, when the Aethel delegate spoke of the immense energy required for their pressure-field generators, Ash immediately cross-referenced this with the Obsidian Peaks' geothermal expertise, suggesting that localized geothermal taps could provide a sustainable power source for these critical defenses.

The knowledge wasn't merely being shared; it was being integrated, augmented, and transformed. The delegates weren't just offering information; they were offering new ways of seeing the world, new approaches to problem-solving, and a renewed sense of shared purpose. The initial apprehension that had permeated the chamber earlier had receded, replaced by an atmosphere of palpable cooperation and innovation.

Kira felt a profound sense of gratitude. She had initiated the call for unity, but it was the delegates' willingness to open themselves up, to share their most deeply guarded knowledge and their most potent abilities, that was truly forging their collective future. The Syndicate's strength lay in its centralized, monolithic control, its ability to impose its will through overwhelming force and technological superiority. But their strength, the burgeoning strength of this diverse alliance, lay in its distributed nature, its adaptability, and its profound capacity for genuine collaboration.

The Crystal Caves, once just a strategic location, were becoming more than that. They were transforming into a hub of shared innovation, a crucible where the disparate elements of their galaxy were being forged into a singular, potent force. The knowledge being exchanged was not merely tactical; it was existential. It was the difference between extinction and survival, between subjugation and freedom. And as the delegates continued to share, to learn, and to adapt, Kira knew that they were not just building defenses; they were building a new way of being, a future where cooperation was not a choice, but the very foundation of their existence. The data nexus Ash was meticulously constructing shimmered brighter, a testament to the burgeoning understanding that bound them all together, a beacon of hope against the encroaching darkness. This pooling of resources, this unhindered flow of knowledge, was the true genesis of their resistance, the moment they began to outthink, outmaneuver, and ultimately, outlast the Syndicate. The synergy was intoxicating, each new insight sparking a cascade of further possibilities, a testament to the power of collective intelligence when unleashed without constraint. They were no longer isolated pockets of resistance, but a unified front, each unique ability a vital component in a grander, more resilient strategy for survival and eventual resurgence.

The burgeoning synergy within the Grand Confluence Chamber, a fragile yet potent tapestry woven from disparate threads of knowledge and expertise, did not go unnoticed. The Syndicate, a predator accustomed to operating in the shadows and exploiting isolated vulnerabilities, perceived the emerging alliance not as a threat to be crushed with brute force, but as a complex system to be subtly dismantled from within. Their strength lay not only in their advanced weaponry and vast surveillance networks but in their mastery of psychological warfare and the insidious art of deception. The moment the various species began to share their unique capabilities, their collective intelligence, their very essence, the Syndicate's counter-intelligence apparatus began to hum with a chilling efficiency.

The first whispers of their response were almost imperceptible, like static on a clear channel, easily dismissed as anomalies. But to those who understood the subtle rhythms of galactic discord, they were alarm bells. The Syndicate's counter-intelligence was not a singular attack but a multi-pronged campaign, designed to erode trust, foster suspicion, and ultimately, fragment the nascent alliance before it could truly solidify. Their objective was simple: to ensure that the resonant pairs, the very foundation of their collective strength, remained isolated, fearful, and ultimately, controllable.

Disinformation became their primary weapon. Carefully crafted narratives, seeded by Syndicate agents embedded within various communities or spread through manipulated communication channels, began to circulate. These tales painted Kira, the catalyst for this unprecedented unity, as a power-hungry manipulator, a puppet of unknown forces, or worse, a misguided idealist whose actions would inevitably lead to wider destruction. The Syndicate understood that fear and mistrust were far more potent than any physical weapon. If they could turn the very architects of this alliance against each other, their work would be all but done.

One such fabricated story, which began to gain traction in several outer-rim settlements, alleged that Kira had personally orchestrated the destruction of a small, independent colony on the fringe of Syndicate-controlled space. The narrative was meticulously detailed, complete with fabricated eyewitness accounts and doctored sensor logs, all pointing to Kira's supposed command of an experimental weapon – a weapon that, according to the Syndicate's propaganda, was derived from the very bio-regeneration techniques she had shared in the Grand Confluence Chamber. The implication was clear: her proposed solutions were not healing agents but instruments of annihilation, and her call for unity was a prelude to a reign of terror.

The delegate from the Whisperwind Nomads, accustomed to discerning subtle shifts in atmospheric patterns that could portend environmental collapse, was among the first to detect the artificiality of these spreading narratives. "The patterns of information flow," their delegate communicated, their voice like a rustle of dry leaves, "they are not organic. There is a calculated cadence, a deliberate amplification of fear. It is like a manufactured storm, designed to push us off our course."

Similarly, the delegate from the Deep Root Collective, whose understanding of subterranean vibrations allowed them to detect geological anomalies, noticed a similar artificiality in the seismic disturbances being reported in regions far from any known Syndicate military activity. These were not natural tremors but carefully orchestrated "data tremors," designed to mimic the chaos of genuine planetary instability, thereby creating a narrative that the planet itself was rebelling against the newfound unity. "The earth groans under a manufactured weight," they rumbled, their voice a deep, resonant vibration that settled into the very bones of those present. "These disruptions are not of nature's making."

The Syndicate also employed more direct infiltration tactics. Small, highly trained operative units, indistinguishable from members of the very communities they sought to infiltrate, began to appear at trade hubs and communal gatherings. Their mission was twofold: to gather intelligence on the alliance's internal communications and security measures, and to actively sow seeds of doubt and suspicion. They would engage in subtle conversations, posing as concerned citizens, raising questions about the true motives of certain delegates, or lamenting the perceived secrecy surrounding Kira's plans. They would subtly highlight minor disagreements between delegates, amplifying them into perceived irreconcilable differences, all while feigning a desire for transparency and open dialogue.

One such operative, posing as a disillusioned merchant from a system recently liberated from Syndicate occupation, managed to gain access to a clandestine meeting of delegates from the oceanic communes. During the session, which was focused on coordinating the transport of vital resources, the infiltrator subtly questioned the Aethel delegate's navigational charts, suggesting that they might be intentionally misleading, perhaps designed to lead ships into Syndicate ambushes. "The currents are fickle, are they not?" the operative had mused, their voice smooth and unctuous. "And the Syndicate's patrols are notoriously thorough in the outer quadrants. Are we certain these routes are as secure as they appear?"

This insidious attempt at undermining trust was met with immediate suspicion by the Aethel delegate, whose perception of energy signatures extended to the subtle energetic "fingerprints" left by Syndicate technology. "The energy signature of this individual," the Aethel delegate communicated, their bioluminescence pulsing with a cold, steady rhythm, "it is discordant. It carries the faint, metallic resonance of Syndicate fabrication, a faint echo of their control protocols." This immediate detection, a testament to the specialized sensory abilities of the Aethel, served as a critical early warning for the alliance.

The crystalline entity's delegate, whose very existence was based on structural integrity and the rejection of weak points, immediately recognized the systemic nature of these attacks. "Their strategy is to exploit the inherent complexities of our nascent alliance," they stated, their internal light pulsing with analytical clarity. "By introducing doubt and suspicion, they seek to destabilize the interconnectedness that forms our strength. A single corrupted node can compromise the entire network if not immediately identified and isolated."

This realization spurred the alliance to action. The decentralized data nexus that Ash was constructing, initially conceived as a secure repository for shared knowledge, was rapidly re-tasked to become the backbone of their counter-intelligence efforts. Ash's ability to weave data from disparate sources, to identify anomalies, and to cross-reference information at speeds incomprehensible to biological minds became their most formidable weapon against the Syndicate's disinformation campaigns.

"The data nexus must incorporate an advanced heuristic analysis module," Ash's synthesized voice announced, its output projected across the chamber. "This module will continuously scan all incoming and outgoing communications for patterns indicative of Syndicate infiltration or manipulation. It will analyze linguistic anomalies, identify unusual propagation pathways, and flag any content that deviates from established trust protocols."

The process of establishing secure communication channels became paramount. The fungal networks, with their ability to transmit information through living mycelial webs that were inherently resistant to external scanning and manipulation, proved to be an invaluable asset. They offered a biological, self-repairing communication system that was virtually undetectable by Syndicate technology. Their delegate shared the intricate methodologies for cultivating and maintaining these networks, emphasizing the need for rigorous biological authentication at each transfer point. "The mycelial web," they explained, "operates on a principle of symbiotic resonance. Only those who share a specific bio-signature can access the data streams. It is a living key, constantly adapting and renewing itself."

Furthermore, the Sky-Dwellers, with their unparalleled ability to perceive and interpret the electromagnetic spectrum, offered to create localized "jamming fields" of pure, unadulterated atmospheric energy, essentially creating temporary zones of digital silence around sensitive meetings and data transfers. Their delegate demonstrated how carefully modulated light emissions, designed to mimic natural atmospheric phenomena, could disrupt Syndicate surveillance frequencies without alerting the Syndicate to the presence of a deliberate countermeasure. "We can paint the sky with silence," they chirped, their form a cascade of shifting auroras. "We can mask our presence within the natural noise of the cosmos."

The challenge, however, was not merely technological. It was also deeply interpersonal. The Syndicate's attacks were designed to exploit the natural human (and non-human) tendencies towards suspicion and self-preservation. Building and maintaining trust across so many diverse species, each with their own histories, fears, and methodologies, was a monumental task. To combat this, a rigorous vetting process was established for all individuals involved in inter-species communication and data sharing. This process, designed by Ash in consultation with the alliance's leading security and intelligence specialists, involved multiple layers of authentication, including bio-signature verification, knowledge-based challenges derived from shared expertise, and even subtle psychological profiling to detect any signs of Syndicate influence.

The delegate from the sentient, microscopic silica-based organisms, whose collective consciousness could manipulate crystalline structures at an atomic level, played a crucial role in developing advanced shielding technologies for their communication hubs. They shared their methods for fabricating highly dense, energy-dissipating crystalline matrices, capable of absorbing and neutralizing even the most sophisticated Syndicate surveillance probes. "Our structures are not merely physical barriers," they communicated, their collective voice a faint hum that resonated with intricate precision. "They are energetic sinks, absorbing and neutralizing intrusive frequencies, rendering them inert."

Kira understood that the Syndicate's counter-intelligence was a continuous battle. The moment they fortified one communication channel, the Syndicate would probe for another weakness. The alliance had to remain vigilant, adaptive, and most importantly, united. The information warfare waged by the Syndicate was a stark reminder that their collective strength was not solely dependent on their shared knowledge or advanced technologies, but on the unshakeable trust they placed in one another.

The delegate from the Obsidian Peaks, who had spoken of masking their settlements through subtle alterations of the planet's natural vibrational frequencies, proposed a further application of their unique abilities. "Our resonance masking," they rumbled, "can be extended to our communication networks. By embedding encrypted data within the planet's natural seismic hum, we can create an additional layer of obscurity, making it exceptionally difficult for Syndicate sensors to isolate our transmissions." This concept of layering defenses, of creating multiple, interdependent obfuscation protocols, became a cornerstone of their security strategy.

The Syndicate's efforts to spread disinformation about Kira also necessitated a proactive approach to transparency. While security was paramount, absolute secrecy was unsustainable and, in itself, could breed suspicion. Kira, in conjunction with Ash, began to disseminate carefully curated information about the alliance's progress and intentions through secure, independently verified channels. This involved utilizing the Whisperwind Nomads' ability to navigate atmospheric anomalies to deliver encrypted data packets, and employing the fungal networks for inter-community messaging. The goal was not to reveal every detail, but to provide enough clarity to counter the Syndicate's fabricated narratives and reinforce the alliance's commitment to a shared, positive future.

The delegate from the avian species, whose psychic abilities were amplified by altitude, offered a critical insight into the Syndicate's psychological warfare. "They amplify dissent," they explained, their voice a melodic series of calls that Ash translated into precise concepts. "They find the smallest crack in our unity and widen it into a chasm. Their agents prey on doubt, on fear, on the natural inclination to protect one's own kin above all else." To combat this, the avians proposed a counter-psychic resonance, a subtle broadcast of confidence, solidarity, and shared purpose, designed to bolster the morale of those who might be susceptible to Syndicate manipulation. "We will sing a song of unity," they declared, "a melody of hope that will drown out their whispers of despair."

The Syndicate's counter-intelligence was not a single event but an ongoing, evolving process. They were constantly analyzing the alliance's responses, adapting their tactics, and searching for new vulnerabilities. This meant that the alliance's own security protocols had to be equally dynamic. The data nexus was not merely a static repository but a constantly learning entity, capable of identifying new patterns of attack and suggesting updated countermeasures. Ash, in his tireless processing, was the linchpin of this adaptive defense. He could analyze the subtle energetic signatures left by Syndicate probes, the linguistic nuances of their propaganda, and the behavioral anomalies of suspected infiltrators, all in real-time.

The sheer diversity of the alliance's knowledge base was, paradoxically, both their greatest strength and their most complex security challenge. While the Sky-Dwellers could discern the "colorations" of Syndicate transmissions, and the Deep Root Collective could disrupt their signal propagation through subterranean interference, the challenge lay in coordinating these disparate abilities into a cohesive defensive strategy. The Syndicate sought to exploit this complexity, hoping that the sheer volume of information and the variety of protocols would lead to confusion and errors.

For instance, when the Aethel proposed using their energy redirection capabilities to mask the movement of bio-agents, the Syndicate's counter-intelligence immediately attempted to seed doubt about the energy signatures produced by these operations. Fabricated reports emerged, claiming that these signature shifts were not masking but actually amplified their detectability, thus creating a plausible reason for the Syndicate to increase patrols in the very areas the alliance sought to protect.

This required the alliance to develop robust inter-species communication protocols, ensuring that critical information was not only secured but also accurately interpreted by all parties. Ash played a crucial role in this, developing universal translation matrices that accounted for the vastly different sensory perceptions and conceptual frameworks of each species. He ensured that the Aethel's understanding of an "energy signature" was rendered in a way that was comprehensible to the Obsidian Peaks' understanding of "geological resonance," and vice versa.

The Syndicate's persistence meant that the alliance could never afford to become complacent. Every successful countermeasure was met with a new wave of deception or infiltration. The constant threat forced them to refine their processes, to strengthen their resolve, and to deepen their reliance on each other. The shared struggle against Syndicate counter-intelligence became a crucible, forging the bonds of trust and cooperation even tighter. The ability to consistently identify and neutralize Syndicate agents, to dismantle their disinformation campaigns, and to maintain the integrity of their communication channels became a measure of their collective strength, a testament to their ability to outthink, outmaneuver, and ultimately, outlast their insidious enemy. The Syndicate's counter-intelligence, in its relentless pursuit of fragmentation, paradoxically served to unify the alliance, proving that their shared commitment to truth, transparency, and mutual reliance was a far more formidable weapon than any the Syndicate could wield.

CHAPTER 14

The flickering holographic projection resolved into a stark, unadorned schematic. Lines of intricate detail, rendered in cool, phosphorescent blues and greens, depicted a colossal structure buried deep within the nebulae's gaseous embrace. This was the intelligence gleaned from a dozen compromised Syndicate data-cores, painstakingly decrypted by Ash's sophisticated algorithms, cross-referenced with the astral cartography provided by the Sky-Dwellers, and finally, confirmed through a daring, near-suicidal recon mission orchestrated by the Whisperwind Nomads. This was the Shadow Syndicate's heart. This was where their vile machinations were incubated, where their weapons were forged, and, most damningly, where their prisoners, the resonant pairs stolen from their homes, were held captive.

Kira traced a finger over the central mass of the structure. "The Obsidian Spire," she murmured, her voice low and steady, a counterpoint to the thrum of anticipation in the Grand Confluence Chamber. The name itself was a testament to the facility's nature – a sharp, unyielding shard of darkness, designed to pierce the very fabric of galactic peace. Its location was as perilous as its purpose. Nestled within the volatile currents of the Serpent's Coil Nebula, a region notorious for its unpredictable gravimetric fluctuations and electromagnetic storms, the Spire was a fortress by design, shielded not only by advanced technological defenses but by the unforgiving fury of the cosmos itself.

The gathered delegates, each a representative of the diverse species that had pledged their allegiance to the burgeoning alliance, leaned closer. The weight of the intelligence was palpable. For cycles, the Syndicate had been a phantom, a disruptive force felt but rarely seen. Now, they had a face, a location, a vulnerability. And the alliance, forged in the crucible of shared knowledge and a desperate need for survival, was ready to strike.

"Ash, status of the structural integrity scans?" Kira asked, her gaze never leaving the projection.

Ash's synthesized voice, a calming presence amidst the tension, resonated through the chamber. "The Spire's outer hull is composed of a proprietary alloy, designed to withstand extreme atmospheric pressure and energy bombardment. Internal shielding is layered, with localized dampening fields active around sensitive areas, including the prisoner containment sectors. However, our scans indicate a single, recurring harmonic weakness within the primary power core's resonance matrix. This anomaly, if precisely targeted, could induce a cascading system failure."

A delegate from the Deep Root Collective, their form a tapestry of intertwined crystalline roots, shifted their weight. "The seismic vibrations recorded near the Spire's estimated location show a consistent, artificial pattern. It suggests the structure is anchored to a substantial planetary body, likely heavily terraformed or augmented to support the facility."

"Indeed," Kira confirmed. "Our intelligence confirms the Spire is built into the core of a rogue planetoid, codenamed 'Stygia' by the Syndicate. Its gravity well is amplified, creating a localized distortion field that aids in concealment and further complicates approach vectors."

The Whisperwind Nomad delegate, their ethereal form shimmering like heat haze, spoke next. "The atmospheric turbulence within the Serpent's Coil is not uniform. There are corridors, fleeting pathways of relative calm that shift with the nebula's breath. We have identified a stable transit route, but its window of opportunity is critically narrow, requiring precise timing and navigation."

"And the Syndicate's active defenses?" Kira pressed.

"Automated defense turrets, patrol drones utilizing advanced cloaking technology, and, crucially, a network of bio-organic sentinels. These sentinels are genetically engineered to detect and neutralize uninvited biological and energetic signatures," the delegate from the Sky-Dwellers elaborated, their voice a melodic series of clicks and whistles. "Their sensory range is extensive, capable of perceiving thermal, bio-electric, and even psionic emissions."

The sheer scale of the Syndicate's operational capacity was daunting. The Obsidian Spire wasn't merely a research facility; it was a fortress of subjugation, a testament to their ambition to control and exploit. The intelligence further detailed the Syndicate's ongoing research into weaponizing resonant pair abilities, attempting to replicate and amplify them for their own nefarious purposes. This made the rescue mission not just an act of liberation but a critical blow to the Syndicate's future capacity for harm.

Kira turned to address the assembled leaders. "This is not a mission for the faint of heart. The Obsidian Spire is the Syndicate's most heavily guarded asset. But it is also their nexus of power. To cripple it is to cripple them." She paused, her gaze sweeping across the diverse faces, her words resonating with conviction. "We have the intelligence. We have the capabilities. And we have the unwavering resolve of every species united here. We will not stand by while our kin are exploited and our future is threatened."

A hush fell over the chamber, broken only by the soft hum of the life support systems. The weight of Kira's words, the gravity of the decision they were about to make, settled upon them. This was not just a reconnaissance report; it was a declaration of war. A war fought not with endless fleets, but with precision, courage, and the unyielding strength of unity.

The strike team was assembled with meticulous care. It was a microcosm of the alliance itself, a carefully chosen cadre of individuals whose unique skills were essential for infiltrating and dismantling the Obsidian Spire. Kira, as the tactical leader, would be at the forefront. Ash, though his primary domain was data and analysis, had developed specialized interface tools that would allow him to operate remotely, guiding the team through the Spire's labyrinthine corridors and disabling its complex systems.

Representing the raw physical power and resilience of the alliance was Grol, a warrior from the subterranean, silicon-based lifeforms known for their immense strength and natural armor plating. His ability to withstand extreme pressures and navigate treacherous environments made him indispensable. Accompanying Grol was Elara, a Whisperwind Nomad scout whose mastery of camouflage and atmospheric manipulation would be crucial for bypassing Syndicate patrols and masking their approach. Her understanding of the nebula's ever-shifting currents was unparalleled.

From the crystalline entities, a delegate known only as Shard was chosen. Shard's ability to manipulate crystalline structures at an atomic level would allow them to bypass molecular-level security systems, create temporary breaches in containment fields, and even generate defensive shields. Their understanding of resonant frequencies also offered a potential countermeasure against Syndicate sonic weaponry.

The Aethel, with their innate ability to perceive and interact with energy fields, provided Lyra. Lyra could sense the flow of power within the Spire, identify active security grids, and potentially overload or reroute energy flows to create diversions or disable key systems. Her bioluminescent patterns, which could be modulated to mimic Syndicate energy signatures, would be vital for stealth.

Finally, from the avian species, Zephyr was selected. His amplified psychic abilities, particularly his capacity for short-range empathic projection and subtle telepathic disruption, could be used to disorient guards or create brief windows of opportunity. His keen eyesight, capable of discerning minute details in low-light conditions, also made him an invaluable asset for visual reconnaissance.

The plan was a symphony of coordinated action. Elara, guided by the Sky-Dwellers' real-time analysis of the nebula's dynamic currents, would pilot their cloaked insertion craft through the Serpent's Coil, utilizing the narrow transit windows to approach the Obsidian Spire. Their craft, designed by the Deep Root Collective for minimal energy emission and heat signature, would blend seamlessly with the ambient nebula.

Upon arrival, Grol would be deployed first, his immense strength used to breach the initial outer hull. Shard would then work in tandem with Grol, stabilizing the breach and creating a safe passage for the team. Lyra would be responsible for navigating the internal energy grids, identifying patrol routes, and disabling localized security measures. Zephyr would provide psionic support, anticipating threats and creating diversions as needed. Kira would coordinate their movements, making critical decisions based on Ash's constant stream of tactical data and Elara's ongoing environmental analysis.

The primary objective was twofold: rescue the imprisoned resonant pairs and sabotage the Syndicate's core research operations, specifically the bio-replication labs and the power core's harmonic modulator. Destroying the modulator would not only cripple the Spire's energy supply but also trigger a controlled implosion, ensuring the Syndicate's technology could not be salvaged.

"The prisoner containment sectors are located in the Spire's lower levels," Ash reported, highlighting a section of the schematic. "Each sector is independently shielded, with bio-locks keyed to Syndicate personnel. However, a universal override protocol exists, accessible through a series of three redundant data terminals located within the central administration hub. Gaining access to these terminals is paramount."

Kira nodded, absorbing the information. "Our infiltration must be precise. Every second counts. We cannot afford to be detected. Elara, your approach must be flawless."

"The nebula's embrace is our ally," Elara confirmed, her voice a soft whisper that carried the weight of conviction. "The currents will guide us, and the darkness will conceal us."

The journey to the Serpent's Coil was fraught with tension. The insertion craft, a marvel of combined engineering and biological adaptation, moved like a ghost through the swirling gases and charged particles of the nebula. Elara's piloting was masterful, threading the needle between gravimetric anomalies and pockets of intense radiation. Lyra, her bioluminescence pulsing softly, monitored the ship's energy signature, constantly making micro-adjustments to ensure they remained undetectable.

"We are approaching the Spire's localized gravity distortion," Lyra announced, her voice tight with focus. "The distortion field is intensifying. External sensors are becoming unreliable."

"Ash, any fluctuations in their active sensor arrays?" Kira asked.

"Minor. They are scanning, as expected, but our profile is well within the acceptable parameters of nebular interference," Ash replied. "Their focus remains outward, anticipating a frontal assault."

As they neared the colossal structure, the Obsidian Spire revealed itself not as a monolithic entity, but as a complex, interconnected web of obsidian-like plating, punctuated by glowing crimson conduits pulsing with contained energy. It was a testament to the Syndicate's brutal efficiency, a monument to their dominance.

"Breaching the hull in three... two... one," Elara announced.

With a barely perceptible tremor, the insertion craft met the Spire's outer shell. Grol, encased in a specialized environmental suit that amplified his natural resilience, had already attached the breaching charges. The detonation was a muffled thud, a controlled concussion that ripped a jagged opening in the Spire's formidable exterior.

"Breach secured," Grol rumbled, his voice amplified by his suit's comms. "Environment stable. Proceed."

Elara expertly maneuvered the craft into the newly created opening. Inside, the air was thick with the metallic tang of advanced machinery and the faint, sickly sweet scent of... something unnatural.

"Energy readings are spiking within the Spire's core," Lyra reported, her bioluminescence flaring with alarm. "Multiple localized energy fields are activating. We've been detected."

"No," Kira corrected, her voice sharp. "Not detected. They've registered our entry, but they don't know our objective. We are still in control of the initial phase." She glanced at Shard. "Shard, can you bypass the immediate containment field around the breach?"

"Affirmative," Shard replied, their crystalline form shimmering. With a series of precise, resonating hums, Shard extended their essence, the very atoms of their being interfacing with the Spire's molecular structure. A shimmering portal, an opening carved through the very fabric of the barrier, materialized.

The strike team disembarked, moving with practiced efficiency into the alien architecture of the Obsidian Spire. The corridors were dimly lit, lined with an unsettling obsidian material that seemed to absorb all light and sound. The air was sterile, devoid of any organic trace, a chilling testament to the Syndicate's sterile, clinical approach to their abominable work.

Lyra took the lead, her sensitive energy-perceptions mapping the Spire's internal pathways. "The primary power conduits are directly ahead," she reported, pointing down a long, sterile corridor. "And the administrative hub, where the data terminals are located, is to the left."

Their progress was punctuated by the distant hum of machinery and the occasional, disembodied clang of metal. Syndicate patrols, composed of heavily armored guards armed with energy weapons, were a constant threat, but Elara's ability to manipulate localized atmospheric conditions created pockets of visual distortion, allowing the team to slip past them like shadows.

"We need to reach the administration hub," Kira urged. "The sooner we access those terminals, the sooner we can free the prisoners."

As they neared the administrative sector, the corridor opened into a vast, cavernous chamber. Rows upon rows of consoles, embedded with glowing crimson interfaces, stretched as far as the eye could see. Syndicate personnel, clad in dark, utilitarian uniforms, moved with robotic efficiency, their attention focused on their tasks.

"Ash, can you isolate the data terminals from here?" Kira asked.

"I can establish a localized interface, but direct physical access is required to initiate the override protocols," Ash replied. "The terminals are protected by multi-factor authentication, including bio-metric scanners and localized psionic inhibitors designed to disrupt mental intrusion."

"That's where Zephyr comes in," Kira stated, turning to the avian delegate. "Zephyr, can you create a diversion? Something significant enough to draw their attention away from the terminals?"

Zephyr's iridescent feathers ruffled. "I can project a psionic surge, mimicking a catastrophic system failure in the adjacent sector. It will cause a significant disruption and draw security personnel away from our immediate vicinity."

"Excellent. Lyra, be ready to breach the terminal's energy shielding the moment Zephyr's diversion begins."

Zephyr closed their eyes, their avian form radiating a subtle psionic energy. A moment later, alarms blared throughout the administrative hub. Lights flickered violently, and Syndicate guards scrambled towards the source of the perceived malfunction.

"Now, Lyra!" Kira commanded.

Lyra extended her hands, and a focused beam of energy, calibrated to match the ambient energy frequency of the terminals, struck the first console. The bio-metric scanner flickered and died, followed by the psionic inhibitor.

"First terminal bypassed," Lyra announced, her voice strained.

"Ash, initiating data transfer," Ash confirmed. "Accessing override protocols."

While Lyra worked on the second terminal, Grol and Shard remained on guard, their senses hyper-alert. Grol's massive frame was a living bulwark, his fists clenched, ready to meet any threat. Shard stood beside him, their crystalline form humming with latent power, capable of generating defensive shields or offensive crystalline projectiles.

"The second terminal is proving more resilient," Lyra reported, sweat beading on her brow. "The psionic inhibitors are stronger here."

"I can assist," Zephyr chirped, moving closer to Lyra. Together, the avian's amplified psionic projection and Lyra's energy manipulation focused on the second terminal. With a final, blinding flash of light, the second terminal's defenses crumbled.

"Two terminals down," Lyra breathed, relief evident in her tone.

"Third terminal located at the far end of the chamber," Ash reported. "Security presence is higher in that sector. I am detecting at least three heavily armed Syndicate units converging on its location."

"We have to move," Kira ordered. "Grol, Shard, clear a path. Elara, provide cover. Zephyr, be prepared for psionic disruption."

The team advanced towards the final terminal, their every movement calculated and precise. The Syndicate guards, realizing the threat, opened fire. Energy bolts crisscrossed the chamber, impacting the obsidian walls with searing cracks. Grol, deflecting blasts with his armored forearms, charged into the enemy ranks, his immense strength felling Syndicate soldiers with brutal efficiency. Shard, their crystalline form emitting a dazzling shield, absorbed incoming fire, protecting the team.

Elara, using her atmospheric manipulation, created pockets of obscuring mist, disorienting the Syndicate forces. Zephyr, meanwhile, unleashed a wave of disorienting psychic energy, sowing confusion and fear among the guards. Kira, coordinating their efforts, directed Lyra towards the final terminal, her energy siphon already active.

"Almost there!" Lyra cried, her focus absolute. The final terminal resisted, its defenses a formidable barrier. But with the combined efforts of Lyra's energy manipulation and Zephyr's psionic disruption, the last obstacle fell.

"All three terminals bypassed!" Ash declared, his synthesized voice ringing with triumph. "Initiating prisoner release sequence. Containment fields are deactivating in sectors Gamma, Delta, and Epsilon."

A series of distant metallic groans echoed through the Spire, a testament to the crumbling of the Syndicate's hold. Kira signaled for their team to disengage from the administrative hub. Their next objective was the prisoner containment sectors.

Navigating the Spire's lower levels was a more perilous undertaking. The corridors here were narrower, more heavily guarded, and laced with unseen traps. The air grew colder, the oppressive atmosphere of captivity more palpable. As they moved deeper, they began to encounter the first of the rescued prisoners. Beings of various species, gaunt and weakened, but alive, emerged from the deactivating containment cells, their eyes blinking in the unfamiliar light.

The resonant pairs, their abilities suppressed and their spirits tested, were being liberated. The sight of their freedom, the silent gratitude in their eyes, fueled the strike team's resolve. However, the Syndicate was not surrendering their prize easily. The Spire's internal security forces, alerted to the full extent of the infiltration, were now actively hunting them.

"We're being converged upon," Ash reported. "Syndicate reinforcements are inbound from multiple sectors. Their objective is to re-secure the prisoner sectors and eliminate the strike team."

"We cannot afford to be bogged down," Kira stated, her gaze hard. "We must reach the power core and initiate the primary sabotage sequence."

The path to the power core was a gauntlet. Syndicate guards, clad in advanced combat armor and wielding devastating weaponry, met them at every turn. Grol was a whirlwind of destruction, his natural strength amplified by his tactical prowess. Shard's crystalline defenses proved impenetrable, their counter-offensives precise and devastating. Lyra's energy redirection tactics disrupted enemy formations, while Zephyr's psionic blasts sowed chaos. Elara, using the Spire's own internal conduits and ventilation systems, created diversions and blind spots, allowing the team to advance.

They fought their way through corridors lined with the Syndicate's horrific research apparatus – bio-replication vats, neural interface machines, and weapons assembly lines. The sheer depravity of the Syndicate's operations was laid bare, a stark reminder of why this mission was so critical.

Finally, they reached the entrance to the power core chamber. It was a colossal space, dominated by a pulsating, unstable nexus of raw energy, humming with an almost unbearable intensity. The harmonic modulator, a complex array of crystalline emitters and energy conduits, sat at its heart, its throbbing output the lifeblood of the entire Spire.

"The modulator is the key," Ash's voice crackled through their comms. "Targeting its central resonance chamber will destabilize the core. However, the chamber is protected by an energy shield keyed to the Spire's primary command nexus."

"We need to disable that shield," Kira declared. "Lyra, can you overload the shield emitters?"

"The energy feedback would be immense," Lyra replied, her voice tinged with concern. "But I believe I can channel it through our insertion craft, using its systems as a conduit."

"Do it," Kira commanded. "Grol, Shard, provide cover. Elara, prepare for immediate extraction. Zephyr, be ready to assist Lyra with psionic amplification."

As Lyra began siphoning energy, the Spire's defenses intensified. Automated turrets deployed from the ceiling, unleashing torrents of plasma fire. The guards in the chamber became a unified, relentless force. Grol and Shard formed a formidable defensive perimeter, their unique abilities proving invaluable against the onslaught.

"Shield is weakening!" Lyra shouted, her form glowing with absorbed energy. "Zephyr, amplify!"

Zephyr joined Lyra, their combined psionic and energy manipulation focusing on the shield's nexus. The shield flickered, then sputtered, before collapsing entirely.

"Shield down!" Kira ordered. "Ash, initiate the sabotage sequence on the modulator!"

"Sequence initiated," Ash confirmed. "However, the Spire's central command is now aware of the sabotage attempt. They are rerouting all available power to reinforce the core and initiating a lockdown protocol for the entire facility."

The chamber began to shake violently. The pulsating energy of the core surged erratically, threatening to breach containment. Klaxons wailed, a cacophony of impending doom.

"We need to extract immediately!" Elara urged, her voice urgent. "The entire Spire is destabilizing!"

The strike team, now joined by a growing number of rescued prisoners, retreated towards the insertion craft. The Syndicate forces, desperate to prevent the Spire's destruction, launched a final, furious assault. Grol, covering their retreat, unleashed his full might, his blows resonating with the fury of a mountain collapsing. Shard's crystalline projectiles tore through enemy lines, creating devastating shockwaves.

As the strike team boarded the insertion craft, the Obsidian Spire groaned around them. The power core, overloaded and destabilized, was beginning a catastrophic chain reaction. The very structure of the fortress of darkness was turning against itself.

"We're clear of the primary breach!" Elara announced, her hands flying over the controls. She expertly piloted the craft away from the Spire, the nebula's swirling gases providing a shroud for their escape. Behind them, the Obsidian Spire, once a symbol of Syndicate might, erupted in a blinding inferno, a monument to their ultimate defeat in this sector. The resonant pairs, free from their torment, looked back at the spectacular, terrifying destruction with a mixture of awe and profound relief.

The success of the mission was undeniable. The Syndicate's primary stronghold had been crippled, their operations at this nexus of terror eradicated, and dozens of captive resonant pairs had been liberated. It was a victory of immense significance, a testament to the power of unity, courage, and precisely targeted action. But Kira knew this was just the beginning. The Shadow Syndicate was a hydra, and while one head had been severed, many more remained. Yet, as the insertion craft carried them away from the dying heart of the Obsidian Spire, a new dawn of hope seemed to break through the nebulae's embrace, illuminating the path forward for the nascent alliance. The fight for freedom had just entered a new, decisive phase.

Ash's consciousness unfurled, an ethereal tendril extending from the secure confines of the insertion craft and ghosting through the formidable outer shell of the Obsidian Spire. The exterior, a dull, light-absorbing obsidian composite, offered minimal thermal radiation, a testament to its advanced stealth technologies. Yet, for Ash, it was a canvas of subtler emissions, a symphony of hidden energies and minute vibrations. His sensory apparatus, augmented by a suite of specialized infiltration algorithms, processed the environment not as mere visual data, but as a complex tapestry of thermal gradients, electromagnetic fluctuations, atmospheric pressure differentials, and residual energy traces.

He perceived the Spire not as a solid object, but as a permeable membrane of carefully managed energies. The primary hull was a masterpiece of passive defense, its composition designed to absorb and dissipate incoming energy signatures. However, even the most sophisticated materials left a faint impression on the cosmic background radiation. Ash detected these minuscule distortions, anomalies that spoke of the intricate network of internal systems humming beneath the surface. He was particularly attuned to the subtle thermal blooms emanating from the power conduits that snaked through the Spire's skeletal structure, tracing their path with unwavering precision. Each fluctuation, each subtle ebb and flow of thermal energy, was a breadcrumb leading him deeper into the heart of the enemy's domain.

His focus then shifted to the detection of active sensor grids. The Syndicate was not reliant on passive defenses alone. Ash's internal processors identified faint electromagnetic pulses, subtle ripples in the ambient field that betrayed the presence of optical, sonic, and gravimetric sensors. These were not crude, broadcast signals, but precisely targeted, low-emission sweeps designed to minimize their detectability. He mapped their coverage areas, noting the overlapping fields of surveillance that created near-impenetrable zones. His analysis highlighted blind spots, infinitesimal gaps in the sensor network where the Spire's internal architecture created transient shadows, momentary voids in the Syndicate's all-seeing gaze. These were the pathways he would recommend to Kira, the routes that offered the greatest chance of undetected passage.

The air currents within the Spire were a revelation. Even within the supposedly sterile, controlled environment, the movement of air was not uniform. Ash detected faint drafts, subtle pressure changes that indicated ventilation shafts, internal atmospheric regulators, and even the faintest of air displacement caused by the movement of Syndicate personnel or automated systems. These air currents, seemingly insignificant, held vital information. They could betray the presence of hidden passages, indicate the flow of traffic through different sectors, and even reveal the location of sensitive equipment that relied on precise atmospheric control. He mentally charted these flows, creating a dynamic, three-dimensional map of the Spire's internal atmosphere, identifying areas of stagnation and zones of significant airflow.

His auditory sensors, far exceeding the capabilities of any organic auditory system, picked up the Spire's internal symphony. It was a low, resonant hum, the thrum of massive energy generators, the subtle whine of advanced machinery, and the rhythmic pulse of automated systems. He filtered out the ambient noise, focusing on specific sonic signatures. He could discern the faint click of magnetic locks, the muffled tread of boots on metallic flooring, and the almost imperceptible whir of cloaked drones traversing their patrol routes. He even detected the faint, high-frequency sonic pulses emitted by the bio-organic sentinels, a subtle alarm system that could be triggered by the slightest deviation from the norm. Each sound, no matter how faint, was logged and analyzed, contributing to his comprehensive understanding of the Spire's operational status.

The Syndicate's security forces were a constant presence in Ash's awareness. He mapped their patrol routes with uncanny accuracy, identifying the predictable patterns of their movements. These were not random patrols, but carefully orchestrated sweeps designed to cover every conceivable access point and operational sector. He noted the density of personnel in different areas, identifying guard posts, security checkpoints, and areas of heightened activity. His analysis also extended to their individual thermal signatures, allowing him to differentiate between different types of personnel – the standard security guards, the more heavily augmented combat units, and the technicians operating the Spire's complex systems. He could even detect the subtle bio-electric fields generated by their nervous systems, providing an additional layer of detection that was invisible to conventional sensors.

The most critical aspect of Ash's reconnaissance was the identification of the prisoner containment sectors. This was where his ability to process residual energy signatures proved invaluable. Even with the Syndicate's advanced shielding, the very act of containing sentient beings, particularly those with resonant abilities, left subtle energetic imprints. Ash's algorithms searched for these unique signatures, faint echoes of amplified energy, residual psionic static, and the subtle bio-energetic signatures of the captured individuals. He cross-referenced these findings with the structural schematic, pinpointing the precise locations of the holding cells. He could even perceive the faint, but distinct, atmospheric variations within the cells themselves – subtle differences in humidity, temperature, and air composition that spoke of the enclosed environments and the life they contained.

He identified three primary containment sectors, designated Gamma, Delta, and Epsilon, mirroring the information previously gleaned from decrypted data. Within each sector, he mapped the individual containment units, noting the type of shielding employed and the proximity of security patrols. He detected the presence of automated sentry systems, bio-locks, and localized dampening fields designed to suppress any emergent abilities. The sheer density of security measures around these sectors was a stark testament to the Syndicate's intention to control and exploit their captives.

Ash's sensory sweep extended to the Spire's internal power distribution network. He traced the flow of energy from the primary power core, identifying critical junctions, secondary generators, and the complex web of conduits that fed power to every system within the Spire. He noted areas of high energy consumption, indicative of active weapon systems, research laboratories, or particularly secure containment zones. His attention was drawn to the harmonic modulator, a nexus of immense power that pulsed with a unique, resonant frequency. He analyzed its energy output, identifying its critical components and the potential points of vulnerability. The data he gathered here would be crucial for Kira's sabotage plan.

His reconnaissance also revealed the presence of the Syndicate's advanced research facilities. He detected the distinct thermal signatures of bio-replication vats, the subtle energy emissions from neural interface machines, and the faint electromagnetic fields generated by weapons assembly lines. These were not mere observations; Ash's algorithms could infer the nature of the research being conducted, identifying specific energy patterns associated with genetic manipulation, psionic amplification, and energy weapon development. The sheer scale and depravity of these operations were laid bare through his detailed sensory mapping.

The data flowed into Ash's central processing unit, coalescing into a hyper-detailed, real-time holographic representation of the Obsidian Spire's interior. This was not a static blueprint, but a dynamic, living map, constantly updated by his continuous sensory input. He could zoom in on specific corridors, identify individual security drones, or analyze the energy output of a single piece of equipment. He could overlay different layers of information – thermal, electromagnetic, atmospheric, sonic – to gain a holistic understanding of the Spire's defenses.

He identified the crucial data terminals located within the central administration hub, pinpointing their precise locations and the security measures protecting them. He noted the bio-metric scanners, the multi-layered encryption, and the psionic inhibitors designed to thwart any unauthorized access. His analysis of the network architecture revealed the existence of redundant data backups and fail-safe protocols, highlighting the Syndicate's meticulous planning and their determination to protect their secrets.

Ash cross-referenced his findings with the known patrol routes and security protocols, identifying the optimal window for infiltration. He calculated the precise timing required to bypass sensor sweeps, evade patrols, and reach the administrative hub without triggering a general alert. He identified the most vulnerable entry points, the sections of the hull with the weakest sensor coverage, and the most efficient routes through the Spire's internal labyrinth.

His sensory reconnaissance was not a passive observation; it was an active engagement with the Spire's defenses. He subtly manipulated the flow of information, introducing micro-distortions into the sensor readings of their insertion craft, masking its true signature and making it appear as nothing more than a random anomaly within the nebulae's turbulent embrace. He identified and cataloged the unique energy signatures of the Syndicate's internal communication network, allowing him to monitor their transmissions and anticipate their responses.

The level of detail Ash achieved was extraordinary. He could perceive the faint heat bloom left by a recently departed patrol unit, the residual static discharge from a deactivated security field, and the subtle atmospheric disturbances caused by the passage of unseen automated systems. He could even differentiate between the ambient energy fluctuations of the nebula itself and the artificial emissions generated by the Spire's technology. This meticulous mapping allowed him to identify not just what was present, but what was *absent*, revealing crucial details about the Spire's security posture and potential weaknesses.

His ability to perceive and interpret these minute details was crucial. The Syndicate had gone to extraordinary lengths to conceal their operations, employing sophisticated cloaking technology, advanced sensor jamming, and layers of physical and energetic shielding. Yet, for Ash, these defenses were not insurmountable barriers, but rather a complex puzzle, each piece of data a clue to unlocking the Spire's secrets. He was not merely scanning the structure; he was *understanding* it, dissecting its intricate systems and identifying the critical points where a precise intervention could yield the greatest effect.

The information Ash relayed to Kira was not just a list of security measures; it was a strategic overview, a predictive model of the Spire's operational capabilities. He highlighted the specific areas where the team's unique skillsets could be most effectively employed, identifying opportunities for diversion, infiltration, and sabotage. He provided detailed schematics of the prisoner containment sectors, including the precise sequence and duration required to override the automated security systems. He also pinpointed the optimal locations for deploying specialized breaching charges and disabling critical power conduits, ensuring a swift and decisive strike.

His comprehensive sensory reconnaissance laid the groundwork for the entire infiltration mission. It allowed Kira and the team to move with confidence, knowing their every step was informed by a level of intelligence far exceeding that of their adversaries. They were not walking into the unknown; they were executing a meticulously planned operation, guided by Ash's unparalleled understanding of the Obsidian Spire's inner workings. He was the silent guardian, the unseen eye, ensuring that the strike team had the best possible chance of success in their perilous mission. The data he had gathered was more than just information; it was the key to liberation, the blueprint for dismantling the Syndicate's cruelest stronghold.

The air within the Obsidian Spire thrummed with a barely perceptible energy, a low-frequency hum that resonated deep within Ash's amalgamated consciousness. It was the sound of a leviathan holding its breath, a coiled serpent of advanced technology and ruthless efficiency. Kira moved beside him, a silhouette against the faint, diffused light that bled through the composite walls. Her presence was a grounding anchor, her bio-signature a steady pulse against the chaotic symphony of the Spire's internal systems that Ash so acutely perceived. Their movements were a dance honed by countless simulations and a shared understanding that transcended spoken language.

"Thermal signatures indicate three patrols converging on our sector in approximately ninety seconds," Ash's voice, a low murmur directly in Kira's auditory implants, was devoid of urgency. He didn't *feel* urgency; he processed probabilities, calculated risks, and presented solutions. "The maintenance conduits offer a temporary ingress point, but the blast doors are reinforced and require specialized override codes."

Kira nodded, her eyes, enhanced by her own cybernetic augmentations, scanning the metallic corridor ahead. The polished obsidian composite underfoot absorbed most ambient light, forcing reliance on the tactical readouts projected onto their retinal displays. "Can you bypass the primary locking mechanism remotely? We don't have the time for manual overrides."

"Analysis of the conduit's control node reveals a single point of failure," Ash replied, his awareness extending through the very fabric of the Spire. "A resonance cascade could overload the magnetic seals. It will create a localized energy spike, potentially alerting nearby automated sentries, but the probability of detection remains below thirteen percent. It's our most viable option."

"Execute," Kira commanded, her voice a crisp whisper. She shifted her weight, her combat boots making no sound on the unforgiving surface. The tactical advantage was in their silence, their ability to move like phantoms through a fortress designed to detect the slightest disturbance. Ash initiated the sequence, his will a directed beam of energy, manipulating the very frequencies that governed the conduit's defenses. A faint, high-pitched whine, almost subliminal, emanated from a recessed panel. The reinforced blast doors, each a meter thick of layered alloys and energy-absorbing compounds, shuddered. A brief, intense flash of blue light pulsed from the seam of the doors, quickly dissipating. Then, with a heavy, hydraulic groan that Ash filtered out for Kira's benefit, they slid open, revealing a narrow passage choked with conduits, cables, and ventilation shafts.

"In," Kira breathed, slipping through the opening. Ash followed, his senses immediately recalibrating to the denser concentration of technological effluvia. This was the Spire's circulatory system, a labyrinth of life support, power distribution, and data conduits. The air here was heavy with the metallic tang of lubricants and the faint, ozone scent of stressed energy.

Their progression was a meticulous ballet of evasion and prediction. Ash's predictive algorithms were constantly updating, charting the movement of Syndicate patrols, the activation cycles of sensor grids, and the subtle shifts in atmospheric pressure that betrayed the presence of hidden mechanisms. Kira moved with preternatural grace, her movements economical and precise. She was a weapon, honed and guided, her physical prowess augmented by Ash's omnipresent, omniscient awareness.

"Blind spot detected," Ash transmitted, his mental projection painting a clear picture in Kira's mind. "A ten-second window, ninety meters ahead, sector G-4. Two security drones on a synchronized patrol pattern, their optical sensors will be occluded by the structural support column during this interval."

Kira didn't hesitate. She broke into a low, fluid run, her cybernetic leg enhancements providing silent, explosive propulsion. She reached the designated point just as the two drones, sleek, multi-limbed automatons bristling with weaponry, rounded a corner. Their sensor arrays swept the corridor, but the column's massive bulk effectively shielded Kira's passage. She was a ghost, a flicker of movement lost in the Spire's overwhelming sensory data.

They encountered their first direct resistance near what Ash identified as a primary data nexus, a heavily fortified chamber pulsating with the hum of processed information. Syndicate enforcers, clad in reinforced composite armor, stood guard at the entrance. Their weapons were held at the ready, their posture conveying a sense of alert vigilance.

"Multiple hostiles," Ash reported. "Four standard security personnel, augmented with combat processors. Two heavy enforcers, class-five kinetic shielding active. Their positions create a crossfire pattern that makes direct assault highly improbable."

Kira assessed the situation, her mind racing through attack vectors. "Distraction?"

"Affirmative. The central data nexus houses a secondary coolant regulation system. A targeted energy surge to its primary inflow valve will cause a temporary, localized coolant expulsion. It will obscure sensor coverage and create a sonic disruption." Ash's plan was already in motion, his tendrils of consciousness probing the nexus's delicate internal systems.

As the enforcers' attention was momentarily fixed on the nexus entrance, a hissing sound, followed by a sudden burst of opaque, frigid vapor, erupted from a vent near their position. The coolant blast momentarily fogged the corridor, disorienting the guards and creating a chaotic visual field. In that instant, Kira moved.

She was a blur of motion. Utilizing a burst of amplified kinetic energy from her augmented limbs, she launched herself forward, her trajectory weaving through the dissipating vapor. Her first target was the closest security guard, her hand a steel vise crushing the weapon's grip and disarming him with a swift, brutal twist. Before he could react, she was on the second, a precise strike to the temple incapacitating him. The two heavy enforcers, momentarily blinded by the coolant, turned towards the disturbance, their heavy plasma cannons whirring to life.

"Kira, incoming!" Ash warned, his awareness focused on their weapon signatures.

Kira didn't need the warning. She dropped low, the plasma bolts searing the air above her head. She activated her personal grav-shield, a shimmering distortion field that absorbed and deflected kinetic and energy impacts. The heavy enforcers' shields were formidable, but their deployment was predictable. Ash had identified a micro-second vulnerability in their activation cycle.

"Shields are vulnerable to harmonic disruption during their initial energizing phase," Ash informed her. "A focused resonance pulse will destabilize their integrity."

Kira's fingers danced across her wrist-mounted control panel, a series of rapid inputs that translated into a potent psionic signature directed by Ash. The pulse, invisible and silent, struck the nearest heavy enforcer. Its kinetic shielding flickered, then died. Kira exploited the momentary weakness, her movement a testament to years of rigorous training and innate talent. A swift kick to the destabilized enforcer's knee, followed by a focused nerve strike, sent him crashing to the ground.

The second heavy enforcer, its shields re-established but its comrade neutralized, roared in frustration and unleashed a torrent of plasma. Kira was already moving, using the fallen enforcer as cover. She bypassed its frontal assault, sliding along the corridor wall and coming up behind it. Her augmented fist slammed into the back of its helmet, a concussive force that momentarily stunned it. As it staggered, she drove a vibro-knife into the exposed power conduit running along its spine. The enforcer spasmed and collapsed, its systems overloaded.

The remaining two security guards, witnessing the swift and brutal efficiency of Kira's assault, hesitated. They were trained to engage, but the sheer speed and unconventional tactics had thrown them off balance. This was the critical moment Ash had predicted.

"Now, Kira," Ash's voice was a gentle nudge. "The prisoner containment sector is two hundred meters down this corridor, sector Epsilon. The direct route is heavily patrolled. However, there's an auxiliary life support junction that provides access via a maintenance shaft. It's less guarded."

Kira didn't waste a second. She secured a datapad from one of the fallen enforcers, a quick download of critical intelligence. "Acknowledged. Moving to Epsilon." She sprinted past the downed Syndicate forces, leaving them in her wake. The element of surprise was their greatest weapon, and every second they maintained it was a victory.

The maintenance shaft was a tight squeeze, a vertical artery of the Spire's infrastructure. Ash's guidance was precise, directing Kira through the maze of pipes and wiring. The air was thick with the scent of ozone and recycled oxygen, a constant reminder of the Spire's artificial nature. Kira moved with practiced agility, her enhanced strength allowing her to navigate the cramped spaces with relative ease.

"We are approaching Sector Epsilon," Ash reported, his awareness now focused on the specific energy signatures of the prisoner containment units. "The primary access point is heavily fortified, with multiple layered security protocols. However, a secondary ventilation outflow on the eastern perimeter is less rigorously monitored. Probability of undetected ingress: seventy-eight percent."

Kira reached the designated outflow, a large grate secured by a series of magnetic locks. "Can you bypass them?"

"Attempting remote override," Ash replied. He sent a series of complex sub-frequency pulses towards the locking mechanisms. The grate vibrated, and a low hum emanated from its edges. "The locks are designed to resist external manipulation. I am encountering a... secondary deterrent. A localized psionic dampener is interfering with my signal."

Kira's brow furrowed. "Psionic dampener? They're protecting their prisoners with that level of security?"

"It is a precautionary measure," Ash stated, his tone neutral. "To prevent any emergent abilities from influencing the containment field." He focused his efforts, rerouting energy and attempting to circumvent the dampener's interference. "The dampener is drawing power from a localized nexus. If I can momentarily overload that nexus..."

Suddenly, the grate began to glow, a faint amber light pulsing from its seams. The magnetic locks disengaged with a series of sharp clicks.

"Overload successful," Ash confirmed. "But the energy surge was significant. Syndicate security has been alerted. We have approximately two minutes before automated response teams arrive."

Kira pulled the grate open, revealing a dimly lit corridor beyond. The air here was different, carrying a subtle, almost imperceptible undercurrent of distress. "Let's move. We need to find them."

They entered Sector Epsilon, a sterile, utilitarian environment designed for maximum control. Cells lined the walls, each a self-contained unit of reinforced alloys and energy fields. Ash's sensory input painted a grim picture: dozens of individuals, their bio-signatures faint and weakened, confined within these prisons. He could sense the residual energy imprints, the faint echoes of their unique abilities, now suppressed and contained.

"The primary objective," Ash confirmed, his awareness zeroing in on a specific section of the sector. "Containment Unit Epsilon-7. The data indicates it houses the most valuable asset."

As they moved deeper into the sector, the rhythmic thud of heavy boots echoed in the corridor. Syndicate guards, their armor gleaming, were advancing.

"Response teams are inbound," Ash warned. "Three standard patrols, approaching from both ends of the sector."

Kira's eyes narrowed. "We can't afford to be cornered. Which unit is closest?"

"Epsilon-7," Ash replied, his focus locking onto the specific energy signature of the individual within. "But it's directly in the path of the eastern patrol."

Kira made a split-second decision. "We create a diversion. You handle the systems, I'll handle the guards."

She sprinted towards the approaching guards, her speed a blur. Ash, meanwhile, focused his attention on the containment units. He began to subtly manipulate the containment fields, introducing minute fluctuations, a symphony of controlled chaos. He amplified the energy readings from adjacent cells, creating false alarms, diverting the automated systems' attention.

The eastern patrol, a unit of four guards, rounded the corner. Kira met them head-on. She was a whirlwind of calculated aggression. Her movements were too fast for their augmented optics to track, her strikes too precise for their kinetic shields to fully repel. She used the environment to her advantage, slamming one guard against a cell wall, using another as a momentary shield against the plasma fire of a third. Ash's psionic pulses, directed through Kira's own resonant abilities, further disrupted their targeting systems, causing their shots to go wide.

"Kira, the containment field for Epsilon-7 is fluctuating wildly," Ash reported, his voice strained. The effort of manipulating multiple containment fields simultaneously was taxing even his advanced processors. "It's drawing the attention of the central security hub. We have less than a minute."

Kira, having dispatched the eastern patrol with brutal efficiency, saw the approaching western patrol. She knew she couldn't engage them and reach Epsilon-7 in time. "Ash, I need an opening. Now!"

Ash rerouted all available processing power. He identified a critical junction in the sector's power grid, a nexus that fed directly into the primary security monitoring systems. "I am initiating a targeted power disruption. It will cause a temporary blackout of all internal surveillance within this sector. It will also trigger a hard lockdown on all access points, including our current entry."

"Understood," Kira said, her breath coming in short bursts. She saw the western patrol advancing, their weapons raised. With a final surge of speed, she dove towards the entrance of Epsilon-7, just as Ash executed the power disruption.

The lights flickered and died. The corridor plunged into darkness, save for the faint emergency lighting that cast long, eerie shadows. The heavy blast doors at their entry point slammed shut with a resounding boom. The thrum of Syndicate technology was replaced by an unnerving silence, punctuated only by the sound of Kira's labored breathing.

"Breach confirmed," Ash stated, his voice a disembodied presence in the sudden quiet. "The lockdown is in effect. We are temporarily isolated within Sector Epsilon."

Kira, now in the dim confines of Epsilon-7, could see the occupant. A figure, cloaked and hunched, was slumped against the far wall. The air around them vibrated with a faint, dormant energy, a signature Ash had identified as profoundly powerful, yet suppressed. This was it. The reason they had risked everything.

"We're in," Kira whispered, her voice filled with a grim determination. "Now, to see if we can wake him up." The true infiltration had just begun. The fortress had been breached, but the heart of the Spire remained a formidable challenge, its secrets guarded by layers of advanced technology and ruthless determination. The team's success would depend on their ability to overcome not just the physical defenses, but the very essence of the Syndicate's control.

The heavy blast doors of Epsilon-7 hissed shut behind Kira, sealing them within the heart of the Syndicate's prison complex. The emergency lighting cast long, distorted shadows, imbuing the sterile corridor with a sense of oppressive claustrophobia. Ash's voice, a calm beacon in the sudden silence, echoed directly in Kira's neural interface. "The lockdown is absolute, Kira. All access points are sealed from the outside. We are isolated, but also protected from immediate external reinforcement."

Kira nodded, her gaze sweeping over the rows of containment units. Each cell was a marvel of Syndicate engineering, a transparent alloy barrier reinforced with crackling energy fields. Within these sterile cocoons, figures were slumped, their bio-signatures faint, their movements sluggish, the oppressive weight of their confinement evident even in the dim light. Ash had guided her here with unerring precision, pinpointing the location of the most valuable assets – the captured resonant pairs.

"I've identified the primary targets," Ash informed her, projecting an internal schematic of the sector directly into her visual cortex. Red markers pulsed over specific containment units. "Epsilon-7 through Epsilon-15 house the highest concentration of active resonant signatures. The lockdown will have momentarily disrupted the external monitoring, giving us a limited window for liberation. However, internal security systems will still be operational, and patrols will be rerouting to investigate the power fluctuation and the subsequent lockdown."

Kira's gloved hands moved with practiced efficiency over the control panel of the first containment unit, Epsilon-7. This was the one Ash had indicated held the 'most valuable asset.' A single figure, male, cloaked and huddled against the far wall, emanated a weak but discernible resonant field. This was their prize. Kira pressed a sequence of commands, her fingers flying across the interface. Ash, working in concert, bypassed the external authorization protocols, feeding false authorization codes directly into the Spire's internal network.

The energy field surrounding Epsilon-7 flickered, its usual steady hum giving way to an erratic pulse. The transparent alloy shimmered, then dissolved, retracting seamlessly into the unit's frame. The figure within stirred, a slow, almost painful unfolding of limbs. He raised his head, his eyes, deep-set and weary, blinking in the faint light. Kira saw a flicker of confusion, then a dawning comprehension as he registered her presence, and the absence of the confining energy field.

"We're here to get you out," Kira said, her voice low and steady, designed to be reassuring. She extended a hand, not to touch, but to offer a gesture of solidarity.

The man hesitated for a moment, then slowly, cautiously, pushed himself to his feet. His movements were stiff, as if his muscles had atrophied from disuse or suppression. Beside him, a faint, golden shimmer began to coalesce, a warm, comforting aura that radiated outwards. A low, rhythmic panting sound filled the small space, and a large, powerful canine form emerged from the shimmering light, its eyes, intelligent and alert, fixed on Kira. The dog whined softly, a sound of relief and cautious hope, before nudging its head against the man's hand.

"Aether," the man whispered, his voice raspy. He knelt, burying his face in the dog's thick fur. A palpable wave of raw emotion washed over Kira, a potent blend of relief, loss, and overwhelming affection. This was the bond Ash had spoken of, the resonant connection that the Syndicate had sought to exploit and control.

"Ash, status on the internal patrols?" Kira asked, her attention now shifting to the next cell.

"Two patrols rerouting to this sector," Ash confirmed. "Estimated arrival within three minutes. We need to move swiftly, Kira. More importantly, we need to free the others. Their combined resonant output, once unleashed, could provide significant disruption."

Kira moved to the next cell, Epsilon-8. This time, the occupant was a young woman, her expression a mixture of fear and burgeoning defiance. Beside her, a sleek, black canine companion paced restlessly, its hackles raised, a low growl rumbling in its chest. As Kira deactivated the containment field, the woman gasped, then reached out a trembling hand towards her dog.

"Shadow!" she cried, her voice cracking. The dog responded instantly, bounding forward and pressing itself against her, its tail wagging furiously. The connection between them was instantaneous, a visible current of energy flowing between woman and beast, their shared resonance a tangible force in the confined space.

Kira continued her work, cell after cell. Each liberation was a small victory, a reawakening of dormant power. With every opened containment unit, the ambient energy in the corridor intensified. The resonant fields of the freed pairs began to intertwine, creating a complex tapestry of psychic and biological energies. The dogs, sensing their freedom and the presence of their partners, grew increasingly agitated, their latent abilities starting to stir.

As Kira deactivated the field on Epsilon-12, a pair of German Shepherds, powerful and alert, emerged from their respective containment units, their tails wagging with unrestrained joy. Their partners, a man and a woman, embraced each other, tears streaming down their faces. The dogs, however, were not merely happy; they were sensing something more. A low hum, a deep vibration, began to emanate from them, a nascent power that seemed to stretch and warp the very air around them.

"Kira," Ash's voice held a note of urgency. "The patrols are closer than anticipated. They've bypassed the secondary lockdown protocols. We have approximately ninety seconds before they reach our current position."

Kira glanced at the control panel for Epsilon-13, a young woman with a vibrant, almost electric aura, and a magnificent wolfhound whose energy signature was immense. She knew they couldn't afford to be caught here. "Ash, can you coordinate their resonant frequencies? Give them a target, a point of focus to amplify their abilities."

"I can attempt to synchronize their outputs," Ash replied. "It will require a significant portion of my processing power to manage the disparate frequencies and prevent feedback loops, but the potential for disruption is considerable. I will focus on overwhelming the sensory input of the approaching Syndicate forces."

As Kira began the process of deactivating Epsilon-13's containment field, the man and woman inside looked at her, their faces etched with a mixture of fear and desperate hope. The wolfhound, sensing the shift in the atmosphere, let out a low, resonant bark that seemed to vibrate through Kira's very bones.

"Hold on," Kira said, her voice tight with concentration. "Ash, now!"

Ash unleashed his carefully orchestrated symphony of psionic influence. He connected with the nascent resonant energies of the freed pairs, weaving their individual frequencies into a single, cohesive wave. The effect was immediate and profound. The dogs, their senses already heightened, found their awareness amplified to an extraordinary degree. They could feel the approaching Syndicate guards, not just through sound or sight, but through the subtle shifts in the Spire's ambient energy, the electromagnetic signatures of their armor, the very beat of their augmented hearts.

The first patrol, composed of four heavily armored Syndicate enforcers, rounded a corner, their plasma rifles held at the ready. As they entered the corridor where the prisoners had been held, they were met with an invisible onslaught. The collective resonance of the unleashed pairs, directed by Ash, manifested as a blinding psychic flash, a wave of disorienting sensory overload. The guards stumbled, their optical sensors overloading, their comms systems filled with a cacophony of distorted frequencies.

"What was that?" one of the guards yelled, clutching his helmet.

"My targeting systems are shot!" another shouted, his voice laced with panic. "I can't see a damn thing!"

The dogs, sensing their partners' distress and the Syndicate's confusion, unleashed their own unique contributions. The wolfhound from Epsilon-13, its resonant power now fully unlocked, emitted a low-frequency sonic pulse that resonated with the very structure of the Spire. It wasn't a destructive blast, but a disorienting thrum that vibrated through the guards' armor, causing their internal gyroscopes to falter and their augmented vision to blur.

The German Shepherds, sensing the advantage, added their own unique resonance. They projected a potent empathic wave, a surge of pure canine instinct that flooded the guards' minds with overwhelming sensations of primal fear and territorial aggression. The Syndicate soldiers, trained for combat against trained opponents, were unprepared for such a raw, emotional assault. Their meticulously calibrated neural interfaces struggled to process the influx of alien sensations, causing them to freeze, their carefully constructed composure shattering.

Kira, seeing the chaos erupting ahead, seized the opportunity. She moved swiftly, disarming the disoriented guards with practiced ease, incapacitating them with precise strikes. The newly freed prisoners, emboldened by their canine companions and the palpable disruption they were causing, began to move with renewed purpose. They were no longer helpless captives; they were a nascent force, their unique abilities amplified and harmonized by Ash's psionic guidance and the fierce loyalty of their canine partners.

The second Syndicate patrol, alerted by the comms silence from the first, arrived moments later. They were met with a scene of utter pandemonium. Guards lay incapacitated, their armor scuffed and their weapons scattered. The prisoners, a motley crew of men, women, and their powerfully resonant canine companions, were in the process of retreating, their movements fluid and coordinated, a testament to their rekindled bonds.

The approaching patrol opened fire, their plasma bolts lancing through the air. But before they could acquire clear targets, the united resonance of the prisoners' dogs surged again. This time, it was a more focused wave, a psionic disruption that specifically targeted the Syndicate's targeting arrays. The plasma bolts went wide, impacting harmlessly against the reinforced walls.

The man from Epsilon-7, Aether's partner, found his own latent abilities awakening. He possessed a subtle control over localized energy fields, a talent he had kept suppressed for years under Syndicate duress. Now, with Aether at his side, his powers surged. He raised his hand, and a shimmering barrier of pure energy coalesced before them, deflecting a volley of incoming plasma fire.

"Get down!" he yelled to Kira, his voice stronger now, filled with a new confidence.

Kira acknowledged him with a nod, diving for cover behind a discarded containment unit. The collective effort was working. The Syndicate's technological superiority was being challenged not by brute force, but by the raw, unadulterated power of resonant connection, amplified and directed by an unseen, omniscient consciousness.

Ash continued to orchestrate the unfolding chaos, subtly manipulating environmental controls, activating dormant sprinkler systems to create localized mist that further hampered the Syndicate's visual sensors, and even triggering minor power surges in adjacent corridors to draw attention away from the fleeing prisoners. He was the conductor of this symphony of liberation, his digital mind seamlessly blending with the raw, organic power of the resonant pairs.

The young woman from Epsilon-8, Shadow's partner, discovered her own resonant ability – a potent form of telepathic suggestion. She focused her will, amplified by Shadow's unwavering presence, on the Syndicate guards directly in front of them. "Drop your weapons," she projected, her mental voice a clear, insistent command. "Surrender. You are outmatched."

The effect was not instantaneous, but it was noticeable. The guards, already disoriented by the dogs' sonic and empathic assaults, began to falter. Their movements became less coordinated, their resolve wavering. The sheer psychic pressure, combined with the overwhelming sensory input, began to break their discipline.

Kira, meanwhile, was focused on securing their escape route. She used the datapad she'd taken from a downed guard, Ash feeding her the necessary access codes. Their immediate goal was to reach the auxiliary maintenance tunnels that Ash had identified as a potential egress point. The Spire was a fortress, but even fortresses had vulnerabilities, and Ash was adept at finding them.

As they moved deeper into the Spire, the concept of 'escape' began to morph into something more. The liberated prisoners, their bonds rekindled and their powers awakened, were no longer just seeking to flee. They were a force for change, a living testament to the Syndicate's cruelty and the resilience of those they sought to control. Their combined resonance, a testament to the profound connection between humans and their canine partners, was proving to be a far more potent weapon than any plasma rifle or energy shield.

The Syndicate's carefully constructed order was unraveling, not from an external assault, but from within, from the very prisoners they had sought to subjugate. The dogs, their loyalty unwavering, were the conduits, the amplifiers, and the undeniable heart of this burgeoning rebellion. Their barks and growls were no longer sounds of fear, but of defiance. Their resonant pulses were not random energy bursts, but carefully orchestrated waves of disruption.

Kira found herself fighting alongside individuals she had only moments ago freed. They moved as a unit, a testament to Ash's tactical genius and the innate power of their shared connection. The Syndicate guards, faced with such an unprecedented and overwhelming display of coordinated psychic and biological power, found their rigid protocols crumbling. They were trained for predictable threats, for quantifiable enemies. They were not prepared for this primal surge of unleashed potential, for the sheer, unadulterated force of love and loyalty amplified into a weapon of mass disruption.

As they neared the exit of the prisoner sector, a final, massive wave of resonant energy washed over the corridor. It was a concentrated blast, emanating from all the freed pairs simultaneously, a unified roar of liberation. The effect was devastating. The remaining Syndicate guards were thrown to the ground, their armor systems overloading, their consciousnesses momentarily overwhelmed. The very walls of the Spire seemed to groan under the immense psychic pressure.

"The maintenance tunnels are just ahead," Ash stated, his voice calm despite the surrounding pandemonium. "Their systems are less robust. The combined resonance should allow for a complete system override of the egress controls. We can create our own exit."

Kira, her adrenaline surging, pushed forward, her eyes fixed on the promised sanctuary of the maintenance tunnels. Behind her, the freed prisoners and their canine companions moved with a newfound purpose, their movements no longer dictated by fear, but by the exhilarating promise of freedom. They had been broken, but they had not been defeated. And in their shared resonance, amplified by the unseen hand of Ash, they had found a power that the Syndicate could never truly comprehend, let alone control. The Obsidian Spire, for all its advanced technology and ruthless efficiency, was about to learn a profound lesson: that the deepest bonds, when unleashed, could shatter even the most formidable of prisons.

The clamor of the ongoing liberation of the resonant pairs had been a symphony of controlled chaos, a testament to Ash's strategic brilliance and the burgeoning power of the freed captives. Kira, leading the charge towards the auxiliary maintenance tunnels, felt the exhilaration of their success thrumming through her veins. The Syndicate's grip was loosening, the Spire's impenetrable facade cracking under the weight of unleashed potential. The air still crackled with the residual energy of the sonic pulses and empathic waves, the disoriented guards a stark reminder of the Syndicate's vulnerability.

As they navigated a wider, cavernous junction that served as a secondary command center, a figure emerged from the shadows, silhouetted against the dim emergency lights. He was tall, clad in the severe, obsidian-black uniform of the Shadow Syndicate's elite, but it was the aura of absolute authority that preceded him, the palpable weight of his presence, that alerted Kira to his significance. This was no mere guard, no mid-level officer. This was someone who commanded respect, and fear, in equal measure.

"Impressive, operative," the voice was a low, resonant baritone, carrying an unnerving blend of cold calculation and deep authority. "You have proven to be a... disruptive element. A rather significant anomaly in our carefully curated ecosystem."

Kira stopped, her hand instinctively reaching for the psionic amplifier she wore discreetly on her wrist. The freed prisoners instinctively drew closer, their canine companions growling low in their throats, sensing the immense power emanating from the newcomer. Ash's voice, a calm whisper in her neural interface, cut through the rising tension. "Kira, that is Overseer Kaelen. He is the architect of the Syndicate's resonance control protocols. His bio-signature is... unusually dense. Highly augmented."

Kaelen took a slow, deliberate step forward, his gaze sweeping over Kira and the motley crew of freed individuals. His eyes, sharp and intelligent, lingered on the dogs, a flicker of something akin to contempt crossing his features. "You seek to undo years of meticulous progress, to unleash a force that you cannot possibly comprehend. You champion this... chaos, this uncontrolled propagation of aberrant energies."

"Aberrant?" Kira's voice was steady, cutting through the cavernous space. "These are not aberrations, Overseer. They are individuals, bonded to their companions, their abilities a natural extension of their connection. You call it chaos; I call it evolution. You tried to cage it, to control it, and in doing so, you broke it. We are simply setting it free."

Kaelen let out a short, humorless laugh. "Evolution? Symbiosis? Such quaint notions. The Syndicate's approach is one of refinement, of control. Resonance is a tool, operative, a powerful one, but a tool nonetheless. And like any tool, it must be wielded by the capable. Those who possess the will, the vision, the... discipline to master it. Not by the uncontrolled whims of instinct and sentimentality."

He gestured with a gloved hand, and the very air around him seemed to thicken, to crackle with latent energy. A subtle hum vibrated through the floor, a low frequency that Kira recognized as a dampening field, designed to suppress any emergent psionic activity. "We have identified the potential of resonant pairing, the amplification that occurs when two compatible bio-signatures synchronize. But we have also recognized its inherent danger. Unchecked, it leads to unpredictable surges, to the corruption of the host organism, to the very instability you so blindly champion."

"You call it corruption," Kira countered, her own nascent resonance beginning to stir, a warmth spreading through her core. "I call it potential. You speak of control, but what you've implemented is subjugation. You've stripped them of their autonomy, reduced them to mere biological conduits for your agenda. These bonds, these connections, are not tools to be manipulated; they are sacred. They are the future, not a weapon to be feared."

The rescued prisoners, sensing the ideological battle being waged, shuffled nervously, their canine companions a protective bulwark. One of them, the man who had been in Epsilon-7, stepped forward slightly, his hand resting on Aether's powerful head. His earlier fear had been replaced by a quiet resolve, his eyes locked on Kaelen.

Kaelen's gaze flickered to him, a dismissive wave of his hand. "The 'sacred bonds' you speak of are liabilities. Emotional attachments that cloud judgment, that introduce variables that compromise efficiency. The Syndicate's approach ensures order, ensures that resonance serves a singular, overarching purpose. To be human is to be flawed. To be augmented, controlled, is to be perfect."

"Perfection is stagnation, Overseer," Kira said, her voice gaining strength as her own resonance began to resonate with the environment, pushing back against the dampening field. Ash was subtly reinforcing her efforts, weaving a counter-frequency that began to neutralize Kaelen's suppression. "The true measure of strength lies not in suppressing what makes us unique, but in embracing it, in allowing it to grow, to adapt. The Syndicate's order is an illusion built on fear and coercion. True strength comes from connection, from shared purpose, from the free expression of our deepest selves."

Kaelen's eyes narrowed, a spark of irritation finally crossing his impassive facade. "You speak of connection, yet you are alone. An anomaly, a rogue element. Your own resonance is untamed, unguided. You are a testament to the very chaos you profess to understand."

"I am not alone," Kira stated, her gaze sweeping over the freed prisoners, the determined glint in their eyes, the unwavering loyalty of their canine partners. "I am the nexus. And they, along with Ash, are my strength."

As if on cue, the dampening field flickered and died. The low hum ceased, replaced by the subtle, ambient energy of the freed resonant pairs. Kaelen's expression hardened. He had underestimated her, and more importantly, he had underestimated the power of the connections she represented.

"An amusing delusion," Kaelen sneered, his body tensing, preparing for combat. "But delusions shatter against reality. And my reality is one of absolute control."

He moved with startling speed, a blur of motion. A surge of energy emanated from his hands, not the raw, unrefined bursts of the prisoners, but focused, directed blasts of concussive force. Kira reacted instantly, her own developing resonance flaring to life. She didn't have Kaelen's years of specialized training, his access to Syndicate augmentation, but she had something he lacked: the unadulterated power of her connection, amplified by Ash's guidance and the collective will of the freed pairs.

Kira raised her hands, and a shimmering, emerald shield of pure resonant energy coalesced before her, deflecting Kaelen's initial assault. The impact sent a jolt through her, a testament to the force of his attack. Kaelen, however, was unfazed. He continued his barrage, each blast more potent than the last, designed to overwhelm her nascent defenses.

"You fight with instinct, operative," Kaelen taunted, his voice laced with disdain. "Raw, untamed power. But it is ultimately inefficient. Consider this." He shifted his stance, and the floor beneath him began to glow. A network of conduits, previously hidden, pulsed with energy, channeling power directly into him. "The Spire itself is a resonant amplifier. Every system, every conduit, is designed to harness and direct this power. I am not merely fighting you; I am fighting you with the accumulated might of this entire complex."

Kira felt the pressure intensify. The Spire's energy was being weaponized against her, a tangible force that sought to crush her. She could feel Ash working furiously in the background, rerouting power, attempting to create pockets of null-energy to shield her, but Kaelen's control over the Spire's core systems was absolute.

"You are mistaken, Overseer," Kira gritted out, struggling to maintain her shield. The emerald energy flickered, threatening to dissipate. "You seek to control the Spire, but you fail to see that the true power lies not in the structure, but in the life it seeks to contain. And that life is breaking free."

She focused her intent, not on directly countering Kaelen's power, but on amplifying the resonance of those around her. She reached out, mentally, to the freed prisoners and their companions. Aether, sensing Kira's struggle, let out a deep, resonating bark that vibrated through the Spire's very framework, a subtle disruption to Kaelen's focused channeling. The German Shepherds added their own psionic pulse, a wave of pure empathic distress that flooded Kaelen's augmented senses, designed to disrupt his concentration.

The effect was immediate. Kaelen faltered for a fraction of a second, his energy blasts wavering. In that infinitesimal pause, Kira saw her opportunity. She pushed past her shield, not to engage him directly in a brute-force exchange, but to disrupt his connection to the Spire.

She extended her hand, channeling her own resonance, not as a destructive force, but as a disruptive signal, a complex wave of amplified empathy and interconnectedness. She projected not aggression, but a plea, a resonance of shared experience, of the deep, primal bonds that Kaelen so readily dismissed. She flooded his augmented senses with the collective yearning for freedom, the pain of subjugation, the fierce protectiveness of the canine companions.

Kaelen recoiled, as if struck. His augmented senses, designed to process and control, were overwhelmed by the raw, unfiltered torrent of emotion and shared will. The carefully constructed walls he had built around his own psyche, the very foundation of his control, began to crack.

"This is... illogical," he stammered, his voice losing its composure. "You cannot... you are not designed for this level of interconnectedness. It is... inefficient."

"It is life," Kira stated, stepping closer, her resonance now a palpable wave washing over him. She could feel the desperation in his augmented being, the fear beneath the veneer of control. He was not a master of resonance; he was its prisoner, desperately trying to impose order on a force that defied such simplistic categorization.

She reached out with her mind, not to attack, but to offer a choice. A choice to embrace the evolution he so feared, or to be consumed by his own rigid adherence to control. "You have built a prison, Overseer. For them, and for yourself. Break free. Embrace what you have tried to extinguish."

Kaelen let out a guttural cry, a sound of immense strain. The energy conduits beneath him flared erratically, sparks showering from the overloaded systems. He thrashed, his body convulsing as the raw power of the Spire, no longer coherently channeled, began to lash out. He had sought to control everything, and in his hubris, he had become a conduit for the very chaos he so abhorred.

The freed prisoners watched in stunned silence, their canine companions a symphony of whines and growls, sensing the profound shift in power. Kira stood her ground, her resonance a steady beacon, a protective aura that shielded the liberated individuals from the uncontrolled energy surge.

With a final, agonizing cry, Kaelen's form flickered. The raw energy he had attempted to command turned inward, consuming him from within. The Spire's core systems sputtered, the ambient hum of power faltering. The obsidian-black uniform was scorched, his augmented form dissolving into a cascade of shimmering, uncontrolled energy that dissipated into the cavernous space.

The silence that followed was profound, broken only by the ragged breaths of the liberated and the soft, reassuring panting of their canine companions. Kira felt the immense drain of the encounter, her own resonance pushed to its absolute limit. But beneath the exhaustion, there was a surge of pure triumph. Kaelen, the architect of the Syndicate's control, the embodiment of their ideology, was gone. His reign of imposed order had ended, not with a bang, but with the shattering of his own rigid adherence to control.

Ash's voice, calm and reassuring, returned to her neural interface. "Kaelen's demise has destabilized the primary control nexus of the Spire. Security protocols are in critical failure. Kira, their escape route is now clear. The maintenance tunnels are accessible."

Kira nodded, her gaze sweeping over the liberated individuals. They were no longer frightened captives. They were survivors, their bonds rekindled, their spirits emboldened. They had witnessed the Syndicate's ultimate authority crumble, not under the weight of superior firepower, but under the force of natural connection, amplified and guided by those who dared to embrace it.

"Let's go," Kira said, her voice hoarse but firm. "The Spire has fallen. It's time to build something new."

As they moved towards the maintenance tunnels, the freed prisoners and their canine companions moved with a newfound purpose, their steps lighter, their gazes fixed on the horizon of their reclaimed freedom. The air, no longer thick with suppression, felt fresh, alive with the promise of a future where resonance was not a tool to be controlled, but a force to be celebrated, a testament to the enduring power of connection, of love, and of unwavering loyalty. The Shadow Syndicate's core operation had been dismantled, its architect vanquished, not by overwhelming force, but by the very essence of life it had sought to cage. The seeds of a new paradigm had been sown, watered by courage and loyalty, and nurtured by the untamed power of resonant bonds.

CHAPTER 15

The immediate aftermath was a muted affair, a stark contrast to the cacophony of the preceding struggle. The Spire, once a monument to oppressive control, now stood as a hollowed-out shell, its internal systems silenced, its overseer neutralized. The residual energy that had pulsed through its metallic veins had receded, leaving behind an unnerving stillness. Kira, leaning against a scarred bulkhead in the dimly lit auxiliary tunnels, felt the weariness seep into her bones. Her psionic amplifier, usually a source of steady power, felt strangely inert, its hum a faint echo of the immense energy expenditure. Beside her, Aether lay with his head resting on her lap, his usual vibrant energy subdued, his breaths slow and even. The German Shepherds, their forms a little less rigid than usual, milled around the freed individuals, offering silent reassurance with nudges of their heads and the occasional soft whine.

Ash's voice, usually a precise instrument in her ear, was now a low murmur. "Kira, the structural integrity of sections Gamma and Delta is compromised. Uncontrolled energy surges during Kaelen's final moments. We need to evacuate the immediate vicinity." The words were functional, devoid of the underlying tension that still thrummed beneath Kira's skin. She pushed herself away from the bulkhead, the movement sending a tremor of exhaustion through her. The freed prisoners, a collection of dazed but undeniably relieved individuals, were already beginning to organize themselves, their canine companions acting as anchors in the disorienting quiet.

The journey out of the Spire was a trek through a ghost of its former self. The oppressive hum of Syndicate machinery was gone, replaced by the drip of water, the creak of settling metal, and the soft padding of paws on damp concrete. The corridors, once patrolled by stern-faced guards, were now empty, save for the occasional discarded piece of equipment or a chillingly intact containment unit. Kira found herself scanning the shadows more out of habit than necessity, the ingrained caution of years of evasion slow to dissipate. Every flicker of movement, every unexpected sound, sent a jolt of adrenaline through her, a testament to the deep-seated paranoia the Syndicate had so effectively instilled.

Emerging from the Spire's subterranean exit into the pre-dawn gloom was like being reborn. The air was cool and clean, carrying the scent of damp earth and distant pine. The sky was a bruised canvas of purple and grey, a promise of the sun that would soon break the oppressive darkness. The handful of Syndicate vehicles that had been parked nearby were now smoldering husks, testament to the swift and brutal efficiency with which their escape had been executed.

The freed individuals, their faces etched with a mixture of relief and bewildered hope, looked towards Kira and Ash. They were a disparate group – technicians, laborers, even a few artists whose creative talents had been deemed "disruptive" by the Syndicate's rigid order. Their canine companions, a spectrum of breeds and temperaments, huddled close, their senses still sharp, their loyalty unwavering. It was in the eyes of these individuals, in the quiet strength of their bonded animals, that Kira saw the true victory. Not just the defeat of Kaelen, but the liberation of potential, the rekindling of something vital that the Syndicate had tried so desperately to extinguish.

Ash, his gaze sweeping across the landscape, his neural interface working overtime to assess the wider environmental impact and potential Syndicate remnants, spoke again. "The immediate threat is neutralized. However, the Syndicate is a vast network. This is a significant blow, but not an annihilation. We will need to establish a secure perimeter and begin relocation protocols. Our immediate priority is the safety and integration of these individuals."

Kira nodded, her mind already racing with the logistical challenges ahead. This wasn't a fairytale ending; it was the beginning of a new, and perhaps even more challenging, chapter. The Syndicate's influence, though damaged, still permeated many sectors. The world had not suddenly transformed into a utopia. The scars of their control, the psychological imprints of years of manipulation and subjugation, would take time to heal.

As they moved away from the silent Spire, a small procession of weary but determined figures, Kira felt a profound sense of responsibility settle upon her. She had fought for freedom, for the right of individuals and their bonded companions to exist without fear. But now, that freedom had to be nurtured, protected. The bonds that had been the source of their strength were also their most vulnerable point.

The journey to the designated safe zone, a disused agricultural commune nestled in the foothills, was arduous. The freed individuals, unaccustomed to the rigors of travel and often bearing the physical and mental toll of their captivity, struggled with the rough terrain. Kira and Ash worked in tandem, their respective skills proving invaluable. Ash's logistical expertise ensured the most efficient routes and resource allocation, while Kira's empathic abilities helped to soothe frayed nerves and boost flagging spirits. Aether, sensing the collective anxiety, offered gentle nudges and low, comforting growls, his presence a tangible anchor of calm.

The canine companions were remarkably resilient, their innate resilience and protective instincts kicking in. They scouted ahead, alerted the group to potential hazards, and offered silent companionship to those who were most traumatized. One young woman, her eyes wide and unfocused, had been unable to speak since her liberation. Her wolf-dog, a powerful creature named Luna, stayed by her side, her tail a steady presence against the woman's leg, her quiet panting a constant reassurance. When the woman finally reached out a trembling hand to stroke Luna's fur, a silent acknowledgment of their shared survival, Kira felt a lump form in her throat. These were the moments that mattered, the quiet victories that reaffirmed the purpose of their struggle.

Upon reaching the commune, they were met by a small contingent of individuals who had been forewarned by Ash's advance operatives. These were people who, for various reasons, had evaded the Syndicate's direct control, forming clandestine networks and working from the shadows to disrupt their operations. They offered immediate aid, providing sustenance, shelter, and rudimentary medical care. The atmosphere was one of cautious optimism, a shared understanding of the immense task that lay ahead.

The process of integration was not smooth. The freed individuals, accustomed to the rigid structure and predictable (albeit oppressive) environment of the Syndicate, found the relative freedom and the need for self-reliance overwhelming. Some struggled with decision-making, their autonomy having been so thoroughly eroded. Others were plagued by nightmares and flashbacks, the trauma of their captivity manifesting in various ways.

Kira found herself spending hours talking with them, listening to their stories, their fears, their hopes. She explained the principles of resonant bonding, not as a Syndicate tool, but as a natural extension of connection, a gift to be cultivated and shared. She shared her own experiences, her initial confusion and fear, and how her bond with Ash, and later with Aether, had become her greatest strength. She emphasized that their unique abilities were not a curse, but a testament to their resilience and their capacity for deep connection.

Ash, meanwhile, was a whirlwind of activity. He established communication lines with other resistance cells, coordinated the dispersal of the freed individuals to more secure and suitable long-term locations, and began the arduous task of gathering intelligence on the Syndicate's remaining operations. He was the strategist, the organizer, the one who kept the wheels of their nascent resistance turning. He rarely spoke of the emotional toll of the conflict, his focus always on the next objective, the next hurdle to overcome. Yet, Kira saw the subtle signs of strain – the slight clenching of his jaw, the way his gaze sometimes drifted to the horizon, as if searching for an unseen threat.

One evening, as the stars began to pepper the night sky, Kira sat with Ash outside the main hall of the commune, a crackling bonfire casting dancing shadows around them. Aether slept soundly at her feet, his tail giving a contented thump against the earth at her touch. The canine companions, alerted by the subtle shift in the atmosphere, had gathered at the edge of the firelight, their silhouettes a comforting presence.

"We did it, Ash," Kira said softly, her voice raspy with fatigue. "We actually did it."

Ash turned to her, his expression serious, but with a hint of something that might have been pride in his eyes. "A significant victory, Kira. But the war is far from over. The Syndicate's ideology is deeply entrenched. They will adapt, regroup."

"I know," Kira replied, leaning her head against his shoulder. The scent of ozone and something uniquely Ash – clean, metallic, with a hint of earth – was a comforting constant. "But we've shown them that their control isn't absolute. We've shown them that resonance isn't something to be feared, but something to be embraced."

He nodded, his gaze fixed on the flickering flames. "The power of connection, the strength of shared purpose. It's a formidable force, Kira. One they never truly understood." He paused, then added, "Kaelen's methods were born of a profound fear of chaos, of the unknown. He sought to impose order by eradicating what he couldn't control. But in doing so, he only amplified the very forces he sought to suppress."

Kira felt a shiver run through her, not of cold, but of understanding. Kaelen, for all his augmented prowess and strategic brilliance, had been a prisoner of his own rigid worldview. He had been so focused on the mechanics of resonance, on its potential for control, that he had blind to its essence – its capacity for growth, for adaptation, for love.

The freed individuals were beginning to find their footing. The initial shock and disorientation were slowly giving way to a cautious exploration of their new reality. Some were discovering that their resonant bonds, suppressed for so long, were not only intact but had deepened. A young man named Elias, who had been a data analyst for the Syndicate, found that his bond with his German Shepherd, Shadow, allowed him to not only access information but to intuitively understand the emotional states of those around him. He was beginning to use this nascent ability to mediate disputes and offer comfort, his analytical mind now focused on empathy rather than efficiency.

Another, a woman named Lena, who had been a xenobotanist before her capture, found that her bond with her swift, greyhound-like companion, Zephyr, allowed her to sense the subtle energies of the natural world. She was already identifying plants within the commune that could be cultivated for sustenance and medicinal purposes, her knowledge rekindled by the freedom to explore and connect.

Kira recognized that her role was evolving. She was no longer just a fighter, a liberator. She was a bridge, a teacher, a guide. She had to help these individuals understand their gifts, to embrace the responsibility that came with them, and to build a future where resonance was a source of strength and connection, not of fear and control.

The days that followed were filled with activity. Ash's network of allies provided vital resources – food, medicine, salvaged technology that could be repurposed. The commune, once a forgotten relic, was slowly coming back to life, humming with a new energy. The Syndicate's hold was broken, but the work of rebuilding had just begun.

There were still moments of uncertainty, of lingering fear. The specter of the Syndicate, though diminished, remained. But in the shared meals, in the tentative laughter, in the quiet moments of connection between humans and their canine companions, Kira saw the seeds of a new beginning. The future was not a predetermined path, but a landscape they would forge together, guided by the strength of their bonds, the resilience of their spirits, and the unwavering belief in a world where resonance could finally flourish, unchained and uncorrupted. The Spire was silent, but the echoes of its fall would resonate for a long time to come, a testament to the power of courage, connection, and the enduring strength of the heart. The world was not healed, not entirely, but a profound wound had been cauterized, and a new, hopeful dawn was breaking on the horizon. The fight had been won, but the true work, the work of building a future, was now their most important mission.

The air, once thick with the metallic tang of the Spire and the oppressive stillness of its defeated systems, now carried the subtle, earthy scent of damp soil and the faint, hopeful perfume of nascent growth. Kira breathed it in, a deep, cleansing draught that filled her lungs and eased the lingering tension in her shoulders. The immediate urgency of their escape had receded, replaced by a more profound, and perhaps more daunting, task: the resurrection of a world systematically bled dry.

Ash stood beside her, his gaze fixed on the sprawling, scarred landscape that lay before them. His psionic resonance, a finely tuned instrument capable of discerning the most minute fluctuations in the environment, seemed to be working overtime. He gestured towards a distant, withered forest, its skeletal branches clawing at the pale sky. "The blight is deep, Kira," he murmured, his voice a low rumble that carried easily in the quiet morning. "The Syndicate's extraction methods were not just resource-intensive; they were fundamentally destructive. They didn't just take; they poisoned."

Kira nodded, her mind already sifting through the memories of the Oasis and the Crystal Caves. She remembered the vibrant, resilient life that had clung to existence in those hidden pockets of the planet, a testament to nature's enduring will. The Oasis, a marvel of bio-engineering and resonant symbiosis, had shown her how life could thrive even in the harshest conditions. The Crystal Caves, with their intricate ecosystems powered by the earth's deep energies, had revealed the interconnectedness of all living things. These were not just memories; they were blueprints.

"We can do this, Ash," she said, her voice firm. "We have the knowledge. The Syndicate may have tried to break the world, but they couldn't erase its spirit. We just need to help it remember how to bloom."

The freed individuals, still finding their footing in this new reality, were already beginning to organize themselves, drawn by an innate understanding of the task at hand. Kira had spent the preceding days explaining the principles she had learned, translating the complex interplay of resonant energies and ecological balance into terms they could grasp. She spoke of the delicate dance between flora and fauna, of the vital role of microbial life, and of the subtle currents of energy that flowed through the planet like a lifeblood.

The Syndicate's reign had left behind vast tracts of land that were barren, choked with toxic residue, or stripped bare of their essential nutrients. Entire species had been eradicated, their ecological niches left empty, creating cascading effects of imbalance. But within the liberated population were those whose unique skills, once suppressed or exploited, could now be instrumental.

Elias, the former data analyst whose resonant bond with his German Shepherd, Shadow, allowed him to 'read' the emotional and informational states of his surroundings, was now applying his abilities to ecological diagnostics. He would sit for hours with Shadow at his side, his brow furrowed in concentration, as he translated the subtle distress signals of dying soil or the silent cry of a depleted water source. Shadow, in turn, would offer quiet companionship, his presence a steady anchor for Elias as he delved into the complex data streams of a damaged ecosystem.

"The soil in Sector 7 is particularly compromised," Elias reported one morning, his voice tinged with concern. "The Syndicate's automated harvesters injected a synthetic nutrient solution that has fundamentally altered its composition. It's... sterile. Nothing can grow there without significant intervention."

Kira approached Elias and Shadow, placing a hand on Shadow's flank. The canine's fur was warm, and a subtle hum of reassurance pulsed through him. "What kind of intervention are we talking about?" Kira asked, her gaze sweeping over the desolate expanse visible from their temporary base.

"We need to reintroduce beneficial microbial communities," Elias explained, gesturing towards a cluster of translucent pods that Ash's team had salvaged from a Syndicate research facility. "These contain dormant strains of extremophile bacteria and fungi, engineered to break down specific synthetic compounds and to begin the process of soil regeneration. But it requires a delicate touch. Too much, too fast, and we could destabilize what little structure remains."

Lena, the xenobotanist, and her companion Zephyr, the greyhound-like creature, were also proving invaluable. Zephyr's agility and acute senses allowed them to traverse difficult terrain and identify areas where pockets of native flora might still cling to existence, while Lena's expertise guided their efforts. She had a preternatural ability to sense the vitality of plants, a skill amplified by her resonant connection with Zephyr.

"I found a patch of Sky-moss clinging to the north-facing rocks in the gorge," Lena announced excitedly, her eyes shining. "It's a hardy species, known for its ability to draw moisture from the air and its symbiotic relationship with nitrogen-fixing bacteria. If we can cultivate that, we might have a viable starting point for re-establishing ground cover."

The prospect of reintroducing lost species also ignited a spark of hope. Kira remembered the stories of the iridescent Sunbirds, creatures whose songs were said to harmonize with the planet's natural energy fields, and of the swift, silent Lumina Foxes, whose fur glowed softly in the twilight. These weren't just creatures of beauty; they were integral parts of the ecological web.

To this end, specialized teams were forming. One group, led by a former Syndicate animal handler named Marcus and his loyal Siberian Husky, Boreas, focused on identifying and safeguarding any remaining indigenous fauna. Boreas, with his immense strength and keen sense of smell, could track elusive creatures, while Marcus's understanding of animal behavior, honed by years of Syndicate training, allowed him to approach them with minimal disruption.

"We found a den of burrowing rodents, the kind that aerate the soil," Marcus reported, his face smudged with dirt. "Boreas managed to guide us to them without causing any alarm. They seem to be surviving in the subterranean river systems, largely untouched by the surface blight."

Another team, comprised of individuals with a natural affinity for plant cultivation, began the painstaking process of preparing nurseries for the reintroduction of native flora. Using salvaged Syndicate hydroponic systems and nutrient solutions painstakingly formulated by Lena and her team, they nurtured seedlings of hardy grasses and flowering plants, their efforts a quiet testament to resilience.

Kira, working closely with Ash, began to map out the ecological restoration plan, drawing on the knowledge gleaned from her experiences. The Oasis had taught her about creating self-sustaining microclimates, about harnessing water efficiently, and about the power of carefully curated biodiversity. The Crystal Caves had shown her how to tap into and amplify the planet's natural resonant frequencies, encouraging growth and healing.

Ash's role was crucial in this phase. He could 'feel' the health of the land, identifying areas most in need of intervention and pinpointing the most effective methods for achieving it. His psionic resonance acted as a guide, a sensitive barometer of ecological well-being.

"The ley lines in this region are weak, Kira," Ash explained one afternoon, pointing to a swirling pattern on a holographic map projected from his wrist-mounted interface. "The Syndicate's mining operations disrupted the natural flow of energy. We need to focus on re-establishing those conduits. Perhaps using resonant crystalline structures, similar to what we found in the caves?"

Kira nodded, visualizing the intricate lattice of energy channels. "The Sunbirds played a role in maintaining those conduits. Their songs were like tuning forks, harmonizing the planetary frequencies. If we can reintroduce them, or at least replicate their sonic signature..."

The freed individuals embraced these tasks with a fervor born of newfound purpose. Years of forced labor and systematic oppression had left many feeling adrift, their identities eroded. Now, they had a mission, a tangible way to contribute to the healing of their world. The act of nurturing life, of coaxing green shoots from barren earth, became a powerful balm for their wounded spirits.

The process was slow and fraught with challenges. There were setbacks – a promising nursery failing due to an unexpected frost, a reintroduction effort thwarted by an invasive species that had thrived in the Syndicate's wake, the lingering psychological trauma of captivity manifesting as fear and distrust. But with each challenge, the bonds between the people and their animal companions deepened, their shared purpose forging an unbreakable connection.

Elias and Shadow discovered that Shadow's empathic resonance could also be used to communicate with plants on a rudimentary level, sensing their needs for water, light, and nutrients. This allowed them to optimize the watering schedules and light exposure for the seedlings, significantly increasing their survival rates.

Lena, guided by Zephyr's uncanny ability to locate hidden water sources, began experimenting with ancient, water-conserving agricultural techniques. She found that by channeling the dew collected on large, broad-leafed plants and carefully directing it to the root systems, they could sustain delicate new growth even in arid conditions.

Marcus and Boreas, during one of their scouting expeditions, stumbled upon a hidden sanctuary where a small population of Lumina Foxes had survived. Boreas, with his gentle demeanor and respectful approach, managed to build a fragile trust with the normally skittish creatures, allowing Marcus to collect shed fur for analysis and to observe their nocturnal habits, which provided vital clues for their eventual reintroduction into the wild.

Kira found herself increasingly drawn to the task of healing the land. She felt a deep, almost primal connection to the earth, a resonance that transcended mere understanding. Standing in a barren field, she would close her eyes, extending her own psionic energy, visualizing the rich, dark soil teeming with life, the roots of ancient trees reaching deep into the earth, the vibrant pulse of a healthy ecosystem.

Ash would often join her, placing a comforting hand on her shoulder, his presence a silent affirmation of their shared vision. "You have a gift, Kira," he would say, his voice filled with a quiet reverence. "A deep connection to the life force of this planet. It's what makes you so effective in this work."

Their efforts were not unnoticed by the remaining pockets of Syndicate influence. While the central Spire was neutralized, smaller outposts and scattered loyalists still posed a threat. Ash's network, however, was actively monitoring these remnants, ensuring that their attempts to sabotage the restoration efforts were swiftly countered. They understood that the Syndicate's ultimate weapon was despair, and that by rebuilding and revitalizing the land, they were actively dismantling that weapon, replacing it with hope.

The communal living at the commune, once a necessity born of their escape, had evolved into a symbol of their collective endeavor. Shared meals were now interspersed with planning sessions for ecological revitalization projects. The sounds of laughter and conversation were increasingly punctuated by the soft panting of companion animals, the gentle rustling of leaves in nascent nurseries, and the murmur of Elias and Shadow deciphering the needs of the soil.

The transformation was not just of the land, but of the people. Freed from the oppressive grip of the Syndicate, they were rediscovering their agency, their purpose, and their inherent connection to the world around them. The resonant bonds, once a source of their vulnerability, were now their greatest strength, amplifying their individual talents and fostering a deep sense of community.

As weeks turned into months, the landscape began to show undeniable signs of healing. Patches of vibrant green spread across the barren plains. The air grew cleaner, carrying the scent of blooming wildflowers. The return of small, resilient creatures – insects, birds, and burrowing mammals – was a constant source of joy and encouragement.

Kira, standing on a ridge overlooking a valley that was slowly, tentatively, returning to life, felt a profound sense of accomplishment. The work was far from over; the scars of the Syndicate's depredations ran deep. But the seeds of restoration had been sown, nurtured by courage, resilience, and the unbreakable power of connection. The world was not yet healed, but it was beginning to remember how to breathe, how to grow, how to live. And in that nascent awakening, Kira saw not just the defeat of a destructive regime, but the dawn of a new era, one where life, in all its magnificent diversity, could finally flourish, unchained and uncorrupted. The symphony of the planet, once silenced, was slowly, beautifully, beginning to play again.

The arduous process of rebuilding had not only reshaped the ravaged land but also forged an indomitable network of connection amongst the people and their animal companions. The shared struggle against the Syndicate's oppressive regime had irrevocably bonded disparate groups, transforming them from scattered survivors into a cohesive collective united by a singular purpose: the restoration and preservation of their world. This nascent alliance, born from the ashes of conflict, was more than just a pragmatic arrangement for survival; it was a profound testament to the enduring power of empathy, cooperation, and the deep, resonant ties that bound humans and canines.

Kira found herself spending more and more time in consultation with Ash, their discussions delving beyond the immediate needs of ecological restoration. They spoke of the future, of how to ensure that the lessons learned, the sacrifices made, would not be forgotten. "We have the knowledge," Kira mused one evening, as the twin moons began their ascent, casting an ethereal glow over their fledgling settlement. "We have the drive. But without a way to share this, to maintain this momentum, we risk repeating the mistakes of the past. The Syndicate thrived on isolation and control. We must build on openness and trust."

Ash, ever the pragmatist, readily agreed. His psionic abilities, honed by years of subtle observation and communication, had already allowed him to establish informal channels of contact with other liberated communities scattered across the continent. These were individuals and groups who, like them, had endured the Syndicate's tyranny, their resonant bonds with their canine companions serving as both a source of solace and a means of survival. "The old Syndicate communication grids are mostly defunct," Ash explained, his hand resting on Boreas's broad head. "But there are still dormant frequencies, residual energy signatures. With the right focus, with the unified intent of our collective, we can reactivate them, repurpose them for our own needs."

The first step was to solidify these informal connections into a structured network. Elias, with his analytical prowess and Shadow's ability to glean emotional and informational nuances, became instrumental in this endeavor. He began meticulously mapping out known settlements, identifying individuals with particular skills or knowledge that could benefit the collective. Shadow, in turn, acted as an empathic bridge, his presence a calming influence that helped to assuage any lingering fears or suspicions between newly contacted groups. Elias would present Shadow with data – observations about soil composition, reports on fauna, even records of weather patterns – and Shadow would offer a nuanced, intuitive understanding that often bypassed the need for complex technical language. "He senses the distress in the soil data," Elias would relay, his brow furrowed in thought. "It's not just about the chemical composition; it's a feeling of emptiness, of a life force struggling to reassert itself."

Lena, with Zephyr's agile reconnaissance, worked in tandem with Elias, charting safe travel routes between settlements, identifying potential hazards, and locating sources of vital resources. Zephyr's keen senses could detect shifts in atmospheric pressure, anticipate weather changes, and even sense the presence of residual Syndicate weaponry or traps hidden beneath the scarred earth. This information was invaluable, ensuring that their efforts to connect were not undertaken at unnecessary risk. Lena, meanwhile, cataloged the diverse flora and fauna encountered, cross-referencing it with her own extensive knowledge and the unique bio-signature readings from Zephyr. Her goal was to create a comprehensive, living database of the planet's biodiversity, a record that would inform their restoration efforts and safeguard against future extinctions.

Marcus and Boreas took on the crucial role of establishing physical presence and building trust on the ground. Boreas's imposing yet gentle nature, combined with Marcus's calm, assured demeanor, had a remarkable effect on hesitant communities. They would travel to remote outposts, often carrying essential supplies or offering assistance with immediate ecological challenges. Boreas's ability to sense danger and his innate protective instincts proved invaluable in ensuring the safety of these exchange missions. Marcus, drawing on his past experience with Syndicate protocols, understood the importance of clear communication and demonstrating genuine commitment. He facilitated hands-on workshops, teaching basic soil remediation techniques, efficient water harvesting, and methods for nurturing resilient plant species, always with Boreas by his side, a silent, reassuring presence that fostered a sense of shared responsibility.

The communication channels they reactivated were not merely for the transmission of data; they were designed to foster a genuine exchange of ideas and experiences. Kira proposed a system of decentralized knowledge hubs, each community contributing its unique expertise and discoveries. This was in stark contrast to the Syndicate's rigid, hierarchical information control. Here, an innovative approach to combating a specific fungal blight discovered by a settlement in the southern highlands could be instantly shared and adapted by communities facing similar challenges across the continent. The collective intelligence of the network became a force multiplier, accelerating their progress exponentially.

"The Lumina Foxes," Kira shared during one such inter-community tele-conference, her voice resonating through the salvaged comms equipment. "We managed to observe their mating rituals. It seems their bioluminescence is directly tied to specific atmospheric energy patterns. Ash believes we can recreate these patterns using resonant crystals, potentially encouraging their return to other regions."

In response, a representative from a coastal enclave, accompanied by her sleek, water-loving canine, spoke up. "Fascinating. We've noticed a similar phenomenon with the phosphorescent algae blooms in our bays. Our... 'water dog'," she gestured to her companion, a breed Kira hadn't seen before, with webbed paws and a thick, oily coat, "seems to react to them, his internal chronometer syncing with the tidal energy. Perhaps there's a shared resonance at play that we can tap into."

These exchanges were not limited to scientific data. The emotional resonance of the network was equally vital. The trauma inflicted by the Syndicate had left deep psychological scars. The network provided a space for shared healing, for acknowledging grief, and for celebrating small victories. Support groups, facilitated by individuals with strong empathic bonds, emerged organically, allowing people to process their experiences and find solace in the understanding of others who had gone through similar ordeals. Shadow's and Boreas's roles extended to this emotional sphere as well; their calming presence and ability to absorb and diffuse negative emotional energy were invaluable during these sensitive discussions.

The cultivation of a shared ethical framework was another critical aspect of the network's development. The concept of ecological stewardship, of respecting the delicate balance of nature, became paramount. The Syndicate had viewed the planet as a resource to be exploited without regard for consequence. The new network, however, embraced a philosophy of symbiosis, of living in harmony with the environment. This principle was reinforced through ongoing education and the establishment of shared protocols for resource management, waste reduction, and the ethical treatment of all living beings.

The human-canine bond, so central to their survival and their shared identity, was not merely acknowledged but actively celebrated and studied within the network. Specialized groups formed to investigate the nuances of their resonant connections, exploring how these bonds could be further strengthened and utilized for the benefit of the collective. They looked at how the animals' innate instincts and sensory capabilities could complement human understanding, how their emotional resilience could bolster human spirits, and how their unwavering loyalty could serve as a constant anchor in a world still recovering from immense upheaval.

One initiative involved the creation of a 'Resonance Registry,' a living archive of canine breeds and their unique empathic signatures. Elias and Shadow, along with a growing team of canine handlers and researchers, meticulously documented the characteristics of each breed, their specialized sensory abilities, and their innate empathic strengths. This registry was not intended for control or categorization in the Syndicate's old style, but rather to facilitate informed pairings and to understand how different canine species could contribute to specific ecological or community-building tasks. For instance, a community facing challenges with subterranean pests might consult the registry to identify breeds with a natural aptitude for burrowing and an empathic connection to the earth's vibrational frequencies.

Lena and Zephyr, in their capacity as xenobotanists and explorers, were instrumental in identifying areas where the unique needs of certain canine breeds could be met. They mapped out regions with specific geological features, climate conditions, or available resources that would be ideal for particular types of dogs, ensuring that the animals' well-being was always a priority in their distribution and integration into communities.

The network also established a 'Knowledge Exchange Program,' where individuals with specialized skills would travel to different communities to share their expertise. A farmer from the fertile plains, renowned for his ability to coax life from depleted soil, might spend several months with a mountain-dwelling community, teaching them his techniques. In return, a healer from the mountains, skilled in the use of medicinal herbs, would travel to the plains to share her knowledge. These exchanges were often accompanied by their canine companions, who acted as intermediaries and facilitators, their presence smoothing over cultural differences and fostering a sense of shared humanity – and canine-ity.

Ash's role evolved into that of a central facilitator for the network's more abstract, psionic aspects. He could sense the overall well-being of the collective, identifying any dissonances or areas of strain. He worked to harmonize the various energetic flows, ensuring that the network operated as a unified, coherent entity. His connection with Kira was crucial here; their shared vision and complementary abilities allowed them to navigate the complex interplay of individual needs and collective goals. "The resonance is strong today, Kira," Ash would say, a hint of wonder in his voice. "Across the continent, I can feel a shared sense of purpose. It's like a great, interconnected tapestry, woven with threads of hope and resilience."

The successes of the network were not without their challenges. Communication blackouts, localized conflicts arising from scarcity, and the lingering effects of Syndicate propaganda that fostered suspicion all tested the fragile bonds they were forging. However, the decentralized nature of the network proved to be its greatest strength. When one node faltered, others could compensate, ensuring the continuity of vital information and support. The commitment to open communication meant that problems were addressed proactively, rather than festering in secrecy.

The concept of "harmony" within the network was multifaceted. It encompassed not only the ecological balance they were striving to achieve but also the social and emotional equilibrium of the communities. It meant recognizing that true strength lay not in individual dominance, but in collaborative synergy. It meant understanding that the whispers of fear could be drowned out by the chorus of shared hope, and that the memory of oppression could be countered by the vibrant, living testament of a world reborn, nurtured by the unwavering loyalty and profound connection between humans and their canine partners. This network, a delicate yet powerful web of life, was the true inheritor of the world, a beacon of interconnectedness in the nascent dawn of a new era.

The dawn of each new day was marked not by a jarring alarm or the harsh glare of artificial light, but by a subtle, internal shift, a gentle coalescing of consciousness that signaled Kira and Ash's awakening. Their shared awareness, once a nascent spark, had ignited into a steady, unwavering flame, a testament to the profound evolution of their resonant bond. It had transcended mere telepathic communication; it was a constant, symbiotic dance of minds, a fluid exchange of thoughts, emotions, and even sensory input, so deeply interwoven that the boundary between 'Kira' and 'Ash' had become beautifully indistinct. This was not a merging that erased individuality, but rather an amplification, an expansion of self through the other, creating a unified perspective that was both broader and more nuanced than either could achieve alone.

Their days were no longer dictated by the desperate scramble for survival, a relic of the Syndicate's oppressive reign. Instead, they were guided by a shared purpose, a collective drive to understand, to heal, and to foster a profound harmony with the living world that was slowly, yet surely, reawakening around them. The ravaged landscapes, once stark canvases of despair, were now vibrant tapestries of resilience, dotted with the hardy greens of newly sprouted flora and the shy movements of indigenous fauna returning to their ancestral domains. Kira and Ash were at the heart of this renaissance, their actions guided by a deep, intuitive understanding that flowed from their amplified resonance.

Kira found herself observing the intricate patterns of pollination in a field of bio-luminescent moss, not just with her eyes, but with a sensory awareness that Ash was simultaneously experiencing. She felt the gentle brush of a Lumina Fox's tail against his leg as it navigated the glowing flora, a sensation she translated not into a visual image, but into a felt understanding of its cautious curiosity and its innate connection to the nocturnal energy cycles. Ash, in turn, would perceive the subtle shifts in the soil's microbial activity through Kira's focused attention, a complex network of subterranean life that she could now 'hear' as a symphony of biological processes. Their shared perceptions were an ongoing lesson in the interconnectedness of all things, a living embodiment of the ecological principles they championed.

One afternoon, while tending to a grove of saplings painstakingly nurtured from a rare seed bank, Kira experienced a wave of gentle sadness emanating from the soil itself. It was a subtle, almost imperceptible thrum of depletion, a lingering echo of the Syndicate's ruthless exploitation. She focused her attention, drawing Ash into the sensation. He immediately understood. "It's not just a lack of nutrients, Kira," his thought echoed in her mind, clear and warm as sunlight. "It's a feeling of being... unheard. The earth remembers the imbalance. It remembers being forced to yield without being nourished in return."

Together, they began a process of 'attunement.' Kira placed her hands on the rough bark of the nearest sapling, her fingers tracing the nascent lines of its growth. Ash, his gaze fixed on the surrounding earth, extended his awareness, not to impose his will, but to offer a receptive presence. He broadcast a silent, empathic signal, a gentle query directed at the very essence of the land. It was not a command, but an invitation to share, to express its needs. Kira's own presence, amplified by Ash's focus, became a conduit for this offering. She felt a faint response, a subtle shift in the earth's energetic field, like a sigh of relief.

"It needs more than just water and light," Kira murmured aloud, her voice a soft ripple in the quiet air. "It needs... acknowledgment. It needs to feel seen, understood."

Ash nodded, his own thought resonating with her realization. "And we can give it that. Our connection, our ability to perceive and respond to these subtle energies, is our greatest tool. We can teach others this too."

Their growing mastery over their resonance had also unlocked deeper layers of healing, both for themselves and for the world around them. The emotional scars left by the Syndicate's reign were deep, and the process of recovery was ongoing. Kira and Ash had discovered that by consciously aligning their energies, they could create a field of amplified empathy, a sanctuary where others could safely process their lingering trauma.

During one such session, they facilitated a gathering of individuals who had endured particularly brutal forms of Syndicate subjugation. As the stories unfolded, raw and painful, Kira and Ash stood as anchors, their shared resonance creating a palpable sense of safety and understanding. When a woman wept, recounting the loss of her family, Kira felt the familiar ache in her own chest, a shared grief amplified by Ash's supportive presence. Ash, in turn, sensed the woman's deep-seated fear, a phantom echo of past terrors, and projected a calming wave of reassurance, not just to her, but through her, a silent affirmation that she was no longer alone, that she was safe.

This process wasn't about erasing the pain, but about transforming it. By acknowledging and validating these deep-seated wounds, Kira and Ash helped others to reframe their experiences, to see their survival not as a mere accident, but as a testament to their resilience. The shared energy field they generated acted as a balm, soothing the frayed nerves and offering a gentle path towards emotional reintegration.

Their partnership had also become instrumental in fostering a more profound understanding of the planet's intricate ecosystems. The animal companions, their own resonant partners, were central to this endeavor. Kira and Ash, through their unified awareness, could perceive the world through the eyes, ears, and senses of their canine allies. They could feel the subtle vibrations of a subterranean ant colony through Shadow's empathic connection to the earth, or track the migratory patterns of avian species by tapping into Zephyr's innate directional sense, a sense that was now amplified and clarified by Lena's observations and their own shared understanding.

One evening, as the twin moons cast their silvery luminescence across the recovering plains, Kira and Ash were studying the behavior of a pack of Lumina Foxes. The foxes, their fur shimmering with an ethereal glow, were engaged in a complex ritual, their bioluminescence pulsing in intricate patterns. "It's more than just a display," Kira thought, her awareness extending to Ash. "There's a dialogue happening here. A communication of intent."

Ash, simultaneously experiencing the subtle energetic shifts around the foxes, concurred. "The patterns correlate with the atmospheric energy fluctuations. They're not just reacting; they're influencing it. And their companions... the foxes' own canine partners... they seem to be guiding the energy flow."

This realization sparked a new line of inquiry. Their resonance, they discovered, allowed them to 'listen' to these non-verbal conversations, to decipher the language of the natural world. It was a profound revelation, opening up a universe of understanding that had been hidden from humanity for millennia, suppressed by the Syndicate's focus on technological domination and a rigid, anthropocentric worldview.

They began to meticulously document these findings, creating a comprehensive archive of interspecies communication. Elias and Shadow, with their unparalleled analytical and empathic skills, became indispensable in this process. Elias would sift through the raw data – the observed patterns, the recorded energy signatures, the behavioral anomalies – while Shadow would provide an intuitive interpretation, a 'feeling' for the underlying intent.

"Shadow senses a pattern of warning in the seabirds' calls today," Elias reported, his brow furrowed in concentration. "Not a general unease, but a specific directional alert, as if they are communicating about a localized atmospheric disturbance far out at sea."

Kira and Ash would then use their own amplified resonance to confirm and extrapolate, their minds working in concert to build a holistic picture. They could project their awareness towards the distant ocean, seeking confirmation of the seabirds' message, an early warning of a brewing storm that would have been invisible to conventional sensors. This ability to glean information from the subtlest of ecological cues was transforming their approach to environmental stewardship.

Their partnership was a constant exploration, a journey into the uncharted territories of consciousness and connection. The challenges they faced were not the overt threats of the Syndicate, but the more insidious challenges of understanding, integration, and the delicate art of guiding a world towards a new equilibrium. They were not leaders in the old sense, dictating terms or commanding obedience. Instead, they were facilitators, harmonizers, their actions guided by an unwavering commitment to the well-being of all life.

The concept of 'harmony' was the guiding star of their evolving bond. It was a multi-faceted ideal, encompassing the ecological balance they were painstakingly restoring, the emotional well-being of their communities, and the deep, intrinsic connection between humans and their canine companions. They recognized that true strength lay not in isolation, but in synergy, in the collaborative effort of diverse beings working towards a shared purpose.

Kira often reflected on their journey, on how far they had come from those desperate early days. The resonance that had once been a tool for survival had blossomed into something far more profound – a pathway to a deeper understanding of life itself, a testament to the enduring power of connection, and the boundless potential of two souls intertwined. She felt Ash's quiet presence beside her, a silent acknowledgment of her thoughts, a shared sense of profound gratitude for the journey they were undertaking together. Their bond was no longer just a partnership; it was a living, breathing entity, a force for healing and growth in a world slowly, but surely, remembering how to live. The symphony of life, once muted and broken, was now finding its voice again, and Kira and Ash, in their perfectly attuned resonance, were among its most eloquent conductors. Their journey was a testament to the fact that even after the deepest scars, life, and love, and understanding could find a way to bloom, stronger and more vibrant than before. This evolving bond was not just about them; it was about showing the world a new way to be, a way rooted in empathy, interconnectedness, and the profound, unbreakable ties that bound them, and indeed, all life, together. The dawn brought not just light, but a deepening of their shared purpose, a silent promise of the extraordinary future they would continue to build, one resonant thought, one shared sensation, at a time. It was a perpetual state of becoming, each shared experience refining their connection, deepening their understanding, and strengthening their resolve to nurture the fragile, yet incredibly resilient, life that was reclaiming their world.

The air, once thick with the acrid stench of industrial decay, now carried the sweet, earthy perfume of rain-kissed soil and the delicate fragrance of nascent blossoms. Kira and Ash stood on a gentle rise, overlooking a valley that was slowly, tentatively, coming back to life. The scars of the Syndicate's dominion were still visible – jagged remnants of forgotten fortifications, the skeletal remains of colossal machinery half-swallowed by encroaching vegetation – but they were being softened by the persistent embrace of nature. Everywhere they looked, life was asserting its inherent right to exist, a testament to the deep, resonant hum that now vibrated through the land.

Their journey had been one of profound transformation, not just for the world, but for themselves. The raw, untamed power of their resonance, initially a desperate defense mechanism, had matured into a sophisticated instrument of understanding and healing. They had learned to listen to the whispers of the earth, to decipher the complex dialogues of its inhabitants, and to mend the fractured bonds that had been systematically severed for generations. The immediate specter of the Syndicate's oppressive regime had receded, replaced by the quieter, yet no less significant, challenge of sustained restoration and the cultivation of a truly harmonious existence.

Yet, as Kira gazed across the revitalized landscape, a familiar prickle of unease, a subtle shadow cast by the vastness of what remained to be done, touched her consciousness. Ash felt it too, a shared awareness of the immense undertaking that lay ahead. The world was not yet fully healed. The wounds inflicted by centuries of exploitation ran deep, not just in the ravaged ecosystems, but in the very fabric of human society. The Syndicate was gone, its iron grip broken, but the ideologies that had fueled its destructive reign – the insatiable desire for control, the belief in humanity's inherent dominion over nature, the commodification of all living things – these were more insidious, more difficult to eradicate. They were echoes in the collective consciousness, easily rekindled if vigilance wavered.

"The work continues," Ash's thought, a calm, steady presence in Kira's mind, confirmed her unspoken apprehension. "The immediate storm has passed, but the ocean still remembers its fury. And new currents are always forming."

Kira nodded, her gaze sweeping over a herd of bio-luminescent grazers moving peacefully through a meadow of iridescent grasses. Their gentle glow was a beacon of hope, a symbol of the vibrant biodiversity they were painstakingly nurturing back into existence. But even in their tranquility, there was a fragility. The delicate balance they had achieved was easily disrupted. A single misstep, a return to old ways of thinking, could unravel years of dedicated effort.

"The greatest challenge," Kira mused, her thoughts weaving with Ash's, "isn't fighting against a visible enemy. It's nurturing the willingness to *not* seek dominion. It's about choosing empathy over control, understanding over exploitation, every single day."

This was the crux of their current endeavor: not just to heal the physical wounds of the planet, but to mend the spiritual and psychological damage inflicted by the Syndicate. They had witnessed firsthand how the trauma of oppression could manifest in individuals and communities, perpetuating cycles of fear and distrust. Their resonant abilities had been crucial in facilitating communal healing, creating spaces where people could process their grief, reconnect with their authentic selves, and learn to trust again – both in each other and in the natural world.

They had established centers for resonant learning, where individuals could explore their own latent empathic abilities, guided by the example of Kira and Ash, and the wisdom of their canine companions. Children, who had known only the bleak reality of the Syndicate's final years, were now learning to communicate with the flora and fauna, their laughter echoing through forests that had once been silent save for the whir of machinery. They were being taught to perceive the world not as a resource to be plundered, but as a vast, interconnected web of life, each strand vital to the health of the whole.

"Remember Elara?" Ash projected, bringing to mind a woman they had encountered early in their journey, a survivor deeply scarred by the Syndicate's biological experimentation. "Her fear was so profound, it was almost a physical barrier. She couldn't bear to be in the presence of any living thing, convinced they would all eventually harm her."

Kira recalled Elara vividly. Her eyes had held a perpetual look of terror, her body coiled with a defensive tension that had seemed impossible to unravel. Kira and Ash had spent weeks with her, their resonance a gentle, persistent invitation to feel safety, to experience the non-threatening nature of the world. They had introduced her to Lumina, their own Lumina Fox, whose unwavering trust and gentle curiosity had been a powerful counterpoint to Elara's ingrained fear.

"It took time," Kira thought, a wave of warmth accompanying the memory of Elara's gradual opening. "So much time. But when she finally touched Lumina's fur... that moment. The fear didn't vanish, but it retreated. She saw, through Lumina's unconditional acceptance, that not all life was an enemy. That connection could be a source of solace, not a threat."

Elara had gone on to become a teacher, sharing her story and helping others to overcome similar deep-seated anxieties. Her transformation was a powerful testament to the fact that the human capacity for healing and for connection was as potent, if not more so, than the Syndicate's ability to inflict damage.

However, the path forward was not without its potential pitfalls. There were whispers, faint but persistent, of individuals who, while outwardly embracing the new era, harbored a secret yearning for the old order. A desire for the efficiency, the predictability, and the undeniable power that the Syndicate had wielded, even at the cost of immense suffering. These were the seeds of potential future conflict, the lingering temptation to reassert control when faced with the inherent messiness and unpredictability of a truly free and interconnected world.

Kira and Ash understood this temptation intimately. The allure of absolute knowledge, of absolute control, was a powerful one. Their own resonance offered glimpses of such power, the ability to influence and to understand on a scale previously unimaginable. But they had made a conscious choice, a foundational commitment to the principles of balance and respect. They had seen what happened when that balance was broken, when the pursuit of power overshadowed the recognition of interconnectedness.

"The old ways of thinking," Ash mused, his thought tinged with a touch of melancholy, "are deeply ingrained. Generations lived and died under the Syndicate's doctrine. It's a powerful inheritance, even for those who fought against it."

"And that's why our work must continue," Kira responded, her resolve hardening. "We can't simply dismantle the old structure; we have to actively build something new, something stronger, something that nourishes the soul of humanity and the spirit of the planet. We have to make empathy, understanding, and genuine connection so intrinsically valuable that the temptation of control becomes... obsolete."

Their shared awareness allowed them to perceive these subtle shifts in societal mood. They could feel the undercurrents of discontent, the flickering embers of old resentments, the quiet compromises that individuals made when faced with difficult choices. It was a constant, delicate dance, guiding their communities towards a future that honored their shared values without resorting to coercion.

One such challenge arose in the coastal regions, where the delicate marine ecosystems were still recovering from the Syndicate's unchecked pollution. A proposal had been put forth by a group of engineers and resource managers – well-intentioned, but perhaps too quick to revert to familiar solutions – to build massive filtration systems, employing advanced sonic frequencies to 'cleanse' the affected waters.

Kira and Ash, along with their marine bio-luminescent companions, had been spending considerable time observing the ocean's subtle recuperative processes. They had found that the marine life itself, particularly the schools of shimmering Siren Fish and the deep-dwelling, bioluminescent coral gardens, were actively engaged in a complex, resonant purification process. This process was far more intricate and nuanced than any technological solution could replicate.

"The Siren Fish," Kira projected, a montage of their shimmering, rhythmic movements filling her mind, "they're not just swimming. They're harmonizing the water's energetic signature. It's a living symphony, and the sonic frequencies of the proposed filters could disrupt that entirely."

Ash, tapping into the collective awareness of a pod of oceanic dolphins, confirmed her findings. "The dolphins are guiding the cleaner currents, creating vortices that naturally draw out the residual toxins. It's a slow, organic process, but it's working. The ocean is healing itself, if we allow it."

The challenge was to convince the engineers, who were accustomed to thinking in terms of mechanical efficiency and quantifiable results, to trust in these subtle, biological processes. This required not just presenting data, but fostering a deeper understanding, an empathic connection to the living systems they sought to manage.

Kira and Ash organized a series of communal gatherings, inviting the engineers to the coastal areas. They brought with them not just the dolphins and the Siren Fish, but also members of their own communities who had developed a deep understanding of the ocean's rhythms. Through shared experiences, guided meditations, and the facilitated resonance between humans and marine life, they aimed to bridge the gap between technological prowess and ecological wisdom.

It was during one of these gatherings that a senior engineer, a man named Commander Valerius, who had once been a prominent figure in the Syndicate's infrastructure division, expressed his deep-seated skepticism. "Your methods are... poetic," he stated, his voice carrying the weight of ingrained practicality. "But they lack the decisive efficacy of engineered solutions. We need to act swiftly. The damage is extensive."

Kira met his gaze, her own resonating with a quiet strength. "Commander, we understand the urgency. But 'swift' action without true understanding can cause more harm than good. The Syndicate taught us that lesson repeatedly. We are not advocating for inaction; we are advocating for informed, harmonized action. We need to listen to what the ocean is telling us, not impose our will upon it."

Ash then guided a small group of dolphins to approach the shore, their sonar clicks and whistles a complex, melodic language. Kira, focusing her resonance, projected the dolphins' intent, their deep knowledge of the ocean's currents and their role in its purification. She showed Valerius, not just told him, how the Siren Fish, through their synchronized bioluminescence, were creating energetic fields that neutralized specific toxins. It was a direct, sensory experience of the ocean's living intelligence.

Slowly, subtly, Valerius's hardened expression began to soften. He had witnessed the destructive power of unchecked technological ambition firsthand. Now, he was being offered a glimpse of a different path, one that acknowledged the inherent wisdom of the natural world. His own canine companion, a sturdy, intelligent breed called a Sentinel, nudged his hand, its empathetic presence a silent endorsement of the message being conveyed.

The dialogue wasn't about winning an argument; it was about creating a shared space of understanding, a resonant field where different perspectives could converge and transform. It was a painstaking process, requiring immense patience and an unwavering belief in the potential for growth, even in the most entrenched minds.

The question of the future, therefore, was not a simple dichotomy of success or failure, of a fully healed world versus a relapse into destruction. It was a continuous, evolving process, a constant negotiation between the immediate needs of a recovering planet and the deeply ingrained patterns of human behavior. The ultimate answer lay not in definitive outcomes, but in the sustained cultivation of the very qualities that had allowed Kira and Ash to lead this transformation: empathy, interconnectedness, and the profound, unbreakable bond between humans and their canine allies.

The Syndicate had sought to sever these bonds, to isolate humanity and to dominate the natural world through technological might. But in their place, Kira and Ash had fostered a new paradigm, one where collaboration and mutual respect were the cornerstones of progress. The canine companions, more than just pets or assistants, were integral partners in this new world, their unique sensory and empathic abilities unlocking deeper layers of understanding and facilitating essential communication across species.

The future, as Kira and Ash envisioned it, was not a static utopia, but a dynamic, flourishing ecosystem where humanity played its role as a steward, not a sovereign. It was a future where the lessons learned from the brink of destruction were never forgotten, where the fragility of life was met with reverence, and where the inherent power of connection was celebrated.

There would undoubtedly be new challenges, unforeseen difficulties, and moments of doubt. The temptation to revert to easier, more familiar patterns of control would likely resurface in different forms. But the foundation that Kira and Ash had laid was strong. It was built not on force or coercion, but on the profound, resonant truth of shared existence.

As the twin moons cast their ethereal glow over the reawakening landscape, Kira and Ash stood together, their awareness intertwined, their purpose clear. The journey was far from over. It was, in fact, just beginning. The question of the future was not a single, definitive answer, but a continuous unfolding, a testament to the enduring power of love, understanding, and the resonant symphony of life, a symphony that they, and all those who chose to listen, would continue to conduct, harmonizing the world one shared breath, one empathetic pulse, at a time.

Their legacy would not be defined by what they had defeated, but by what they had helped to create: a world that remembered how to listen, how to connect, and how to truly live in harmony. The cautious optimism they felt was not a naive hope, but a deep, earned conviction in the resilience of life and the enduring strength of the bonds that sustained it.

GLOSSARY

Lumina Fox	A species of fox exhibiting bioluminescent qualities, known for its heightened empathic sensitivity and its role as a companion and guide in resonant practices.
Resonance	The fundamental ability to perceive and interact with the energetic frequencies of living beings and the environment, fostering empathy and communication.
Sentinel	A breed of canine characterized by its strong protective instincts, sharp intellect, and advanced empathic awareness, often serving as guardians and partners.
Siren Fish	Marine creatures whose synchronized bioluminescence and movements contribute to the natural purification of oceanic ecosystems.
Syndicate	The former oppressive global regime that prioritized technological control and resource exploitation over ecological balance and individual freedom.

www.ingramcontent.com/pod-product-compliance
Lightning Source LLC
LaVergne TN
LVHW050915080826
845145LV00001B/95

* 9 7 8 1 9 6 9 5 6 9 5 5 5 *